# XI
# IRISH AND OVERSEAS

Leon Tolstoy

# THE
# Masterpiece Library of Short Stories

*The Thousand Best Complete Tales of all Times and all Countries*

*Selected by*

## AN INTERNATIONAL BOARD
## OF EMINENT CRITICS

Sir William Robertson Nicoll, LL.D.

Sir Arthur Quiller-Couch
Clement Shorter
George Saintsbury, LL.D.
Richard le Gallienne
Brander Matthews, Litt.D.

Sir Frederick Wedmore
Sir Edmund Gosse, C.B., LL.D.
W. P. Trent, LL.D.
Carl Van Doren
Thomas Seccombe

*Edited by*

## Sir J. A. Hammerton

# XI.  IRISH AND OVERSEAS

LONDON
THE EDUCATIONAL BOOK COMPANY LIMITED

**Special Edition in 10 double-volumes
issued by Allied Newspapers, Ltd.,
in association with The Educational
Book Co. Ltd.**

# Editorial Board

# Editorial Note

A SHORT story may be a mere anecdote of three hundred words or a work of ten or fifteen thousand. In content it may be anything from a glimpse of character, an incident, to a highly finished picture of life. But it should be a complete work of imagination, its effect achieved with a minimum of personages and events.

TO select the best thousand examples was a task that could be achieved only on arbitrary lines. As to length, three thousand words was the ideal average, but this excluded some of the finest stories, so exceptions had to be allowed. National characteristics also had consideration. Another test was the value of a story as illustrating the development of the art.

PROBLEMS of arrangement were not entirely solved by classification according to the country of each writer's origin. This puts Richard Steele into the Irish volume and separates those ideal literary partners Agnes and Egerton Castle. But it is the best possible arrangement for the work, and the index makes reference easy. The inclusion of a series of stories of the War became possible when the War itself ruled out all modern German work.

A WORD as to the method of selection. The General Editor prepared a trial list of titles which were submitted to all the members of the Editorial Board, who rejected and added according to their individual tastes and knowledge. These individual lists were then collated and the final list evolved. The thousand stories selected are therefore representative of the combined opinion of the whole group of editors. A very few modifications of the final list were made necessary by difficulties of copyright and considerations of Anglo-Saxon taste in certain translations from foreign literatures.

MOST of the foreign stories have been specially translated, and all copyrights, in both stories and translations, the use of which authors and publishers have courteously permitted, are duly credited at the end of each volume.     J. A. H.

# Contents of Volume XI

# THE IRISH STORY-
## TELLERS

THE territorial classification of the authors represented in this Library results in the present volume starting off with three of the most famous names in English literature, none of which might immediately occur to the mind in thinking of " The Irish Story-Tellers." And, of course, if we omit the Gaelic school, Irish literature is essentially a part of English literature : there is no Irish short story as distinct from the English short story. A considerable proportion of the tales in the following pages will be found to have no association whatever with scenes of Irish life, although they contain a very interesting collection of short fictions which are both the work of Irish authors and inspired by Irish life and character.

**STEELE**

In association with Addison the name of Richard Steele (1672–1729) takes us back to one of the most memorable periods of English letters. In those early years of the eighteenth century the short story was still a somewhat elusive and undeveloped literary form : it was the great day of the essay. Such fictions as Steele wrote are therefore examples of the transition stage from the essay to the tale, and may be described as essay-stories. " Inkle and Yarico," one of the best examples of these, is the artistic expansion of an anecdote, told with a subtle charm of simplicity which lifts it out of the journalism of the day into the realm of enduring things. It has a further claim to inclusion here, as stated by its author, in that it is the counterpart to the classic story " The Widow of Ephesus " (see Volume I). In " Sir Roger de Coverley's

Wooing " we scent the fragrance of a vanished day and find the short story as a vehicle for the portrayal of character already adequate in form even though the method is still that of the essay.

## STERNE

As an illustration of the triumph of style over matter, no more delightful piece could be quoted than the " Story of Le Fevre," by Laurence Sterne (1713–1768). This, of course, is one of those few exceptions in the Library where a short complete tale has been chosen from a long work of fiction, " The Story of Le Fevre " being culled from *Tristram Shandy*. It contains a minimum of incident, but what a world of kindly nature stands revealed in the reading of these half-dozen pages ! They recall curiously to the present writer something of the emotional satisfaction with which he first read Pierre Loti's wonderful description of Sylvestre's leave-taking, in *Pêcheur d'Islande*, an incident of the most ordinary kind, which by the sheer genius of the author's literary treatment is transmuted into a triumph of art.

## GOLDSMITH

Oliver Goldsmith (1728–1774), who was born just a year before Sir Richard Steele died, is yet another of the great writers of the past whose works provide us with specimens of the essay-story. Entirely typical of this is "The History of the Man in Black," presenting in the form of a brief fiction a philosophic view of life that is tinged with cynicism but must be accepted as a true commentary on human hypocrisy. " The Soldier's Story," by the same author, is not a short story at all in the strict modern sense, but comes very near to being a picaresque " novel in a nutshell." It is a wonderfully compressed narrative of vagabond life, valuable as a picture of the times and pathetic in its simplicity : reasons which have been held sufficient to justify its inclusion in this collection. Another form of early short story is also taken from the works of Goldsmith, who in " Alcander and Septimius " provides an example of the apologue notable for a certain classic stiffness but also for charm of style and some ingenuity of plot.

## MARIA EDGEWORTH

One of the classic writers of Ireland is Maria Edgeworth (1767–1849), yet though her name is associated with numerous short stories it is found on critical analysis of these that few of them possess the qualities necessary for admission to such an assembly as the present, while those that do have suffered from the prolixity of their time. From her children's stories, however, one is selected that must be familiar to many readers. Somewhat naïve both in plot and telling, " The Purple Jar " has a charm of childish days which marks it out for memory. When we turn to "The City of the Demons" we touch the work of a very remarkable Irishman whose name was at one time familiar to English readers by reason of its association with *Blackwood's* and *Fraser's*. William Maginn, who was born in Cork, 1793, and died in London, August 20, 1842, was one of the most variously gifted of Irishmen and seemed to possess every quality except the ability to order his own affairs wisely, resembling in this his more famous countryman, Goldsmith. In " The City of the Demons" Maginn is also bent upon the apologue, but this time it is of the Eastern type, always the more acceptable, and with great skill he has caught the quaintness of the oriental manner.

## SAMUEL LOVER AND OTHERS

There is a complete change both of spirit and atmosphere in the next story of our series, " Frank Kennedy," by W. Hamilton Maxwell (1794–1850). Here we have an admirably constructed short story in the historical manner. Maxwell was probably the first of our writers to develop the military novel, which in the hands of James Grant became so widely popular. His *Stories of Waterloo*, from which " Frank Kennedy " is taken, is a work that has been curiously neglected by the reprinters of our standard authors, who have found ready audiences for much matter of far less literary and historic value. With Samuel Lover (1797–1868) we arrive at an author who is Irish of the Irish. All his writings were aimed at expressing Irish character in an Irish way, and immensely popular though he was as recently as fifty or sixty years ago, much that he wrote now seems to belong to a very remote day. Humour is a quality curiously apt to go out of fashion unless it be entirely of the mind. Lover's story of " The Gridiron " is just a good old Irish anecdote told in a rollicking manner reminiscent of " Handy Andy," and the humour of it happens to be quite fresh, in which it differs from most of his other short stories. Here one might have expected an example from William Carleton, whose tales of the Irish peasantry used to be so popular ; but careful examination of his work has failed to discover an example suitable for inclusion, as they lack both invention and narrative art, and are told with unnecessary circumlocution. There is movement and literary grace, however, in " The Story of Généviève," by Mrs. Anna Jameson (1797–1860), whose *Characters of Shakespeare's Women* is still a popular classic. This is an old-fashioned romantic fiction and not the less charming on that account, but the author was evidently distrustful of her power to illustrate movement by dialogue, in which the real art of the short story abides.   There is the true Irish flavour in " Daniel O'Rourke," the first of two excellent stories by Crofton Croker (1798–1854), famous as a folklorist and author of *Fairy Legends and Traditions of the South of Ireland*.   The *Quarterly* said aptly of " Daniel O'Rourke " : " It is a fine Dutch picture of nightmare ; rivalling in its way the sublimed vision of Burns."   Croker's other story, " The Lady of Gollerus," is a fairy tale of sorts, racy of the Irish fisher folk, and might well have served as germ of the idea which Mr. H. G. Wells used with so much humour and ingenuity in " The Lady from the Sea."

## BANIM—GRIFFIN—LEVER

An author of considerable popularity in the days of the " Annuals " was John Banim (1798–1842), whose *Tales of the O'Hara Family* had quite a vogue.   The two examples of his work here are chosen almost as much for their historical value as for their literary qualities. " The Stolen Sheep " is a good straightforward tale of the hungry times in Ireland, and has both atmosphere and movement ; while " The Churchyard Watch," though it cannot be considered an artistic success, is historically important, and from the literary point of view interesting as realising a situation full of tragic possibilities which, in the hands of a more skilled or indeed any present-day story-writer, could be developed with thrilling effect.   Gerald Griffin (1803–1846) was a young Irishman of much literary promise, whose story *The Collegians* has still a certain popularity as the *Colleen Bawn*.   " The Dilemma of Phadrig," an excellent peasant tale, is the best example of Griffin's work in the short story.   The fairy doctor plays the part of the Medicine Man of the savages, and the way out of the situation realised by the story-teller is of a piece with the superstition of the times in which it was written.   " A Hero-Worshipper," by Charles James Lever (1809–1872), introduces one of the most notable figures among modern Irish authors. Lever's famous stories, such as " Harry Lorrequer," " Charles O'Malley," and half a dozen others which the reader will readily remember, did in many ways for Ireland what the Waverley Novels did for Scotland.   Lever was one of the great novelists in his splendid virility, his breadth of view, his rich imagination, and the vigour of his style.   He belonged to the grand school of novel writers that flourished in mid-Victorian days and the tradition of which is being maintained by none of our contemporary writers.   " A Hero-Worshipper " is selected from his volume *Cornelius O'Dowd*, which consists chiefly of stories and sketches originally contributed to *Blackwood's*, and in this we have the real stuff : clever characterisation, brisk and confident narrative, rich humour.

## FROM SHERIDAN LE FANU TO FRANK MATHEW

In the middle years of last century and particularly among Irish and Scottish writers ghost stories and tales of the supernatural were so frequently forthcoming that there must have been a wide demand for them. Among the Irish writers who penned many tales of the supernatural was the novelist Sheridan Le Fanu (1814–1873), and he fortunately combined with an ability to thrill his readers an admirable sense of humour, both qualities being well illustrated in " The Ghost and the Bone-Setter." Canon Sheehan (1852–1913) never had any considerable popularity among English readers, but his name and works are treasured among his countrymen and co-religionists, and " A Thorough Gentleman " will show that he could tell an interesting story and display at the same time a certain sardonic wit. In Frankfort Moore (1855–1931) we seem to touch our own day for the first time. One of the most popular of modern authors, Moore was a good Irishman who wrote tales of many lands and different times, but always seemed to move with most confident step in the gallant days of the seventeenth and eighteenth centuries. " The Comedy of the Old Love " is typical of his very distinguished gifts of story-telling. And what a piece of perfect beauty in the realm of the fairy story is " The Birthday of the Infanta," from Oscar Wilde's *House of Pomegranates*. " Maureen's Fairing," by Jane Barlow (1860–1917), is a good example of that delightful writer's work, which was always essentially Irish in inspiration and in manner. Mrs. Hinkson (Katharine Tynan, 1861–1931), on the other hand, was an Irish novelist of wide popularity, who most usually sought her scenes and characters elsewhere than in her native land. Her two stories here reprinted, " At the Spotted Lamb " and " The Meeting in the Library," are happily contrasted, the one being touched with romance and gaiety and the other awakening deeper emotions. " Richard Dehan " (1864–1932) was another brilliant novelist of Irish origin who drew but little upon her native land for the scenes and characters of her books. " Richard Dehan " had written much and well in the way of the short story long before winning fame as a " full-length " novelist, and " A Nursery Tea," for invention, characterisation, and smoothness of form, is probably as good a short story of its length as one could find. Mr. Shan Bullock (*b.* 1865) is an admirable Irish writer who has gone back to the scenes of his youth for most of his tales, and is probably discovered at his best in such examples as the two from " Ring o' Rushes " included in this volume. Frank Mathew (1865–1924) also sought to interpret Irish life and character in the same way, and it would be difficult to find other two such perfect idylls of Ireland as " The Reverend Peter Flannery " and " A Connemara Miracle," selected from his delightful book *At the Rising of the Moon*.

## W. B. YEATS AND OTHERS

No living writer, of course, has done more to revivify in Ireland a sense of the old national things than her most eminent living poet, Mr. W. B. Yeats (b. 1865). Chiefly in the theatre he has sought to effect that national literary revival which others have been quick to turn to political ends. " The Twisting of the Rope," which is selected from his *Tales of Red Hanrahan*, is a poet's way of telling an old folk story, and very charming and characteristic it must be pronounced. It is rather in favour of our territorial classification that Mrs. Agnes Castle (d. 1922), whom we usually think of as part author with her husband, Egerton Castle, of the daintiest " costume " romances set in old English scenes, should appear, when bracketed with her fellow-countrymen in this volume, as the author of an essentially Irish and very beautiful and moving short story. Seumas MacManus, of course, is Irish to the core in all his writings, and has confined himself to the telling of tales of his native countryside. He could not have done better, as his gifts for this particular and desirable work are high, and if he has not won, or tried to win, a wide audience in the other British Isles for his tales of Irish peasantry, he has achieved both fame and popularity with the much wider reading public of the United States. " The Bewitched Fiddle," delightfully told as it is and full of humour, is probably based upon some old story which its author heard in his boyhood, and " The Resurrection of Dinny O'Dowd," so admirably narrated, has no doubt germinated from some popular local story of the people. A pure work of the imagination and a short story of true tenderness and real beauty is the late Mrs. Shorter's " Priscilla." Dora Sigerson Shorter was one of the sweetest singers of Ireland and a lady who burned with the intensest enthusiasm for all things Irish. In her all too short life she won a measure of fame with her poetry which will endure and grow, for she had vision and music, and perhaps the attraction of her poetry has a little obscured her remarkable work in prose, of which *The Father Confessor and Other Stories* is sufficient to mark the writer out from the ordinary ruck of story-tellers. It is from that volume that the beautiful story of " Priscilla " is reprinted.

## SOMERVILLE AND ROSS

Probably no popular writers of our time are more representative of their native country in the mind of the reading public than the two gifted Irish ladies who have added so considerably to the gaiety of our literature under the style of " E. Œ. Somerville and Martin Ross." *The Experiences of an Irish R.M.* is one of the modern classics of humour and the life joyous. All the writings of these admirable literary partners are informed with the best of high spirits and a fresh and lively wit.  " Martin Ross " was the pen-name of Miss Violet Florence Martin, who died in December 1915, and whose biography has been so sympathetically written by her surviving colleague.  " The House of Fahy " illustrates their delightful art at its best, and to the few who are unacquainted with their work it is a certain appetiser for more, while to those who are familiar with it the story will stand a second or a third or even a fourth reading, which is the real " acid test " of merit.   In a totally different way from these gay chroniclers of one of the most fascinating aspects of Irish country life, Mr. Daniel Corkery, an Irish writer of more recent reputation, is equally interpretative of his native land.   The greyer things of Ireland, the shadowed lives of its poorer classes, have found in him an exponent whose art is entirely admirable and whose sympathy is profound.   Humour of the deeper sort, of course, is by no means absent even from the tragic side of Irish life, and there is a pleasant touch of it in " The Breath of Life," but " The Child Saint " is of sentiment all compact.   Each is a perfect study in its way and representative of Mr. Corkery's very fine work, *A Munster Twilight*.

## LORD   DUNSANY

There is nothing at all that is Irish in the very remarkable work of Lord Dunsany unless it be the wonderful imaginative qualities of his tales. He holds a place in our later literature that is unique, and he is a master of the most beautiful and sensuous style.   One reads his books as much for their manner as for their matter, and the least thing that he has written has distinction :  he is essentially an artist in words.   Lord Dunsany's effects are all achieved with an ideal economy of description, and yet there is no touch that seems lacking to the completeness of the picture he sets out to paint.   The group of selections from his various writings here given will serve well to show the wide range of his imagination from the weird fancy of " Mallington Moor " and the sardonic humour of " Coronation of Mr. Thomas Shap " to the biting satire of " The Hen."

J. A. H.

## SIR RICHARD STEELE
1672–1729

# THE STORY OF INKLE AND YARICO

ARIETTA is visited by all persons of both sexes, who have any pretence to wit and gallantry. She is in that time of life which is neither affected with the follies of youth, nor infirmities of age; and her conversation is so mixed with gaiety and prudence, that she is agreeable both to the young and the old. Her behaviour is very frank, without being in the least blamable: and as she is out of the track of any amorous or ambitious pursuits of her own, her visitants entertain her with accounts of themselves very freely, whether they concern their passions or their interests. I made her a visit this afternoon, having been formerly introduced to the honour of her acquaintance by my friend Will Honeycomb, who has prevailed upon her to admit me sometimes into her assembly, as a civil inoffensive man. I found her accompanied with one person only, a commonplace talker, who, upon my entrance, arose, and after a very slight civility sat down again; then, turning to Arietta, pursued his discourse, which I found was upon the old topic of constancy in love. He went on with great facility in repeating what he talks every day of his life; and with the ornaments of insignificant laughs and gestures, enforced his arguments by quotations out of plays and songs, which allude to the perjuries of the fair, and the general levity of women. Methought he strove to shine more than ordinarily in his talkative way, that he might insult my silence, and distinguish himself before a woman of Arietta's taste and understanding. She had often an inclination to interrupt him, but could find no opportunity, till the larum cease of itself, which it did not till he had repeated and murdered the celebrated story of the Ephesian Matron.

Arietta seemed to regard this piece of raillery as an outrage done to her sex; as indeed I have always observed that women, whether out of a nicer regard to their honour, or what other reason I cannot tell, are more sensibly touched with those general aspersions which are cast upon their sex, than men are by what is said of theirs.

When she had a little recovered herself from the serious anger she was in, she replied in the following manner:

" Sir, when I consider how perfectly new all you have said on this subject is, and that the story you have given us is not quite two thousand years old, I cannot but think it a piece of presumption to dispute it with you; but your quotations put me in mind of the fable of the lion and the man. The man walking with that noble animal, showed him, in the ostentation of human superiority, a sign of a man killing a lion. Upon which, the lion said very justly, ' We lions are none of us painters, else we could show a hundred men killed by lions for one lion killed by a man.' You men are writers, and can represent us women as unbecoming as you please in your works, while we are unable to return the injury. You have twice or thrice observed in your discourse that hypocrisy is the very foundation of our education; and that an ability to dissemble our affections is a professed part of our breeding. These and such other reflections are sprinkled up and down the writings of all ages by authors, who leave behind them memorials of their resentment against the scorn of particular women, in invectives against the whole sex. Such a writer, I doubt not, was the celebrated Petronius, who invented the pleasant aggravations of the frailty of the Ephesian lady; but when we consider this question between the sexes, which has been either a point of dispute or raillery ever since there were men and women, let us take facts from plain people, and from such as have not either ambition or capacity to embellish their narrations with any beauties of imagination. I was the other day amusing myself with Ligon's *Account of Barbadoes*; and, in answer to your well-wrought tale, I will give you (as it dwells upon my memory) out of that honest traveller, in his fifty-fifth page, the history of Inkle and Yarico.

" ' Mr. Thomas Inkle, of London, aged twenty years, embarked in the Downs, on the good ship called the *Achilles*, bound for the West Indies, on the 16th June, 1647, in order to improve his fortune by trade and merchandise. Our adventurer was the third son of an eminent citizen, who had taken particular care to instil into his mind an early love of gain, by making him a perfect master of numbers, and consequently giving him a quick view of loss and advantage, and preventing the natural impulses of his passions by prepossession towards his interests. With a mind thus turned, young Inkle had a person every way agreeable, a ruddy vigour in his countenance, strength in his limbs, with ringlets of fair hair loosely flowing on his shoulders. It happened, in the course of the voyage, that the *Achilles*, in some distress, put into a creek on the main of America, in search of provisions. The youth, who is the hero of my story, among others went on shore on this occasion. From their first landing they were observed by a party of Indians, who hid themselves in the woods for that purpose. The English unadvisedly marched a great distance from the shore into the country, and were intercepted by the natives, who slew the greatest number of them. Our adventurer escaped among others, by flying into a forest. Upon his coming into a remote and pathless part of the wood, he threw himself, tired and breathless, on a little hillock, when an Indian maid rushed from a thicket behind him. After the first surprise they appeared mutually agreeable to each other. If the European was highly charmed with the limbs, features, and wild graces of the naked American; the American was no less taken with the dress, complexion, and shape of an European, covered from head to foot. The Indian grew immediately enamoured of him, and consequently solicitous for his preservation. She therefore conveyed him to a cave, where she gave him a delicious repast of fruits, and led him to a stream to slake his thirst. In the midst of these good offices, she would sometimes play with his hair, and delight in the opposition of its colour to that of her fingers: then open his bosom, then laugh at him for covering it. She was, it seems, a person of distinction, for she every day came to him in a different dress, of the most beautiful shells, bugles,[1] and bredes.[2] She likewise brought him a great many spoils, which her other lovers had presented to her, so that his cave was richly adorned with all the spotted skins of beasts, and most party-coloured feathers of fowls, which that world afforded. To make his confinement more tolerable, she would carry him in the dusk of the evening, or by the favour of moonlight, to unfrequented groves and solitudes, and show him where to lie down in safety, and sleep amidst the falls of waters and melody of nightingales. Her part was to watch and hold him awake in her arms, for fear of her countrymen, and wake him on occasions to consult his safety. In this manner did the lovers pass away their time, till they had learned a language of their own, in which the voyager communicated to his mistress how happy he should be to have her in his country, where she should be clothed in such silks as his waistcoat was made of, and be carried in houses drawn by horses, without being exposed to wind or weather. All this he promised her the enjoyment of, without such fears and alarms as they were there tormented with. In this tender correspondence these lovers lived for several months, when Yarico, instructed by her lover, discovered a vessel on the coast, to which she made signals; and in the night, with the utmost joy and satisfaction, accompanied him to a ship's crew of his countrymen bound to Barbadoes. When a vessel from the main arrives in that island, it seems the planters come down to the shore, where there is an immediate market of the Indians and other slaves, as with us of horses and oxen.

" To be short, Mr. Thomas Inkle, now coming into English territories, began seriously to reflect upon his loss of time, and to weigh

---

[1] Beads.                    [2] Braids.

with himself how many days' interest of his money he had lost during his stay with Yarico. This thought made the young man very pensive, and careful what account he should be able to give his friends of his voyage. Upon which consideration, the prudent and frugal young man sold Yarico to a Barbadian merchant; notwithstanding that the poor girl, to incline him to commiserate her condition, told him that she was with child by him: but he only made use of that information to rise in his demands upon the purchaser.' "

I was so touched with this story (which I think should be always a counterpart to the Ephesian Matron) that I left the room with tears in my eyes, which a woman of Arietta's good sense did, I am sure, take for greater applause than any compliments I could make her.

# SIR ROGER DE COVERLEY'S WOOING

### Sir Richard Steele

The first of our society is a gentleman of Worcestershire, of ancient descent, a baronet, his name Sir Roger de Coverley. His great grandfather was inventor of that famous country-dance which is called after him. All who know that shire are very well acquainted with the parts and merits of Sir Roger. He is a gentleman that is very singular in his behaviour, but his singularities proceed from his good sense, and are contradictions to the manners of the world only as he thinks the world is in the wrong. However, this humour creates him no enemies, for he does nothing with sourness or obstinacy; and his being unconfined to modes and forms makes him but the readier and more capable to please and oblige all who know him. When he is in town he lives in Soho Square.

It is said, he keeps himself a bachelor by reason he was crossed in love by a perverse beautiful widow of the next county to him. Before this disappointment, Sir Roger was what you call a fine gentleman, had often supped with my lord Rochester and Sir George Etherege, fought a duel upon his first coming to town, and kicked Bully Dawson in a public coffee-house for calling him youngster. But being ill-used by the above-mentioned widow, he was very serious for a year and a half; and though, his temper being naturally jovial, he at last got over it, he grew careless of himself and never dressed afterwards; he continues to wear a coat and doublet of the same cut that were in fashion at the time of his repulse, which, in his merry humours, he tells us, had been in and out twelve times since he first wore it. . . .

He is now in his fifty-sixth year, cheerful, gay, and hearty, keeps a good house in both town and country; a great lover of mankind; but there is such a mirthful cast in his behaviour, that he is rather beloved than esteemed. His tenants grow rich, his servants look satisfied, all the young women profess love to him, and the young men are glad of his company. When he comes into a house he calls the servants by their names, and talks all the way upstairs to a visit. I must not omit that Sir Roger is a justice of the *Quorum*; that he fills the chair at a quarter-session with great abilities, and three months ago gained universal applause by explaining a passage in the game-act. . . .

I mentioned a great affliction which my friend Sir Roger had met with in his youth; which was no less than a disappointment in love. It happened this evening that we fell into a very pleasing walk at a distance from his house. As soon as we came into it,

" It is," quoth the good old man, looking round him with a smile, " very hard that any part of my land should be settled upon one who has used me so ill as the perverse widow did; and yet I am sure I could not see a sprig of any bough of this whole walk of trees, but I should reflect upon her and her severity. She has certainly the finest hand of any woman in the world. You are to know this was the place wherein I used to muse upon her; and by that custom I can never come into it, but the same tender sentiments revive in my mind, as if I had actually walked with that beautiful creature under these shades. I have been fool enough to carve her name on the bark of several of these trees; so unhappy is the condition of men in love, to attempt the removing of their passion by the methods which serve only to imprint it deeper. She has certainly the finest hand of any woman in the world."

Here followed a profound silence, and I was not displeased to observe my friend falling so naturally into a discourse, which I had ever before taken notice he industriously avoided. After a very long pause he entered upon an account of this great circumstance in his life, with an air which I thought raised my idea of him above what I had ever had before; and gave me the picture of that cheerful mind of his before it received that stroke which has ever since affected his words and actions. But he went on as follows:

" I came to my estate in my twenty-second year, and resolved to follow the steps of the most worthy of my ancestors who have inhabited this spot of earth before me, in all the methods of hospitality and good neighbourhood, for the sake of my fame; and in country sports and recreations, for the sake of my health. In my twenty-third year I was obliged to serve as sheriff of the county;

and in my servants, officers, and whole equipage, indulged the pleasure of a young man (who did not think ill of his own person) in taking that public occasion of showing my figure and behaviour to advantage.

" You may easily imagine to yourself what appearance I made, who am pretty tall, rid[e] well, and was very well dressed, at the head of a whole county, with music before me, a feather in my hat, and my horse well bitted. I can assure you I was not a little pleased with the kind looks and glances I had from all the balconies and windows as I rode to the hall where the assizes were held. But when I came there, a beautiful creature in a widow's habit sat in court to hear the event of a cause concerning her dower. This commanding creature (who was born for destruction of all who behold her) put on such a resignation in her countenance, and bore the whispers of all around the court with such a pretty uneasiness, I warrant you, and then recovered herself from one eye to another, till she was perfectly confused by meeting something so wistful in all she encountered, that at last, with a murrain to her, she cast her bewitching eye upon me. I no sooner met it, but I bowed like a great surprised booby; and knowing her cause to be the first which came on, I cried like a captivated calf as I was,

" ' Make way for the defendant's witnesses.'

" This sudden partiality made all the county immediately see the sheriff also was become a slave to the fine widow. During the time her cause was upon trial she behaved herself, I warrant you, with such a deep attention to her business, took opportunities to have little billets handed to her counsel, then would be in such a pretty confusion, occasioned, you must know, by acting before so much company, that not only I but the whole court was prejudiced in her favour; and all that the next heir to her husband had to urge was thought so groundless and frivolous, that when it came to her counsel to reply, there was not half so much said as every one besides in the court thought he could have urged to her advantage.

" You must understand, sir, this perverse woman is one of those unaccountable creatures that secretly rejoice in the admiration of men, but indulge themselves in no further consequences. Hence it is that she has ever had a train of admirers, and she removes from her slaves in town to those in the country, according to the seasons of the year. She is a reading lady, and far gone in the pleasures of friendship; she is always accompanied by a confidant, who is witness to her daily protestations against our sex, and consequently a bar to her first steps towards love, upon the strength of her own maxims and declarations.

" However, I must needs say this accomplished mistress of mine has distinguished me above the rest, and has been known to declare Sir Roger de Coverley was the tamest and most human of all the brutes in the country. I was told she said so by one who thought he rallied me; but upon the strength of this slender encouragement, of being thought least detestable, I made new liveries, new-paired my coach-horses, sent them all to town to be bitted, and taught to throw their legs well, and move all together, before I pretended to cross the country and wait upon her.

" As soon as I thought my retinue suitable to the character of my fortune and youth, I set out from hence to make my addresses. The particular skill of this lady has ever been to inflame your wishes, and yet command respect. To make her mistress of this art, she has a greater share of knowledge, wit, and good sense, than is usual, even among men of merit. Then she is beautiful beyond the race of women. If you won't let her go on with a certain artifice with her eyes and the skill of beauty, she will arm herself with her real charms, and strike you with admiration instead of desire. It is certain that if you were to behold the whole woman, there is that dignity in her aspect, that composure in her motion, that complacency in her manner, that if her form makes you hope, her merit makes you fear. But then again, she is such a desperate scholar, that no country-gentleman can approach her without being a jest.

" As I was going to tell you, when I came to her house I was admitted to her presence with great civility; at the same time she placed herself to be first seen by me in such an attitude as I think you call the posture of a picture, that she discovered new charms, and I at last came towards her with such an awe as made me speechless. This she no sooner observed but she made her advantage of it, and began a discourse to me concerning love and honour, as they both are followed by pretenders, and the real votaries to them. When she had discussed these points in a discourse, which I verily believe was as learned as the best philosopher in Europe could possibly make, she asked me whether she was so happy as to fall in with my sentiments on these important particulars. Her confidant sat by her, and upon my being in the last confusion and silence, this malicious aid of hers, turning to her, says, ' I am very glad to observe Sir Roger pauses upon this subject, and seems resolved to deliver all his sentiments upon the matter when he pleases to speak.' They both kept their countenances, and after I had sat half an hour meditating how to behave before such profound casuists, I rose up and took my leave.

" Chance has since that time thrown me very often in her way, and she as often has directed a discourse to me which I do not understand. This barbarity has kept me ever at a distance from the most beautiful object my eyes ever beheld. It is thus also she deals with all mankind, and you must make love to her, as you would conquer the Sphinx, by posing her. But were she like other women, and that there were any talking to her, how constant must the pleasure of that man be who could converse with a creature——

" But after all, you may be sure her heart is fixed on some one
or other; and yet I have been credibly informed; but who can
believe half that is said! After she had done speaking to me, she
put her hand to her bosom, and adjusted her tucker. Then she
cast her eyes a little down upon my beholding her too earnestly.
They say she sings excellently: her voice in her ordinary speech
has something in it inexpressibly sweet. You must know I dined
with her at a public table the day after I first saw her, and she
helped me to some tansy in the eye of all the gentlemen in the
country: she has certainly the finest hand of any woman in the
world. I can assure you, sir, were you to behold her, you would
be in the same condition; for as her speech is music her form is
angelic. But I find I grow irregular while I am talking of her;
but indeed it would be stupidity to be unconcerned at such perfection. Oh the excellent creature, she is as inimitable to all women
as she is inaccessible to all men."

I found my friend begin to rave, and insensibly led him towards
the house, that we might be joined by some other company; and
am convinced that the widow is the secret cause of all that inconsis-
tency which appears in some parts of my friend's discourse; though
he has so much command of himself as not directly to mention her,
yet according to that of Martial, which one knows not how to
render in English, *Dum tacet hanc loquitur.* I shall end this paper
with that whole epigram, which represents with much humour my
honest friend's condition:

> Let *Rufus* weep, rejoice, stand, sit, or walk,
> Still he can nothing but of *Nævia* talk;
> Let him eat, drink, ask questions, or dispute,
> Still he must speak of *Nævia*, or be mute.
> He writ to his father, ending with this line,
> I am, my lovely *Nævia*, ever thine.

# LAURENCE STERNE

1713–1768

# THE STORY OF LE FEVRE

MY uncle Toby was one evening sitting at his supper, when the landlord of a little inn in the village came into the parlour, with an empty phial in his hand, to beg a glass or two of sack:

" 'Tis for a poor gentleman—I think of the army," said the landlord, " who has been taken ill at my house four days ago, and has never held up his head since, or had a desire to taste anything till just now, that he has a fancy for a glass of sack and a thin toast;—I think, said he, taking his hand from his forehead, it would comfort me.—

" If I could neither beg, borrow, nor buy such a thing," added the landlord, " I would almost steal it for the poor gentleman, he is so ill.—I hope in God he will still mend," continued he,—" we are all of us concerned for him."

" Thou art a good-natured soul, I will answer for thee," cried my uncle Toby, " and thou shalt drink the poor gentleman's health in a glass of sack thyself,—and take a couple of bottles, with my service, and tell him he is heartily welcome to them, and to a dozen more if they will do him good.

" Though I am persuaded," said my uncle Toby, as the landlord shut the door, " he is a very compassionate fellow, Trim, yet I cannot help entertaining a high opinion of his guest too; there must be something more than common in him, that in so short a time should win so much on the affections of his host ":—

" And of his whole family," added the corporal, " for they are all concerned for him."

" Step after him," said my uncle Toby, " do, Trim, and ask if he knows his name."

" I have quite forgot it, truly," said the landlord, coming back into the parlour with the corporal, " but I can ask his son again."

" Has he a son with him then? " said my uncle Toby.

" A boy," replied the landlord, " of about eleven or twelve years of age; but the poor creature has tasted almost as little as his father; he does nothing but mourn and lament for him night and day: he has not stirred from the bedside these two days."

My uncle Toby laid down his knife and fork, and thrust his plate from before him as the landlord gave him the account; and Trim, without being ordered, took it away without saying one word, and in a few minutes after brought him his pipe and tobacco.

"Stay in the room a little," said my uncle Toby. "Trim!" said my uncle Toby, after he had lighted his pipe and smoked about a dozen whiffs—Trim came in front of his master and made his bow—my uncle Toby smoked on, and said no more. "Corporal!" said my uncle Toby; the corporal made his bow—my uncle Toby proceeded no farther, but finished his pipe.

"Trim!" said my uncle Toby, "I have a project in my head, as it is a bad night, of wrapping myself up warm in my roquelaure, and paying a visit to this poor gentleman."

"Your honour's roquelaure," replied the corporal, "has not once been had on since the night before your honour received your wound, when we mounted guard in the trenches before the gate at St. Nicholas; and besides it is so cold and rainy a night, that what with the roquelaure, and what with the weather 'twill be enough to give your honour your death, and bring on your honour's torment in your groin."

"I fear so," replied my uncle Toby; "but I am not at rest in my mind, Trim, since the account the landlord has given me. I wish I had not known so much of this affair," added my uncle Toby, "or that I had known more of it: how shall we manage it?"

"Leave it, an' please your honour, to me," quoth the corporal; "I'll take my hat and stick, and go to the house and reconnoitre, and act accordingly; and I will bring your honour a full account in an hour."

"Thou shalt go, Trim," said my uncle Toby, "and here's a shilling for thee to drink with his servant."

"I shall get it all out of him," said the corporal, shutting the door.

My uncle Toby filled his second pipe; and had it not been that he now and then wandered from the point, with considering whether it was not full as well to have the curtain of the tenaille a straight line as a crooked one, he might be said to have thought of nothing else but poor Le Fevre and his boy the whole time he smoked it.

It was not till my uncle Toby had knocked the ashes out of his third pipe that Corporal Trim returned from the inn, and gave him the following account:—"I despaired at first," said the corporal, "of being able to bring back to your honour any kind of intelligence concerning the poor sick lieutenant."

"Is he in the army then?" said my uncle Toby.

"He is," said the corporal.

"And in what regiment?" said my uncle Toby.

"I'll tell your honour," replied the corporal, "everything straight forwards, as I learned it."

"Then, Trim, I'll fill another pipe," said my uncle Toby, "and not interrupt thee till thou hast done; so sit down at thy ease, Trim, in the window seat, and begin thy story again."

The corporal made his old bow, which generally spoke as plain as a bow could speak it—*your honour is good*:—and having done that, he sat down as he ordered, and began the story to my uncle Toby over again in pretty nearly the same words.

" I despaired at first," said the corporal, " of being able to bring back any intelligence to your honour about the lieutenant and his son; for when I asked where his servant was, from whom I made myself sure of knowing everything which was proper to be asked,——"

" That's a right distinction, Trim," said my uncle Toby.

" I was answered, and please your honour, that he had no servant with him; that he had come to the inn with hired horses, which, on finding himself unable to proceed (to join, I suppose, the regiment), he had dismissed the morning after he came.—If I get better, my dear, said he, as he gave his purse to his son to pay the man, we can hire horses from hence.—But alas! the poor gentleman will never get from hence, said the landlady to me, for I heard the death-watch all night long; and when he dies the youth his son will certainly die with him; for he is broken-hearted already.

" I was hearing this account," continued the corporal, " when the youth came into the kitchen, to order the thin toast the landlord spoke of;—but I will do it for my father myself, said the youth. Pray let me save you the trouble, young gentleman, said I, taking up a fork for that purpose, and offering him a chair to sit down by the fire, whilst I did it.—I believe, sir, said he, very modestly, I can please him best myself.—I am sure, said I, his honour will not like the toast the worse for being toasted by an old soldier. The youth took hold of my hand, and instantly burst into tears."

" Poor youth! " said my uncle Toby, " he has been bred up from an infant in the army, and the name of a soldier, Trim, sounded in his ears like the name of a friend;—I wish I had him here."

" I never, in the longest march," said the corporal, " had so great a mind to my dinner as I had to cry with him for company; what could be the matter with me, an' please your honour? "

" Nothing in the world, Trim," said my uncle Toby, blowing his nose, " but that thou art a good-natured fellow."

" When I gave him the toast," continued the corporal, " I thought it was proper to tell him I was Captain Shandy's servant, and that your honour (though a stranger) was extremely concerned for his father: and that if there was anything in your house or cellar "—(" and thou mightest have added my purse too," said my uncle Toby)—" he was heartily welcome to it: he made a very low bow (which was meant to your honour), but no answer, for his heart was so full—so he went upstairs with the toast.—I warrant you, my dear, said I, as I opened the kitchen door, your father will be well again. Mr. Yorick's curate was smoking a pipe by the kitchen fire; but said not a word, good or bad, to comfort the youth. I thought it wrong," added the corporal.

" I think so too," said my uncle Toby.

" When the lieutenant had taken his glass of sack and toast he felt himself a little revived, and sent down into the kitchen to let me know that in about ten minutes he should be glad if I would step upstairs. I believe, said the landlord, he is going to say his prayers, for there was a book laid upon the chair by his bedside, and as I shut the door I saw his son take up a cushion. I thought, said the curate, that you gentlemen of the army, Mr. Trim, never said your prayers at all.—I heard the poor gentleman say his prayers last night, said the landlady, very devoutly, and with my own ears, or I could not have believed it.—Are you sure of it? replied the curate. A soldier, an' please your reverence, said I, prays as often (of his own accord) as a parson; and when he is fighting for his king, and for his own life, and for his honour too, he has the most reason to pray to God of any one in the whole world."

" 'Twas well said of thee, Trim," said my uncle Toby.

" But when a soldier, said I, an' please your reverence, has been standing for twelve hours together in the trenches, up to his knees in cold water, or engaged, said I, for months together in long and dangerous marches—harassed, perhaps, in his rear to-day—harassing others to-morrow—detached here—countermanded there—resting this night out upon his arms—beat up in his shirt the next—benumbed in his joints—perhaps without straw in his tent to kneel upon—may say his prayers *how* and *when* he can. I believe, said I,—for I was piqued," quoth the corporal, " for the reputation of the army,—I believe, an' please your reverence, said I, that when a soldier gets time to pray, he prays as heartily as a parson, though not with all his fuss and hypocrisy."

" Thou shouldest not have said that, Trim," said my uncle Toby, " for God only knows who is a hypocrite, and who is not: at the great and general review of us all, corporal, at the day of judgment (and not till then), it will be seen who have done their duties in this world, and who have not; and we shall be advanced, Trim, accordingly." " I hope we shall," said Trim.

" It is in the Scripture," said my uncle Toby; " and I will show it thee to-morrow; in the meantime, we may depend upon it, Trim, for our comfort," said my uncle Toby, " that God Almighty is so good and just a governor of the world, that if we have but done our duties in it, it will never be inquired into whether we have done them in a red coat or a black one." " I hope not," said the corporal.

" But go on, Trim," said my uncle Toby, " with thy story."

" When I went up," continued the corporal, " into the lieutenant's room, which I did not do till the expiration of the ten minutes, he was lying in his bed, with his head raised upon his hand, with his elbow upon the pillow, and a clean white cambric handkerchief beside it. The youth was just stooping down to take up the cushion upon which I suppose he had been kneeling. The book was laid upon the bed; and as he rose, in taking up the cushion with one hand, he reached out his other to take it away at the same time.—Let it remain there, my dear, said the lieutenant. He did not offer to speak to me till I had walked up close to his bedside.—If you be Captain Shandy's servant, said he, you must present my thanks to your master, with my little boy's thanks along with them, for his courtesy to me: if he was of Levens', said the lieutenant—I told him your honour was—Then, said he, I served three campaigns with him in Flanders, and remember him,— but 'tis most likely, as I had not the honour of any acquaintance with him, that he knows nothing of me. You will tell him, however, that the person his good-nature has laid under obligation to him is one Le Fevre, a lieutenant in Angus'—but he knows me not, said he a second time, musing :—possibly he may my story, added he—Pray tell the captain I was the ensign at Breda, whose wife was most unfortunately killed with a musket shot, as she lay in my arms in my tent.—I remember the story, an' please your honour, said I, very well. Do you so? said he, wiping his eyes with his handkerchief, then well may I. In saying this he drew a little ring out of his bosom, which seemed tied with a black ribbon about his neck, and kissed it twice. Here, Billy, said he.—The boy flew across the room to the bedside, and falling down upon his knee, took the ring in his hand, and kissed it too, then kissed his father, and sat down upon the bed and wept."

" I wish," said my uncle Toby, with a deep sigh, " I wish, Trim, I was asleep."

" Your honour," replied the corporal, " is too much concerned; shall I pour your honour out a glass of sack to your pipe? "

" Do, Trim," said my uncle Toby.

" I remember," said my uncle Toby, sighing again, " the story of the ensign and his wife, with a circumstance his modesty omitted; and particularly well that he, as well as she, on some account or other (I have forgot what) was universally pitied by the whole regiment;—but finish the story thou art on."

" 'Tis finished already," said the corporal, " for I could stay no longer, so wished his honour a good-night: young Le Fevre rose from off the bed, and saw me to the bottom of the stairs: and as we went down together, told they had come from Ireland, and were on their route to join the regiment in Flanders. But, alas! " said the corporal, " the lieutenant's last day's march is over."

" Then what is to become of his poor boy? " cried my uncle Toby.

It was to my uncle Toby's eternal honour—though I tell it only for the sake of those who, when cooped in betwixt a natural and a positive law, know not for their souls which way in the world to turn themselves—that, notwithstanding my uncle Toby was warmly engaged at that time in carrying on the siege of Dendermond, parallel with the allies, who pressed theirs on so vigorously that they scarce allowed him time to get his dinner:—that nevertheless he gave up Dendermond, though he had already made a lodgment upon the counterscarp;—and bent his whole thoughts towards the private distresses at the inn: and, except that he ordered the garden gate to be bolted up, by which he might be said to have turned the siege of Dendermond into a blockade, he left Dendermond to itself, —to be relieved or not by the French king as the French king thought good; and only considered how he himself should relieve the poor lieutenant and his son. That kind Being, who is a friend to the friendless, shall recompense thee for this.

" Thou hast left this matter short," said my uncle Toby to the corporal, as he was putting him to bed, " and I will tell thee in what, Trim. In the first place, when thou madest an offer of my services to Le Fevre,—as sickness and travelling are both expensive, and thou knewest he was but a poor lieutenant, with a son to subsist as well as himself out of his pay, that thou didst not make an offer to him of my purse; because, had he stood in need, thou knowest, Trim, he had been as welcome to it as myself."

" Your honour knows," said the corporal, " I had no orders."

" True," quoth my uncle Toby,—" thou didst very right, Trim, as a soldier, but certainly very wrong as a man.

" In the second place, for which, indeed, thou hast the same excuse," continued my uncle Toby,—" when thou offeredst him whatever was in my house, thou shouldst have offered him my house too. A sick brother officer should have the best quarters, Trim; and if we had him with us, we could tend and look to him.—— Thou art an excellent nurse thyself, Trim, and what with thy care of him, and the old woman's, and his boy's, and mine together, we might recruit him again at once, and set him upon his legs.——

" In a fortnight or three weeks," added my uncle Toby, smiling, " he might march."

" He will never march, an' please your honour, in this world," said the corporal.

" He *will* march, said my uncle Toby, rising up from the side of the bed, with one shoe off.

" An' please your honour," said the corporal, " he will never march, but to his grave."

" He *shall* march," cried my uncle Toby, marching the foot which had a shoe on, though without advancing an inch, " he shall march to his regiment." " He cannot stand it," said the corporal.

" He shall be supported," said my uncle Toby.

"He'll drop at last," said the corporal, "and what will become of his boy?"

"He shall not drop," said my uncle Toby, firmly.

"A-well-a-day! do what we can for him," said Trim, maintaining his point,—"the poor soul will die."

"He shall not die, by God!" cried my uncle Toby.

The accusing spirit, which flew up to heaven's chancery with the oath, blushed as he gave it in; and the recording angel, as he wrote it down, dropped a tear upon the word, and blotted it out for ever.

My uncle Toby went to his bureau, put his purse into his breeches pocket, and having ordered the corporal to go early in the morning for a physician, he went to bed, and fell asleep.

The sun looked bright the morning after to every eye in the village but Le Fevre's and his afflicted son's; the hand of death pressed heavy upon his eyelids; and hardly could the wheel at the cistern turn round its circle, when my uncle Toby, who had rose up an hour before his wonted time, entered the lieutenant's room, and without preface or apology sat himself down by the chair at the bedside, and independently of all modes and customs opened the curtain in the manner of an old friend and brother officer would have done it, and asked him how he did,—how he had rested in the night,—what was his complaint,—where was his pain,—and what he could do to help him; and, without giving him time to answer any one of the inquiries, went on and told him of the little plan which he had been concerting with the corporal the night before for him.

"You shall go home directly, Le Fevre," said my uncle Toby, "to my house, and we'll send for a doctor to see what's the matter, —and we'll have an apothecary,—and the corporal shall be your nurse;—and I'll be your servant, Le Fevre."

There was a frankness in my uncle Toby—not the effect of familiarity, but the cause of it—which let you at once into his soul, and showed you the goodness of his nature. To this there was something in his looks, and voice, and manner, superadded, which eternally beckoned to the unfortunate to come and take shelter under him, so that before my uncle Toby had half finished the kind offers he was making to the father, had the son insensibly pressed up close to his knees, and had taken hold of the breast of his coat, and was pulling it towards him. The blood and spirits of Le Fevre, which were waxing cold and slow within him, and were retreating to their last citadel, the heart—rallied back,—the film forsook his eyes for a moment;—he looked up wishfully in my uncle Toby's face;—then cast a look upon his boy; and that ligament, fine as it was, was never broken.

Nature instantly ebbed again; the film returned to its place; the pulse fluttered—stopped—went on, throbbed—stopped again— moved—stopped. Shall I go on? No.

# OLIVER GOLDSMITH
1728–1774

# THE HISTORY OF THE MAN IN BLACK

My father, the younger son of a good family, was possessed of a small living in the church. His education was above his fortune, and his generosity greater than his education. Poor as he was, he had his flatterers still poorer than himself; for every dinner he gave them, they returned an equivalent in praise; and this was all he wanted. The same ambition that actuates a monarch at the head of an army, influenced my father at the head of his table; he told the story of the ivy-tree, and that was laughed at; he repeated the jest of the two scholars and one pair of breeches, and the company laughed at that; but the story of Taffy in the sedan chair, was sure to set the table in a roar: thus his pleasure increased in proportion to the pleasure he gave; he loved all the world, and he fancied all the world loved him.

As his fortune was but small, he lived up to the very extent of it; he had no intentions of leaving his children money, for that was dross; he was resolved they should have learning; for learning, he used to observe, was better than silver or gold. For this purpose he undertook to instruct us himself; and took as much pains to form our morals as to improve our understanding. We were told that universal benevolence was what first cemented society; we were taught to consider all the wants of mankind as our own; to regard the *human face divine* with affection and esteem; he wound us up to be mere machines of pity, and rendered us incapable of withstanding the slightest impulse made either by real or fictitious distress; in a word, we were perfectly instructed in the art of *giving away* thousands, before we were taught the more necessary qualifications of *getting* a farthing.

I cannot avoid imagining, that thus refined by his lessons out of all my suspicion, and divested of even all the little cunning which Nature had given me, I resembled, upon my first entrance into the busy and insidious world, one of those gladiators who were exposed with armour in the amphitheatre at Rome. My father, however, who had only seen the world on one side, seemed to triumph in my superior discernment; though my whole stock of wisdom consisted in being able to talk like himself upon subjects that once were useful, because they were then topics of the busy world; but that now were utterly useless, because connected with the busy world no longer.

The first opportunity he had of finding his expectations disappointed, was at the very middling figure I made in the university; he had flattered himself that he should soon see me rising into the foremost rank in literary reputation, but was mortified to find me utterly unnoticed and unknown. His disappointment might have been partly ascribed to his having overrated my talents, and partly to my dislike of mathematical reasonings at a time when my imagination and memory, yet unsatisfied, were more eager after new objects, than desirous of reasoning upon those I knew. This did not, however, please my tutors, who observed indeed, that I was a little dull; but at the same time allowed, that I seemed to be very *good-natured*, and had no harm in me.

After I had resided at college seven years my father died, and left me—his blessing. Thus shoved from shore without ill-nature to protect, or cunning to guide, or proper stores to subsist me in so dangerous a voyage, I was obliged to embark in the wide world at twenty-two. But, in order to settle in life, my friends *advised* (for they always advise when they begin to despise us), they advised me, I say, to go into orders.

To be obliged to wear a long wig, when I liked a short one, or a black coat, when I generally dressed in brown, I thought was such a restraint upon my liberty, that I absolutely rejected the proposal. A priest in England is not the same mortified creature with a bonze in China; with us, not he that fasts best, but eats best, is reckoned the best liver; yet I rejected a life of luxury, indolence, and ease, from no other consideration but that boyish one of dress. So that my friends were now perfectly satisfied I was undone; and yet they thought it a pity for one who had not the least harm in him, and was so very good-natured.

Poverty naturally begets dependence, and I was admitted as flatterer to a great man. At first I was surprised that the situation of a flatterer at a great man's table could be thought disagreeable; there was no great trouble in listening attentively when his lordship spoke, and laughing when he looked round for applause. This even good manners might have obliged me to perform. I found, however, too soon, that his lordship was a greater dunce than myself; and from that very moment flattery was at an end. I now rather aimed at setting him right, than at receiving his absurdities with submission; to flatter those we do not know is an easy task; but to flatter our intimate acquaintances, all whose foibles are strongly in our eye, is drudgery insupportable. Every time I now opened my lips in praise, my falsehood went to my conscience; his lordship soon perceived me to be very unfit for service: I was therefore discharged, my patron at the same time being graciously pleased to observe, that he believed I was tolerably good-natured, and had not the least harm in me.

Disappointed in ambition, I had recourse to love. A young lady, who lived with her aunt, and was possessed of a pretty fortune in her own disposal, had given me, as I fancied, some reason to expect success. The symptoms by which I was guided were striking. She had always laughed with me at her awkward acquaintance, and at her aunt among the number; she always observed, that a man of sense would make a better husband than a fool, and I as constantly applied the observation in my own favour. She continually talked, in my company, of friendship and the beauties of the mind, and spoke of Mr. Shrimp my rival's high-heeled shoes with detestation. These were circumstances which I thought strongly in my favour; so, after resolving and re-resolving, I had courage enough to tell her my mind. Miss heard my proposal with serenity, seeming at the same time to study the figures of her fan. Out at last it came. There was but one small objection to complete our happiness; which was no more than—that she was married three months before to Mr. Shrimp, with high-heeled shoes! By way of consolation, however, she observed that, though I was disappointed in her, my addresses to her aunt would probably kindle her into sensibility; as the old lady always allowed me to be very good-natured, and not to have the least share of harm in me.

Yet, still I had friends, numerous friends, and to them I was resolved to apply. O Friendship! thou fond soother of the human breast, to thee we fly in every calamity; to thee the wretched seek for succour; on thee the care-tired son of misery fondly relies; from thy kind assistance the unfortunate always hopes relief, and may be ever sure of—disappointment. My first application was to a city scrivener, who had frequently offered to lend me money when he knew I did not want it. I informed him that now was the time to put his friendship to the test; that I wanted to borrow a couple of hundreds for a certain occasion, and was resolved to take it up from him.

" And pray, Sir," cried my friend, " do you want all this money? "

" Indeed I never wanted it more," returned I.

" I am sorry for that," cries the scrivener, " with all my heart; for they who want money when they come to borrow, will always want money when they should come to pay."

From him I flew with indignation to one of the best friends I had in the world, and made the same request.

" Indeed, Mr. Drybone," cries my friend, " I always thought it would come to this. You know, Sir, I would not advise you but for your own good; but your conduct has hitherto been ridiculous in the highest degree, and some of your acquaintance always thought you a very silly fellow. Let me see—you want two hundred pounds. Do you only want two hundred, Sir, exactly? ''

'' To confess a truth,'' returned I, '' I shall want three hundred; but then I have another friend from whom I can borrow the rest.''

'' Why, then,'' replied my friend, '' if you would take my advice (and you know I should not presume to advise you but for your own good), I would recommend it to you to borrow the whole sum from that other friend; and then one note will serve for all, you know.''

Poverty now began to come fast upon me; yet instead of growing more provident or cautious as I grew poor, I became every day more indolent and simple. A friend was arrested for fifty pounds; I was unable to extricate him except by becoming his bail. When at liberty he fled from his creditors, and left me to take his place: in prison I expected greater satisfactions than I had enjoyed at large. I hoped to converse with men in this new world, simple and believing like myself, but I found them as cunning and as cautious as those in the world I had left behind. They spunged up my money whilst it lasted, borrowed my coals and never paid for them, and cheated me when I played at cribbage. All this was done because they believed me to be very good-natured, and knew that I had no harm in me.

Upon my first entrance into this mansion, which is to some the abode of despair, I felt no sensations different from those I experienced abroad. I was now on one side of the door, and those who were unconfined were on the other: this was all the difference between us. At first, indeed, I felt some uneasiness, in considering how I should be able to provide this week for the wants of the week ensuing; but after some time, if I found myself sure of eating one day, I never troubled my head how I was to be supplied another. I seized every precarious meal with the utmost good humour; indulged no rants of spleen at my situation; never called down heaven and all the stars to behold me dining upon an half-penny-worth of radishes; my very companions were taught to believe that I liked salad better than mutton. I contented myself with thinking, that all my life I should either eat white bread or brown; considered that all that happened was best; laughed when I was not in pain; took the world as it went, and read Tacitus often, for want of more books and company.

How long I might have continued in this torpid state of simplicity I cannot tell, had I not been roused by seeing an old acquaintance, whom I knew to be a prudent blockhead, preferred to a place in the Government. I now found that I had pursued a wrong track, and that the true way of being able to relieve others, was first to aim at independence myself; my immediate care, therefore, was to leave my present habitation, and make an entire reformation in my conduct and behaviour. For a free, open, undesigning deportment, I put on that of closeness, prudence and economy. One of the most heroic actions I ever performed, and for which I shall praise myself as long as I live, was the refusing half-a-crown to an old acquaintance, at the time when he wanted it, and I had it to spare; for this alone I deserve to be decreed an ovation.

I now, therefore, pursued a course of uninterrupted frugality, seldom wanted a dinner, and was consequently invited to twenty. I soon began to get the character of a saving hunks that had money, and insensibly grew into esteem. Neighbours have asked my advice in the disposal of their daughters, and I have always taken care not to give any. I have contracted a friendship with an alderman, only by observing, that if we take a farthing from a thousand pounds, it will be a thousand pounds no longer. I have been invited to a pawnbroker's table, by pretending to hate gravy; and am now actually upon treaty of marriage with a rich widow, for only having observed that the bread was rising. If ever I am asked a question, whether I know it or not, instead of answering, I only smile and look wise. If a charity is proposed, I go about with the hat, but put nothing in myself. If a wretch solicits my pity, I observe that the world is filled with imposters, and take a certain method of not being deceived, by never relieving. In short, I now find the truest way of finding esteem, even from the indigent, is *to give away nothing, and thus have much in our power to give.*

# THE SOLDIER'S STORY

### OLIVER GOLDSMITH

ACCIDENTALLY meeting some days ago a poor fellow begging at one of the outlets of this town, with a wooden leg, I was curious to learn what had reduced him to his present situation; and after giving him what I thought proper, desired to know the history of his life and misfortunes, and the manner in which he was reduced to his present distress. The disabled soldier, for such he was, with an intrepidity truly British, leaning on his crutch, put himself into an attitude to comply with my request, and gave me his history as follows:—

" As for misfortunes, Sir, I cannot pretend to have gone through more than others. Except the loss of my limb, and my being obliged to beg, I don't know any reason, thank Heaven, that I have to complain; there are some who have lost both legs and an eye: but, thank Heaven, it is not quite so bad with me.

" My father was a labourer in the country, and died when I was five years old; so I was put upon the parish. As he had been a wandering sort of man, the parishioners were not able to tell to what parish I belonged, or where I was born; so they sent me to another parish, and that parish sent me to a third; till at last it was thought I belonged to no parish at all. At length, however, they fixed me. I had some disposition to be a scholar, and had actually learned my letters; but the master of the workhouse put me to business as soon as I was able to handle a mallet.

" Here I lived an easy kind of a life for five years; I only wrought ten hours in the day, and had my meat and drink provided for my labour. It is true, I was not suffered to stir far from the house, for fear I should run away: but what of that? I had the liberty of the whole house, and the yard before the door, and that was enough for me.

" I was next bound out to a farmer, where I was up both early and late, but I ate and drank well, and liked my business well enough, till he died. Being then obliged to provide for myself, I was resolved to go and seek my fortune. Thus I lived, and went from town to town, working when I could get employment, and starving when I could get none; and might have lived so still; but happening one day to go through a field belonging to a magistrate, I spied a hare crossing the path just before me. I believe the devil put it in my head to fling my stick at it: well, what will you have on it? I killed the hare, and was bringing it away in triumph, when the Justice himself met me: he called me a villain, and collaring me, desired I would give an account of myself.

" I began immediately to give a full account of all that I knew of my breed, seed, and generation; but though I gave a very long account, the Justice said, I could give no account of myself; so I was indicted, and found guilty of being poor, and sent to Newgate, in order to be transported to the Plantations.

" People may say this and that of being in gaol; but for my part I found Newgate as agreeable a place as ever I was in, in all my life. I had my belly-full to eat and drink, and did no work; but alas, this kind of life was too good to last for ever! I was taken out of prison after five months, put on board of a ship, and sent off with two hundred more. Our passage was but indifferent, for we were all confined in the hold, and died very fast, for want of sweet air and provisions; but for my part, I did not want meat, because I had a fever all the way: Providence was kind; when provisions grew short, it took away my desire of eating. When we came ashore, we were sold to the planters. I was bound for seven years, and as I was no scholar, for I had forgot my letters, I was obliged to work among the negroes; and served out my time, as in duty bound to do.

" When my time was expired, I worked my passage home, and

glad I was to see Old England again, because I loved my country.
O liberty, liberty, liberty, that is the property of every Englishman, and I will die in its defence.   I was afraid, however, that I
should be indicted for a vagabond once more, so did not much
care to go into the country, but kept about town, and did little
jobs when I could get them.   I was very happy in this manner for
some time; till one evening, coming home from work, two men
knocked me down, and then desired me to stand still.   They belonged to a press-gang; I was carried before the Justice, and as I
could give no account of myself (that was the thing that always
hobbled me) I had my choice left, whether to go on board a
man-of-war, or list for a soldier.   I chose to be a soldier; and in
this post of a gentleman I served two campaigns, was at the battle
in Flanders, and received but one wound through the breast, which
is troublesome till this day.

" When the peace came on, I was discharged; and as I could
not work, because my wound was sometimes painful, I listed for a
landman in the East India Company's service.   I here fought the
French in six pitched battles; and verily believe, that if I could
read or write, our captain would have given me promotion, and
have made me a corporal.   But that was not my good fortune.   I
soon fell sick, and when I became good for nothing, got leave to
return home again with forty pounds in my pocket, which I saved
in the service.   This was at the beginning of the present war, so I
hoped to be set on shore, and to have the pleasure of spending my
money; but the Government wanted men, and I was pressed again,
before ever I could set foot on shore.

" The boatswain found me, as he said, an obstinate fellow: he
swore that I understood my business perfectly well, but that I
pretended sickness merely to be idle; God knows, I knew nothing
of sea-business; he beat me without considering what he was about.
But still my forty pounds was some comfort to me under every
beating: the money was my comfort, and the money I might have
had to this day; but that our ship was taken by the French, and
so I lost it all.

" Our crew was carried into a French prison, and many of them
died, because they were not used to live in a gaol; but for my part,
it was nothing to me, for I was seasoned.   One night, however, as
I was sleeping on the bed of boards, with a warm blanket about
me (for I always loved to lie well), I was awaked by the boatswain,
who had a dark lantern in his hand.

" ' Jack,' says he to me, ' will you knock out the French sentry's
brains? '

" ' I don't care,' says I, striving to keep myself awake, ' if I
lend a hand.'

" ' Then follow me,' says he, ' and I hope we shall do business.'

" So up I got, and tied my blanket, which was all the clothes I had, about my middle, and went with him to fight the Frenchman; we had no arms; but one Englishman is able to beat five French at any time; so we went down to the door, where both the sentries were posted, and rushing upon them, seized their arms in a moment and knocked them down. From thence, nine of us ran together to the quay, and seizing the first boat we met, got out of the harbour, and out to sea; we had not been here three days before we were taken up by an English privateer, who was glad of so many good hands; and we consented to run our chance. However, we had not so much luck as we expected. In three days we fell in with a French man-of-war, of forty guns, while we had but twenty-three; so to it we went. The fight lasted for three hours, and I verily believe we should have taken the Frenchman, but, unfortunately, we lost almost all our men, just as we were going to get the victory. I was once more in the power of the French, and I believe it would have gone hard with me, had I been brought back to my old gaol in Brest; but by good fortune, we were retaken, and carried to England once more.

" I had almost forgot to tell you, that in this last engagement I was wounded in two places; I lost four fingers of the left hand, and my leg was shot off. Had I the good fortune to have lost my leg and use of my hand on board a king's ship, and not a privateer, I should have been entitled to clothing and maintenance during the rest of my life, but that was not my chance; one man is born with a silver spoon in his mouth, and another with a wooden ladle. However, blessed be God, I enjoy good health, and have no enemy in this world that I know of, but the French, and the Justice of Peace."

Thus saying, he limped off, leaving us in admiration of his intrepidity and content.

# ALCANDER AND SEPTIMIUS

### Oliver Goldsmith

ATHENS, even long after the decline of the Roman empire, still continued the seat of learning, politeness, and wisdom. The emperors and generals, who in these periods of approaching ignorance still felt a passion for science, from time to time added to its buildings, or increased its professorships. Theodoric, the Ostrogoth, was of the number: he repaired those schools which barbarity was suffering to fall into decay, and continued those pensions to men of learning which avaricious governors had monopolised to themselves.

In this city, and about this period, Alcander and Septimius were fellow-students together. The one the most subtle reasoner of all the Lyceum; the other the most eloquent speaker in the Academic Grove. Mutual admiration soon begot an acquaintance, and a similitude of disposition made them perfect friends. Their fortunes were nearly equal, their studies the same, and they were natives of the two most celebrated cities in the world; for Alcander was of Athens, Septimius came from Rome.

In this mutual harmony they lived for some time together, when Alcander, after passing the first part of his youth in the indolence of philosophy, thought at length of entering into the busy world, and as a step previous to this, placed his affections on Hypatia, a lady of exquisite beauty. Hypatia showed no dislike to his addresses. The day of their intended nuptials was fixed, the previous ceremonies were performed, and nothing now remained but her being conducted in triumph to the apartment of the intended bridegroom.

An exultation in his own happiness, or his being unable to enjoy any satisfaction without making his friend Septimius a partner, prevailed upon him to introduce his mistress to his fellow-student, which he did with all the gaiety of a man who found himself equally happy in friendship and love. But this was an interview fatal to the peace of both; for Septimius no sooner saw her but he was smit with an involuntary passion. He used every effort, but in vain, to suppress desires at once so imprudent and unjust. He retired to his apartment in inexpressible agony; and the emotions of his mind in a short time became so strong, that they brought on a fever, which the physicians judged incurable.

During this illness Alcander watched him with all the anxiety of fondness, and brought his mistress to join in those amiable offices of friendship. The sagacity of the physicians, by this means, soon discovered the cause of their patient's disorder; and Alcander, being apprised of their discovery, at length extorted a confession from the reluctant dying lover.

It would but delay the narrative to describe the conflict between love and friendship in the breast of Alcander on this occasion; it is enough to say that the Athenians were at this time arrived at such refinement in morals, that every virtue was carried to excess. In short, forgetful of his own felicity, he gave up his intended bride, in all her charms, to the young Roman. They were married privately by his connivance; and this unlooked-for change of fortune wrought as unexpected a change in the constitution of the now happy Septimius. In a few days he was perfectly recovered, and set out with his fair partner for Rome. Here, by an exertion of those talents of which he was so eminently possessed, he in a few years arrived at the highest dignities of the state, and was constituted the city judge, or pretor.

Meanwhile Alcander not only felt the pain of being separated from his friend and mistress, but a prosecution was also commenced against him by the relations of Hypatia, for his having basely given her up, as was suggested, for money. Neither his innocence of the crime laid to his charge, nor his eloquence in his own defence, was able to withstand the influence of a powerful party. He was cast, and condemned to pay an enormous fine. Unable to raise so large a sum at the time appointed, his possessions were confiscated, himself stripped of the habit of freedom, exposed in the market-place, and sold as a slave to the highest bidder.

A merchant of Thrace becoming his purchaser, Alcander, with some other companions of distress, was carried into that region of desolation and sterility. His stated employment was to follow the herds of an imperious master; and his skill in hunting was all that was allowed him to supply a precarious subsistence. Condemned to hopeless servitude, every morning waked him to a renewal of famine or toil, and every change of season served but to aggravate his unsheltered distress. Nothing but death or flight was left him, and almost certain death was the consequence of his attempting to flee. After some years of bondage, however, an opportunity of escaping offered: he embraced it with ardour, and travelling by night, and lodging in caverns by day, to shorten a long story, he at last arrived in Rome. The day of Alcander's arrival Septimius sat in the forum administering justice; and hither our wanderer came, expecting to be instantly known and publicly acknowledged. Here he stood the whole day among the crowd, watching the eyes of the judge, and expecting to be taken notice of; but so much was he altered by a long succession of hardships, that he passed entirely without notice; and in the evening, when he was going up to the pretor's chair, he was brutally repulsed by the attending lictors. The attention of the poor is generally driven from one ungrateful object to another; night coming on, he now found himself under a necessity of seeking a place to lie in, and yet knew not where to apply. All emaciated and in rags as he was, none of the citizens would harbour so much wretchedness, and sleeping in the streets might be attended with interruption or danger: in short, he was obliged to take up his lodging in one of the tombs without the city, the usual retreat of guilt, poverty, or despair.

In this mansion of horror, laying his head upon an inverted urn, he forgot his miseries for a while in sleep; and virtue found on this flinty couch more ease than down can supply to the guilty.

It was midnight when two robbers came to make this cave their retreat, but happening to disagree about the division of their plunder, one of them stabbed the other to the heart, and left him weltering in blood at the entrance. In these circumstances he was found next morning, and this naturally induced a further inquiry.

The alarm was spread, the cave was examined, Alcander was found sleeping, and immediately apprehended and accused of robbery and murder. The circumstances against him were strong, and the wretchedness of his appearance confirmed suspicion. Misfortune and he were now so long acquainted, that he at last became regardless of life. He detested a world where he had found only ingratitude, falsehood, and cruelty, and was determined to make no defence. Thus, lowering with resolution, he was dragged, bound with cords, before the tribunal of Septimius. The proofs were positive against him, and he offered nothing in his own vindication; the judge, therefore, was proceeding to doom him to a most cruel and ignominious death, when, as if illumined by a ray from heaven, he discovered, through all his misery, the features, though dim with sorrow, of his long-lost, loved Alcander. It is impossible to describe his joy and his pain on this strange occasion; happy in once more seeing the person he most loved on earth, distressed at finding him in such circumstances. Thus agitated by contending passions, he flew from his tribunal, and, falling on the neck of his dear benefactor, burst into an agony of distress. The attention of the multitude was soon, however, divided by another object. The robber who had been really guilty was apprehended selling his plunder, and, struck with a panic, confessed his crime. He was brought bound to the same tribunal, and acquitted every other person of any partnership in his guilt. Need the sequel be related? Alcander was acquitted, shared the friendship and the honours of his friend Septimius, lived afterwards in happiness and ease, and left it to be engraved on his tomb, that " no circumstances are so desperate which Providence may not relieve."

# MARIA EDGEWORTH

1767–1849

# THE PURPLE JAR

ROSAMOND, a little girl about seven years old, was walking with her mother in the streets of London. As she passed along she looked in at the windows of several shops, and saw a great variety of different sorts of things, of which she did not know the use, or even the names. She wished to stop to look at them, but there was a great number of people in the streets, and a great many carts, carriages, and wheelbarrows, and she was afraid to let go her mother's hand.

" Oh, mother, how happy I should be," she said, as she passed a toy-shop, " if I had all these pretty things! "

" What, all! Do you wish for them all, Rosamond? "

" Yes, mamma, all."

As she spoke they came to a milliner's shop, the windows of which were decorated with ribands and lace, and festoons of artificial flowers.

" Oh, mamma, what beautiful roses! Won't you buy some of them? "

" No, my dear."

" Why? "

" Because I don't want them, my dear."

They went a little further, and came to another shop, which caught Rosamond's eye. It was a jeweller's shop, and in it were a great many pretty baubles, ranged in drawers behind glass.

" Mamma, will you buy some of these? "

" Which of them, Rosamond? "

" Which? I don't know which; any of them will do, for they are all pretty."

" Yes, they are all pretty, but of what use would they be to me? "

" Use! Oh, I am sure you could find some use or other for them if you would only buy them first."

" But I would rather find out the use first."

" Well, then, mamma, there are buckles; you know that buckles are useful things, very useful things."

43

" I have a pair of buckles; I don't want another pair," said her mother, and walked on.

Rosamond was very sorry that her mother wanted nothing. Presently, however, they came to a shop which appeared to her far more beautiful than the rest. It was a chemist's shop, but she did not know that.

" Oh, mother, oh! " cried she, pulling her mother's hand; " look, look! blue, green, red, yellow, and purple! Oh, mamma, what beautiful things! Won't you buy some of these? "

Still her mother answered as before, " Of what use would they be to me, Rosamond? "

" You might put flowers in them, mamma, and they would look so pretty on the chimney-piece. I wish I had one of them."

" You have a flower-pot," said her mother, " and that is not a flower-pot."

" But I would use it for a flower-pot, mamma, you know."

" Perhaps if you were to see it nearer, if you were to examine it, you might be disappointed."

" No, indeed, I'm sure I should not; I should like it exceedingly."

Rosamond kept her head turned to look at the purple vase till she could see it no longer.

" Then, mother," said she, after a pause, " perhaps you have no money."

" Yes, I have."

" Dear me, if I had money I would buy roses and boxes and buckles and purple flower-pots and everything." Rosamond was obliged to pause in the midst of her speech.

" Oh, mamma, would you stop a minute for me? I have got a stone in my shoe; it hurts me very much."

" How came there to be a stone in your shoe? "

" Because of this great hole, mamma—it comes in there; my shoes are quite worn out. I wish you would be so very good as to give me another pair."

" Nay, Rosamond, but I have not money enough to buy shoes and flower-pots and buckles and boxes and everything."

Rosamond thought that was a great pity. But now her foot, which had been hurt by the stone, began to give her so much pain that she was obliged to hop every other step, and she could think of nothing else. They came to a shoemaker's shop soon afterwards.

" There, there! Mamma, there are shoes; there are little shoes that would just fit me, and you know shoes would be really of use to me."

" Yes, so they would, Rosamond. Come in."

She followed her mother into the shop.

Mr. Sole, the shoemaker, had a great many customers, and this shop was full, so they were obliged to wait.

" Well, Rosamond," said her mother, " you don't think this shop so pretty as the rest? "

" No, not nearly; it is black and dark, and there are nothing but shoes all round; and, besides, there's a very disagreeable smell."

" That smell is the smell of new leather."

" Is it? Oh! " said Rosamond, looking round, " there is a pair of little shoes; they'll just fit me, I'm sure."

" Perhaps they might; but you cannot be sure till you have tried them on, any more than you can be quite sure that you would like the purple vase *exceedingly,* till you have examined it more attentively."

" Why, I don't know about the shoes, certainly, till I have tried, but, mamma, I am quite sure that I should like the flower-pot."

" Well, which would you rather have, a jar or a pair of shoes? I will buy either for you."

" Dear mamma, thank you—but if you could buy both? "

" No, not both."

" Then the jar, if you please."

" But I should tell you, that in that case I shall not give you another pair of shoes this month."

" This month! that's a very long time indeed! You can't think how these hurt me; I believe I'd better have the new shoes. Yet, that purple flower-pot. Oh, indeed, mamma, these shoes are not so very, very bad! I think I might wear them a little longer, and the month will soon be over. I can make them last till the end of the month, can't I? Don't you think so, mamma? "

" Nay, my dear, I want you to think for yourself; you will have time enough to consider the matter whilst I speak to Mr. Sole about my clogs."

Mr. Sole was by this time at leisure, and whilst her mother was speaking to him, Rosamond stood in profound meditation, with one shoe on and the other in her hand.

" Well, my dear, have you decided? "

" Mamma!—yes—I believe I have. If you please, I should like to have the flower-pot; that is, if you won't think me very silly, mamma."

" Why, as to that I can't promise you, Rosamond; but, when you have to judge for yourself, you should choose what would make you happy, and then it would not signify who thought you silly."

" Then, mamma, if that's all, I'm sure the flower-pot would make me happy," said she, putting on her old shoe again; " so I choose the flower-pot."

" Very well, you shall have it; clasp your shoe and come home."

Rosamond clasped her shoe and ran after her mother. It was not long before the shoe came down at the heel, and many times she was obliged to stop to take the stones out of it, and she often limped with pain! But still the thoughts of the purple flower-pot prevailed, and she persisted in her choice.

When they came to the shop with the large window, Rosamond felt much pleasure upon hearing her mother desire the servant, who was with them, to buy the purple jar and bring it home. He had other commissions, so he did not return with them. Rosamond, as soon as she got in, ran to gather all her own flowers, which she kept in a corner of her mother's garden.

" I am afraid they'll be dead before the flower-pot comes, Rosamond," said her mother to her, as she came in with the flowers in her lap.

" No, indeed, mamma, it will come home very soon, I daresay. I shall be very happy putting them into the purple flower-pot."

" I hope so, my dear."

The servant was much longer returning home than Rosamond had expected; but at length he came, and brought with him the long-wished-for jar. The moment it was set down upon the table, Rosamond ran up to it with an exclamation of joy; " I may have it now, mamma? "

" Yes, my dear, it is yours."

Rosamond poured the flowers from her lap upon the carpet and seized the purple flower-pot.

" Oh, dear, mother! " cried she, as soon as she had taken off the top, " but there's something dark in it which smells disagreeably. What is it? I didn't want this black stuff."

" Nor I, my dear."

" But what shall I do with it, mamma? "

" That I cannot tell."

" It will be of no use to me, mamma."

" That I cannot help."

" But I must pour it out and fill the flower-pot with water."

" As you please, my dear. That was more than I promised you, my dear; but I will lend you a bowl."

The bowl was produced, and Rosamond proceeded to empty the purple vase. But she experienced much surprise and disappointment on finding, when it was entirely empty, that it was no longer a *purple* vase. It was a plain white glass jar, which had appeared to have that beautiful colour merely from the liquor with which it had been filled.

Little Rosamond burst into tears.

" Why should you cry, my dear? " said her mother; " it will be of as much use to you now as ever for a flower-pot."

" But it won't look so pretty on the chimney-piece. I am sure, if I had known that it was not really purple, I should not have wished to have it so much."

" But didn't I tell you that you had not examined it; and that perhaps you would be disappointed? "

" And so I am disappointed indeed. I wish I had believed you at once. Now I had much rather have the shoes, for I shall not be able to walk all this month; even walking home that little way hurt me exceedingly. Mamma, I will give you the flower-pot back again, and that purple stuff and all, if only you'll give me the shoes."

" No, Rosamond; you must abide by your own choice; and now the best thing you can possibly do is to bear your disappointment with good humour."

" I will bear it as well as I can," said Rosamond, wiping her eyes, and she began slowly and sorrowfully to fill the vase with flowers.

But Rosamond's disappointment did not end here. Many were the difficulties and distresses into which her imprudent choice brought her before the end of the month.

Every day her shoes grew worse and worse, till at last she could neither run, dance, jump, nor walk in them.

Whenever Rosamond was called to see anything, she was detained pulling her shoes up at the heels, and was sure to be late.

Whenever her mother was going out to walk, she could not take Rosamond with her, for Rosamond had no soles to her shoes; and at length, on the very last day of the month, it happened that her father proposed to take her with her brother to a glass-house, which she had long wished to see. She was very happy; but, when she was quite ready, had her hat and gloves on, and was making haste downstairs to her brother and father, who were waiting for her at the hall door, the shoe dropped off. She put it on again in a great hurry, but, as she was going across the hall, her father turned round.

" Why are you walking slip-shod? No one must walk slip-shod with me. Why, Rosamond," said he, looking at her shoes with disgust, " I thought that you were always neat; go, I cannot take you with me."

Rosamond coloured and retired.

" Oh, mamma," said she, as she took off her hat, " how I wish that I had chosen the shoes! They would have been of so much more use to me than that jar; however, I am sure, no, not quite sure, but I hope I shall be wiser another time."

# WILLIAM MAGINN
1793-1842

# THE CITY OF THE DEMONS

In days of yore there lived in the flourishing city of Cairo a Hebrew rabbi, by name Jochonan, who was the most learned of his nation. His fame went over the East, and the most distant people sent their young men to imbibe wisdom from his lips. He was deeply skilled in the traditions of the fathers, and his word on a disputed point was decisive. He was pious, just, temperate, and strict; but he had one vice—a love of gold had seized upon his heart, and he opened not his hand to the poor. Yet he was wealthy above most, his wisdom being to him the source of riches. The Hebrews of the city were grieved at this blemish on the wisest of their people; but though the elders of the tribes continued to reverence him for his fame, the women and children of Cairo called him by no other name than that of Rabbi Jochonan the miser.

None knew so well as he the ceremonies necessary for initiation into the religion of Moses; and consequently the exercise of those solemn offices was to him another source of gain. One day, as he walked in the fields about Cairo, conversing with a youth on the interpretation of the law, it so happened that the angel of death smote the young man suddenly, and he fell dead before the feet of the Rabbi, even while he was yet speaking. When the Rabbi found that the youth was dead, he rent his garments and glorified the Lord. But his heart was touched, and the thoughts of death troubled him in the visions of the night. He felt uneasy when he reflected on his hardness to the poor, and he said, " Blessed be the name of the Lord! The first good thing that I am asked to do, in that holy name, will I perform "; but he sighed, for he feared that some one might ask of him a portion of his gold. While yet he thought upon these things, there came a loud cry at his gate.

" Awake, thou sleeper! " said the voice, " awake! A child is in danger of death, and the mother hath sent me for thee, that thou mayst do thine office."

" The night is dark and gloomy," said the Rabbi, coming to his casement, " and mine age is great; are there not younger men than I in Cairo? "

" For thee only, Rabbi Jochonan, whom some call the wise, but whom others call Rabbi Jochonan the miser, was I sent. Here is gold," said he, taking out a purse of sequins, " I want not thy labour for nothing. I adjure thee to come, in the name of the living God."

So the Rabbi thought upon the vow he had just made, and he groaned in spirit, for the purse sounded heavy.

" As thou hast adjured me by that name, I go with thee," said he to the man, " but I hope the distance is not far. Put up thy gold."

" The place is at hand," said the stranger, who was a gallant youth in magnificent attire. " Be speedy, for time presses."

Jochonan arose, dressed himself, and accompanied the stranger, after having carefully locked up all the doors of his house, and deposited his keys in a secret place—at which the stranger smiled.

" I never remember," said the Rabbi, " so dark a night. Be thou to me as a guide, for I can hardly see the way."

" I know it well," replied the stranger with a sigh, " it is a way much frequented, and travelled hourly by many; lean upon mine arm, and fear not." They journeyed on; and though the darkness was great, yet the Rabbi could see when it occasionally brightened that he was in a place strange to him. " I thought," said he, " I knew all the country for leagues about Cairo, yet I know not where I am. I hope, young man," said he to his companion, " that thou hast not missed the way "; and his heart misgave him.

" Fear not," returned the stranger. " Your journey is even now done," and, as he spoke, the feet of the Rabbi slipped from under him, and he rolled down a great height. When he recovered, he found that his companion had fallen also, and stood by his side.

" Nay, young man," said the Rabbi, " if thus thou sportest with the grey hairs of age, thy days are numbered. Woe unto him who insults the hoary head! " The stranger made an excuse, and they journeyed on some little further in silence. The darkness grew less, and the astonished Rabbi, lifting up his eyes, found that they had come to the gates of a city which he had never before seen. Yet he knew all the cities of the land of Egypt, and he had walked but half an hour from his dwelling in Cairo. So he knew not what to think, but followed the man with trembling.

They soon entered the gates of the city, which was lighted up as if there were a festival in every house. The streets were full of revellers, and nothing but a sound of joy could be heard. But when Jochonan looked upon their faces, they were the faces of men pained within; and he saw, by the marks they bore, that they were Mazikin.[1] He was terrified in his soul; and, by the light of

[1] Demons.

the torches, he looked also upon the face of his companion, and, behold! he saw upon him too the mark that showed him to be a Demon. The Rabbi feared excessively—almost to fainting; but he thought it better to be silent, and sadly he followed his guide, who brought him to a splendid house, in the most magnificent quarter of the city.

" Enter here," said the Demon to Jochonan, " for this house is mine. The lady and the child are in the upper chamber "; and, accordingly, the sorrowful Rabbi ascended the stair to find them.

The lady, whose dazzling beauty was shrouded by melancholy beyond hope, lay in bed; the child, in rich raiment, slumbered on the lap of the nurse, by her side.

" I have brought to thee, light of my eyes! " said the Demon, " Rebecca, beloved of my soul! I have brought thee Rabbi Jochonan the wise, for whom thou didst desire. Let him, then, speedily begin his office; I shall fetch all things necessary, for he is in haste to depart."

He smiled bitterly as he said these words, looking at the Rabbi; and left the room, followed by the nurse.

When Jochonan and the lady were alone, she turned in the bed towards him, and said: " Unhappy man that thou art! knowest thou where thou hast been brought? "

" I do," said he, with a heavy groan; " I know that I am in a city of the Mazikin."

" Know then, further," said she, and the tears gushed from eyes brighter than the diamond, " know then, further, that no one is ever brought here unless he hath sinned before the Lord. What my sin hath been imports not to thee, and I seek not to know thine. But here thou remainest for ever—lost, even as I am lost." And she wept again. The Rabbi dashed his turban on the ground, and tearing his hair, exclaimed, " Woe is me! Who art thou, woman, that speakest to me thus? "

" I am a Hebrew woman," said she, " the daughter of a doctor of the laws, in the city of Bagdad; and being brought hither, it matters not how, I am married to a prince among the Mazikin, even him who was sent for thee. And that child, whom thou sawest, is our first-born, and I could not bear the thought that the soul of our innocent babe should perish. I therefore besought my husband to try to bring hither a priest, that the law of Moses (blessed be his memory!) should be done; and thy fame, which has spread to Bagdad, and lands further towards the rising of the sun, made me think of thee. Now my husband, though great among the Mazikin, is more just than the other Demons; and he loves me, whom he hath ruined, with a love of despair. So he said that the name of Jochonan the wise was familiar unto him, and that he knew thou wouldst not be able to refuse. What thou hast done, to give him power over thee, is known to thyself."

" I swear, before Heaven," said the Rabbi, " that I have ever diligently kept the law, and walked steadfastly according to the traditions of our fathers from the day of my youth upward. I have wronged no man in word or deed, and I have daily worshipped the Lord; minutely performing all the ceremonies thereto needful."

" Nay," said the lady, " all this thou mightest have done, and more, and yet be in the power of the Demons. But time passes, for I hear the foot of my husband mounting the stair. There is one chance of thine escape."

" What is that? O lady of beauty! " said the agonised Rabbi.

" Eat not, drink not, nor take fee or reward while here; and as long as thou canst do thus, the Mazikin have no power over thee, dead or alive. Have courage, and persevere."

As she ceased from speaking, her husband entered the room, followed by the nurse, who bore all things requisite for the ministration of the Rabbi. With a heavy heart he performed his duty, and the child was numbered among the faithful. But when, as usual, at the conclusion of the ceremony, the wine was handed round to be tasted by the child, the mother, and the Rabbi, he refused it, when it came to him, saying:

" Spare me, my lord, for I have made a vow that I fast this day; and I will eat not, neither will I drink."

" Be it as thou pleasest," said the Demon; " I will not that thou shouldst break thy vow "; and he laughed aloud.

So the poor Rabbi was taken into a chamber looking into a garden, where he passed the remainder of the night and the day, weeping and praying to the Lord that He would deliver him from the city of Demons. But when the twelfth hour came, and the sun was set, the Prince of the Mazikin came again unto him and said:

" Eat now, I pray thee, for the day of thy vow is past "; and he set meat before him.

" Pardon again thy servant, my lord," said Jochonan, " in this thing. I have another vow for this day also. I pray thee be not angry with thy servant."

" I am not angry," said the Demon; " be it as thou pleasest, I respect thy vow ": and he laughed louder than before.

So the Rabbi sat another day in his chamber by the garden, weeping and praying. And when the sun had gone behind the hills the Prince of the Mazikin again stood before him, and said:

" Eat now, for thou must be an hungered. It was a sore vow of thine "; and he offered him daintier meats.

And Jochonan felt a strong desire to eat, but he prayed inwardly to the Lord, and the temptation passed, and he answered:

" Excuse thy servant yet a third time, my lord, that I eat not. I have renewed my vow."

" Be it so then," said the other; " arise, and follow me."

The Demon took a torch in his hand, and led the Rabbi through
winding passages of his palace to the door of a lofty chamber,
which he opened with a key that he took from a niche in the
wall.   On entering the room Jochonan saw that it was of solid
silver, floor, ceiling, walls, even to the threshold and the door-
posts.   And the curiously-carved roof and borders of the ceiling
shone in the torch-light as if they were the fanciful work of frost.
In the midst were heaps of silver money, piled up in immense urns
of the same metal, even over the brim.

" Thou hast done me a serviceable act, Rabbi," said the
Demon;   " take of these what thou pleasest; aye, were it the
whole."

" I cannot, my lord," said Jochonan.   " I was adjured by thee
to come hither in the name of God; and in that name I came, not
for fee or for reward."

" Follow me," said the Prince of the Mazikin; and Jochonan
did so into an inner chamber.   It was of gold, as the other was of
silver.   Its golden roof was supported by pillars and pilasters of
gold, resting upon a golden floor.   The treasures of the kings
of the earth would not purchase one of the four-and-twenty vessels
of golden coins which were disposed in six rows along the room.
No wonder! for they were filled by the constant labours of the
Demons of the mine.   The heart of Jochonan was moved by avarice
when he saw them shining in yellow light, like the autumnal sun,
as they reflected the beams of the torch.   But God enabled him
to persevere.

" These are thine," said the Demon; " one of the vessels which
thou beholdest would make thee richest of the sons of men—and
I give thee them all."

But Jochonan refused again; and the Prince of the Mazikin
opened the door of a third chamber, which was called the Hall
of Diamonds.   When the Rabbi entered he screamed aloud, and
put his hands over his eyes, for the lustre of the jewels dazzled him,
as if he had looked upon the noonday sun.   In vases of agate were
heaped diamonds beyond numeration, the smallest of which was
larger than a pigeon's egg.   On alabaster tables lay amethysts,
topazes, rubies, beryls, and all other precious stones, wrought by
the hands of skilful artists, beyond power of computation.   The
room was lighted by a carbuncle, which from the end of the hall
poured its ever-living light, brighter than the rays of noontide,
but cooler than the gentle radiance of the dewy moon.   This was
a sore trial on the Rabbi; but he was strengthened from above,
and he refused again.

" Thou knowest me then, I perceive, O Jochonan, son of Ben-
David," said the Prince of the Mazikin; " I am a Demon who would
tempt thee to destruction.   As thou hast withstood so far, I tempt

thee no more.  Thou hast done a service which, though I value it
not, is acceptable in the sight of her whose love is dearer to me
than the light of life.  Sad has been that love to thee, my Rebecca!
Why should I do that which would make thy cureless grief more
grievous?  You have yet another chamber to see," said he to
Jochonan, who had closed his eyes, and was praying fervently to
the Lord, beating his breast.

Far different from the other chambers, the one into which the
Rabbi was next introduced was a mean and paltry apartment
without furniture.  On its filthy walls hung innumerable bunches
of rusty keys of all sizes, disposed without order.  Among them,
to the astonishment of Jochonan, hung the keys of his own house,
those which he had put to hide when he came on this miserable
journey, and he gazed upon them intently.

" What dost thou see," said the Demon, " that makes thee look
so eagerly?    Can he who has refused silver, and gold, and
diamonds, be moved by a paltry bunch of rusty iron? "

" They are mine own, my lord," said the Rabbi, " them will I
take if they be offered me."

" Take them, then," said the Demon, putting them into his
hand; " thou mayst depart.  But, Rabbi, open not thy house only
when thou returnest to Cairo, but thy heart also.  That thou didst
not open it before was that which gave me power over thee.  It
was well that thou didst one act of charity in coming with me
without reward, for it has been thy salvation.  Be no more Rabbi
Jochonan the miser."

The Rabbi bowed to the ground, and blessed the Lord for his
escape.  " But how," said he, " am I to return, for I know not
the way? "

" Close thine eyes," said the Demon.  He did so, and, in the
space of a moment, heard the voice of the Prince of the Mazikin
ordering him to open them again.  And behold, when he opened
them, he stood in the centre of his own chamber, in his house at
Cairo, with the keys in his hand.

When he recovered from his surprise, and had offered thanks-
givings to God, he opened his house and his heart also.  He gave
alms to the poor, he cheered the heart of the widow, and lightened
the destitution of the orphan.  His hospitable board was open to
the stranger, and his purse was at the service of all who needed
to share it.  His life was a perpetual act of benevolence, and the
blessings showered upon him by all were returned bountifully
upon him by the hand of God.

But people wondered, and said, " Is not this the man who was
called Rabbi Jochonan the miser?   What hath made the change? "

And it became a saying in Cairo.  When it came to the ears of
the Rabbi he called his friends together, and he avowed his former
love of gold, and the danger to which it had exposed him, relating

all which has been above told, in the hall of the new palace that he built by the side of the river, on the left hand, as thou goest down the course of the great stream. And wise men, who were scribes, wrote it down from his mouth, for the memory of mankind, that they might profit thereby. And a venerable man, with a beard of snow, who had read it in these books, and at whose feet I sat, that I might learn the wisdom of the old time, told it to me.

And I write it in the tongue of England, the merry and the free, on the tenth day of the month Nisan, in the year according to the lesser supputation, five hundred ninety and seven, that thou mayst learn good thereof. If not, the fault be upon thee.

# WILLIAM HAMILTON MAXWELL
### 1792-1850

# FRANK KENNEDY

MY father left the carabineers some years before the Irish rebellion of ninety-eight. Like greater warriors, the crop of laurels he collected in that celebrated corps was but a short one. It is true he had seen service: his sword, like Butler's knight's, of " passing worth," had been unsheathed in executing " warrants and exigents "; and more than once he had stormed a private distillery, under the leading of a desperate gauger.

He was, however, a stout slashing-looking fellow, and found favour in my mother's sight. She had reached the wrong side of thirty; consequently she made but a short resistance, and bestowed her hand and fortune on the bold dragoon. My mother was an heiress, but the estate of Killnacoppal owed " a trifle of money ": now *a trifle* in Connaught is sometimes a sweeping sum; and you cannot safely calculate on rents in Connemara being paid exactly to the day.

I never exhibited precocity of intellect; but before I was sixteen I discovered that our establishment occasionally suffered from a scarcity of specie. At these times my father was sure to be afflicted with cold or rheumatism, and never left the house; and I suppose, for fear of disturbing him, the hall door was but seldom opened, and then only to a particular friend; while an ill-favoured tradesman or suspicious-looking stranger received their commands in the briefest manner from an upper window.

What was to be done with me had cruelly puzzled both my parents: and whether I should ornament the church, or benefit the revenue, was for a long time under consideration. The law, however, held out more promising prospects than either; and it was decided that I should be bound to an attorney.

Duncan Davidson, of Dorset Street, Dublin, was married to my father's sister. He was of Scotch descent, and like that " thinking people " from whom he sprung, he held " a hard grip of the main chance." Duncan was wealthy and childless, and if he could be induced to bring me up at his feet, God knows what might be the consequence. My father accordingly made the application, and the gracious Duncan consented to receive me for a time *on trial*.

What a bustle there was in Killnacoppal when my uncle's letter arrived! Due preparations were made for my departure; and as the term of my absence was computed at seven years, I had to take a formal and affectionate leave of my relatives to the fifteenth degree of consanguinity. My aunt Macan, whose cat's leg I had unfortunately dislocated, and who had not spoken to me since Candlemas, was induced to relent on the occasion, and favoured me with her blessing and a one-pound note, although she had often declared she never could banish the idea from her mind but that I should travel at the public expense, if my career were not finished in a more summary manner.

I arrived safely in Dublin—and awful were my feelings when first ushered into the presence of my uncle Duncan. He was a short fat man, in a brown coat and flax-coloured scratch-wig, perched upon a high office stool. Considering his dimensions, I used to marvel much how he managed to get there. Holding out his forefinger, which I dutifully grasped, he told me to be steady and attentive, and that my aunt would be happy to see me upstairs. On leaving the room, I heard him softly remark to the head clerk, that he did not much like my appearance, for that I had " a wild eye in my head."

I was duly put to the desk, and the course of trial was not flattering to me, or satisfactory to my intended master. It was allowed on all hands that my writing was abominable; and my spelling, being untrammelled by rules, was found in many material points to differ from modern orthographers. Nor was I more successful in comparing deeds—my desk and stool were unluckily placed beside a window which looked into a narrow court, and a straw-bonnet maker occupied the opposite apartment. She was pretty, and I was naturally polite—and who with a rosy cheek before him would waste a look upon a tawny skin of parchment?  I mentally consigned the *deed* to the devil, and let the copy loose upon the world " with all *its* imperfections on its head."

The first trial was nearly conclusive—for never before had such a lame and lamentable document issued from the office of the punctilious Duncan. I had there omitted setting forth " one hundred dove-cots," and, for ought I know, left out " one hundred castles," to keep them company. My uncle almost dropped from his perch at the discovery; and Counsellor Roundabout was heard to remark that a man's life was not safe in the hands of such a delinquent. I was on the point of getting my *congé*, and free permission to return to the place from whence I came; but my aunt—good easy woman —interfered, and Duncan consented to give me a farther trial, and employ me to transport his bag to the courts and his briefs to the lawyer.

Any drudgery for me but the desk. With suitable instructions the bag was confided to me, and for three days it came back safely. On the fourth evening I was returning; the bag was unusually full, and so had been my uncle's admonitions for its security. I had got half-way down Capel Street, when whom should I see on the other side of the way but Slasher Mac Tigue?

The Slasher was five akin to my mother, and allowed to be the greatest buck at the last fair of Ballinasloe—and would he acknowledge me, loaded as I was like a Jew clothesman? What was to be done? I slipped the accursed bag to a ragged boy—promised him some halfpence for his trouble—prudently assured him that his cargo was invaluable—told him to wait for me at the corner, and next moment was across the street, with a fast hold of the Slasher's right hand.

The Slasher—peace to his ashes! for he was shot *stone dead* in the Phœnix Park—we never well understood the quarrel in Connemara, and it was said there that the poor man himself was not thoroughly informed on the subject—appeared determined to support his justly-acquired reputation at the late fair of Ballinasloe. Not an eye in Capel Street but was turned on him as he swaggered past. His jockey boots—I must begin below—were in the newest style; the top sprang from the ankle-bone, and was met midleg by short tights of tea-coloured leather; three smoothing-iron seals and a chain that would manacle a deserter dangled from the fob; his vest was of amber kerseymere, gracefully sprinkled with stars and shamrocks; his coat sky-blue, with basket buttons, relieved judiciously with a purple neckcloth, and doeskin gloves; while a conical hat with a leaf full seven inches broad topped all. A feeble imitation of the latter article may still be seen by the curious, in a hatter's window, No. 71 in the Strand, with a label affixed thereto, denominating it " *Neck or Nothing.*"

Lord, how proud I felt when the Slasher tucked me under his arm! We had already taken two turns—the admiration of a crowded thoroughfare—when I looked round for my bag-holder; but he was not visible. I left my kinsman hastily, ran up and down the street, looked round the corners, peered into all the public-houses; but neither bag nor boy was there. I recollected my uncle's name and address were written on it, and the urchin might have mistaken his instructions and carried the bag home. Off I ran, tumbled an apple basket in Bolton Street, and spite of threats and curses, held on my desperate course, until I found myself, breathless, in my uncle's presence.

He sternly reproached me for being dilatory.

" What had detained me? Here had been Counsellor Leatherhead's servant waiting this half-hour for his papers;—bring in the bag." I gaped at him, and stuttered that I supposed it had been already here; but it would certainly arrive shortly. Question and answer followed rapidly, and the fatal truth came out—*the bag was*

*lost!*—for the cad, advertised of the value of his charge, had retreated the moment I turned my back; and although on investigation he must have felt much disappointed at the result of his industry, yet, to do him justice, he lost no time in transferring the
papers to the tobacconist and pocketing the produce of the same.

For some moments Duncan's rage prevented him from speaking.
At last he found utterance;—'' Heaven and earth! '' he exclaimed;
'' was there ever such a villain?   He was ruined:—all the Kilgobbin title-deeds—Lady Splashboard's draft of separation—papers
of satisfaction for sixteen mortgages of Sir Phelim O'Boyl!—What
was to be done? ''

I muttered that I supposed I should be obliged to give Sir Phelim
satisfaction myself.

'' O! curse your satisfaction,'' said my uncle; '' these are your
Connaught notions, you desperate do-no-good.   What an infernal
business to let any one from that barbarous country into my house!
Never had but two clients in my life on the other side of the
Shannon.   I divorced a wife for one; and he died insolvent the very
day the decree was pronounced, and costs and money advanced
went along with him to the devil.   The other quarrelled with me for
not taking a bad bill for my demand, and giving a large balance
over my claim, in ready cash.   I threatened law, and he threatened
flagellation.   I took courage and sent down a writ; and the sheriff
returned a *non est inventus*, although he was hunting with him for
a fortnight.   I ran him to execution and got *nulla bona* on my
return.   As a last resource I sent a man specially from Dublin: they
tossed him in a blanket, and forced him to eat *the original*; and he
came back, half dead, with a civil intimation that if I ever crossed
the bridge of Athlone, the defendant would drive as many slugs
through my body as there were hoops on a wine-pipe! ''

I could not help smiling at the simile: the client was a wag; for
my uncle in his personal proportions bore a striking resemblance to
a quarter-cask.

'' But run, every soul of you,'' he continued, '' and try to get
some clue by which we may trace the papers.''

Away clerk and apprentice started; but their researches were unsuccessful; many a delicate cut of cheese was already encased in
my Lady Splashboard's separation bill; and the Kilgobbin title-
deeds had issued in subdivisions from the snuff-shop, and were
making a rapid circle of the metropolis.

My aunt's influence was not sufficient to obtain my pardon, and
mollify the attorney; and I was despatched, per mail, to that *re-
fugium peccatorum*, as Duncan styled Connemara.

The gentle auditor may anticipate that on my return no fatted
calf was killed; nor was there '' joy in Aztlan,'' as the poet-laureate
has it.   I re-entered Kilnacoppal without beat of drum—and indeed
my demeanour on this occasion was so modest that I had been in

undisturbed possession of the front attic for two whole days before my worthy parents were advertised that I had retired from the study of the law, with no future intention to " stick to the woolsack."

To communicate the abrupt termination of my forensic pursuits to my aunt Macan was an affair of nice and delicate management. When acquainted with the unhappy incident which had drawn down the wrath of my uncle Duncan, she particularly inquired " if there had been any money in the lost bag," and requested to see the last " Hue and Cry."

God knows whether I should have been enabled to weather the gale of family displeasure, as my aunt had again resumed the mantle of prophecy, when, luckily for me, the representation of the county of Galway became vacant by the sudden decease of Sir Barnabas Bodkin; the honest gentleman being smothered in a hackney-coach returning *comfortable* from a corporation dinner at Morrison's.

On this distressing event being known, Mr. Denis Darcey, of Carrig-a-howley Castle, *declared himself*. He was strongly supported by Mr. Richard Martin, the other member; and his address, from the pen of the latter gentleman, was circulated without delay. In it he set forth his family and pretensions: pledged himself to support Catholic emancipation and the repeal of still fines;— humanely recommended his opponent to provide himself with a coffin previous to the opening of the poll;—professed strong attachment to the House of Brunswick, and the Church by ʼaw established; and promised to use his utmost exertions to purify the penal code, by making accidents in duelling amount to justifiable homicide: and abduction of heiresses and dogs, felony without benefit of clergy.

A person of Denis Darcey's constitutional principles was a man after my father's own heart: the Killnacoppal interest was accordingly given him, and I was despatched at the head of sixscore freeholders, " good men and true," untrammelled with tight shoes or tender consciences, to give our " most sweet voices," in the ancient town of Galway.

But I was not entrusted with this important command without receiving full instructions for my conduct on the occasion. My father, no doubt, would have led the Killnacoppal legion to the hustings in person, had it not happened that the sheriff was on the other side; and, therefore, his public appearance within the bailiwick of that redoubted personage would have been a dangerous experiment. " Frank," said my father, " don't overdo the thing: poll your men *twice*! and more cannot be expected; but mind the outwork, for it's there the *tinints* will shine."

I obeyed him to the letter; and without personal vanity, I ascribe the happy return of my esteemed friend Denis Darcey to the unwearied exertions of the freeholders of Killnacoppal. What between pelting the military, smashing the booths, and scattering the tallies, we managed to keep up such confusion that our adversaries could hardly bring forward a man. If dispersed by a charge of cavalry here, we were rallied in a few minutes in the next street, cracking heads and crashing windows: if routed by the Riot Act and a row of bayonets, before the sheriff was well round the corner we had a house pulled down to the tune of " Hurrah for Killnacoppal! "

At last, all human means being found unavailable by our opponents to bring in a freeholder, the booths were closed, and Mr. Denis Darcey declared duly elected.

After such feats, how could it be wondered at that I was

> courted and caressed,
> High placed in halls a welcome guest;

seated within seven of the chairman at the election dinner, drank wine with the new member, toasted by the old one, I mean Dick Martin—and embraced by Blakes, Brownes, and Bodkins in endless variety?—Nor did the reward of " high desert " end here; for in the next gazette I was appointed to a lieutenancy in the South Mayo militia.

With very different feelings I now returned to my maternal mansion—*I*, who had left the little lawyer in Dorset Street in disgrace, and been happy to effect a sort of felonious re-entry of the premises at Killnacoppal—I now came home a conqueror; an hundred blackthorns rattled above my head; an hundred voices yelled " *Kinnidy* for ivir! "—a keg of poteen was broached before the door; a stack of turf was blazing in the village; and all was triumph and exultation. We had brought back, of course, the usual assortment of broken bones, left some half-score damaged skulls to be repaired at the expense of the county, and carried back one gentleman totally defunct, who had been suffocated by tumbling dead drunk into a bog-hole. My fame had travelled before me, and my aunt Macan had taken to her bed not from vanity, but " vexation of spirit."

My leave of absence expired, and I set out to join my regiment. My mother consulted the Army List, and discovered she had divers relatives in my corps; for there was scarcely a family from Loughrea to Belmullet with whom she was not in some way connected. Some of her relations in the South Mayoo she mentioned as being rather remote; but there was Captain Rattigan: his father, Luke Rattigan of Rawnacreeva, married Peter Fogarty's third daughter; and Peter Fogarty and my aunt Macan were cousins-german.

No doubt the gallant captain would know and acknowledge the relationship, and take that lively interest in my welfare which was natural; but, for fear of mistakes, she wrote a letter of introduction with me, having very fortunately danced fifteen years before with the said Mr. Rattigan, at a fair ball at Ballinasloe.

For the second time I left my father's house. The headquarters of the regiment were in Naas, and there I arrived in safety; was recognized by Captain Rattigan; presented by him in due form to the colonel; introduced to the corps; paid plate and band-fund fees; dined at the mess; got drunk there as became a soldier of promise, and was carried home to my inn by a file of the guard, after having overheard the fat major remark to my kinsman—

" Rat, that boy of yours will be a credit to the regiment; for as I'm a true Catholic, he has taken off three bottles of Page's port, and no doubt he'll improve."

A year passed over—I conducted myself creditably in all regimental matters, touching drill duty and drinking, when an order suddenly came for a detachment to march to Ballybunnion; in the neighbourhood of which town the pleasant part of the population were amusing themselves nightly in carding middlemen, and feathering tithe proctors. Captain Rattigan's company (in which I was an unworthy lieutenant) was selected for this important service.

The morning I left Naas for Ballybunnion will be a memorable day in the calendar of my life. My cousin Rattigan frequently boasted, after dinner, that " he was under fifty, and above five feet three "; but there were persons in the corps who alleged that he was above the former and under the latter:—but let that pass —he is now, honest man, quietly resting at Craughane churchyard, with half a ton weight of Connemara marble over him, on which his virtues and his years are recorded.

Now, without stopping to ascertain minutely the age and height of the departed, I shall describe him as a thick square-shouldered undersized man, having a short neck and snub-nose—the latter organ fully attesting that Page's port was a sound and well-bodied liquor. The captain, on his pied pony, rode gallantly on at the head of " his charge " : I modestly followed on foot—and late in the evening we marched in full array down the main street of Ballybunnion, our fife and drum playing to the best of their ability the captain's favourite quick step, " *I'm over young to marry yet.*"

My kinsman and I were peaceably settled over our wine, when the waiter announced that a gentleman had called upon us. He was shown up in proper form; and having managed by depressing his person, which was fully six feet four inches, to enter the apartment he announced himself as Mr. Christopher Clinch; and in a handsome speech declared himself to be an ambassador from the stewards of the Ballybunnion coterie; which coterie being to be holden that evening, he was deputed to solicit the honour of our company on this occasion. Captain Rattigan returned our acknowledgments duly; and he and the ambassador having discussed a cooper of port within a marvellous short period, separated with many squeezes of the hand, and ardent hopes of a future acquaintance.

There was a subject my kinsman invariably dwelt upon whenever he had transgressed the third bottle—it was a bitter lamentation over the numerous opportunities he had suffered to escape of making himself comfortable for life, by matrimony. As we dressed together, for we were cantoned in a double-bedded room, Rat was unusually eloquent on the grand mistake of his earlier days, and declared his determination of even yet endeavouring to amend his youthful error, and retrieve lost time.

The commander's advice was not lost upon me. I took unusual pains in arraying myself for conquest, and in good time found myself in the ballroom, with thirty couples on the floor all dancing " for the bare life " that admired tune of " *Blue bonnets over the border.*"

The attention evinced in his visit to the inn by Mr. Christopher Clinch was not confined to a formal invitation; for he assured us on our arrival that two ladies had been expressly kept disengaged for us. Captain Rattigan declined dancing, alleging that exercise flurried him, and he could not abide a red face, it looked so very like dissipation. I, whose countenance was fortunately not so inflammable as my kinsman's, was marshalled by Mr. Clinch to the head of the room.

" He was going," he said, " to introduce me to Miss Jemima O'Brien—lady of first connections—large fortune when some persons at present in possession dropped off—fine woman—much followed—sprightly—off-handed—fond of military men. Miss O'Brien, Captain Kennedy." I bowed—she ducked—seized my offered hand, and in a few minutes we were going down the middle like two-year-olds for " the Kirwans." Nor had Captain Rattigan been neglected by the master of the ceremonies: he was snugly seated in a quiet corner at cribbage, a game the commander delighted in, with an elderly gentlewoman, whom my partner informed me was her aunt.

Miss O'Brien was what Rattigan called *a spanker*. She was dressed in a blue silk lute-string gown, with a plume of ostrich feathers, flesh-coloured stockings, and red satin shoes. She had the usual assortment of beads and curls, with an ivory fan and a well-scented handkerchief.

She was evidently a fine-tempered girl; for, observing my eye rest on an immense stain upon her blue lute-string, she remarked with a smile " that her aunt's footman had spilled some coffee on her dress, and to save him from a scolding, she had assured the dear old lady that the injury was trifling, and that it would be quite unnecessary to detain her while she should change her gown: it was quite clear she never could wear it again; but her maid and the milliner would be the gainers. Amiable creature!—the accident did not annoy her for a second.

The first dance had concluded, when the long gentleman whispered softly over my shoulder how I liked " the heiress "? *The heiress!*—I felt a faint hope rising in my breast which made my cheek colour like a peony. Rattigan's remorse for neglected opportunities rushed to my mind. Had my lucky hour come? And had I actually an heiress by the hand for nine-and-twenty couples? We were again at the head of the room, and away we went—she cutting and I capering, until we danced to the very bottom, " *The wind that shakes the barley!* "

I had placed Miss O'Brien with great formality on a bench, when Rattigan took me aside:—" Frank, you're a fortunate fellow, or it's your own fault—found out all from the old one—lovely creature —great catch—who knows?—strike while the iron is hot," etc., etc., etc.

Fortune indeed appeared to smile upon me. By some propitious accident all the men had been provided with partners, and I had *the heiress* to myself. " She was, she confessed, romantic—she had quite a literary turn; spoke of Lady Morgan's *Wild Irish Girl*; she loved it—doted upon it;—and why should she not? for Lieutenant-colonel Cassidy had repeatedly sworn that Glorvina was written for herself ";—and she raised her fan.

The conscious blush to hide.

Walter Scott succeeded—I had read in the *Galway Advertiser* a quotation from that poet, which the newspaper had put in the mouth of a travelling priest, and alleged to have been spoken by him in a charity sermon, which I now fortunately recollected and repeated. Miss O'Brien responded directly with that inflammatory passage,—

In peace love tunes the shepherd's reed.

" And could she love? "—I whispered with a look of tender inquietude. " She could; she had a heart, she feared, too warm for her happiness: she was a creature of imagination—all soul—all sympathy. She could wander with the man of her heart from

Egypt's fires to Zembla's frost."

There was no standing this. I mustered all my resolution— poured out an unintelligible rhapsody—eternal love—life gratefully devoted—permission to fall at her feet—hand—heart—fortune!

She sighed deeply—kept her fan to her face for some moments— and, in a voice of peculiar softness, murmured something about " short acquaintance," with a gentle supplication to be allowed time for ten minutes to consult her heart. Rat again rushed to my mind; procrastination had ruined him; I was obdurate—pressed—raved—

ranted—till she sighed, in a timid whisper, that she was mine for ever!

Heavens!—was I awake?—did my ears deceive me? The room turned topsy-turvy—the candles danced a reel—my brain grew giddy—*it was true—absolutely true*; *Jemima O'Brien* had consented to become *Mrs. Kennedy*!

Up came Captain Rattigan, as my partner left me for an instant to speak to her aunt. Rat was thunderstruck—cursed his fate, and complimented mine.

"But, zounds! Frank, you must stick to her. Would she run away with you? These d—— lawyers will be tying up the property, so that you cannot touch a guinea but the half-year's rent—may be inquiring about settlements, and ripping up the cursed mortgages of Killnacoppal. At her, man,—they are all on the move. I'll manage the old one: mighty lucky, by-the-by, at cribbage. Try and get the heiress to be off—to-morrow, if possible—early hour. Oh! murder—how I lost my time!"

All was done as the commander directed. Rat kept the aunt in play while I pressed the heiress hard—and so desperately did I portray my misery, that, to save my life, she humanely consented to elope with me at twelve o'clock next day.

Rattigan was enraptured. What a chance for a poor lieutenant—as he shrewdly observed, from the very unpretending appearance of Mrs. Cogan's mansion, that "my aunt's" purse must be a long one. We settled ourselves joyfully at the inn fire—ordered two bottles of mulled port—arranged all for the elopement—clubbed purses—sum total not burdensome—and went to bed drunk and happy.

Next morning—the morning of that day which was to bless me with fortune and a wife, Captain Rattigan and I were sitting at an early breakfast, when, who should unexpectedly arrive but Cornet Bircham, who was in command of a small party of dragoons in Ballybunnion, and an old acquaintance of my kinsman. "How lucky!" whispered Rat; "he has been quartered here for three months, and we shall hear the particulars of the O'Briens from him."

While he spoke the trooper entered. "Ah! Ratty, old boy, how wags the world?—Just heard you had been sent here to exterminate carders—cursed scoundrels!—obliged me to leave a delightful party at Lord Tara's; but, Rat, we'll make them smoke for it."

"Mr. Bircham, my cousin Kennedy. Come, Cornet, off with the scimitar and attack the congo. Any news stirring?"

"Nothing but a flying report that you had determined on sobriety and forsworn a drop beyond the third bottle;—but that shake in your claw gives a lie direct to the tale. And you were dancing, Rat, last night. How did the carnival or coterie go off? Any wigs lost or gowns tattered? Any catastrophe?"

" Why, no—pleasant thing enough—some fine women there."

" Were there, faith? Why, Rat, you're a discoverer; for such a crew as figured at the last one, mortal eye never looked upon."

" I only particularly noticed one—by Jove, a fine woman!—a Miss O'Brien."

" Miss *Jemmy* O'Brien, as the men call her. Why, Rat, what iniquity of yours has delivered you into the hands of the most detestable harpy that ever infested country quarters? "

" Detestable harpy! "—Rat and I looked cursedly foolish. " Bircham—hem!—are you sure you know the lady? "

" Know the lady! to be sure I do. Why, she did me out of an ivory fan one unlucky wet day that the devil tempted me to enter Mrs. Cogan's den. Phoo! I'll give you what the beadle calls ' marks and tokens.' Let me see.—Yes—I have it—blue dress, cursedly splashed with beer—she says coffee; soiled feathers, and tricked out like a travelling actress."

I groaned audibly—it was Jemima to a T:—Captain Rattigan looked queer.

" My dear Bircham—hem!—you know among military men— hem!—honourable confidence may be reposed—hem! My young friend here danced with her—represented as an heiress to him——"

" By a cursed hag who cheats at cribbage, and carries off negus by the quart."

" True bill, by ——! " ejaculated the Captain. " Complained eternally of thirst and the heat of the room, and did me regularly out of thirty shillings."

" Ha! ha! ha!—Rat, Rat, and wert thou so soft, my old one? "

" But, Birchy," said the Captain, " the devil of it is, my young friend—little too much wine—thought himself in honourable hands, and promised her——"

" A new silk gown—ah, my young friend, little didst thou know the Jezebel. But it was a promise obtained under false pretences— she told you a cock-and-bull story about Lady Morgan—sported Scott—dealt out Tom Moore by the yard—all false pretences. See her damned before I would buy her a yard of riband. What a pirate the woman is! "

Rat jumped off his chair, drew his breath in, and gulped out— " A gown! Zounds, man, he promised to marry her! "

Up jumped Bircham.—" To marry her! Are you mad, or are you hoaxing? "

" Serious, by St. Patrick," said Rat.

" Why then it's no longer a joke. You are in a nice scrape. I beg to tell you that Jemmy O'Brien is as notorious as Captain Rock. She has laid several fools under contribution, and has just returned from Dublin, after taking an action against a little drunken one-eyed Welsh major, whom her aunt got, when intoxicated, to sign some paper or promise of marriage. The major, like a true gentleman, retrieved his error by suspending himself in his lodgings the day before the trial; and it is likely that *Jem* and her aunt will be in gaol, for the law expenses.''

Rat and I were overwhelmed, and looked for some minutes in silence at each other. At last I told Bircham the whole affair. The dragoon was convulsed with laughter—'' So,'' said he, '' at twelve o'clock the gentle *Jemmy* is to be spirited away. But come, there's no time to lose—sit down, Rat, get a pen in thy fist, and I'll dictate and thou inscribe.''

'' MADAM—Having unfortunately, at the request of his afflicted family, undertaken the case of Lieutenant Kennedy of the South Mayo regiment, I beg to apprise you that the unhappy gentleman is subject to occasional fits of insanity. Fearing from his mental malady that he may have misconducted himself to your amiable niece last night at the coterie, I beg on the part of my poor friend (who is tolerably collected this morning) to say that he is heartily sorry for what has occurred, and requests the lady will consider anything he might have said only as the wanderings of a confirmed lunatic!—I am, Madam, etc., your obedient servant,

'' TERENCE RATTIGAN, Capt. S— M— Militia.
'' To Mrs. Cogan, etc.''

How very flattering this apology was to me I submit to the indulgent auditor. I was indubitably proven to have been an ass overnight, and I must pass as a lunatic in the morning. We had barely time to speculate on the success of Bircham's curious epistle, when my aunt Cogan's answer arrived with due promptitude. The Cornet separated the wet wafer with a '' Faugh! '' and holding the billet at arm's length, as if it exhibited a plague-spot, he favoured us with the contents, which were literally as follows:

'' CAPTIN RATIGIN.
'' SIR—I have red your paltrey appollogey for your nephew's breech of promis. I beg to tell you that a lady of the family of Clinch will not submit to be ensulted with impunnitey. My neece is packed and reddy; and if your friend does not appear according to apointment, he will shortly here as will not plase him, from yours to command,

'' HONOR COGAN, otherwise CLINCH.
'' Hawthorne Cotage, Friday morning.''

Twelve o'clock passed—and we waited the result of Mrs. Cogan's threats, when the waiter showed up a visitor, and Mr. Christopher Clinch, the prime cause of all our misfortunes, presented himself. He persisted in standing, or more properly stooping—for the ceiling was not quite six feet from the floor—coughed—hoped his interference might adjust the mistake, as he presumed it must be on the part of Lieutenant Kennedy, and begged to inform him that Miss Jemima O'Brien was ready to accompany the said Mr. Kennedy, as last night arranged. Captain Rattigan took the liberty to remark that he, the captain, had been very explicit with Mrs. Cogan, and requested to refer to his letter, in which Mr. Kennedy's sentiments were fully conveyed, and, on his part, to decline the very flattering proposal of Miss Jemima O'Brien.

Mr. Clinch stated that an immediate change of sentiment on the part of Mr. Kennedy was imperative, or that Mr. K. would be expected to favour him, Mr. C., with an interview in the Priest's Meadow. Captain Rattigan acknowledged the request of Mr. Clinch to be a very reasonable alternative, and covenanted that Mr. Kennedy should appear at the time and place mentioned; and Mr. Clinch was then very ceremoniously conducted downstairs by the polite commander.

Through motives of delicacy, I had at the commencement of the interview retired to the next apartment; and as the rooms were only separated by a boarded partition, I overheard through a convenient chink, with desperate alarm, Captain Rattigan giving every facility to my being shot at in half an hour in the Priest's Meadow. No wonder then Rat found me pale as a spectre, when bursting into the room he seized me by the hand, and told me he had brought this unlucky business to a happy termination. He, the captain, dreaded that Jemima would have been looking for legal redress; but, thank God, it would only end in a duel.

I hinted at the chance of my being shot.

" Shot! " exclaimed my comforter, " why, what the deuce does that signify? If indeed you had been under the necessity of hanging yourself, like the one-eyed major, it would have been a hardship. No funeral honours—no decent wake—but smuggled into the earth like a half-bale of contraband tobacco;—but, in your case, certain of respectable treatment—reversed arms—dead march— and Christian burial:—vow to God, quite a comfort to be shot under such flattering circumstances! Frank, you have all the luck of the Rattigans about you! "—and, opening the door, he halloed—" Myke—Myke Boyle, bring down *the pace-makers* to the parlour."

In a few seconds I heard the captain and his man busily at work, and by a number of villainous clicks, which jarred through my system like electricity, I found these worthies were arranging the commander's *pace-makers* for my use in the Priest's Meadow.

At the appointed hour I reached the ground, which was but a short distance from the inn. Rattigan and Bircham accompanied me, and Myke Boyle followed with *the tools*. Mr. Christopher Clinch and his friends were waiting for us; and a cadaverous-looking being was peeping through the hedge, whom I afterwards dis-

covered to be the village apothecary, allured thither by the hope
of an accident, as birds of prey are said to be collected by a chance
of carrion.

The customary bows were formally interchanged between the
respective belligerents—the ground correctly measured—pistols
squibbed, loaded, and delivered to the principals. I felt very queer
on finding myself opposite a truculent fellow of enormous height,
with a pair of projecting whiskers upon which a man might hang
his hat, and a pistol two feet long clutched in his bony grasp.
Rattigan, as he adjusted my weapon, whispered, " Frank, jewel,
remember the hip-bone; or, as the fellow's a —— of a length,
you may level a trifle higher "; and, stepping aside, his coadjutor
pronounced in an audible voice—" One!—two! !—*three* ! ! ! "

Off went the pistols. I felt Mr. Clinch's bullet whistle past my
ear, and saw Captain Rattigan next moment run up to my antagonist and inquire " if he was much hurt." Heavens!—how delightful! I had brought the engagement to a glorious issue by neatly
removing Mr. Clinch's trigger-finger, and thereby spoiling his
shooting for life.

With a few parting bows we retired from the Priest's Meadow,
leaving Christopher Clinch a job for the vampire apothecary, and
a fit subject for the assiduities of Mrs. Cogan and the gentle
Jemima.

If Captain Rattigan had registered a rash vow against port wine,
it is to be lamented, for never were three gentlemen of the sword
more completely done up at an early hour of the evening than we.

Next day we were informed that Clinch was tolerably well, and
that their attorney had been closeted with the ladies of Hawthorn
Cottage. We held a council of war, and while debating on the
expediency of my retiring on leave to Connemara, where I might
set *Jemmy* and her lawyer at defiance, the post brought us intelligence that " a turn-out for the line was wanted "; and if I could
muster the necessary number, I should be exchanged into a regular
regiment.

Off Rat and I started for Naas, and with little difficulty succeeded
in making up the quota; and the first intimation the prototype of
Glorvina received of our movements was being seduced to the
window by the drums, as I marched past Hawthorn Cottage, with
as choice a sample of " food for gunpowder " as ever left Ballybunnion. I saluted the once-intended Mrs. Kennedy with great
respect; the fifers struck up " *Fare you well, Killeavey* "; and Captain Rattigan, who accompanied me the first day's march, ejaculated, as he looked askance at this second Ariadne, " May the devil
smother you, Jemima O'Brien! "

I have a mighty affection for the army, and, therefore, I sup-
plicate young soldiers never to propose for a lady in a public ballroom the first night they arrive in country quarters, and to shun,

as they would the *chorea viti,* that seductive tune, called " *The wind that shakes the barley!* "—and, finally, to give no credence whatever to any apology offered for a soiled silk unless they have perpetrated the offence in person, or have seen it committed in their own actual presence.

SAMUEL LOVER

THE GRIDIRON

# SAMUEL LOVER

1797–1868

# THE GRIDIRON

A CERTAIN old gentleman in the west of Ireland, whose love of the ridiculous quite equalled his taste for claret and fox-hunting, was wont, upon certain festive occasions when opportunity offered, to amuse his friends by drawing out one of his servants who was exceedingly fond of what he termed his " thravels," and in whom a good deal of whim, some queer stories, and, perhaps more than all, long and faithful services, had established a right of loquacity.

He was one of those few trusty and privileged domestics, who, if his master unheedingly uttered a rash thing in a fit of passion, would venture to set him right.

If the squire said, " I'll turn that rascal off," my friend Pat would say, " throth you won't, sir "; and Pat was always right, for if any altercation arose upon the subject-matter in hand, he was sure to throw in some good reason, either from former service —general good conduct—or the delinquent's " wife and childher," that always turned the scale.

But I am digressing. On such merry meetings as I have alluded to, the master, after making certain " approaches," as a military man would say, as the preparatory steps in laying siege to some extravaganza of his servant, might, perchance, assail Pat thus:

" By the by, Sir John " (addressing a distinguished guest), " Pat has a very curious story, which something you told me to-day reminds me of. You remember, Pat " (turning to the man, evidently pleased at the notice paid to himself)—" you remember that queer adventure you had in France? "

" Throth I do, sir," grins forth Pat.

" What! " exclaims Sir John, in feigned surprise. " Was Pat ever in France? "

" Indeed he was," cries mine host; and Pat adds, " Ay, and farther, plase your honour."

" I assure you, Sir John," continues mine host, " Pat told me a story once that surprised me very much, respecting the ignorance of the French."

" Indeed ! " rejoins the baronet. " Really, I always supposed the French to be a most accomplished people."

" Throth, then, they're not, sir," interrupts Pat.

" Oh, by no means," adds mine host, shaking his head emphatically.

" I believe, Pat, 'twas when you were crossing the Atlantic? " says the master, turning to Pat with a seductive air, and leading into the " full and true account "—(for Pat had thought fit to visit North Amerikay, for " a raison he had," in the autumn of the year ninety-eight).

" Yes, sir," says Pat, " the broad Atlantic," a favourite phrase of his, which he gave with a brogue as broad almost as the Atlantic itself.

" It was the time I was lost in crassin' the broad Atlantic, comin' home," began Pat, decoyed into the recital; " whin the winds began to blow, and the sae to rowl, that you'd think the *Colleen Dhas* (that was her name) would not have a mast left.

" Well, sure enough, the masts went by the board at last, and the pumps was choaked (divil choak them for that same), and av coorse the wather gained an us, and throth, to be filled with water is neither good for man or baste; and she was sinkin' fast, settlin' down, as the sailors calls it, and faith I never was good at settlin' down in my life, and I liked it then less nor ever. Accordingly we prepared for the worst, and put out the boat, and got a sack o' bishkits, and a cashk o' pork, and a kag o' wather, and a thrifle o' rum aboord, and any other little mathers we could think iv in the mortial hurry we wor in—and, faith, there was no time to be lost, for my darlint, the *Colleen Dhas*, went down like a lump o' lead, afore we wor many sthrokes o' the oar away from her.

" Well, we dhrifted away all that night, and next mornin' we put up a blanket an the ind av a pole as well as we could, and thin we sailed illigant, for we dar'n't show a stitch o' canvas the night before, bekase it was blowin' like murther, savin' your presence, and sure it's the wondher of the world we worn't swallyed alive by the ragin' sae.

" Well, away we wint for more nor a week, and nothin' before our two good-looking eyes but the canophy iv heaven, and the wide ocean—the broad Atlantic—not a thing was to be seen but the sae and the sky: and though the sae and the sky is mighty purty things in themselves, throth they're no great things whin you've nothin' else to look at for a week together—and the barest rock in the world, so it was land, would be more welkim.

" And then, sure enough, throth, our provisions began to run low, the bishkits, and the wather, and the rum—throth that was gone first of all—God help uz!—and oh! it was thin that starvation began to stare us in the face. ' Oh, murther, murther, captain, darlint,' says I, ' I wish we could see land anywhere,' says I.

" ' More power to your elbow, Paddy, my boy,' says he, ' for sitch a good wish, and, throth, it's myself wishes the same.'

" ' Oh,' says I, ' that it may plaze you, sweet queen in heaven —supposing it was only a dissolute island,' says I, ' inhabited wid Turks, sure they wouldn't be such bad Christhans as to refuse uz a bit and a sup.'

" ' Whisht, whisht, Paddy,' says the captain; ' don't be talkin' bad of any one,' says he; ' you don't know how soon you may want a good word put in for yourself, if you should be called to quarthers in th' other world all of a suddent,' says he.

" ' Thrue for you, captain, darlint,' says I—I called him darlint, and made free wid him, you see, bekase disthress makes uz all equal—' thrue for you, captain, jewel—God betune uz and harm, I owe no man any spite '—and, throth, that was only thruth.

" Well, the last bishkit was sarved out, and, by gor, the wather itself was all gone at last, and we passed the night mighty cowld. Well, at the brake o' day the sun riz most beautiful out o' the waves, that was as bright as silver and as clear as cryshthal.

" But it was only the more crule upon uz, for we wor beginnin' to feel terrible hungry; when all at wanst I thought I spied the land—by gor, I thought I felt my heart up in my throat in a minnit, and ' Thundher and turf, captain,' says I, ' look to leeward,' says I.

" ' What for? ' says he.

" ' I think I see the land,' says I. So he ups with his bring-'um-near (that's what the sailors call a spy-glass, sir), and looks out, and, sure enough, it was.

" ' Hurrah! ' says he, ' we're all right now; pull away, my boys,' says he.

" ' Take care you're not mistaken,' says I; ' maybe it's only a fog-bank, captain, darlint,' says I.

" ' Oh, no,' says he, ' it's the land in airnest.'

" ' Oh, then, whereabouts in the wide world are we, captain? ' says I; ' maybe it id be in Roosia or Proosia, or the Garman Oceant,' says I.

" ' Tut, you fool,' says he, for he had that consaited way wid him—thinkin' himself cleverer nor any one else—' tut, you fool,' says he; ' that's France,' says he.

" ' Tare an ouns,' says I, ' do you tell me so? And how do you know it's France it is, captain, dear,' says I.

" ' Bekase this is the Bay o' Bishky we're in now,' says he.

" ' Throth, I was thinkin' so myself,' says I, ' by the rowl it has; for I often heerd av it in regard o' that same '; and, throth, the likes av it I never seen before nor since, and, with the help o' God, never will.

" Well, with that my heart begun to grow light, and when I

seen my life was safe, I began to grow twice hungrier nor ever
—so says I, ' Captain, jewel, I wish we had a gridiron.'

" ' Why, then,' says he, ' thundher and turf,' says he, ' what
put a gridiron into your head? '

" ' Bekase I'm starvin' with the hunger,' says I.

" ' And sure, bad luck to you,' says he, ' you couldn't ate a
gridiron,' says he, ' barrin you wor a pelican o' the wilderness,'
says he.

" ' Ate a gridiron! ' says I.   ' Och, in throth, I'm not such a
gommoch all out as that, anyhow.   But sure if we had a gridiron
we could dress a beefsteak,' says I.

" ' Arrah! but where's the beefsteak? ' says he.

" ' Sure, couldn't we cut a slice aff the pork? ' says I.

" ' By gor, I never thought a' that,' says the captain.   ' You're
a clever fellow, Paddy,' says he, laughin'.

" ' Oh, there's many a thrue word said in joke,' says I.

" ' Thrue for you, Paddy,' says he.

" ' Well, then,' says I, ' if you put me ashore there beyant '
(for we were nearin' the land all the time), ' and sure I can ask
thim for to lind me the loan of a gridiron,' says I.

" ' Oh, by gor, the butther's comin' out o' the stirabout in
airnest now,' says he.   ' You gommoch,' says he, ' sure I towld
you before that's France—and sure they're all furriners there,'
says the captain.

" ' Well,' says I, ' and how do you know but I'm as good a
furriner myself as any o' thim? '

" ' What do you mane? ' says he.

" ' I mane,' says I, ' what I towld you, that I'm as good a
furriner myself as any o' thim.'

" ' Make me sinsible,' says he.

" ' By dad, maybe that's more nor me, or greater nor me, could
do,' says I; and we all began to laugh at him, for I thought I'd
pay him off for his bit o' consait about the Garman Oceant.

" ' Lave aff your humbuggin,' says he, ' I bid you, and tell me
what it is you mane at all, at all.'

" ' Parly-voo frongsay? ' says I.

" ' Oh, your humble sarvant,' says he.   ' Why, by gor, you're
a scholar, Paddy.'

" ' Throth, you may say that,' says I.

" ' Why, you're a clever fellow, Paddy,' says the captain, jeerin'
like.

" ' You're not the first that said that,' says I, ' whether you joke
or no.'

" ' Oh, but I'm in airnest,' says the captain.   ' And do you tell
me, Paddy,' says he, ' that you spake Frinch? '

" ' Parly-voo frongsay? ' says I.

" ' By gor, that bangs Banagher, and all the world knows
123*

Banagher bangs the devil. I never met the likes o' you, Paddy,' says he. ' Pull away, boys, and put Paddy ashore, and maybe we won't get a good bellyfull before long.'

" So, with that, it was no sooner said nor done—they pulled away and got close into shore in less than no time, and run the boat up in a little creak; and a beautiful creek it was, with a lovely white sthrand, an illigant place for ladies to bathe in the summer; and out I got, and it's stiff enough in my limbs I was afther bein' cramped up in the boat, and perished with the cowld and hunger; but I conthrived to scramble an, one way or the other, towards a little bit iv a wood that was close to the shore, and the smoke curlin' out of it, quite timpting like.

" ' By the powdhers o' war, I'm all right,' says I; ' there's a house there '—and sure enough there was, and a parcel of men, women, and childher, ating their dinner round a table quite convainent. And so I wint up to the dure, and I thought I'd be very civil to thim, as I heerd the Frinch was always mighty p'lite intirely —and I thought I'd show them I knew what good manners was.

" So I took off my hat, and making a low bow, says I, ' God save all here,' says I.

" Well, to be sure, they all stopt ating at wanst, and begun to stare at me, and faith they almost looked me out of countenance —and I thought to myself it was not good manners at all—more be token from furriners, which they call so mighty p'lite; but I never minded that, in regard of wantin' the gridiron; and so says I, ' I beg your pardon,' says I, ' for the liberty I take, but it's only bein' in disthress in regard of ating,' says I, ' that I make bowld to throuble yez, and if you could lind me the loan of a gridiron,' says I, ' I'd be entirely obleeged to ye.'

" By gor, they all stared at me twice worse nor before, and with that, says I (knowing what was in their minds), ' Indeed it's thrue for you,' says I; ' I'm tathered to pieces, and God knows I look quare enough, but it's by raison of the storm,' says I, ' which dhruv us ashore here below, and we've all starvin',' says I.

" So then they began to look at each other agin, and myself, seeing at wanst dirty thoughts was in their heads, and that they tuk me for a poor beggar comin' to crave charity—with that, says I, ' Oh! not at all,' says I, ' by no manes; we have plenty o' mate ourselves, there below, and we'll dhress it,' says I, ' if you would be plased to lind us the loan of a gridiron,' says I, makin' a low bow.

" Well, sir, with that, throth, they stared at me twice worse nor ever, and faith I began to think that maybe the captain was wrong, and that it was not France at all, at all; and so says I—' I beg pardon, sir,' says I, to a fine ould man, with a head of hair as white as silver—' maybe I'm undher a mistake,' says I, ' but I

thought I was in France, sir; aren't you furriers? ' says I—
Parly-voo frongsay? '

" ' We, munseer,' says he.

" ' Then would you lind me the loan of a gridiron,' says I, ' if
you plase? '

" Oh, it was thin that they stared at me as if I had siven heads;
and faith myself began to feel flusthered like, and onaisy—and so,
says I, making a bow and scrape agin, ' I know it's a liberty I
take, sir,' says I, ' but it's only in the regard of bein' cast away,
and if you plase, sir,' says I, ' Parly-voo frongsay? '

" ' We, munseer,' says he, mighty sharp.

" ' Then would you lind me the loan of a gridiron? ' says I,
' and you'll obleege me.'

" Well, sir, the old chap begun to munseer me, but the divil a
bit of a gridiron he'd gie me; and so I began to think they were all
neygars, for all their fine manners; and, throth, my blood began
to rise, and says I, ' By my sowl, if it was you was in disthress,'
says I, ' and if it was to ould Ireland you kem, it's not only the
gridiron they'd give you if you ax'd it, but something to put an it
too, and a dhrop of dhrink into the bargain, and cead mille failte."

" Well, the word cead mille failte seemed to stchreck his heart,
and the ould chap cocked his ear, and so I thought I'd give him
another offer, and make him sinsible at last; and so says I, wanst
more, quite slow, that he might undherstand—' Parly—voo—
frongsay, munseer? '

" ' We, munseer,' says he.

" ' Then lind me the loan of a gridiron,' says I, ' and bad scran
to you.'

" Well, bad win' to the bit of it he'd gi' me, and the ould chap
begins bowin' and scrapin', and said something or other about a
long tongs.

" ' Phoo!—the devil sweep yourself and tongs,' says I, ' I don't
want a tongs at all, at all; but can't you listen to raison,' says I—
' Parly-voo frongsay? '

" ' We, munseer.'

" ' Then lind me the loan of a gridiron,' says I, ' and howld
your prate.'

" Well, what would you think but he shook his owld noddle, as
much as to say he wouldn't; and so says I, ' Bad cess to the likes
o' that I ever seen—throth if you were in my country, it's not
that-a-way they'd use you; the curse o' the crows on you, you ould
sinner,' says I; ' the divil a longer I'll darken your dure.'

" So he seen I was vexed, and I thought, as I was turnin' away,
I seen him begin to relint, and that his conscience throubled him;
and says I, turnin' back, ' Well, I'll give you one chance more—
you owld thief—are you a Chrishthan at all, at all?—are you a
furriner,' says I, ' that all the world calls so p'lite? Bad luck to

you; do you undherstand your own language?—Parly-voo frong-say? ' says I.

" ' We, munseer,' says he.

" ' Then, thundher and turf,' says I, ' will you lind me the loan of a gridiron? '

" Well, sir, the divil resave the bit of it he'd gi' me—and so with that, ' The curse o' the hungry on you, you owld negardly villain,' says I; ' the back o' my hand and the sowl o' my foot to you; that you may want a gridiron yourself yet,' says I; ' and wherever I go, high and low, rich and poor shall hear o' you,' says I; and with that I lift them there, sir, and kem away—and in throth it's often since that I thought that it was remarkable.''

# MRS. ANNA JAMESON
1794–1860

# THE STORY OF GÉNÉVIÈVE

*L'ART de bien conter* is still a Frenchman's most admired talent. Our handsome and interesting beau, Edmonde, piques himself on this accomplishment, and is a " conteur " by profession. He related to us in the Tuileries, yesterday, the following anecdote, with infinite grace of elocution, and considerable effect, spite of his odd falsetto voice. The circumstances occurred at the time Le Noir was minister of the police: I forget the year.

Geneviève de Sorbigny was the last of a noble family: young, beautiful, and a rich heiress, she seemed born to command all this world could yield of happiness. When left an orphan, at an early age, instead of being sent to a convent, as was then the universal custom, she was brought up under the care of a maternal aunt, who devoted herself to her education, and doated on her with an almost exclusive affection.

Geneviève resided in the country with her aunt till she was about sixteen; she was then brought to Paris to be united to the marquis of ——; it was a mere marriage *de convenance,* a family arrangement entered into when she was quite a child, according to the *ancien régime*; and, unfortunately for Geneviève, her affianced bridegroom was neither young nor amiable; yet more unfortunately it happened that the marquis's cousin, the Baron de Villay, who generally accompanied him in his visits of ceremony, possessed all the qualities in which *he* was deficient; being young and singularly handsome, " amiable," " spirituel." While the marquis, with the good breeding of that day, was bowing and paying his devoirs to the aunt of his intended (*sa future*), the young baron, with equal success, but in a very different style, was captivating the heart of the niece. Her extreme beauty had charmed him at the first glance, and her partiality, delicately and involuntarily betrayed, subdued every scruple, if he ever entertained any; and so, in the usual course of things, they were soon irretrievably and *éperdument* in love with each other.

Geneviève, to much gentleness of character, united firmness. The preparations for the marriage went on; the trousseau was bought; the jewels set; but the moment she was aware of her own sentiments she had courage enough to declare to her aunt that, rather than give her hand to the marquis, whom she detested past all her terms of detestation, she would rather throw herself into a nunnery, and endow it with her fortune. The poor aunt was thrown, by this unexpected declaration, into the utmost amazement and perplexity; she was *au désespoir*; such a thing had never been heard of or contemplated: but the tears of Géneviève prevailed; the marriage, after a long negotiation, was broken off, and the baron appeared publicly as the suitor of Génevieve. The marquis politely challenged his cousin, and owed his life to his forbearance; and the duel, and the cause of it, and the gallantry and generosity of De Villay, rendered him irresistible in the eyes of all the women in Paris, while to the heart of Génevieve he became dearer than ever.

To gain the favour of the aunt was now the only difficulty; she had ever regarded him with ill-concealed aversion and suspicion. Some mystery hung over his character; there were certain reports whispered relative to his former life and conduct which it was equally difficult to discredit and to disprove. Besides, though of a distinguished family, he was poor, most of his ancestral possessions being confiscated or dissipated; and his father was notoriously a *mauvais sujet*. All these reports and representations appeared to the impassioned Génevieve mere barbarous calumnies, invented to injure her love; and regarding herself as the primal cause of these slanders, they rather added to the strength of her attachment. A reluctant consent was at last wrung from her aunt, and Génevieve was united to her lover.

The château of the baron was situated in one of the wildest districts of the wild and desolate coast of Bretagne. The people who inhabited the country round were a ferocious, half-civilised race, and, in general, desperate smugglers and pirates. They had been driven to this mode of life by a dreadful famine and the oppressions of the provincial tax-gatherers, and had pursued it partly from choice, partly from necessity. They had carried on for near half a century a constant and systematic warfare against the legal authorities of the province, in which they were generally victorious. No revenue officer or *exempt* dare set his foot within a certain district; and when the tempestuous season, or any other accident, prevented them from following their lawless trade on the sea, they dispersed themselves through the country in regularly organised bands, and committed the most formidable depredations, extending their outrages even as far as St. Pol. Such was their desperate courage, the incredible celerity of their movements, and the skill of their leaders, that though a few stragglers had been occasionally shot, all attempts to take any of them alive, or to penetrate into their secret fastnesses, proved unavailing.

The baron had come to Paris for the purpose of representing the disturbed state of his district to the government and procuring an order from the minister of the interior to embody his own tenantry and dependants into a sort of militia for the defence of his property, and for the purpose of bringing these marauders to justice, if possible. He was at first refused, but after a few months' delay, money and the interest of Généviève's family prevailed; the order was granted, and he prepared to return to his château. The aunt and all her friends remonstrated against the idea of exposing his young wife to such revolting scenes, and insisted that she should be left behind at Paris; to which he agreed with seeming readiness, only referring the decision to Généviève's own election. She did not hesitate one moment; she adored her husband, and the thought of being separated from him in this early stage of their union was worse than any apprehended danger; she declared her resolution to accompany him. At length the matter was thus compromised: they consented that Généviève should spend four months of every year in Bretagne, and the other eight at Paris, or at her uncle's château in Auvergne; in fact, so little was known then in the capital of what was passing in the district provinces that Généviève only, being prepared by her husband, could form some idea of what she was about to encounter.

On their arrival the peasantry were immediately armed, and the château converted into a kind of garrison, regularly fortified. A continual panic seemed to prevail through the whole household, and she heard of nothing from morning till night but the desperate deeds of the marauders and the exploits of their captain, to whom they attributed more marvellous atrocities than were ever related of Barbone, or Blue Beard himself. Généviève was at first in constant terror; finding, however, that week after week passed and the danger, though continually talked of, never appeared, she was rather excited and *désennuyée* by the continual recurrence of these alarms. She would have been perfectly happy in her husband's increasing and devoted tenderness, but for his frequent absences in pursuit of the smugglers either on sea or on shore, and the dangers to which she fancied him exposed: but even those absences and these dangers endeared him to her, and kept alive all the romantic fervour of her attachment. He was not only the lord of her affections, but the hero of her imagination. The time allotted for her stay insensibly passed away; the four months were under different pretences prolonged to six, and then, her confinement drawing near, it was judged safest to defer her journey to Paris till after her recovery.

Généviève in due time became the mother of a son; an event which filled her heart with a thousand delicious emotions of gratitude, pride, and delight. It seemed to have a very different and most inexplicable effect on her husband the baron's behaviour. He became gloomy, anxious, abstracted, and his absences, on various pretexts, more frequent than ever; but what appeared most painful and incomprehensible to Geneviève's maternal feelings was his indifference to his child. He would hardly be persuaded even to look at it, and if he met it smiling in its nurse's arms, would perhaps gaze for a moment, then turn away as from an object which struck him with a secret horror.

One day as Geneviève was sitting alone in her dressing-room, fondling her infant, and thinking mournfully on this change in her husband's conduct, her femme-de-chambre, a faithful creature who had been brought up with her, and accompanied her from Paris, came into the room, pale as ashes; and throwing herself at her feet, told her that, though regard for her health had hitherto kept her silent, she could no longer conceal the dreadful secret which weighed upon her spirits. She then proceeded to inform the shuddering and horror-struck Geneviève that the robbers who had excited so much terror, and were now supposed to be at a distance, were then actually in the château: that they consisted of the very servants and immediate dependants, with the baron himself at their head. She supposed they had been less on their guard during Geneviève's confinement; and many minute circumstances had at first awaked, and then confirmed her suspicions. Then embracing her mistress's knees, she besought her, for the love of Heaven, to return to Paris instantly, with those of her own attendants on whom she could securely depend, before they were all murdered in their beds.

Geneviève, as soon as she had recovered from her first dizzy horror and astonishment, would have rejected the whole as a dream, and impossible fiction. She thought upon her husband, on all that her fond heart admired in him, and all that till lately she had found him—his noble form, his manly beauty, his high and honourable bearing, and all his love, his truth, his tenderness for her—and could *he* be a robber, a ruffian, an assassin? No; though her woman's attachment and truth were beyond suspicion, her tale too horribly consistent for disbelief, Geneviève would trust to her own senses alone to confirm or disprove the hideous imputation. She commanded her maid to maintain an absolute silence on the subject and leave the rest to her.

The same evening the baron informed his wife that he was obliged to set off before light next morning in pursuit of a party of smugglers who had landed at St. Paul; and that she must not be surprised if she missed him at an early hour. His absence, he assured her, would not be long: he should certainly return before the evening. They retired to rest earlier than usual. Geneviève, as it may be imagined, did not sleep, but she lay perfectly still as if in a profound slumber. About the middle of the night she heard her husband softly rise from his bed and dress himself; and taking his pistols he left the room. Geneviève rushed to the window which overlooked the courtyard, but there neither horses nor attendants were waiting; she flew to another window which commanded the back of the château—there, too, all was still; nothing was to be seen but the moonlight shadows on the pavement. She hastily threw round her a dark cloak or wrapper, and followed her husband, whose footsteps were still within hearing, It was not difficult, for he walked slowly, stopping every now and then, listening, and apparently irresolute; he crossed the court and several outbuildings, and part of the ruins of a former château, till he came to an old well which, being dry, had long been disused and shut up, and moving aside the trap-door which covered the mouth of it, he disappeared in an instant. Généviève with difficulty suppressed a shriek of terror. She followed, however, with a desperate courage, groped her way down the well by means of some broken stairs, and pursued her husband's steps, guided only by the sound on the hollow damp earth. Suddenly a distant light and voices broke upon her eye and ear; and stealing along the wall, she hid herself behind one of the huge buttresses which supported the vault above; she beheld what she was half prepared to see—a party of ruffians, who were assembled round a board drinking. They received the baron with respect as their chief, but with sullen suspicious looks, and an ominous silence. Généviève could distinguish among the faces many familiar to her, which she was accustomed to see daily around her, working in the gardens or attending in the château; among them the concierge, or house-steward, who appeared to have some authority over the rest. The wife of this man was the nurse of Généviève's child. The baron took his seat without speaking. After some boisterous conversation among the rest, carried on in an unintelligible dialect, a quarrel arose between the concierge and another villain, both apparently intoxicated; the baron attempted to part them, and the uproar became general. The whole was probably a preconcerted plan, for from reproaching each other they proceeded to attack the baron himself with the most injurious epithets; they accused him of a design to betray them; they compared him to his father, the old baron, who had never flinched from their cause, and had at last died in it; they said they knew well that a large party of regular troops had lately arrived at Saint-Brieu, and they insisted it was with his knowledge, that he was about to give them up to justice, to make his own peace with government, etc.

The concierge, who was by far the most insolent and violent of these mutineers, at length silenced the others, and affecting a tone of moderation he proposed, and his proposal was received with an approving shout, that the baron should give up his infant son into the hands of the band; that they should take him to the island of Guernsey, and keep him there as a pledge of his father's fidelity till the regular troops were withdrawn from the province. How must

the mother's heart have trembled and died away within her! She
listened breathless for her husband's reply. The baron had hitherto
with difficulty restrained himself, and attempted to prove how
absurd and unfounded was their accusation, since his safety was
involved in theirs, and he would, as their leader, be considered as
the greatest criminal of all. His eyes now flashed with fury; he
sprung upon the concierge like a roused tiger, and dragged him by
the collar from amid the mutinous group. A struggle ensued, and
the wretch fell, stabbed to the heart by his master's hand; a crowd
of ferocious faces then closed around the baron—Généviève heard
—saw no more—her senses left her.

When she recovered she was in perfect silence and darkness, and
felt like one awakening from a terrible dream; the first image which
clearly presented itself to her mind was that of her child in the
power of these ruffians, and their daggers at her husband's throat.
The maddening thought swallowed up every other feeling, and lent
her for the moment strength and wings; she rushed back through
the darkness, fearless for herself; crossed the court, the galleries;—
all was still: it seemed to her affrighted imagination that the château
was forsaken by its inhabitants. She reached her child's room,
she flew to his cradle and drew aside the curtain with a desperate
hand, expecting to find it empty; he was quietly sleeping in his
beauty and innocence: Généviève uttered a cry of joy and thank-
fulness, and fell on the bed in strong convulsions.

Many hours elapsed before she was restored to herself. The first
object she beheld was her husband watching tenderly over her, her
first emotion was joy for his safety—she dared not ask him to
account for it. She then called for her son; he was brought to her,
and from that moment she would never suffer him to leave her.
With the quick wit of a woman, or rather with the prompt resolution of a mother trembling for her child, Généviève was no sooner
sufficiently recovered to think than she had formed her decision and
acted upon it; she accounted for her sudden illness and terrors
under pretence that she had been disturbed by a frightful dream:
she believed, she said, that the dulness and solitude of the château
affected her spirits, that the air disagreed with her child, and that
it was necessary that she should instantly return to Paris. The
baron attempted first to rally and then to reason with her: he consented—then retracted his consent; seemed irresolute—but his affections finally prevailed over his suspicions, and preparations were
instantly made for their departure, as if he intended to accompany
her.

Putting her with her maid and the child into a travelling carriage,
he armed a few of his most confidential servants, and rode by her
side till they came to Saint-Brieu: he then turned back in spite of
all her entreaties, promising to rejoin her at Paris within a few days.
He had never during the journey uttered a word which could

betray his knowledge that she had any motive for her journey but that which she avowed; only at parting he laid his finger expressively on his lip, and gave her one look full of meaning: it could not be mistaken; it said, " Généviève! your husband's life depends on your discretion, and he trusts you." She would have thrown herself into his arms, but he gently replaced her in the carriage, and remounting his horse, rode back alone to the château.

Généviève arrived safely at Paris, and commanded her maid, as she valued both their lives, and on pain of her eternal displeasure, not to breathe a syllable of what had passed, firmly resolved that nothing should tear the terrible secret from her own breast: but the profound melancholy which had settled on her heart, and her pining and altered looks, could not escape the eyes of her affectionate aunt; and her maid, either through indiscretion, timidity, or a sense of duty, on being questioned, revealed all she knew, and more than she knew. The aunt, in a transport of terror and indignation, sent information to the governor of the police, and Le Noir instantly summoned the unfortunate wife of the baron to a private interview.

Généviève, though taken by surprise, did not lose her presence of mind, and at first she steadily denied every word of her maid's deposition; but her courage and her affection were no match for the minister's art: when he assured her he had already sufficient proof of her husband's guilt, and promised, with jesuitical equivocation, that if she would confess all she knew his life should not be touched, that due regard should be had for the honour of his family and hers, and that he (Le Noir) would exert the power which he alone possessed to detach him from his present courses and his present associates without the least publicity or scandal—she yielded, and on this promise being most solemnly reiterated and confirmed by an oath, revealed all she knew.

In a short time afterwards the baron disappeared, and was never heard of more. In vain did his wretched wife appeal to Le Noir and recall the promise he had given: he swore to her that her husband still *lived*, but more than this he would not discover. In vain she supplicated, wept, offered all her fortune for permission to share his exile if he were banished, his dungeon if he were a prisoner— Le Noir was inexorable.

Généviève, left in absolute ignorance of her husband's fate, tortured by a suspense more dreadful than the most dreadful certainty, by remorse and grief which refused all comfort, died brokenhearted: what became of the baron was never known.

I could not exactly learn the fate of his son: it is said that he lived to man's estate, that he took the name of his mother's family, and died a violent death during the Revolution.

# THOMAS CROFTON CROKER
1798–1854

# DANIEL O'ROURKE

PEOPLE may have heard of the renowned adventures of Daniel O'Rourke, but how few are there who know that the cause of all his perils, above and below, was neither more nor less than his having slept under the walls of the Phooka's tower! I knew the man well; he lived at the bottom of Hungry Hill, just at the right-hand side of the road as you go towards Bantry.

An old man was he at the time that he told me the story, with grey hair and a red nose: and it was on June 25, 1813, that I heard it from his own lips, as he sat smoking his pipe under the old poplar tree, on as fine an evening as ever shone from the sky. I was going to visit the caves in Dursey Island, having spent the morning at Glengariff.

"I am often *axed* to tell it, sir," said he, "so that this is not the first time. The master's son, you see, had come from beyond foreign parts in France and Spain, as young gentlemen used to go, before Buonaparte or any such was heard of; and sure enough there was a dinner given to all the people on the ground, gentle and simple, high and low, rich and poor. The *ould* gentlemen were the gentlemen, after all, saving your honour's presence. They'd swear at a body a little, to be sure, and maybe give one a cut of a whip now and then, but we were no losers by it in the end; and they were so easy and civil, and kept such rattling houses, and thousands of welcomes; and there was no grinding for rent, and few agents; and there was hardly a tenant on the estate that did not taste of his landlord's bounty often and often in the year;—but now it's another thing: no matter for that, sir, for I'd better be telling you my story.

"Well, we had everything of the best, and plenty of it; and we ate, and we drank, and we danced, and the young master by the same token danced with Peggy Barry, from the Bohereen—a lovely young couple they were, though they are both low enough now. To make a long story short, I got, as a body may say, the same thing as tipsy almost, for I can't remember ever at all, no ways, how it was I left the place: only I did leave it, that's certain. Well,

I thought, for all that, in myself, I'd just step to Molly Cronohan's, the fairy-woman, to speak a word about the bracket heifer that was bewitched; and so as I was crossing the stepping-stones of the ford of Ballyasheenough, and was looking up at the stars and blessing myself—for why? it was Lady-day—I missed my foot, and souse I fell into the water. ' Death alive! ' thought I, ' I'll be drowned now! '

" However, I began swimming, swimming, swimming away for the dear life, till at last I got ashore, somehow or other, but never the one of me can tell how, upon a *dissolute* island.

" I wandered and wandered about there, without knowing where I wandered, until at last I got into a big bog. The moon was shining as bright as day, or your fair lady's eyes, sir (with your pardon for mentioning her), and I looked east and west, and north and south, and every way, and nothing did I see but bog, bog, bog; —I could never find out how I got into it; and my heart grew cold with fear, for sure and certain I was that it would be my *berrin* place. So I sat down upon a stone, which, as good luck would have it, was close by me, and I began to scratch my head and sing the *Ullagone*—when all of a sudden the moon grew black, and I looked up, and saw something for all the world as if it was moving down between me and it, and I could not tell what it was. Down it came with a pounce, and looked at me full in the face; and what was it but an eagle? as fine a one as ever flew from the kingdom of Kerry.

" So he looked at me in the face, and says he to me, ' Daniel O'Rourke,' says he, ' how do you do? '

" ' Very well, I thank you, sir,' says I; ' I hope you're well '; wondering out of my senses all the time how an eagle came to speak like a Christian.

" ' What brings you here, Dan? ' says he.

" ' Nothing at all, sir,' says I; ' only I wish I was safe home again.'

" ' Is it out of the island you want to go, Dan? ' says he.

" ' 'Tis, sir,' says I; so I up and told him how I had taken a drop too much; and fell into the water; how I swam to the island; and how I got into the bog and did not know my way out of it.

" ' Dan,' says he after a minute's thought, ' though it is very improper for you to get drunk on Lady-day, yet as you are a decent sober man, who 'tends mass well, and never flings stones at me nor mine, nor cries out after us in the fields—my life for yours,' says he; ' so get up on my back, and grip me well for fear you'd fall off, and I'll fly you out of the bog.'

" ' I am afraid,' says I, ' your honour's making game of me; for who ever heard of riding a-horseback on an eagle before? '

" ' 'Pon the honour of a gentleman,' says he, putting his right foot on his breast, ' I am quite in earnest; and so now either take my offer or starve in the bog; besides, I see that your weight is sinking the stone.'

" It was true enough as he said, for I found the stone every minute going from under me. I had no choice; so thinks I to myself, faint heart never won fair lady, and this is fair persuadance:—' I thank your honour,' says I, ' for the loan of your civility, and I'll take your kind offer.'

" I therefore mounted upon the back of the eagle, and held him tight enough by the throat, and up he flew in the air like a lark. Little I knew the trick he was going to serve me. Up, up, up— God knows how far up he flew.

" ' Why, then,' said I to him—thinking he did not know the right road home—very civilly, because why?—I was in his power entirely;—' sir,' says I, ' please your honour's glory, and with humble submission to your better judgment, if you'd fly down a bit, you're now just over my cabin, and I could be put down there, and many thanks to your worship.'

" ' *Arrah*, Dan,' said he, ' do you think me a fool? Look down in the next field, and don't you see two men and a gun? By my word it would be no joke to be shot this way, to oblige a drunken blackguard that I picked up off of a *could* stone in a bog.'

" ' Bother you,' said I to myself, but I did not speak out, for where was the use? Well, sir, up he kept flying, flying, and I asking him every minute to fly down, and all to no use.

" ' Where in the world are you going, sir? ' says I to him.

" ' Hold your tongue, Dan,' says he; ' mind your own business, and don't be interfering with the business of other people.'

" ' Faith, this is my business, I think,' says I.

" ' Be quiet, Dan,' says he; so I said no more.

" At last where should we come to but to the moon itself. Now you can't see it from this, but there is, or there was in my time, a reaping-hook sticking out of the side of the moon, this way (drawing the figure thus ☾ on the ground with the end of his stick).

" ' Dan,' said the eagle, ' I'm tired with this long fly; I had no notion 'twas so far.'

" ' And my lord, sir,' said I, ' who in the world *axed* you to fly so far—was it I? Did not I beg, and pray, and beseech you to stop half an hour ago? '

" ' There's no use talking, Dan,' said he; ' I'm tired bad enough, so you must get off and sit down on the moon until I rest myself.'

" ' Is it sit down on the moon? ' said I; ' is it upon that little round thing, then? why then, sure, I'd fall off in a minute, and be *kilt* and split, and smashed all to bits: you are a vile deceiver— so you are.'

" ' Not at all, Dan,' said he; ' you can catch fast hold of the reaping-hook that's sticking out of the side of the moon, and 'twill keep you up.'

" ' I won't then,' said I.

" ' Maybe not,' said he quite quiet. ' If you don't, my man, I shall just give you a shake, and one slap of my wing, and send you down to the ground, where every bone in your body will be smashed as small as a drop of dew on a cabbage-leaf in the morning.'

" ' Why, then, I'm in a fine way,' said I to myself, ' ever to have come along with the likes of you '; and so giving him a hearty curse in Irish, for fear he'd know what I said, I got off his back with a heavy heart, took a hold of the reaping-hook, and sat down upon the moon; and a mighty cold seat it was, I can tell you that.

" When he had me there fairly landed, he turned about on me, and said, ' Good-morning to you, Daniel O'Rourke,' said he, ' I think I've nicked you fairly now. You robbed my nest last year ' ('twas true enough for him, but how he found it out is hard to say), ' and in return you are freely welcome to cool your heels dangling upon the moon like a cockthrow.'

" ' Is that all, and is this the way you leave me, you brute you! ' says I. ' You ugly unnatural *baste,* and is this the way you serve me at last? Bad luck to yourself, with your hook'd nose, and to all your breed, you blackguard.'

" 'Twas all to no manner of use; he spread out his great big wings, burst out a-laughing, and flew away like lightning. I bawled after him to stop; but I might have called and bawled for ever without his minding me. Away he went, and I never saw him from that day to this—sorrow fly away with him! You may be sure I was in a disconsolate condition, and kept roaring out for the bare grief, when all at once a door opened right in the middle of the moon, creaking on its hinges as if it had not been opened for a month before—I suppose they never thought of greasing 'em—and out there walks—who do you think but the man in the moon himself? I knew him by his bush.

" ' Good-morrow to you, Daniel O'Rourke,' said he: ' how do you do? '

" ' Very well, thank your honour,' said I. ' I hope your honour's well.'

" ' What brought you here, Dan? '' said he. So I told him how I was a little overtaken in liquor at the master's, and how I was cast on a *dissolute* island, and how I lost my way in the bog, and how the thief of an eagle promised to fly me out of it, and how instead of that he had fled me up to the moon.

" ' Dan,' said the man in the moon, taking a pinch of snuff, when I was done, ' you must not stay here.'

" ' Indeed, sir,' says I, ' 'tis much against my will I'm here at all; but how am I to go back? '

" ' That's your business,' said he, ' Dan : mine is to tell you that here you must not stay, so be off in less than no time.'

" ' I'm doing no harm,' says I, ' only holding on hard by the reaping-hook lest I fall off.'

" ' That's what you must not do, Dan,' says he.

" ' Pray, sir,' says I, ' may I ask how many you are in family that you would not give a poor traveller lodging : I'm sure 'tis not so often you're troubled with strangers coming to see you, for 'tis a long way.'

" ' I'm by myself, Dan,' says he; ' but you'd better let go the reaping-hook.'

" ' Faith, and with your leave,' says I, ' I'll not let go the grip, and the more you bids me, the more I won't let go—so I will.'

" ' You had better, Dan,' says he again.

" ' Why, then, my little fellow,' says I, taking the whole weight of him with my eye from head to foot, ' there are two words to that bargain; and I'll not budge, but you may if you like.'

" ' We'll see how that is to be,' says he; and back he went, giving the door such a great bang after him (for it was plain he was huffed) and I thought the moon and all would fall down with it.

" Well, I was preparing myself to try strength with him, when back again he comes with the kitchen cleaver in his hand, and without saying a word, he gives two bangs to the handle of the reaping-hook that was keeping me up, and *whap!* it came in two.

" ' Good-morning to you, Dan,' says the spiteful little old black-guard when he saw me cleanly falling down with a bit of the handle in my hand : ' I thank you for your visit, and fair weather after you, Daniel.'

" I had not time to make any answer to him, for I was tumbling over and over, and rolling and rolling at the rate of a fox-hunt. ' God help me,' says I, ' but this is a pretty pickle for a decent man to be seen in at this time of night; I am now sold fairly.'

" The word was not out of my mouth, when whiz! what should fly by close to my ear but a flock of wild geese, all the way from my own bog of Ballyasheenough, else how should they know *me*? The *ould* gander, who was their general, turning about his head, cried out to me, ' Is that you, Dan? '

" ' The same,' said I, not a bit daunted now at what he said, for I was by this time used to all kinds of *bedevilment*, and, besides, I knew him of *ould*.

" ' Good-morrow to you,' says he, ' Daniel O'Rourke; how are you in health this morning? '

" ' Very well, sir,' says I, ' I thank you kindly,' drawing my breath, for I was mightily in want of some. ' I hope your honour's the same.'

" ' I think 'tis falling you are, Daniel,' says he.

" ' You may say that, sir,' says I.

" ' And where are you going all the way so fast? ' said the gander.

" So I told him how I had taken the drop, and how I came on the island, and how I lost my way in the bog, and how the thief of an eagle flew me up to the moon, and how the man in the moon turned me out.

" ' Dan,' said he, ' I'll save you; put out your hand and catch me by the leg, and I'll fly you home.'

" Sweet is your hand in a pitcher of honey, my jewel,' says I, though all the time I thought in myself that I don't much trust you; but there was no help, so I caught the gander by the leg, and away I and the other geese flew after him as fast as hops.

" We flew, and we flew, and we flew, until we came right over the wide ocean. I knew it well, for I saw Cape Clear to my right hand sticking up out of the water.

" ' Ah! my lord,' said I to the goose, for I thought it best to keep a civil tongue in my head anyway, ' fly to land, if you please.'

" ' It is impossible, you see, Dan,' said he, ' for a while, because you see we are going to Arabia.'

" ' To Arabia? ' said I; ' that's surely some place in foreign parts, far away. Oh, Mr. Goose! why then, to be sure, I'm a man to be pitied among you.'

" ' Whist, whist, you fool,' said he, ' hold your tongue; I tell you Arabia is a very decent sort of place, as like West Carbery as one egg is like another, only there is a little more sand there.'

" Just as we were talking a ship hove in sight, scudding so beautiful before the wind: ' Ah! then, sir,' said I, ' will you drop me on the ship, if you please? '

" ' We are not fair over it,' said he.

" ' We are,' said I.

" ' We are not,' said he. ' If I dropped you now, you would go splash into the sea.'

" ' I would not,' says I: ' I know better than that, for it's just clean under us, so let me drop now at once.'

" ' If you must, you must,' said he. ' There, take your own way '; and he opened his claw, and faith he was right—sure enough I came down plump into the very bottom of the salt sea! Down to the very bottom I went, and I gave myself up then for ever, when a whale walked up to me, scratching himself after his night's sleep, and looked me full in the face, and never the word did he say, but lifting up his tail he splashed me all over again with the cold salt water, till there wasn't a dry stitch upon my whole carcass; and I heard somebody saying—'twas a voice I knew too—' Get up, you drunken brute, off of that '; and with that I woke up, and there was Judy with a tub full of water, which she was splashing all over me,—for, rest her soul! though she was a good wife, she never could bear to see me in drink, and had a bitter hand of her own!

" ' Get up,' said she again; ' and of all places in the parish would no place *sarve* your turn to lie down upon but under the *ould* walls of Carrigaphooka? an uneasy resting I am sure you had of it.'

" And sure enough I had; for I was fairly bothered out of my senses with eagles, and men of the moon, and flying ganders, and whales, driving me through bogs, and up to the moon, and down to the bottom of the green ocean. If I was in drink ten times over, long would it be before I'd lie down in the same spot again, I know that."

# THE LADY OF GOLLERUS

THOMAS CROFTON CROKER

ON the shore of Smerwick harbour, one fine summer's morning, just at daybreak, stood Dick Fitzgerald " shoghing the dudeen," which may be translated, smoking his pipe.   The sun was gradually rising behind the lofty Brandon, the dark sea was getting green in the light, and the mists, clearing away out of the valleys, went rolling and curling like the smoke from the corner of Dick's mouth.

" 'Tis just the pattern of a pretty morning," said Dick, taking the pipe from between his lips, and looking towards the distant ocean, which lay as still and tranquil as a tomb of polished marble. " Well, to be sure," continued he, after a pause, " 'tis mighty lonesome to be talking to one's self by way of company, and not to have another soul to answer one—nothing but the child of one's own voice, the echo!   I know this, that if I had the luck, or maybe the misfortune," said he with a melancholy smile, " to have the woman, it would not be this way with me!—and what in the wide world is a man without a wife?   He's no more surely than a bottle without a drop of drink in it, or dancing without music, or the left leg of a scissors, or a fishing-line without a hook, or any other matter that is no ways complete.—Is it not so? " said Dick Fitzgerald, casting his eyes towards a rock upon the strand, which, though it could not speak, stood up as firm and looked as bold as ever Kerry witness did.

But what was his astonishment at beholding, just at the foot of that rock, a beautiful young creature combing her hair, which was of a sea-green colour; and now the salt water shining on it appeared in the morning light, like melted butter upon cabbage.

Dick guessed at once that she was a Merrow, although he had never seen one before, for he spied the *cohuleen driuth,* or little enchanted cap, which sea-people use for diving down into the ocean, lying upon the strand near her; and he had heard that if once he could possess himself of the cap she would lose the power of going away into the water: so he seized it with all speed, and she, hearing the noise, turned her head about as natural as any Christian.

When the Merrow saw that her little diving-cap was gone, the salt tears—doubly salt, no doubt, from her—came trickling down her cheeks, and she began a low mournful cry with just the tender voice of a new-born infant. Dick, although he knew well enough what she was crying for, determined to keep the *cohuleen driuth,* let her cry never so much, to see what luck would come out of it. Yet he could not help pitying her; and when the dumb thing looked up in his face, and her cheeks all moist with tears, 'twas enough to make any one feel, let alone Dick, who had ever and always, like most of his countrymen, a mighty tender heart of his own.

" Don't cry, my darling," said Dick Fitzgerald; but the Merrow, like any bold child, only cried the more for that.

Dick sat himself down by her side, and took hold of her hand by way of comforting her. 'Twas in no particular an ugly hand, only there was a small web between the fingers, as there is in a duck's foot; but 'twas as thin and as white as the skin between egg and shell.

" What's your name, my darling? " says Dick, thinking to make her conversant with him; but he got no answer; and he was certain sure now, either that she could not speak, or did not understand him: he therefore squeezed her hand in his, as the only way he had of talking to her. It's the universal language, and there's not a woman in the world, be she fish or lady, that does not understand it.

The Merrow did not seem much displeased at this mode of conversation; and, making an end of her whining all at once—" Man," says she, looking up in Dick Fitzgerald's face, " man, will you eat me? "

" By all the red petticoats and check aprons between Dingle and Tralee," cried Dick, jumping up in amazement, " I'd as soon eat myself, my jewel! Is it I eat you, my pet? Now, 'twas some ugly ill-looking thief of a fish put that notion into your own pretty head, with the nice green hair down upon it, that is so cleanly combed out this morning! "

" Man," said the Merrow, " what will you do with me if you won't eat me? " Dick's thoughts were running on a wife: he saw, at the first glimpse, that she was handsome; but since she spoke, and spoke, too, like any real woman, he was fairly in love with her. 'Twas the neat way she called him man that settled the matter entirely.

" Fish," says Dick, trying to speak to her after her own short fashion; " fish," says he, " here's my word, fresh and fasting, for you this blessed morning, that I'll make you Mistress Fitzgerald before all the world, and that's what I'll do."

" Never say the word twice," says she, " I'm ready and willing to be yours, Mister Fitzgerald; but stop, if you please, till I twist up my hair." It was some time before she had settled it entirely to her liking; for she guessed, I suppose, that she was going among strangers, where she would be looked at. When that was done, the Merrow put the comb in her pocket, and then bent down her head and whispered some words to the water that was close to the foot of the rock.

Dick saw the murmur of the words upon the top of the sea, going out towards the wide ocean, just like a breath of wind rippling along, and, says he, in the greatest wonder, " Is it speaking you are, my darling, to the salt water? "

" It's nothing else," says she, quite carelessly, " I'm just sending word home to my father not to be waiting breakfast for me; just to keep him from being uneasy in his mind."

" And who's your father, my duck? " says Dick.

" What! " said the Merrow, " did you never hear of my father? he's the king of the waves, to be sure! "

" And yourself, then, is a real king's daughter? " said Dick, opening his two eyes to take a full and true survey of his wife that was to be. " Oh, I'm nothing else but a made man with you, and a king your father—to be sure he has all the money that's down in the bottom of the sea! "

" Money," repeated the Merrow, " what's money? "

" 'Tis no bad thing to have when one wants it," replied Dick; " and maybe now the fishes have the understanding to bring up whatever you bid them? "

" Oh, yes," said the Merrow, " they bring me what I want."

" To speak the truth then," said Dick, " 'tis a straw bed I have at home before you, and that, I'm thinking, is no ways fitting for a king's daughter; so if 'twould not be displeasing to you, just to mention, a nice feather bed, with a pair of new blankets—but what am I talking about? maybe you have no such things as beds down under the water? "

" By all means," said she, " Mr. Fitzgerald—plenty of beds at your service. I've fourteen oyster beds of my own, not to mention one just planting for the rearing of young ones."

" You have," says Dick, scratching his head and looking a little puzzled. " 'Tis a feather bed I was speaking of—but clearly, yours is the very cut of a decent plan, to have bed and supper so handy to each other, that a person when they'd have the one need never ask for the other." However, bed or no bed, money or no money, Dick Fitzgerald determined to marry the Merrow, and the Merrow had given her consent. Away they went, therefore, across the strand, from Gollerus to Ballinrunnig, where Father Fitzgibbon happened to be that morning.

" There are two words to this bargain, Dick Fitzgerald," said his reverence, looking mighty glum. " And is it a fishy woman you'd marry?—the Lord preserve us!—Send the scaly creature home to her own people, that's my advice to you, wherever she came from."

Dick had the *cohuleen driuth* in his hand, and was about to give it back to the Merrow, who looked covetously at it, but he thought for a moment, and then says he:

" Please, your reverence, she's a king's daughter."

" If she was the daughter of fifty kings," said Father Fitzgibbon, " I tell you, you can't marry her, she being a fish."

" Please, your reverence," said Dick again, in an undertone, " she's as mild and beautiful as the moon."

" If she was as mild and as beautiful as the sun, moon, and the stars, all put together, I tell you, Dick Fitzgerald," said the priest, stamping his right foot, " you can't marry her, she being a fish! "

" But she has all the gold that's down in the sea only for the asking, and I'm a made man if I marry her: and," said Dick, looking up slily, " I can make it worth any one's while to do the job."

" Oh! that alters the case entirely," replied the priest; " why, there's some reason now in what you say: why didn't you tell me this before?—marry her by all means, if she was ten times a fish. Money, you know, is not to be refused in these bad times, and I may as well have the hansel of it as another that maybe would not take half the pains in counselling you that I have done."

So Father Fitzgibbon married Dick Fitzgerald to the Merrow, and, like any loving couple, they returned to Gollerus well pleased with each other. Everything prospered with Dick—he was at the sunny side of the world; the Merrow made the best of wives, and they lived together in the greatest contentment.

It was wonderful to see, considering where she had been brought up, how she would busy herself about the house, and how well she nursed the children, for at the end of three years there were as many young Fitzgeralds—two boys and a girl. In short, Dick was a happy man, and so he might have continued to the end of his days if he had only the sense to take proper care of what he had got; many another man, however, beside Dick, has not had wit enough to do that.

One day when Dick was obliged to go to Tralee, he left the wife minding the children at home after him, and thinking she had plenty to do without disturbing his fishing-tackle.

Dick was no sooner gone than Mrs. Fitzgerald set about cleaning up the house, and chancing to pull down a fishing-net, what should she find behind it, in a hole in the wall, but her own *cohuleen driuth*.

She took it out and looked at it, and then she thought of her father the king, and her mother the queen, and her brothers and sisters, and she felt a longing to go back to them.

She sat down on a little stool and thought over the happy days she had spent under the sea; then she looked at her children, and thought on the love and affection of poor Dick, and how it would break his heart to lose her. " But," says she, " he won't lose me entirely, for I'll come back to him again, and who can blame me for going to see my father and my mother after being so long away from them? "

She got up and went towards the door, but came back again to look once more at the child that was sleeping in the cradle. She kissed it gently, and, as she kissed it, a tear trembled for an instant in her eye, and then fell on its rosy cheek. She wiped away the tear, and turning to the eldest, the little girl, told her to take good care of her brothers, and to be a good child herself, until she came back. The Merrow then went down to the strand. The sea was lying calm and smooth, just heaving and glittering in the sun, and she thought she heard a faint sweet singing, inviting her to come down. All her old ideas and feelings came flooding over her mind, Dick and her children were at the instant forgotten, and, placing the *cohuleen driuth* on her head, she plunged in.

Dick came home in the evening, and, missing his wife, he asked Kathleen, his little girl, what had become of her mother, but she could not tell him. He then inquired of the neighbours, and he learned that she was seen going towards the strand with a strange-looking thing like a cocked hat in her hand. He returned to his cabin to search for the *cohuleen driuth*. It was gone, and the truth now flashed upon him.

Year after year did Dick Fitzgerald wait expecting the return of his wife, but he never saw her more. Dick never married again, always thinking that the Merrow would sooner or later return to him, and nothing could ever persuade him but that her father the king kept her below by main force; " for," said Dick, " she surely would not of herself give up her husband and her children."

While she was with him, she was so good a wife in every respect, that to this day she is spoken of in the tradition of the country, as the pattern for one under the name of THE LADY OF GOLLERUS.

# JOHN BANIM
### 1798–1842

# THE STOLEN SHEEP

THE Irish plague, called typhus fever, raged in its terrors. In almost every third cabin there was a corpse daily. In every one, without an exception, there was what had made the corpse—hunger. It need not be added that there was poverty, too. The poor could not bury their dead. From mixed motives, of self-protection, terror, and benevolence, those in easier circumstances exerted themselves to administer relief in different ways. Money was subscribed (then came England's munificent donation—God prosper her for it!), wholesome food, or food as wholesome as a bad season permitted, was provided; and men of respectability, bracing their minds to avert the danger that threatened themselves, by boldly facing it, entered the infected house, where death reigned almost alone, and took measures to cleanse and purify the close-cribbed air and the rough, bare walls.

In the early progress of the fever, before the more affluent roused themselves to avert its career, let us cross the threshold of an individual peasant. His young wife lies dead; his second child is dying at her side; he has just sunk into a corner himself, under the first stun of disease, long resisted. The only persons of his family who have escaped contagion, and are likely to escape it, are his old father, who sits weeping feebly upon the hob, and his first-born, a boy of three or four years who, standing between the old man's knees, cries also for food.

We visit the young peasant's abode some time after. He has not sunk under " the sickness." He is fast regaining his strength, even without proper nourishment; he can creep out of doors and sit in the sun. But in the expression of his sallow and emaciated face there is no joy for his escape from the grave, as he sits there alone, silent and brooding. His father and surviving child are still hungry —more hungry, indeed, and more helpless than ever; for the neighbours who had relieved the family with a potato and a mug of sour milk are now stricken down themselves, and want assistance to a much greater extent than they can give it.

" I wish Mr. Evans was in the place," cogitated Michaul Car-

roll; " a body could spake forn'ent him, and not spake for nothin',
for all that he's an Englishman; and I don't like the thoughts o'
goin' up to the house to the steward's face—it wouldn't turn kind
to a body.  May be he'd soon come home to us, the masther himself."

Another fortnight elapsed.  Michaul's hope proved vain.  Mr.
Evans was still in London; though a regular resident on his small
Irish estate since it had come into his possession, business unfortunately—and he would have said so himself—now kept him an
unusually long time absent.  Thus disappointed, Michaul overcame
his repugnance to appear before the " hard " steward.  He only
asked for work, however.  There was none to be had.  He turned
his slow and still feeble feet into the adjacent town.  It was market-
day, and he took up his place among a crowd of other claimants
for agricultural employment, shouldering a spade, as did each of his
companions.

Many farmers came to the well-known " stannin," and hired men
at his right and at his left, but no one addressed Michaul.  Once or
twice, indeed, touched perhaps by his sidelong looks of beseeching
misery, a farmer stopped a moment before him, and glanced over
his figure; but his worn and almost shaking limbs giving little
promise of present vigour in the working field, worldly prudence
soon conquered the humane feeling which started up towards him
in the man's heart, and, with a choking in his throat, poor Michaul
saw the arbiter of his fate pass on.

He walked homeward, without having broken his fast that day.
" Bud, *musha,* what's the harm o' that," he said to himself; " only
here's the ould father, an' *her* pet boy, the weenock, without a
pyatee either.  Well, *asthore,* if they can't have the pyatees, they
must have betther food—that's all; ay "—he muttered, clenching
his hands at his sides, and imprecating fearfully in Irish—" an' so
they must."

He left his house again, and walked a good way to beg a few
potatoes.  He did not come back quite empty-handed.  His father
and his child had a meal.  He ate but a few himself; and when he
was about to lie down in his corner for the night, he said to the old
man across the room:

" Don't be a-cryin' to-night, father, you and the child there;
bud sleep well, and ye'll have the good break'ast afore ye in the
mornin'."

" The good break'ast, *ma-bauchal*?[1]  A-then, an' where 'ill id
come from? "

" A body promised it to me, father."

" *Avich!* Michaul, an' sure it's fun you're making of us, now, at
any rate.  Bud, the good night, a *chorra,*[2] an' my blessin' on your
head, Michaul; an' if we keep trust in the good God, an' ax His

[1] My boy.　　　　　　　　[2] Term of endearment.

blessin' too, mornin' an' evenin', gettin' up an' lyin' down, He'll be a friend to us at last: that was always an' ever my word to you, poor boy, since you was at the years o' your own weenock, now fast asleep at my side; an' it's my word to you now; *ma-bauchal*; an' you won't forget id; and there's one sayin' the same to you, out o' heaven, this night—herself, an' her little angel-in-glory by the hand, Michaul *a-vourneen*."

Having thus spoken in the fervent and rather exaggerated, though everyday, words of pious allusion of the Irish poor man, old Carroll soon dropped asleep, with his arms round his little grandson, both overcome by an unusually abundant meal. In the middle of the night he was awakened by a stealthy noise. Without moving, he cast his eyes round the cabin. A small window, through which the moon broke brilliantly, was open. He called to his son, but received no answer. He called again and again: all remained silent. He arose, and crept to the corner where Michaul had lain down. It was empty. He looked out through the window into the moonlight. The figure of a man appeared at a distance, just about to enter a pasture-field belonging to Mr. Evans.

The old man leaned back against the wall of the cabin, trembling with sudden and terrible misgivings. With him the language of virtue which we have heard him utter, was not cant. In early prosperity, in subsequent misfortunes, and in his late and present excess of wretchedness he had never swerved in practice from the spirit of his own exhortations to honesty before men, and love for, and dependence upon God, which, as he had truly said, he had constantly addressed to his son since his earliest childhood. And hitherto that son had, indeed, walked by his precepts, further assisted by a regular observance of the duties of his religion. Was he now about to turn into another path? to bring shame on his father in his old age? to put a stain on their family and their name, " the name that a rogue or a bould woman never bore "? continued old Carroll, indulging in some of the pride and egotism for which an Irish peasant is, under his circumstances, remarkable. And then came the thought of the personal peril incurred by Michaul; and his agitation, incurred by the feebleness of age, nearly overpowered him.

He was sitting on the floor, shivering like one in an ague fit, when he heard steps outside the house. He listened, and they ceased: but the familiar noise of an old barn door creaking on its crazy hinges came on his ear. It was now day-dawn. He dressed himself, stole out cautiously, peeped into the barn through a chink of the door, and all he had feared met full confirmation. There, indeed, sat Michaul, busily and earnestly engaged, with a frowning brow and a haggard face, in quartering the animal he had stolen from Mr. Evans's field.

The sight sickened the father—the blood on his son's hands, and all. He was barely able to keep himself from falling. A fear, if not a dislike, of the unhappy culprit also came upon him. His unconscious impulse was to re-enter their cabin unperceived, without speaking a word; he succeeded in doing so; and then he fastened the door again and undressed, and resumed his place beside his innocent grandson.

About an hour afterwards, Michaul came in cautiously through the still open window, and also undressed and reclined on his straw, after glancing towards his father's bed, who pretended to be asleep. At the usual time for arising, old Carroll saw him suddenly jump up, and prepare to go abroad. He spoke to him, leaning on his elbow.

"And what *hollg*[1] is on you now, *ma-bauchal*? "

"Going for the good break'ast I promised you, father dear."

"An' who's the good Christhthan 'ill give id to us, Michaul? "

"Oh, you'll know that soon, father: now, a good-bye "—he hurried to the door.

"A good-bye, then, Michaul; bud, tell me, what's that on your hand? "

"No-nothin'," stammered Michaul, changing colour, as he hastily examined the hand himself; "nothin' is on id: what could there be? " (Nor was there, for he had very carefully removed all evidence of guilt from his person; and the father's question was asked upon grounds distinct from anything he then saw.)

"Well, *avich*, an' sure I didn't say anything was on it wrong; or anything to make you look so quare, an' spake so sthrange to your father, this mornin';—only I'll ax you, Michaul, over agin, who has took such a sudd'n likin' to us, to send us the good break'ast?—an' answer me sthraight, Michaul—what is id to be, that you call it so *good*? "

"The good mate, father "—he was again passing the threshold.

"Stop! " cried his father; " stop, an' turn fornent me. Mate?— the good mate?—What 'ud bring mate into our poor house, Michaul? Tell me, I bid you again an' again, who is to give id to you? "

"Why, as I said afore, father, a body that——"

"A body that thieved id, Michaul Carroll! " added the old man, as his son hesitated, walking close up to the culprit; " a body that thieved id, an' no other body. Don't think to blind me, Michaul. I am ould, to be sure; but sense enough is left in me to look round among the neighbours, in my own mind, an' know that none of 'em that has the will has the power to send us the mate for our break'ast in an honest way. An' I don't say, outright, that you had the same thought wid me when you consented to take it from a thief—I don't mean to say that you'd go to turn a thief's receiver, at this hour o' your life, an' afther growin' up from a boy to a man

[1] What are you about.

widout bringin' a spot o' shame on yourself, or on your weenock, or on one of us. No; I won't say that. Your heart was scalded, Michaul, an' your mind was darkened, for a start; an' the thought o' getting comfort for the ould father an' for the little son made you consent in a hurry, widout lookin' well afore you, or widout lookin' up to your good God."

"Father, father, let me alone! don't spake them words to me," interrupted Michaul, sitting on a stool, and spreading his large and hard hands over his face.

"Well, thin, an' I won't, *avich;* I won't;—nothin' to throuble you, sure: I didn't mean id;—only this, *a-vourneen,* don't bring a mouthful o' the bad, unlucky victuals into this cabin; the pyatees, the wild berries o' the bush, the wild roots o' the arth, will be sweeter to us, Michaul; the hunger itself will be sweeter; an' when we give God thanks afther our poor meal, or afther no meal at all, our hearts will be lighter, and our hopes for to-morrow sthronger, *avich-ma-chree,* than if we faisted on the fat o' the land, but couldn't ax a blessin' on our faist."

"Well, thin, *I* won't, either, father; I won't: an' sure you have your way now. I'll only go out a little while from you—to beg; or else, as you say, to root down in the ground, with my nails, like a baste-brute, for our break'ast."

"My vourneen you are, Michaul, an' my blessin' on your head; yes, to be sure, *avich,* beg, an I'll beg wid you—sorrow a shame is in that—no, but a good deed, Michaul, when it's done to keep us honest. So come; we'll go among the Christhthans together. Only, before we go, Michaul, my own dear son, tell me—tell one thing."

"What, father? " Michaul began to suspect.

"Never be afraid to tell me, Michaul Carroll, *ma-bauchal?* I won't—I can't be angry wid you now. You are sorry; an' your Father in heaven forgives you, and so do I. But you know, *avich,* there would be danger in quitting the place widout hiding every scrap of anything that could tell on us."

"Tell on us! What can tell on us? " demanded Michaul; "what's in the place to tell on us? "

"Nothin' in the cabin, I know, Michaul; but——"

"But what, father? "

"Have you left nothing in the way, out there? " whispered the old man, pointing towards the barn.

"Out there? Where? What? What do you mean at all, now, father? Sure you know it's your ownsef has kep me from as much as laying a hand on it."

"Ay, to-day mornin'; bud you laid a hand on it last night, *avich,* an' so——"

"*Curp-an-duoul!* " imprecated Michaul—" this is too bad, at any rate; no, I didn't—last night—let me alone, I bid you, father."

"Come back again, Michaul," commanded old Carroll, as the son once more hurried to the door: and his words were instantly obeyed. Michaul, after a glance abroad, and a start, which the old man did not notice, paced to the middle of the floor, hanging his head and saying in a low voice, "Hushth now, father—it's time."

"No, Michaul, I will not hushth; an' it's not time; come out with me to the barn."

"Hushth!" repeated Michaul, whispering sharply: he had glanced sideways to the square patch of strong morning sunlight on the ground of the cabin, defined there by the shape of the open door, and saw it intruded upon by the shadow of a man's bust leaning forward in an earnest posture.

"Is it in your mind to go back into your sin, Michaul, an' tell me you were not in the barn, at daybreak, the mornin'?" asked his father, still unconscious of a reason for silence.

"Arrah, hushth, ould man!" Michaul made a hasty sign towards the door, but was disregarded.

"I saw you in id," pursued old Carroll sternly: "ay, and at your work in id, too."

"What's that you're sayin', ould Peery Carroll!" demanded a well-known voice.

"Enough to hang his son," whispered Michaul to his father, as Mr. Evans's land-steward, followed by his herdsman and two policemen, entered the cabin. In a few minutes afterwards the policemen had in charge the dismembered carcase of the sheep, dug up out of the floor of the barn, and were escorting Michaul, handcuffed, to the county gaol, in the vicinity of the next town. They could find no trace of the animal's skin, though they sought attentively for it; and this seemed to disappoint them and the steward a good deal.

From the moment that they entered the cabin, till their departure, old Carroll did not speak a word. Without knowing it, as it seemed, he sat down on his straw bed, and remained staring stupidly around him, or at one or another of his visitors. When Michaul was about to leave the wretched abode, he paced quickly towards his father, and holding out his ironed hands, and turning his cheek for a kiss, said, smiling miserably, "God be wid you, father dear."

Still the old man was silent, and the prisoner and all his attendants passed out on the road. But it was then that the agony of old Carroll assumed a distinctness. Uttering a fearful cry, he snatched up his still sleeping grandson, ran with the boy in his arms till he overtook Michaul; and, kneeling down before him in the dust, said:

"I ax pardon o' you, *avich*—won't you tell me I have id afore you go? An' here, I've brought little Peery for you to kiss; you forgot *him, a-vourneen*."

" No, father, I didn't," answered Michaul, as he stooped to kiss the child; an' get up, father, get up; my hands are not my own, or I wouldn't let you do that afore your son. Get up, there's nothin' for you to throuble yourself about; that is, I mean, I have nothin' to forgive you: no, but everything to be thankful for, an' to love you for; you were always an' ever the good father to me; an'——"

The many strong and bitter feelings which till now he had almost perfectly kept in, found full vent, and poor Michaul could not go on. The parting from his father, however, so different from what it had promised to be, comforted him. The old man held him in his arms and wept on his neck. They separated with difficulty.

Peery Carroll, sitting on the roadside after he lost sight of the prisoner, and holding his screaming grandson on his knees, thought the cup of his trials was full. By his imprudence he had fixed the proof of guilt on his own child; that reflection was enough for him, and he could indulge it only generally. But he was yet to conceive distinctly in what dilemma he had involved himself as well as Michaul.

The policemen came back to compel his appearance before the magistrate; and when the little child had been disposed of in a neighbouring cabin, he understood, to his consternation and horror, that he was to be the chief witness against the sheep-stealer. Mr. Evans's steward knew well the meaning of the words he had overheard him say in the cabin, and that if compelled to swear all he was aware of, no doubt would exist of the criminality of Michaul in the eyes of a jury.

" 'Tis a sthrange thing to ax a father to do," muttered Peery, more than once, as he proceeded to the magistrate's; " it's a very sthrange thing."

The magistrate proved to be a humane man. Notwithstanding the zeal of the steward and the policemen, he committed Michaul for trial, without continuing to press the hesitating and bewildered old Peery into any detailed evidence; his nature seemed to rise against the task, and he said to the steward:

" I have enough of facts for making out a committal; if you think the father will be necessary on the trial, subpœna him."

The steward objected that Peery would abscond, and demanded to have him bound over to prosecute, on two sureties, solvent and respectable. The magistrate assented; Peery could name no bail; and consequently he also was marched to prison, though prohibited from holding the least intercourse with Michaul.

The assizes soon came on. Michaul was arraigned; and, during his plea of "not guilty," his father appeared, unseen by him, in the gaoler's custody, at the back of the dock, or rather in an inner dock. The trial excited a keen and painful interest in the court, the bar, the jury-box, and the crowds of spectators. It was universally known that a son had stolen a sheep, partly to feed a starving father; and that out of the mouth of that father it was now sought to condemn him.

" What will the old man do? " was the general question which ran through the assembly: and while few of the lower orders could contemplate the possibility of his swearing to the truth, many of their betters scarcely hesitated to make out for him a case of natural necessity to swear falsely.

The trial began. The first witness, the herdsman, proved the loss of the sheep and the finding the dismembered carcass in the old barn. The policemen and the steward followed to the same effect, and the latter added the allusions which he had heard the father make to the son upon the morning of the arrest of the latter. The steward went down from the table. There was a pause, and complete silence, which the attorney for the prosecution broke by saying to the crier deliberately, " Call Peery Carroll."

" Here, sir," immediately answered Peery, as the goaler led him by a side door out of the back dock to the table. The prisoner started round; but the new witness against him had passed for an instant into the crowd.

The next instant old Peery was seen ascending the table, assisted by the gaoler and by many other commiserating hands, near him. Every glance fixed on his face. The barristers looked wistfully up from their seats round the table; the judge put a glass to his eye and seemed to study his features attentively. Among the audience there ran a low but expressive murmur of pity and interest.

Though much emaciated by confinement, anguish, and suspense, Peery's cheeks had a flush, and his weak blue eyes glittered. The half-gaping expression of his parched and haggard lips was miserable to see. And yet he did not tremble much, nor appear so confounded as upon the day of his visit to the magistrate.

The moment he stood upright on the table he turned himself fully to the judge, without a glance towards the dock.

" Sit down, sit down, poor man," said the judge.

" Thanks to you, my lord, I will," answered Peery, " only, first I'd ax you to let me kneel, for a little start "; and he accordingly did kneel, and after bowing his head, and forming the sign of the cross on his forehead, he looked up, and said, " My Judge in heaven above, 'tis you I pray to keep me to my duty, afore my earthly judge, this day—amen "—and then, repeating the sign of the cross, he seated himself.

The examination of the witness commenced, and humanely proceeded as follows—the counsel for the prosecution taking no notice of the superfluity of Peery's answers.

" Do you know Michaul, or Michael, Carroll, the prisoner at the bar? "

" Afore that night, sir, I believed I knew him well; every

thought of his mind, every bit of the heart in his body: afore that night, no living creatur could throw a word at Michaul Carroll, or say he ever forgot his father's renown, or his love of his good God; an' sure the people are afther telling you by this time how it came about that night—an' you, my lord—an' ye, gintlemen—an' all good Christhthans that hear me;—here I am to help to hang him— my own boy, and my only one—but, for all that, gintlemen, ye ought to think of it; 'twas for the weenock and the ould father that he done it;—indeed, an'deed, we hadn't a pyatee in the place; an' the sickness was among us, a start afore; it took the wife from him, and another babby; an' id had himself down, a week or so beforehand; an' all that day he was looking for work, but couldn't get a hand's turn to do; an' that's the way it was; not a mouthful for me an' little Peery; an', more betoken, he grew sorry for id, in the mornin', an' promised me not to touch a scrap of what was in the barn,—ay, long afore the steward and the peelers came on us, —but was willin' to go among the neighbours an' beg our break- fast, along wid myself, from door to door, sooner than touch it."

" It is my painful duty," resumed the barrister, when Peery would at length cease, " to ask you for closer information. You saw Michael Carrol in the barn that night? "

" *Musha*—The Lord pity him and me—I did, sir."

" Doing what? "

" The sheep between his hands," answered Peery, dropping his head, and speaking almost inaudibly.

"I must still give you pain, I fear; stand up, take the crier's rod, and if you see Michael Carrol in court lay it on his head."

" *Och, musha, musha,* sir, don't ax me to do that! " pleaded Peery, rising, wringing his hands, and for the first time weeping —" och, don't, my lord, don't, and may your own judgment be favourable, the last day."

" I am sorry to command you to do it, witness, but you must take the rod," answered the judge, bending his head close to his notes, to hide his own tears; and, at the same time, many a veteran barrister rested his forehead on the edge of the table. In the body of the court were heard sobs.

" Michaul, *avich*! Michaul, *a corra-ma-chree*! " exclaimed Peery, when at length he took the rod, and faced round to his son, " is id your father they make to do it, *ma-bauchal*? "

" My father does what is right," answered Michael, in Irish.

The judge immediately asked to have his words translated; and when he learned their import, regarded the prisoner with satis- faction.

" We rest here, my lord," said the counsel, with the air of a man freed from a painful task. The judge instantly turned to the jury- box:

" Gentlemen of the jury, that the prisoner at the bar stole the

sheep in question, there can be no shade of moral doubt. But you
have a very peculiar case to consider. A son steals a sheep that his
own famishing father and his own famishing son may have food.
His aged parent is compelled to give evidence against him here for
the act. The old man virtuously tells the truth, and the whole
truth, before you and me. He sacrifices his natural feelings—and
we have seen that they are lively—to his honesty, and to his religious sense of the sacred obligations of an oath. Gentlemen, I will
pause to observe that the old man's conduct is strikingly exemplary, and even noble. It teaches all of us a lesson. Gentlemen,
it is not within the province of a judge to censure the rigour of the
proceedings which have sent him before us. But I venture to anticipate your pleasure that, notwithstanding all the evidence given,
you will be enabled to acquit that old man's son, the prisoner at
the bar. I have said there cannot be the shade of a moral doubt
that he has stolen the sheep, and I repeat the words. But, gentlemen, there is a legal doubt, to the full benefit of which he is entitled.
The sheep has not been identified. The herdsman could not venture to identify it (and it would have been strange if he could)
from the dismembered limbs found in the barn. To his mark on
its skin, indeed, he might have positively spoken; but no skin has
been discovered. Therefore, according to the evidence, and you
have sworn to decide by that alone, the prisoner is entitled to your
acquittal. Possibly, now that the prosecutor sees the case in its
full bearing, he may be pleased with this result."

While the jury, in evident satisfaction, prepared to return their
verdict, Mr. Evans, who had but a moment before returned home,
entered the court, and becoming aware of the concluding words of
the judge, expressed his sorrow aloud that the prosecution had
ever been undertaken, that circumstances had kept him uninformed
of it, though it had gone on in his name; and he begged leave
to assure his lordship that it would be his future effort to keep
Michaul Carroll in his former path of honesty, by finding him honest
and ample employment, and, as far as in him lay, to reward the
virtue of the old father.

While Peery Carroll was laughing and crying in a breath, in the
arms of his delivered son, a subscription, commenced by the bar,
was mounting into a considerable sum for his advantage.

# THE CHURCHYARD WATCH

### John Banim

The dead are watched lest the living should prey on them!—
'Tis a strange alliance—of the living with Death—that his kingdom
and sovereignty may remain untrenched upon. In different parts
of England we have seen watch-houses, almost entirely composed
of glass, built in lonesome churchyards, of which generally the
parish sexton, and perhaps his dog (ill-fated among men and
dogs!), are the appointed nightly tenants, with liberty, ceded or
taken, to leave their dull lamp in the watch-box, and roam, here
and there, at their pleasure, among the graves, until daylight.

What stern necessities man forces upon man! There can scarce
be a more comfortless lot, or, making allowance for the almost inborn shudderings of the human heart, a more appalling one, than
that of the poor grave-scooper or bell-puller who is thus doomed
to spend his nights summer and winter. Habit, indeed, may
eventually blunt the first keenness of his aversion, if not terror:
he may serve a due apprenticeship to horrors, and learn his trade.
After a thousand secret and unowned struggles to seem brave and
indifferent, he may at last grow callously courageous. His flesh
may cease to creep as he strides on, in his accustomed round, over
the abodes of the silent and mouldering, and hears his own
dull footstep echoed through the frequent dreary hollowness
beneath.

But what has he gained, now, beyond the facility of earning his
wretched crust for himself and his crying infants!—We have seen
and spoken with such an unhappy being, who seemed to have lost,
in the struggle which conquered nature's especial antipathy (nature
in a breast and mind, like his, at least), most of the other sym-
pathies of his kind. He had a heavy, ox-like expression of face; he
would scarce speak to his neighbours (although *we* contrived to
make him eloquent) when they passed him at his door, or in the
village street; his own children feared or disliked him, and did
not smile nor whisper in his presence.

We have watched him go into the churchyard, at his usual hour,
after nightfall; and as he began to stalk about there, the ghastly
sentinel of the dead, he appeared to be in closer fellowship with
them than with the fair existence which he scarce more than
nominally shared. It was said, indeed, that, upon his initiation, at

a tender age and under peculiar circumstances, into his profession
of churchyard watchman, temporary delirium prepared him for its
regular and steady pursuit ever since; and that, although he showed
no symptoms of distinct insanity, when we knew him, the early
visitation had left a gloom on his mind, and a thick, nerveless
insensibility in his heart, which then, at forty-five, formed his
character.

In fact we learned a good deal about him, for every one talked
of him—and, as has been hinted, much of that good deal from
himself, to say nothing of his wife, in his absence; and if he did not
deliberately invent fables of his past trials, for the purpose of grati-
fying a little spirit of mockery of our undisguised interest, as mad
as the maddest bedlamite he must have been upon the occasion
alluded to: nay, to recount, with a grave face (as he did), the
particulars of the delusions of his time of delirium, did not argue
him a very sound-minded man at the moment he gave us his
confidence.

We are about to tell his story, at length, in our own way, however; that is, we shall try to model into our own language (particularly the raving parts) what his neighbours, his spouse, and his
own slow-moving and heavy lips have, from time to time, supplied
us with.

He was the only child of an affectionate and gentle-mannered
father who died when he was little more than a boy, leaving him
sickly and pining.   His mother wept a month, mourned three
months more—and was no longer a widow.   Her second husband
proved a surly fellow, who married her little fortune rather than
herself, as the means of keeping his quart pot filled, almost from
morning to night, at the village Tap, where he played good fellow
and politician to the expressed admiration of all his companions.

He had long been the parish sexton, and took up his post, night
after night, in the churchyard.   Little fear had he of what he might
see there; or he had outgrown his fears; or, if he thought or felt of
the matter, the lonely debauch which he was known to make in
that strange banquet-place served to drug him into obliviousness.
He deemed his duty—or he said and swore he did—only a tiresome
and slavish one, and hated it just as he hated daily labour.   And
—as he declared and harangued at the Tap—he had long ago forsworn it, only that it paid him well; but now that his marriage
made his circumstances easier, he was determined to drink alone
in the churchyard no longer: and he fed an idle, useless lad at
home, who with his dog—as idle as he—roamed and loitered about,
here and there, and had never yet done a single thing to earn their
bread.

But it was full time that both were taught the blessings of
industry; and he would teach them;—and—now that he thought
of it—why should not Will take his place in the watch-box, and so

keep the shillings in the family?   His friends praised his views, one
and all, and he grew thrice resolved.

Returned the next morning from his nocturnal charge, he reeled
to bed in solemn, drunken determination.   He arose, towards
evening, only half-reclaimed by sleep to ordinary sense, and set
about his work of reformation.   He ate his meal in silence, turned
from the table to the fire without a word, looked at the blaze, grimly
contemplative, then grumbling suddenly at his wife:

" And where is that truant now? " he asked: " down by the
marshes with his cur, I suppose; or gone a-nutting, or lying
stretched in the sun, the two idlers together; what!—and must I
work and work, and strive and strive—I, I, for ever—and will he
never lend me a hand? go where he likes, do what he likes, and
laugh and fatten on my labour? "

" Master Hunks," said the wife, " Will is sickly, and won't fatten
on either your labour or mine—not to talk of his own;—you know
'tis a puny lad, and wants some favour yet awhile; with God's help
and ours he may be stronger soon."

Will and dog here came in.   From what followed, this evening,
it will be seen that the ill-fated lad promised, in early youth, to be
of an open, kindly, intelligent character, very different indeed
from that in which we found him husked up at five-and-
forty.

He saluted his stepfather, and sat down quietly near the fire.
His poor dumb companion—friend of his boyhood, and his father's
gift—coiled himself up before the blaze, and prepared to surrender
his senses to happy sleep, interspersed with dreams of all the sports
he had enjoyed with his master that day.

Hunks, his eye glancing from one object of dislike to the other,
kicked the harmless brute, who jumped up, yelping in pain and
bitter lamentation, and ran for shelter under Will's chair.   Will's
pale cheek broke out into colour, his weak eye sparkled, his feeble
voice arose shrilly, and he asked—" Why is my poor dog
beaten? "

" The lazy cur! " said Hunks—" he was in my way, and only
got paid for idleness."

" 'Twas ill done," resumed Will—" he was my father's dog, and
my father gave him to me; and if my father were alive and well,
he would not hurt him, nor see him hurt! "   Tears interrupted this
sudden fit of spirit.

" Cur, as much as he is! " retorted Hunks—" do you put upon
me, here at my own fireside?   *You* are the idler—you—and he
only learns of you—and I hadn't ought to have served him out,
and you so near me."

" It has been God's will," said the boy, " to keep my strength
from me."

" Be silent and hear me! " roared Hunks—" this is your life,

I say—playing truant for ever—and what is mine and your own good mother's here? ''

'' Master Hunks,'' pleaded the wife—'' God knows I don't grudge nothing I can do for my poor Will's sake.''

'' And you—not a word from you either, Missis! '' grunted Hunks—'' I am put upon by one and t'other of you—ye sleep in comfort every night, and leave me to go a-watching, out o' doors, there, in all weathers; but stop a bit, my man, it sha'n't be this way much longer; I'll have my natural rest in my bed, some time or other, and soon; and you must earn it for me.''

'' How, father? how can I earn it? '' asked Will—'' I would if I could—but how? I haven't learnt no trade, and you know as well as any one knows it, I am not able to work in the fields or on the roads or get my living any one way.''

'' Then you can sit still and watch—that's light work,'' muttered Hunks.

'' Watch! '' cried mother and son together—'' watch what? and where? or whom? ''

'' The dead folk in the churchyard.''

'' Heaven defend me from it! '' cried poor Will, clasping his hands and falling back in his chair.

'' Ay, and this very night,'' continued the despot—'' this very night you shall mount guard in my place, and I shall have my lawful sleep, what the whole parish cries shame on me for not having months ago.''

'' Master Hunks, 'twill kill the boy! '' cried the mother.

'' Missis—don't you go for to cross me so often! ''—remonstrated her husband with a fixed look, which, short as they had been one flesh, she had reason to understand and shrink at.—'' Come, my man, stir yourself; 'tis time you were at the gate; the church clock has struck; *they will expect us* ''—he interrupted himself in a great rage, and with a great oath—'' but here I keep talking, and the cur never minds a word I say!—Come along! ''

'' Don't lay hands on him! '' screamed the mother as he strode towards the boy—'' what I have often told you has come to pass, Master Hunks—you have killed him! ''

Hunks scoffed at the notion, although, indeed, Will's hands had fallen helplessly at his side, and his chin rested on his breast, while his eyes were closed, and his lips apart. But he had only become insensible from sheer terror acting on a weak frame. Sighs and groans soon gave notice of returning animation. His mother then earnestly besought their tyrant to go on his night's duty, and, at least till the following night, leave her son to her care. Half in fear of having to answer for a murder, incredulously as he pretended to speak, Hunks turned out of the house, growling and threatening.

'' Is he gone? '' asked Will, when he regained his senses—'' gone not to come back? ''—and having heard his mother's gentle assurances, he let his head fall on her shoulder, weeping while he continued:

'' Mother, mother, it would destroy the little life I have! I could not bear it for an hour! The dread I am in of it was born with me! When I was a child of four years I had dreams of it, and I remember them to this day; they used to come in such crowds round my cradle! As I grew up you saw and you know my weakness. I could never sit still in the dark, nor even in the daylight out of doors in lonesome places. Now in my youth—a lad—almost a man—I am ashamed to speak of my inward troubles. Mother, you do not know me—I do not know myself! I walk out sometimes down by the river, and, listening to the noise of the water over the rocks, where it is shallow, and to the rustling of the trees as they nod in the twilight, voices and shrieks come round me— sometimes they break in my ears—and I have turned to see what thing it was that spoke, and thought some grey tree at my side had only just changed and become motionless, and seemed as if a moment before it had been something else, and had a tongue, and said the words that frightened me!—Oh, it was but yester evening I ran home from the river-side, and felt no heart within me till I had come in here to the fireside, and seen you moving near me!

'' You know the lone house all in ruins upon the hill—I fear it, mother, more than my tongue can tell you! I have been taken through it, in my dreams, in terrible company, and here I could describe to you its bleak apartments, one by one—its vaults, pitch dark, and half-filled with stones and rubbish, and choked up with weeds—its winding, creeping staircases, and its flapping windows —I know them all, though my feet never yet crossed its threshold! —Never, mother—though I have gone near it, to enter it, and see if what I had dreamt of it was true—and I went in the first light of the morning; but when close by the old doorway, the rustle of the shrubs and weeds startled me, and I thought—but sure *that* was fancy—that some one called me in by name—and then I turned and raced down the hill, never looking back till I came to the meadow-ground where cows and sheep are always grazing, and heard the dogs barking in the town, and voices of the children at play! ''

'' Will, my king,'' said his mother soothingly, '' this is all mere childishness at your years. God is above us and around us; and even if evil and strange things are allowed to be on earth, He will shield us from all harm. Arouse up like a man; for, indeed, your time of boyhood is passing—nay, it has passed with other lads not much older; only you have been poorly and weakly from your cradle, Will. Come, go to sleep; and before you lie down, pray for better health and strength to-morrow.''

" To-morrow! " he repeated—" and did my stepfather say anything of to-morrow? "

His mother answered him evasively, and he resumed,—" Oh, how I fear to-morrow!—oh, mother, you have loved me, and you do love me—for my weakness, my ill-health, and my dutifulness—and you loved my father—oh, for his sake as well as mine, mother, keep me from what I am threatened with!—keep me from it, if you would keep me alive another day! "

He went into his little sleeping apartment, stricken to the very soul with supernatural fears.

After spending a miserable night, he stole out of the house next morning and wandered about the private walks adjacent to the town until he thought his stepfather might have arisen and taken his usual walk to the Tap. But as the lad was about to re-enter the house, Hunks met him at the threshold. Will shrunk back; to his surprise and comfort, however, his fears now seemed ill-founded. The man bade him good-morrow in as cheerful and kind a tone as he could command, shook his hand, tapped him on the head, and left the house. Delighted, though still agitated, Will sought his mother within doors, told her his good omens, and spent a happy day. At dinner, too, notwithstanding Hunks' presence, the mother and son enjoyed themselves, so amiable had the despot become, at least in appearance.

When their meal was over, Hunks, as if to attain the height of civility, invited Will to go out with him for a walk by the river—" and let's have Barker (Will's dog) for company," continued Hunks; " he may show us sport with a rat, or such like, Will."

Accordingly, the three strolled out together, Will leading the way by many a well-known sedge or tuft of bushes, or undermined bank, the resorts of the water-rat, and sometimes of the outlaw otter; and Barker upheld his character, by starting, hunting down, and killing one of the first-mentioned animals. As twilight came on, they turned their faces towards the little town. They entered it. Its little hum of life was now hushed; its streets were silent, and almost deserted; its doors and windows barred and bolted, and the sounds of the rushing river and the thumping mill were the only ones which filled the air. The clock pealed ten as they continued their way. Hunks had grown suddenly silent and reserved. They passed the old Gothic church, and now were passing the gate which led into its burial-ground. Hunks stopped short. His grey, bad eye fell on the lad—" Will," he said, " I be thinking we've walked enough for this time."

" Enough, indeed,—and thank you for your company—and good-night, father," answered Will, trying to smile, though he began to tremble.

" Good-night then, my man—and here be your watch-light,"—and Hunks drew a dark lantern from his huge pocket.

" Nay, I want no light home," said Will; " I know the way so well; and 'tis not very dark; and you know you can't do without it on your post."

" My post? " Hunks laughed villainously—" your post, you mean, Will; take it; I be thinking I shall sleep sound to-night without a dead-light—as if I were a corpse to need it. Come along."

" You cannot have the heart to ask me! " cried Will, stepping back.

" Pho, my man "—Hunks clutched him by the shoulder with one hand, with the other unlocked the gate and flung it open—" In with you; you'll like it so in a few nights, you'll wish no better post; the dead chaps be civil enough; only treat them well, and let them walk awhile, and they make very good company." He dragged Will closer to the gate.

" Have mercy! " shrieked the wretched lad, trying to kneel, " or kill me first, father, to make me company for them, if that will please you."

" Get in! " roared the savage—" get in!—ay, hollo out, and twist about, so, and I'll pitch your shivering carcass half-way across the churchyard! "—he forced him in from the gate—" stop a bit, now—there be your lantern "—he set it down on a tombstone— " so, good-night—yonder's your box—just another word—don't you be caught strolling too near the murderer's corner over there, or you may trip and fall among the things that turn and twine on the ground, like roots of trees, to guard him."

With a new and piercing shriek, Will clung close to his fell tormentor. Hunks, partially carrying into effect a threat he had uttered, tore the lad's hands away, tossed him to some distance, strode out at the gate, locked it, and Will was alone with horror.

At first an anguish of fear kept him stupefied and stationary. He had fallen on a freshly-piled grave, to which mechanically his fingers clung and his face joined, in avoidance of the scene around. But he soon recollected what clay it was he clung to, and at the thought he started up, and, hushed as the sleepers around him, made some observations. High walls quite surrounded the churchyard, as if to part him from the habitable world. His lamp was burning upon the tombstone where Hunks had placed it—one dim red spot amid the thick darkness. The church clock now tolled eleven. It ceased; his ears ached in the resumed silence, and he listened and stared about him for what he feared. Whispers seemed to arise near him. He ran for his lamp, snatched it up, and instinctively hurried to the watch-box. Oh, he wished it made of solid rock!—it was chiefly framed of glass, useless as the common air to his terrors! He shut his eyes and pressed his palms upon them—vain subterfuge! The fevered spirit within him brought before his mind's vision worse things than the churchyard could yawn up, were all that superstition has fancied of it true. He looked out from his watch-box in refuge from himself.

That evening a half-moon had risen early, and, at this moment, was sinking in gathering clouds behind distant hills. As he vaguely noticed the circumstance, he felt more and more desolate. Simultaneously with the disappearance of the planet, the near clock began again to strike—he knew what hour! Each stroke smote his ear as if it would crack the nerve; at the last he shrieked out delirious! He had a pause from agony, then a struggle for departing reason, and then he was at rest.

At daybreak his stepfather found him asleep. He led him home. Will sat down to breakfast, smiling, but did not speak a word. Often during the day his now brilliant eye turned to the west; but why, his mother could not tell; until, as the evening made up her couch of clouds there, drawing around her the twilight for drapery, he left the house with an unusually vigorous step, and stood at the gate of the churchyard. Again he took up his post. Again the hour of twelve pealed from the old church, but now he did not fear it. When it had fully sounded he clapped his hands, laughed, and shouted.

The imaginary whispers he had heard the previous night—small, cautious whispers—came round him again, first from a distance, then nearer and nearer. At last he shaped them into words:

" Let us walk," they said—" though he watches us, he fears us." *He!*—'twas strange to hear the dim dead speak to a living man of himself! the maniac laughed again at the fancy, and replied to them:

" Ay, come! appear! I give leave for it. Ye are about in crowds, I know, not yet daring to take up your old bodies till I please; but, up with them!—Graves, split on, and yield me my subjects! for am I not king of the churchyard? Obey me!—ay, now your mouths gape—and what a yawning!—are ye musical, too?—a jubilee of groans!—out with it, in the name of Death!— blast it about like giants carousing! "

" Well blown!—and now a thousand heads popped up at once —their eyes fixed on mine, as if to ask my further leave for a resurrection; and they know I am good-humoured now, and grow upward, accordingly, like a grove of bare trees that have no sap in them. And now they move; passing along in rows, like trees, too, that glide by one on a bank, while one sails merrily down the river—and all stark staring still: and others stand bolt upright against their own headstones to contemplate. I wonder what they think of! Move! move! young, old, boys, men, pale girls, and palsied grandmothers—my churchyard can never hold 'em! And yet how they pass each other from corner to corner! I think they make their way through one another's bodies, as they do in the grave. They'll dance anon. Minuets, at least. Why, they begin already!—and what partners!—a tall, genteel young officer takes out our village witch of the wield—she that died at Christmas—and our last rector smirks to a girl of fifteen—ha, ha! yon tattered little fellow is a radical, making a leg to the old duchess!—music! music!—Go, some of you that look on there, and toll the dead bell! Well done! they tie the murderer to the bell-rope by the neck (though he was hanged before), and the bell swings out merrily! but what face is here? ''

It was the vision of a child's face, which he believed he caught staring at him through the glass of his watch-box—the face of an only brother who had died young. The wretch's laughter changed into tears and low wailings. By the time that his mother came to seek him, just at daybreak, he was, however, again laughing; but in such a state as to frighten mirth from her heart and lips till the day she died. As has been said, symptoms of positive insanity did not long continue to appear in his words or actions; yet when he recovered, there was still a change in him—a dark and disagreeable change, under the inveterate confirmation of which, the curious student of human nature may, at this moment, observe him in his native village.

# GERALD GRIFFIN
1803–1840

# THE DILEMMA OF PHADRIG

" THERE'S no use in talken about it, Phadrig. I know an I feel that all's over wit me. My pains are all gone, to be sure—but in place o' that, there's a weight like a quern stone down upon my heart, an I feel it blackenen within me. All I have to say is—think o' your own Mauria when she's gone, an be kind to poor Patcy."

" Ah, darlen, don't talk that way—there's hopes yet—what'll I do, what'll the child do witout you? "——

" Phadrig, there's noan. I'm goen fast, an if you have any regard for me, you won't say anythin that'll bring the thoughts o' you an him between me an the thoughts o' heaven, for that's what I must think of now. An if you marry again——"

" Oh, Mauria, honey, will you kill me entirely? Is it *I'll* marry again? "

——" If it be a thing you should marry again," Mauria resumed, without taking any notice of her husband's interruption, " you'll bear in mind that the best mother that ever walked the ground will love her own above another's. It stands with raisin an natur. The gander abroad will pull a strange goslen out of his own flock; and you know yourself, we could never get the bracket hen to sit upon Nelly O'Leary's chickens, do what we could. Everything loves its own. Then, Phadrig, if you see the floury potaties—an the top o' the milk—an the warm seat be the hob—an the biggest bit o' meat on a Sunday goen away from Patcy—you'll think o' your poor Mauria, an do her part by him; just quietly, and softly, an without blamen the woman—for it is only what's nait'rel, an what many a stepmother does without thinking o' themselves. An above all things, Phadrig, take care to make him mind his books and his religion, to keep out o' bad company, an study his readin-made-aisy, and that's the way he'll be a blessing an a comfort to you in your old days, as I once thought he would be to me in mine."

Here her husband renewed his promises in a tone of deep affliction.

" An now for yourself, Phadrig. Remember the charge that's upon you, and don't be goen out venturen your life in a little canvas canoe, on the bad autumn days, at Ballybunion; nor wit foolish boys at the Glin and Tarbert fairs;—an don't be so wake-minded as to be trusten to card-drawers, an fairy doctors, an the like; for it's the last word the priest said to me was, that you were too superstitious, and that's a great shame an a heavy sin. But tee you![1] Phadrig, dear, there's that rogue of a pig at the potaties over——"

Phadrig turned out the grunting intruder, bolted the hurdle-door, and returned to the bedside of his expiring helpmate. That tidy housekeeper, however, exhausted by the exertion which she had made to preserve, from the mastication of the swinish tusk, the fair produce of her husband's conacre of white-eyes, had fallen back on the pillow and breathed her last.

Great was the grief of the widowed Phadrig for her loss—great were the lamentations of her female friends at the evening wake—and great was the jug of whisky-punch which the mourners imbibed at the mouth, in order to supply the loss of fluid which was expended from the eyes. According to the usual cottage etiquette, the mother of the deceased, who acted as mistress of the ceremonies, occupied a capacious hay-bottomed chair near the fireplace—from which she only rose when courtesy called on her to join each of her female acquaintances as they arrived, in the death-wail which (as in politeness bound) they poured forth over the pale piece of earth that lay coffined in the centre of the room. This mark of attention, however, the old lady was observed to omit with regard to one of the fair guests—a round-faced, middle-aged woman, called Milly Rue—or Red Milly, probably because her head might have furnished a solution of the popular conundrum, " Why is a red-haired lady like a sentinel on his post? "

The fair Milly, however, did not appear to resent this slight, which was occasioned (so the whisper went among the guests) by the fact that she had been an old and neglected love of the new widower. All the fiery ingredients in Milly's constitution appeared to be comprehended in her glowing ringlets—and those, report says, were as ardent in hue as their owner was calm and regulated in her temper. It would be a cold morning, indeed, that a sight of Milly's head would not warm you—and a hot fit of anger which a few tones of her kind and wrath-disarming voice would not cool. She dropped, after she had concluded her " cry," a conciliating curtsey to the sullen old lady, took an unobtrusive seat at the foot of the bed, talked of the " notable " qualities of the deceased, and was particularly attentive to the flaxen-headed little Patcy, whom she held in her lap during the whole night, cross-examining him in his reading and multiplication, and presenting him, at part-

[1] To you! Beware!

ing, in token of her satisfaction at his proficiency, with a copy of *The Seven Champions of Christendom,* with a fine marble cover and pictures.  Milly acted in this instance under the advice of a prudent mother, who exhorted her, "whenever she thought o' maken presents, that way, not to be layen her money out in cakes or gingerbread, or things that would be ett off at wanst, an no more about them or the giver—but to give a strong toy, or a book, or somethen that would last, and bring her to mind now and then, so as that when a person 'ud ask where they got that, or who gev it, they'd say, 'from Milly Rue,' or 'Milly gev it, we're obleest to her,' an be talken an thinken of her when she'd be away.''

To curb in my tale, which may otherwise become restive and unmanageable—Milly's deep affliction and generous sympathy made a serious impression on the mind of the widower, who more than all was touched by that singularly accidental attachment which she seemed to have conceived for little Patcy.  Nothing could be farther from his own wishes than any design of a second time changing his condition; but he felt that it would be doing a grievous wrong to the memory of his first wife if he neglected this opportunity of providing her favourite Patcy with a protector, so well calculated to supply her place.  He demurred a little on the score of true love, and the violence which he was about to do his own constant heart —but like the bluff King Henry, his conscience—"aye—his conscience,"—touched him, and the issue was that a roaring wedding shook the walls which had echoed to the wail of death within the few preceding months.

Milly Rue not only supplied the place of a mother to young Patcy, but presented him in the course of a few years with two merry play-fellows, a brother and a sister.  To do her handsome justice, too, poor Mauria's anticipations were completely disproved by her conduct, and it would have been impossible for a stranger to have detected the stepson of the house from any shade of undue partiality in the mother.  The harmony in which they dwelt was unbroken by any accident for many years.

The first shock which burst in with a sudden violence upon their happiness was one of a direful nature.  Disease, that pale and hungry fiend who haunts alike the abodes of wealth and of penury; who brushes away with his baleful wing the bloom from beauty's cheek, and the balm of slumber from the pillow of age; who troubles the hope of the young mother with dreams of ghastliness and gloom, and fears that come suddenly, she knows not why nor whence; who sheds his poisonous dews alike on the heart that is buoyant and the heart that is broken; this stern and conquering demon scorned not to knock, one summer morning, at the door of Phadrig's cow-house, and to lay his iron fingers upon a fine milch-cow, a sheeted-stripper which constituted (to use his own emphatic phrase) the poor farmer's " substance," and to which he might have applied the well-known lines which run nearly as follows:

> She's straight in her back, and thin in her tail;
> She's fine in her horn, and good at the pail;
> She's calm in her eyes, and soft in her skin;
> She's a grazier's without, and a butcher's within.

All the " cures " in the pharmacopoeia of the village apothecary were expended on the poor animal, without any beneficial effect; and Phadrig, after many conscientious qualms about the dying words of his first wife, resolved to have recourse to that infallible refuge in such cases—a fairy doctor.

He said nothing to the afflicted Milly about his intention, but slipped out of the cottage in the afternoon, hurried to the Shannon side near Money Point, unmoored his light canvas-built canoe, seated himself in the frail vessel, and fixing his paddles on the *towl-pin*, sped away over the calm face of the waters towards the isle of Scattery, where the renowned Crohoore-na-Oona, or Connor-of-the-Sheep, the Mohammed of the cottages, at this time took up his residence. This 'mysterious personage, whose prophecies are still commented on among the cottage circles with looks of deep awe and wonder, was much revered by his contemporaries as a man " who had seen a dale "; of what nature those sights or visions were was intimated by a mysterious look, and a solemn nod of the head.

In a little time Phadrig ran his little canoe aground on the sandy beach of Scattery, and, drawing her above high-water mark, proceeded to the humble dwelling of the gifted Sheep-shearer with feelings of profound fear and anxiety. He passed the lofty round tower—the ruined grave of St. Senanus, in the centre of the little isle—the mouldering church, on which the eye of the poring antiquary may still discern the sculptured image of the two-headed monster, with which cottage tradition says the saint sustained so fierce a conflict on landing in the islet—and which the translator of Odranus has vividly described as " a dragon, with his fore-part covered with huge bristles, standing on end like those of a boar; his mouth gaping wide open with a double row of crooked, sharp tusks, and with such openings that his entrails might be seen; his back like a round island, full of scales and shells; his legs short and hairy, with such steely talons, that the pebble-stones, as he ran along them, sparkled—parching the way wherever he went, and making the sea boil about him where he dived—such was his excessive fiery heat." Phadrig's knees shook beneath him when he remembered this awful description—and thought of the legends of Lough Dhoola, on the summit of Mount Callon, to which the hideous animal was banished by the saint, to fast on a trout and a half per diem to the end of time; and where, to this day, the neighbouring fishermen declare that, in dragging the lake with their nets, they find the half trout as regularly divided in the centre as if it were done with a knife and scale.

While Phadrig remained with mouth and eyes almost as wide open as those of the sculptured image of the monster which had fascinated him to the spot, a sudden crash among the stones and dock-weed in an opposite corner of the ruin made him start and yell as if the original were about to quit Lough Dhoola on parole of honour, and use him as a relish after the trout and a half. The noise was occasioned by a little rotund personage, who had sprung from the mouldering wall, and now stood gazing fixedly on the terrified Phadrig, who continued returning that steady glance with a half-frightened, half-crying face—one hand fast clenched upon his breast, and the other extended, with an action of avoidance and deprecation. The person of the stranger was stout and short, rendered still more so by a stoop, which might almost have been taken for a hump—his arms hung forward from his shoulders, like those of a long-armed ape—his hair was grey and bushy, like that of a wanderoo—and his sullen grey eye seemed to be inflamed with ill-humour—his feet were bare and as broad 'as a camel's—and a leathern girdle buckling round his waist secured a tattered grey frieze riding-coat, and held an enormous pair of shears, which might have clipped off a man's head as readily, perhaps, as a lock of wool. This last article of costume afforded a sufficient indication to Phadrig that he stood in the presence of the awful object of his search.

" Well! an who are *you*? " growled the Sheep-shearer, after surveying Phadrig attentively for some moments.

The first gruff sound of his voice made the latter renew his start and roar for fright; after which, composing his terrors as well as he might, he replied, in the words of Autolycus, " I am only a poor fellow, sir."

" Well! an what's your business with me? "

" A cure, sir, I wanted for her. A cow o' mine that's very bad inwardly, an we can do nothen for her; an I thought may be you'd know what is it ail'ded her—an prevail on THEM " (this word was pronounced with an emphasis of deep meaning) " to leave her to uz."

" Huth! " the Sheep-shearer thundered out, in a tone that made poor Phadrig jump six feet backwards with a fresh yell, " do you daare to spake of *them* before me. Go along! you villyan o' the airth, an wait for me outside the church, an I'll tell you all about it there; but, first—do you think I can get the *gentlemen* to do anything for me *gratish*—without offeren 'em a trate or a haip'orth? "

" If their honours wouldn't think two tin-pennies and a fi'penny bit too little.—It's all I'm worth in the wide world."

" Well! we'll see what they'll say to it. Give it here to me. Go now—be off with yourself—if you don't want to have 'em all a-top o' you in a minnit."

This last hint made our hero scamper over the stones like a startled fawn; nor did he think himself safe until he reached the spot where he had left his canoe, and where he expected the coming of the Sheep-shearer; conscience-struck by the breach of his promise to his dying Mauria, and in a state of agonising anxiety with respect to the lowing patient in the cow-house.

He was soon after rejoined by Connor-of-the-Sheep.

" There is one way," said he, " of saving your cow—but you must lose one of your childer if you wish to save it."

"O Heaven presarve uz, sir, how is that, if you plase? "

" You must go home," said the Sheep-shearer, " and say nothen to anybody, but fix in your mind which o' your three childer you'll give for the cow; an when you do that, look in his eyes, an he'll sneeze, an don't you bless him, for the world. Then look in his eyes again, an he'll sneeze again, an still don't think o' blessen him, be any mains. The third time you'll look in his eyes he'll sneeze a third time—an if you don't bless him the third time, he'll die—but your cow will live."

" An this is the only cure you have to gi' me? " exclaimed Phadrig, his indignation at the moment overcoming his natural timidity.

" The only cure.—It was by a dale to do I could prevail on them to let you make the choice itself."

Phadrig declared stoutly against this decree, and even threw out some hints that he would try whether or no Shaun Lauther, or Strong John, a young rival of the sheep-shearing fairy doctor, might be able to make a better bargain for him with the " gentlemen."

" Shaun Lauther! " exclaimed Connor-of-the-Sheep, in high anger—" Do you compare me to a man that never seen any more than yourself?—that never saw so much as the skirt of a dead man's shroud in the moonlight—or heard as much as the moanen of a sowlth [1] in an old graveyard? Do you know me?—Ask them that do—an they'll tell you how often I'm called up in the night, and kep posten over bog an mountain, till I'm ready to drop down with the sleep,—while few voices are heard, I'll be bail, at Shaun Lauther's windey—an little knollidge given him in his drames. It is then that I get mine. Didn't I say before the King o' France was beheaded that a blow would be struck wit an axe in that place, that the sound of it would be heard all over Europe?—An wasn't it true? Didn't I hear the shots that were fired at Gibaralthur, an tell it over in Dooly's forge, that the place was relieved that day? —an didn't the news come afterwards in a month's time that I toult nothen but the truth? "

[1] Bodiless spirit.

Phadrig had nothing to say in answer to this overwhelming list of interrogatories—but to apologise for his want of credulity, and to express himself perfectly satisfied.

With a heavy heart he put forth in his canoe upon the water and prepared to return. It was already twilight, and as he glided along the peaceful shores he ruminated mournfully within his mind on the course which he should pursue. The loss of the cow would be, he considered, almost equivalent to total ruin—and the loss of any one of his lovely children was a probability which he could hardly bear to dwell on for a moment. Still it behoved him to weigh the matter well. Which of them, now—supposing it possible that he could think of sacrificing any—which of them would he select for the purpose? The choice was a hard one. There was little Mauria, a fair-haired, blue-eyed little girl—but he could not, for an instant, think of losing her, as she happened to be named after his first wife; her brother, little Shamus, was the least useful of the three, but he was the youngest—" the child of his old age—a little one! " his heart bled at the idea; he would lose the cow, and the pig along with it, before he would harm a hair of the darling infant's head. He thought of Patcy—and he shuddered and leaned heavier on his oars, as if to flee away from the horrible doubt which stole into his heart with that name. It must be one of the three, or the cow was lost for ever. The two first-mentioned he certainly would not lose—and Patcy; Again he bade the fiend begone, and trembling in every limb, made the canoe speed rapidly over the tide in the direction of his home.

He drew the little vessel ashore and proceeded towards his cabin. They had been waiting supper for him, and he learned with renewed anxiety that the object of his solicitude, the milch-cow, had rather fallen away than improved in her condition during his absence. He sat down in sorrowful silence with his wife and children to their humble supper of potatoes and thick milk.

He gazed intently on the features of each of the young innocents as they took their places on the suggan chairs that flanked the board. Little Mauria and her brother Shamus looked fresh, mirthful, and blooming from their noisy play in the adjoining paddock, while their elder brother, who had spent the day at school, wore— or seemed, to the distempered mind of his father, to wear a look of sullenness and chagrin. He was thinner, too, than most boys of his age—a circumstance which Phadrig had never remarked before. It might be the first indications of his poor mother's disease, consumption, that were beginning to declare themselves in his constitution; and if so, his doom was already sealed—and whether the cow died or not, Patcy was certain to be lost. Still the father could not bring his mind to resolve on any settled course, and their meal proceeded in silence.

Suddenly the latch of the door was lifted by some person outside, and a neighbour entered to inform Phadrig that the agent to his landlord had arrived in the adjacent village for the purpose of driving matters to extremity against all those tenants who remained in arrear. At the same moment, too, a low moan of anguish from the cow outside announced the access of a fresh paroxysm of her distemper, which it was very evident the poor animal could never come through in safety.

In an agony of distress and horror the distracted father laid his clenched fingers on the table, and looked fixedly in the eyes of the unsuspecting Patcy. The child sneezed, and Phadrig closed his lips hard, for fear a blessing might escape him. The child at the same time, he observed, looked paler than before.

Fearful lest the remorse which began to awake within his heart might oversway his resolution, and prevent the accomplishment of his unnatural design, he looked hurriedly a second time into the eyes of the little victim. Again the latter sneezed, and again the father, using a violent effort, restrained the blessing which was struggling at his heart. The poor child drooped his head upon his bosom, and letting the untasted food fall from his hand, looked so pale and mournful as to remind his murderer of the look which his mother wore in dying.

It was long—very long—before the heart-struck parent could prevail on himself to complete the sacrifice. The visitor departed; and the first beams of a full moon began to supplant the faint and lingering twilight which was fast fading in the west. The dead of the night drew on before the family rose from their silent and comfortless meal. The agonies of the devoted animal now drew rapidly to a close, and Phadrig still remained tortured by remorse on the one hand, and by selfish anxiety on the other.

A sudden sound of anguish from the cow-house made him start from his seat. A third time he fixed his eyes on those of his child —a third time the boy sneezed—but here the charm was broken.

Milly Rue, looking with surprise and tenderness on the fainting boy, said, " Why, then, Heaven bless you, child!—it must be a cold you caught, you're sneezen so often."

Immediately the cow sent forth a bellow of deep agony, and expired; and at the same moment a low and plaintive voice outside the door was heard, exclaiming, " And Heaven bless you, Milly! and the Almighty bless you, and spare you a long time over your children! "

Phadrig staggered back against the wall—his blood froze in his veins—his face grew white as death—his teeth chattered—his eyes stared—his hair moved upon his brow, and the chilling damp of terror exuded over all his frame. He recognised the voice of his first wife; and her pale, cold eye met his at that moment, as her shade flitted by the window in the thin moonlight, and darted on him a glance of mournful reproach. He covered his eyes with his hands, and sunk, senseless, into a chair; while the affrighted Milly, and Patcy, who at once assumed his glowing health and vigour, hastened to his assistance.  They had all heard the voice, but no one saw the shade nor recognised the tone excepting the conscience-smitten Phadrig.

# CHARLES JAMES LEVER

1806–1872

# A HERO-WORSHIPPER

JEAN PAUL tells us that there never was a nature yet formed without its vein of romance—that the most realistic and commonplace people we have ever met have their moods of romance, and that the cord, however little we may suspect it, runs through the woof of all humanity.

I am not able to affirm that he is right; but certainly a little incident which has just occurred to me leads me to believe that there are cases of the affection in natures and temperaments in which nothing would have led me to suspect them. I need not be told that it is the men who have a most worldly character who are often seen marrying portionless wives; that traits of self-sacrifice and devotion are being continually displayed by cold, ungenial, and, to all seeming, unimpressionable people. What I was not prepared for was to find that hero-worship could find a place in the heart of a hard, money-getting, money-lending fellow, whose ordinary estimate of humanity was based less on what they were than what they had. I own that I had no other clue to the man's nature than that furnished by a few lines of a newspaper advertisement, which set forth his readiness to advance sums from one hundred to five hundred pounds on mere personal security, and at a most moderate rate of interest. And though the former amounted to obligations, the breach of which would have reduced one to bondage, and the latter varied from eighty to a hundred and thirty per cent., he was so pleasant-looking, so chatty, so genially alive to the difficulties that beset youth, so forgivingly merciful to wasteful habits and ways, that I took to him from the moment I saw him, and signed my four bills for fifty each, and took up my hundred and eighteen pounds off the table with the feeling that at last I had found in an utter stranger that generous trustfulness and liberality I had in vain looked for amongst kindred and relatives.

We had a pint of madeira to seal the bargain. He told me in a whisper it was a priceless vintage. I believe him. On a rough calculation, I think every glass I took of it cost me forty-seven pounds some odd shillings. It is not, however, to speak of this event that I desire here. Mr. Nathan Joel and I ceased after a while to be the dear friends we swore to be over that madeira. The history of those four bills, too complicated to relate, became disagreeable. There were difficulties—there were renewals—there were protests—and there was a writ. Nathan Joel was—no matter what. I got out of his hands after three years by ceding a reversion worth five times my debt, with several white hairs in my whiskers, and a clearer view of gentlemen of the Jewish persuasion than I had ever picked up out of Ecclesiasticus.

A good many years rolled over—years in which I now and then saw mention of Mr. Joel as a plaintiff or an opposing creditor—once or twice as assignee, too. He was evidently thriving. Men were living very fast, smashes were frequent, and one can imagine the coast of Cornwall rather a lucrative spot after a stormy equinox. I came abroad, however, and lost sight of him; a chance mention, perhaps, in a friend's letter, how he had fallen into Joel's hands— that Joel advanced or refused to advance the money—something about cash, was all that I knew of him, till t'other evening the landlord of the little inn near my villa called up to ask if I knew anything of a certain Mr. Nathan Joel, who was then at his inn, without baggage, money, papers, or effects of any kind, but who, on hearing my name, cried out with ecstasy, " Ah! he knows me. You've only to ask Mr. O'Dowd who I am, and he'll satisfy you at once."

" So," thought I, " Joel! the Lord hath delivered thee into my hands, and now, what sort of vengeance shall I take? Shall I ignore you utterly, and declare that your claim to my acquaintance is a gross and impudent fraud? Shall I tell the innkeeper I disown you? " If this was my first thought, it soon gave way—it was so long since the rascal had injured me, and I had cursed him very often for it since then. It was his nature too; *that* also ought to be borne in mind. When leeches cease sucking they die, and very probably moneylenders wither and dry up when they are not abstracting our precious metals.

" I'll go over and see if it be the man I know," said I, and set off at once towards the inn. As I went along, the innkeeper told me how the stranger had arrived three nights back, faint, weary, and exhausted, saying that the guide refused to accompany him after he entered the valley, and merely pointed out the road and left him. " This much I got out of him," said the landlord, " but he is not inclined to say more, but sits there wringing his hands, and moaning most piteously."

Joel was at the window as I came up, but seeing me he came to the door. " Oh, Mr. O'Dowd," cried he, " befriend me this once, sir. Don't bear malice, nor put your foot on the fallen, sir. Do pity me, sir, I beseech you."

The wretched look of the poor devil pleaded for him far better than his words. He was literally in rags, and such rags, too, as seemed to have once been worn by another, for he had a brown peasant jacket and a pair of goatskin breeches, and a pair of shoes fastened round his ankles with leather thongs.

" So," said I, " you have got tired of small robberies and taken to the wholesale line. When did you become a highwayman? "

" Ah, sir," cried he, " don't be jocose, don't be droll. This is too pitiful a case for laughter."

I composed my features into a semblance of decent gravity, and after a little while induced him to relate his story, which ran thus:

Mr. Joel, it appeared, who for some thirty years of life had taken a very practical view of humanity, estimating individuals pretty much like scrip, and ascribing to them what value they might bring in the market, had suddenly been seized with a most uncommon fervour for Victor Emmanuel, the first impulse being given by a " good thing he had done in Piedmontese fives," and a rather profitable investment he had once made in the Cavour Canal. In humble gratitude for these successes, he had bought a print of the burly monarch, whose bullet head and bristling moustaches stared fiercely at him from over the fireplace, till by mere force of daily recurrence he grew to feel for the stern soldier a sentiment of terror dashed with an intense admiration.

" Talk of Napoleon, sir," he would say, " he's a humbug—an imposition—a wily, tricky, intriguing dodger. If you want a great man, a man that never knew fear, a man that is above all flimsy affectations, a man of the heroic stamp—there he is for you!

" As for Garibaldi, he's not to be compared to him. Garibaldi was an adventurer, and made adventure a career; but here's a king; here's a man who has a throne, who was born in a palace, descended from a long line of royal ancestors, and instead of giving himself up to a life of inglorious ease and self-indulgence, he mounts his horse and heads a regiment, sir. He takes to the field like the humblest soldier in his rank, goes out, thrashes the Austrians, drives them out of Milan, hunts them over the plains of Lombardy, and in seven days raises the five per cents. from fifty-one and a half to eighty-two and a quarter ' for the account.' Show me the equal of that in history, sir. There's not another man in Europe could have done as much for the market."

His enthusiasm knew no bounds; he carried a gold piece of twenty francs, with the King's image, to his watch-chain, and wore small coins with the cross of Savoy in his breast, as shirt-studs. An ardour intense as this is certain to bear its effects. Mr. Joel had often promised himself a trip to the Continent, of which he knew nothing beyond Paris. He took, then, the season of autumn, when the House was up, and money-lending compara-

tively dull, and came abroad. He told his friends he was going to
Vichy; he affected a little gout. It was a disease gentlemen
occasionally permitted themselves, and Mr. Joel was a rising man,
and liked to follow the lead of persons of condition. Very different, however, was his object; his real aim was to see the great
man whose whole life and actions had taken such an intense hold
on his imagination. To see him, to gaze on him, to possess himself
fully of the actual living traits of the heroic sovereign; and if by
any accident, by any happy chance, by any of those turns of
capricious fortune which now and then elevate men into a passing
greatness, to get speech of him!—this Mr. Joel felt would be an
operation more overwhelmingly entrancing than if Spanish bonds
were to be paid off in full, or Poyais fives to be quoted at par in
the market.

It is not impossible that Mr. Joel believed his admiration for the
*Re Galantuomo* gave him a *bona fide* and positive claim on that
monarch's regard. This is a delusion by no means rare: it possesses a large number of people, and influences them in their conduct to much humbler objects of worship than a king on his throne.
Sculptors, authors, and painters know something of what I mean,
and not uncommonly come to hear how ungraciously they are
supposed to have responded to an admiration of which it is possible
they never knew, and which it would be very excusable in them
if they never valued. The worshipper, in fact, fancies that the
incense he sends up as smoke should come back to him in some
shape substantial. However this may be, and I am not going to
persist further on my reader's attention, Mr. Joel got to imagine
that Victor Emmanuel would have felt as racy an enjoyment at
meeting with *him*, as he himself anticipated he might experience
in meeting the King. It goes a very long way in our admiration of
any one to believe that the individual so admired has a due and
just appreciation of ourselves. We start at least with one great
predisposing cause of love—an intense belief in the good sense and
good taste of the object of our affections.

Fully persuaded, then, that the meeting would be an event of
great enjoyment to each, the chief difficulty was to find a '' mutual
friend,'' as the slang has it, to bring them into the desired relations.

This was really difficult. Had King Victor Emmanuel been an
industrial monarch, given to cereals, or pottery, gutta-percha,
cotton, or corrugated iron, something might have been struck out
to present him with as pretext for an audience. Was he given to
art, or devoted to some especial science?—a bust, a bronze, or a
medal might have paved the way to an interview. The King,
however, had no such leanings, and whatever his weaknesses, there
were none within the sphere of the money-changer's attributions;
and as Mr. Joel could not pretend that he knew of a short cut to
Venice, or a secret path that led to the Vatican, he had to abandon

all hopes of approaching the monarch by the legitimate roads.

"See him I must, speak to him I will," were, however, the vows he had registered in his own heart, and he crossed the Alps with this firm resolve, leaving, as other great men before him have done, time and the event to show the way where the goal had been so firmly fixed on.

At Turin he learned the King had just gone to Ancona to open a new line of railroad. He hastened after him, and arrived the day after the celebration to discover that His Majesty had left for Brindisi. He followed to Brindisi, and found the King had only stopped there an hour, and then pursued his journey to Naples. Down to Naples went Mr. Joel at once, but to his intense astonishment, nobody there had heard a word of the King's arrival. They did not, indeed, allege the thing was impossible; but they slily insinuated that, if His Majesty had really come, and had not thought proper to make his arrival matter of notoriety, they, as Italians, Neapolitans *surtout*, knew good manners better than to interfere with a retirement it was their duty to respect. This they said with a sort of half-droll significancy that puzzled Mr. Joel much, for he had lived little in Italy, and knew far more about Cremorne than the Casino!

Little dubious sentences, shallow insinuations, half-laughing obscurities, were not weapons to repel such a man as Joel. His mind was too steadfastly intent on its object to be deterred by such petty opposition. He had come to see the King, and see him he would. This same speech he made so frequently, so publicly, and so energetically, that at the various cafés which he frequented, no sooner was he seen to enter than some stranger to him—all were strangers—would usually come up in the most polite manner, and express a courteous hope that he had been successful, and had either dined with His Majesty or passed the evening with him. It is needless to say that the general impression was that poor Mr. Joel was a lunatic, but as his form of the malady seemed mild and inoffensive, his case was one entirely for compassion and pity.

A few, however, took a different view. They were of the police, and consequently they regarded the incident professionally. To their eyes, Joel was a Mazzinian, and came out specially to assassinate the King. It is such an obvious thing to the official mind that a man on such an errand would attract every notice to his intentions beforehand, that they not alone decided Joel to be an intended murderer, but they kept a strict record of all the people he accidentally addressed, all the waiters who served, and all the hackney cabmen who drove him, while the telegraphic wires of the whole kingdom vibrated with one name, asking, Who is Joel? trace Joel; send some one to identify Joel. Little poor Joel knew all this time that he had been photographed as he sat eating his oysters, and that scraps of his letters were pasted on a large piece of pasteboard in the Ministry of Police, that his hand-writing might be shown under his varied attempts to disguise it.

One evening he sat much later than was his wont at a little open-air café of the St. Lucia quarter. The sky was gloriously starlit, and the air had all the balmy softness of the delicious south. Joel would have enjoyed it and the cool drink before him intensely, if it were not that his disappointed hopes threw a dark shadow over everything, and led him to think of all that his journey had cost him in cash, and all in the foregone opportunities of discounts and usuries.

A frequenter of the café, with whom he had occasionally exchanged greetings, sat at the same table; but they said little to each other, the stranger being evidently one not given to much converse, and rather disposed to the indulgence of his own thoughts in silence.

" Is it not strange," said Joel, after a long pause, " that I must go back without seeing him? "

A half-impatient grunt was all the reply, for the stranger was well weary of Joel and his sorrows.

" One would suppose that he really wanted to keep out of my way, for up to this moment no one can tell me if he be here or not."

Another grunt.

" It is not that I have left anything undone, Heaven knows. There isn't a quarter of the town I have not walked, day and night, and his is not a face to be mistaken; I'd know him at a glance."

" And what in the devil's name do you want with him when you have seen him? " exclaimed the other, angrily. " Do you imagine that a king of Italy has nothing better to do with his time than grant audiences to every idle John Bull whose debts or doctors have sent him over the Alps? " This rude speech was so fiercely delivered, and with a look and tone so palpably provocative, that Joel at once perceived his friend intended to draw him into a quarrel, so he finished off his liquor, took up his hat and cane, and with a polite *felice sera, Signor,* was about to withdraw.

" Excuse me," said the stranger, rising, with a manner at once obsequious and apologetic. " I entreat you to forgive my rude and impatient speech. I was thinking of something else, and forgot myself. Sit down for one moment, and I will try and make you a proper reparation—a reparation you will be satisfied with. You want to see the King, and you desire to speak with him: both can be done with a little courage; and when I say this, I mean rather presence of mind—*aplomb,* as the French say—than anything like intrepidity or daring. Do you possess the quality I speak of? "

" It is my precise gift—the essential feature of my character," cried Joel in ecstasy.

" This, then, is the way—and mind I tell you this secret on the

faith that as an English gentleman you preserve it inviolate—
' parole Inglese,' is a proverb with us, and we have reason to believe that it deserves its signification."

Joel swore to observe the bond, and the other continued:

"The King, it is needless to tell you, detests state and ceremonial; he abhors courtly etiquette, and the life of a palace is to
him the slavery of the galleys. His real pleasure is the society of
a few intimates, whom he treats as equals, and with whom he dis-
courses in the rough dialect of Piedmont, as it is talked in the camp
by his soldiers. Even this amount of liberty is, however, sometimes not sufficient for this bold native spirit; he longs for more
freedom—for, in fact, that utter absence of all deference, all
recognition of his high estate, which followers never can forget;
and to arrive at this, he now and then steals out at night and
gains the mountains, where, with a couple of dogs and a rifle, he
will pass two, three, perhaps four days, sharing the peasant's
fare and his couch, eating the coarsest food, and sleeping on straw,
with a zest that shows what a veritable type of the medieval baron
this Count of Savoy really is, and by what a mistake it is that he
belongs to an age where the romance of such a character is an
anachronism!

" You may feel well astonished that nobody could tell you where
he is—whether here or at Turin, at Bologna, at Florence, or
Palermo. The fact is, they don't know; that's the real truth—not
one of them knows; all they are aware of is that he is off—away on
one of those *escapades* on which it would be as much as life is worth
to follow him; and there is La Marmora, and there sits Minghetti,
and yonder Della Rovere, not daring to hint a syllable as to the
King's absence, nor even to hazard a guess above a whisper
as to when he will come back again. Now I can tell you where he
is—a mere accident put me in possession of the secret. A *fattore*
of my brother's came up yesterday from the Terri di Lavoro, and
told how a strange man, large, strong-boned, and none over bland-
looking, had been quail-shooting over the Podere for the last two
days; he said he was a wonderful shot, but cared nothing about his
game, which he gave freely away to any one he met. I made him
describe him accurately, and he told me how he wore a tall high-
crowned hat—a ' calabrese ' as they call it—with a short peacock's
feather, a brown jacket all covered with little buttons, leather
small-clothes ending above the knees, which were naked, light
gaiters, half-way up the leg, his gun slung at his back, pistols in
his belt, and a *couteau-de-chasse* without a scabbard hung by a
string to his waist-belt; he added that he spoke little, and that little
in a strange dialect; probably Roman or from the Marches.

" By a few other traits he established the identity of one whose
real rank and condition he never had the slightest suspicion of.
Now, as the King is still there, and as he told the Paroco of the

little village at Catanzaro that he'd send him some game for his
Sunday dinner, which he meant to partake of with him, you have
only to set out to-night, reach Nola, where, with the aid of a pony
and a carratella, you will make your way to Raniglia, after which,
three miles of a brisk mountain walk—nothing to an Englishman—
you'll arrive at Catanzaro, where there is a little inn.  He calls
there every evening, coming down the valley from St. Agata, and
if you would like to meet him casually, as it were, you have only
to set out a little before sunset and stroll up the gorge; there you'll
find him."  The stranger went on to instruct Mr. Joel how he
should behave to the distinguished unknown—how, while carefully
avoiding all signs of recognition, he should never forget that he
was in the presence of one accustomed to the most deferential
respect.

" Your manner," said he, " must be an artful blending of easy
politeness with a watchful caution against over-familiarity; in fact,
try to make him believe that you never suspect his great rank, and
at the same time take care that in your own heart you never
forget it.  Not a very easy thing to do, but the strong will that has
sent you so far will doubtless supply the way to help you further ";
and with a few more such friendly counsels he wished Joel success
and a good-night, and departed.

Mr. Joel took his place in the " rotondo " of the diligence—no
other was vacant—and set off that night in company with two
priests, a gendarme, and a captured galley-slave, who was about
to show the officers of justice where a companion of his flight had
sought concealment.  The company ate and drank, smoked villainous tobacco, and sang songs all night, so that when Joel reached
Nola he was so overcome with fatigue, headache, and sickness, that
he had to take to bed, where the doctor who was sent for bled him
twice, and would have done so four or five times more, if the
patient, resisting with the little strength left him, had not put him
out of the room and locked the door, only opening it to creep downstairs and escape from Nola for ever.  He managed with some
difficulty to get a place in a baroccino to Raniglia, and made the
journey surrounded with empty wine-flasks, which required extreme
care and a very leisurely pace, so that the distance, which was but
eighteen miles, occupied nearly as many hours.  It took him a full
day to recruit at Raniglia, all the more since the rest of the
journey must be made on foot.

" I own, sir," said Mr. Joel, whom I now leave to speak for
himself, " it was with a heavy heart I arose that morning and
thought of what was before me.  I had already gone through
much fatigue and considerable illness, and I felt that if any mishap
should befall me in that wild region, with its wild-looking semi-
savage inhabitants, the world would never hear more of me.  It
was a sad way to finish a life which had not been altogether un-

successful, and I believe I shed tears as I fastened on my knap-sack and prepared for the road. A pedlar kept me company for two miles, and I tried to induce him to go on the whole way with me to Cantanzaro, but he pointed to his pack, and said, ' There are folk up there who help themselves too readily to such wares as I carry. I'd rather visit Catanzaro with an empty pack than a full one.' He was curious to learn what led *me* to visit the place, and I told him it was to see the fine mountain scenery and the great chestnut and cork woods of which I had heard so much. He only shook his head in reply. I don't know whether he dis-believed me, or whether he meant that the journey would scarce repay the fatigue. I arrived at Catanzaro about three in the afternoon. It was a blazing hot day—the very air seemed to sparkle with the fiery sun's rays, and the village, in regular Italian fashion, was on the very summit of a mountain, around which other mountains of far greater height were grouped in a circle. Every house was shut up, the whole population was in bed, and I had as much difficulty in getting admission to the inn as if I had come at midnight.''

I will not trouble my reader to follow Mr. Joel in his description of or comment upon Italian village life, nor ask him to listen to the somewhat lengthy dialogue that took place between him and the priest, a certain Don Lertoro, a most miserable, half-famished fel-low, with the worst countenance imaginable, and a vein of ribaldry in his talk that, Mr. Joel declared, the most degraded creature might have been ashamed of.

By an artful turn of the conversation, Joel led the priest to talk of the strangers who occasionally came up to visit the mountain, and at last made bold to ask, as though he had actually seen him, who was the large, strong-boned man, with a rifle slung behind him : he did not look like a native of these parts.

'' Where did you meet him? '' asked the priest with a furtive look.

'' About a mile from this,'' said Joel; '' he was standing on the rock over the bridge as I crossed the torrent.''

'' *Che Bestia!* '' muttered Don Lertoro, angrily; but whether the compliment was meant for Joel or the unknown did not appear. Unwilling to resume the theme, however, he affected to busy him-self about getting some salad for supper, and left Joel to himself.

While Joel sat ruminating, in part pleasantly, over the craft of his own address, and in part dubiously, thinking over Don Ler-toro's exclamation, and wondering if the holy man really knew who the stranger was, the priest returned to announce the supper.

By Joel's account, a great game of fence followed the meal, each pushing the other home with very searching inquiries, but Joel candidly declaring that the Don, shrewd as he was, had no chance with him, insomuch as that, while he completely baffled the other

as to what led him there, how long he should remain, and where
go to afterwards, he himself ascertained that the large heavy-boned
man with the rifle might usually be met every evening about sunset
in the gorge coming down from St. Agata; in fact, there was a little
fountain about three miles up the valley which was a favourite
spot of his to eat his supper at—" a spot easily found," said the
priest, " for there are four cypress trees at it, and on the rock
overhead you'll see a wooden cross, where a man was murdered
once."

This scarcely seemed to Joel's mind as a very appetising element;
but he said nothing, and went his way. As the day was drawing to
a close, Mr. Joel set out for the fountain. The road, very beautiful and picturesque as it was, was eminently lonely. After leaving
the village he never saw a human being; and though the evening
was deliciously fine, and the wild flowers at either side scented the
air, and a clear rivulet ran along the roadside with a pleasant
murmur, there was that in the solitude and silence, and the tall
peaked mountains, lone and grim, that terrified and appalled him.
Twice was he so overcome that he almost determined to turn
back and abandon the expedition.

Onward, however, he went, encouraging himself by many little
flatteries and compliments to his own nature. How bold he was!
how original! how unlike other money-lenders! what manifest
greatness there must be somewhere in the temperament of one like
him, who could thus leave home and country, security, and the
watchful supervision of Scotland Yard, to come into the wild
mountains of Calabra, just to gratify an intellectual craving!
These thoughts carried him over miles of the way, and at last he
came in sight of the four cypress trees; and as he drew nigh, sure
enough there was the little wooden cross standing out against the
sky; and while he stopped to look at it, a loud voice, so loud as to
make him start, shouted out, " *Alto là*—who are you? "

Mr. Joel looked about him on every side, but no one was to be
seen. He crossed the road, and came back again, and for a
moment he seemed to doubt whether it was not some trick of his
own imagination suggested the cry, when it was repeated still
louder; and now his eyes caught sight of a tall, high-crowned hat,
rising above the rank grass on a cliff over the road, the wearer
being evidently lying down on the sward. Joel had but time to
remove his hat courteously, when the figure sprang to his feet,
and revealed the person of an immense man. He looked gigantic
on the spot he stood on, and with his stern, flushed features, and
enormous moustaches, turned fiercely upwards at the points, recalled
to Mr. Joel the well-known print over his chimneypiece at home.
" Where are you going? " cried he, sternly.

" Nowhere in particular, sir. Strolling to enjoy my cigar," replied Joel, trembling.

"Wait a moment," said the other, and came clattering down the cliff; his rifle, his pistols, and his ammunition pouches making a terrific uproar as he came.

"You came from Catanzaro—were there any gendarmes there when you left?"

"None, sire: not one," said Joel, who was so overcome by the dignity of the gentleman that he forgot all his intended reserve.

"No lies, no treachery, or, by the precious tears of the Madonna, I'll blow your brains out."

"Your Majesty may believe every word I utter in the length and breadth of the Peninsula; you have not a more devoted worshipper."

"Did you see the priest, Don Lertoro?"

"Yes, sire; it was *he* told me where I should find Your Majesty, at the well, here, under the cypress trees."

"*Scioccone!*" cried the stranger; but whether the epithet was meant for Joel or the curé did not appear. A very long and close cross-examination ensued, in which Joel was obliged not merely to explain who he was, whence he came, and what he came for, but to narrate a variety of personal circumstances which at the time it seemed strange His Majesty would care to listen to—such as the amount of money he had with him, how much more he had left behind at Naples, how he had no friends in that capital, nor any one like to interest themselves about him if he should get into trouble, or require to be assisted in any way. Apparently the King was satisfied with all his replies, for he finished by inviting him to partake of some supper with him; and, producing a small basket from under the brushwood, he drew forth a couple of fowls, some cheese, and a flask of wine. It was not until he had drunk up three large goblets of the wine that Joel found himself sufficiently courageous to be happy. At last, however, he grew easy, and even familiar, questioning His Majesty about the sort of life he led, and asking how it was that he never fell into the hands of brigands.

Nothing could be more genial or good-humoured than the King; he was frankness itself; he owned that his life might possibly be better; that, on the whole, his father confessor was obliged to bear a good deal from him; and that all his actions were not in strictest conformity with church discipline.

"You ought to marry again; I am persuaded, sir," said Joel, "it would be the best thing you could do."

"I don't know," said the other, thoughtfully. "I have a matter of seven wives as it is, and I don't want any more."

"Ah! Your Majesty, I guess what you mean," said Joel, winking; "but that's not what I would suggest. I mean some strong political connection—some alliance with a royal house, Russian or Bavarian, if, indeed, Austrian were not possible."

"On the whole," said Joel, " I found that he didn't much trust any one; he thought ill of Louis Napoleon, and called him some hard names; he was not over-complimentary to the Pope; and as for Garibaldi, he said they had once been thick as thieves, but of late they had seen little of each other, and, for his part, he was not sorry for it. All this time, sir," continued Joel, " His Majesty was always fancying something or other that I wore or carried about me; first it was my watch, which I felt much honoured by his deigning to accept; then it was my shirt-studs, then my wrist-buttons, then my tobacco-pouch, then my pipe, a very fine meer-schaum, and at last, to my intense astonishment, my purse, whose contents he actually emptied on the table, and counted out before me, asking me if I had not any more about me, either in notes or bills, for it seemed a small sum for a ' Milordo,' so he called me, to travel with.

" Whatever I had, however, he took it—took every carlino of it —saying, ' There's no getting any change up here—there are no bankers, my dear Signor Joel; but we'll meet at Naples one of these days, and set all these things to rights.'

" I suppose the wine must have been far stronger than I thought; perhaps, too, drinking it in the open air made it more heady; then the novelty of the situation had its effect—it's not every day that a man sits hobnobbing with a king. Whatever the reason, I became confused and addled, and my mind wandered. I forgot where I was. I believe I sang something—I am not sure what— and the King sang, and then we both sang together; and at last he whistled with a silver call-whistle that he wore, and he gave me in charge to a fellow—a ragged rascally-looking dog he was—to take me back to Cantanzaro; and the scoundrel, instead of doing so, led me off through the mountains for a day and a half, and dropped me at last at Reccone, a miserable village, without tasting food for twelve hours. He made me change clothes with him, too, and take his dirty rags, this goat-skin vest and the rest of it, in-stead of my new tweed suit; and then, sir, as we parted, he clapped me familiarly on the shoulder, and said, ' Mind me, *amico mio,* you're not to tell the padrone, when you see him, that I took your clothes from you, or he'll put a bullet through me. Mind *that,* or you'll have to settle your scores with one of my brothers.'

" ' By the padrone you perhaps mean the King,' said I, haughtily.

" ' King, if you like,' said he, grinning; ' we call him " Ninco Nanco ": and now that they've shot Pilone, and taken Stoppa, there's not another brigand in the whole of Italy to compare with him.' Yes, sir, out came the horrid truth. It was Ninco Nanco, the greatest monster in the Abruzzi, I had mistaken for Victor Em-manuel. It was to him I had presented my watch, my photo-graph, my seal-ring, and my purse with forty-two napoleons.

Dirty, ragged, wretched, in tatters, and famished, I crept on from village to village till I reached this place yesterday evening, only beseeching leave to be let lie down and die, for I don't think I'll ever survive the shame of my misfortune, if my memory should be cruel enough to preserve the details.''

'' Cheer up, Joel; the King is to review the National Guard to-day. I'll take care that you shall have a good place to see him, and a good dinner afterwards.''

'' No, sir; I'll not go and look at him. Ninco Nanco has cured me of hero-worship. I'll go back to town and see after the exchanges. The sovereigns that come from the mint are the only ones I mean to deal with from this day forward.''

# JOSEPH SHERIDAN LE FANU
1814-1873

# THE GHOST AND THE BONE-SETTER

*Extract from the MS. papers of the late Rev. Francis Pudcell of Drumcoolagh*

I TELL the following particulars, as nearly as I can recollect them, in the words of the narrator. It may be necessary to observe that he was what is termed a well-spoken man, having for a considerable time instructed the ingenious youth of his native parish in such of the liberal arts and sciences as he found it convenient to profess —a circumstance which may account for the occurrence of several big words in the course of this narrative, more distinguished for euphonious effect than for correctness of application. I proceed, then, without further preface, to lay before you the wonderful adventures of Terry Neil.

" Why, thin, 'tis a quare story, an' as thrue as you're sittin' there; and I'd make bould to say there isn't a boy in the seven parishes could tell it better nor crickther than myself, for 'twas my father himself it happened to, an' many's the time I heerd it out iv his own mouth; an' I can say, an' I'm proud av that same, my father's word was as incredible as any squire's oath in the counthry; and so signs an' if a poor man got into any unlucky throuble, he was the boy'id go into the court an' prove; but that doesn't signify—he was as honest and as sober a man, barrin' he was a little bit too partial to the glass, as you'd find in a day's walk; an' there wasn't the likes of him in the counthry round for nate labourin' an' *baan* diggin'; and he was mighty handy entirely for carpenther's work, and mendin' ould spudethrees, an' the likes i' that. An' so he tuk up with bone-settin', as was most nathural, for none of them could come up to him in mendin' the leg iv a stool or a table; an' sure, there never was a bone-setter got so much custom—man an' child, young an' ould—there never was such breakin' and mendin' of bones known in the memory of man. Well, Terry Neil—for that was my father's name—began to feel his heart

136

growin' light, and his purse heavy; an' he took a bit iv a farm in Squire Phelim's ground, just undher the ould castle, an' a pleasant little spot it was; an' day an' mornin' poor crathurs not able to put a foot to the ground, with broken arms and broken legs, id be comin' ramblin' in from all quarters to have their bones spliced up. Well, yer honour, all this was as well as well could be; but it was customary when Sir Phelim id go anywhere out iv the country, for some iv the tinants to sit up to watch in the ould castle, just for a kind of compliment to the ould family—an' a mighty unplisant compliment it was for the tinants, for there wasn't a man of them but knew there was something quare about the ould castle. The neighbours had it that the squire's ould grand-father, as good a gintleman—God be with him—as I heer'd, as ever stood in shoe-leather, used to keep walkin' about in the middle iv the night, ever sinst he bursted a blood-vessel pullin' out a cork out iv a bottle, as you or I might be doin', and will too, please God—but that doesn't signify. So, as I was sayin', the ould squire used to come down out of the frame, where his picthur was hung up, and to break the bottles and glasses—God be merciful to us all—an' dthrink all he could come at—an' small blame to him for that same; and then if any of the family id be comin' in, he id be up again in his place, looking as quite an' as innocent as if he didn't know anything about it—the mischievous ould chap.

" Well, yer honour, as I was sayin', one time the family up at the castle was stayin' in Dublin for a week or two; and so, as usual, some of the tinants had to sit up in the castle, and the third night it kem to my father's turn. ' Oh, tare an' ouns! ' says he unto himself, ' an must I sit up all night, and that ould vaga-bone of a sperit, glory be to God,' says he, ' serenadin' through the house, an' doin' all sorts iv mischief? ' However, there was no gettin' aff, and so he put a bould face on it, an' he went up at nightfall with a bottle of pottieen, and another of holy wather.

" It was rainin' smart enough, an' the evenin' was darksome an' gloomy, when my father got in; an' what with the rain he got, an' the holy wather he sprinkled on himself, it wasn't long till he had to swally a cup iv the pottieen, to keep the cowld out iv his heart. It was the ould steward, Lawrence Connor, that opened the door —and he an' my father wor always very great. So when he seen who is was, an' my father tould him how it was his turn to watch in the castle, he offered to sit up along with him; an' you may be sure my father wasn't sorry for that same. So says Larry:

" ' We'll have a bit iv fire in the parlour,' says he.

" ' An' why not in the hall? ' says my father, for he knew that the squire's picthur was hung in the parlour.

" ' No fire can be lit in the hall,' says Lawrence, ' for there's an ould jackdaw's nest in the chimney.'

" ' Oh, thin,' says my father, ' let us stop in the kitchen, for it's
125*

very unproper for the likes iv me to be sittin' in the parlour,' says he.

" ' Oh, Terry, that can't be,' says Lawrence; ' if we keep up the ould custom at all, we may as well keep it up properly,' says he.

" ' Divil sweep the ould custom! ' says my father—to himself, do ye mind, for he didn't like to let Lawrence see that he was more afeard himself.

" ' Oh, very well,' says he. ' I'm agreeable, Lawrence,' says he; and so down they both wint to the kitchen, until the fire id be lit in the parlour—an' that same wasn't long doin'.

" Well, yer honour, they soon wint up again, an' sat down mighty comfortable by the parlour fire, and they beginned to talk, an' to smoke, an' to dhrink a small taste iv the pottieen; and, more-over, they had a good rousin' fire o' bogwood and turf, to warm their shins over.

" Well, sir, as I was sayin', they kep' convarsin' an' smokin' together most agreeable, until Lawrence beginn'd to get sleepy, as was but nathural for him, for he was an ould sairvint man, an' was used to a great dale iv sleep.

" ' Sure it's impossible,' says my father, ' it's gettin' sleepy you are? '

" ' Oh, divil a taste,' says Larry; ' I'm only shuttin' my eyes,' says he, ' to keep out the parfume o' the tibacky smoke, that's makin' them wather,' says he. ' So don't you mind other people's business,' says he, stiff enough, for he had a mighty high stomach av his own (rest his sowl), ' and go on,' says he, ' with your story, for I'm listening',' says he, shuttin' down his eyes.

" Well, when my father seen spakin' was no use, he went on with his story. By the same token, it was the story of Jim Sooli-van and his ould goat he was tellin'—an' a plisant story it is—an' there was so much divarsion in it, that it was enough to waken a dormouse, let alone to pervint a Christian goin' asleep. But, faix, the way my father tould it, I believe there never was the likes heerd sinst nor before, for he bawled out every word av it, as if the life was fairly lavin' him, thryin' to keep ould Larry awake; but, faix, it was no use, for the hoorsness came an him, an' before he kem to the end of his story Larry O'Connor beginned to snore like a bagpipes.

" ' Oh, blur an' agres,' says my father, ' isn't this a hard case,' says he, ' that ould villain, lettin' on to be my friend, and to go asleep this way, an' us both in the very room with a sperit,' says he. ' The crass o' Christ about us! ' says he; and with that he was goin' to shake Lawrence to waken him, but he just remim-bered if he roused him, that he'd surely go off to his bed, an' lave him complately alone, an' that id be by far worse.

" ' Oh thin,' says my father, ' I'll not disturb the poor boy. It id be neither friendly nor good-nathured,' says he, ' to tormint him while he is asleep,' says he; ' only I wish I was the same way myself,' says he.

" An' with that he beginned to walk up an' down, an' sayin' his prayers, until he worked himself into a sweat, savin' your presence. But it was all no good; so he dthrunk about a pint of sperits, to compose his mind.

" ' Oh,' says he, ' I wish to the Lord I was as asy in my mind as Larry there.  Maybe,' says he, ' if I thried I could go asleep '; an' with that he pulled a big armchair close beside Lawrence, an' settled himself in it as well as he could.

" But there was one quare thing I forgot to tell you.   He couldn't help, in spite av himself, lookin' now an' thin at the picthur, an' he immediately obsarved that the eyes av it was follyin' him about, an' starin' at him, an' winkin' at him, wheriver he wint.  ' Oh,' says he, when he seen that, ' it's a poor chance I have,' says he; ' an' bad luck was with me the day I kem into this unforthunate place,' says he.   ' But any way there's no use in bein' freckened now,' says he; ' for if I am to die, I may as well parspire undaunted,' says he.

" Well, your honour, he thried to keep himself quite an' asy, an' he thought two or three times he might have wint asleep, but for the way the storm was groanin' an' creakin' through the great heavy branches outside, an' whistlin' through the ould chimleys iv the castle.  Well, afther one great roarin' blast iv the wind, you'd think the walls iv the castle was just goin' to fall, quite an' clane, with the shakin' iv it.  All av a suddint the storm stopt, as silent an' as quite as if it was a July evenin'.  Well, your honour, it wasn't stopped blowin' for three minutes, before he thought he hard a sort iv a noise over the chimleypiece; an' with that my father just opened his eyes the smallest taste in life an' sure enough he seen the ould squire gettin' out iv the picthur, for all the world as if he was throwin' aff his ridin' coat, until he stept out clane an' complate, out av the chimley-pieces, an' thrun himself down an the floor.  Well, the slieveen ould chap—an' my father thought it was the dirtiest turn iv all—before he beginned to do anything out iv the way, he stopped for a while to listen wor they both asleep; an' as soon as he thought all was quite, he put out his hand an' tuk hould iv the whiskey bottle, an' dhrank at laste a pint iv it.  Well, your honour, when he tuk his turn out iv it, he settled it back mighty cute entirely, in the very same spot it was in before.  An' he beginned to walk up an' down the room, lookin' as sober an' as solid as if he never done the likes at all.  An' whinever he went apast my father, he thought he felt a great scent of brimstone, an' it was that that freckened him entirely; for he knew it was brimstone that was burned in hell, savin' your presence.  At any rate, he often heerd it from Father Murphy, an' he had a right to know what belonged to it—he's dead since, God rest him. Well, your honour, my father was asy enough until the sperit kem past him; so close, God be marciful to us all, that the smell in the sulphur tuk the breath clane out iv him; an' with that he tuk such a fit iv coughin', that it al-a-most shuk him out iv the chair he was sittin' in.

" ' Ho, ho! ' says the squire, stoppin' short about two steps aff, an' turnin' round facin' my father, ' is it you that's in it?—an' how's all with you, Terry Neil? '

" ' At your honour's sarvice.' says my father (as well as the fright id let him, for he was more dead than alive), ' an' it's proud I am to see your honour to-night,' says he.

" ' Terence,' says the squire, ' you're a respectable man ' (an' it was thrue for him), ' an industhrious, sober man, an' an example of inebriety to the whole parish,' says he.

" ' Thank your honour,' says my father, gettin' courage, ' you were always a civil-spoken gintleman, God rest your honour.'

" ' *Rest* my honour? ' says the sperit (fairly gettin' red in the face with the madness), ' Rest my honour? ' says he. ' Why, you ignorant spalpeen,' says he, ' you mane, niggarly ignoramush,' says he, ' where did you lave your manners? ' says he. ' If I *am* dead, it's no fault iv mine,' says he; ' an' it's not to be thrun in my teeth at every hand's turn, by the likes iv you,' says he, stampin' his foot an the flure, that you'd think the boords id smash undther him.

" ' Oh,' says my father, ' I'm only a foolish, ignorant poor man,' says he.

" ' You're nothing else,' says the squire; ' but any way,' says he, ' it's not to be listenin' to your gosther, nor convarsin' with the likes iv you, that I came *up*—down I mane,' says he—(an' as little as the mistake was, my father tuk notice iv it). ' Listen to me now, Terence Neil,' says he; ' I was always a good masther to Pathrick Neil, your grandfather,' says he.

" ' 'Tis thrue for your honour,' says my father. ' And, more-over, I think I was always a sober, riglar gintleman,' says the squire.

" ' That's your name, sure enough,' says my father (though it was a big lie for him, but he could not help it).

" ' Well,' says the sperit, ' although I was as sober as most men—at laste as most gintelmin,' says he; ' an' though I was at different periods a most extempory Christian, and most charitable and inhuman to the poor,' says he; ' for all that I'm not as asy where I am now,' says he, ' as I had a right to expect,' says he.

" ' An' more's the pity,' says my father. ' Maybe your honour id wish to have a word with Father Murphy? '

" ' Hould your tongue, you misherable bliggard,' says the squire; ' it's not iv my sowl I'm thinkin'—an' I wondther you'd have the impitence to talk to a gintelman consarnin' his sowl; and when

I want *that* fixed,' says he, slappin' his thigh, ' I'll go to them that knows what belongs to the likes,' says he. ' It's not my sowl,' says he, sittin' down opposite my father; ' it's not my sowl that's annoyin' me most—I'm unasy on my right leg,' says he, ' that I bruk at Glenvarloch cover the day I killed black Barney.' My father found out afther, it was a favourite horse that fell undher him, afther leapin' the big fence that runs along by the glin. ' I hope,' says my father, ' your honour's not unasy about the killin' iv him? '

" ' Hould your tongue, ye fool,' said the squire, ' an' I'll tell you why I'm unasy on my leg,' says he. ' In the place where I spend most iv my time,' says he, ' except the little leisure I have for lookin' about me here,' says he, ' I have to walk a great dale more than I was ever used to,' says he, ' and by far more than is good for me either,' says he; ' for I must tell you,' says he, ' the people where I am is ancommonly fond iv cowld wather, for there is nothin' betther to be had; an', moreover, the weather is hotter than is altogether plisant,' says he; ' and I'm appinted,' says he, ' to assist in carryin' the wather, an' gets a mighty poor share iv it myself,' says he, ' an' a mighty throublesome, wearin' job it is, I can tell you,' says he; ' for they're all iv them surprisin'ly dthry, an' dthrinks it as fast as my legs can carry it,' says he; ' but what kills me intirely,' says he, ' is the wakeness in my leg,' says he, ' an' I want you to give it a pull or two to bring it to shape,' says he; ' and that's the long an' the short iv it,' says he.

" ' Oh, plase your honour,' says my father (for he didn't like to handle the spirit at all), ' I wouldn't have the impidence to do the likes to your honour,' says he; ' it's only to poor crathurs like myself I'd do it to,' says he.

" ' None iv your blarney,' says the squire. ' Here's my leg,' says he, cockin' it up to him—' pull it for the bare life,' says he; ' an' if you don't, by the immortal powers I'll not lave a bone in your carcish I'll not powdher,' says he.

" When my father heerd that, he seen there was no use in pur- tendin', so he tuk hould iv the leg, an' he kep' pullin' an' pullin', till the sweat, God bless us, beginned to pour down his face.

" ' Pull, you divil! ' says the squire.

" ' At your sarvice, your honour,' says my father.

" ' Pull harder,' says the squire. My father pulled like the divil.

" ' I'll take a little sup,' says the squire, rachin' over his hand to the bottle, ' to keep up my courage,' says he, lettin' an to be very wake in himself intirely. But, as cute as he was, he was out here, for he tuk the wrong one. ' Here's to your good health, Terence,' says he; ' an' now pull like the very divil.' An' with that he lifted the bottle of holy wather, but it was hardly to his mouth, whin he let a screech out, you'd think the room id fairly split with it, an' made one chuck that sent the leg clane aff his body in my father's hands. Down wint the squire over the table, an' bang wint my father half-way across the room on his back, upon the flure. Whin he kem to himself the cheerful mornin' sun was shinin' through the windy shutthers, an' he was lyin' flat an his back, with the leg iv one of the great ould chairs pulled clane out iv the socket an' tight in his hand, pintin' up to the ceilin', an' ould Larry fast asleep, an' snorin' as loud as ever. My father wint that mornin' to Father Murphy, an' from that to the day of his death he never neglected confission nor mass, an' what he tould was betther believed that he spake av it but seldom. An', as for the squire, that is the sperit, whether it was that he did not like his liquor, or by rason iv the loss iv his leg, he was never known to walk agin."

## CANON P. A. SHEEHAN
### 1852–1913

# A THOROUGH GENTLEMAN

SOME time towards the end of the Parliamentary session, 188–, I found myself in London, on the way to Switzerland. I was not long in the great Babylon when I knocked up against an old schoolmate, now developed into an august Member of the British Parliament. It was in the evening, the place was the Strand; and I remember well what an impression it made upon me when, as we strolled up and down the crowded thoroughfare, he pointed out to me group after group of Irish Members moving quietly along in twos and threes, clearly strangers in a strange land. It was a day off (Wednesday, I think), and I expressed my surprise that they should not seize the opportunity to scatter themselves, and enjoy the hospitality of many houses which would be glad to open their doors to them. My friend smiled.

" There is not one house in London to-night," he said, " that would entertain them; and what is more, not one of them would accept such entertainment if proffered. It is war time; and in war you don't sit down to dinner with your enemies."

It impressed me deeply. My heart went out to these Irish guerilleros, isolated and banned on the London streets.

" That reminds me," said my friend, " you and I are not at war, though we had many a tough battle in days gone by. Come along here; I know a cosy corner where we can dine."

We left the Strand, and he took me along until we came to a modest, but evidently quite new, little French café off Oxford Street. It was pretty full when we entered. There was but one table vacant, far over in a dim, dusky corner, and we at once made our way towards it.

" We get an excellent dinner here," he said, " and at a singularly moderate price."

He lifted his hand, and the waiter came over.

Just then a tall, straight, gentlemanly figure entered the room, and placing his hat upon a rack, he looked around inquiringly. My friend, the Member, caught his eye, and whispering to me:

" That's P——, one of our men, Member for the E—— Division,
C—— County," he whistled, and put up his hand.

The gentleman, without divesting himself of his overcoat, came
slowly towards us, and when he had come quite close, my friend
discovered his mistake.

" I beg a thousand pardons," he said.  " In the dusk I quite
mistook you for a friend and Parliamentary colleague."

"A most happy mistake," said the gentleman, removing his
gloves.  " May I be allowed to take advantage of it?  I perceive
there is no other table unoccupied."

It was awkward; but what can an Irishman do but be civil?  My
friend said we would both be most happy to have his company,
and he at once in a most peremptory, gentlemanly manner ordered
soup.

He was quite tall, bald on the crown of his head; he wore a
short thick beard, slightly silvered with grey, and he looked excessively delicate.  His cheeks were sunken, the cheek-bones quite
apparent, and his eyes glowed as the eyes of a consumptive patient
enlarge and shine with the progress of the disease.  There was a
curious blending of hauteur and deference in his manner; and a
strange odour exhaled from his clothes, which I could not for a
considerable time define.

He took his soup rather too hastily, I thought; and then he
rubbed his bread around and around the plate, and ate it almost
ravenously.

" He has lived abroad," I thought.  " That is not an English
custom."

When the waiter brought fish, he sent back the tiny morsel, and
looking at the carte, he said:  " I see salmon here.  Bring me a
large slice of salmon, and sauce—mind, sauce! "

Then turning to my friend he said in an altered tone:  " So I have
the honour of dining with a Member of Parliament? "  My friend
bowed.

" I have been in pretty high society," he said, picking up some
crumbs and eating them, " nay, I have enjoyed Her Majesty's
hospitality, but I have never aspired to be a Member of the
Legislature.  It is a great honour, sir, to be allowed to dine with
you; and I perceive, or rather I presume, you are both Irish? "

" Yes, we are Irish," said my friend laconically.

" Now," said the stranger, taking up his fork and breaking the
salmon cutlet before him, " I do not share the insular and narrow
prejudices of my countrymen against the Irish.  I have been lately
the guest of one of your excellent countrymen.  He maintained
the national reputation for hospitality.  In fact if I could complain
of anything, it would be that he was almost too pressing in his
attentions.  But to resume.  I am a travelled man; I have seen all
races and peoples and tongues; and I have learned to distinguish—

what, do you think? Races? No!—all races are alike. I have learned to distinguish a gentleman from a cad! "

Somehow, we felt flattered; and we launched at once into a most amiable discussion on the peculiarities of nations and races; and there was a singular unanimity in our opinions. We thoroughly agreed that there were gentlemen in every country, even amongst the Turks, and when these were mentioned, the stranger became quite heated.

" The Turks? " he said. " Why, they are the cream of civilisation. Every Turk is a gentleman. They are the only race which, as a race—I am not speaking of individuals merely—maintain dignity, reserve, courtesy. A Turk never presumes, is never disturbed, is always calm, serene, dignified. And if you want to see the perfection of family life, get, if you can, at Cairo or Alexandria, an invitation from some Sheik to his house, and there—well," he continued, " I must not tell. It would be ungentlemanly—a breach of hospitality."

He ate ravenously, voraciously; but I set it down to his Oriental experiences. He drank nothing, and refused the bottle of Margaux which my friend pushed towards him. " He is a Mussulman," I said to myself. " See, he avoids wine, and he is *so* enthusiastic."

In the intervals of the courses, he spoke as rapidly as he had eaten, giving us details of all his travels in Mexico, Guatemala, on the banks of the Ganges, and the Nile. He had marvellous powers of description, and when he talked about the charms of the Desert, the great dark night hanging down with its rich clusters of stars over the Bedouin tents, evening on the Ganges, the sun setting behind the Pyramids, etc., I began to feel that, after all, a man must travel to know. But, then, his pale, emaciated features, stooped shoulders, and short cough told another tale. " You have gained by your travels," I said, " but you have lost somewhat. Your health appears to have suffered."

" Quite so," he replied, " I *have* suffered."

" I perceive," said my friend, " that you are using iodine." The stranger's fingers were stained a deep brownish red, and his finger-nails were rough and jagged.

" Sir," said he, " you are a Sherlock Holmes. Every night, for many weeks, I have had to use tincture of iodine for my lungs."

This gave me the clue to the singular odour I had noticed hanging around his clothes as he entered.

" And you are using creosote? " I remarked.

" Sir," he said, " you are a brother detective. Yes, I have been using creosote, or coal-tar in some form."

Just here the waiter came round, switching on the electric lamps. The stranger looked slightly disconcerted, and bending across the table he whispered: " You are in possession of the table, sir, and have the right to interfere. Would you kindly tell this waiter to leave us in the dusk? My eyes have suffered from the glare of the desert sands, and that abominable light is particularly hurtful.''

The request seemed strange, but my friend complied.

'' You don't wish for the light, sir? '' the waiter said.

'' No, we have light enough,'' said the Member.

'' I beg your par'n, sir,'' said the waiter, '' but this gentleman belongs to your party? ''

'' Well, ye—es,'' said the Member. '' We have dined together.''

'' Oh, all right, sir,'' said the waiter. '' We only wanted to know.''

The stranger was not disconcerted in the least. He slewed his chair around, sipped his coffee carefully, lit a proffered cigar, and said: '' Now, there's another instance of the vast gulf that separates Oriental from Occidental civilisation. You noticed that impertinent question? That would be impossible in the East! just as impossible as that a mere servant should be allowed, nay, compelled to wear the garments of civilisation, and these—the full dress of a gentleman. You perceive the incongruity? Now, in the East, a slave—and that *cochon* is but a slave—would have approached with deference, salaaming to the ground, lifted your right foot, and placed it on his head, salaamed again, and then protested that you were a son of the Prophet, that sunshine was your shadow, that your eyes lighted the stars at night, and that he, your most humble and adoring subject, would think himself privileged to die a thousand deaths at your bidding.''

'' But that's all bunkum,'' said my friend the Member.

''Bunkum? Yes,'' echoed the stranger. '' I am not sure,'' he continued very slowly, as if he had been deeply pained at the expression, but was too gentlemanly to resent it, '' that I would have used the expression. But it *is* expressive; and your remark is quite correct. But is not *bunkum* the oil of life? This old, decrepit, worn-out civilisation would have been shaken to pieces long ago, and after creaking and moaning enough to make angels or lost angels weep, would have collapsed and lain still for ever were it not for bunkum. What is ' Your Majesty? ' Bunkum. 'Your Royal Highness? ' Bunkum. ' Your Grace? ' Bunkum. ' My Lord? ' Bunkum. When the nurse takes the pink and puling baby, who has wandered hither from eternity, to the admiring father and calls it ' a cherub,' ' an angel ' it is bunkum. And when the headstone declares that a paragon of all the virtues lies here, it is bunkum. Did it ever occur to you, my dear friend, as you sat on the green benches in the House of Commons and heard a Cabinet Minister address one of your party, which, as you know, he cordially detests, and would sweep into Gehenna without compunction as ' my honourable and learned friend,' that this was bunkum? The only person in your august assembly that is not a lay-figure is the Speaker. No one dare address bunkum to him.

He is ' Sir '—no more; but that is the title of a gentleman.''

My friend the Member was calmly chuckling to himself at this delightful attack on Society in general, and the Mother of Parliaments in particular.

'' Where, then, comes in the difference between Oriental and Occidental bunkum? '' continued the stranger, between every furious puff of his cigar.

'' Mark! the expression is not mine. I hold you responsible for it. Well, the difference is, that the Orientals are consistent; you are not. The Oriental never forgets himself, never breaks into anger, is never insolent. He does not call you ' Son of the Prophet ' to your face and grimace behind your back. He does not welcome you effusively to his house; and, when you are leaving, say: ' Praised be Allah, what a riddance! ' He may sometimes, under great provocation, cheat you in a bargain, but it is always done in a gentlemanly manner; and if he does put laudanum in your coffee, at least he calls upon Allah to protect you. But here, whilst you retain all the bunkum—pardon me, the expression is your own— of the East, everything else is vulgar, plebeian, monkeyish; and it reveals itself in such awful *bêtises* as that wretched creature was just now guilty of. But here he comes again, the slave of the lamp and the napkin! ''

The waiter approached and proffered to my friend the Member the bill on a salver. As he did so, I saw him give a searching look on the stranger. The latter threw aside the stump of his cigar, and reaching over he said eagerly: '' Is my account here? ''

'' Yes,'' said the waiter irreverently; '' the entire account is on that bill.''

'' Then I shall pay for all,'' said the stranger, fumbling in a side-pocket.

The Member had placed a sovereign on the salver and beckoned the waiter away.

'' I cannot allow this, sir,'' said the stranger, deeply offended. '' It would be most ungentlemanly to permit a perfect stranger to discharge my debts.''

'' I wouldn't have taken the liberty,'' said the Member, '' but you didn't resent it when I said we belonged to the same party. Besides it is a way we Irish have.''

'' Yes, I perceive,'' said the gentlemanly stranger, and sank into a brown study.

The receipted bill was brought, the waiter tipped, and we stood up to depart, when, in a pitiful way, the stranger stopped us. '' Gentlemen,'' he said, '' please be seated one moment, if I may detain you.''

He had turned away his head, and it sank low on his breast. The café was empty. The waiters had gone into the kitchen as there was nothing further to be done.

" Your generosity has overpowered me," he said at length. " I don't know where to begin my confession."

Then, as if he were doing a desperate thing and should do it quickly, he said: " You have entertained a gentleman, and—a gaol-bird. I had just come out of prison, starved, emaciated, dying, and—to die! For God is my witness, I was about to seek my bed to-night in the Thames. But, as I passed this place I said, ' I shall dine like a gentleman once more, and then——' "

He paused for a moment, as if trying to remember his feelings.

" You may ask why I was in gaol or a gaol-bird, which implies so much more. It were a tedious story; but I may say at once that I have never been guilty of an ungentlemanly act. I have never done anything beyond what is done every day and night by the *élite* of this city. But you will say I have lied to you, and that is not gentlemanly. No! I have not lied. I have equivocated. I said I had enjoyed Her Majesty's hospitality. So I have. I said that I had been entertained by one of your countrymen, and that he was too pressing in his attentions. It is true. Rourke, or Crooke, or something else, was my warder. I have said that I used iodine. It is true. But that stain," he pointed to his thumb and fingers, " is not iodine. It is oakum. And the prison odour that clings around me still is not creosote, as your learned friend conjectured, but the odour of tarred rope. You will object that it was not gentlemanly to come in here and order dinner, knowing that I had not the means of paying for it. Bismillah! Is it not done every day hundreds of times in this city by your greatest swells? No gentleman pays for such trifles as dinner or habiliments. He pays for a box at the opera, or a diamond; but for a dinner? Oh no! Of course I know that if I had not had the good fortune to meet you, I should have been flung out upon the pavement and copped instantly. But, then, why quarrel with good fortune? I never do. If I had been copped I should sleep to-night on a dry board instead of the slime of the river. That would have been one gain. But I would have lost an excellent dinner. Well! there's the equilibrium of things."

He stood up. " I now go to my doom; but with the sublime consciousness that I have dined as a gentleman, with gentlemen. And now, one favour more. May I take this cigar? "

The Member nodded. The gentlemanly stranger lighted the cigar leisurely, and smoked for a second or two.

" The favour is this," he said. " To perfect the compliment by allowing me to accompany you to the door. I see these wretched slaves have come in again and are watching us."

" Come along," said the Member. At the door, under the pitiless glare of the pale electric light, all was visible. The soiled collar, the blue melton overcoat white at the elbows and seams, the yellow tips of the fingers showing through the shabby and broken gloves, the silk hat brown and broken—all told their tale.

The stranger turned and said: " Gentlemen, I must not intrude on you any longer. I beg once more to thank you. May Allah protect you! " Then, lifting his shabby hat, he said to my friend, " *Ave Cæsar Imperator! moriturus te saluto!* " [1] He strolled leisurely down the crowded thoroughfare, and the odour of the cigar filled the air.

I couldn't help laughing. " That was a bad sell," I said.

" Never mind," said the Member, " you have dined with a gentleman." I did not know how true were his words, until in after years, long after his death, I learned that my friend the Member had that evening parted with his last sovereign to entertain a stranger and a felon.

[1] " Hail, Emperor and Cæsar! I, about to die, salute you! " The salutation of the gladiators in the arena.

# F. FRANKFORT MOORE
1855–1931

# THE COMEDY OF THE OLD LOVE

## A STORY OF NELL GWYN

### I

" MADAM ELLEN'S *levée* is at this hour, is't not? " said the Duke
of Buckingham to one of the many lackeys who formed a bowing
line, suggesting a row of scarlet poppies yielding to a persistent
wind, as he entered the splendid ante-room to the great *salon*,
decorated—rather too profusely—in the latest French style, in
Madam Eleanor Gwyn's house in Pall Mall.

" Madam Ellen is at the point of descending, your Grace," replied the major-domo.

" I am the earliest of her visitors," said the Duke. " Will there
be a large attendance to-day? "

" Madam does not limit the attendance at her *levées*, your
Grace. 'Tis at the card-tables in the evening that only a few are
admitted," said the major-domo.

" H'm, I shall wait," remarked his Grace.

The major-domo bowed; not without a due sense of his own
importance, as well as of the importance of the visitor.

The Duke strolled about the rooms with smiles that varied as his
eye caught the various objects of decoration scattered with ludicrous
profusion about the *salon*. Side by side with a masterpiece of
French workmanship was a wretched thing of pasteboard and paint,
presented to Nell Gwyn by one of the playhouse carpenters. A
pair of bronze gilt candelabra worth a fortune stood on pedestals of
wood emblazoned with coloured paper. Nell Gwyn's taste was
eccentric—to be more exact it might be said to be extremely
inclusive.

The Duke was hugely amused, nor was his impression changed
when he glanced round, hearing the swish of the *portières*, and saw
at the point of entering the lower *salon* two beautiful ladies—their

charms were so amply displayed as to place no tax upon the imagination of his Grace. No two ladies of the Court were more generous in this way than the Duchess of Cleveland—lately the Countess of Castlemaine—and the Duchess of Portsmouth—lately the exquisite Madame de Querouaille, the gift of the French king to the English Court.

" We have not come soon enough," whispered the Duchess of Portsmouth to her Grace of Cleveland.

" Oil and vinegar," murmured the Duke; " a piquant salad for Nelly."

" Ah, Duke, you are early in offering your duty to Madam Ellen, are you not? " said the Duchess of Cleveland quite pleasantly —for her—as the Duke bowed lower than any lackey.

" If I am arraigned on such a charge, I shall claim the privilege of having your Grace beside me in the dock," said he.

" I' faith, we are early," said the Duchess of Portsmouth; " but the Park in the morning is very sweet."

" So that your Grace was compelled to seek an antidote in Nell Gwyn's house? " suggested the Duke.

" And we have found one," cried the Duchess.

" Nay, madam, I said not that you needed an antidote to sweetness; were you not in the companionship of the Duchess of Cleveland? " said the Duke, smiling.

" The Duke of Buckingham hath been round the coffee-houses already. That accounts for his wit," said the Duchess of Cleveland.

" His Grace's wit is of such a quality as proves beyond doubt that none of the coffee-house wits are early risers," remarked the other lady.

" If they are not, madam, they cannot certainly excuse themselves on the ground that they sat up late at a party of the Duchess of Portsmouth's," said the Duke.

" Nay, my parties are not always dull: your Grace is sometimes absent," said the Duchess of Portsmouth.

" That is how I come to be alive to-day. And I fly from your Grace's presence now so that I may be alive to-morrow," cried he, bowing as he passed out through the curtains.

" I'm afraid we must have him as an ally," said the Duchess of Cleveland.

" I think," said the other, " you will find some difficulty in securing as an ally one whose enmity you have cultivated for several years."

" Bah! I can do what I please with men."

The other smiled. Her smile was very irritating—it had the elements of a shrug about it. She only remarked, however, " What can be keeping our friend, Madam Ellen? "

" This orange-woman's brat gives herself the airs of an Empress," said the Duchess of Portsmouth. Then, turning suddenly

at the sound of the curtain rings, she cried, " Ah, dear Madam
Ellen.  What a picture of grace! "

" A picture of grace! " echoed the other.

" Ah, then we are the Three Graces that Mr. Dryden told me of
—her Grace the Duchess of Portsmouth, her Grace the Duchess of
Cleveland, and me—grace personified by the grace of—of your
Graces," cried Nell.  Then glancing critically from one to the other
of her visitors, she remarked, " I wonder how much of the
grace of God there is among the three of us?  Dr. Ken, the
Canon of Winchester, would have no difficulty appraising it,
I fancy."

" The wretch that would not let you lodge in his house," said
the Duchess of Cleveland, with well-simulated indignation.

" Ay, that was Dr. Ken.  But your Graces have not honoured
me with this visit to talk about clergymen."

" Nay, 'tis but a visit of friendship, madam; and converse on
theology is no promoter of friendships," said the Duchess of
Cleveland.

" Though Madam Ellen's heart is generous enough to make impossible even a quarrel with her on theology," said the other.

" Oh, your Grace overwhelms me," cried Nell, sinking in a
curtsey.

" Ah, 'tis true indeed, but alas! generosity may sometimes lead
one astray," said the Duchess of Cleveland.

" Is it worth while discussing a point which cannot possibly
affect your Grace? " asked Nell.

" Nay, 'tis but in connection with this freak of yours—this
hospital for old soldiers, dear child.  Are you not urging the King
to an act of foolish generosity? " said her Grace.

" 'Tis not generosity, madam; 'tis but simple justice," cried
Nell.

" Think of the money that it will cost—thousands—tens of
thousands," said the French lady.

" Less than His Majesty would throw away in a year upon one
of us," replied Nell.

" One of us—one of—oh, yes; of course, but—well, we need it,"
said her Grace of Cleveland.

" We are not so needy as the poor men who fought for the
King and his house."

" Ah, true—true; but I fear that the people will not submit to
the enormous cost of maintaining your hospital," said the Duchess
of Cleveland.

" When they submitted to the King's granting you the revenues
of the post-office, they will submit to anything," said Nell.

Her Grace of Cleveland took an angry step in the direction of
Nell, but Nell stood her ground, and the Duchess refrained from
saying the words which had sprung to her lips.  She gave a laugh

that rang very hollow, and some moments had passed before she said:

" Look you, Madam Ellen; if you agree to cease urging on the King to waste upon this hospital the money which he would certainly spend upon us, we promise you that within a year you shall be made a Duchess."

" I will promise you this, madam: I will not cease to urge the King to build this hospital even though his courtiers should be left beggars," cried Nell. " And as for your bribe—we have enough Duchesses in this realm to last us for a while. I am Nell Gwyn, daughter of the people, and I seek not to be known by any other name. Every one knows that I am on the side of the English people against all the world. But you, Duchess of Cleveland— you, Madame de Querouaille, are you on the side of the King of England or the King of France? "

" Bah! the King of France is stronger than the King of England," cried the Frenchwoman.

" Yes; but the people of England are stronger than both. Beware of the people of England, Madame de Querouaille," said Nell.

" They are *canaille*, and you—you are one of them, Nell Gwyn," cried the Duchess of Portsmouth.

" Insolent baggage! " shrieked the other Duchess. " You shall die in the gutter from which you sprang, and your boy—ah, you think that the King will be fool enough to ennoble the brat. I know better. He will die a——"

Nell sprang toward her, and she wisely retreated.

" If you say that word which is trembling on your lips, I will tear out the tongue that framed it," said Nell in a whisper. " Take yourself out of my house, foul-mouthed creature! "

" We are properly repaid for putting ourselves on a level with an orange-girl," cried the Frenchwoman.

" The King shall learn of this," cried the Duchess of Cleveland.

" Tell it to your King, the King of France," cried Nell, as the two ladies dashed through the *portière*.

Left alone in the *salon*, Madam Ellen paced the room excitedly for some time. Then she struck her hands together, crying, " As God is my witness, I will never cease to urge the King to build the hospital. Honours—what care I for honours?—for duchess-ships?. The honours of dishonour. Nay, I ask only the honour of having it said of me that I helped on this work for England's soldiers."

The ante-room had by this time become crowded with courtiers anxious to profit by doing her the honour of attending her *levée*.

Through the curtain came a still young officer. He bowed low, and she greeted him cordially.

" Ah, Colonel Churchill, you have not forgotten me in your foreign wars."

" How would that be possible, madam? "

" I cannot conceive it for myself. No man who remembers himself so well as Colonel Churchill does could forget Nell Gwyn. How can I be of help to you, Colonel? "

He went close to her.

" Dear madam, General Crosby is very ill——"

" Ah, I thought that my old friend remembered himself. Well, better that than that he should forget himself. Sir, the King shall hear of your merits before the breath is out of poor Crosby's body."

" With what words——"

" Good morning to you, Colonel—General Churchill."

He retired, bowing low, having kissed her hand, and made way for an elderly gentleman who had come forward.

" Ah, my Lord, I have not been honoured by a visit from your Lordship since—was it since you begged of me to ask the King to make you Warden of the Meres? " said she. " And what help can I be to your Lordship at this time? "

" Madam, 'tis not for myself; I would die, madam, rather than ask favours for myself," he replied with firmness.

" But you have a son."

" The finest young fellow that lives, though I am his father, madam."

" That is not his fault, my Lord. Is it in the Royal Scots or the Life Guards you wish him placed? "

" The Life Guards, dear madam. We are a poor but proud family, madam. Merit only hath advanced us. My boy would scorn to ask for favours if he once got a start. The Life Guards, dear madam—and, if possible, a captaincy. I may depend on your good word? A thousand thanks. We come of a proud stock, madam. We are poor but proud, madam—my son——"

" His name shall be put before His Majesty, my Lord."

The fine old fellow bent low over her hand. Going to the door, he glared back scornfully at the crowd, and muttered, " Pack of sycophants—pack of sycophants! "

She had not heard the petitions of more than half of them when a strange and incongruous figure appeared at the entrance—a middle-aged lady dressed in incomparable finery, but suggesting, among her silks and feathers, the jackdaw masquerading as a peacock. She was remonstrating with the major-domo with great fluency—the fluency of Lewknor Lane.

" Why shouldn't I see my daughter at any hour I please, fellow? " she was asking.

Madam Ellen laughed, and dismissed her Court.

" 'Tis my lady mother," she cried. " What post can she come to ask for? Ladies and gentlemen, you may all depend on my good word on your behalf. Come now, mother, and tell me all that you have to tell. Heavens, madam, do not tell me that you wish to be made Mistress of the Robes—or Master of the Horse."

"Not me—not me," said Mrs. Gwyn, eyeing the disappearing Court until she was alone with her daughter.

"I breathe again," said Nell. "But I scarce knew that you were journeying hither to-day. 'Tis an honour and a surprise as well; and i' faith, now that I come to think on't, the surprise is a deal greater than the honour. If you say you haven't come hither for more money, my surprise will be unbounded."

"I'm not come for money, though a trifle would be welcome," said the mother when Nelly had shown her the way into one of the rooms opening off a corridor at one side of the hall.

"I have met with an old friend of yours this day, Nell," said the mother, "and he is coming hither."

"An old friend! I' faith, good mother, 'tis the young friends are more to my taste. The savour of Lewknor Lane doth not smell sweet."

"Oh, ay, but you once wasn't so dainty a madam."

"'Twere vain to deny it, mother, since it can be urged against me that I became your daughter. Whom say you that you met to-day?"

"What should you say if I told you that his name was Dick Harraden?"

"What, Dick! Dick! Dick Harraden!"

Nell had sprung to her feet, and had grasped her mother by the shoulder, eagerly peering into her face.

After a moment of silence following her exclamation, she gave her mother a little push in the act of taking her hand off her shoulder, and threw herself back in her own chair again with a laugh.

"What should I say, do you ask me?" she cried. "Well, I should say that you were a liar, good mother."

"I'm no liar," said the mother. "'Twas Dick himself I met face to face."

"It puzzles me to see wherein lies your hope of getting money from me by telling me such a tale," said Nell.

"I want not your money—at least, not till the end of the month or thereabouts. I tell you I saw Dick within the hour."

"'Twas his ghost. You know that when he threw away his link he took to the sea and was drowned in a storm off the Grand Canary. What did the seafaring man tell us when I asked him if he had seen Dick?"

"A maudlin knave he was—a very maudlin knave to come with such a tale."

"But he said he had sailed in the same ship as Dick, and that it had gone down with all aboard save only himself."

"Oh, ay; and he wept plentifully when he saw how you wept—ay, the knave! For I saw Dick with these eyes within the hour."

"Oh, mother—and you told him—no, you dursn't tell him——"

" He had just this morning come to London from the Indies, and it was good luck—or ill-luck may be—that made him run against me. He plied me with question after question—all about Nell—his Nell, he called you, if you please."

" His Nell—ah, mother! his Nell! Well, you told him——"

" I told him that you would never more need his aid to buy footgear. Lord! Nell, do you mind how he bought you the worsted stockings when you were nigh mad with the chilblains? "

" And you told him. . . . For God's sake say what you told him."

" I didn't mention the King's name—no, I'm loyal to His Majesty, God save him! I only told him that you had given up selling oranges in the pit of Drury Lane, and had taken to the less reputable part of the house, to wit, the stage."

" Poor Dick! he didn't like to hear that. Oh, if he had stayed at home and carried his link as before, all would have been well."

" What is the wench talking about? Well—all would have been well? And is not all well, you jade? 'Twere rank treason to say else. Isn't this room, with its gilded looking-glasses and painted vases, pretty well for one who has been an orange-girl? The King is a gentleman—and a merry gentleman too. Well, indeed! "

" But Dick—what more did you say to him, mother? "

" I asked him after himself, to be sure. I' faith, the lad hath prospered, Nell. He will tell you all himself."

" What! you told him where I dwelt? "

" I meant it not, Nelly; but he had it from me before I was aware. But he knows nothing. He will have no time to hear of the King and the King's fancies before he sees you."

" He is coming hither, then? No, he must not come; oh, he shall not come. Mother, you have played me false."

" I? Oh, the wench is mad! False? What could I say, girl, when he pressed me? "

" You could have said that I was dead—that would have been the truth. The girl he knew is dead. He must not come to this house."

" Then give your lackeys orders not to admit him and all will be well."

" I'll not see him. Did he say he'd come soon? "

" Within the hour, he said."

Instinctively Nell looked at her reflection in a mirror.

" I'll not see him," she repeated.

" That gown will do well enough for one just returned from the Indies," said the mother.

" Oh, go away; go away," cried her daughter. " You have done enough mischief for one morning. Why could not you have let things be? Oh, go away; go away! "

" Oh, yes; I'll go. And you'll see him, too; no fear about that. And so good-day to you, good Mistress Eve."

She made a mock curtsey and marched out of the room.

Her daughter watched her departure, and only when she had disappeared burst into a laugh. In a moment she was grave once again. She remained seated without changing her attitude or expression for a long time. At last she sprang to her feet, saying out loud:

" What a fool thou art, friend Nell, to become glum over a boy sweetheart—and a link-boy, of all boys. But I'll not see him. 'Twere best not. He'll hear all soon enough, and loathe me as at times I loathe myself. No, no; not so much as that—not so much as that: Dick had always a kind heart. No, I'll not see him."

She went resolutely to the bell-pull, but, when there, stood irresolute with the ornamental ring of brass in her hand for some moments before pulling it. She gave it a sudden jerk, and when it was responded to by a lackey, she said:

" Should a man call, asking to see me, within the next hour, he is to be told—with civility, mind you; he is a gentleman—that— that I am in this room, and that I will see him for five minutes— only five minutes, mind you, sirrah."

" And the man—the gentleman—is to be admitted, madam? "

" Certainly—for five minutes."

" Your ladyship will regulate the time? "

" Go away, you numskull! How could I regulate the time? I'm no astronomer."

" Madam, I meant but to inquire if you are to be interrupted at the end of five minutes."

" I gave you no such instruction, sirrah. It is enough for you to carry out the instruction I gave you. Carry it out and yourself into the bargain."

The man bowed and withdrew.

When he had gone Nelly laughed again, but suddenly became graver even than she had yet been.

" What have I done? " she cried. " Oh, there never was so great a fool as me. No, no; I'll not see him. I have as kind a heart as Dick, and I'll prove it by not seeing him."

And yet, when she had her hand on the lock of the door, she stood irresolute once again for some moments. Then she went out with a firm step, her intention being to countermand in the hall the instructions she had given to the servant in the parlour; but in the hall she found herself face to face with her old friend Sir Charles Sedley. He had brought her a bunch of violets.

" The satyr offers flowers to Aurora," said the courtier, bowing as gracefully as a touch of rheumatism permitted him.

" And Aurora was so fond of flowers that she accepted them even from the most satiric of satyrs," said Nell, sinking into a curtsey.

They were standing apart from the group of servants in the hall.
Nell Gwyn had pretended that she was about to ascend the stairs,
but loitered on the second step with her right elbow resting on the
oak banister while she smelt at the violets with her head poised
daintily as she looked with eyes full of mischief and mirth at the
courtier standing on the mat.

Suddenly Nell straightened herself as she looked down the hall
towards the door—she started and dropped her violets. All the
mischief and mirth fled from her eyes as a man was admitted, with
some measure of protestation, by the porter. He was a young man
with a very brown face, and he carried no sword, only the hanger
of a sailor; his dress was of the plainest.

Before Sir Charles had time to turn to satisfy himself as to the
identity of the man at whom Nell was gazing so eagerly, she had
run down the hall and seized the new-comer by both hands, crying:
" Dick—Dick—it is you yourself, Dick, and no ghost! "

" No ghost, I dare swear, Nell," cried the man in a tone that
made the candles in the chandelier quiver. " No ghost, but—oh,
Lord, how you've grown, Nell! Why, when I burnt my last link
seeing you home you was only so high." He put his hand within
a foot of the floor.

"And you, too, Dick! Why! you're a man now—you'll grow
no more, Dick," cried Nell, still standing in front of him with his
hands fast clasped in her own. Suddenly, recollecting the servants
who were around, she dropped his hands saying: " Come along
within, Dick, and tell me all your adventures since last we were
together."

" Lord! Adventures! You don't know what you've set yourself down for, Nell. If I was to tell you all I should be in your
company for at least a week."

She led him past Sir Charles Sedley without so much as glancing
at the courtier, and the new-comer had no eyes for any one save
Nell. A servant threw open the door of the room where she had
been with her mother, and the two entered.

Sir Charles took snuff elaborately, after he had replaced his hat
on his head.

" If His Majesty should arrive, let him know that I am in the
long parlour," he said to a servant as he walked toward a door
on the left.

He paused for a space with his hand on the handle of the door,
for there came from the room into which Nell Gwyn and Dick
Harraden had gone a loud peal of laughter—not a solo, but a
duet.

He turned the handle.

So soon as he had disappeared there came a second ripple of
laughter from the other room, and the lackeys lounging in the hall
laughed too.

II

Within the room Nell was seated on the settee and Dick Harraden by her side. She had just reminded him of the gift of the worsted stockings which he had made to her when he was a linkboy and she an orange-girl in Drury Lane. They had both laughed when she had pushed out a little dainty shoe from beneath her gown, as she said:

" Ah, Dick, 'tis not in worsted my toes are clad now. I have outgrown your stockings."

" Not you, Nell! " he cried. " By the Lord Harry! your feet have got smaller instead of larger during these years—I swear to you that is so."

" Ah, the chilblains do make a difference, Dick," said she; " and you never saw my feet unless they were covered with chilblains. Lord! how you cried when you saw my feet well covered for the first time."

" Not I—I didn't cry. What was there to cry about, Nell? " he said.

She felt very much inclined to ask him the same question at that moment, for his face was averted from her, and he had uttered his words spasmodically.

" Poor Dick! you wept because you had eaten nothing for three days in order to save enough to buy my stockings," she said.

" How know you that? " he cried, turning to her suddenly.

" I knew it not at the time," she replied, " but I have thought over it since."

" Think no more of it, Nell. Oh, Lord, to think that I should live to see Nell again! No—no. I'll not believe it. That fine lady that I see in the big glass yonder cannot be Nell Gwyn."

" Oh, Dick, would any one but Nell Gwyn remember about Nell Gwyn's chilblains? "

" Hearsay—mere hearsay, my fine madam! "

" By what means shall I convince you that I'm the Nell you knew? Let me see—ah, I know. Dick, I'll swear for you; you know well that there was no one could match me in swearing. Let me but begin."

" Oh, Lord! not for the world. You always knew when to begin, Nell, but you ne'er knew when to stop. And how doth it come that you haven't forgot the brimstone of the Lane, Nelly, though you have become so mighty fine a lady? "

" 'Snails, Dick, the best way to remember a language is to keep constantly talking it."

" But in silks and satins? "

" Oh, I soon found that I only needed to double the intensity of my language in the Lane in order to talk the mother-tongue of fashion."

" If swearing make the fine lady you'll be the leader of the town, Nell, I'll warrant. But don't say that you doubled your language—that would be impossible."

" Oh, would it indeed? "

" Not so? Then, for God's sake, don't give me a sample of what you reached in that way, for I've only lived among the pirates and buccaneers of the Indies since."

" Then I'll e'en spare thee, Dick; but take warning: don't provoke me. You wouldn't provoke a pirate whose guns you knew to be double-shotted. Don't say that I'm not Nell Gwyn for all my silks and lace. Why, man, doth oatmeal porridge cease to be porridge because it's served in a silver platter? Did your salt pork turn to venison when you ate it off the gold plate that you stole from the chapels? "

" Lord, Nell, I wasn't a pirate."

" What! Didn't you say just now that you had been among pirates and buccaneers in the Indies? "

" I was among them, but not of them."

" You mean to say that you were neither a pirate nor a buccaneer? "

" Neither."

" Then all I can say is that I'm mightily ashamed of you, Dick. I counted on your being at least a pirate. Don't say that you became a merchant; I never could abide dishonesty, Dick."

" Well, no; I never became just a merchant, Nell—at least, not the sort of merchant that merchants would call a merchant."

" Oh, then there's some hope for you yet, Dick. We may be friends still."

" Friends? Well, I should say so. What did I work for, do you think, through all these years? What did I lay up a store of guineas for—guineas and Spanish doubloons and pieces of eight for——? "

" And you have made a fortune, Dick? Think of that! Ah, I fear that you must have been a regular merchant after all; only regular merchants make fortunes in these days."

" Ay, but some irregular ones do pretty fairly for themselves."

" And you were somewhat irregular, I dare swear? "

" Well, I wasn't regularly irregular, dear; only by fits and starts. Ah, what I said to myself was: I've put the stockings on Nell, but I've to get new shoes for her yet. That's what gave me the strength of ten men—working for those new shoes, Nell."

" Poor Dick! and now when you come home you find that I am already provided for."

Again she showed him the dainty tips of her shoes.

" Those are fair-weather shoes, Nell," he cried.

" Ay, that they are, Dick," she assented with a note of sadness in her voice.

"But what I would offer you would stand the stress of all weather—fair or foul, Nell."

"I believe you, Dick, with all my heart. I know what you had to offer me; but it's too late now—too late, Dick."

"Too late? What do you mean, girl?"

The look that came into his face frightened her. She threw herself back on the settee and laughed loudly for a minute or two.

"That's what I mean," she cried, tilting up her toes until they were on a level with his knees. "What else could I mean than that I'm already sufficiently shod? Even Nell Gwyn can't wear more than one pair of shoes at one time, Dick. It's rather a pity, but it's an ill that must be borne! Now tell us about yourself, Dick. Tell us how you fought with pirates and buccaneers—above all, tell us what the Spanish Main is."

"The Spanish Main—why it's the Spanish Main to be sure—south of the Indies—a good place for trade, and a good place for pirates. But you, Nell; I wonder if you meant anything by saying that I had come back too late? I thought, you know, when I met your mother——"

"Oh, I want to hear about the fighting—the buccaneers. I don't want to hear about my mother. I hear enough about her. You fought the pirates? Well, next to being a pirate yourself that's the best thing."

"Well, if you must know, I got about me a few score of lads—most of them were stout Irish lads—who were sold to the plantations by Cromwell."

"The monster!"

"Ay, we made up a fine crew, I can tell you. Our plan was to do no pirating on our own behalf, but only to attack the pirates when they had a deckload of spoil. Taking from thieves isn't stealing, is it, Nell?"

"No, that's business."

"A bit irregular it may be, as I said just now; but bless you, Nelly, it was like sermon-preaching compared to some sorts of business that thrive mightily at the Indies. Anyhow, here I am to-day, sound and hearty, Nell, with a pretty nice fortune made already, and more to come—here I am, ready and willing to buy you the best pair of shoes in London town, and every other article of attire you may need for the next dozen—ay, the next fifty years."

"Dick—Dick!"

"Isn't it true that you were always my sweetheart, Nell? Didn't you say that you would never marry another? Well, you've kept your word so far—your mother told me that."

"Ah, that's the worst of it."

"The worst of it! That's the best of it, Nelly; for though a fine lady living in a mansion like this—why it might be a palace—the King himself might come here."

"The King—you've heard that—that the King——" She grasped him fiercely by the sleeve, and was eagerly peering into his face.

He burst out laughing, but suddenly checked himself.

"The King—the King—what was there for me to hear?" he asked in a low voice. "I only arrived from Bristol port in the morning. How could I hear anything? I don't want to hear anything except to hear you say that you haven't broken your promise—that you haven't married any one else."

"Oh, go away, Dick—go away!" she cried, burying her face on the arm of the settee.

He got upon his feet slowly and painfully, and stood over her.

"Why should I go away?" he asked in the same grave voice. "If I love you—and you know I do—and if you love me—and I believe that you do—it is not for me to go away. Ah, is it possible that you have given your promise to marry some one else! Don't weep, Nell; that's it, I see, and it can be made all right. Is that it, dear?"

"No, no. Oh, go away—go away, and never return to make me feel how miserable I am!"

"I'll not go away. There's some mystery about you and this house, and I'll not go before I fathom it."

She looked up and saw him standing there with his arms folded.

She leapt up so quickly that she almost seemed to spring into his arms. He thought so at any rate, and was about to clasp her when she caught both of his hands in her own, gazing tearfully—eagerly—wistfully into his face.

"Dick—dear Dick," she said, "if you love me still—and I know you do—you will leave me now. Oh, you should never have come here—I did not mean you to come; but, if you love me, Dick, you will leave me now—leave me and go into the nearest coffee-house and ask of the first man you see there who is Nell Gwyn—what is Nell Gwyn. If you return to me after that, then—then, Dick, I swear to you that I'll marry you—there will be none to stay us then—none to come between—the King himself shall not come between us."

He gripped her hands fiercely, his face close down to hers.

"By God, I'll do it!" he said through his set teeth. "I'll do it. You have put it upon me. I know that I shall hear nothing but what is good of you, and I'll return to claim you as sure as there's a sun in heaven."

He dropped her hands, snatched up his hat, and walked firmly to the door. When there he turned slowly and looked back at her. She was standing pale and lovely where he had left her. Her eyes were upon his face.

He flung himself through the door, and she fell on her knees beside the settee, burying her face in one of its cushions.

For some minutes nothing was heard in the room but the sound of her sobs; but then the silence was broken by a shout outside—a shout and the noise of a scuffle. Cries of " Hold him back! Hold him back! " came from the servants, mixed with some full-bodied imprecations in other voices. Nell started to her feet as the door of the room was all but crashed in, and she was standing with a startled look on her face as the door was flung wide, and Dick Harraden hurled a limp antagonist into the room.

" He shall eat his words—every foul word he uttered he shall swallow in the presence of Nell herself," cried Dick, and then Nell recognised Sir Charles Sedley as the man who was standing panting, with a broken sword in his hand, by her side, facing Dick.

" For God's sake, Dick!—Sir Charles—what has happened? "

The courtier was too breathless to speak—he signified so much very pleasingly to Nell.

" The cowardly knave! " panted Dick. " But I swore that I'd make him eat his words, and by the Lord Harry I'll keep my oath."

" Sir Charles, pray—oh, Dick! "

" Dick me no Dicks, Nell, until this popinjay has gone down on his knees before you and asked your pardon for his foul words," cried Dick. " Down you go, my gentleman, were you fifty times Sir Charles! "

" For Heaven's sake, Nell, keep that fire-eater at a distance," gasped Sir Charles. " He's fit for Bedlam."

" Stand where you be, Dick," said Nell. " What said Sir Charles Sedley to give you offence? "

" He said that you—no, I'll hang in chains in Execution Dock before I repeat the lie—but he'll take it back—every word, if I have to wring his neck."

Dick was with difficulty kept at a distance.

" Did he say aught about the King and me? " asked Nell in a low voice.

" It was, I swear, a most unhappy *contretemps*, Nell," said Sir Charles, smiling in a somewhat constrained way. " How could I know that there was one man in England who didn't know how splendid, yet how natural, a conquest the charms of Mistress Eleanor Gwyn have achieved? "

" Then you only spoke the truth, Sir Charles," said Nell.

" God above us! "

Dick staggered back and grasped the frame of a chair to support himself.

There was a long silence.

He took a faltering step or two towards where she stood in the middle of the room.

" I see it all now," he said in a low voice. " I see it all. This house—the lackeys in scarlet—the King's servants—they are the

King's servants, and you—you, Nell, are the King's—oh, God—let me die—let me die! This is what I came home for—you told me to go to the first coffee-house—I didn't need to go so far. Oh, Nelly, if I had come home to stand beside the green hillock of your grave I could have borne it—but this—this! "

He dropped into a chair and covered his face with his hands. His sobbing was the only sound in the room.

After a long pause he got slowly upon his feet.

" I'm going away," he said. " My heart is broken, Nell—my heart is broken. Good-bye, Nell."

" Good-bye, Dick."

She had not moved from the middle of the room. She did not hold out a hand to him. He walked slowly to the door. Then he turned round.

" I humbly ask your pardon, sir," he said to Sir Charles.

" Sir," said the courtier, " I honour you more than any living man."

" Nell—Nell—come to me—come away with me—come to my arms, Nell," cried the man, holding out his hands to her from where he stood.

Sir Charles watched her face. He saw it light up for a moment. Her hands moved; she was going to him.

No, she only looked at the man who loved her and was ready to offer her everything, and said:

" Dick, I have a boy in a cradle upstairs."

There was another long pause before Dick whispered the words: " God bless thee, Nell! "

Then the door was flung wide in his face by a lackey who bowed to the ground as he ushered in a rather plain-faced man wearing a diamond star and a broad blue sash as well as a diamond garter.

Nell sank in a curtsey and Sir Charles Sedley made an obeisance. Dick remained unmoved.

" Ha—what have we here? " said the stranger. " I' faith, a pretty family picture! Who may you be, good sir? " he asked of Dick.

" Who may you be? " asked Dick.

" Well, who I may be in a year or two the Lord and Nelly only know—she says a merry pauper. But who I am is easier said; I happen just now to be the King."

Dick stood unmoved.

" Then I could tell you what you are, sir," said Dick.

" Not half as well as I could tell you, my friend," said the King.

" I wonder if your Majesty ever hears the truth," said Dick.

" Seldom; any time I do it comes from the lips of Nelly yonder," replied the King. " And by my soul, sir, I would rather hear the truth from Nelly than a lie from the most honourable of my subjects."

" Profligate! " cried Dick.

" I answer to that name, sir; what then? " said the King.

" What then? God only can reply to your ' What then? ' The answer rests with Him. He will not forget to answer you when His time comes."

" Even so," said the King in a low tone, bending his head.

Sir Charles had moved round the settee and had opened the door. He touched Dick on the elbow. Dick started for a moment, and then stalked through the door. Sir Charles went out with his face turned toward the King.

" A straightforward fellow, but as conceited as a Puritan, Nell," cried the King, with a laugh.

But Nell had sunk once more on her knees beside the settee, and her face was, as before, buried in the cushion.

" Ha, what's this, Nelly? What's amiss? " said the King, bending over her.

" Oh, go away—go away; I never want to see you again. You heard the word—Profligate! Profligate! "

" I'll go away, Nell, so soon as I pass to you the two papers which I hold in my hand."

" I want no papers. I want to be alone."

" Come, dear child. See if you will like your new plaything."

He pushed before her one of the two papers which he held.

She glanced at it without rising, and without taking it from him. Suddenly she put out a hand to it.

" What? " she cried. She was now on her feet. " You have done it for me—all for me! The hospital to be built at Chelsea. Oh, my liege! "

" Now the other paper," said the King.

She took it from him.

" Ah, Royal Letters Patent—our boy—our Charlie—Duke of St. Albans! Oh, my liege—my King—my love for ever! "

She sank on her knees, and, catching his hand, covered it with kisses—with kisses and tears.

# OSCAR WILDE
1856–1900

# THE BIRTHDAY OF THE INFANTA

IT was the birthday of the Infanta. She was just twelve years of age, and the sun was shining brightly in the gardens of the palace.

Although she was a real Princess and the Infanta of Spain, she had only one birthday every year, just like the children of quite poor people, so it was naturally a matter of great importance to the whole country that she should have a really fine day for the occasion. And a really fine day it certainly was. The tall striped tulips stood straight up upon their stalks, like long rows of soldiers, and looked defiantly across the grass at the roses, and said: " We are quite as splendid as you are now." The purple butterflies fluttered about with gold dust on their wings, visiting each flower in turn; the little lizards crept out of the crevices of the wall, and lay basking in the white glare; and the pomegranates split and cracked with the heat, and showed their bleeding red hearts. Even the pale yellow lemons, that hung in such profusion from the mouldering trellis and along the dim arcades, seemed to have caught a richer colour from the wonderful sunlight, and the magnolia trees opened their great globe-like blossoms of folded ivory, and filled the air with a sweet heavy perfume.

The little Princess herself walked up and down the terrace with her companions, and played at hide-and-seek round the stone vases and the old moss-grown statues. On ordinary days she was only allowed to play with children of her own rank, so she had always to play alone, but her birthday was an exception, and the King had given orders that she was to invite any of her young friends whom she liked to come and amuse themselves with her. There was a stately grace about these slim Spanish children as they glided about, the boys with their large-plumed hats and short fluttering cloaks, the girls holding up the trains of their long brocaded gowns, and shielding the sun from their eyes with huge fans of black and silver. But the Infanta was the most graceful of all, and the most tastefully attired, after the somewhat cumbrous fashion of the day. Her robe was of grey satin, the skirt and the wide puffed sleeves heavily embroidered with silver, and the stiff corset studded with rows of fine pearls. Two tiny slippers with big pink rosettes peeped out beneath her dress as she walked. Pink and pearl was her great gauze fan, and in her hair, which like an aureole of faded gold stood out stiffly round her pale little face, she had a beautiful white rose.

From a window in the palace the sad melancholy King watched them. Behind him stood his brother, Don Pedro of Aragon, whom he hated, and his confessor, the Grand Inquisitor of Granada, sat by his side. Sadder even than usual was the King, for as he looked at the Infanta bowing with childish gravity to the assembling courtiers, or laughing behind her fan at the grim Duchess of Albuquerque who always accompanied her, he thought of the young Queen, her mother, who but a short time before—so it seemed to him—had come from the gay country of France, and had withered away in the sombre splendour of the Spanish court, dying just six months after the birth of her child, and before she had seen the almonds blossom twice in the orchard, or plucked the second year's fruit from the old gnarled fig-tree that stood in the centre of the now grass-grown orchard. So great had been his love for her that he had not suffered even the grave to hide her from him. She had been embalmed by a Moorish physician, who in return for this service had been granted his life, which for heresy and suspicion of magical practices had been already forfeited, men said, to the Holy Office, and her body was still lying on its tapestried bier in the black marble chapel of the Palace, just as the monks had borne her in on that windy March day nearly twelve years before. Once every month the King, wrapped in a dark cloak and with a muffled lantern in his hand, went in and knelt by her side calling out, " *Mi reina! Mi reina!* " and sometimes breaking through the formal etiquette that in Spain governs every separate action of life, and sets limits even to the sorrow of a King, he would clutch at the pale jewelled hands in a wild agony of grief, and try to wake by his mad kisses the cold painted face.

To-day he seemed to see her again, as he had seen her first at the Castle of Fontainebleau, when he was but fifteen years of age, and she still younger. They had been formally betrothed on that occasion by the Papal Nuncio in the presence of the French King and all the Court, and he had returned to the Escurial bearing with him a little ringlet of yellow hair, and the memory of two childish lips bending down to kiss his hand as he stepped into his carriage. Later on had followed the marriage, hastily performed at Burgos, a small town on the frontier between the two countries, and the grand public entry into Madrid with the customary celebration of high mass at the Church of La Atocha, and a more than usually solemn *auto-da-fé,* in which nearly three hundred heretics, amongst whom were many Englishmen, had been delivered over to the secular arm to be burned.

Certainly he had loved her madly, and to the ruin, many thought, of his country, then at war with England for the possession of the empire of the New World. He had hardly ever permitted her to be out of his sight; for her he had forgotten, or seemed to have forgotten, all grave affairs of State; and, with that terrible blindness that passion brings upon its servants, he had failed to notice that the elaborate ceremonies by which he sought to please her did but aggravate the strange malady from which she suffered. When she died he was, for a time, like one bereft of reason. Indeed, there is no doubt but that he would have formally abdicated and retired to the great Trappist monastery at Granada, of which he was already titular Prior, had he not been afraid to leave the little Infanta at the mercy of his brother, whose cruelty, even in Spain, was notorious, and who was suspected by many of having caused the Queen's death by means of a pair of poisoned gloves that he had presented to her on the occasion of her visiting his castle in Aragon. Even after the expiration of the three years of public mourning that he had ordained throughout his whole dominions by royal edict, he would never suffer his ministers to speak about any new alliance, and when the Emperor himself sent to him, and offered him the hand of the lovely Archduchess of Bohemia, his niece, in marriage, he bade the ambassadors tell their master that the King of Spain was already wedded to Sorrow, and that though she was but a barren bride he loved her better than Beauty; an answer that cost his crown the rich provinces of the Netherlands, which soon after, at the Emperor's instigation, revolted against him under the leadership of some fanatics of the Reformed Church.

His whole married life, with its fierce, fiery-coloured joys and the terrible agony of its sudden ending, seemed to come back to him to-day as he watched the Infanta playing on the terrace. She had all the Queen's pretty petulance of manner, the same wilful way of tossing her head, the same proud curved beautiful mouth, the same wonderful smile—*vrai sourire de France* indeed—as she glanced up now and then at the window, or stretched out her little hand for the stately Spanish gentlemen to kiss. But the shrill laughter of the children grated on his ears, and the bright pitiless sunlight mocked his sorrow, and a dull odour of strange spices, spices such as embalmers use, seemed to taint—or was it fancy?—the clear morning air. He buried his face in his hands, and when the Infanta looked up again the curtains had been drawn, and the King had retired.

She made a little *moue* of disappointment, and shrugged her shoulders. Surely he might have stayed with her on her birthday. What did the stupid State affairs matter? Oh had he gone to that gloomy chapel, where the candles were always burning, and where she was never allowed to enter? How silly of him, when the sun was shining so brightly, and everybody was so happy! Besides, he would miss the sham bull-fight for which the trumpet was already sounding, to say nothing of the puppet-show and the other wonderful things. Her uncle and the Grand Inquisitor were much more sensible. They had come out on the terrace, and paid her nice compliments. So she tossed her pretty head, and taking Don Pedro by the hand, she walked slowly down the steps towards a long pavilion of purple silk that had been erected at the end of the garden, the other children following in strict order of precedence, those who had the longest names going first.

A procession of noble boys, fantastically dressed as *toreadors*, came out to meet her, and the young Count of Tierra-Nueva, a wonderfully handsome lad of about fourteen years of age, uncovering his head with all the grace of a born hidalgo and grandee of Spain, led her solemnly in to a little gilt and ivory chair that was placed on a raised dais above the arena. The children grouped themselves all round, fluttering their big fans and whispering to each other, and Don Pedro and the Grand Inquisitor stood laughing at the entrance. Even the Duchess—the Camerera-Mayor as she was called—a thin, hard-featured woman with a yellow ruff, did not look quite so bad-tempered as usual, and something like a chill smile flitted across her wrinkled face and twitched her thin bloodless lips.

It certainly was a marvellous bull-fight, and much nicer, the Infanta thought, than the real bull-fight that she had been brought to see at Seville, on the occasion of the visit of the Duke of Parma to her father. Some of the boys pranced about on richly-caparisoned hobby-horses brandishing long javelins with gay streamers of bright ribands attached to them; others went on foot waving their scarlet cloaks before the bull, and vaulting lightly over the barrier when he charged them; and as for the bull himself, he was just like a live bull, though he was only made of wicker-work and stretched hide, and sometimes insisted on running round the arena on his hind legs, which no live bull ever dreams of doing. He made a splendid fight of it too, and the children got so excited that they stood up upon the benches, and waved their lace handkerchiefs and cried out: *Bravo toro! Bravo toro!* just as sensibly as if they had been grown-up people. At last, however, after a prolonged combat, during which several of the hobby-horses were gored through and through, and their riders dismounted, the young Count of Tierra-Nueva brought the bull to his knees, and having obtained permission from the Infanta to give the *coup de grâce*, he plunged his wooden sword into the neck of the animal with such violence that the head came right off, and disclosed the

126*

laughing face of little Monsieur de Lorraine, the son of the French Ambassador at Madrid.

The arena was then cleared amidst much applause, and the dead hobby-horses dragged solemnly away by two Moorish pages in yellow and black liveries, and after a short interlude, during which a French posture-master performed upon the tight-rope, some Italian puppets appeared in the semi-classical tragedy of *Sophonisba* on the stage of a small theatre that had been built up for the purpose. They acted so well, and their gestures were so extremely natural, that at the close of the play the eyes of the Infanta were quite dim with tears. Indeed some of the children really cried, and had to be comforted with sweetmeats, and the Grand Inquisitor himself was so affected that he could not help saying to Don Pedro that it seemed to him intolerable that things made simply out of wood and coloured wax, and worked mechanically by wires, should be so unhappy and meet with such terrible misfortunes.

An African juggler followed, who brought in a large flat basket covered with a red cloth, and having placed it in the centre of the arena, he took from his turban a curious reed pipe, and blew through it. In a few moments the cloth began to move, and as the pipe grew shriller and shriller two green and gold snakes put out their strange wedge-shaped heads and rose slowly up, swaying to and fro with the music as a plant sways in the water. The children, however, were rather frightened at their spotted hoods and quick darting tongues, and were much more pleased when the juggler made a tiny orange-tree grow out of the sand and bear pretty white blossoms and clusters of real fruit; and when he took the fan of the little daughter of the Marquess de Las-Torres, and changed it into a blue bird that flew all round the pavilion and sang, their delight and amazement knew no bounds. The solemn minuet, too, performed by the dancing boys from the church of Nuestra Señora del Pilar, was charming. The Infanta had never before seen this wonderful ceremony which takes place every year at Maytime in front of the high altar of the Virgin, and in her honour; and indeed none of the royal family of Spain had entered the great cathedral of Saragossa since a mad priest, supposed by many to have been in the pay of Elizabeth of England, had tried to administer a poisoned wafer to the Prince of the Asturias. So she had known only by hearsay of " Our Lady's Dance," as it was called, and it certainly was a beautiful sight. The boys wore old-fashioned court dresses of white velvet, and their curious three-cornered hats were fringed with silver and surmounted with huge plumes of ostrich feathers, the dazzling whiteness of their costumes, as they moved about in the sunlight, being still more accentuated by their swarthy faces and long black hair. Everybody was fascinated by the grave dignity with which they moved through the intricate figures of the dance, and by the elaborate grace of their slow gestures, and stately bows, and when they had finished their performance and doffed their great plumed hats to the Infanta, she acknowledged their reverence with much courtesy, and made a vow that she would send a large wax candle to the shrine of Our Lady of Pilar in return for the pleasure that she had given her.

A troop of handsome Egyptians—as the gipsies were termed in those days—then advanced into the arena, and sitting down cross-legs, in a circle, began to play softly upon their zithers, moving their bodies to the tune, and humming, almost below their breath, a low dreamy air. When they caught sight of Don Pedro, they scowled at him, and some of them looked terrified, for only a few weeks before he had had two of their tribe hanged for sorcery in the market-place at Seville, but the pretty Infanta charmed them as she leaned back peeping over her fan with her great blue eyes, and they felt sure that one so lovely as she was could never be cruel to anybody. So they played on very gently and just touching the cords of the zithers with their long pointed nails, and their heads began to nod as though they were falling asleep. Suddenly, with a cry so shrill that all the children were startled and Don Pedro's hand clutched at the agate pommel of his dagger, they leapt to their feet and whirled madly round the enclosure beating their tambourines, and chaunting some wild love-song in their strange guttural language. Then at another signal they all flung themselves again to the ground and lay there quite still, the dull strumming of the zithers being the only sound that broke the silence. After they had done this several times, they disappeared for a moment and came back leading a brown shaggy bear by a chain, and carrying on their shoulders some little Barbary apes. The bear stood upon his head with the utmost gravity, and the wizened apes played all kinds of amusing tricks with two gipsy boys who seemed to be their masters, and fought with tiny swords, and fired off guns, and went through a regular soldier's drill just like the King's own bodyguard. In fact the gipsies were a great success.

But the funniest part of the whole morning's entertainment was undoubtedly the dancing of the little Dwarf. When he stumbled into the arena, waddling on his crooked legs and wagging his huge misshapen head from side to side, the children went off into a loud shout of delight, and the Infanta herself laughed so much that the Camerera was obliged to remind her that although there were many precedents in Spain for a King's daughter weeping before her equals, there were none for a Princess of the blood royal making so merry before those who were her inferiors in birth. The Dwarf, however, was really quite irresistible, and even at the Spanish Court, always noted for its cultivated passion for the horrible, so fantastic a little monster had never been seen. It was his first appearance, too. He had been discovered only the day before,

running wild through the forest, by two of the nobles who happened to have been hunting in a remote part of the great cork-
wood that surrounded the town, and had been carried off by them
to the Palace as a surprise for the Infanta; his father, who was a
poor charcoal-burner, being but too well pleased to get rid of so ugly
and useless a child. Perhaps the most amusing thing about him
was his complete unconsciousness of his own grotesque appearance.
Indeed he seemed quite happy and full of the highest spirits. When
the children laughed, he laughed as freely and as joyously as any
of them, and at the close of each dance he made them each the
funniest of bows, smiling and nodding at them just as if he was
really one of themselves, and not a little misshapen thing that
Nature, in some humorous mood, had fashioned for others to mock
at. As for the Infanta, she absolutely fascinated him. He could
not keep his eyes off her, and seemed to dance for her alone, and
when at the close of the performance, remembering how she had
seen the great ladies of the Court throw bouquets to Caffarelli, the
famous Italian treble, whom the Pope had sent from his own chapel
to Madrid that he might cure the King's melancholy by the sweetness of his voice, she took out of her hair the beautiful white rose,
and partly for a jest and partly to tease the Camerera, threw it to
him across the arena with her sweetest smile, he took the whole
matter quite seriously, and pressing the flower to his rough coarse
lips he put his hand upon his heart, and sank on one knee before
her, grinning from ear to ear, and with his little bright eyes
sparkling with pleasure.

This so upset the gravity of the Infanta that she kept on laughing long after the little Dwarf had run out of the arena, and
expressed a desire to her uncle that the dance should be immediately repeated. The Camerera, however, on the plea that the
sun was too hot, decided that it would be better that her Highness
should return without delay to the Palace, where a wonderful feast
had been already prepared for her, including a real birthday cake
with her own initials worked all over it in painted sugar and a
lovely silver flag waving from the top. The Infanta accordingly
rose up with much dignity, and having given orders that the little
Dwarf was to dance again for her after the hour of siesta, and conveyed her thanks to the young Count of Tierra-Neuva for his
charming reception, she went back to her apartments, the children
following in the same order in which they had entered.

Now when the little Dwarf heard that he was to dance a second
time before the Infanta, and by her own express command, he
was so proud that he ran out into the garden, kissing the white rose
in an absurd ecstasy of pleasure, and making the most uncouth
and clumsy gestures of delight.

The Flowers were quite indignant at his daring to intrude into their beautiful home, and when they saw him capering up and down the walks, and waving his arms above his head in such a ridiculous manner, they could not restrain their feelings any longer.

" He is really far too ugly to be allowed to play in any place where we are," cried the Tulips.

" He should drink poppy-juice, and go to sleep for a thousand years," said the great scarlet Lilies, and they grew quite hot and angry.

" He is a perfect horror! " screamed the Cactus. " Why, he is twisted and stumpy, and his head is completely out of proportion with his legs. Really he makes me feel prickly all over, and if he comes near me I will sting him with my thorns."

" And he has actually got one of my best blooms," exclaimed the White Rose-Tree. " I gave it to the Infanta this morning myself, as a birthday present, and he has stolen it from her." And she called out: " Thief, thief, thief! " at the top of her voice.

Even the red Geraniums, who did not usually give themselves airs, and were known to have a great many poor relations themselves, curled up in disgust when they saw him, and when the Violets meekly remarked that though he was certainly extremely plain, still he could not help it, they retorted with a good deal of justice that that was his chief defect, and that there was no reason why one should admire a person because he was incurable; and, indeed, some of the Violets themselves felt that the ugliness of the little Dwarf was almost ostentatious, and that he would have shown much better taste if he had looked sad, or at least pensive, instead of jumping about merrily, and throwing himself into such grotesque and silly attitudes.

As for the old Sundial, who was an extremely remarkable individual, and had once told the time of day to no less a person than the Emperor Charles V. himself, he was so taken aback by the little Dwarf's appearance, that he almost forgot to mark two whole minutes with his long shadowy finger, and could not help saying to the great milk-white Peacock, who was sunning himself on the balustrade, that every one knew that the children of Kings were Kings, and that the children of charcoal-burners were charcoal-burners, and that it was absurd to pretend that it wasn't so; a statement with which the Peacock entirely agreed, and indeed screamed out, " Certainly, certainly," in such a loud, harsh voice, that the gold-fish who lived in the basin of the cool splashing fountain put their heads out of the water, and asked the huge stone Tritons what on earth was the matter.

But somehow the Birds liked him. They had seen him often in the forest, dancing about like an elf after the eddying leaves, or crouched up in the hollow of some old oak-tree, sharing his nuts with the squirrels. They did not mind his being ugly a bit. Why, even the nightingale herself, who sang so sweetly in the orange groves at night that sometimes the Moon leaned down to listen, was not much to look at after all; and, besides, he had been kind to them, and during that terribly bitter winter, when there were no berries on the trees, and the ground was as hard as iron, and the wolves had come down to the very gates of the city to look for food, he had never once forgotten them, but had always given them crumbs out of his little hunch of black bread, and divided with them whatever poor breakfast he had.

So they flew round and round him, just touching his cheek with their wings as they passed, and chattered to each other, and the little Dwarf was so pleased that he could not help showing them the beautiful white rose, and telling them that the Infanta herself had given it to him because she loved him.

They did not understand a single word of what he was saying, but that made no matter, for they put their heads on one side, and looked wise, which is quite as good as understanding a thing, and very much easier.

The Lizards also took an immense fancy to him, and when he grew tired of running about and flung himself down on the grass to rest, they played and romped all over him, and tried to amuse him in the best way they could. " Every one cannot be as beautiful as a lizard," they cried; " that would be too much to expect. And, though it sounds absurd to say so, he is really not so ugly after all, provided, of course, that one shuts one's eyes, and does not look at him." The Lizards were extremely philosophical by nature, and often sat thinking for hours and hours together, when there was nothing else to do, or when the weather was too rainy for them to go out.

The Flowers, however, were excessively annoyed at their behaviour, and at the behaviour of the birds. " It only shows," they said, " what a vulgarising effect this incessant rushing and flying about has. Well-bred people always stay exactly in the same place, as we do. No one ever saw us hopping up and down the walks, or galloping madly through the grass after dragon-flies. When we do want change of air, we send for the gardener, and he carries us to another bed. This is dignified, and as it should be. But birds and lizards have no sense of repose, and indeed birds have not even a permanent address. They are mere vagrants like the gipsies, and should be treated in exactly the same manner." So they put their noses in the air, and looked very haughty, and were quite delighted when after some time they saw the little Dwarf scramble up from the grass, and make his way across the terrace to the palace.

" He should certainly be kept indoors for the rest of his natural life," they said. " Look at his hunched back, and his crooked legs," and they began to titter.

But the little Dwarf knew nothing of all this. He liked the birds and the lizards immensely, and thought that the flowers were the most marvellous things in the whole world, except of course the Infanta, but, then, she had given him the beautiful white rose, and she loved him, and that made a great difference. How he wished that he had gone back with her! She would have put him on her right hand, and smiled at him, and he would have never left her side, but would have made her his playmate, and taught her all kinds of delightful tricks. For though he had never been in a palace before, he knew a great many wonderful things. He could make little cages out of rushes for the grasshoppers to sing in, and fashion the long jointed bamboo into the pipe that Pan loves to hear. He knew the cry of every bird, and could call the starlings from the tree-top, or the heron from the mere. He knew the trail of every animal, and could track the hare by its delicate foot-prints, and the boar by the trampled leaves. All the wild-dances he knew, the mad dance in red raiment with the autumn, the light dance in blue sandals over the corn, the dance with white snow-wreaths in winter, and the blossom-dance through the orchards in spring. He knew where the wood-pigeons built their nests, and once when a fowler had snared the parent birds, he had brought up the young ones himself, and had built a little dovecot for them in the cleft of a pollard elm. They were quite tame, and used to feed out of his hands every morning. She would like them, and the rabbits that scurried about in the long fern, and the jays with their steely feathers and black bills, and the hedgehogs that could curl themselves up into prickly balls, and the great wise tortoises that crawled slowly about, shaking their heads and nibbling at the young leaves. Yes, she must certainly come to the forest and play with him. He would give her his own little bed, and would watch outside the window till dawn, to see that the wild horned cattle did not harm her, nor the gaunt wolves creep too near the hut. And at dawn he would tap at the shutters and wake her, and they would go out and dance together all the day long. It was really not a bit lonely in the forest. Sometimes a Bishop rode through on his white mule, reading out of a painted book. Some-times in their green velvet caps, and their jerkins of tanned deer-skin, the falconers passed by, with hooded hawks on their wrists. At vintage-time came the grape-traders, with purple hands and feet, wreathed with glossy ivy and carrying dripping skins of wine; and the charcoal-burners sat round their huge braziers at night, watching the dry logs charring slowly in the fire, and roasting chestnuts in the ashes, and the robbers came out of their caves and made merry with them. Once, too, he had seen a beautiful procession winding up the long dusty road to Toledo. The monks went in front singing sweetly, and carrying bright banners and crosses of gold, and then, in silver armour, with matchlocks and pikes, came the soldiers, and in their midst walked three barefooted men, in strange yellow dresses painted all over with wonderful figures, and carrying lighted candles in their hands. Certainly there was a great deal to look at in the forest, and when she was tired he would find a soft bank of moss for her, or carry her in his arms, for he was very strong, though he knew that he was not tall. He would make her a necklace of red bryony berries, that would be quite as pretty as the white berries that she wore on her dress, and when she was tired of them, she could throw them away, and he would find her others. He would bring her acorn-cups and dew-drenched anemones, and tiny glow-worms to be stars in the pale gold of her hair.

But where was she? He asked the white rose, and it made him no answer. The whole Palace seemed asleep, and even where the shutters had not been closed, heavy curtains had been drawn across the windows to keep out the glare. He wandered all round looking for some place through which he might gain an entrance, and at last he caught sight of a little private door that was lying open. He slipped through, and found himself in a splendid hall, far more splendid, he feared, than the forest, there was so much more gilding everywhere, and even the floor was made of great coloured stones, fitted together into a sort of geometrical pattern. But the little Infanta was not there, only some wonderful white statues that looked down on him from their jasper pedestals, with sad blank eyes and strangely smiling lips.

At the end of the hall hung a richly embroidered curtain of black velvet, powdered with suns and stars, the King's favourite devices, and broidered on the colour he loved best. Perhaps she was hiding behind that? He would try at any rate.

So he stole quietly across and drew it aside. No; there was only another room, though a prettier room, he thought, than the one he had just left. The walls were hung with a many-figured green arras of needle-wrought tapestry representing a hunt, the work of some Flemish artists who had spent more than seven years in its composition. It had once been the chamber of *Jean le Fou*, as he was called, that mad King who was so enamoured of the chase, that he had often tried in his delirium to mount the huge rearing horses, and to drag down the stag on which the great hounds were leaping, sounding his hunting-horn, and stabbing with his dagger at the pale flying deer. It was now used as the council-room, and on the centre table were lying the red portfolios of the ministers, stamped with the gold tulips of Spain, and with the arms and emblems of the house of Hapsburg.

The little Dwarf looked in wonder all round him, and was half afraid to go on. The strange silent horsemen that galloped so swiftly through the long glades without making any noise, seemed to him like those terrible phantoms of whom he had heard the charcoal-burners speaking—the Comprachos, who hunt only at night, and if they meet a man, turn him into a hind, and chase him. But he thought of the pretty Infanta, and took courage. He wanted to find her alone, and to tell her that he too loved her. Perhaps she was in the room beyond.

He ran across the soft Moorish carpets, and opened the door. No! She was not here either. The room was quite empty.

It was a throne-room, used for the reception of foreign ambassadors, when the King, which of late had not been often, consented to give them a personal audience; the same room in which, many years before, envoys had appeared from England to make arrangements for the marriage of their Queen, then one of the Catholic sovereigns of Europe, with the Emperor's eldest son. The hangings were of gilt Cordovan leather, and a heavy gilt chandelier with branches for three hundred wax lights hung down from the black and white ceiling. Underneath a great canopy of gold cloth, on which the lions and towers of Castile were broidered in seed pearls, stood the throne itself, covered with a rich pall of black velvet studded with silver tulips and elaborately fringed with silver and pearls. On the second step of the throne was placed the kneeling-stool of the Infanta, with its cushion of cloth of silver tissue, and below that again, and beyond the limit of the canopy, stood the chair for the Papal Nuncio, who alone had the right to be seated in the King's presence on the occasion of any public ceremonial, and whose Cardinal's hat, with its tangled scarlet tassels, lay on a purple *tabouret* in front. On the wall, facing the throne, hung a life-sized portrait of Charles V. in hunting-dress, with a great mastiff by his side, and a picture of Philip II. receiving the homage of the Netherlands occupied the centre of the other wall. Between the windows stood a black ebony cabinet, inlaid with plates of ivory, on which the figures from Holbein's Dance of Death had been graved—by the hand, some said, of that famous master himself.

But the little Dwarf cared nothing for all this magnificence. He would not have given his rose for all the pearls on the canopy, nor one white petal of his rose for the throne itself. What he wanted was to see the Infanta before she went down to the pavilion, and to ask her to come away with him when he had finished his dance. Here, in the Palace, the air was close and heavy, but in the forest the wind blew free, and the sunlight with wandering hands of gold moved the tremulous leaves aside. There were flowers, too, in the forest, not so splendid, perhaps, as the flowers in the garden, but more sweetly scented for all that; hyacinths in early spring that flooded with waving purple the cool glens, and grassy knolls; yellow primroses that nestled in little clumps round the gnarled roots of the oak-trees; bright celandine, and blue speedwell, and irises lilac and gold. There were grey catkins on the hazels, and the foxgloves drooped with the weight of their dappled bee-haunted cells.

The chestnut had its spires of white stars, and the hawthorn its pallid moons of beauty. Yes: surely she would come if he could only find her! She would come with him to the fair forest, and all day long he would dance for her delight. A smile lit up his eyes at the thought, and he passed into the next room.

Of all the rooms this was the brightest and the most beautiful. The walls were covered with a pink-flowered Lucca damask, patterned with birds and dotted with dainty blossoms of silver; the furniture was of massive silver, festooned with florid wreaths, and swinging Cupids; in front of the two large fire-places stood great screens broidered with parrots and peacocks, and the floor, which was of sea-green onyx, seemed to stretch far away into the distance. Nor was he alone. Standing under the shadow of the doorway, at the extreme end of the room, he saw a little figure watching him. His heart trembled, a cry of joy broke from his lips, and he moved out into the sunlight. As he did so, the figure moved out also, and he saw it plainly.

The Infanta! It was a monster, the most grotesque monster he had ever beheld. Not properly shaped, as all other people were, but hunchbacked, and crooked-limbed, with huge lolling head and mane of black hair. The little Dwarf frowned, and the monster frowned also. He laughed, and it laughed with him, and held its hands to its sides, just as he himself was doing. He made it a mocking bow, and it returned him a low reverence. He went towards it, and it came to meet him, copying each step that he made, and stopping when he stopped himself. He shouted with amusement, and ran forward, and reached out his hand, and the hand of the monster touched his, and it was as cold as ice. He grew afraid, and moved his hand across, and the monster's hand followed it quickly. He tried to press on, but something smooth and hard stopped him. The face of the monster was now close to his own, and seemed full of terror. He brushed his hair off his eyes. It imitated him. He struck at it, and it returned blow for blow. He loathed it, and it made hideous faces at him. He drew back, and it retreated.

What is it? He thought for a moment, and looked round at the rest of the room. It was strange, but everything seemed to have its double in this invisible wall of clear water. Yes, picture for picture was repeated, and couch for couch. The sleeping Faun that lay in the alcove by the doorway had its twin brother that slumbered, and the silver Venus that stood in the sunlight held out her arms to a Venus as lovely as herself.

Was it Echo? He had called to her once in the valley, and she had answered him word for word. Could she mock the eye as she mocked the voice? Could she make a mimic world just like the real world? Could the shadows of things have colour and life and movement? Could it be that——? He started, and taking from his breast the beautiful white rose, he turned round and kissed it. The monster had a rose of its own, petal for petal the same! It kissed it with like kisses, and pressed it to its heart with horrible gestures.

When the truth dawned upon him, he gave a wild cry of despair, and fell sobbing to the ground. So it was he who was misshapen and hunchbacked, foul to look at and grotesque. He himself was the monster, and it was at him that all the children had been laughing, and the little Princess who he had thought loved him—she too had been merely mocking at his ugliness, and making merry over his twisted limbs. Why had they not left him in the forest, where there was no mirror to tell him how loathsome he was? Why had his father not killed him, rather than sell him to his shame? The hot tears poured down his cheeks, and he tore the white rose to pieces. The sprawling monster did the same, and scattered the faint petals in the air. It grovelled on the ground, and, when he looked at it, it watched him with a face drawn with pain. He crept away, lest he should see it, and covered his eyes with his hands. He crawled, like some wounded thing, into the shadow, and lay there moaning.

And at that moment the Infanta herself came in with her companions through the open window, and when they saw the ugly little Dwarf lying on the ground and beating the floor with his clenched hands, in the most fantastic and exaggerated manner, they went off into shouts of happy laughter, and stood all round him and watched him.

" His dancing was funny," said the Infanta; " but his acting is funnier still. Indeed he is almost as good as the puppets, only of course not quite so natural." And she fluttered her big fan, and applauded.

But the little Dwarf never looked up, and his sobs grew fainter and fainter, and suddenly he gave a curious gasp, and clutched his side. And then he fell back again, and lay quite still.

" That is capital," said the Infanta, after a pause; " but now you must dance for me."

" Yes," cried all the children, " you must get up and dance, for you are as clever as the Barbary apes, and much more ridiculous."

But the little Dwarf made no answer.

And the Infanta stamped her foot, and called out to her uncle, who was walking on the terrace with the Chamberlain, reading some despatches that had just arrived from Mexico, where the Holy Office had recently been established. " My funny little dwarf is sulking," she cried; " you must wake him up, and tell him to dance for me."

They smiled at each other, and sauntered in, and Don Pedro stooped down, and slapped the Dwarf on the cheek with his em-

broidered glove. " You must dance," he said, " *petit monstre*.
You must dance. The Infanta of Spain and the Indies wishes to be
amused."

But the little Dwarf never moved.

" A whipping master should be sent for," said Don Pedro
wearily, and he went back to the terrace. But the Chamberlain
looked grave, and he knelt beside the little Dwarf, and put his hand
upon his heart. And after a few moments he shrugged his shoulders, and rose up, and having made a low bow to the Infanta, he
said:

" *Mi bella Princesa,* your funny little dwarf will never dance
again. It is a pity, for he is so ugly that he might have made
the King smile."

" But why will he not dance again? " asked the Infanta, laughing.

" Because his heart is broken," answered the Chamberlain.

And the Infanta frowned, and her dainty rose-leaf lips curled in
pretty disdain. " For the future let those who come to play with
me have no hearts," she cried, and she ran out into the garden.

# JANE BARLOW

1860-1917

# MAUREEN'S FAIRING

" WELL, good-night to you kindly, ma'am," said Mrs. Halpin to
Mrs. O'Dell, who had escorted her guest to the gap in the low
furzy bank, which formed her entrance gate. As the two old
women stood at it, they were looked down upon by almost the
whole height of a dark mountain, whose purple summit was crested
and jagged like the battlements of a thunder-cloud; for the white
and russet cabin had been set only a little way up the first climbing
slope. Across the narrow valley they confronted a range of hills
softer and greener, whose ridge still rose into the light of the summer sun-setting; but the valley itself was full of long shadows, and
its windings ended to right and left in a faint haze, paler and dimmer than the melting gyres of blue smoke.

" I dunno what to say to it at all," said Mrs. O'Dell, who
having discussed the situation thoroughly with her gossip indoors
was naturally inclined to reopen the subject at the last moment.
" Not a soul, so to spake, to be doin' a hand's turn about the
place, except meself, that hasn't as much strength left in me as
you'd put on the point of a knife. Sure it's to wrack and ruin
we're goin' as aisy as a hose runnin' away down hill. And as for
the rint—after gettin' no price for our fine heifer——"

" 'Deed then, ma'am," said Mrs. Halpin, " I always said you
were a cruel unlucky woman, wid your poor son and the wife took
on you that way, and the grand-daughter not able for anythin',
bein' dark, the crathur, the Lord may pity her. But there's that
brother of hers now—sure Rody's a big grown lad, and if he was
worth a thraneen at all, he might be keepin' things together for the
two of yous."

" Is it Rody? Ah, now, I wouldn't say he was too bad-manin'
a poor lad whatever," said Rody's grandmother; " but sorra the
ha'porth of use. Moonin' about the place he'll be from mornin'
till night, and what he'll ha' got done at the end of it the dear
knows, only it isn't a stroke of work. Bedad, it's surprisin' the
sinse he hasn't got, and he no stookawn, mind you, all the time.
Ready enough he is at the book-learnin'. Some talk he has of the

school-master findin' him a place off away at Kilmacrum, but I
wouldn't think he'll ever go for to be lavin' Maureen; and it's lost
she'd be widout him. Rael good he is to her, I'll say that for
him. He'd be hard set to make more of her if she could see
from this to the land of Agypt and back agin.''

'' Sure, woman dear, it's quare world entirely,'' said Mrs. Halpin, resorting to general propositions for lack of any more particularly appropriate, '' and the longer you live in it, the quarer
it seems to be gettin'. You'd ha' thought you'd be apt to grow
used to it, och wirra, it's the other way round. . . . But, musha,
there's himself creepin' home,'' she continued, pointing to a figure
on the road a little way below. '' I must be steppin' along after
him, for if he come to our place afore me, like enough he might
have it in blazes over our heads, and he fiddlin' with the fire; he's
that foostherin' and feeble these times, poor man.''

'' Somewhiles,'' said Mrs. O'Dell, '' it seems to me the whole of
us together's no betther than the black ould flies, when it's near
winther on them, and they do be crawlin' about on their legs just
for the name of keepin' alive. Och, but I'll be glad meself to creep
into me bed now as soon as the childher come in. These fine
evenin's they're mostly sittin' up above there at the ould Rath;
and they've such contintment together, the crathurs, that I haven't
the heart to be bawlin' them in, as long as there's a shadow
of light in the air at all.''

To the old Rath a short length of steep path led up through a
screen of stunted oaks and beeches. It was a circular space of
smooth green turf, marked out by curved banks of the same material, now worn down to a very unobtrusively artificial aspect.
Here and there they were fortified by bushes of thorn and briar,
but in one place they had crumbled into a wide gap, giving on the
mountain slope, rougher ground with tussocks and clumps of coarse
grass and furze and bracken. About this time Rody O'Dell and
his twin sister, Maureen, who was blind, were sitting under a
sloe bush nearly opposite to the gap. Rody looked as if he had
on a burnished copper skullcap, his red hair was so short and
sleek, and his grey eyes were light and bright; but Maureen was
black-haired, and her eyes were much the colour of the wild violets
which she had sometimes gathered, though never seen. She had
now pulled a spike of foxglove blooms, and was poking her
finger down their speckled throats with an air of enjoyment. Her
touch was so fine that it only pilfered a little gold dust from each
without hurt to the frailest filament. Rody was whittling away
at a snaggy piece of a stick.

'' Themselves had a right to be in it soon,'' Maureeen said
presently; and Rody replied: '' Sure they'll be comin' this now,
no fear.'' However, the girl listened, and the boy looked for
some minutes more, and nothing seemed to arrive. Then both of

them exclaimed at once with suppressed eagerness: " Here they are." There was not apparently much cause for excitement. Ordinarily sharp ears might never have noticed the faint rustling among the drier fern-fronds; ordinarily keen eyes might have overlooked in the thickening light the whisked glimpses of white and brown, scuttling from clump to clump; and, in fact, it was after all merely the rabbits coming out to play in the dusk. Yet the event had plainly deep interest for the two O'Dells. Rody left off whittling his stick, and kept a close watch on the scampering rushes, while Maureen sat still with the expression of one who expects news. At last she said: " Is there plinty of them comin' to-night, Rody? " " Ay is there," he said; " sure the place is thick wid them along under the big bohalawns."

" Ah, now that's great," said Maureen, with a sigh of satisfaction, for she, of course, knew as well as possible that these golden-tufted rag-weeds are especially sacred to the little people, and may be orthodoxly associated with their proceedings. " And what 'ud you think they're goin' to be at to-night, Rody? " she asked again after a short silence.

" Just let me see," said Rody, staring hard in among the curved bracken-stalks and flat furze-boughs. " I'll tell you what—I declare to goodness, it looks like as if it was a fair they were having —ay, bedad, and it is so; a cattle fair, no less, wid every manner of little baste a-dhrivin' out to it. Och, but that bates all."

" Good luck to them then," said Maureen, " that's grand entirely. Sure you never seen the likes of it before. And what sort of crathurs is the fairy bastes? "

" Sure just the one thing wid what cattle we have ourselves," said Rody, " only the quarest little bigness on them that ever you beheld. Be jabers now, there's a drove of bullocks after goin' by, and scarce a one of them the size of a *keerhogue* (clock). The whole of them 'ud trot aisy on the palm of me hand."

" Och, glory be to goodness to think of that. And is there any horses and sheep in it, and pigs? "

" Plinty, bedad. Is it pigs? Faix, here's littler feller comin' along wid a couple, and he is as drunk as a fiddler, or I might say ould Dan Cosby that I seen dhroppin' in a hape off the car yisterday below Letterdrum."

" I never heard tell the good people 'ud be drinkin'," said Maureen, looking rather scandalised.

" Ah, well, sure maybe he's only lettin' on. But what 'ud you suppose they've got be way of cattle-pens? The peelin's of the apple you had aitin' here last night. They've set it up on an end in a ring like, and where it doesn't raich quite far enough, they've joined it wid dandelion stalks as iligant as you plase."

" 'Deed, now, that's a fine invintion whatever. It's themselves do be rael cute."

" And here's a fairy man and a boy, and they ladin' a big
sturk of a shaggy ould bull.   Be the same token, they'll have their
own work wid him, for a crosser lookin' ould divil I niver set eyes
on.   Bedad, if he was as big as he's little, he'd be apt to be doin'
destruction on all before him; but sure you could lift him between
your finger and thumb, same as if it was a dowlduff; and suppose
he tried hornin' you, 'twould be no more than a sort of prickle."
To illustrate this, Rody broke off a sloe-thorn, and gently prodded
the back of his sister's hand.   " There, you might think that was
him," he said, " and he lettin' a weeny roar—*moo-oo-ah*—like
a hummin' bee goin' by in the air."

" And the hair on him 'ud be somethin' as soft and furry
feelin'," said Maureen reflectively.   " Them fairy bastes must be
gay little crathurs.   Rody, I wish to goodness 'twould stay summer wid us all the year round, the way we'd get the chance to be
watchin' for them ivery evenin'.   But go on tellin' me what all else
they have."

" Musha, all manner of iverythin'.   Here's a one of them jiggin'
along on a terrible fine sorrel horse, a thrifle higher-standin' then
a big grasshopper.   Thunder and turf!   More power to your
honour's elbow—sure there was a troop of pigs and such thrapesin'
in front of him that put him past his patience, so he up and lep
clane over the back of a *bonyeen* (young pig), and it's after fright-
enin' a little ould woman till she's let a pair of chickens flutther
out of her basket on her—troth you might think they were a couple
of specklety moths flickerin' over the grass—and now the whole
lot's high-skyin' after them as hard as they can pelt be way of
catchin' them. . . .   Och, and to see the rate a flock of wee black-
faced sheep's racin' round and round a stalk of hemlock, wid
their bit of a colley doin' his endeavours to turn them; but they're
past his conthrol."

" It's quare that I don't hear e'er a bark out of him," said
Maureen, " for when they're drivin' the sheep on the hills over
beyond there, I hear them yap-yappin' the length of the day, and
themselves as far off as you'd run in an hour or more."

" But sure there aren't many could bate you at hearin', Maureen," said Rody, " and you don't considher what a scrapeen of a
crathur it is.   A good-sized ladybird might as well be settin' up
for a dog.   He couldn't rise a noise 'ud raich that far, not if he
barked wid ivery bone in his body."

" Sure not at all," Maureen said acquiescently, being wont to
regard Rody's utterances as conclusively oracular.   Still her face
kept its listening expression, and in a minute she said: " There—
I heard somethin' that time."

She was not mistaken.   But when the approaching sounds
strengthened into distinctness, they proved to be caused by very
merely a mortal.   Across the tussocky slope came a tall young

man in a sailor's blue jersey, with a black woollen cap on his head, and in his hand a redly wrapped-up bundle. As he passed along, rabbits dived out of sight all around, but bobbed up again almost before the parted bracken-fronds had swung together.

"Why, it's Christy M'Kenna," said Rody. "I seen him yisterday down below. What the mischief's bringin' him here?" Rody's tone implied dissatisfaction with the event, whatever the cause might have been, and Maureen looked half inclined to run away like the rabbits; but she compromised the matter by drawing her little heather-green shawl further over her black hair, and shrinking into the shadow of the sloe-bush.

"Good evenin' to yous," said Christy, coming up to the bank. "Well, Rody, did you get anythin' of a dacint price for the little heifer? 'Twas but a slack fair." There was nothing repellent or formidable in the good-humoured bronze of Christy's visage, and his voice struck Maureen as being rather reassuringly pleasant, though she feared that it would scare away the fairy folk.

"Och, she wint chape enough; cattle was down to nothin' at all," Rody replied, with some grumpy indifference of tone. He had resumed his whittling, and just now slashed at a rough knot with so little dexterity that the knife slipped out of his hand, and went flying into the tangle at his feet, an accident which added to his discomposure.

"Is it watchin' the rabbits you were?" said Christy. "There's a great gatherin' of them out on the hill-side to-night. You could have knocked them over handy wid a stick comin' through the furzes."

As Rody was groping on his hands and knees for his knife, he could not answer promptly, and before he had spoken, Maureen said, as if startled into speech: "Rabbits? I niver heard tell there were any in it. Sure it's the *fairies* there are in among the bushes, and that's what we're lookin' at."

Christy laughed a little. "Begorrah, thin, I think the rabbits has put them out of it this night, body and bones," he said, "for ne'er a sign of a *sheogue* did I notice at all at all."

"Rody sez the place is full of them," said Maureen. "Isn't it, Rody?"

Her appeal placed Rody in a painful dilemma. He did not wish to undeceive her, yet he was loth to profess a belief which might seem ridiculous to the much-travelled Christy, while again pride on his sister's behalf made him shrink from obviously humouring her in the presence of a stranger. Under other circumstances the difficulty might have been got over by his mother wit, but at the moment he was out of temper, which sorely blunts the edge of shrewdness; and he adopted, perhaps, the most ill-judged course he could have chosen when he said to Christy in what he supposed to be an aside: "Arrah now, man alive, can't you whisht gabbin' about rabbits? '' For Maureen's quick ears caught the words, and they filled her with dismayed suspicion. She leaned forward, saying anxiously and eagerly: '' But the good people come to the Rath here 'most ivery fine evenin'—sure, Rody, you haven't been only humbuggin' me all these times? ''

But Rody remained guiltily silent, while Christy, perplexed at the girl's evident distress, answered as discreetly as he could in his ignorance of its cause: '' Well, at all evints, them crathurs was all I seen about just now: but sure there might aisy ha' been an odd fairy or so through them, and I niver notice it. They'll do no harm anyway, here or there.''

This philosophic view of the matter was not consolatory to Maureen. She rose to her feet, and stood for a moment with drooping head. '' I wish,'' she said without looking up, '' I wish I had the sight of me eyes, the way that people couldn't be makin' a fool of me.'' Then she turned slowly away, and sat down again on the bank at a little distance. I think she had lost something more than her evening's entertainment, and faith in Rody—certain vague dreams based upon traditions of wonderful cures wrought by the good people when found in a kindly mood, a chance that might happen to anybody one of those days. The two young men eyed each other ruefully through the gathering dusk. Said Christy in an undertone: '' What ails her at all? ''

'' Botheration to it,'' said Rody, '' sure you see, she not havin' her sight, we do be at a loss now and agin for a bit of diversion; so I used to get tellin' her quare ould invintions, whin the rabbits come out here of an evenin', lettin' on to her 'twas the fairies were in it, and this way and that way. And, bedad, now themselves is the comical little divils, wid their thricks and their capers, and that's no lie,'' he added, as if in self-defence. Strange as the freak of conscience may appear, it is a fact that on nights when no rabbits were to be seen, he had never reported any fairy doings. '' She'd take a won'erful pleasure in hearin' about anythin' off the common like; but she won't now that she knows 'twas only romancin'. And I doubt she's a thrifle vexed, the crathur,'' Rody said, glancing compunctiously towards his sister.

'' Ah, now, that's a rael bad job,'' said Christy, with unfeigned concern. '' Faith, if I'd known, I'd ha' liefer lost a month's pay than to be spoilin' her stories on her. But, sure, if it's a fancy she has for hearing curious things, I meself could be tellin' her plenty that 'ud surprise her finely, and as thrue, more be token, as the sky over our heads. Why, what 'ud you say to an affair I seen, maybe a little better than a couple of months ago,'' Christy went on, raising his voice, not unintentionally, '' and we sailin' home from the United States? A big hill, the full size of one of them forninst us, swimmin' along on the say, and ivery bit of it nothin' but clane ice, as clear and as green as the deep wather;

the same as if you could be buildin' up a great hape o' rowlin' waves, and the top of it all white, powdered wid snow, like as if it was settlin' to foam over the edges. That's quare now? And a grand watherfall leppin' right down from the heighth of it, wid the sun turnin' it all the colours in the rainbow, till the sparklin' of it 'ud 'most——''

An indignant murmur from Rody cut him short: '' Musha, man, where'd be the sinse of blatherin' about rainbows sparklin', to her that's had niver a chance to see a shine out of the sun in all her life's days? Sure, when I'm tellin' her aught, I keep describin' the things accordin' to the littleness and bigness of them, and the feelin' and shapes they have; and so she gets some sort of notion what I'm talkin' about. But you may let the sun alone.''

Upon this a crestfallen silence succeeded Christy's traveller's tale. Presently, however, his face brightened with a sudden thought, and he began to unknot a corner of his bundle. '' Whethen now, only I was stookawn enough to nearly disremember it,'' he said. '' I've somethin' here she might belike take a fancy to.'' He extricated a beautiful tropical shell, whose lily-white whorls were lined with a flush of wild-rose pink. '' Wouldn't you think she might be pleased handlin' that? '' he said. '' And the say hummin' it has in it she could hear as well, in course, as another.''

'' She might, may be,'' Rody said doubtfully; and Christy considered himself encouraged to try the experiment. Going over to Maureen, he touched her hand softly with the shell, saying in his most persuasive manner: '' Just thry the feel of that in your hand, mavourneen. I'm afther showin' it to your brother there, and he's in great admiration of it.''

Maureen took the shell, and ran her fingers swiftly along the delicate outlines, fine in texture as a blossom, and firm as marble. A happier look stole into her face. '' What at all is it? '' she said.

'' Sure it's just a sort of shell. I picked it up meself one day off the strand near the town of Kingston in Jamaicy. Lyin' it was in the sand, that's as soft there as fine male, and as hot as if it was gettin' a bake in the oven. But hold it to your ear a minute —so, that a-way—and you'll hear somethin' 'ill surprise you.''

'' Saints above! '' said Maureen, listening, not without awe. '' It's like the win' blustherin' by when you're under the tree branches, wid a sound of the chapel-bell through it, as if 'twas near blown away, and somethin' else besides—I dunno what.''

'' That's the taste of the say-waves roarin'; it's kep' inside it. Och, now, you wouldn't be askin' me to take it back? Keep it yourself, jewel, and then you can be hearin' it hummin' wheniver you like. I've plinty more the same, only diff'rint pattrons. Some of them's as round and as shiny as a chiny bowl, and some's the shape of grand big saucers. And I've a string of bades, the iligantest blue colour—och, no matter about that—but they're that smooth you could scarce hold them from slippin' out of your hand. And I've the quarest sort of a big ball, that looks to be wound round and round wid threads of silk as thin as cobwebs; and what's inside of it I can't say, but if you shake it, you'll hear it rattlin' like a *glugger* (bad egg). It's somethin' rael uncommon, I'm thinkin'. So, if you'd e'er a fancy to see them, I'd step over and bring them to-morra, wid all the pleasure in life. I lost me ship be raison of me father bein' took bad last week, and I'm stoppin' a while wid me sister down at Letterdrum. May be them things 'ud divert you a bit.''

"Ay would they," Maureen said softly.

At this moment a shrill and querulous call came quavering up the hill: "Childher, musha, good gracious, childher, is it sittin' out there you'd be till the sun's risin', and keepin' me waitin' up for you, wid the head noddin' off me shoulders?''

"There's granny lettin' a screech to us," said Rody, standing up from his search for his knife, and glad to end what seemed to him an unlucky evening. "We had a right to be goin' in.''

"Well, I'll step over here to-morra wid the whole of them," Christy said to Maureen, "about this time, or perhaps in the mornin' if I can; but I'll bring them, at any rate.''

"They'll be grand," said Maureen. "And—and I'd like to hear tell, mind you, about the big ice hill, wid the watherfall on it, and all. Sure I know well enough about the sun shinin'. It's only the way Rody will be talkin'," she said, with rather ungrateful disparagement. Indeed, from henceforth, I believe, Rody, regarded as her oracle, may be said to have fallen dumb.

One fine rose-latticed evening, a few weeks later, old Mrs. O'Dell had another gossip with her neighbour, Mrs. Halpin, standing at her door. "Ay, indeed, it's a great thing for us entirely," said she in reply to a congratulatory remark. "The M'Kennas is a rael dacint family, and Christy has a bit of money saved that he's willing to put in the farm. And Rody's got a fine place down below at Athbeg, that he's goin' to after the weddin'. Och, now, who'd ha' iver thought of such a thing happenin' Maureen, the crathur? Sure I sez to Christy himself, when he was talkin' to me about it: 'Goodness help you, lad,' sez I, 'and what at all will you be doin' wid only a dark wife to keep house for you?' And sez he to me: 'Bedad, ma'am, I'll tell you that aisy, if you'll tell me what I'm to do widout her; for me soul to the saints, if I know, be any manner of manes.' That's what he said. Christy's always plisant. There, that's the three of them comin' along the lane. Ay, sure it's great good luck altogether.''

# KATHARINE TYNAN
## (MRS. HINKSON)
### 1861–1931

# AT THE SPOTTED LAMB

MRS. LUMLEY at The Spotted Lamb had a gentleman in her best rooms, the like of whom did not often come to Rosegarland. He had arrived by the coach from London on a Tuesday, and had now for three weeks been Mrs. Lumley's lodger.

He dressed modestly in garments of Quaker grey or snuff-brown, but the suits were cut with distinction. His hair had been powdered the day he came and tied in a queue with ribbons: but powder will not last for ever, and there were no perruquiers in Rosegarland village, so the gentleman's brown hair, dusty from the powder or perhaps from the passage of time, had come in view.

He wore flowered waistcoats, magnificent although sober, and his linen was of the finest. His coat and breeches, although of woollen stuff, were of a fineness that exceeded silk. It was a pity, said Mrs. Lumley, who was a kind soul, to see how the garments had been stuffed headlong into his travelling-bag. Under her kind hands they had somewhat recovered from their evil treatment, being laid away with lavender bags between the folds in the bow-shaped chest of drawers and the mahogany wardrobe, great enough to have held all Bluebeard's wives.

Rosegarland village lies pleasantly upon a hill. The strange gentleman's bedroom—he called himself Mr. Jones—stood endways to the valley. The window of one of its closets looked over the valley, and at night the songs of the nightingales came in by it. Across the fireplace, which was laid with tiles representing the parable of the Prodigal Son, was another closet, a powdering-closet, which did not admit a chink of light, and was hung with clothes-pegs and shelved to the roof.

The powdering-closet interested Mr. Jones. Mrs. Lumley was very ready to talk about it. Many a lady had had her head dressed there in Squire Alvanley's time, when there were hunt-balls and the like at The Spotted Lamb. That was thirty years ago, and the Place had been shut up these many years. It was another world without the Alvanleys.

Mr. Jones seemed to like to listen to Mrs. Lumley's simple rustic talk, her tales of the great days that were over. She was often afraid that her lodger might be bored and might depart as suddenly as he had come. Every Friday the coach passed through Rosegarland on its way to town; and she breathed more freely when the horn was blown and the four greys clattered on their way, since the danger was over for another week.

It was May, and the valley was full of newly-opened leaves, whitethorn in blossom, and the songs of thrush and blackbird, to say nothing of the nightingales at night. At night, too, if you climbed the hilly road to Rosegarland, the glow-worms were all alight amid the starwort and speedwells of the grassy banks. Every little wood and coppice was sky-blue with the dancing hyacinths. The woods, which you might walk a hundred times and every time take a new road, were heavenly in their first freshness of green, and full of the whisperings and mysteries of young love.

" And how long might your honour be pleased to stay? " Mrs. Lumley asked timidly after one of their conversations. She had taken a fancy to her lodger. What if his face was lined, his cheeks too purple and a little flaccid, his eyes dusty and tired, he had a way with the women that made them devoted to him. In spite of his premature ageing he was still a fine, handsome man, with an elegant figure and an air of distinction. And he had beautiful manners; Rosegarland had never dreamt of such manners.

" Stay! " he repeated, with a frown that had no displeasure in it. " Why, stay for ever, my good soul."

" For ever, sir! " Mrs. Lumley could not believe in her own good fortune. " Your honour means to stay with us for ever? "

" Could I do better? "

He waved his hand towards the window of the sitting-room which was open on an orchard all rosy with blossom. A troop of little black pigs grunted and squealed in the grass, which lay under a shower of the blossom. Stocks and gillyflowers in great scented clumps grew under the window, and the air was spicy with their smell.

" Could I do better? St. James's has nothing to show like this."

It was the first suggestion he had made that he was a man of fashion, though Mrs. Lumley, with her memories of the Alvanleys and their fine friends, had never doubted it.

" Ah but, sir," she said, " the winter will come and 'twill not be so pretty. Your honour will go back to town then."

" Not I. I am sick of the town. I want the simplicities of life. There will be beauties in winter—a sky of rose and lilac over there beyond the Alvanleys' chimney-stacks and a flight of crows upon it. And the brooks cutting channels in the roads when the

" And Margery's child lived? "

" As good and bonny a maid as any in the country. Many lads go courting at Redstreak Farm for all that Dick Stone's not such good company."

A few days later Mr. Jones came back from one of his long solitary walks, and entered the kitchen of The Spotted Lamb with so blithe a step that Mrs. Lumley, who was making cowslip wine, looked up at him in wonder.

" Your honour has liked the walk? " she said.

" It is a land of apples and roses," he answered; " and I have drunk milk from the hands of Hebe herself. I should be a sour fellow to complain."

" Your honour looks well on it. Ten years have rolled off your age since the day the Flying Mercury left your honour at my door."

" Why, I have been bathing my face in May dew. How old would you take me to be, Mrs. Lumley? Fifty? Forty-five? Forty?—I am no more than forty, and I feel young enough for bridegroom to a girl of eighteen. Your air does wonders. The Wells would be deserted if the fine folks only knew."

After that he would break into snatches of song as he moved about the house that brought a smile to Mrs. Lumley's lips, for she had grown fond of her lodger.

> Dolly's neck is white as curds,
> With a golden freckle or two;
> Dolly's voice is like the birds
> In the pastures, in the dew;
> Dolly laughs with Prue and Phyllis,
> And her laugh's a shower of lilies.

" Lord, what a pretty song, sir," she said once, " and your honour's self has a voice like a bird's. You sing as if your heart was in it."

" The song was made," said Mr. Jones, " on a milkmaid that was the sweetest thing the songmaker had ever seen. She was taking butter from a churn, and her arms were stripped high above her elbows, and they were white as the milk. She had a head of black curls with a thought of a pansy in their jet; her eyes, too, were black, but her face was milk and roses; she had two dimples —what would not a woman of fashion have given for them?— and a round white chin; and she wore a pink wrapper; and because the day was hot she had left her neck bare—the sweetest neck. She made the man think on his old love, but she was his old love's daughter; and he loved her, as he had loved her mother, at first sight.

> Pink is Dolly's only wear;
> Dolly's eyes are black as sloes:
> Dolly's always fresh and fair
> From her top-knot to her toes."

He broke again into the cheerful singing.

" The song might have been made on Dolly Stone of Redstreak Farm," said Mrs. Lumley. " But, lord, 'tis fitter for a lad to make than a man who had wooed the girl's mother. 'Twould be foolishness in a man of his age."

" Lads don't know how to love," said Mr. Jones, frowning. " They are in love with their own image, like the golden Hyacinthus. It takes an older man to love."

He went away then and sang no more for the day. But the next day he was singing again; and presently, coming in on Mrs. Lumley as she was making a candy of May-blossom, he nearly made the good woman drop her pan with its fragrant contents, so surprised was she at the fineness of his appearance.

He was dressed in pearl-grey silk, with lace ruffles and jewelled buttons; he had silk stockings and shoes with red heels to them; and his three-cornered hat was worn rakishly. Nor did his clothes look too gay for his years, for some magic of the sweet country had wrought a subtle alteration in the man.

The crow's-feet had passed away from his eyes and they were bright, as though he had washed them in euphrasy. His cheeks, which had had the stain of wine in them, had grown clear since he had lived plainly. His face and figure and gait had become tonic, braced-up, as though he had found a fountain of youth in these wilds and had drunk deep of it.

" Well! "

He smiled at the good woman's open-mouthed admiration.

" You are like a bridegroom, sir."

" Well, who knows but that I may be one before the summer is out? "

He went off twirling his cane and singing; and the same song was on his lips perpetually in the weeks that followed, while the sweet spring turned round to summer.

> Dolly dabbles fingers brown
>   In the whitest milk that flows;
> Dolly wears a rosy gown,
>   Smells of roses as she goes.

It was always Dolly: always and for ever Dolly.

It was not long before the gossip of the village came to Mrs. Lumley, and she knew that the Dolly of the song was the Dolly of Redstreak Farm. It seemed that Mr. Jones had made friends with glum Dick Stone, who was well pleased that his daughter should marry a gentleman. And about the girl herself no one seemed to know. Young Oliver Buckenham of Meadowsweet Farm had been courting her before Mr. Jones came; but now they had quarrelled, and no one thought it strange that she should have thrown over Oliver for her splendid new lover, although he was middle-aged.

And for the matter of that he grew younger every day, although he could not hope to have the smooth cheek and thick yellow hair of a lad like Oliver. Yet Oliver grew old while his fortunate rival grew young, and sang no more to his team of horses nor as he mowed the hay; and people hardly knew him for the same merry fellow who had been as blithe as the lark.

One day when Mr. Jones was absent, as he usually was the greater part of the day, two gentlemen rode up to The Spotted Lamb and asked if such a one, describing him, had lodgings in the village.

" It will be Mr. Jones," said Mrs. Lumley. " If your honours would be pleased to wait. He generally returns about this hour."

The gentlemen gave their horses to be fed and watered, and while they waited for Mr. Jones they ordered and consumed a meal of Mrs. Lumley's cold roast beef and fresh garden salad, with home-brewed ale; and were so free with their money and so finely dressed and had such a way with the serving-maids of the house that the good woman set them down in her mind as highwaymen. Of course that would explain the mystery about Mr. Jones and why a retired place like Rosegarland was best suited to him. But she was grieved to think that it was so; for however gallant highwaymen might be and adored by the girls, they were meat for the gallows if they were caught.

When Mr. Jones came in suddenly upon them, his eyes flashed, and the old gloom fell upon his face, and when they cried out, laughing, that at last they had run him to earth he fell to swearing at them, so that Mrs. Lumley shut the door hastily, for Mr. Jones had been so gentle in speech that she had sometimes doubted that he was a man of fashion; and his new violence troubled her.

For more than two hours there was the sound of much argument from the parlour, and Mrs. Lumley learned, because there was a cupboard in her store-closet adjoining where the wall was thin, that they were trying to prevail upon Mr. Jones to go with them, urging upon him that some one, whose name she could not catch, was inconsolable without him. But to that Mr. Jones answered bitterly that that person had no loyalty to any one except in so far as he or she ministered to his pleasures. Moreover, that he was tired of that person's insolence, being a better man than he; that he had loved him once but loved him no longer; and finally that he would never return. And the same he asserted with a round oath and a blow of his clenched fist on the table that made Mrs. Lumley jump at the other side of the partition.

The two gentlemen rode away at sundown, calling back to Mr. Jones, who stood bareheaded in the road to see them go, that he would soon tire of his stay in Arcady and come back to town. He was gloomy for that evening, but the next day he was as merry as ever, and for many days following.

His clothes had come down from town, many chests of them, by the coach; and he hardly ever seemed to wear the same suit two days running. His attire was the delight and admiration of the village, and Mrs. Lumley never saw him but with uplifted eyes and hands of admiration.

One day as he passed out he paused and asked her if she remembered what she had said about the song of Dolly and him that made it, and how it was fitter for a lad than a mature man.

" Do you think still," he asked, " that she would prefer a rustic lad in homespuns, with hay in his hair and smelling of his occupation, before a town gallant."

" Why, it would depend, sir, on whether she had a true heart," said Mrs. Lumley simply.

" Might not her heart be true to the gallant as well? " he asked, and then went out without waiting for an answer.

Being a lover, he was a creature of whims and moods; and the evening following he came in with a dejected air, and put his hand on Mrs. Lumley's shoulder.

" You were right," said he, " when you said that the clock of Time could never be turned backward. If I could make a bargain to sell my soul to get my youth back, I would do it."

" Don't say such things, sir," pleaded Mrs. Lumley, almost tearfully. " As for talking about the clock of Time, that I never did; I leave such things to my betters."

It was now the time when the wild roses hung all the hedgerows, and the faint sweet scent of them was like wine in the air. The honeysuckle, too, was out, golden as honey and as sweet; and the rank sweetness of the elder-blossom was everywhere. The hay lay new in the meadows and the corncrake was silent at last in the moonlit nights. The time of the nightingale was over; and soon the year would be sober and would carry the air of a matron, although she was now in the flush of youth.

And Mr. Jones had the air of a triumphant lover. He and Dolly were to be made man and wife in July; and every one seemed to have forgotten Oliver Buckenham except Mrs. Lumley, who had a compassionate heart, and had come on the lad, face downwards in the honeyed swathes of the hay, one day as she took the short-cut by Wood-End to the village of Farley.

" Shall we have a hauling home of the bride to The Spotted Lamb, your honour? " she asked of Mr. Jones.

He went with his head so much in the air those days that it might well be he had thought of nothing so practical as the roof that was to cover himself and his bride. But he had thought of it, and a fine sensation there was when it was known that Alvanley Place had come into his hands, and was to be made ready for Dick Stone's daughter. Many people, though they had liked pretty

Dolly, thought it little short of a scandal that she was to sit in old Madam Alvanley's seat.

There were others who said that Dick Stone had got more joy of the marriage than his daughter, and that pretty Dolly's roses were withering. But if it was so her infatuated lover saw nothing of it.

> Dolly's mouth is filled with pearls,
>     Damask roses on her cheek;
> 'Mid her dimples and her curls
>     Love himself plays hide-and-seek.

The song of Dolly was for ever on his lips; but Mrs. Lumley smiled no longer. She had never known good to come of such unequal marriages, and the memory of Oliver Buckenham's attitude, as though he lay on the rack, troubled her.

One morning in the dews and scents of the hour before dawn she heard a horse clatter furiously through the village.

" It will be Mrs. Stiles at the Leas," she said to herself, " and John Stiles is riding for the midwife. I pray the poor soul may not be mortal bad; he rode at such a rate."

But it was not Mrs. Stiles, for John Stiles was in for his beer next morning and reported his wife still up and doing.

Mr. Jones went off as usual about half an hour before noon, " walking on air," said the gossips, who leant through the door of The Spotted Lamb to look after him.

About twelve o'clock there was another sensation, for a magnificent coach with postilions and footmen drove up to The Spotted Lamb; and the postilions and footmen and coachmen all had powdered heads, and were dressed in liveries of gold and scarlet, fine enough for a duke or the Lord Mayor of London.

One gentleman rode in the coach. He wore no powder, but his head of curls fell about his handsomely fleshy face; and his clothes were even finer than Mr. Jones had made them used to at The Spotted Lamb.

Mrs. Lumley went out all curtseys to the side of the coach. The gentleman asked for Mr. Jones and was told he was out; he then asked if he might have a private sitting-room to await his return.

The Spotted Lamb, and indeed the village for the matter of that, was all in a flutter. The servants who came with the coach soon told the name of their master. Mrs. Lumley was quite overcome, and vowed that nothing would induce her to enter the parlour where he waited, because she would surely faint on approaching him.

So she had hartshorn to her nose, and in the safe hiding-place of her store-closet lay back in a chair, listening to the impatient pacing to and fro of those august feet.

At last word was brought to her that Mr. Jones was returning. She hastened out as fast as her trembling feet would carry her to warn him of who awaited him. But he passed her by without a word. What had come to him? The good woman could have screamed outright at his face that put even her news out of her head.

It was fallen in a mass of haggard lines and shadows. If ever despair sat on a face it sat there. Although he would not wait for her to speak he walked slowly and heavily. His white silk coat was stained as though he had lain with it in the grass before the dews were dried. The lace at his wrists was torn, and dangled in a few shreds. Blood trickled down his chin where he had bitten his lip through.

"Lord love your honour, what has happened to you?" she cried, mother-tenderness awake in her heart.

He went on as though he had not heard her and passed within the parlour whence so often she had heard the song of Dolly.

The door closed slowly. She heard the shout inside:

"Why, Jack, I have come for you!"

Then the door closed.

She flew to the store-closet and laid her ear to the wall, where a day or two before she had discovered a tiny hole from which a knot of wood had fallen out.

"I spoke in anger, but now I withdraw it. Dear Jack, the wine is sour without you. There is no one to set the table in a room. Almack's is deserted. The pretty women are inconsolable. Come back with me to the town. You look as though you were tired of your country whim."

"I will go where you like." Mr. Jones's voice had the strangest sound of suffering. "Only let me make a hasty toilet; I am not fit to be seen with your Highness."

"You won't escape me again?—then I shall let you go. Upon my honour, Jack, I was deucedly sorry I said it. I can't make excuses even to you, though I love you, man. It shall not occur again, I promise you on the word of a prince."

"I had forgotten it, I assure your Highness."

The voice of utmost dejection brought the tears to Mrs. Lumley's kind eyes.

An hour later the splendid coach was again at the door of The Spotted Lamb. Mr. Jones had clad himself in the sober fineness of his early days. The blood was washed from his lip. He looked no worse now than care-worn and old.

Mrs. Lumley was in tears. Mr. Jones was coming back no more. A man would be sent to fetch away his belongings. He had left more gold on the table than would pay for a year's lodging, and Mrs. Lumley did not care to take it up.

Just at the last he paused in the narrow inn passage where the Great Person preceded him, and turned aside into the little brown parlour. There had been stocks and gillyflowers when he came:

there were now Mary-lilies and the last of the roses. A sheaf of lilies in the brown room was sharp as the flash of an angel's sword.

"After all," he said, "you were wise, you kind soul. She chose the lad and rode with him at daybreak. Good-bye!"

He kissed her cheek and was gone. Coach and horses, coachman, footmen, postilions were gone, like a fairy-tale, into a cloud of dust. The crowd of villagers, who had stood about in an awestruck gaping, might well believe that those tremendous events had happened to Rosegarland only in a dream.

# THE MEETING IN THE LIBRARY

## Katharine Tynan

The Library was little frequented except by the curious. It was rather inaccessible for those who would consult its learning, out-of-the-way, with slums grown up about it. For the mere idler it had no interest at all: the newest book its shelves held was two hundred years old.

The Librarian had something of a sinecure. This hot summer afternoon the garden invited him. The Library overlooked the Deanery garden, and the Librarian used to walk there sometimes in his slackest hours with the Dean's daughter. It might be said that his hours were always slack. They were short too, for the Library closed at dusk. No provision for reading by artificial light had ever been made there.

This day of June the Librarian came in hastily. The walk had taken more time than he knew and he was to dine at the Deanery at eight o'clock. He had to go home and dress first. The golden pollen of the lilies between which he had been walking with the Dean's daughter was on his coat. He dismissed the porter, went into the Library, locked up his desk, whistling in a glad, quick way, something after the manner of the blackbird in the cedar outside, took the great bunch of keys, locked the Library door behind him, and went home.

He had not noticed in one of the recesses a young man asleep with his head upon his arms, his arms upon a table in the window overlooking the garden.

The green twilight came after the rose and violet. The evening star shone out in the green and the young moon came after. Lights sprang up in the Deanery house across the garden. The birds went to sleep and the scent of the lilies grew stronger in the dew; for

the country was close at hand and the dews yet drenched the
Deanery garden as though it were a meadow.

The scent of lilies was strong as a narcotic. Humphrey
Brandon's head fell sideways in his sleep, revealing his face. It
was a fair, handsome face and a good one, although the mouth,
sweet as it was, lacked firmness. The forehead, white above its
line of sunburn, wore a frown. A name broke from his lips,
" Amaryllis "; another name, " Margaret." The frown grew
deeper, a look of pain scored the young handsome face in its
sleep.

Master Humphrey Brandon had been sleeping ill of late, or his
slumbers had not now been so profound in spite of his hard pillow
and the evident uneasiness of his thoughts.

He had come into the Library on his way back from a garden-
party where he had had an exquisite hour with Amaryllis. Only
six weeks before her disturbing presence had troubled his life—a
gay, enchanting, bewildering presence. He and Amaryllis had
strayed away from the rest of the company by a pond, had fed the
ducks, and afterwards rowed in a crazy boat among the water-
lilies. How Amaryllis had laughed! She had taken off her hat—
an airy pink thing wreathed with roses—and had pinned a white
and golden water-lily here and there among the roses. Her golden-
brown curls clustering about her small head were as alluring as a
baby's. Her violet eyes under dark lashes; her pert little white
nose and firm white chin; the red lips innocently smiling over little
perfect teeth; the milk-white throat above the falling lace collar:
all these beauties had so bewitched him that he had forgotten
Margaret.

Once away from Amaryllis he had remembered. And it was not
the first time he had forgotten; not the first time by many that he
had remembered.

Margaret was the fair saint of his boyish dreams. She was six
years his senior, and she had meant to him all of calm and rest and
soothing the world possessed. She had been something of a religion
to him.

They were not declared lovers, but Humphrey Brandon had
always been sure that one day he would ask his saint to become
mere woman for him and that she would stoop into his arms.
Then had come—Amaryllis. He knew that if he should go to
Margaret and tell her about Amaryllis she would bless him as she
had always blessed him, and would bid him bring the girl to her
that she might love her as well.

But though he had no fear on that score, yet he was not sure that
he wanted to go to Margaret with his tale. Just now he was bewitched, bedevilled, when Amaryllis came in view. The hem of
her muslin skirt, the point of her little high-heeled shoe, were
things to fall down before. He had hardly ever looked lower than

Margaret's eyes, those true eyes, with immortal lights steady in them.

He wanted Amaryllis, and yet he was quite sure that his eternal need would be for Margaret.

Perhaps if he gave his passion for Amaryllis the rein it would fall as dead as scattered rose-petals in a little while and his heart would return to Margaret, if indeed it had ever strayed from her.

Such thoughts and trouble at his own frailty had kept him awake of nights. He was not of the stuff of which sinners are made. He could not palter with his conscience light-heartedly.

If he waited—the hurt to Amaryllis would be nothing. He had heard her laugh with a new lover before he was out of hearing. It was perhaps her gay indifference, her light, sweet, untouched coldness of nature which made her charm for him. She was as virginal as a rose-bud and as lovely. Certainly Amaryllis would not suffer.

A hundred times he made up his mind to drift with the tide, a hundred times unmade it. That last laugh of Amaryllis had flung him into torments of jealousy this afternoon. But he would not turn back. He was on his way to Margaret. Only first he must rest and grow calm, for her tender, faithful eyes would discover the traces of recent conflict on his face. And where could a better place be found to rest than the Library? So he had turned in there and fallen asleep, worn out by sleeplessness and emotion, lulled by the fragrance of the lilies and the warmth of the drowsy air, full of the humming of innumerable bees.

He awoke cold, with the dews from the garden upon his hair, and in a sleepy bewilderment. The moon was gone now; and there was only a dusky fragrance, sown with a million stars, outside the open window. The place had been in darkness but for a faint light, a light that wavered hither and thither.

He rose stiffly and looked beyond the recess. There was a figure holding a candle in its hand going from shelf to shelf, taking out a book and replacing it.

While he looked, the figure turned its head and lifted the candle high to see him the better.

What an odd figure it was! It was that of a man about sixty, dressed in clerical garb of an ancient cut with white bands, and wearing on its head a bagwig. Humphrey Brandon stared. The strange person looked at him with a piercing gaze from cavernous eyes. The face was ivory pale and was furrowed with the track of storms. Bitterness and desolation were in its expression.

" So you have awakened, sir," the visitor said grimly.

" I don't know how I came to fall asleep," answered Humphrey Brandon apologetically. " I suppose you are—the Dean? "

" I am the Dean," the other replied.

" I must have slept some time." Humphrey Brandon looked

at his watch. " By Jove! half-past twelve! It was only half-past six when I came in. How did I come to do it? I was on my way to keep—an appointment."

" With Amaryllis or with Margaret? "

Humphrey Brandon stared at the sardonic face.

" How do you know? " he began, stammering.

" I am no wizard," the other replied. " You talked in your sleep. Amaryllis—Margaret: no scale could have balanced them more evenly." The hue of guilt crept into Humphrey Brandon's face. His lashes, dark and curling like a girl's, fell on his cheeks.

" You are a coxcomb," said the old man severely, putting down the candle in its old-fashioned candlestick on the Librarian's desk.

Some wild impulse to make confession and ask counsel came over the young man. He flung himself with a reckless air into one of the worn leather-covered chairs. " Perhaps I am," he said humbly. " Anyhow, Mr. Dean, you are ghostly—and I need ghostly counsel." The Dean snuffed the candle with a whimsical smile on his full lips. " It is your duty to help erring mortals. Will you not take the chair opposite to mine and listen to me? "

The Dean took the chair and dropped his cheek upon his hand. The bag-wig fell either side his face. Humphrey Brandon stared at him. Who was it he was like as he sat so? Some baffling memory played about the young man's mind and eluded him. He forgot it then, fascinated by the eyes in their cavernous hollows. They were burning as though they needed the slaking of tears. The face was the face of one deeply unhappy.

It was easier to pour out the tale of his vacillation to such a face. When he had finished there was a pause. Then the man opposite him sighed so hollowly that the young man started.

" I said you were a coxcomb," said the Dean, " but you are only a fool. You must go back to Margaret. Not for all the Amaryllises in the world would you break Margaret's heart. And you would break it, though she might live for twenty years after it was broken and show you always a smiling face. There are such women."

Humphrey Brandon, a creature of impulses, sprang to his feet, would have taken the Dean's hand if it had not been hidden somewhere in the folds of the gown, and cried out that the Dean was right: he would return to Margaret, and see Amaryllis no more till Margaret was his wife.

" It was fortunate I met you, sir," he said. " While I slept my soul was tossed about on a rack of pain. Dreams are heavy things."

" Do I not know them? " replied the Dean. " Dreams, aye, and wakings. Over in yonder Deanery I have had such pangs as you could not dream of. There was a night when the torchlights burned in the church." He seemed as though he would have said more, but he broke off abruptly.

"Let me at least thank you," said the lad.

"If I have saved another soul from a crime like my own. . . ." Again the voice died off in a hollow sighing.

"Well, I shall be saying good-night, or rather good-morning," said the younger man, abashed, as though he looked on some suffering he had no right to see.

"Why, we are locked in," he said in surprise after trying the door. " But you have the key, Mr. Dean? "

"I have no key. You must wait till the Librarian comes in the morning."

"But you? You were locked in with me. How careless the Librarian must be."

"I am often here through the hours of the night."

"Ah, well, I shall go the garden way. I can drop from the window and scale the gates. See, it is morning. How the sky trembles! "

All of a sudden he thought that the Library with its ancient books smelt mouldily; it was the air of graves and charnel-houses. The east indeed was trembling like a multitude of wings. A bird called from the cedar and was answered by a drowsy twittering. He touched an ivy leaf and his hand was wet with dew. He could see the lilies glimmering in the dark of the garden. Their smell came sharp and fresh. He was going to Margaret, and he felt as though this were his wedding morning.

With his hand on the sill, in act to drop, he turned his face to say good-bye. But what had happened to the Dean? He was standing as he had seen him first with the candle in his hand. But surely he was fading, fading into mists and dreams. A mere grey outline of a figure was there now, with only the eyes of it alive. As he stood staring they too went out and the Library was in darkness.

# RICHARD DEHAN
1864–1932

# A NURSERY TEA

THE driver of the rakish yellow dog-cart, hired from The Bluntell Arms, a white-faced tavern opposite the railway terminus four miles away, pulled up the lean-barrelled chestnut mare at a sign from the passenger, and touched the brim of his dusty bowler hat as the gentleman got down at the park gates of Fawncourt. The lodge-keeper's wife came out, wiping the soap-suds from her wrinkled hands, and opened the great wrought-iron gates for the visitor, and he passed in under the shield of the three wyverns rampant, and the cross crosslets, and the proud motto, *Sic fidem teneo*. He saw the gilding was tarnished and the metal rusted, and that one of the weather-stained limestone wyverns on the gate pillars had lost a leg, and he had a disgusted eye for the newly-washed garments of both sexes hung unblushingly to dry upon the rhododendrons as he threw the lodge-woman a shilling and walked rapidly into the avenue.

The park was rough and wild, and full of ancient, rugged oaks and beeches, the gardens were a sweet wilderness of autumn roses and tall white lilies within rankly-flourishing box borders. And then came the house—a Tudor building of ancient red brick, faced with creamy stone, standing on fair uncut lawns, drowsing in the rich black shadows flung by ancient cedars and giant yews.

The gentleman—a personable figure of a man—tall, lean, square-shouldered, and fashionably dressed—mounted the two wide steps shadowed by the double-columned portico, and would have rung the bell or plied the heavy copper knocker, but that he perceived in time the door was ajar. He pushed it with his stick and went into a vestibule paved with black and white Italian marble. A long oaken bench, dark with time, ran along the wall, dust obscured its polish at either end, in the middle was a clean patch. Here rested a man's hat, a sunburnt straw with a soiled London University ribbon. A hunting-crop, badly used, lay on the floor. And clumping boot-soles came clattering downstairs. The cold blue eyes lifted as the door in the screen swung open and calmly inspected the face of the newcomer, a short, weather-beaten man of forty-five in a well-worn Norfolk suit of grey tweed.

" This is not yours, I think? " The voice was cultivated and rather musical, the tone languid and chill.

The short man picked up his old hunting-crop and put on the scorched hat. Then he looked at his watch, a handsome gold chronometer attached to a shabby strap, and clacked his tongue against his palate, and slipped the watch back into his pocket, and was going out into the fragrant sunshine when a question from the other stopped him.

" Are you Mr. Fladwheat's agent? "

" I am—not," said the short man in tweeds shortly.

" You don't happen to belong to the Estate Office at W——? "

" No."

" Pardon me. Not by any chance a representative of the *County Chronicle*—are you? "

" Not by any chance."

" Then," persisted the tall, well-dressed gentleman with the thin lips and cold blue eyes, " if I may venture upon another question, What were you doing upstairs? "

The short man in tweeds was plainly annoyed. His weather-beaten face grew red as he turned upon the persistent stranger.

" You want to know what I was doing upstairs? Visiting an old patient."

" Indeed. Then—you are—I presume you are—the medical practitioner who succeeded to old Dr. Carberry's practice——"

" Fifteen years ago, Sir Wilfrid."

The tall, thin gentleman frowned.

" A man who wants to preserve an incognito ought not to be the image of his father," said the Doctor coolly. " I met the late Baronet—in my business capacity—twelve years ago. He had run down with some friends for the shooting—an attack of rheumatic gout——"

" My father was a chronic sufferer from rheumatic gout in his later years," said the late Baronet's successor. " It touched his heart towards the end. He let the old place get into a devil of a state," he commented in a low, absent voice. " And the people who have rented it for shooting have made bad worse. And, now——"

" And now it is on the market," said the Doctor raspingly.

" Continuing the realisation of my—my—of my late father's estate," said the other, sweeping his cold eyes back from the sunny world outdoors to the wall immediately above the Doctor's head. " Messrs. Bewis and Moseley will sell the property for me at Tokenhouse-yard on Saturday next at twelve. The reserve price of the mansion-house, gardens, and park-land is seventeen thousand. So, Doctor, if you contemplate an investment——" He shrugged in infinite contempt.

" I'm a poor man," the Doctor flashed back, " but if I had the money I would buy Fawncourt to-morrow. Not to save it from the creditors." Sir Wilfrid Bluntell, drawing diagrams on the dusty pavement with the end of his slim umbrella, raised his eyebrows interrogatively, still perusing the wall above the Doctor's head. " Not for my own sake—what are historic bricks and ancient acres and three-hundred-year-old oaks to me? Not for my wife's sake —I'm a confirmed bachelor—but for *hers*." He jerked his worn hunting-crop towards the heavy beams and ancient mouldings of the ceiling.

" Might one be permitted to ask who *she* is? " said the Baronet's smooth voice.

" She is my patient," said the Doctor shortly. " You know her —or you have good reason to! And her name is Hannah Brown."

Sir Wilfrid's cold blue eyes dropped from the wall above his head and questioned him. " Hannah Brown. . . . Do you mean Nurse Brown? . . . Nurse Brown! . . . Why . . . I thought she . . . I supposed she was dead, like Hurst, the butler, and all the other old people. Alive! . . . By Jove! she must be a hundred if she's a day."

" As a fact, she is ninety," said the Doctor.

Sir Wilfrid went on without hearing. " She was laundry-maid in my grandfather's time, she nursed my father, he was always ' Master Reginald ' to her, the pattern-boy held up to us "—he grinned a little. " She was head nurse when we—when we were kids. Nurse Hannah Brown—Nurse Brown." His face was creased into quite a boyish smile. His cold eyes had a twinkle. " How I used to worry her—up to all kinds of mischief, and dragging Gerry——" He broke off. " What you tell me is very interesting," he added nonchalantly. " I must go up and see the old lady before I leave. Frankly, I ran down to look over the old house before the sale; there are several bits of rare old china and carved oak presses which would fetch rattling prices at Christie's. As for books—the library was a desert in my time, with *Spectators* for palm-trees and Malory's *King Arthur*—the one well not brackish Do you happen to know——"

" I happen to know one thing," said the Doctor stiffly, " and that concerns my patient."

" Nothing much the matter there, I hope? " said Sir Wilfrid.

" Old age," blurted out the Doctor with resentful eyes, gleaming through his spectacles, " and poverty and semi-starvation. Will you understand what I mean to convey, Sir Wilfrid Bluntell, or do you mean to play a comedy of ignorance with me? Since Sir Reginald left Fawncourt fifteen years ago, with glib promises and kind words, and hearty handshakes, and all the pinchbeck trash that she has always taken for pure gold, not a penny of her poor pension of £30, once her yearly wage, has ever been paid. But for charity, sir—*charity*—she would have died of want, and so I tell you to your face! "

" Your method of communicating the intelligence is offensive," said Sir Wilfrid, " but I give you credit for meaning well. As to Nurse Brown, I should have thought that in her seventy-four years of service she would have managed to save, to put by, to accumulate a considerable provision——"

The Doctor was foaming now. He gesticulated wildly with the hand that held his hunting-crop, and his small angry eyes snapped sparks. " So she had. Aye, aye! ' Saved,' ' put by,' ' accumulated ' some £700. Hurst—old Hurst, the butler—made her buy Consols—she'd be getting some £21 the year—enough to keep body and soul together—just—her pension being forgotten by the family."

" Well? "

" Well! " The Doctor was now at white heat. " What else could one expect? Mind, she never uttered one complaint—I wormed the story out of her, inch by inch. The year before Sir Reginald died, down comes Mr. Gerald Bluntell——"

" My brother Gerald? "

" Yes. By the Lord! and proud would I be if he was mine. She cried for joy when he came to pay her a visit in the old nursery in the east wing there, and asked her to make him tea—in the same little old brown teapot he remembered. Boyhood's recollections—old tie—present troubles—pressing creditors to satisfy, no use going to Sir Reginald—ruin impending, in fact, which might be averted by a sum of ready money—nothing less than £700——"

" Spare me the *réchauffage* of Mr. Bluntell's misdeeds," said Sir Wilfrid, with a slight protesting gesture of his gloved hand. " As to his usage of this old servant of our family, it is strictly in accordance with his character. I say no more and no less. My own affairs are—somewhat in confusion. All property that is not strictly entailed upon my son is to be sold. I cannot restore the old woman's money—even if I would. And I live in Paris; I have no home to offer her here. But when she is removed from Fawncourt—and it is necessary and advisable that she should go at once—a home shall be found for her in the village. She is already indebted to you for certain kind offices, I understand; perhaps you would not object to take charge of this? "

But the Doctor waved away the crackling £5 note.

" Give it her yourself, my good sir, since I understand your intention is to look in upon the poor old forgotten creature. But unless you desire to be guilty of her death say nothing about removing her to another home. This house has been her home for seventy-four years. She blossomed in its prime, and has fallen into decay with it. Ninety years old, and incredibly frail and feeble, she has not stirred out of the old nursery in the east wing for ten years or more. Pulse a mere thread—the heart's action liable to stop at any moment. . . . That she should have lived so long, and under such conditions, is a marvel, but there's lasting stuff in good old yeoman stock unvitiated by centuries of aristocratic vice and high-bred intemperance. Now remember—I have warned you! "

The Doctor's overworked straw hat was dabbed upon his head, the Doctor's heavy boots clumped away in the direction of the stable.

Sir Wilfrid shrugged his shoulders and pushed open the heavy wrought door in the carved screen, which would have to go with the other fixtures, otherwise . . . " Worth £1,000," he said, with a little vexed whistle, as he passed through the semi-gloom of the hall, with its trophies of the chase and stands of rusted armour, and began the ascent of the great oaken staircase in a shaft of silvery-golden sunlight falling from the high mullioned windows on the landing. He mounted another staircase, the carpet under his feet ageing as he climbed, and turned down a well-remembered passage lighted by leaded casements. This was the oldest portion of the house. There were double doors at the passage-end, covered with faded green baize. They parted as Sir Wilfrid looked, and a rosy-cheeked country girl in a print dress and sun-bonnet came out, carrying a cup and plate. Her brown eyes widened at the sight of the strange gentleman; she dipped a curtsey, village style, as she slid by. Sir Wilfrid guessed her to be a niece or daughter of the caretaker. He went into the room.

It was low-pitched, panelled shoulder-high with blackened oak, and the plaster of walls and ceiling was cracked and browned with age, and mouldy in patches with damp. There was a lofty oaken chimneypiece, its pillars and centre-board scored with generations of initials burned in by childish hands, probably with the same little worn, bent poker that had always hung on a corner of the rusty, wrought-iron guard. Three casemented windows, whose cracked or broken panes had been pasted over with paper and rag, gave outlook to the south upon quiet, sloping lawns, browned with the fallen needles from giant cedars, whose sun-gilded trunks made the pillars of a Druid temple, roofed with their spreading boughs and sombre, spice-smelling foliage. And the door of an inner room, once the night-nursery, stood open, revealing three little rusty cot-beds in a row, and a heavy wooden cradle, with a broken rocker. A small fire burned between the wide hobs of the Queen Anne grate, and a small kettle sang upon it just as it used to sing, and Nurse Brown sat in a red-covered winged chair, her frail, old hands, with their idle knitting-pins, lying placid in her lap, her peaked chin sunk in the hollow of her bosom. There was no doubt of the " poverty," the " privations " of which the Doctor had spoken.

The man who looked on her had been her nursling and her darling, her tyrant and her god, as had his father before him. Some long atrophied fibre stirred in his cold, narrow heart, his hard eyes softened and grew kind. He felt almost tender towards this old, worn-out link with the old worn-out days. At the same time he shrank almost with dread from the idea of touching her. To be hugged, to be wept over!—the thought was almost unbearable; and yet he had sat upon those knees and kissed those withered lips, forty-five years ago. Nurse Brown had been a personable, buxom woman then, with brown hair only getting grey under her smart lace cap, and singularly bright, black eyes. A little smack of the country-side had flavoured her speech, plenty of good, shrewd common sense was wont to be upon her tongue, a homely humour modified her outlook upon the world, a homely loyalty was in her single-hearted belief in the goodness, virtue, nobility, beauty of every individual member of the Bluntell family, the " flower of the flock," as she repeatedly assured his descendants, having been her own first nursling, Master Reginald. Now, here she sat, that faithful-looking soul—forgotten, bereft, unpitied. . . . It was a damned shame—a——

But Nurse Brown's bright, black eyes were open and looking at him.

" Master Wilfrid. . . . My own dear boy! "

Nurse Brown had got out of her chair somehow, and ran towards him, feebly and with outstretched hands. He caught them in his as she stumbled and seemed about to fall. They seemed to dissolve in his grasp for very frailness as he led her back to her chair. She shed a few tears there. The sight of him was good for sore eyes, she said, as she wiped her own.

" And you're the first to come, as I knew you would, Master Wilfrid." Her voice was a little tremulous, and thinner, but very like the voice that Sir Wilfrid remembered. He pulled up a chair and sat down, smiling, for the languid cynicism and flippant indifference of his former mood had fallen from him. He felt, sitting in the old Fawncourt nursery with the humble, homely creature at whose knee he had faltered his first petition to a Father in heaven, that it would have been well if his children had had a better earthly one.

" And you're the first. The eldest always sets an example. . . . When I look up and see you—There! I says, as was promised, my dear boy. And then Miss Gertrude and Master Gerald—and I forget what came next; but Him as the Rector comes regular to read about and talk of—and may He bless him for being that good to an old useless woman—He never breaks His word."

" She wanders a little," thought the man, as the brief, ecstatic smile faded from the keen-featured old face and a look of distress took its place. " Poor old soul! " Aloud he asked, " What is the matter? "

" The bit o' fire . . . going black out under the kettle . . . this day of all days, when my three children will be a-wanting o' their tea." There was a quaver in the old voice that heralded tears, and Sir Wilfrid made haste to say:

" Don't worry. Leave it to me—I'll make it burn up all right."

" Maybe there's a bit o' wood in the cupboard side of chimney," said Nurse Brown, cheering. " Mrs. Pretty, the caretaker, she brings me a bundle every now an' then, or send it by her little gell, A good gell, Rhoda is, but too fond o' ribbons to please me. Do ye be careful, Master Wilfrid—you was always so venturesome wi' matches."

Sir Wilfrid, with an appearance of great absorption in the task, had found and stuck some little bits of dry apple-wood under the kettle, and was now drawing up the leaping spirelets of wavering green flame by dexterous use of a silk handkerchief.

" A fire's a treat to me," said Nurse Brown, " in these pinched days; though I've nothing to complain of—don't ye ever dream that, Master Wilfrid. There has been family i'barrassments—law troubles and such—or my Master Reginald—the first of them I nursed—would niver have forgot me. My Miss Gertrude! "

She had risen and stood upright, holding by the arm of her chair, her bright eyes fixed upon the door.

" There is nothing," said Sir Wilfrid. " You fancied you heard a footstep, that was all."

But Nurse Brown was obstinate, if the term can be applied to anything so feeble and soft and frail.

" Bless the boy! " she said with a gentle laugh, " does he suppose I don't know my own sweet girl's footstep from out among them all?—and there are hundreds of footsteps in this house, dear, of folks I know, and used to know, and others, dear, that were before me. Now it draws nearer. And now it's in the corridor —not so light as when she was a young thing and danced because she was too full o' life to walk—but a firm, free step. . . . Now the swing-doors, and now—her knock. Oh, my dear love, come in! "

Some one had actually knocked, and Sir Wilfrid leapt up, oversetting his chair, and breaking its worm-eaten back. The door opened, and a handsome woman crossed the threshold, and, with a little cry, stepped forward and embraced Nurse Brown, whose shrunken figure almost vanished amongst her chiffons and laces.

" You dear old, old thing! " the newcomer gushed, and kissed the wrinkled cheek in a delicate, pecking, Society way. " Now, don't cry," she said, " I haven't much time to spend here." Then she recognised the tall, lean figure of the elder brother, whose cold blue eyes and thin, straight features bore much resemblance to her own. " Wilfrid! You here? How odd! " she uttered, with a little agitated catch of her breath.

" How are you, Gertrude? " he said, awkwardly for him, and came to her, offering his hand. She smiled wryly as she took it, for he had commanded his wife to " drop Gertrude " when Mrs. Consterdine had elected to burn her boats and leave her husband for Lord Vibart, and the sum total of Wilfrid's own conjugal errors had but recently been added up by a British jury.

" Poor Millicent! " Lady Vibart had commented, " spending all that time and all that money in getting twelve men to agree that Wilfrid is to keep his distance—when he has never done anything else." Now she said, in response to her brother's stiff greeting, " Oh, clinking! and so is Vibart, thanks," and she smiled again, more naturally, as she unwound the latest thing in automobile veils and tossed it upon the table.

" You came down by road, I see? " her brother said.

" In Savarny's ' Napier,' " returned Lady Vibart, looking straight into her brother's eyes. " I had seen in yesterday's *Times* that Fawncourt was to be sold. I had had an idea that I should like to see the old place again—and—here I am."

" You have not brought Savarny? " said Sir Wilfrid.

" I have left him at The Stag and Arrow in the village," Lady Vibart said, " trying to order luncheon in what he believes to be English learned from me."

" I hope you will draw the line at learning from him any more of what you believe to be French," said Sir Wilfrid.

Lady Vibart showed her excellent white teeth in response and dropped a little mocking curtsey.

" *Merci, mon cher!* The caution comes admirably well from you! "

" Hush! " he said.

But thrust, parry, and riposte had glanced beside the true heart that had loved these worldly ones from birth. " Come, sit you down, my dear love," said Nurse Brown, fondling the jewelled hand that had grown cold between hers. " And, Master Wilfrid, you should never speak unkind to your sister. I mind, and so should you, how she cried outside the door when you was down wi' the measles, and broke open her money-box to buy you a new fishing-rod when you got well."

A less unfriendly look was interchanged between both pairs of cold blue eyes. The woman's glance asked, " Is she quite childish? "

The man replied:

" Far from it. She only occasionally confuses the Present with the Past."

The quavering old voice rose again:

" You'll kiss each other, dears, like a good boy and girl. Otherwise the tea won't draw and there'll be no sugar on the bread-and-butter."

" You always used to say that, you dear old thing, when we were naughty," Lady Vibart cried. She straightened the poor shabby cap and patted the old, worn, veinous hands. " And where is the tea? I'm parched—simply."

" Drat my head—I've never wetted it! " The Nurse Brown of the past was revivified from the ashes of the present. She sprang erect, renewed, to minister to her nurslings' needs. Age fell from her like a discarded shawl. Spellbound they sat and watched her as she bustled to the cupboard where the caddy lived; it was the little black japanned one they remembered of old. She drew a crusty loaf from a biscuit-tin, she produced butter from a jam-pot, she conjured from various hiding-places plates, cups, knives, teaspoons, a teapot, sugar. To and fro, to and fro between the table and the cupboard and the fireplace the bent figure journeyed, intent on service, unconscious of toil. The kettle boiled, the teapot was warmed, the infusion made. Triumphantly she bade them draw to the table, spread with all her scanty store.

" And manners, my dearies, remember. If I'm humble myself, I know how my betters should behave. Yes, Master Wilfrid, you may cut the bread. Miss Gertrude likes to butter it—there'll only be brown sugar on the second slice. When you're grand grown man and woman you'll remember how happy you made yourselves in the old Fawncourt nursery, with Nurse Brown, and a bit o' bread-and-butter, and a cup o' tea."

" Dear old thing! I have often—often remembered it," said Lady Vibart with a sigh.

" And so has Master Wilfrid . . . and so has my boy Gerald. There! to think of me forgetting my boy. Whatever can have come to him? "

Nurse rose as though to run in search.

" Sit down . . ." said Sir Wilfrid, falling unconsciously into schoolboy idiom in humouring her. " Gerry's all right. You'll see him presently, as safe as houses."

" Oh, Will! " his sister protested below her breath.

" He's watching the fallow deer, or the big pike in the pond, with them big bright eyes of his," said Nurse Brown, putting the teapot to stand on the hob for " her boy," and reserving a Benjamin's portion of bread-and-butter. " The Lord behears the prayers I put up that no harm may come to him. When you grows up, Master Wilfrid, love, you'll have your seat in the House of Commons like your grandfather, and make the longest and grandest speeches, you will, on every subject that can be brought up, without committing your party, as I've heard it called, to anything

whatsumever. But Master Gerry will be a—what do they call
the gentleman with the laurel wreath as Queen Victoria pays thousands a year to for writing poetry? "

"Laureate," suggested Lady Vibart.

"And that's what my sweet boy will be, Heaven ever bless
him!" said Nurse proudly. "You'll be married, Miss Gerty,
dear, before Master Gerry is crowned; but mark my words, the
day will come. And you'll be only less proud of your brother then
than you will be of your husband. He'll be dark-complexioned as
you are fair, and you'll bring the dear babe down to Fawncourt to
get the country air and sleep in the old nursery; and a good mother
you'll make, love, that are that fond of your dolls to-day."

"My God, my God!" broke from Lady Vibart in a suffocated
voice, "why was I so mad as to come here? Why——? "

"Pull yourself together," said Sir Wilfrid, leaning to her ear.
" Brave it out—lie, act as women can. It is the one thing we can
do for her—never to let her guess the truth. Do you know what
she has suffered at our hands? Gerald stole her savings, our father
ceased to pay her poor pension long before he died——"

"Impossible! Oh, Will, say it is not true!"

"I—damn me for it!—forgot her. So did you."

"I—I am afraid I did!" admitted Lady Vibart.

Sir Wilfrid went on: "But for the Doctor's charity—but for
the Doctor's help she would have *died*. What's that? "

"That " was another step upon the landing, a new touch upon
the rattling handle of the door. Lady Vibart rose with a little cry
of recognition. Sir Wilfrid sat still as stone.

"Shut the door behind you, Master Gerald, there's my own
boy," said Nurse in a tone of calm authority, "and put down
your hat, and come to the table. Your tea's a-waiting and your
bread-and-butter's cut."

"And I'm confoundedly hungry and infernally thirsty," said
the prodigal, accepting the invitation.

"Don't let me hear you make use of grown gentlemen's bad
language again, Master Gerald," warned Nurse Brown, returning
from the hob, teapot in hand, "or I shall be compelled to put
you to bed without your tea. Make room for your brother, do,
Miss Gerty, and hand him the bread-and-butter."

"She's awfully old!" said Gerald Bluntell under his breath.
" It frightens me to look at her—by Jove, it does! "

"I am glad to hear you have so much conscience left," said
Lady Vibart icily.

"What do you mean? What the—what do you mean? "
snarled the prodigal.

"Now, that's not pretty, Master Gerald, my lamb, to talk to
your sister so," said Nurse Brown, and the lamb subsided with a
scowl. "And you know he was a weakly babe, Miss Gerty, and

your dear, sweet mother, my blessed lady now with Them above—made you promise to be a kind elder sister to your little brother. I can see my lady now, leaning back amongst her great embroidered pillows, with her big, bright eyes shining like stars, and her colour as pink as roses, and the little lace shawl—French lace, hundreds of years old—tied over her lovely head. And every night she prayed on her two knees that her three children might grow up good.''

The shadows without had grown longer, the sunlight mellower and less intense. An owl, waking from the daylight's sleep, swooped noiselessly from one tree into another, and the shrill, alarmed protest of an angry mother-bird followed on the predatory visit.

'' She'll be afeard for her nestlings, poor thing! '' said Nurse Brown, who had returned to the red arm-chair, after offering that throne successively to each of her visitors, '' and well she may. They be silly-looking, hook-nosed things by day, they owls, though bodeful and dreadsome enough on moonlight nights, the screechers specially. I had a nursery-maid in your dear father's time, my children, that was mortal afeard o' owls. Rhoda Pretty, the gell as does my bit o' marketing, be her granddaughter, and nigh as skeery. Eh, dears, what days they was to be sure! The head nurse, whose place I got after, and me as second, the nursery-maid, and a scrubbing-maid, that was the nursery staff. And Sir Reginald, the loveliest boy with the flaxenest curls that ever was a nurse's pride. None of his children had his pretty ways or his tender heart—though I say it to your faces, dears! ''

'' Fancy the old governor! '' said the prodigal under his breath, '' with pretty ways and a tender heart. Good Lord! '' he chuckled drearily.

'' Bless him! I thought he never would a-done mourning over the leg o' mutton for the nursery dinner that had once belonged to a live sheep.'' Nurse Brown's flow of reminiscence was interrupted by a yawn.

''We have tired you,'' said Lady Vibart gently, drawing a stool to the side of the red arm-chair. She remembered Savarny, waiting at the inn in the village, she wished intensely to escape from the stinging memories and gnawing regrets that lived under the roof of Fawncourt—she bitterly upbraided herself for having had the idiocy to come; and yet—she looked at the prodigal, and refrained from taking leave. Some latent instinct of protection towards the feeble, childish, trusting creature who had already suffered plunder at his greedy hands—might suffer it again—awakened in her. Tardy gratitude for all the wealth of love, all the treasures of loyalty and fidelity hung like despised garlands about such worthless necks, outpoured at such shapeless feet of vulgar clay, moistened her cold eyes and melted her frozen heart. She gulped a little sob and fumbled for her handkerchief—an absurd square inch of gossamer cambric, bordered with a frill. She did not waste time in regretting the past, but she wished that things had been different! Dim-eyed, she reached forth to touch the withered hand, and found it covered by another—Wilfrid's! and the prodigal Gerald was sitting on a ragged hassock at Nurse Brown's feet.

" This is like blessed old times," said Nurse Brown, " wi' all my children round me. 'Twas promised—and I knew the promise would be kept—as I should have this good hour—and now it has come to me. All my children—that is, saving one. And him——"

" What was that? "

" What was what, Miss Gerty, dear? " asked Nurse.

Lady Vibart had uttered the exclamation. " It is quite absurd," she said with a little empty laugh, " and I know my nerves must have played me a trick, but a child in a little old-fashioned white pelisse and tartan sash actually peeped in at us just now from the old night-nursery."

" A neighbour's child—possibly the caretaker's," said Sir Wilfrid, clearing his throat.

" Perhaps. . . . Ah! there it is again. No, it has gone! "

" A white embroidered frock and a Rob-Roy sash and yellow curls, pale, like ripe barley, not gold, like corn, had he? " said Nurse Brown, smiling wisely inside her cap-border.

" That's the kiddy," assented the prodigal. " I saw him as well as Gerty. Looked round the door and laughed . . . and then dodged back again. I hear him chuckling now, I'm almost certain."

" Take no notice, and maybe he'll come out," said Nurse. " 'Twould be hard if my own boy were kep' back, when the promise was for all. By-and-by, when the sun has wested and the shadows get longer, he'll grow more venturesome. I've heerd him behind my chair—ah! a many, many times; but when I turns, sweet love, he's always hiding. Tell me if you sees him again, dear! "

" She means our father," Sir Wilfrid whispered to Lady Vibart.

Nurse Brown—strangely keen of hearing and alert of perception in this her hour of joy—gave a little triumphant laugh.

" To be sure! My own boy—the first of all I nursed—who should I mean else? It's wonderful the love a woman can feel for them she never bore. Even if ye had grown up warped and blighted, cold-hearted, bad-natured, wicked, instead of noble, good, grand, 'twould be all the same to me. What I lulled to sleep in my old arms and saw thrive under my fostering, could I ever come to hate it? And that's how the Lord above looks upon His children. Eh, loves, 'tis getting dark."

A flash of lightning pierced the gathering gloom with a shaft of fierce blue radiance, and a rushing pattering sound of heavy rain followed the dull boom of distant cloud-artillery.

"When this is over I must positively escape," reflected Lady Vibart, and the panes streamed and the roof-gutters vomited. The half-admitted dread of the lonely journey through the deserted corridors, down the wide desolate staircases, the semi-conscious fear of meeting—something! made her draw her laces and chiffons closer about her, and hope that Wilfrid would in decency propose to see her to the door. As for Gerald, how could she hope to prevent him from carrying out whatever purpose he had in view? If he chose to remain—remain he must. The results of the raid would be discouraging enough to prevent his making another, and to-morrow—welcome to-morrow!—she would send Nurse enough money to keep the dear old thing in comfort for a decent time. But how dark it was! and how the rain poured and beat against the casements and clanked upon the flagstones of the terrace far below! Cool earth-odours, spicy cedar-smells stole in from the wet outer world mingling with the suggestions of dry-rot, the palpable hints of mice, the dampness that the little dying fire in the Queen Anne grate had no power to conquer. She shivered. A vision rose before her of drear, wet autumns, long, freezing winters, nipping, piercing springs spent in this place, alone, by this old, old feeble woman. Scarce fed, clothed in garments as ancient as her remembrances, less lasting than her faithful love. A rigor of cold and horror seized her, she shivered again, setting her teeth, and shutting her eyes and hands. In the increasing gloom so acute was her sense of desolation that she moved nearer to her brother Wilfrid, and was sensible that he drew closer to her. At last she touched his shoulder, and he put his arm about her. And the Prodigal, presuming but unrebuked, leaned his fast grizzling head against his sister's knee. So like, but so different to, the group that had gathered here in the old days when they were "Will" and "Gerty" and "Gerry" to each other, and Fawncourt was their Paradise, into which no serpent had entered yet. So changed and yet so much the same, they sat together now. A common love had stirred in their cold breasts, however faintly, a common sympathy had moved them, a regret had been shared, a remorse had stung them equally; an unacknowledged awe, a secret terror of unknown powers that might be gathering round them in the shadows united them in a common bond. Children again, they huddled together in the semi-obscurity—these three who were to go upon their way so shortly, uttering cold farewells, never to meet again on earth. They stilled their breathing and listened, and could have sworn to footsteps on the stairs, to voices in the corridors, to strains of music—once to a burst of laughter—that came pealing upwards from the locked-up, shuttered dining-room. Time passed, the rain had ceased, the sun had set, and the sky was a lake of pale rosy yellow behind the black umbrage of the dripping cedars.

" What a strange shadow—there upon the floor . . ."

One of the three Bluntells had spoken, or none. The uttered words might have been the crystallised thought of all three brains. But Nurse made answer:

" It be, my love. It have frightened me by times when it took shape like that. Whether 'tis the shadow of the gable over window or what else I never guess. Black, and long and heavy, with an edge of clear light. And the shape of a bier. And a figure on it with a face; there now—it's edge to me! And I seems sometimes to know whose it is, and sometimes not. Last time it came it were my boy, your dear father, Sir Reginald, lie there so still. And now——! See, dear loves, it be a woman . . . a-lying like a carved stone queen upon a monument, a-waiting for the Last Trump to stir the dust an' bid the dry bones live. And but that I never was so grand, my children, I'd say it were myself."

Silence again fell and the rose-yellow sky grew grey, a north wind swayed the cedar branches, and the last drops trickled from the gargoyle-mouthed roof gutters. The last spark of the fire died out, the cold shadows gathered closer. Then Lady Vibart called out suddenly in sharp alarm:

" How strangely she is breathing! Strike a light, if either of you have matches. Nurse! Nurse Brown! "

" I will send for the Doctor," said Sir Wilfrid hurriedly, as the vesta scraped and flared and burned out, and the hand that he had lifted fell inertly from his own. But the bright black eyes opened a moment later, and——

" My boy a-crying," said Nurse. " Why frightened of the dark, my love, and me so near? I'm a-coming, Master Reginald! I'm a-coming, my love. . . . That were the promise, after long waiting—as I should go—wi' all my—children by. The Lord bless my dear loves, my kind loves—that came before—the end! "

The worn old body quivered, and the last breath went out in a happy sigh, as Nurse laid down the burden of her many years, and went upon her way.

# SHAN F. BULLOCK

B. 1865

# THEY THAT MOURN

BUNN market was over, its hurry and haggle. In corners and quiet spots of the big market-yard, you saw men and women carefully counting their little stores of silver, testing the coins with their teeth, knotting them firmly in red pocket-handkerchiefs, finally stowing them away in their long wide pockets as cautiously as though every sixpence were a diamond. In the streets, people were leisurely moving towards the shops, where tills were rattling, and counters teeming, and trade, for a few hours, mightily flourishing after its whole six days of blissful stagnation.

A cart laden with butter, chiefly in firkins, issued from the market-yard gate, a man between the shafts, one at either wheel, two pulling behind, all noisily endeavouring to keep the cart from running amuck downhill into the river. Close behind, like chief mourners after a hearse, one might fancy, came Tim Kerin and Nan his wife; a battered, slow-footed couple, heavily burdened with the big load of their years, white haired both of them, and lean as greyhounds. Heavily they shuffled along in their clumsy boots; the man with one arm across his back, the other swinging limply; the woman holding up her skirt with one hand, and gripping with the other the handle of an empty basket; both looking fixedly over the tail-board of the cart at the few pounds of butter for which they had slaved hard for weeks, and for which, after hours of haggling, they had just received a few most precious shillings. Fixedly they watched it, and mournfully almost, as though they were bidding it a last farewell.

They passed through the gate, straggled across the footpath, and silently watched the cart zigzag down the street, run presently against the kerb, and, amid great shouting, discharge its contents into the packing-house.

" Faith," said Tim, across his shoulder, " 'twas cliverly done. I wonder, some day, they don't break their necks." He wagged his head dubiously; Nan tucked up her skirt; the two turned their faces uphill, and set out to share their profits with the shops. The butter was gone, and sorrow go with it: 'twas a heartbreak.

Tim Kerin's share of the profits was a shining sixpence, reluctantly tendered to him by Nan his wife, who now walked a couple of steps behind him, with eighteenpence shut tight in her hand, and the remainder of the butter-money (only a shilling or two) tied fast in a cotton bag and safely stowed away in the neck of her linsey-woolsey dress. Threepence of Tim's sixpence was to buy tobacco, a penny might go in the purchase of a weekly newspaper, a penny would buy a pair of whangs (leather laces) for his boots; the penny remaining, when all those luxuries had been honestly paid for, would buy a whole tumblerful of frothing porter. A whole tumblerful! At sight of it, with his mind's eye, Tim's lips dried and his feet went quicker over the cobble stones.

Nan's lips were tight, her brow wrinkled. She was figuring. It would take her to be powerful 'cute to fill her basket with the value of eighteenpence. Och, the lot o' things she wanted: tea, sugar, bacon, a herring for the Sunday's dinner, a bit o' white bread—and—and supposing there were a penny or two over (with knowing bargaining there might be), was it likely, now, that Mr. Murphy, the draper, would let her have cheap a yard of narrow soiled lace to go round the border of her nightcaps? Twopence might do, threepence would be sure to—— Aw, glory be to goodness, did anybody ever hear of such romancin', such extravagance? Sure it was runnin' wild her wits were! Threepence for lace indeed!

A friend stepped from behind a cart and caught Nan by the arm. What! was it pass a neighbour like that Mrs. Kerin would do? Pass her ouldest friend, Mrs. Brady, as if she were a milestone, and never pass the time of day, or tell how she sold her butter, or how the world was using herself? "Och, och, Mrs. Kerin," moaned Mrs. Brady, "what have I done to ye at all, at all?"

Nan stopped and put out her hand; then volubly began explaining: sure, sorrow the sight of Mrs. Brady she had seen; sure, she never passed a neighbour without speaking; sure, 'twas walking along romancin' she was, figuring in her head, seeing how far she could make the few shillings go. "An' how are you, ma'am?" asked Nan, when full pardon for her oversight had been generously given and gratefully received. "How are you an' all your care?"

Swiftly the two old heads bobbed together; ceaselessly the tongues began to wag; freely the full tide of their softly drawling speech flowed gurgling round the little nothings of their little world.

Meanwhile, Tim, his sixpence hot in his palm, had taken a turn through the throng of the streets; had questioned his neighbours about sales and prices (just as though his pockets bulged with bank-notes); had spelt out the time on the big market-house clock as he stood by the town pump listening to the hoarse drone of a ballad singer; and now, on the sidewalk of Main Street, stood dreamily looking through a shop window at a pile of newspapers which stood precariously among an array of tobacco pipes and sweet bottles. If he bought a paper, Tim was thinking, he would have a whole week's diversion o' nights; if he didn't buy it, he would save the price of another tumblerful o'—— A heavy hand fell on his shoulder.

" Hello, Tim," said his neighbour, Shan Grogan; " havin' a wee squint at the sugar-sticks is it, ye are? "

" Aw ay," answered Tim, turning; " aw ay! I was just lookin' at the papers there, an' wonderin' what an ojus lot o' news they give us nowadays for a penny. Enough to keep one goin' for a week. Powerful it is."

" Yis," said Shan; " it's a wonderful world. But aisy, Tim; ha' ye been to the Post lately? "

" Naw," said Tim.

" Well, look in there if you're passin', me son. The lassie that sells the stamps asked me to tell ye. Away quick; mebbe she'll give ye news for nothin'."

" Now, now," answered Tim. " I'm obliged to ye, Shan; I'm obliged to ye. Now, now," he repeated to himself, as he shuffled off along the pavement; " now, now. Is Shan havin' a wee joke, I wonder? " he said; and coming to the post-office doubtfully sidled in.

" Me name is Kerin, Miss," he said to the clerk, very humbly as to one of the representatives of mighty Government itself, " Tim for Christian; an' they tell me ye'd mebbe be havin' somethin' for me? "

The girl handed him a letter bearing the Chicago postmark, stamped in one of the bottom corners, and carrying its address thence right up to the top of the envelope. Tim bore it tenderly to the door and carefully inspected it; then took it back to the counter.

" Whose countersign might that be, Miss, if ye please? " he asked, and placed his thumb over the postmark. Humbly he asked; curtly he was answered.

" Chicago? " said Tim. " Ay, ay! I'm obliged to ye, Miss; I'm obliged to ye. May the Lord be good to ye, an' send ye a duke for a husband. Good-day to ye, Miss," said he; then, with his hand deep in his pocket and the letter in his hand, stepped out into the street and went off in search of Nan.

It's from Padeen, he kept thinking to himself, as he walked joyfully along, his feet clattering loosely on the pavement, his old face turning here and there, watching for his wife; it's from Padeen, sure as ever was. Aw! but he was glad. Aw! but Nan would be glad. So long it was, ages and ages ago, since they heard from him. 'Twasn't Padeen's hand-write—naw! but sure it might have altered; everything altered in the Big Country. Ay! 'twas only poor ould Ireland that kept the same—never any worse, never any better. But where was Nan? Sure she ought to be in the shops. He was dying to find her. Up and down he went; at last found her still bobbing heads at the top of Bridge Street with her friend Mrs. Brady.

" Aw, it's here ye are, Nan? " said he, coming up. " An' me huntin' the town for ye. It's yourself is well, Mrs. Brady, I'm hopin'? That's right, that's right."

His voice came strangely broken and shrill; his eyes danced like a child's; still his hand gripped the letter in his pocket.

" What's the matter, Tim? " whispered Nan. " Is it news ye have? "

" Ay, ay," he answered. " Come away till I tell ye; come away."

He turned and, with Nan at his heels, set off almost at a run downhill towards the river. Aw! but his heart was thumpin'.

" Aisy, Tim," cried Nan behind him; " aisy, man, or me breath—me breath——"

Without answering, or slackening his pace, Tim went on, turned through the butter-market gate, crossed the empty yard, came to the furthermost corner of one of the long low sheds, and there halted, with his face to the wall. Aw! but his heart was thumpin'. Presently, Nan came to him, panting and flurried.

" What is it, Tim? " she asked; " what is it? "

Slowly Tim brought out his letter, and, holding it by both hands, let his wife look at it.

" It's—it's from Padeen! " cried she; " it's from Padeen! "

" Yis," said Tim; " yis. It's not his hand-write; but—but it must be from him."

" Aw, glory be to God! " cried Nan. " Glory be to God! Sure it's ages since we heard from the boy, ages! "

She put down her basket, and, with her head between Tim's shoulder and the wall, looked fixedly at the envelope. Aw! but she was glad to see it. Such a time it was since they had heard from Padeen! A whole two years it was, come Christmas, since the last letter came, with that money order in it, an' the beautiful picture of Padeen himself, dressed out in his grand clothes, with a gold chain across his waistcoat, and a big gold ring on his finger. A whole two years almost. And now maybe——

" Aw, Tim, open it quick," she panted; " open it quick! "

" Mebbe," said Tim, " we'd better wait till we get home. The light's bad, an'——"

" No—no, Tim! No—no; it'd kill me to wait."

" Ay? " said Tim; then slowly drew his knife from his pocket and tenderly cut open the top of the envelope. His fingers trembled greatly as he fumbled with the enclosure. Nan's hand went quick to her heart.

" Aw, quick, Tim! " she cried. " Quick, quick! "

" Don't—don't flooster me, woman," said Tim; " I can't—can't——" The next moment his shaking old fingers held a sheet of notepaper, and a black-edged card on which, in large letters, beneath a long silvern cross, were the words: PATRICK KERIN.

Nan fell back a step; her fingers clutched at her dress over her heart. Tim's knife clattered upon the stones, and the envelope fluttered down. For a while they stood there silent, dread-stricken. At last Nan spoke. " Read, Tim," she said. " Read! "

" I—I can't."

" Ye must, Tim; it's better. Let us know the worst, for God's sake! Read, Tim."

" I—I——," Tim began; then quickly opened the sheet. " It's—it's too dark here," he mumbled; " I—I want me specs."

" Read what ye can, Tim—an' quick, for God's sake! "

So Tim, still with his face to the wall, raised the letter to catch the light, and began to read:

CHICAGO CITY, U.S.A.

DEAR—DEAR MISTER KERIN,—*It is my—my sad duty to in-form you that your son Patrick died* (" Aw, Padeen, Padeen! ") *of ty—typhus here on the 2nd of this month at twelve o'clock a.m.* (" God's mercy! " cried Nan). *As his oldest friend, I was with him at the end. He died in peace. He was buried at his request in —— Cemetery. I—I send you something to—to keep . . .*

" Aw, I can read no more," said Tim, with a groan; " it's too dark. I can read no more. Me poor ould Padeen! "

Nan turned and looked vacantly across at the busy street, dry-eyed and grey-faced. Ah! her poor Padeen, dead and buried away among the strangers, dead and buried, and never, never would she see him again, never hear his voice, never grip his hand! Dead, dead! her big, handsome, noble son . . .

She turned to Tim and caught him by the sleeve.

" Come away home, Tim," she said. " Come away wi' me."

Tim looked at her.

" Ah! Nan, Nan," he said, as the big tears sprang to his eyes. " Nan, me girl, but it's hard! "

" Ah yis," said she, and lifted her basket; " but come away, Tim, come away. Home's the best place for us."

" Yis," said Tim, wiping his eyes with his hand. " Yis, Nan."

Then, Nan leading the way and Tim shuffling after, the two old people (mourners now in real earnest) crossed the yard; and at the gate Nan halted.

" I think," said she, as Tim came up, " I think we can manage this week wi'out the bits o' groceries. Sure they're only luxuries anyway. I'll go an' see if Mr. Murphy can find me a bit o' crape for me bonnet. Yis."

" Do," said Tim. " Do, Nan; an' when you're about it," he said, taking his sixpence from his pocket and handing it to her, " ye may as well get me a bit for me hat. Ay! sure I can do wi'out me tabaccy for one week. Aw yis! Away quick, Nan; an' hurry back, me girl, hurry back."

So Nan turned up towards the market-house; but Tim went downhill towards the bridge; and when, presently, Nan came to him, carrying her little packet of crape in her big basket, Tim's head was bowed over the parapet and he was mumbling tearfully: " Aw, me poor Padeen, me poor Padeen! "

Nan plucked at his sleeve.

" Come away home, Tim," she said; " come away." And at the word Tim raised his head, dried his eyes, and set off slowly after Nan up the long, dusty road that wearily led towards home.

# TH' OULD BOY

### SHAN F. BULLOCK

BELOW in the kitchen, the plebeians were making merry with quip and crank, pipe and glass, as they sat round the walls and here and there over the floor in the warmth of the great peat fire; their laughter and chatter (subdued though it was, or tried to be) was heard distinctly above in the little parlour, where, round a well-spread table, sat a select company—the *élite* of the wake, you might say—gravely stirring their tea, eating their ham, discoursing on the merits and virtues (now, many of them, first brought to light) of the man who ofttimes had made merry at that very table, and now lay stark and lonely in a room beyond the kitchen.

" Ay, ay," sobbed the widow from her place behind the tea-cups; " it's God's truth; he was the generous heart an' the tender. Och, the heart av a child! "

The spoons clinked dolefully round the cups; the men solemnly wagged their heads; the women sniffed and, to conquer emotion, tried buttered toast.

" How often, here in this very room," the widow went on, " did I hear him spake the word. Ay, ay! An' 'twas the great gift o' prayer he had. Ah, ye all know it."

" Ay, ay," went the voices; " we do, we do; 'twas powerful, powerful! "

" An' now he's tuk from us—tuk, tuk," cried the widow; " gone an' left us to struggle alone wi' Satan. Ah, dear, dear! ''

The men were bent over their plates, the women biting their lips; it was blessed relief when the hard, level voice of Red John went out through the doleful assembly.

'' It's truth ye say, ma'am,'' said John; '' an' may your man be safe in glory (*Amen—Amen,* went the voices). But for yourself, have no fear o' Satan an' all his works: next time he makes bold to struggle wi' ye, just ax him if he remembers Red John: that'll settle him.''

With one accord, all eyes were raised and turned wonderingly towards the bottom of the table, where, one hand thrust carelessly into his waistcoat pocket, the other idly playing with his knife, sat Red John: a big man he was, red-headed, and with a strong, impassive face. '' You're all wonderin'? '' he went on, raising his eyes. '' Well, ye needn't. I say to ye all once more: next time Satan tries strugglin', just mention me: that'll finish him.''

Swiftly vanished sorrow and dole; the men found their big, coarse voices; the women pocketed their handkerchiefs: all, even the widow herself, called on John to explain.

'' Ye mean to say ye never heard? '' asked John. '' No? Well, well. Such is life; an' meself has told the story a score o' times. No odds. Here ye are. An' mind,'' he added, shaking his finger, '' no interruptions, an' no sayin' I'm a liar when I'm done. . . . Of course, ma'am; of course I'll wait a minute in welcome; an' just ax them down there to keep their bulls' voices quiet. Ye know,'' he went on, as the widow went out for a moment (carrying tobacco, or a bottle, or something, for the plebeians in the kitchen), '' it'll niver do to let the poor thing fret. Och, no; an' there's nothin' like a story to keep the heart from care. . . . Back again, ma'am? Well, then, 'twas like this: One day—ay, years ago—word came to me that Long Bob was runnin' a brewin' o' poteen. Now, when Long Bob brews, I'm off; for let him use treacle, or malt, or whatever he chooses, there's no man these parts (an' I've interviewed a few) can make stuff to grip your tongue like he can. No matter. Soon as I heard word, off I went, for I wanted no dregs; an' after a three-mile pull in the cot at last came to a wee island out in the lake, and there, in the middle o' the scrub an' the stones, was me darlint Still firin' away; an' round it a party o'—Well, never mind, there was more than *one* there I knew, an' all made me welcome. Ah, 'twas great stuff that; with a whiff off it like the middle o' a haystack, an' not a bite in a gallon of it. . . . Och, och, ma'am, *is* there anything behind ye there in the press? Sure a toothful'd send the words *flowin'* out o' me. . . . That's right, that's right. *Hurroo!* Now, now, only a toothful I said, ma'am; well, so be it. I'll do me endeavours.

'' Well,'' Red John went on, when the company had drunk the

widow's health and wished her long life, "I pass by all that happened there, just sayin' that we had great times, an' that when about dusk I set out for home I held a tidy sup besides the two lemonade bottles full in me tail pocket. It was a cowld night, an' ye know it's lonesome work draggin' a cot about a lake: so I'll not deny but mebbe I *did* wet me lips once or twice on the way; an' I'll acknowledge straight that when I landed it took more than a drop to take the stiffness out o' me joints. But mark me, ma'am, an' all o' ye, ye mus'n't run away wi' the notion that I was fuddled; I held me share, but I was as steady on me pins when I stepped out home as I am the night, an' as clear in the head as yourself, ma'am; long life to ye an' your very good health. . . . *Me smilin' little Cruiskeen lawn, lawn, lawn*," sang John in chorus with the plebeians in the kitchen, beating time with his tumbler on the table —*Me smilin' lit-tle Crui-skeen lawn!*

"'Twas about eleven o'clock—more or less, I'll not say as I'm strivin' for the truth, when I got home. Mary an' the childer were all in bed, an' there was a glimmer in the lamp, an' a pot o' porridge waitin' for me over a snug fire; so down I sits an' makes me supper; then lights the pipe and was goin' over (meanin' to make meself comfortable) to hang me coat on the back o' the door when, badness to me, if I didn't catch sight o' the neck o' a bottle stickin' out o' the tail pocket. 'Och, och,' says I, scratchin' me head, 'but it's the sore temptation, och, och! I wonder now would a wee sup hurt one?' An' afore I could make up me mind, the cork was out o' the bottle an' with some o' the poteen in a mug I was over by the dresser liftin' a sup o' water out of a can that stood on the floor.

"Now you'll attend to this, ma'am, an' the rest o' ye; for it's here the fun begins an' it's here I'll be truthfuller than ever. Just as I was stoopin' to get the water, there was a shakin' in the house, an' a blue flash that kind o' dazzled me; an' with that I turns round sharp—when, lo and behold ye, there, sittin' by the fire, wi' his legs crossed an' him lookin' straight at me, was as fine a lookin' gentleman as ever I clapped eyes on. All dressed in black he was, wi' a big cloak fallin' to the ground, an' a top hat, if ye please; an' his hair black, an' his face shaved, an' sorrow a smell o' jewelry on his person. Arrah, Lord save us, thinks I to meself, who are ye at all, an' where did ye come from? An', somehow, the way he sat there that cool, an' the *divilish* way he looked at me set me shakin'; if it hadn't been for the sup in the mug I'd ha' dropped on the floor. But the poteen gave me courage; an' wi' that I minded me manners an' spakes out.

"'Good evenin', sir,' says I; 'it's pretty late ye'll be?' He looked straight at me, keepin' his legs crossed, an' not one word he answered. Then, thinkin', maybe, he was hard o' hearin' I spakes again. 'Good evenin', sir,' says I; 'is it missed your way ye have the night? ' But sorrow a word; there he sat in the chair —just as ye are yourself, ma'am, beggin' pardon an' meanin' no comparisons; an' never moved hand or foot or budged a lip. So I scratched me head an' cast about what I was to do; for I couldn't keep standin' there like a fool, an' I was afraid to move. What in glory, thinks I, am I to do? Then all of a sudden the thought struck me; an' round I turns to the coat hangin' on the back o' the door, an' takes th' other lemonade bottle out o' the pocket. ' Axin' your pardon, sir,' says I, ' but if it's not makin' bold, could I offer ye the least taste just to keep the raw from your bones? '

" Not a word he answered; but, thinks I, there's a twinkle in your eye, me boy, that looks as if you'd be partial to a drop; an' ye all know a nod's as good as a wink to a blind horse. So, keepin' an eye on him over me shoulder, I turned an' got another mug off the dresser, an' mixin' a tidy dose I went across the floor an' offered it t' him. Like a lamb, sirs, he took it; gulped it down an' smacked his lips on the last drop. But see here, ma'am; may I never see light! if the draught didn't turn into blue blazes in his throat. Ye laugh? Well, don't then, if it isn't at your own ignorance. Laugh! troth most o' ye'll see worse than that after ye die." And John winked over his glass at the company.

" Well, thunder an' turf, thinks I to meself, what kind of a customer is this? Sure if he'd be sociable even it 'd not be so bad. Howsomede'er, thinks I, I'll make meself at home by me own fire; an' down I plops on a stool fornenst him, pulls out the cutty, fills it, an' lights up. After a couple o' whiffs I wipes the shank on me coat an' offers it to him.

" ' Mebbe you'd like a draw? ' says I, holdin' the cutty to him across the hearth; ' people these parts say it goes well wi' poteen.'

" He reached out an' tuk it, knocked the ashes off it, an' put it in his mouth. May death have me, ma'am, if the sight didn't parch me tongue! Every whiff o' him was a blue strame o' fire; an' ye could see blue blazes dancin' over the pipe; an' the eyes o' him glared like a cat's in the dark. An' he never moved a limb; just sat there as unconcerned as ever in his black suit, movin' his lips an' whiffin' out them infernal blue strames.

" ' Ah, great powers! ' says I; ' what are ye at all, at all? Why are ye here? Why are ye here? '

" An' with that, for I was frightened powerful, I tumbled off the stool, an' with an odious clatter went crash among the pots an' pot-hooks. An' the next thing I hears is Mary gettin' out o' bed in the room above an' liftin' the latch to come an' see what was up.

" She drew back immediately she seen some one wi' me—by good luck the gentleman had his back to her; an' in a minute or two down she comes in her petticoats—savin' your presence, ladies all— an' wid a shawl round her shoulders. ' What's the matter,

John? ' says she, kind o' frightened like, an' standin' behind the boy-o, sittin' there like a graven image smokin' away.

" ' Nothin',' says I.

" ' But I was woke out o' me sleep wi' a shockin' clatter? ' says she.

" ' Ye were,' says I, ' right enough. I stumbled over the pot there.'

" ' You're late? ' says she.

" ' I am,' says I.

" ' What kep' ye,' says she.

" ' Aw, nothin' particular,' says I. Just made a *kaley* or two. The gentleman there lost his way in the bog, an' he's warmin' himself before he starts out again.'

" All the time we were discoorsin', I was winkin' at Mary to spake to the boy-o; for I thought it powerful *un*genteel to stand there wi'out addressin' him. At last, she comes round, an' drops a curtsy, an' says she, in a haltin' kind o' way, not a bit like Mary's usual style o' talkin', for, as ye all know, she's blessed wi' the gift o' the gab:

" ' Savin' your presence, sir,' says she, ' for appearin' in these duds afore ye; but—I—was loth—to wait—long—for I was a—fraid somethin' bad had ha—happened when I heard—heard——'

" Not another word could she get out; I could see her eyes openin' wide, an' her jaw droppin', an' she fell a-tremblin'. For the boy-o just riz his eyes 'n looked at her; kept them hard on her, an' never moved a muscle, nor spoke a word, nor stopped puffin' blue blazes out o' me ould cutty.

" All of a sudden Mary turns to me, white as a corpse, an' says she: ' God in Heaven! John Graham, who's this? An' what's goin' to happen to us at all? '

" I couldn't answer; an' I thought Mary was goin' into a fit.

" ' Look at the mouth o' him,' shouts she, ' blue flames comin' out o' it! An' his nose! An' look at his eyes! Aw, God help us! '—an' she lets a screech; ' *look at his feet! Cloots—cloots! It's the divil himself!* ' An' with that she tears from the kitchen up into her room an' bolts the door. I was fair flabbergasted. What could I do? Thinks I, what brings th' ould boy to my fireside? I rubs me head an' looks hard at him; then gets up, an' creepin' to the table empties the lemonade bottle down me throat. Boys, but poteen's the darlin' stuff; it put a new heart in me; an' cleared me head; an' made me feel fit to fight twenty divils. Off I peels me waistcoat; tucks up me shirt sleeves, an' spits on me hands: then up I steps to Mister Divil.

" ' Ye ould ragamuffin,' says I, an' whacks me fists in his face, ' what brings ye roamin' like a roarin' lion to decent Prodestan' houses? Did ye ever hear tell o' Red John Graham,' says I, ' that hits man or divil like the kick o' a horse? Look at the face o' him, then,' an' I glares straight at him; ' look at him,' says I, ' ye tarnation ould scarecrow; look an' tremble, Mister Beelzebub! Ye're in the wrong house the night, ye flamin' ould tinker ye! ' says I. ' Your kind isn't here, Apollyon. I'm Red John, me boy, that fears neither man nor divil. Let me at your face,' says I—an' from the bedroom comes Mary's voice shoutin': ' *Hurroo, John! Pelt the ould vagabond. Pepper him, John.*' ' *I will, Mary,*' I shouts; ' *I will.* Come out. Stand up. Give me three minutes at your wizened countenance till I leave ye a laughin' stock for your own angels.'

" Then I made a grab," shouted John, knocking his chair over as he jumped up, and upsetting his tumbler as he made a false clutch at his neighbour's hair. " I made a grab at the head o' him just like that.

" ' *Come out!* ' roars I. ' *Come out an' be kilt!* ' An' with the word I fell on me head in the corner over an empty chair."

" Gone? " cried the widow. " He was gone? "

" Ay," answered John; " when I came to there was no one there but Mary, flingin' water over me an' roarin' *meila murther.*"

" Prime," went up the voices. " It's prime. Bully for you, John. Tight boy, John." Then, from halfway down the table, came the voice of a sceptic.

" Well," it said, " in me own experience I've known poteen do *quare* things; but never before this night did I hold it responsible for makin' a man the biggest liar at a wake. Is there no one else? Och, is there no one else? Can no one tell a sober lie for a change? "

John leant over the table towards the sceptic. " Young man," he said, " ye call me a liar, an' ye say I was drunk. Your years, an' the house we're in, 'll excuse ye this time; but never again, mind. An' if you, or any other person here, repeats such things, I'll take ye home an' prove me words by sittin' ye in the very chair th' ould boy sat in: an' I'll give ye the wiggin' I meant for him into the bargain."

# FRANK MATHEW
1865–1924

# THE REVEREND PETER FLANNERY

My friend the Reverend Peter Flannery is the sternest-looking and the gentlest of men. To look at him you would fancy he had spent a fierce life; but the truth is that he has lived in a wilderness and that in his broad parish of Moher there is not a mouse afraid of him.

I first met him in an hotel at Lisdoonvarna. One night there was singing, and a big, truculent old priest sang in his turn:

> When we went a-gipsying,
> A long time ago.

He was very serious and hoarse. With his grim face and white hair he looked the last man in the world to " go a-gipsying." Afterwards I came to know Peter, and spent many evenings with him in the little house where he lives with an old housekeeper of singular ugliness and a turbulent small boy known as Patrick Flannery. I found him absurdly simple, a man knowing nothing of the world and troubling himself little about anything beyond the borders of Moher; but though he is so unpretending he has deep respect for his dignity as a parish priest. On one of those evenings in his naked little parlour he told me the story of the only adventure of his life.

A small island with a ruined house on it lies near the shore of the most desolate part of the parish; at high tide it is ringed with white jumping waves, but at ebb it is set in a black rim of rocks. A miser was strangled there for his money by his daughter, seventy years ago, so the house is known for miles around as the " House of the Murder." Then it was a headland, but afterwards the encroaching sea cut it off from the coast. The Moher folk say the island is haunted by the ghost of an old man with a choked face and with purple foam on his lips, and is given up to the Evil Spirits.

One stormy winter's night, nearly twelve years ago now, Peter Flannery was riding back from visiting a dying woman near Liscan-

nor. It was raining, the wind was dead against him; he had seldom
been out on such a night though his life-work took him on many
a wild lonely ride. As he reached the Liscannor Cross-roads his
horse stopped, and a heart-broken voice came from under the trees.

" Remember the Dark Man! For God's sake remember the
Dark Man! " He knew that it was Andy Lonergan, the " Dark
Man "—that is, the blind man—who haunted that place day and
night.

" Is that yourself, Andy? " said he.

" 'Tis so, your reverence, but 'tis the black night to be abroad,
sure the Banshee is keenin' on th' island."

" The Banshee, is it? I know, I know, and manny's the time
I've heard that same, Andy. There's never a rough night without
her."

" Is it the wind ye mane, father? I know the wind's cry if
annyone, but 'twasn't only that on th' island to-night; 'twas a
woman's voice, sometimes 'twas like a child's. There'll be sore
hearts in Moher the morn."

" Ah well, Andy! manny's the queer thing ye've heard in your
time," said Peter, and he rode homewards, but Andy's words kept
in his head. Now, the blind man was half crazed, yet dared not
lie about the Banshee; perhaps there was some poor soul out on
the island. At last he turned his horse; as he rode back past the
Cross-roads he called out, " Are ye there, Andy? " but no answer
came. The horse seemed to have strong objections to going sea-
ward, and Peter himself had misgivings; he is a Clare man, the son
of a Ballyvaughan fisherman, and though of course he does not
believe in the Banshee, yet would rather not have gone where there
was any chance of meeting her. Then he thought—suppose Andy
was fooling him! He could fancy the blind man sitting hidden
and grinning at him as he rode back past the Cross-roads. It would
be a fine joke in Moher; he flushed at such irreverence.

Then he reached the shore, and dismounting fastened his horse
to a wall, and walked down across the slipping shingle, crunching
it under foot; he was tripped by tangles of seaweed, and stumbled
over a fishing coracle, could see scarcely a yard in front of him.
" 'Tis a blind man's holiday," he thought. " Faith, Dark Andy
could see as much as I can, and why couldn't McCaura leave his
coracle in a sensible place? " He went to the water's edge, the
foam splashed over him, he could see nothing but the white flashes
of breakers and was deafened by the noise. A few minutes of this
was enough; he turned back with a smile at the absurdity of his
going out there at that time of night. " There's no fool like an
old one," he said; then stopped to listen again, and in a pause
(when the wind seemed to be taking breath for a howl) heard a
child's cry from the island. How could a baby be on the island in
a hurricane, when there was not a soul for miles around would go

there for love or money at any time? His misgivings rushed back with uncanny legends of lost souls bound on the winds or imprisoned in the waves that always keep racing towards the land yet always break before reaching it. This might be some Devil's trap. True, he could exorcise the Devil, but would rather not.

He waited during the new howl of the wind—it seemed endless— then in the next pause heard the child's voice again; it was an unmistakably human squall. " 'Tis a child, sure enough," he said, " an' a strong one at that." The question for him was not how did the baby get on the island, but how was he to get it off? McCaura's cabin was a mile away across the bog, and on such a night no one would be out except Dark Andy, who would be worse than useless. The only thing was to go out to the island himself, so he groped his way to the coracle.

Now a coracle is a sort of punt, a shallow frame covered with tarpaulin, a ticklish craft, but it can live in the wildest sea, though as Peter said—" 'Tis always on the look-out for a chance to drown ye." He shouldered it as one to the manner born. Many a day and night had he spent afloat in the time when he was a fisher-boy; he thought how often since then he had longed to put out to sea, only his mighty dignity as a parish priest forbade it. His old bones were stiff, but he was as strong as ever.

Well, to cut a long story short, he launched that coracle and reached the island, not without risky and hard work. Dragging the coracle ashore, he made his way to the ruined house; the roof had fallen in, the windows were gone, only the walls were left. He could see nothing, but the child's cry guided him, and then in a corner he found a woman lying huddled on a heap of fallen plaster and laths; her face was to the wall, her left arm clutched a tiny baby. He knelt down by her and touched her forehead—she was dead. By her dress he knew she came from the Arran Islands. Perhaps she had been brought to the " House of the Murder " to keep the birth secret; or perhaps the fishers bringing her to the mainland had been caught by the gale, and could place her in no better shelter in the time of her trouble. Now the Arran folk were familiar to him, many were of his kindred; he must have known this woman from her babyhood, and as a slip of a girl running barefoot on the hills. He turned her face to him, but could only see it dimly; it was much changed too, and half hidden by wet hair. Then the thought came that he had no right to pry into her secret; he laid her head back reverently. She lay there with her face to the wall as if she had died in shame.

He took the baby and chafed it, wrapping his woollen comforter round it; he thought it was dying—his knowledge of babies was small—so he decided to baptize it at once. There was no lack of water, for the rain was still falling in torrents, so he filled a cup that was lying with some untasted food by the mother, and baptized

that whining infant as reverently and solemnly as if he had been
in a great cathedral.

It must have been a strange scene in the " House of the Murder "
—the gaunt old man dripping from the rain and the sea, holding
the baby tenderly and awkwardly, with the body of the mother
lying beside them.  He gave the baby the name Patrick, the first
that came to him, " *Pathricius, ego te baptizo*," and so forth in his
queer Latin brogue, and the small new Christian howled dismally,
and the gale answering howled outside.  Then he unbuttoned the
breast of his greatcoat and fastened the baby inside—so that only
its ridiculous red face could be seen—and started for home.  Crossing more easily this time, he found his old horse huddled in dumb
resignation under the lee of the wall, and rode home through the
storm at a good pace with a light heart.  Every now and then the
child cried to show that the life was in it, and then he tried to quiet
it tenderly with " Be hushed now, vick machree, son of my heart!
Ah! be sthill, Pathrick.  Be aisy, ye cantankerous little cur! "

There was great work that night in the little house, when the
old priest and his housekeeper welcomed their guest.  And when
the baby was cosily asleep, Peter got into his big arm-chair and
mixed himself a steaming tumbler of punch—for no man values
punch more, though of course in strict moderation—and he felt he
deserved it to-night.  " An' would ye believe it? " and at this
point of his story his voice shook with pathos—" would ye believe
it, at th' instant when I was putting it to me lips the clock sthruck
twelve, and so I couldn't taste a dhrop, not a single dhrop! "  For
if he had tasted it after midnight he could not have said Mass.
This was a lame ending to his one adventurous night.  The baby
was kept in the priest's house, and, when the gale went down, the
mother's body was brought from the island and buried; I think
Father Peter found afterwards who she was, though her name never
passed his lips.

For nearly twelve years " Pathrick " has ruled the priest's house,
thriving under the rough tenderness of Peter Flannery.  Meanwhile
Peter has led always the same life, rising in the early morning to
say Mass in the cold chapel before a scanty congregation of women;
many of them pray aloud with shut eyes and entire disregard of
their neighbours, and Patrick now serves him as clerk, looking
very serious in his little white surplice, like a Cupid in a monk's
cowl.

Then he rides on his sick-calls, miles and miles away through
the bogs and over the hills, for he goes at any hour of the day or
night to any one who chooses to summon him; or he walks down
to the school—where he usually finds Patrick standing in the corner
with his face to the wall, in disgrace—or he goes his rounds through
the Village of Moher.  Many a time have I seen him striding down
the Village " like an executioner," and the dirty little ragged

children running to meet him and snuggling their smeared faces against his long coat. The first time babies see him they yell as if he was the Devil; but the next time they would yell louder still if he forgot to fondle them. Many a time have I seen him standing in the street, beleaguered by a cluster of women, scowling nervously over them and looking to see if there is any chance of rescue; while they all talk at once, quarrelling among themselves:

" Ah! Peggy Lonergan, dacint woman, be whisht, can't ye? "

" Mary Ronan, I take shame o' ye to be throublin' the holy priest so. Won't ye be lettin' me have a single word wid him? "

And now in the evenings he has something to dream about, and when he sits alone by the fire in his naked parlour, smoking his old pipe—with his tumbler of punch smoking too, to keep him company—he dreams of the great future of Patrick Flannery. He sees that urchin grow up a model, go to Maynooth and win prizes there, rise rapidly in the Church, and even become a Bishop. It is true Pat will have to change greatly before them, for it is a queer Bishop he would make now; but time works wonders and Pat has a good heart.

Peter hears him preaching the great sermons himself has never preached to the great congregations he has never seen. And he thinks that " His Lordship Docthor Flannery " has a pleasing sound, that Bishop Flannery will be loved by all, that blessings will go with him; it is he that will have an eye for true worth and never let a plain man spend his life in a wilderness while smoother-tongued men have all they want. But at this point the dream breaks, for he knows in his heart that he would be sorry to leave his wilderness; so when the clock strikes nine he slowly finishes his punch, knocks out the ashes from his pipe and goes up the steep stairs to his bedroom, quavering in his hoarse voice,

When we went a-gipsying,
A long time ago.

# A CONNEMARA MIRACLE

## Frank Mathew

SOME said big John Murnane was the laziest man in Connemara, others called him a surly dog; but I always liked him. He had some excuse for his laziness and surliness. When I knew him first he was active enough. He used then to begin the day in the brightest of tempers, and if he had been let sit in peace and sunshine would have remained merry, but work undermined his cheerfulness.

128*

His farm lay high above Leenane at the head of the Killeries, a creek walled in by mountains, in the heart of the Irish Highlands.

Two roads wind down to the creek, one lower by Finigan's shebeen and one by Murnane's farm.  In those days I half envied him; he had a pretty little wife, a neat home, and three pigs, while I owned neither a pig nor a wife; he had no vain ambition and asked nothing better than to live and die at home in that wilderness.

But when I visited Connemara again, years later, things had changed with him; he had met with ill-luck, and had lost heart. A bank holding his little money had failed, his crops had failed too, his last pig had died; everything had gone badly with him. He spent half his time at the shebeen, and had a dangerous look. To make matters worse, he was to be turned out of his farm—had quarrelled with his landlord; for a true Galway-man always quarrels with the man best able to thrash him.  Murnane was full of fight, his mother used to say of him that he was never at rest except when he was fighting, and of course he knew that some one else must be responsible for his misfortunes, so he laid the blame at his landlord's door.

His landlord was my friend Shane Desmond, who in those days was always at war with his tenants.  Here I thought were the makings of a tragedy—a lawless district, an unruly peasantry, and a hated landlord.

Well, that summer my stay in Connemara was brief, and soon after I left, Murnane came to the turning-point of his life.  I have the story from his own lips.

In November, when the days grew short and the nights dark, there was a rumour in the shebeens near Leenane that some of " the boys " were coming from Desmond's estate in Clare, a fishing-boat would bring them from Liscannor to the Killeries and take them back without any one being the wiser, and their trip might mend matters.

One boisterous evening, Murnane was standing at his window watching his wife trudging heavily up the mountain road.  All day the wind had been hissing drearily through the mountains; now it was snarling and yelping like fighting dogs.  There was a veil of rain wavering on the grey crescent of sea.

He had spent hours that day at the shebeen.  As he watched his wife he thought in a muddled way how pretty she was when she was young though now she was a plain little woman; he thought of the time when he first caught her in his arms, down yonder where the Owen-Erriff runs by the Devil's Mother Mountain—" I love ye, Molly Joyce! tell me now, are ye listenin' to me, mavourneen dheelish!  I love ye! "—then of their life, of the careless years, of his losses and troubles, of the heavy evenings he spent smoking by the dull light of the turf fire alone with her in this cabin, then of the loud nights in the shebeen, and of the dreary times at home after. She seemed to get so silent and dull, he was tired of her worried face, sick of her frightened way of watching him.

Though he knew that she was a kind little woman, and that she loved him like a dog, he had grown hard and cold with her. Only that evening he had told her roughly to stop making a hare of herself, moping and poking about doing nothing, and to get out of that and to spend the night at her father's; and she, knowing the little use of speaking to him, had gone silently. He felt half sorry for his roughness as he watched her; after all she was a good soul and they had been happy together once. But now that he was to lose his last belongings why should he keep her? how could he when he couldn't? She must go back to her own folk who were well-to-do—for those parts—while he went out to try his luck in the world.

Then he walked up and down his cabin. It looked wretched; the turf fire on the hearth had smouldered, the whitewashed walls were blackened by smoke, they had little on them but a big crucifix, there was little furniture left. He remembered it bright and home-like; now it would be unroofed, he would be penniless and homeless unless Desmond was shot that night.

For the boat had come from Liscannor, and when Desmond drove back from Carrala, " the boys " were to wait for him on the lower road. If he came by the upper road, Murnane would see him, and was to put a light in his window; then they would change their ambush.

At the best, Murnane's thoughts were not clear. Now he kept thinking, over and over again, sure 'twas no harm lighting a candle, 'twas no business of his whatever the boys below might do; then, 'twas his chance of revenge, sure the man deserved to be killed; then, if only he was going to hit Desmond himself 'twould be different, but 'twas cowardly just lighting a candle; then, 'twas a black job after all.

Outside the twilight was fading; the wind was working itself into a rage with uncanny cries. Was that the wind or the shriek of the Banshee? It was said that lost souls were chained on the wind, surely there were human cries in it now: why were the dead abroad to-night?

The landscape was blotted out. Then the moon began to rise and the backs of the mountains rose out of the darkness. Then he saw their steep walls and the winding lane of slaty water between them.

There was a glimmer of silver over Muilrea; the moon floated into sight with milky-edged clouds round her; a path of light crossed the water, and three streams glittered on the Blue Gable Mountain. The moon seemed to shine out with strange suddenness; the jagged top of Muilrea stood black against her, making her look as if a ragged piece had been torn from her. He stared till the light dazzled him; then turned away.

The black crucifix on the wall opposite was shown plainly by the moonlight; the face of its figure was bent forward as if watching him. He had prayed before it so often all his life. It had seen him a baby in the cradle, a child dandled by his mother, a man bringing home his bride. Here in this cabin, this one room where his life had been centred, the crucifix hung as a silent witness. He thought of his misery; sure he had cause to hate the man. Still that sad face was watching him, he could not bear it, must take the crucifix down. Placing a bench under, he reached to the nail fastening the top and wrenched it out.

The moon was covered. The cross leant forward in the darkness. He turned his head away to shun the bent face; and groping, tugged out the nail at the foot. The cross seemed as heavy as lead, he dared not look at it; placing it in the corner—face downward—he covered it with a cloth.

Then he stood again at the window. The moon shone out, and the wind lurched drunkenly against the door, with an echo of singing from the shebeen, the chorus of " Crúiscin Lan " (The Little Full Jug):

> Is gradh mo croidhe a cuilin ban ban ban
> Is gradh mo croidhe a cuilin ban.

He could fancy the crowded smoky room, the glowing turf fire, and old Pat Finigan singing with a jolly flushed face; and those other men listening too, crouching behind the low wall.

There was a stain of rust on his right hand and he thought it was blood, rubbed it but it was dry, felt as if a curse had fallen on him. Then came a pause between the gusts, and he heard the ring of hoofs on the stony road. At once he turned back to light the candle, took it with a shaky hand: then on the wall where the cross had been, saw a dazzling white cross.

He staggered back with his eyes fixed on it: it was a miracle, a last warning. He dashed the candle on the ground, and crunched it under foot into the earthen floor.

The moon was drowned by the clouds and left the cabin pitch dark. The wind crashed against the door again. He unlatched the door, it was dashed open—he could not breathe—tried to pull it to after him but could not, some unseen hand seemed dragging it. The wind swirled through the cabin and flung the cloth from the prostrate crucifix.

The next morning was calm, with a stainless sky. Molly came trudging down the mountain road from her father's farm, her heart heavy with foreboding. All that night she had been crying and praying. The glory of the morning, the rare colouring of the mountains, the green crescent of sea, were nothing to her.

As she reached the door of the cabin she saw her man sitting by the hearth with his head bent forward on his hands. The crucifix was gone from its place. It had been fixed there when the walls had been shining with fresh whitewash, now they were blackened, but where it had hung the wall remained white in the shape of a cross.

" Is it you, asthore? " he said, came to meet her, put his hands on her shoulders, and drew her close to him.

" It's a hard world 'tis, mavourneen, but we'll bear God's will together, Molly dear."

# W. B. YEATS

B. 1865

# THE TWISTING OF THE ROPE

HANRAHAN was walking the roads one time near Kinvara at the fall of day, and he heard the sound of a fiddle from a house a little way off the roadside. He turned up the path to it, for he never had the habit of passing by any place where there was music or dancing or good company, without going in. The man of the house was standing at the door, and when Hanrahan came near he knew him and he said: " A welcome before you, Hanrahan, you have been lost to us this long time." But the woman of the house came to the door and she said to her husband: " I would be as well pleased for Hanrahan not to come in to-night, for he has no good name now among the priests, or with women that mind themselves, and I wouldn't wonder from his walk if he has a drop of drink taken." But the man said, " I will never turn away Hanrahan of the poets from my door," and with that he bade him enter.

There were a good many neighbours gathered in the house, and some of them remembered Hanrahan; but some of the little lads that were in the corners had only heard of him, and they stood up to have a view of him, and one of them said: " Is not that Hanrahan that had the school, and that was brought away by Them? " But his mother put her hand over his mouth and bade him be quiet, and not be saying things like that. " For Hanrahan is apt to grow wicked," she said, " if he hears talk of that story, or if any one goes questioning him." One or another called out then, asking him for a song, but the man of the house said it was no time to ask him for a song, before he had rested himself; and he gave him whiskey in a glass, and Hanrahan thanked him and wished him good health and drank it off.

The fiddler was tuning his fiddle for another dance, and the man of the house said to the young men, they would all know what dancing was like when they saw Hanrahan dance, for the like of it had never been seen since he was there before. Hanrahan said he would not dance, he had better use for his feet now, travelling as he was through the five provinces of Ireland. Just as he said that, there came in at the half-door Oona, the daughter of the house, having a few bits of bog deal from Connemara in her arms for the fire. She threw them on the hearth and the flame rose up, and showed her to be very comely and smiling, and two or three of the young men rose up and asked for a dance. But Hanrahan crossed the floor and brushed the others away, and said it was with him she must dance, after the long road he had travelled before he came to her. And it is likely he said some soft word in her ear, for she said nothing against it, and stood out with him, and there were little blushes in her cheeks. Then other couples stood up, but when the dance was going to begin, Hanrahan chanced to look down, and he took notice of his boots that were worn and broken, and the ragged grey socks showing through them; and he said angrily it was a bad floor, and the music no great things, and he sat down in the dark place beside the hearth. But if he did, the girl sat down there with him.

The dancing went on, and when that dance was over another was called for, and no one took much notice of Oona and Red Hanrahan for a while, in the corner where they were. But the mother grew to be uneasy, and she called to Oona to come and help her to set the table in the inner room. But Oona, that had never refused her before, said she would come soon, but not yet, for she was listening to whatever he was saying in her ear. The mother grew yet more uneasy then, and she would come nearer them, and let on to be stirring the fire or sweeping the hearth, and she would listen for a minute to hear what the poet was saying to her child. And one time she heard him telling about white-handed Deirdre, and how she brought the sons of Usnach to their death; and how the blush in her cheeks was not so red as the blood of kings' sons that was shed for her, and her sorrows had never gone out of mind; and he said it was maybe the memory of her that made the cry of the plover on the bog as sorrowful in the ear of the poets as the keening of young men for a comrade. And there would never have been that memory of her, he said, if it was not for the poets that had put her beauty in their songs. And the next time she did not well understand what he was saying, but as far as she could hear it had the sound of poetry though it was not rhymed, and this is what she heard him say: " The sun and the moon are the man and the girl, they are my life and your life, they are travelling and ever travelling through the skies as if under the one hood. It was God made them for one another. He made your life and my life before the beginning of the world, he made them that they might go through the world, up and down, like the two best dancers that go on with the dance up and down the long floor of the barn, fresh and laughing, when all the rest are tired out and leaning against the wall."

The old woman went then to where her husband was playing cards, but he would take no notice of her, and then she went to a

woman of the neighbours and said: " Is there no way we can get
them from one another? " and without waiting for an answer she
said to some young men that were talking together: " What good
are you when you cannot make the best girl in the house come out
and dance with you? And go now the whole of you," she said,
" and see can you bring her away from the poet's talk." But
Oona would not listen to any of them, but only moved her hand
as if to send them away. Then they called to Hanrahan and said
he had best dance with the girl himself or let her dance with one
of them. When Hanrahan heard what they were saying he said:
" That is so, I will dance with her; there is no man in the house
must dance with her but myself."

He stood up with her then, and led her out by the hand, and
some of the young men were vexed, and some began mocking at
his ragged coat and his broken boots. But he took no notice, and
Oona took no notice, but they looked at one another as if all the
world belonged to themselves alone. But another couple that had
been sitting together like lovers stood out on the floor at the same
time, holding one another's hands and moving their feet to keep
time with the music. But Hanrahan turned his back on them as if
angry, and in place of dancing he began to sing, and as he sang
he held her hand, and his voice grew louder, and the mocking of
the young men stopped, and the fiddle stopped, and there was
nothing heard but his voice that had in it the sound of the wind.
And what he sang was a song he had heard or had made one time
in his wanderings on Slieve Echtge, and the words of it as they
can be put into English were like this:

> O Death's old bony finger
> Will never find us there
> In the high hollow townland
> Where love's to give and to spare;
> Where boughs have fruit and blossom
> At all times of the year;
> Where rivers are running over
> With red beer and brown beer.
> An old man plays the bagpipes
> In a gold and silver wood;
> Queens, their eyes blue like the ice,
> Are dancing in a crowd.

And while he was singing it Oona moved nearer to him, and the
colour had gone from her cheek, and her eyes were not blue now,
but grey with the tears that were in them, and any one that saw
her would have thought she was ready to follow him there and
then from the west to the east of the world.

But one of the young men called out: " Where is that country
he is singing about? Mind yourself, Oona, it is a long way off,
you might be a long time on the road before you would reach to
it." And another said: " It is not to the Country of the Young

you will be going if you go with him, but to Mayo of the bogs."
Oona looked at him then as if she would question him, but he
raised her head in his hand, and called out between singing and
shouting: " It is very near us that country is, it is on every side;
it may be on the bare hill behind it is, or it may be in the heart
of the wood." And he said out very loud and clear: " In the
heart of the wood; oh, death will never find us in the heart of the
wood. And will you come with me there, Oona? " he said.

But while he was saying this the two old women had gone outside
the door, and Oona's mother was crying, and she said: " He has
put an enchantment on Oona. Can we not get the men to put him
out of the house? "

" That is a thing you cannot do," said the other woman, " for
he is a poet of the Gael, and you know well if you would put a poet
of the Gael out of the house, he would put a curse on you that
would wither the corn in the fields and dry up the milk of the cows,
if it had to hang in the air seven years."

" God help us," said the mother, " and why did I ever let him
into the house at all, and the wild name he has! "

" It would have been no harm at all to have kept him outside,
but there would great harm come upon you if you put him out by
force. But listen to the plan I have to get him out of the house by
his own doing, without any one putting him from it at all."

It was not long after that the two women came in again, each of
them having a bundle of hay in her apron. Hanrahan was not
singing now, but he was talking to Oona very fast and soft, and
he was saying: " The house is narrow but the world is wide, and
there is no true lover that need be afraid of night or morning or
sun or stars or shadows of evening, or any earthly thing." " Hanrahan," said the mother then, striking him on the shoulder, " will
you give me a hand here for a minute? " " Do that, Hanrahan,"
said the woman of the neighbours, " and help us to make this hay
into a rope, for you are ready with your hands, and a blast of
wind has loosened the thatch on the haystack."

" I will do that for you," said he, and he took the little stick in
his hands, and the mother began giving out the hay, and he twisting
it, but he was hurrying to have done with it, and to be free again.
The women went on talking and giving out the hay, and encouraging him, and saying what a good twister of a rope he was, better
than their own neighbours or than any one they had ever seen.
And Hanrahan saw that Oona was watching him, and he began to
twist very quick and with his head high, and to boast of the readiness of his hands, and the learning he had in his head, and the
strength in his arms. And as he was boasting, he went backward,
twisting the rope always till he came to the door that was open
behind him, and without thinking he passed the threshold and was
out on the road. And no sooner was he there than the mother

made a sudden rush, and threw out the rope after him, and she shut the door and the half-door and put a bolt upon them.

She was well pleased when she had done that, and laughed out loud, and the neighbours laughed and praised her. But they heard him beating at the door, and saying words of cursing outside it, and the mother had but time to stop Oona that had her hand upon the bolt to open it. She made a sign to the fiddler then, and he began a reel, and one of the young men asked no leave but caught hold of Oona and brought her into the thick of the dance. And when it was over and the fiddle had stopped, there was no sound at all of anything outside, but the road was as quiet as before.

As to Hanrahan, when he knew he was shut out and that there was neither shelter nor drink nor a girl's ear for him that night, the anger and the courage went out of him, and he went on to where the waves were beating on the strand.

He sat down on a big stone, and he began swinging his right arm and singing slowly to himself, the way he did always to hearten himself when every other thing failed him. And whether it was that time or another time he made the song that is called to this day " The Twisting of the Rope," and that begins, " What was the dead cat that put me in this place," is not known.

But after he had been singing a while, mist and shadows seemed to gather about him, sometimes coming out of the sea, and sometimes moving upon it. It seemed to him that one of the shadows was the queen-woman he had seen in her sleep at Slieve Echtge; not in her sleep now, but mocking, and calling out to them that were behind her: " He was weak, he was weak, he had no courage." And he felt the strands of the rope in his hand yet, and went on twisting it, but it seemed to him as he twisted that it had all the sorrows of the world in it. And then it seemed to him as if the rope had changed in his dream into a great water-worm that came out of the sea, and that twisted itself about him, and held him closer and closer, and grew from big to bigger till the whole of the earth and skies were wound up in it, and the stars themselves were but the shining of the ridges of its skin. And then he got free of it, and went on, shaking and unsteady, along the edge of the strand, and the grey shapes were flying here and there around him. And this is what they were saying, " It is a pity for him that refuses the call of the daughters of the Sidhe, for he will find no comfort in the love of the women of the earth to the end of life and time, and the cold of the grave is in his heart for ever. It is death he has chosen; let him die, let him die, let him die."

# AGNES CASTLE

D. 1922

# ROSANNA

SITTING by the fire we were, smoking our bits of pipes, just him and me together, when, of a sudden, he turns on me an' he says: "Da," he says, "it's about time I was thinking of taking a wife," says he.

"An' is that the way wid ye? " I says. "Troth, an' I'm thinking as much meself this long time. Sure it's scandalising discomfirture we're living in," I says, "ever since poor auld Maria went and died on us,—the Lord be merciful to her soul! Your poor mother,—the Lord be merciful to her!—she'd be like to tear the eyes out of them sluts of girls this minute,—the blessed saint in Heaven, that she is! Thrue for ye, me boy, it's a wife we want, and who'd be the wan to look out but yourself, since it's the auld fellow I'm getting, entirely. And who'll it be? " says I, that innicent, niver suspecting he'd be so undutiful as to be making his choice unbeknownst to me—let alone that same grand choice! "Who'll be it? " I axes him. "What would ye say to Miss Condren at the Cross Roads? It's thrue she's a long nose of her own; but what's that? She's the rale auld family."

"What 'ud I say to Miss Condren? " cries he. "It's making game o' me ye are, I think. What 'ud I say to Judy Condren? " says he, grinning at me wid all his white teeth an' thim clinched over his pipe. "Sure, if I saw that long nose of hers poking about here—' Take your snipe's beak out of this house,' that's what I'd say to her."

"Then it's one of them thriftless Roches ye've got in your mind," says I; "not but what auld Roche is a dacent feller, an' the girls has fine figures of their own, I'm not denying. But it's not much fortune they'd be bringing a boy."

"Is it I," he cried, " 'd take up wid one of them? Bedad, I'm surprised at ye for mintioning them at all! What would I be doing with such flithereens, streeling about wid their ribbins an' their feathers an' the impident airs of them? "

"Then it'll be Mary Cassidy, I'll be bound," says I.

"No such thing," says he; "she's been walking wid Jim Nolan this month past."

"Will it be Miss O'Donnell? " says I.

"It will not," says he; "I'd rather go single all me days."

"Well, in the name of God," says I, "who is it to be, thin? May be it's a town-girl ye're set on after all. There's Miss Hinnegan at the hotel,—it's not the family connection I'd choose for ye, Johnny, the O'Moores have never wedded wid trade yet—but they do be sayin' it's rolling in gold she'll be when auld Hinnegan dies. She'll not say no to ye, Johnny. Troth, and I was noticing them were quare looks she was giving ye last Saturday after the pig-fair."

"An' what sort of looks would ye have her give anny wan wid them crass eyes of hers," says me young man, an' he takes his pipe out of his mouth an' bursts out laughing. "Sure, God help her, she can't look one way widout lookin' the other. She'd be the right sort to put things straight for us."

At that I bid him lave off his moidering thricks, for I knew it was humbugging me, he was, an' not a bit of marrying on him. An' he never answered me back a word, but was spacheless, playing a chune on the stem of his pipe wid his fingers, an' puffing at it, an' it black out. An' thin he says: "It's not money we want wid a wife; ye're a warm man, father—an' it's not beholden to a slip of a girl we'd be—you an' me."

"It's aisy talking that-a-way," says I, "but it 'ud be no use at all, at all, for a fine young feller like yourself to go taking up wid a body that hadn't enough to keep herself. It 'ud not be respectable," says I, "not what your father's son was rared up to."

"An' as for family," says he, kind of dreamy, as if he had not heard me, "isn't it the rale auld stock we are ourselves? O'Moores of Moorestown, discindints of Rory O'Moore,—king's blood," says he, "an' what's Roches, an' Condrens, an' O'Donnells to that? It's no sort of use to try and ally ourselves wid thim as'll match us," says he; "an' why? Because they're not to be found—that's why. We'll mate to plaze ourselves," he says, as bould as brass; "an' what we want is a little young crathur wid a heart full of love; a little weeshy, dawshy, coaxing bit of a thing wid eyes the colour of violets, that would swally ye'r heart alive and niver let it out again; an' a head full of curls that would drive a boy wild just to look at! "

"What sort of blasphemious talk is that out of ye? " cries I, interrupting him. "It's meself ye'll have wild in a minute or two," for I didn't fancy the looks of him, wid his head on one side an' a kind of silly smile on him. "What in the whole wide worrld's upon ye? " says I. "Spake out, man, or I'll drag the tongue out of yer jaws an' make you tell the thrut that-a-way."

He turns upon me wid his hands on his knees, an' his face the colour of the peeonies in the garden beyant. "Da," he says, an' rasps his throat; "Father," he says an' thin out he bursts. "You've no right," he says, "to be casting up at her thim rogues

and vagabonds of parints of hers! Shure her mother isn't her
mother at all, on'y her stepmother; an' as for her father—bad
scran to him—he's the greatest bla'guard between this and Dublin. However, it's not fair," says he, " to be goin' on this way,
for sure it's niver themselves they are, at all, but blind drunk every
day of the week, an' Sundays into the bargain. But as for herself,
it's the purty little crathur she is, like an angel from heaven, her
that's niver seen nothing but hell's wickedness since the day she
was born. She doesn't rightly know how to set about anything yit,
an' if she is a Protestant it's on'y because she know no betther.
She learnt no wickedness off anny of thim, an' troth it's a Catholic
she'll be the minute she's told how."

" Tare an' ages," says I, " ye murthering villain, hold yer
tongue! Hold yer tongue, you spawn of hell, an' tell me the name
of her widout another word! "

He was white now from red he was before, but his impidence
was beyond everything. " It's Rosanna Moriarty," he says.

Well, I let a screech—I have a quick kind of temper, not a bad
one, mind ye, but hasty-like. My poor mother—God be merciful
to her!—manny's the time she'd tell us of the day I nearly mur-
thered her wid the pitaty knife, an' I but seven years of age; an'
the day I had me little sisther—God be merciful to her, that's poor
auld Maria, I mean—strangled wid her apron-strings for letting me
little pet rabbits run away. Blue in the face she was, an' I pulling
at the strings as hard as I could! We used to be kilt wid the
laughing, talking of it. But I was always the rale good Catholic,
an' sure me blood was up entirely. I was like to kill him dead
that minute, break his head open on him, an' small blame to me.
But I controlled meself. Wid a moighty effort I kep' calm.
" Johnny O'Moore," I says, " ye black, onfilial, heathen scrawn
of a bla'guard scamp, mintion that name in my hearing again an'
I'll have yer life, as sure as you stand there."

Wid that he says no more, an' I says no more, nor was the
subject as much as remarked upon between us till the next time
he had impidence enough to dare, an' that was the very week
after.

What did that owdacious rogue of a Moriarty go for to do, but die
on us all of a suddent in the Delirious Trimmings, as the Docthur
called it—a real roaring fit of drunkenness—an' his limb of a wife,
she takes to her heels an' off wid her out of the place, sorra a one
knew where, an' the little schemer of a Rosanna left behind on our
hands together wid the corpse an' a power of debts.

It was auld Jim Roche first gave us the news; an' says he:
" It's rale bad Rosanna is, the crathur! Sure they can't get her
away from the poor fella' at all, an' neither bite nor sup has crossed
her lips this blessed day. It 'ud break your heart to see her, with
them purty red curls of hers hanging every way, and them big black

eyes of hers swollen up wid the crying. An' him the bitther bad father!"

An' then I see me fine young man start up from his corner an' off wid him widout a word.

Sure I knew the way it 'ud be. Some one would be offering to take in the girl out of charity, an' me fella' would have to be keeping up them sperrits of hers an' consoling of her an' wiping away all them tears—him as cute as a pet fox from the day he was weaned! But there's two on us can be cute, thinks I, an' out of the place she goes, or my name's not Larry O'Moore. There's the workhouse for her, an' the likes of her, beyant in the town. She'll be fed, an' warmed, an' clothed dacenter there than ever she's been in her life, an' my money helping to do it into the bargain. But I'll not have her left here to be bringing disgrace into my family. So I just says a word to Jim Roche, an' then I took a bit of a stroll, an' wint here and there, an' dropt into this wan an' that, an' be jabers I gave them all the hint. There isn't wan but 'ud be afeard to fall out wid me for they, most of them, owes me a bit an' I've been a good friend to them in the bad times. An', to tell the thrut, I'm plisanter as a friend than as an enemy.

Av course not a boy of them let on he understood what I was dhriving at: they wouldn't be that onpolite, an' I wouldn't have misdemeaned meself by speaking too plain. But, lonnies, it's aisy to say a good deal when you're saying nothin' at all, and when I came home, sure, I knew I had settled the young gintleman's nonsense for him, for as grand as he thought himself.

The auld cuckoo-clock had gone twelve (an' it's twenty minutes late regular) before Johnny came back that night. A rale warm spring night it was, black and moist, an' all his curls were plastered down his cheeks wid the way he'd been stravaguing round.

I was sitting waiting for him, smoking me pipe wid a peaceful soul, for it was a good stroke of work I had done the day, an' so I kep' telling meself, when in he bursts like a wild fella.

"Father," says he, "I've tauld ye I wanted to marry Rosanna Moriarty; an' I mean to marry her," he says.

"Och, listen to him," says I, scornful; "sure it's wandering in his speech, he is!"

"Father," he says, rale earnest and eager, "I've always been a good son to you. I've never been drunk nor contradictious, an' when other young men would have gone off an' seen the world, I've kep' at home an' worked an' helped you. In the name of God," says he, pitiful-like, "do not drive me to be undutiful now! Oh, father, it is a poor little innocent thing she is, an' it's alone and desolate she is, an' by Heaven," he cries, "this is a hard cruel worrld! There's not one of them 'll give her a shelter or a crust this blessed night; an' on'y for auld Kitty who's sittin' and wakin' the corpse, the poor crathur 'ud be alone wid the dead this minute—enough to drive her distracted entirely! But give your consent to our wedding," he cries, " an' then it's who'll have her, I'll be bound. The cauld-hearted scoundrels as could shut their doors on her that way—why, it's fighting for her they'll be then! But I'll be even wid them yet, the whole lot of them, whatever black curse of cruelty has come over them, at all, at all."

I was puffing away at my pipe, an' for the life of me I could not but give an agreeable smile to meself, thinking it was the rale proper kind of respect I was held in all over the place; not but that I knew there was not one of them as 'ud dare to go agin me.

When he sees me smile, he stops suddent and gives me a quare look. " Father," says he, " I see what you have been after. God forgive you," he says, " but it's a wicked man you are."

" Whisht, now, don't be goin' on," says I; " you will live to thank me yet."

" An' what is to become of that poor young crathur? " says he, quite quiet; " have ye thought of that? She cannot live alone in that auld tumble-down place, an' her that purty an' little, an' black Mac (divel take him!) wid his eye on her this many a day. What is to become of her, father? "

" Let her go to the workhouse," says I; " she need not fear black Mac there, for they keep them away from each other fast enough, the young boys an' the young girls too. They will be coming, no doubt, to bury the father from the Union to-morrow; let them take the daughter too; it's the right place for her."

Wid that, he lets the awfullest oath ever ye heard. " She'll not go there," he says, " so long as I'm alive."

" May I ax what you intend to do, then? " says I, very polite.

" I have tauld you already," says he; " I intend to marry her."

" An' may I inquire what yez are going to live on then? For I warn ye fair," says I, in a white rage—for I seen by the obstinate look of him that he was set on his wickedness—" I warn ye," says I, " that across this thrashle ye will niver step once ye take up wid that Protestant slut of Moriarty's; nor a penny of me money ye will never see, neither now nor when I am gone."

" Is that your last word? " says he, an' stands up.

" It's me last word," says I, " as I'm a living man."

" Then, good-bye, father," says he.

" Good-bye," says I, " an' me curse upon you," says I. " My father's curse on the two of yez! "

Well, out he stamps widout as much as another word, an' I sits by the fire thinking it's home again he'll be before I can turn round. Sure an' I never thought he'd have thrown me over that-a-way, an' him an' me always together from the time he was a babby. But the turf itself burnt white under my eyes, an' the dawn broke that cauld an' desolate into the room, but sorra a bit of him come back to me. An' for three days I heard no news

of him, an' sure I was that dark an' down in meself not wan dared
to speak to me. The fellers was afraid to tell me the thrut, an' to
be plain wid ye, I was not, so to say, encouraging to conversation. Bedad, I would not let them think I cared a halfpenny what
that scoundrel of a boy was up to, when he chose to go against his
father that rate.

He niver came home to me, an' I axed no questions of nobody.
But on the Thursday it was, Mrs. Malony (his Rivirence's housekeeper, a contrary fidget of an auld woman she is) stops me just as
I was passing the door. " Oh, Mr. O'Moore," she cries, in that
mincing way of hers, " what is this I hear about Johnny? " she
says. " Father O'Hara will be fit to be tied," she says, " when
he comes back from visiting His Holiness at Rome."

" What may ye have heard, ma'am? " says I. " For it's little I
know or want to know about him."

" Oh," she says, throwing up her eyes like an auld hen in a fit,
" oh, Mr. O'Moore, sir, do not ax me; I couldn't defile my tongue
by speaking of it."

" Well, an' that happens to come right," says I, " for I don't
want to hear. Though if you can reconcile it to your conscience to
be keeping the thrut from his own father, it is surprised at ye I am,
Mrs. Malony, an' that's all I have got to say."

Sure, it was just itching the auld girl was to tell me the bad
news. " Is it possible you don't know, Mr. O'Moore? " she says.
" Oh dear, how can I bring meself to discourse of such a scandal!
It is the real saint we all thought Mr. Johnny, an' him so good in
the choir, an' so regular at the Stations. Och, the shame of it! "
she says. " Father O'Hara will be leppin' mad, he will! But
there's little shame about either of them," she says, " going about
that brazen, an' buying things together—set up house they have
as bold as man an' wife—the like was niver seen hereabouts before.
Set up house in that ruinacious auld cabin of Moriarty's, an' him
not a week dead yet. And she, the dirthy Protestant. Now if
she'd been a Catholic itself—Och, it's a terrible visitation to the
place, an' the remarks of the folks, an' the illusions, an' the jokes,—
it's shocking altogether! Could not ye speak to your son, now? "

" Mrs. Malony," says I, an' I niver turned a hair, " he is no
longer anny son of mine, an' I will thank ye to remember it. I
have cast him off," I says; " he is no O'Moore, at all, at all, to be
bringing disgrace upon the name of them that has been kings in
the land. An' as for that other," says I, " I'm wondering how
ye have the face to mintion her to me! " Wid that I made her an
iligant bow an' left her.

Well, that was the cruel, hard time for me. And, as if they'd
given each other the word, sure every one in the place had something to say to me about them, wonst it was out that I knew their
goings on. This boy told me wan thing, an' that boy would tell

another, till it is distracted I was. An' sure did not one up to me an' says he: " Ye'd better let them be married off at worst," says he, " an' save the shame of it." I struck him prostrate for that same, for as auld as I am. " I will let them go to hell together," says I.

If only Father O'Hara had been back home, but it's visiting His Holiness in Rome he was, an' not expected for another week.

Sunday was the rale disgraceful day. On my entry into the chapel, before I could as much as kneel down, I hears a kind of stir in the place behind me, an' I sees all them rows of Roche girls nudging each other and tossing their heads. An' there was a kind of titter among the boys, an' auld Biddy Flannagan, the crathur, who always kneels in the middle just before the rails, where she can have a good view of his Rivirence an' plenty of room to be rocking herself about, looks over her shoulder, an' snorts like an auld say-pig, an' rolls her eyes that wild-like I thought she was struck wid an apple-complex. An' then what should I see but my young gentleman marching up the chapel, an' Miss Moriarty, if ye plaze, alongside of him in a bran new black gown, an' a white sun-bonnet—he looking neither to right nor left, an' she watching him with them saucer eyes, that had done all the mischief. An' when he salutes the altar, she gives a little dip beside him, the heathen! He kneels down at the end of the bench an' she inside. An' in a minute or two out comes little Father Jo, the curate from town beyant, who says Mass of a Sunday when Father O'Hara is away; an' glad I was to see him, for the cheeks was burning off of me. When he done the Gospel, an' he had off wid his vestment, an' come to the altar-steps to read out the notices an' every one was quiet listening to what he was going to say, if the first things he lets out is not the banns of marriage between John O'Connell O'Moore of Moorestown in this parish an' Rosanna Moriarty of Mount Pleasant in the same! Begorrah, the whole place was swimming round wid me. Spacheless I was, an' all I could do was just to look at them, thinking it 'ud be a wonder if the auld flags would not open and swalley them up.

Himself was sitting like a lamb, niver stirring hand nor foot, his eyes fixed rale pious on the alther, as if butther would not melt in his mouth. An' she, wid her sun-bonnet tumbled off them red curls of hers, as rosy over the impident face of her as ye plaze, wid a kind of dimple coming an' going on one side of her cheek that was just bursting wid smiles as anny one could see. At the sight of them I don't know what came over me, bit I gives a kind of bawl, and ups on me feet. " Your Rivirence," says I, " I forbid them banns."

An' Father Jo, who was rambling on quite aisy, stops as if he had been shot. " What's that? " says he, very sharp—you could have heard a pin drop. But my blood was up, an' the whole place looking at me. " I forbid them banns," I says; " an' if your Rivirence wants to know about the impidiment, sure there she is, an' sorra a bit of spiritual relation either, but a real Orange heretic, an' not a bit of shame on her, the dirthy streel, shamming prayer beside the poor boy she has deluded entirely—an' her breaking all the Commandments this minute. She'll not wed him, I'll have her know it."

" This is very onseemly," says Father Jo, as pink as a babby to the roots of his hair; " I cannot have this disturbance in the chapel," he says.

" But your Rivirence," says I, " didn't ye give it out this minute? ' If any one is aware,' says you, and sure——"

" Whisht! " says he; " this is scandalising behaviour."

" An' it is that same, yer Rivirence," says I, " but that's no fault of mine."

" Sit down," says he; " I'll see ye after Mass in the vestry."

An' Johnny niver a word out of him, but sitting there like a statue. I sees her crudle up to him like a child, an' now an' agin she shoots a look at me out of her eyes that was swalleying up her face—too big was they entirely. And what wid one thing an' another, I felt that mad, that it's not a prayer I said that day.

Well, I gives Father Jo a bit o' me mind in the vestry; but not a ha'-porth of good could I get out of him. " Ye must speak to Father O'Hara," says he, " for I cannot interfere."

An' when I got out of the chapel, och, to hear them all talking! " What's the meaning of her coming to chapel wid him, and her a Protestant? " says one. " Why it's converting her he is," says another, and wid that they were all fit to die wid laughing. An' didn't that scrawn of hell, black Mac, catch up the pair of them on the road, an' out with some of his impidence, an' did not Johnny an' he have the grandest set-to that ever was seen in these parts, an' did not Johnny give him such a pair of black eyes that the folks do be talking about it still? The finest shindy ever they saw, they tell me : but sure, I could not be taking pleasure out of anything wid the shame of the world upon me.

Well, on Tuesday evening, as I was sitting down to me bit of a supper, on the stroke of ten o'clock, who should come tearing in upon me but Father O'Hara himself. It is the holy show he was with the grime an' the smuts of the railway on the pale face of him, an' his long white hair hanging wild-like over his eyes. " What is this I hear," he says, widout as much as reaching me his hand, " what is this I hear about Johnny? " I was right glad to tell him the story, but when I had finished I thought he was going to murther me entirely. Rale wicked, he was, an' I as innercent as the babe unborn.

" You onnatural man," says he, " an' can ye sit there and tell me in cold blood that you have drove these unfort'nit children into sin? Och, God help us all," he cries, " that I should have come home to this! I have been among yez forty years come Christmas an' I have had the grief of the world over yez all, God knows," he says. " An' manny an' manny a time I have seen yez break our Divine Master's holy commandments; manny a time, my poor flock, I have had to weep over yez and for yez. I have seen yez fighting, an' injuring, an' cheating each other, an' seen yez in jail an' in throuble, an' known in me sorrowful soul that the sentence of the law was just. When we had that terrible murther here," he went on, " 'tis fifteen year ago now, on'y for the grace of God an' His powerful consolation an' the sight of the poor sinner's beautiful penitence, sure I must have died of the agony in me heart, for it is the heart of a father I have to yez all. But niver," he says, " niver before in all the days I have been among yez have anny of my children fell into such sin as this. An' to think it should be the child of me predelection, little Johnny," he cries, his voice breaking wid the sorrow, " him that was my pride an' my joy, him that your sainted wife, Laurence O'Moore, laid in me arms wid her last dying effort! Oh, man," he goes on, turning on me again, " I hold you responsible before the throne of God for all the guilt that lies on the souls of that poor boy an' girl to-night."

An' not bit of reason wud he hear from me. Priests an' women is that-a-way where the young folks is concerned: they do be forgetting the Fourth Commandment altogether. I could not pacify him at all, at all. " Come wid me," he says, " come this minute, an' let us seek these childer. Not another night will I consent to let them stray without the Fold. Come, Laurence," he says, " in the name of your God, I command you; come and repair in so far as His mercy will permit the cruel wrong you have done! "

Nothing would serve him but I must set out wid him into the night beyant that very instant. An' on'y that I was afeared for his sake, on account of the state he was in, an' him such an auld man an' so frail, sure I had niver have demeaned meself by going a step.

But out he runs me, an' down the lane, an' across the village— thanks to goodness there was none about—an' up the bit of bog to the shanty, where Johnny had set up wid his light-of-love. The moon burst out of the clouds; there was a soft wind blowing round us, an' his Rivirence's face shone as pale as death wid all the white locks round it, an' him skimming along like a hare, so that I was hard set to keep up wid him. Well, we soon come in sight of Mount Pleasant. There it stood in the moonlight, wid the thatch falling off the roof, an' the mud of the walls crumbling away, the miserablest, most God-forsaken hole of a place I ever see. An' as I thought of my on'y son disgracing himself by coming down to such a residence, I could not help it, but I let a curse on the pair of them.

His Rivirence whisks round an' lifts his hand, an' then he clutches
me with one hand by the arm, an' points wid the other. " See
yonder! " he says, wid a kind of strangled whisper. " See yonder,
you sinful man! " An' he pointed to a black heap lying in the
shade of the hovel across the door; an' then he motioned me back,
so stern I durst not disobey him, an' himself went forward up to it.

" Johnny, my poor child," he says—his voice was like a cooing
dove's—" Johnny, my poor child, what are ye lying out there
for? "

An' Johnny, for Johnny it was, sleeping like a tramp on the bare
turf, he up like a shot, an' rubbed his eyes, an' stared at Father
O'Hara like wan daft. " Oh, your Rivirence," says he, reproach-
ful like, " sure you would not have me lying widin wid the poor
little girl, an' the holy words not spoken over us yet! " An' his
Rivirence he beat his hands together, and fell upon the fella's neck
and sobbed aloud. " I thank God," he cries, " I thank God! "

" Father O'Hara, is it you? " cries Johnny, that surprised and
as if he had just waked out of a dream. " Oh, father, we have
wanted ye sore, an' it's the cruel time we have had! An' it's the
cruel things that people have said of us, an' she as innicent as the
flowers of the field. Sure she does not know what they do be
meaning. My heart's been fit to break," he says.

An' then his Rivirence let a shout for me. " Come here," he
says, " Laurence O'Moore, an' bless your good son, an' give praise
to the Father above that kep' him and his bride from sin, when his
earthly father would have driven them into it. Come here an' tell
him that ye have seen the hardness of your heart, an' repented.
Tell him that he an' the good little girl he has chosen for his wife
will be welcome to your hearth. An' in the meantime," he says,
" Rosanna shall come to my house; an' Johnny, me boy, it's meself will give the wedding-feast." An' after that what could I do?

# SEUMAS MACMANUS

B. 1868

# THE BEWITCHED FIDDLE

FAIX, it's a good long wheen of years since it happened now. It was ould Jimmy Higgerty, that was uncle to Mickey acrass there, reharsed the passage to me. An' it was ould Jimmy himself, more betoken, that was the cause of the whole affair—for Jimmy, ye know, was what we call a canny man, very knowin' intirely, an' up to all sorts of saicrets that you nor me nor one belonging to us, thanks be to Providence, knows nothin' at all, at all about. Jimmy was right-han' man with the fairies; an' if ye'd believe all the stories ye hear goin' he come through some quare things, too, in his day —used to be out, they say, as reg'lar as the sun set, an' away ridin' aist an' waist with the good people, an' gettin' insight into their ways of workin'; an' sure it's meself that rec'le'ts if there was only a bit of a year-oul' calve sick from one end of the barony to the other, it was nothin' but post haste for Jimmy Higgerty to cure it— an', sure enough, when Jimmy put the charm on it, it either lived or died afther; there was no middle coorse.

Well, howsomiver, in Jimmy's day there was in Doorin a one Solomon Casshidy; an' the same Solomon in his young days was a thrifle wild—the fact is (to kill the hare at a blow), Solomon was the completest rascal ivir run on two feet, an' was a parable for the counthry. Christenin', weddin', wake, funeral, patthern, fair, or market nivir wint off complete without Solomon Casshidy; dance, raffle, or spree of any sort, shape, or patthern nivir missed Solomon Casshidy, who, by the way, was the very life an' sowl of the gatherin's; an' people would as soon think of doin' without the fiddler at one of these merry-makin's as without Solomon Casshidy. An' that just put me in mind that Solomon was the dandy hand at the fiddle; the bate of him wasn't to be got between cock-crow an' candlelight the longest day in June. He would charm the heart of a whin-bush; arrah, good luck to your wit, man, he'd actially make the fiddle spake! They say it was as good as a sarcus to hear how he'd handle it.

But poor Solomon, good luck to him, soon came to the end of his tether, an', afther takin' all the fun he could out of the worl', he, as himself said, turned over a new laif an' begun to look at the other side of the picther. An' I'm thinkin' whatsomiver he seen on the other side of it must have been deuced onpleasant, for the rollickin', singin', laughin, fiddlin', reckless, ne'er-do-well Solomon pulled a face on him the length of a tailyer's lapboord, an' if any of his ould comrades attimpted to make him convarsible on the fun that was goin' in any quarther of the counthry, Solomon would dhrop his jaws, an' fetch a groan would frighten a corp'; an' "My fren'," he would say, " this is all vanity, vanity! Life is hollow, an' these frivolities are only snares spread in our paths by the divil."

Anyhow, Solomon was an althered man, an' where he would go formerly to honour the Sabbath by a rousin' game of *caman* with the good boys, he was now seen makin' his way to the meetin'-house with a Bible anondher his arm the size of a salt-box, an' as many hime-books as would set up a hawker in a daicent way of thradin', an' he obsarvin' naither to the right nor to the left, but away a thousand miles ahead of him, as if he was always thryin' to make out the way to heaven somewhere in the skies foreninst him; an' where he would of another time be makin' his way across the counthry, maybe to the shouldher of Srual mountain for a spree, with the fiddle anondher his coat, ye might now meet him in the dusk of the evenin', still with the fiddle ondher the coat, but on a far betther errand—goin' to some prayer-meetin' at Inver, or Killymard, or Ballywell, or the divil only knows where; he wouldn't go within an ass's roar of a raffle-house; an' if you tould him there was to be a dance or any other wee divarshin in sich and sich a place he'd strive to put the breadth of a townlan' betwixt him an' it, for he said the divil was chained to the back-stone of any house that there was a hornpipe played in.

Well, one evenin', it was in October, an' jist about night-fallin', Solomon was makin' his way for Billy Knox's of the head of the Glibe, where a great and very pious man, one Bartholomew Binjamin Rankin, was to hold a prayer-meetin' for the benefit of all the well-disposed sinners in that sthretch of counthry; an' throth, it seems to me that, onless the Glibe's changed mortially within the last jinnyration, there must have been a daicent quantity of sinners in them same parts. But, as I was sayin', Solomon was this evenin' on the good arrand, with his fiddle peepin' out from ondher his coat—for ye see, Solomon's ould practice whin he was a sinner come in handy now that he was a saint, an' no prayer-meetin' could be held without Solomon's fiddle to steady the voices, when they joined to sing the himes. She was a splendid piece of a fiddle, an' Solomon, when he turned over the new laif, was goin' out to brak her neck across the nixt ditch, when he remimbered how she might come in handy this way, so he said to himself (as he tould afther), that " he'd make the occasion of his sins a steppin'-stone to new vartues, an' cause her that was hairtofore jiggin' him down to the place below, now fiddle him into heaven.''

He thought to himself this evenin' that he'd jist light the pipe to keep him company as he jogged on, so where do ye think he'd dhrop into, on purpose to light it, but ould Jimmy Higgerty's, the fairyman's, that I rehearsed to ye about before. On layin' '' Pagganinny,'' as he called the fiddle, down on a stool, whilst he was puttin' a screed of coal to the pipe, Jimmy Higgerty lifted her, an' dhrawin' the bow acrass her, he took a bar of a lively tune out of her, when Solomon jumped up as if he was sthruck.

'' Higgerty, me good man,'' he says, '' you have shocked me. Thim vain airs,'' siz he, '' has been long unknown to that fiddle, an' I trusted that she would nivir more be an insthrument that the divil would gamble for sowls on. Paice, paice, and dhraw not the bow in idle vanity again! ''

'' Arrah, good morra to ye,'' siz Jimmy, that way back to him, '' but it's delicate yer narves must have got intirely, lately. Throth, Misther Casshidy, I seen the time this wouldn't frighted ye one bit ''; an' all at oncet he sthruck up, '' Go to the divil an' shake yerself,'' while poor Solomon stood thrimblin' in the middle of the flure like a man with the aguey. While Jimmy finished up with a flourish that would have delighted Solomon the days he was at himself (for, be the same token, Solomon was no miss at handlin' the bow naither), he cut some quare figures with his left han' three times over the fiddle, an' handin' it to Solomon, he says, '' May ye nivir have more raison to be frightened than by a jig from the same fiddle—*that's all I say!* ''

Poor Solomon didn't know the hidden mainin' of them words, or it would have made him look crooked; nor he didn't know naither that Jimmy had put *pisherogues* on the fiddle; but all the same he took it from him with a glum look enough, and afther praichin' an edifyin' sarmon on frivolities, an' death an' jedgment, to Jimmy Higgerty, he betook him on the road again.

There was a wondherful congregation of the sinners an' saints of the Glibe—but the sinners had the best of it anyhow, in regards to numbers—in Bill Knox's that night. An' Bartholomew Binjamin Rankin was there, an' it was as good as a sarmin in itself just to get one glance at his face. There was as much holiness an' piety in it, ye'd a'most think, as would save the sowls of a whole barony. Solomon, who now got all sorts an' sizes of respect, as bein' a reformed sinner, an' was looked up to with ten times as much honour and rivirence as was paid to them that was saints all their life, got a sait, as was usual, beside the praicher. An' it's himself that was proud, an' he'd look down on the common crowd below with a most pityin' look on his face. An' the well-disposed ones in the congregation would look up at Solomon an' then give a groan that ye might hear at Srual; an' Solomon would look down on the sinners an' give another groan that ye might hear him at Barnesmore; an' then both Solomon an' the sinners would look up at the rafthers, an' give a groan that ye might hear at Muckish. Afther some time, when they had got faistin' their sowls fairly well on Solomon, a hime was called out, a very solemn one. "An'," says the praicher, lookin' at Solomon, "our saintly brother here, of whom aich and ivery heart in this gatherin' feels proud, an' whose pious ways are the glorification, admiration, an' edifycation of every true Christian since he gave up his ungodly life, an' turned onto the path of righteousness—brother Solomon will give us the keynote, an' lend us the aid of his unmusical box, throughout."

Brother Solomon, be me socks, dhrew a face on him the length of his own fiddle, as if he was thinkin' of his own unworthiness, poor man, an' says:

" It affords me a pious pleasure to dhraw my bow ondher the circumstances—that bow which so often snared me into the divil's sarvice; but I thank God with my heart that I have long since departed from my wicked, wicked, unspaikably vile an' sinful ways; an' this han' has long since forgotten them vain and ungodly airs that at one time occupied every spare moment of my then on-Christian life—long since, I say, have I buried deep in obliveen every remimbrance of thim wicked tunes, an' the cunnin' of my han' is now only used for a far loftier an' betther purpose. Bretherin, I shall begin."

And Solomon dhraws the bow across the fiddle, an' of all the himes tunes which was prented, what do ye think does he sthrike up? " Go to the divil an' shake yerself! " Och, it's as thrue as I'm tellin' it to ye. But, *ochón*, if there wasn't consternation in that house, I'm a gintleman! Solomon himself stopped suddent, for all the world lookin' like a stuck pig; an' he looked at the praicher, an' the praicher looked at him, and the congregation looked at both of them, and then Solomon prayed from his heart as he nivir prayed afore, that the Lord in His marcy might make the flure open and swallow him. The flure, though, as I suppose ye have guessed, did not open, but Bartholomew Binjamin's mouth did, an' he sayed, siz he:

" Bretherin! bretherin! this is a sad fallin' away! Alas! alas! Who should have thought that Brother Solomon, the deformed sinner, would have returned to his ould godless coorses! The rulin' passion, my dear bretherin, is so sthrong in him—waxin' sthrong with new sthrength—that he has onvoluntarily bethrayed the divil that has again got hould on him. Bretherin, let us pray for him! "

An' in a jiffey the thundersthruck congregation were on their knees prayin' like Trojans for the delivery of poor Solomon from the divil. Solomon, of course, for appairance' sake, had to take to his knees, too, but between you an' me, it's meself's afeard that all the prayers he said would not fetch him very far on the way to the first milestone that leads to heaven. I'll wager whoivir heerd him, that his prayers were sweet ones, that the divil might saize ould Jimmy Higgerty an' carry him off body an' bones, an' give him a toastin' on a special griddle down below. When they thought they had prayed long enough, an' that the divil was gone out of Solomon, they got up to their feet again, and they turned up the whites of their eyes till Bartholomew Binjamin announced that they would oncest more put Brother Solomon's faith to the test, to see if he had profited by the few minutes' sperritial recreation that they had indulged in. Solomon lifted the bow, an' afore he started he turned up the whites of his eyes in the usual fashion, as if he was lookin' for guidance, but in his heart he was only callin' down another black curse on Jimmy Higgerty.

" Bretherin! " siz he, as solemn as a judge—" Bretherin! The temper " (by which he meant the divil of coorse) " possessed the fiddle, and not my humble self; in witness whereof just attind to the solemn an' addyfyin' air I will now produce for ye." An' down comes the bow on the fiddle, an' up starts that beautiful jig tune, " The Siege of Carrick! "

Och, tarnation to me waistcoat, but there was sich a scene in two minnits as would charm a dancin' masther! When Solomon played the first bar of it, he could as soon comb his head with his toes as he could stop it. But that wasn't the best of it. Bartholomew Binjamin, instead of goin' into a cowld dead faint, as one would expect, begun to shuffle his feet in a suspicious way, an' afore ye'd say " thrapsticks " he was weltin' the flure like the broth of a boy, tearin' away at the jig like the ould Nick! An' in the squintin' of yer eye there wasn't a sowl anondher the roof, man, woman, or child, saint or sinner, that wasn't whackin' away at it like the forties, iviry man of them leatherin' the flure like a thrasher, jumpin' up till their heads would a'most sthrike the rafters, an' yellin' like red Injins, whilst me brave Solomon played like a black, put new life into the fiddle at ivery squeak, an' gave the jiggers whativer wee encouragement that he could spare time from the fiddle for:

" Come, boys, yez haven't fair play to foot it properly here. Yez is the finest set at a jig that I have faisted me eyes on since I give up me ungodly ways, an' it would be a pity for not to give yez ivery privilege—it's a fine clear moonlight, an' we'll go outside where we'll have room an' fair play at it. Come along, me mirry, mirry lads! " An' Solomon fiddled away out of the dure, an' the whole congregation leapt an' flung an' jigged it out in all possible an' onpossible shapes afther him. Och, they say it was a sight for sore eyes to see the capers that the party cut; ivery man jack of them tryin' to see who could be crazier than his naybour; an' out they got that way on the road, like a lunatic asylum turned loose for a holiday; an' Solomon headed down the road in the direction of Donegal, while the whole counthryside turned out when they

heard the yellin' an' fiddlin' an' prancin', an' seein' Solomon
headin' them with the fiddle, an' Bartholomew Binjamin fillin'
the front rank in company with his two feet, an' he jiggin' it
away at the rate of a christenin'! The people were first inclined
to laugh, but be the powdhers the nixt thing they done was join
in themselves, an' foot it away afther the fiddle ninety-nine times
crazier than the congregation. An' hot foot they kept it goin', up
hill an' down dale, over height an' hollow, with fresh batches
joinin' in at ivery lane an' turn, an' Solomon, the boy, layin' into
the fiddle at a rate as if he was gettin' a salary for it; an', be
the boots, by the time they raiched the foot of the road, you niver
seen in all your born days a harvest fair or a Repale meetin' as
big as it was!

Here Solomon turned to the left, with the purcession still jiggin'
it afther him, an' he nixt got onto the lane that leads up to the
Killymard ould graveyard, an' over the stile, in among the graves
with the mirry company brakin' their necks over, afther him; an'
when they got in here, Solomon made thracks for a nate dandy bit
of a tombstone in the centre of the yard, an' upon it he h'isted himself, with Bartholomew Binjamin up beside him, whilst the remainder of the party reshumed their attitudes all roun' about, an'
they fightin' like wild cats to see who would get purcession of the
tombstones, for they saw they were as good as barn-doors for
dancin' on. An' throgs, there might be purty good dancers there,
but divil resave the one of them that Solomon and Bartholomew
Binjamin couldn't take the shine out of. They had a bran' new
tombstone, the pick an' choice of all in the yard, an' if they didn't
do it in royal style, an' cut a copy to the crowd, call me a cuckoo!

But what would ye have of it, but the nixt man lands on the
scene was Sandy Montgomery, the Recthor. He was passin' the
road, an' seein' the fun in the graveyard, he come up in a t'un-
dherin' passion to horsewhip iviry mother's sowl of them. But,
sweet good luck to ye, if he didn't jump up on the fiddler's tombstone, an' catchin' Bartholomew Binjamin by the han', foot it away,
likewise.

An' it would have gone on to daylight in the mornin', if ould Jimmy
Higgerty, the rascal, who followed the fun the whole way from the
Glibe, for the purpose of tastifyin' to it—if he hadn't come behin'
Solomon an' tould him to kick up his right heel, dhraw his left
thumb three times over the sthrings of the fiddle, an' look over his
left shouldher at the moon, an' then see what music he'd take out
of it. No sooner sayed nor done; an' all at once the tune changed
to a hime tune, all mournful, an' iviry heel in the graveyard was
paralysed. Ivery sowl of them looked at one another like they
wor wakenin' out of a dhraim.

Solomon himself dhrew up, an' he gave a bewildhered look all
roun' him, an' then looked at Sandy Montgomery, who was standin'

forenenst him on the stone, an' he as pale as a sheet.  Ivery man of the three on the tombstone gave themselves up as lost men, ruinated intirely, out an' out, afther makin' such spectacles of themselves for the counthry.  The Recthor lost conthrol of himself completely, an' puttin' his fist anondher Solomon's nose, he says:

" Ye common scoundhril, ye; ye've made me disgrace my cloth, ye cut-throat villain——"

But afore he could get out another word, Solomon, who had some of the spunk of his early days in him still, and was a thrifle hasty, besides that his dandher was riz in regards to the purty pickle he was in—Solomon ups with the fiddle, an' dhrawin' it roun' his head with a swing, he takes the Recthor across the noddle an' knocked him a'most into kingdom come, away off the tombstone.  But, my hearty, in swingin' the fiddle, doesn't he catch Bartholomew Binjamin, who was standin' behind him, a nate little bit of a knock on the skull.  So, now turnin' round to apologise to him, Bartholomew Binjamin ups with his fist an' plants it undher Solomon's nose, too, for he was just commencin' a norration.

" Ye mane, onprincipled, ungodly bla'guard! "

But Solomon couldn't stand this neither.  He says to himself he might as well be hung for a sheep as a lamb, and that when he knocked down a Recthor, he might with an asier conscience knock down a praicher.  So he took the praicher a wallop with the fiddle that left him sprawlin' in the Recthor's lap with his heels uppermost, and Solomon leapt from the tombstone, an' off through the crowd for the bare life, wallopin' them right an' left.  They all slunk home afther a while with their tails between their legs, but poor Solomon was the worst of all.  He made " Pagganinny " into smithereens—what remained of her.  An' he didn't lift his head for twelve months afther.

# THE RESURRECTION OF DINNY O'DOWD

## Seumas MacManus

In the parish of Pulbochog where me father's people come from there's many a man strugglin' for sthraws, bekase the rents are that big, and the farms that small—but there's wan man, and only wan, who is as ondependent as a prince—and as well-to-do after his own fashion—and that's Manis O'Dowd.  And Manis is as he is, bekase he houlds his bit of land free of all rent while grass grows, and water runs, and crows put out their tongue.

How he comes to be this way is a great story, in throth, and a dhroll wan.

Manis's father that is now, was Cormac, and his father again was Dinny O'Dowd, or Dinny the Ghost, as he was known till the day of his death. And him it was that got for the wee farm the privilege of goin' rent free for ever and a day.

I dar' say it's a good four score of years ago now since Dinny the Ghost (as he wasn't named just then), mainin' for to be both good till himself and good till his farm, marri'd a wan Molshie M'Connell from the next parish, in the hopes that she'd fetch him both favour and fortune. But God help poor Dinny, the fortune she fetched him was the clothes on her back and a bad temper; and Molshie wasn't the third night in the house till Dinny seen the coat-tails of Paice pass out of his doore.

But me brave Dinny struggled with Molshie and the wurrl' as best he could for three years. But the rent was high and hard to pay, and for farm produce there was next to no price at all; so that debts and difficulties begun to hail on the poor divil. And to make bad worse, there riz bad blood atween him and the man marched him, Big Denis M'Cue, about a right-o'-way, which got so bitter that to save his skin he had to go afore the magistrates and swear his life again Big Dinis, who threatened to murdher him afore br'akfast some mornin'. But instead of mendin' matthers this only made things worse; the M'Cues now s'ore be all the Saints in the Almanac that they'd never get a paiceful night's sleep till they'd see Dinny O'Dowd's blood flowin'.

" By this and by that," says Dinny till himself at last, " this must end. This climate isn't 'hol'some for me, so I'll thry a change." Without lettin' sowl or sinner know, he made up he'd slip off unknownst, and away till Amirikay. " Me wife and me neighbours 'ill maybe both be better of their tempers be the time I come back, and I'll arn as much money as 'ill lift me out o' me difficulties."

No sooner did night fall that selfsame day than he went out to fother the cows (be pretence); but me brave Dinny took the road in rale 'arnest, to push for a sayport and sail for the Lan' of Liberty. But he wasn't three fields from the house when he met a beggar-man that he gave a shillin' to swap clothes with him—so it would be the harder to detect him when the wife would rise the hewin'-cry afther him. That done, then wanst away and aye away, me brave Dinny wasn't seen or heard of more.

But for the misfortunate poor beggarman 'twas the black hour that he took Dinny's shillin' and swapped clothes with him! For where did the divil temp' his steps only across M'Cue's lan', over the very right-o'-way that riz all the bad blood. And who (as the divil would still have it) should be convaynient but Big Dinis M'Cue himself, with a tarrific bludgeon of a stick in his han'. And, " Well, bad luck to you, O'Dowd! " says he, knowin' Dinny in the dark (as he thought) be the hat and sleeved waistcoat and whole rig-out —" Bad luck seize you, O'Dowd," says he, " for a provokin' ruffian! Take that! " and he tumbled the beggar with wan blow of his bludgeon; and he never spoke more, he was as dead as an iron dog. Big Dinis he went lookin' for help, and himself and his brother atween them hoisted the corp on their shoulders, and marched with him across hedge and hill till they come to Mondar-rig, where they tied stones to it, and sunk it in the deepest boghole they could find. Then says they, " The Lord be thankit! Dinny O'Dowd's over and done with; and we'll have paice and a right-o'-way all to ourselves for the time to come."

Next mornin' the *gar* went roun' that Dinny O'Dowd was a-missin', went out to fother the cows and didn't come home las' night, and Molshie was disthracted. And some sayed this, and some more sayed that; but it wasn't long till most of them agreed that Dinny had bid good-bye to hardships and hard-livin', and gone to the river and dhrownded himself; and the M'Cues sayed they had seen a man of his height and appearance goin' in the direction of the river las' night. But when the river was dragged and the country screenged and sarched from end to wynd, thrace or thrack wasn't got of him. And poor Molshie was left to mourn and to manage as best she might.

And poorly enough she did manage for wan year and for longer. As Big Dinis M'Cue's land lay into her own, and as she was sorely in need of a man to care her farm and Big Dinis just as sorely in need of a woman to care his house, people thought it 'ud be *a go* atween them. Dinis, in throth, begun to show Molshie attention enough—but she, of course, hadn't sartain enough proof that Dinny was dead. When, as luck would have it, just near on the score of the second twelvemonth after Dinny's departure, doesn't a man who was barrowin' turf in the bog discover a corp lyin' in wan of the holes. The word was passed, and when the people crowded to see it, though the faytures was gone, all his neighbours at wanst recog-nised Dinny O'Dowd be the oul' grey hat and the sleeved waistcoat with brassy buttons, and every article of apparel. Even Lanty Meehan, the shoemaker, could swear to his high-lows and the patches he put on the uppers. Poor Molshie come, wailin', and recognised him too, and cried over him her hearty fill, as if there had never afore been a wife so grieved afther a man.

Well, a hasty wake and a hurried funeral it got, and they hid it away as fast as they could.

Poor Dinny, poor man, he reached Amerikay all safe and in good time, and went to work in the lead works, where he wrought hard and very hard for twelve months, and then lost his health complete be lead poisonin', and had to take to his bed, where he lay atween life and daith for near twelve months more. And as soon as he found fit to put a foot in under him he got up; and as his only hope of life was to get to Irelan' again, a few of his friends put as much together as bought him a ticket, and sent him off.

When Dinny landed he was noways unlike a very far-gone ghost: as white as bleached lint, only the eyes of him was sunk in his head and black round about, and the skin only hangin' from his bones. "But what I feel worst," says he till himself, lookin' down at his rags, "is the ondaicent clothes I have—they'd disgrace a scarecrow." Hot-foot, then, he started for home; and when he came near where he'd be known, he waited till night fell on him sooner nor be seen comin' back from America in such duds. And when night did fall, on he went, and for his own house as smooth as he could, takin' the fields for it, instead of the roads, so no wan would see him. And behold ye, when he climbed in of his own garden what does he find, where Molshie had put them to get the air, only his own daicent oul' rig that he'd swapped with the beggar two years ago. "Thank God!" says Dinny, "for it's Him put them my way." And without any more ado off him he peels his own string o' rags and gets into the sleeved waistcoat with the brassy buttons, and claps his own brave oul' grey hat on his head. "Molshie, the knave, must a made the poor beggarman give them up," says he; "but it stands me good sarvice she did."

Now, as fortune would have it, this was only the third night afther the berral, and Big Dinis had strolled into Molshie's to comfort her, and settle up wee mathers about the weddin'—which was now fixed upon for sartain, and to take place as soon as they could daicently think of houldin' it. And the both of them were sittin' purty close together, love-makin', when me brave Dinny advanced and looked in of the winda! The first thing upset them then was an onearthly yell without; and the next thing the doore burstin' in, and Dinny O'Dowd that they had turned the sods on, three days afore, Dinny, in his oul' sleeved waistcoat, and lookin' more daithly than any dead man, jumped into the middle of the floore!

Molshie she gave a scream out of her, and fainted dead away. Big Dinis M'Cue, with his mouth open, lost the power to aither move or spaik, till Dinny, shakin' a bony fist undher his nose, says, "Ye murtherin' villian!" which was a common word of abuse of his—"Ye murtherin' villian, M'Cue! I'll niver rest until I see ye in the hangman's hands!" Big Dinis with that got the power of his lungs and his leg all of a suddent, and lettin' a bawl out of him like a calf a-sthranglin', he dives atween Dinny's legs, and flew like a weaver's shuttle through the doore.

Poor Molshie was in a rale bad way, and every time she opened her eyes and saw Dinny's white face and the sleeved waistcoat with the brassy buttons bendin' over her, she went off in another faint again. Says Dinny, " The woman'll die dead of the fear o' me onless I send in some of the neighbours to bring her to." So out he went and down the road to Neilis Lainaghan's, and he heerd big noise and fiddlin' as he come till it—for there was a dance in Neilis's, and all the countryside was gathered. Dinny lifted the latch and walked into the middle of them, and that ins'ant there was a scraim in this corner of the house, and a yell in that, and a groan in the other, and a racket and a rush all over, and a crush and a dive for the doore; and in less time than I say it Dinny was standin' alone by himself, barrin' for half-a-dozen fainted women and girls that was lyin' among broken chairs; and every minute there was wan of these women comin' to, and, seein' Dinny, givin' another scraim and goin' off.

" Well, bad cess to yous, wan and all! " says Dinny, afther he'd stood in speechless wonderment for five minutes—" The worst of bad snuff to yous, wan and all! Is the wurl' gone mad, or what's come over Pulbochog anyhow, that the sight of a man come back afther two years sends every wan helther-skelther like frightened hares in a harvest-fiel'? "

But it was goin' from bad to worse with the faintin' women; so, off he had to take himself, and fare further. But behould ye, there wasn't a hut or house he come till that wasn't as emp'y as if the plague had cleaned them out; and he could only hear the shouts of the people as they were hurryin' and scurryin' far over the face of the country. " Musha, and may the divil dhrive yous to the facthory where they brew bad luck! " says he, turnin', and makin' for home again.

Intil his own byre he went—for he'd got enough of Molshie for wan evenin'—and threw himself down to sleep under the cow's head; and slep' purty hearty.

Now, when Dinny left home first, the lan' had been in arrears ov rent, and it had been gettin' deeper intil it since he left; and the landlord had at last just got a decree again' Molshie, and had ordhered the bailiff to go to Molshie's, and seize something on the decree. So, it was on this very mornin' I'm talkin' of that the bailiff had made up to come on his decree. " I'll be there," says he, " afore Molshie is out and about, and I'll have me seizure lifted and carried off with small throuble." So, close afther the screek of day he come, and walked intil the byre. " Here's a cow," says he, " 'ill be good for ten poun' off the decree," and walked forrid to the baste's head to liberate her. And that minute up jumped Dinny, and naturally flew for the fellow's throat. But, my sorra, the bailiff, when he got the first gleek of him and seen who it was, didn't wait, but let out of him a yell and a howl, and sprung for the door, and away, and never waited or stopped till he had put hills behind him.

Dinny prayed bad prayers on the bailiff that had come to seize

his only cow, and on the lan'lord that sent him, and then he
started out hot-foot and never stopped or stayed till he was at the
lan'lord's house. The bailiff had reached there long ahead of him,
and when he toul' the lan'lord that he didn't lift the decree bekase
Dinny O'Dowd's ghost had riz at the cow's head, and spouted fire
at him from both mouth and nosthrils, the lan'lord gave him no
end of abuse for an *amadan* and an ediot, and swore he'd dismiss
him and have *a man* in his place afore the sun set.

But behould ye! the lan'lord was only warmin' up to it, and the
poor bailiff, with his teeth still chatterin', takin' all insults as
compliments, when the doore opens and Dinny steps in.

The tongue stood still in the lan'lord's mouth, and the hair riz
on his head at the sight, and the poor bailiff give a howl and dived
in under the lan'lord's chair.

" Small wonder yous is mortially ashamed of yerselves," Dinny
thunders at them, " for to go for to take away a lone woman's
cow! "

" It was—it was all a mistake," says the lan'lord, when he got
his tongue—" It was all a great mistake, entirely," says he, " and
I'm very, very sorry for it, and it'll never occur again, Misther
O'Dowd," says he, him thremblin' like a sally leaf, and the colour
of the limewall in the face.

" Ay, *Misther* O'Dowd—no less," says Dinny till himself.
" Troth the lan'lords has been improvin' in their manners since I
left the country." And then says he, spaikin' out, " I'm glad to
hear ye say it. For in faith I thought it was a cold welcome to a
man comin' back afther bein' two years gone from yous."

" Oh, then, Misther O'Dowd, we're—we're—we're glad to see
ye back. I suppose ye're goin' round to see all the neighbours
afore ye go again; so, I'll not be delayin' ye. Good mornin',"
says the lan'lord.

" Not so quick, be yer laive, sir," says Dinny. " I seem about
as welcome to the neighbours as to yerself and yer bailiff; they all
screech, and show me their heels, whatever the divil's the matter
with them."

The lan'lord was thryin' to be as plaisin' as possible. " Oh,"
says he, " Misther O'Dowd, that's all only bekase we arn't *used*
to you yet."

" Plaise God, then, it'll not be my fault for the time to come,"
says Dinny, " or yous 'ill get used to me."

" Oh, Misther O'Dowd, don't say that," says the lan'lord,
beseechin' him.

" What the divil do *you* mane, now? " says Dinny.

" I mane," says the other, " I mane that—that—Oh, ye know
what I mane. I mane that, of course, we're very glad entirely to
see ye; but—but we think ye'd maybe be better and happier *where
ye were*," says he.

" Happier! " says Dinny. " Look at me! Look at me! Ye're now lookin' at a man that suffered hell since he went away."

The poor bailiff give a screech from in under the chair, and the lan'lord give another screech.

" Plaise, Misther O'Dowd, if ye go away from here, I'll do anything at all to sarve ye."

" I only ax sparin's, and I'll bring ye here inside wan twelve-month, and count ye down, every sovereign I owe ye, even if I have to rob the divil to get it."

" Oh, no, no, no! Plaise, no! Don't bring me any money. I forgive ye every penny ye owe me, and I'll make ye out a clear resait up till this day, if ye promise to put it in your pocket, and depart in paice."

" Oh, ye ginerous man! " says Dinny, overcome with such onexpected goodness. " I'll niver forget that act to ye. And for the time to come, as sure as ever galeday comes round, ye'll find me the first man here in the mornin', with me rent to ye."

" Oh, no! Oh, no, plaise! " says the lan'lord. " Don't come with any rent to me, ever. I'll here and now fill ye out a resait up till the year of ten thousand and nothin'—just to save ye the throuble and worry of comin' back."

And there and then, without more ado, he fills out a resait to say that " the undhersigned, Dinny O'Dowd, has paid me every penny of rent ever due again' his farm in Pulbochog, or that ever will be due against it, up till and includin' the year ten thousand and nothin'. "

And the dumbfoundhered Dinny takes this from the lan'lord's thrimblin' hand, and pockets it, and walks off.

But he didn't see man or mortial, sowl or sinner, nor couldn't know what happened to them, till he come as far as the chapel; and this he found panged with people to the door. For, the way of it was, Molshie, by the advice of the neighbours, had axed for a Mass to be sayed that Dinny's soul might get rest, and all the parish had gathered, to join their prayers.

Into the chapel poor Dinny walks; and the minute they saw him, the congregation let wan howl out o' them that near carried the roof off the buildin', and they made such a rush for the three doors that it was a marcy they didn't take the sidewalls with them; and Dinny found himself alone in the chapel with the priest.

The same priest was a purty courageous man, and he actually walked forrid to Dinny and addhressed him—commandin' him in the Name to say what was a-throuble to him to fetch him back here.

" A-throuble to me! " says Dinny. " I knew nothin' but throuble since I left here."

" To yer shame be it said, Dinny O'Dowd," says the priest. " It wasn't for want of warnin's enough from me, ye went asthray."

" Thrue for ye—thrue for ye, father," says Dinny. " And it's often when I was sufferin' that I sayed the same to meself."

" Well, well, it's me is the sorry man for ye, Dinny O'Dowd. But it's too late to lament now. Is there anything I can do for ye? " says the priest.

" Yes, yer reverence, can ye tell me why these people loses their wits and runs like the Roe wather when they see me? " says Dinny.

" Oh, that's only natural," says the priest. " They'll not be content till ye're gone again. So hurry yerself."

" Till I'm gone! But I'm come to remain," says Dinny.

" Come! come! " says the other, " ye can't do that, ye know."

" And why not, may I ax? " says Dinny.

" There's no whys in it," says the other. " If ye have anything on yer mind, or any requist to ax, ax it and go."

" Well, upon my veracity, that is a cool way to thrait wan who expected a wee bit of welcome and pleasure afther two years of torture," says Dinny.

" Ye're afther confessin' ye 'arned it," says the priest.

" But I've made up my mind to turn a new laif," Dinny said.

" It's too late now if ye had made up yer mind to turn a whole grove," says the priest. " There's no second chance in your wurrl," says he. " So, right about face now," says he, " and march; or if ye don't do it of yer own free will, I'll soon find a means of makin' ye."

Poor Dinny, poor man, was sore put about at this traitment. But, says he, " It 'ud puzzle ye to take stockin's off a barefooted man. How am I to go without either money or mains? "

" Come! none of yer nadiums," says the priest, " go the way ye come."

" I come in *The Irish Maiden*," says he, " to Darry, and had to pay smartly for it."

" What do ye mane? " says the priest, says he; and he puts his hand on Dinny, and feels him. " Aren't ye a dead man, sir? " says he.

But, faix, the grip of Dinny didn't at all feel like what a ghost should be, to the priest's mighty wondherment; and he never let go of him till he marched him out of the chapel, and along the road, hearin' Dinny's story as they went. The people they were crouchin' on the hills watchin' them both, and waitin' to see Dinny go off like a puff o' smoke. But that they didn't see.

The priest marched Dinny straight home to Molshie, and toul' her it wasn't Dinny's ghost at all, but Dinny himself. But Molshie tuk her heels with her away from the house, and wild horses wouldn't dhrag her back again. She'd never come, she said, to live with a ghost.

An' she was as good as her word; and in troth Dinny didn't br'ak his heart with the grief, either.

Big Dinis M'Cue, when he got the fright, never stopped runnin' till he reached the polis barracks, and give himself up for the murdher.

Dinny O'Dowd himself tuk a holiday to attend the hangin'. And, happy as he was that day, he was never a day less so till he died, and left his freehould to his son Cormac, a child Molshie left with him; and Cormac left it to his son again, Manis; and as I sayed, Manis and his freehould are flourshin' in Pulbochog at this day. And may they long continue so.

# DORA SIGERSON SHORTER
1872–1918

# PRISCILLA

PRISCILLA was dead, and all the women of the village had come
to her waking. They moved about the big house where she had
lived so long and so quietly as though they had never seen it
before; and they never had, without Priscilla.

They moved silently, or came together in little groups to talk
about her. They seemed as much amazed as sorry. Who could
imagine Priscilla dead? Surely she was the oldest woman in the
village; and yet she seemed not so very old; but no one remembered the village without her, and no one remembered her young.
Perhaps she had entered into their lives unnoticed, and only when
she came to her womanhood had taken her place in their sight, as
a little unknown seedling will one day become a tree and landmark.

Perhaps in the great house she had passed her shadowy girlhood,
and only became a personage when her uncle died, leaving her his
sole and only heir. Then she crept forth, and her fading hands
drew the hearts of the people towards her.

Was she rich? Who can say? The black, barrack-like house,
with its neglected garden, had no air of wealth about it; but never
a child or woman came to Priscilla for help and went away empty-
handed. Some said that for this reason the house grew more
desolate as it grew old—that pictures and silver and ornaments
vanished one by one.

But others would have it that Priscilla had a box of money in her
room, corded, sealed, and locked. For true it was that such a box,
to all appearance, was there, as Ann O'Ruark, who nursed her
once in an illness, could tell.

Now she lay dead, and it seemed to the women of the little
village as though something marvellous had happened—as though
the old round tower they looked upon every morning when they
opened their doors had crumpled in the night, or as though the
church bell they depended upon to awaken them at six had forgotten to ring, leaving them late and bewildered. True, she might
have been ill, or gone away on a visit, or vanished for a time.
But to die! No one ever thought that of Priscilla after all those

years. Why, even now the children from the cottages were
running down the street on the stroke of five to meet her coming
from her Saturday's marketing with something hidden for them
in her pocket. Yet they had been told she would come up the
narrow street no more. Yes, even now poor cripple Janie Doyle
was turning her face to the window to be ready for the smile and
cheery word that always met her. Yet she too knew Priscilla
would never pass again.

All the women there sitting at her wake felt that to-morrow they
would put on their shawls and run to tell Priscilla their joys and
sorrows, or to ask her advice, as they had done all the time since
they became aware she *was*. And Priscilla would be lying with
that strange smile upon her face, so far removed from them.

Was she so very old—Priscilla? Hers was a face you could not
imagine had ever been young. Wrinkled and fallen away, you
could not fix and fill it with youth.

Once she had said to a child, " I was light as a bird when I was
young as you "; and the little one had gone away troubled at the
lie. She knew, as all the children did, that Priscilla had never,
never been young.

Though Priscilla knew everything of everybody, nobody knew
anything of Priscilla, except, of course, that she was an old maid—
as any one of the name of Priscilla must be. Why, the very sound
of it was enough to tell how prim, how neat, how old-maidish she
was. No one could have imagined her with a lover. Many a time
the village women had sat and talked of Priscilla, what she must
have been like as a girl—if she ever had been a girl: the primmest
of little girls, who always had her hair smooth and lessons learnt:
a girl with large feet and high, buttoned boots, with every button
fastened in its place; thin legs, of course; a waist that had never
known tight-lacing; straight hair, first in a plait and later a tight
coil at the back of her smooth head; a high white forehead, intelligent grey eyes, a rather large and rather pink nose, a pleasant
mouth, thin neck and breast, long arms, large nervous hands.
Yes, that must have been Priscilla, if ever she had been a girl. But
there was no lover in the setting of Priscilla's girlhood. No, she
hated men, and rough boys the natty Priscilla must have
always shunned, nor could she, with her cleverness, ever have
admired the developing youth.

Yes, she hated men and all their sex; she was hardly kind to
little boys—they were cruel to her cats, she would say. But the
girl babies, how she loved them! There was never a birth in the
village where she was not first visitor to the new arrival. And if it
was a boy, she would look close into the little red face till he raised
his voice and howled. Then she would laugh. " Shout for it and
you will get it, my lad; only shout long enough and you will get
it." Then she would press a golden pound into his little fist and

leave him.  But if it was a girl, she would take it in her arms, and
if it was crying it would stop that minute.  She would drop a tear
upon it, perhaps, and whisper things into its little unconscious ears.
When she was leaving she would put a guinea into its hands, with
the words, " For your sad heart, my girl, for your sad heart."
So the baby would be added to her list of loves.

But she liked best the lovelorn maidens who would come to her
with their stories.  They were indeed for her heart of hearts.  Many
a sorrowful soul that had forgotten how to be proud would after
consulting with her become strong again, and win the lover back
by flaunting who had grown weary of too patient a love.

The house was built like one that had never been intended to
hold the young; dark, gloomy, rambling.  Priscilla was the only
one to whom it seemed a fitted background.

The little children who braved its awfulness would hasten, afraid
of its silence, from passage to passage till they reached Priscilla,
every minute expecting a horrible something belonging to the mould
and age to spring upon them from each dark place.  Only the
mysterious cupboards with hidden sweets and jams, found nowhere
else, could tempt them to come.  And it took three of them to do
it, clinging together, and stopping often with shrieks that were not
all laughter, but served to fill the dusty silence.

When Priscilla died there turned up from somewhere a far-
removed cousin—a stern, middle-aged woman, who looked at the
world through smoked glasses; and no doubt the world looked grey
to her.  She had no tears, no smiles, no sentiments, only the hardness of middle life, which has left the softness of youth behind and
not yet reached the softness of age.  She was a business-like person,
and ordered everything and everybody as if she had lived all her
life in Priscilla's house.  The people wondered if she would get
Priscilla's box of treasure; but, of course, there was no one else.
The cousin was making herself busy, pretending to be concerned
for Priscilla.  Why had she not come before to take care of her?
She wanted to blame somebody for not calling in a doctor.  But
she ought to know Priscilla would not have the doctor.  She had
a perfect horror of the doctor, and would never see him, or speak
of him.  There was only one doctor in the village—an old man,
as old as Priscilla, it might be—a married man with grown-up sons
and daughters, now married themselves and doing well.  Once a
neighbour had spoken of the doctor to Priscilla.  It was to repeat
a story of his past, a story of a lonely girl he had jilted almost on
their wedding-day, and how the girl had vanished and been heard
of no more; but that had not happened in the village, and so the
village was not interested in the particulars.  When Priscilla heard
the story she rose from her seat and went to the window without a
word.  So the neighbour thought she was weary, and changed the
subject from men and their misdeeds, but she did make a parting

remark to the effect that the doctor and his wife never got on
together. She was surprised when Priscilla said, in a voice so sweet
and far away she hardly heard it, " Poor lad! poor lad! "

Priscilla would not have the doctor come near her when she
lived, but when she died he had to be called in. People who
watched him coming were surprised to see him falter, he ought to
have been so used to death. And yet he came like one most cruelly
afraid. He stood at the door of the room where she lay for a few
moments, as though unable to enter. Then he pushed the door
open and went as if with an effort. When he reached her bedside he stood silent, looking upon her face. And there were those
there who thought they had heard him whisper, " Priscilla! " and
then louder, as though she must hear, " Priscilla! "

But Priscilla was dead, and all the village had come to her wake;
two nights they had sat up, and this was the third. The will had
been read—such as it was; for there was little to leave to anybody.
Yet every one had had a trifle, the house had gone to the cousin,
but there was no money to speak of—nothing more except the
little wooden box, corded, locked, and sealed—the box that must
contain the body of the fortune. The cousin's fingers had been
on the cords, the eyes of the village women had been turned to it,
waiting for it to open, when they were told it was to be buried with
her. What an idea! Whoever heard of a box being buried in a
tomb? Who would ever have thought she would have carried away
what she could no longer want? Who would have imagined Priscilla a miser?

The crowd had all gone to the dining-room at the end of the
long passage in the west wing, and the cousin was sitting alone in
the room with the box; upstairs Priscilla was lying, and she would
never know—never know the seals were broken and the knots
undone. Surely, it was no harm to open and look in—no, not to
touch a single penny, since she was such a screw—only to open.
No box was ever yet buried by a woman unopened. The lid lay
loose.

The cousin sat back a moment, then went upon her knees and
raised the cover. She saw the contents were wrapped in white
paper. She pulled it off and drew forth what came to her hand.
Astonishment was upon her face, for first there came a dress—a
white satin dress—then a long veil, then a wreath of orange blossoms. Shoes, gloves, and underwear, all lace and ribbons, all sewn
by hand in tiny stitches, surely Priscilla's own. What was this
the cousin had stumbled on unawares? A wedding outfit, Priscilla's wedding outfit, breathing the breath of years, lavender and
age. How time had ruined all, as it had destroyed Priscilla's love-
story! How was it the cousin never knew of this prepared wedding? Where or who was the man? She had known little of
Priscilla when she was young, only that she was fatherless and

motherless, and that an uncle had taken charge of her; that she had grown up between the grey walls of her uncle's quiet, lonely house and a convent school, where she had spent half her time. Always unnoticed, silent, and companionless, was it because there was no one who cared enough about her to draw her from her solitude? There was something, the cousin fancied she half-remembered, something of a scandal of Priscilla and a young doctor, something about love-letters and stolen meetings discovered at the convent. Was it possible Priscilla had returned home to work her wedding outfit, while the young doctor had forgotten his promise and married money while she was still awaiting him? But it was a vague memory, and might not have been her.

The cousin bent above the box. Nothing else; no money—not a penny. Ah! here was a key to the story, a bundle of old letters —love-letters, for were they not tied by a silken bow? Poor Priscilla!

As she took them into her hands she fancied she heard the sound of a woman sobbing far away; it might be upstairs with the dead. Some friend of Priscilla's, no doubt. She turned the letters over in her hands. She wished that wild crying would stop. It disturbed her. She laid her fingers upon the beknotted strings, then hesitated. Should she dare spy into the secrets of the helpless dead? But curiosity was strong; she loosed the ribbons. At the same time a wild cry resounded through the room. She sprang to her feet, the letters in her hands, and looked fearfully around. There was no one there. It must have been outside. Yes; it came from the floor above—from Priscilla's room—long, sad, and awful; the sound of a woman's wild grief.

The cousin thrust the letters into her pocket, and ran down the hall, calling to the people to hurry to the room above. She called to them to bring hot blankets and restoratives, that Priscilla was not dead, that she had waked in terror, finding herself decked out for death. And all the time she was shouting to them she was running up the long staircase and down the corridors to the room where the crying came from. Then she called, " Priscilla, I am coming; don't be afraid; Priscilla, I am coming." She imagined Priscilla sitting up in her grave-clothes, half mad with terror at her position. When she touched the handle of the door the crying ceased. She opened it, and stood half-fainting upon the threshold. In her coffin lay Priscilla stiff and dead, her hands clasped as they had been when she was laid there, her face unchanged, the great room empty —death everywhere.

The cousin stood dumb at the door, the women crowding about her with hot blankets and restoratives. " It was a mistake," she said; and pushing them back, closed the door.

She went downstairs to the room where the trunk lay, and drawing the letters from her pocket placed them back unopened where she had found them. With reverent hands she laid the wedding things one by one in their place, and when she had finished she sealed and corded the box.

When Priscilla went to her sleeping-place the next day, there was borne by her side a little trunk, and it was laid at her feet in the cold vault that held so many dead.

# E. Œ. SOMERVILLE AND
# MARTIN ROSS

# THE HOUSE OF FAHY

NOTHING could shake the conviction of Maria that she was by nature and by practice a house dog. Every one of Shreelane's many doors had, at one time or another, slammed upon her expulsion, and each one of them had seen her stealthy, irrepressible return to the sphere that she felt herself so eminently qualified to grace. For her the bone, thriftily interred by Tim Connor's terrier, was a mere diversion; even the fruitage of the ashpit had little charm for an accomplished *habitué* of the kitchen. She knew to a nicety which of the doors could be burst open by assault, at which it was necessary to whine sycophantly; and the clinical thermometer alone could furnish a parallel for her perception of mood in those in authority. In the case of Mrs. Cadogan she knew that there were seasons when instant and complete self-effacement was the only course to pursue; therefore when, on a certain morning in July, on my way through the downstairs regions to my office, I saw her approach the kitchen door with her usual circumspection, and, on hearing her name enunciated indignantly by my cook, withdraw swiftly to a city of refuge at the back of the hay-rick, I drew my own conclusions.

Had she remained, as I did, she would have heard the disclosure of a crime that lay more heavily on her digestion than her conscience.

" I can't put a thing out o' me hand but he's watching me to whip it away! " declaimed Mrs. Cadogan, with all the disregard of her kind for the accident of sex in the brute creation. " 'Twas only last night I was back in the scullery when I heard Bridget let a screech, and there was me brave dog up on the table eating the roat beef that was after coming out from the dinner! "

" Brute! " interjected Philippa, with what I well knew to be a simulated wrath.

" And I had planned that bit of beef for the luncheon," continued Mrs. Cadogan in impassioned lamentation, " the way we wouldn't have to inthrude on the cold turkey! Sure he has it that dhragged, that all we can do with it now is run it through the mincing machine for the Major's sandwiches."

At this appetising suggestion I thought fit to intervene in the deliberations.

" One thing," I said to Philippa afterwards, as I wrapped up a bottle of Yanatas in a Cardigan jacket and rammed it into an already apoplectic Gladstone bag, " that I do draw the line at, is taking that dog with us. The whole business is black enough as it is."

" Dear," said my wife, looking at me with almost clairvoyant abstraction, " I could manage a second-evening-dress if you didn't mind putting my tea-jacket in your portmanteau."

Little, thank Heaven! as I know about yachting, I knew enough to make pertinent remarks on the incongruity of an ancient 60-ton hireling and a fleet of smart evening-dresses; but none the less I left a pair of indispensable boots behind, and the tea-jacket went into my portmanteau.

It is doing no more than the barest justice to the officers of the Royal Navy to say that, so far as I know them, they cherish no mistaken enthusiasm for a home on the rolling deep when a home anywhere else presents itself. Bernard Chute had unfortunately proved an exception to this rule. During the winter, the invitation to go for a cruise in the yacht that was in process of building for him hung over me like a cloud; a timely strike in the builder's yard brought a respite, and, in fact, placed the completion of the yacht at so safe a distance that I was betrayed into specious regrets, echoed with an atrocious sincerity by Philippa. Into a life pastorally compounded of Petty Sessions and lawn-tennis parties, retribution fell when it was least expected. Bernard Shute hired a yacht in Queenstown, and one short week afterwards the worst had happened, and we were packing our things for a cruise in her, the only alleviation being the knowledge that, whether by sea or land, I was bound to return to my work in four days.

We left Shreelane at twelve o'clock, a specially depressing hour for a start, when breakfast has died in you, and lunch is still remote. My last act before mounting the dogcart was to put her collar and chain on Maria and immure her in the potato-house, whence, as we drove down the avenue, her wails rent the heart of Philippa and rejoiced mine. It was a very hot day, with a cloudless sky; the dust lay thick on the white road, and on us also, as, during two baking hours, we drove up and down the long hills and remembered things that had been left behind, and grew hungry enough to eat sandwiches that tasted suspiciously of roast beef.

The yacht was moored in Clountiss Harbour; we drove through the village street, a narrow and unlovely thoroughfare, studded with public-houses, swarming with children and poultry, down through an ever-growing smell of fish, to the quay.

Thence we first viewed our fate, a dingy-looking schooner, and the hope I had secretly been nourishing that there was not wind enough for her to start, was dispelled by the sight of her topsail going up. More than ever at that radiant moment—as the reflection of the white sail quivered on the tranquil blue, and the still water flattered all it reproduced, like a fashionable photographer—did I agree with George Herbert's advice, " Praise the sea, but stay on shore."

" We must hail her, I suppose," I said drearily. I assailed the *Eileen Oge,* such being her inappropriate name, with desolate cries, but achieved no immediate result beyond the assembling of some village children round us and our luggage.

" Mr. Shute and the two ladies was after screeching here for the boat awhile ago," volunteered a horrid little girl, whom I had already twice frustrated in the attempt to seat an infant relative on our bundle of rugs. " Timsy Hallahane says 'twould be as good for them to stay ashore, for there isn't as much wind outside as'd out a candle."

With this encouraging statement the little girl devoted herself to the alternate consumption of gooseberries and cockles.

All things come to those who wait, and to us arrived at length the gig of the *Eileen Oge,* and such, by this time, were the temperature and the smells of the quay that I actually welcomed the moment that found us leaving it for the yacht.

" Now, Sinclair, aren't you glad we came? " remarked Philippa, as the clear green water deepened under us, and a light briny air came coolly round us with the motion of the boat.

As she spoke, there was an outburst of screams from the children on the quay, followed by a heavy splash.

" Oh, stop! " cried Philippa in an agony; " one of them has fallen in! I can see its poor little brown head! "

" 'Tis a dog, ma'am," said briefly the man who was rowing stroke.

" One might have wished it had been that little girl," said I, as I steered to the best of my ability for the yacht.

We had traversed another twenty yards or so, when Philippa, in a voice in which horror and triumph were strangely blended, exclaimed, " She's following us! "

" Who? The little girl? " I asked callously.

" No," returned Philippa; " worse."

I looked round, not without a prevision of what I was to see, and beheld the faithful Maria swimming steadily after us, with her brown muzzle thrust out in front of her ripping through the reflections like a plough.

" Go home! " I roared, standing up and gesticulating in fury that I well knew to be impotent. " Go home, you brute! "

Maria redoubled her efforts, and Philippa murmured uncontrollably:

" Well, she *is* a dear! "

Had I had a sword in my hand I should undoubtedly have slain Philippa; but before I could express my sentiments in any way, a violent shock flung me endways on top of the man who was pulling stroke. Thanks to Maria, we had reached our destination all unawares; the two men, respectfully awaiting my instructions, had rowed on with disciplined steadiness, and, as a result, we had rammed the *Eileen Oge* amidships, with a vigour that brought Mr. Shute tumbling up the companion to see what had happened.

" Oh, it's you, is it? " he said, with his mouth full. " Come in; don't knock! Delighted to see you, Mrs. Yeates; don't apologise. There's nothing like a hired ship after all—it's quite jolly to see the splinters fly—shows you're getting your money's worth. Hullo! who's this? "

This was Maria, feigning exhaustion, and noisily treading water at the boat's side.

" What, poor old Maria? Wanted to send her ashore, did he? Heartless ruffian! "

Thus was Maria installed on board the *Eileen Oge,* and the element of fatality had already begun to work.

There was just enough wind to take us out of Clountiss Harbour, and with the last of the out-running tide we crept away to the west. The party on board consisted of our host's sister, Miss Cecilia Shute, Miss Sally Knox, and ourselves; we sat about in conventional attitudes in deck chairs and on adamantine deck bosses, and I talked to Miss Shute with feverish brilliancy, and wished the patience-cards were not in the cabin; I knew the supreme importance of keeping one's mind occupied, but I dared not face the cabin. There was a long, almost imperceptible swell, with little queer sea-birds that I have never seen before—and trust I never shall again—dotted about on its glassy slopes. The coast-line looked low and grey and dull, as, I think, coast-lines always do when viewed from the deep. The breeze that Bernard had promised us we should find outside was barely enough to keep us moving. The burning sun of four o'clock focussed its heat on the deck; Bernard stood up among us, engaged in what he was pleased to call " handling the stick," and beamed almost as offensively as the sun.

" Oh, we're slipping along," he said, his odiously healthy face glowing like copper against the blazing blue sky. " You're going a great deal faster than you think, and the men say we'll pick up a breeze once we're round the Mizen."

I made no reply; I was not feeling ill, merely thoroughly disinclined for conversation. Miss Sally smiled wanly, and closing her eyes, laid her head on Philippa's knee. Instructed by a dread free-masonry, I knew that for her the moment had come when she could no longer bear to see the rail rise slowly above the horizon, and with an equal rhythmic slowness sink below it. Maria moved restlessly to and fro, panting and yawning, and occasionally rearing

herself on her hind-legs against the side, and staring forth with
wild eyes at the headachy sliding of the swell. Perhaps she was
meditating suicide; if so I sympathised with her, and since she was
obviously going to be sick I trusted that she would bring off the
suicide with as little delay as possible. Philippa and Miss Shute
sat in unaffected serenity in deck chairs, and stitched at white things
—tea-cloths for the *Eileen Oge*, I believe, things in themselves a
mockery—and talked untiringly, with that singular indifference to
their marine surroundings that I have often observed in ladies who
are not sea-sick. It always stirs me afresh to wonder why they
have not remained ashore; nevertheless, I prefer their tranquil and
total lack of interest in seafaring matters to the blatant Vikingism
of the average male who is similarly placed.

Somehow, I know not how, we crawled onwards, and by about
five o'clock we had rounded the Mizen, a gaunt spike of a headland
that starts up like a boar's tusk above the ragged lips of the Irish
coast, and the *Eileen Oge* was beginning to swing and wallop in the
long sluggish rollers that the American liners know and despise. I
was very far from despising them. Down in the west, resting on
the sea's rim, a purple bank of clouds lay awaiting the descent of
the sun, as seductively and as malevolently as a damp bed at a
hotel awaits a traveller.

The end, so far as I was concerned, came at tea-time. The meal
had been prepared in the saloon, and thither it became incumbent
on me to accompany my hostess and my wife. Miss Sally, long
past speech, opened, at the suggestion of tea, one eye, and disclosed
a look of horror. As I tottered down the companion I respected
her good sense. The *Eileen Oge* had been built early in the sixties,
and head-room was not her strong point; neither, apparently, was
ventilation. I began by dashing my forehead against the frame of
the cabin door, and then, shattered morally and physically, entered
into the atmosphere of the pit. After which things, and the sight
of a plate of rich cake, I retired in good order to my cabin, and
began upon the Yanatas.

I pass over some painful intermediate details and resume at the
moment when Bernard Shute woke me from a drugged slumber to
announce that dinner was over.

" It's been raining pretty hard," he said, swaying easily with the
swing of the yacht; " but we've got a clinking breeze, and we ought
to make Lurriga Harbour to-night. There's good anchorage there,
the men say. They're rather 'a lot of swabs, but they know this
coast, and I don't. I took 'em over with the ship all standing."

" Where are we now? " I asked, something heartened by the
blessed word " anchorage."

" You're running up Sheepskin Bay—it's a thundering big bay;
Lurriga's up at the far end of it, and the night's as black as the
inside of a cow. Dig out and get something to eat, and come on

deck—— What! no dinner?"—I had spoken morosely, with closed eyes—" Oh, rot! you're on an even keel now. I promised Mrs. Yeates I'd make you dig out. You're as bad as a soldier officer that we were ferrying to Malta one time in the old *Tamar*. He got one leg out of his berth when we were going down the Channel, and he was too sick to pull it in again till we got to Gib!"

I compromised on a drink and some biscuits. The ship was certainly steadier, and I felt sufficiently restored to climb weakly on deck. It was by this time past ten o'clock, and heavy clouds blotted out the last of the afterglow, and smothered the stars at their birth. A wet warm wind was lashing the *Eileen Oge* up a wide estuary; the waves were hunting her, hissing under her stern, racing up to her, crested with the white glow of phosphorus, as she fled before them. I dimly discerned in the greyness the more solid greyness of the shore. The mainsail loomed out into the darkness, nearly at right angles to the yacht, with the boom creaking as the following wind gave us an additional shove. I know nothing of yacht sailing, but I can appreciate the grand fact that in running before a wind the boom is removed from its usual sphere of devastation.

I sat down beside a bundle of rugs that I had discovered to be my wife, and thought of my whitewashed office at Shreelane and its bare but stationary floor, with a yearning that was little short of passion. Miss Sally had long since succumbed; Miss Shute was tired, and had turned in soon after dinner.

" I suppose she's overdone by the delirious gaiety of the afternoon," said I acridly, in reply to this information.

Philippa cautiously poked forth her head from the rugs, like a tortoise from under its shell, to see that Bernard, who was standing near the steersman, was out of hearing.

" In all your life, Sinclair," she said impressively, " you never knew such a time as Cecilia and I have had down there! We've had to wash *everything* in the cabins, and remake the beds, and *hurl* the sheets away—they were covered with black finger-marks —and while we were doing that, in came the creature that calls himself the steward, to ask if he might get something of his that he had left in Miss Shute's ' birthplace '! and he rooted out from under Cecilia's mattress a pair of socks and half a loaf of bread!"

" Consolation to Miss Shute to know her berth has been well aired," I said, with the nearest approach to enjoyment I had known since I came on board; " and has Sally made any equally interesting discoveries?"

" She said she didn't care what her bed was like; she just dropped into it. I must say I am sorry for her," went on Philippa; " she hated coming. Her mother made her accept."

" I wonder if Lady Knox will make her accept *him*!" I said. " How often has Sally refused him, does any one know?"

" Oh, about once a week," replied Philippa; " just the way I kept on refusing you, you know! "

Something cold and wet was thrust into my hand, and the aroma of damp dog arose upon the night air; Maria had issued from some lair at the sound of our voices, and was now, with palsied tremblings, slowly trying to drag herself on to my lap.

" Poor thing, she's been so dreadfully ill," said Philippa. " Don't send her away, Sinclair. Mr. Shute found her lying on his berth not able to move; didn't you, Mr. Shute? "

" She found out that she was able to move," said Bernard, who had crossed to our side of the deck; " it was somehow borne in upon her when I got at her with a boot-tree. I wouldn't advise you to keep her in your lap, Yeates. She stole half a ham after dinner, and she might take a notion to make the only reparation in her power."

I stood up and stretched myself stiffly. The wind was freshening, and though the growing smoothness of the water told that we were making shelter of some kind, for all that I could see of land we might as well have been in mid-ocean. The heaving lift of the deck under my feet, and the lurching swing when a stronger gust filled the ghostly sails, were more disquieting to me in suggestion than in reality, and, to my surprise, I found something almost enjoyable in rushing through darkness at the pace at which we were going.

" We're a small bit short of the mouth of Lurriga Harbour yet, sir," said the man who was steering, in reply to a question from Bernard. " I can see the shore well enough; sure I know every yard of wather in the bay——"

As he spoke he sat down abruptly and violently; so did Bernard, so did I. The bundle that contained Philippa collapsed upon Maria.

" Main sheet! " bellowed Bernard, on his feet in an instant, as the boom swung in and out again with a terrific jerk. " We're ashore! "

In response to this order three men in succession fell over me while I was still struggling on the deck, and something that was either Philippa's elbow, or the acutest angle of Maria's skull, hit me in the face. As I found my feet the cabin skylight was suddenly illuminated by a wavering glare. I got across the slanting deck somehow, through the confusion of shouting men and the flapping thunder of the sails, and saw through the skylight a gush of flame rising from a pool of fire around an overturned lamp on the swing-table. I avalanched down the companion and was squandered like an avalanche on the floor at the foot of it. Even as I fell, McCarthy the steward dragged the strip of carpet from the cabin floor and threw it on the blaze; I found myself, in some unexplained way, snatching a railway rug from Miss Shute and applying it to the same purpose, and in half-a-dozen seconds we had smothered the flame and were left in total darkness. The most striking feature of the situation was the immovability of the yacht.

"Great Ned!" said McCarthy, invoking I know not what heathen deity, "is it on the bottom of the say we are? Well, whether or no, thank God, we have the fire quinched!"

We were not, so far, at the bottom of the sea, but during the next ten minutes the chances seemed in favour of our getting there. The yacht had run her bows upon a sunken ridge of rock, and after a period of feminine indecision as to whether she were going to slide off again, or roll over into deep water, she elected to stay where she was, and the gig was lowered with all speed, in order to tow her off before the tide left her.

My recollection of this interval is but hazy, but I can certify that in ten minutes I had swept together an assortment of necessaries and knotted them into my counterpane, had broken the string of my eyeglass, and lost my silver matchbox; had found Philippa's curling-tongs and put them in my pocket; had carted all the luggage on deck; had then applied myself to the manly duty of reassuring the ladies, and had found Miss Shute merely bored, Philippa enthusiastically anxious to be allowed to help to pull the gig, and Miss Sally radiantly restored to health and spirits by the cessation of movement and the probability of an early escape from the yacht.

The rain had, with its usual opportuneness, begun again; we stood in it under umbrellas, and watched the gig jumping on its tow-rope like a dog on a string, as its crew plied the labouring oar in futile endeavour to move the *Eileen Oge*. We had run on the rock at half-tide, and the increasing slant of the deck as the tide fell brought home to us the pleasing probability that at low water —viz. about 2 A.M.—we should roll off the rock and go to the bottom. Had Bernard Shute wished to show himself in the most advantageous light to Miss Sally he could scarcely have bettered the situation. I looked on in helpless respect while he whom I had known as the scourge of the hunting-field, the terror of the shooting-party, rose to the top of a difficult position and kept there, and my respect was, if possible, increased by the presence of mind with which he availed himself of all critical moments to place a protecting arm round Miss Knox.

By about 1 A.M. the two gaffs with which Bernard had contrived to shore up the slowly heeling yacht began to show signs of yielding, and, in approved shipwreck fashion we took to the boats, the yacht's crew in the gig remaining in attendance on what seemed likely to be the last moments of the *Eileen Oge*, while we, in the dinghy, sought for the harbour. Owing to the tilt of the yacht's deck, and the roughness of the broken water round her, getting into the boat was no mean feat of gymnastics. Miss Sally did it like a bird, alighting in the inevitable arms of Bernard; Miss Shute followed very badly, but, by innate force of character, successfully;

Philippa, who was enjoying every moment of her shipwreck, came last, launching herself into the dinghy with my silver shoe-horn clutched in one hand, and in the other the tea-basket. I heard the hollow clank of its tin cups as she sprang, and appreciated the heroism with which Bernard received one of its corners in his waist. How or when Maria left the yacht I know not, but when I applied myself to the bow oar I led off with three crabs, owing to the devotion with which she thrust her head into my lap.

I am no judge of these matters, but in my opinion we ought to have been swamped several times during that row. There was nothing but the phosphorus of breaking waves to tell us where the rocks were, and nothing to show where the harbour was except a solitary light, a masthead light, as we supposed. The skipper had assured us that we could not go wrong if we kept " a westerly course with a little northing on it "; but it seemed simpler to steer for the light, and we did so. The dinghy climbed along over the waves with an agility that was safer than it felt; the rain fell without haste and without rest, the oars were as inflexible as crowbars, and somewhat resembled them in shape and weight; nevertheless, it was Elysium when compared with the afternoon leisure of the deck of the *Eileen Oge*.

At last we came, unexplainably, into smooth water, and it was at about this time that we were first aware that the darkness was less dense than it had been, and that the rain had ceased. By imperceptible degrees a greyness touched the back of the waves, more a dreariness than a dawn, but more welcome than thousands of gold and silver. I looked over my shoulder and discerned vague bulky things ahead; as I did so, my oar was suddenly wrapped in seaweed. We crept on; Maria stood up with her paws on the gunwale, and whined in high agitation. The dark objects ahead resolved themselves into rocks, and without more ado Maria pitched herself into the water. In half a minute we heard her shaking herself on shore. We slid on; the water swelled under the dinghy, and lifted her keel on to grating gravel.

" We couldn't have done it better if we'd been the Hydrographer Royal," said Bernard, wading knee-deep in a light wash of foam, with the painter in his hand; " but all the same, that masthead light is some one's bedroom candle! "

We landed, hauled up the boat, and then feebly sat down on our belongings to review the situation, and Maria came and shook herself over each of us in turn. We had run into a little cove, guided by the philanthropic beam of a candle in the upper window of a house about a hundred yards away. The candle still burned on, and the anæmic daylight exhibited to us our surroundings, and we debated as to whether we could at 2.45 A.M. present ourselves as objects of compassion to the owner of the candle. I need hardly say that it was the ladies who decided on making the attempt, having, like most of their sex, a courage incomparably superior to ours in such matters; Bernard and I had not a grain of genuine compunction in our souls, but we failed in nerve.

We trailed up from the cove, laden with emigrants' bundles, stumbling on wet rocks in the half-light, and succeeded in making our way to the house. It was a small two-storeyed building, of that hideous breed of architecture usually dedicated to the rectories of the Irish Church; we felt that there was something friendly in the presence of a pair of carpet slippers in the porch, but there was a hint of exclusiveness in the fact that there was no knocker and that the bell was broken. The light still burned in the upper window, and with a faltering hand I flung gravel at the glass. This summons was appallingly responded to by a shriek; there was a flutter of white at the panes, and the candle was extinguished.

" Come away! " exclaimed Miss Shute, " it's a lunatic asylum! "

We stood our ground, however, and presently heard a footstep within, a blind was poked aside in another window, and we were inspected by an unseen inmate; then some one came downstairs, and the hall door was opened by a small man with a bald head and a long sandy beard. He was attired in a brief dressing-gown, and on his shoulder sat, like an angry ghost, a large white cockatoo. Its crest was up on end, its beak was a good two inches long and curved like a Malay kris; its claws gripped the little man's shoulder. Maria uttered in the background a low and thunderous growl.

" Don't take any notice of the bird, please," said the little man nervously, seeing our united gaze fixed upon this apparition; " he's extremely fierce if annoyed."

The majority of our party here melted away to either side of the hall door, and I was left to do the explaining. The tale of our misfortunes had its due effect, and we were ushered into a small drawing-room, our host holding open the door for us, like a nightmare footman with bare shins, a gnome-like bald head, and un unclean spirit swaying on his shoulder. He opened the shutters, and we sat decorously round the room, as at an afternoon party, while the situation was further expounded on both sides. Our entertainer, indeed, favoured us with the leading items of his family history, amongst them the facts that he was a Dr. Fahy from Cork, who had taken somebody's rectory for the summer, and had been prevailed on by some of his patients to permit them to join him as paying-guests.

" I said it was a lunatic aslyum," murmured Miss Shute to me.

" In point of fact," went on our host, " there isn't an empty room in the house, which is why I can only offer your party the use of this room and the kitchen fire, which I make a point of keeping burning all night."

He leaned back complacently in his chair, and crossed his legs;

then, obviously remembering his costume, sat bolt upright again. We owed the guiding beams of the candle to the owner of the cockatoo, an old Mrs. Buck, who was, we gathered, the most paying of all the patients, and also, obviously, the one most feared and cherished by Dr. Fahy. '' She has a candle burning all night for the bird, and her door open to let him walk about the house when he likes,'' said Dr. Fahy; '' indeed, I may say her passion for him amounts to dementia. He's very fond of me, and Mrs. Fahy's always telling me I should be thankful, as whatever he did we'd be bound to put up with it! ''

Dr. Fahy had evidently a turn for conversation that was un-affected by circumstance; the first beams of the early sun were lighting up the red chair covers before the door closed upon his brown dressing-gown, and upon the stately white back of the cockatoo, and the demoniac possession of laughter that had wrought in us during the interview burst forth unchecked. It was most painful and exhausting, as such laughter always is; but by far the most serious part of it was that Miss Sally, who was sitting in the window, somehow drove her elbow through a pane of glass, and Bernard, in pulling down the blind to conceal the damage, tore it off the roller.

There followed on this catastrophe a period during which reason tottered and Maria barked furiously. Philippa was the first to pull herself together, and to suggest an adjournment to the kitchen fire that, in honour of the paying-guests, was never quenched, and, respecting the repose of the household, we proceeded thither with a stealth that convinced Maria we were engaged in a rat hunt. The boots of paying-guests littered the floor, the débris of their last repast covered the table; a cat in some unseen fastness crooned a war song to Maria, who feigned unconsciousness and fell to scientific research in the scullery.

We roasted our boots at the range, and Bernard, with all a sailor's gift for exploration and theft, prowled in noisome purlieus and emerged with a jug of milk and a lump of salt butter. No one who has not been a burglar can at all realise what it was to roam through Dr. Fahy's basement storey, with the rookery of paying-guests asleep above, and to feel that, so far, we had repaid his confidence by breaking a pane of glass and a blind, and putting the scullery tap out of order. I have always maintained that there was something wrong with it before I touched it, but the fact remains that when I had filled Philippa's kettle no human power could prevail upon it to stop flowing. For all I know to the contrary it is running still.

It was in the course of our furtive return to the drawing-room that we were again confronted by Mrs. Buck's cockatoo. It was stand-ing in malign meditation on the stairs, and on seeing us it rose, without a word of warning, upon the wing, and with a long screech

flung itself at Miss Sally's golden-red head, which a ray of sunlight
had chanced to illumine. There was a moment of stampede, as
the selected victim, pursued by the cockatoo, fled into the drawing-
room; two chairs were upset (one, I think, broken), Miss Sally
enveloped herself in a window curtain, Philippa and Miss Shute
effaced themselves beneath a table; the cockatoo, foiled of its prey,
skimmed, still screeching, round the ceiling. It was Bernard who,
with a well-directed sofa-cushion, drove the enemy from the room.
There was only a chink of the door open, but the cockatoo turned
on his side as he flew, and swung through it like a woodcock.

We slammed the door behind him, and at the same instant there
came a thumping on the floor overhead, muffled, yet peremptory.

" That's Mrs. Buck! " said Miss Shute, crawling from under the
table; " the room over this is the one that had the candle in it."

We sat for a time in awful stillness, but nothing further happened,
save a distant shriek overhead, that told the cockatoo had sought
and found sanctuary in his owner's room. We had tea *sotto voce*,
and then, one by one, despite the amazing discomfort of the drawing-room chairs, we dozed off to sleep.

It was at about five o'clock that I woke with a stiff neck and an
uneasy remembrance that I had last seen Maria in the kitchen. The
others, looking, each of them, about twenty years older than their
age, slept in various attitudes of exhaustion. Bernard opened his
eyes as I stole forth to look for Maria, but none of the ladies awoke.
I went down the evil-smelling passage that led to the kitchen stairs,
and, there on a mat, regarding me with intelligent affection, was
Maria; but what—oh what was the white thing that lay between
her forepaws?

The situation was too serious to be coped with alone. I fled
noiselessly back to the drawing-room and put my head in; Bernard's
eyes—blessed be the light sleep of sailors!—opened again, and there
was that in mine that summoned him forth. (Blessed also be the
light step of sailors!) We took the corpse from Maria, withholding
perforce the language and the slaughtering that our hearts ached
to bestow. For a minute or two our eyes communed. " I'll get the
kitchen shovel," breathed Bernard; " you open the hall door! "

A moment later we passed like spirits into the open air, and on
into a little garden at the end of the house. Maria followed us,
licking her lips. There were beds of nasturtiums, and of purple
stocks, and of marigolds. We chose a bed of stocks, a plump bed,
that looked like easy digging. The windows were all tightly shut
and shuttered, and I took the cockatoo from under my coat and hid
it, temporarily, behind a box border. Bernard had brought a
shovel and a coal scoop. We dug like badgers. At eighteen inches
we got down into shale and stones, and the coal scoop struck work.
" Never mind," said Bernard; " we'll plant the stocks on top of
him."

It was a lovely morning, with a new-born blue sky and a light northerly breeze. As we returned to the house, we looked across the wavelets of the little cove and saw, above the rocky point round which we had groped last night, a triangular white patch moving slowly along. "The tide's lifted her!" said Bernard, standing stock still. He looked at Mrs. Buck's window and at me. "Yeates!" he whispered, "let's quit!"

It was now barely six o'clock, and not a soul was stirring. We woke the ladies and convinced them of the high importance of catching the tide. Bernard left a note on the hall table for Dr. Fahy, a beautiful note of leave-taking and gratitude, and apology for the broken window (for which he begged to enclose half-a-crown). No allusion was made to the other casualties. As we neared the strand he found an occasion to say to me: "I put in a postscript that I thought it best to mention that I had seen the cockatoo in the garden, and hoped it would get back all right. That's quite true, you know! But look here, whatever you do, you must keep it all dark from the ladies——"

At this juncture Maria overtook us with the cockatoo in her mouth.

# DANIEL CORKERY

# THE BREATH OF LIFE

THE opera company which I had accompanied as first violinist on so many tours suddenly collapsing, I found myself rather unexpectedly out of an engagement. I communicated with my society, and after a day's delay I was ordered to go at once to Clonmoyle.

I was in the worst of humours. Clonmoyle was one of those places in Ireland which, instead of increasing in size and importance as places ought, seem to have become accustomed to doing the very opposite. Once a city, it was now but a straggling town. What had brought an opera company to try its fortunes there I could make no guess at, yet there it was, and with difficulties accumulating about it. Here was I myself, for instance, in Clonmoyle because the manager had found it impossible to supplement his scanty travelling orchestra with local players; and several others as well as I had had to travel day and night to be in time for the opening performance. Only one local musician had been dug up; and of him this story.

In everything he stood apart from us. He was old, well over sixty, however young in appearance. He was large and heavy in build, easy-going, ruminative. We, the others in the band, were rather meagre, high-strung, irritable, worried—as is the way of our tribe; on this trip particularly so (consider my own case: a first-class violinist in such surroundings!). He, on the other hand, smiled the whole day long, and his voice whispered rather than spoke. It did not seem to trouble him that the old ramshackle theatre was mouldy, damp, foul-smelling. He did not seem to notice the cruel draughts that swept us while we played, and benumbed our fingers. It made no difference to him if the manager was in a vile temper over the receipts, and our conductor still worse, his rheumatism playing old Harry with him.

At our first rehearsal I discovered he could not play in tune. ' I'm in for it! '' I said, for a week of such fellowship I knew only too well would leave me a wreck. And even as I said this I saw the conductor staring hard at where the two of us were sitting side by side; was it possible he thought it was I who was playing like

that! He might well have thought so, for my companion's face
was not a guilty face; how any one could play so consistently flat
and still smile was a problem beyond me. Yes, Ignatius O'Byrne,
such was his name, still smiled and still flattened. The fact is, he
was the happiest man alive; it was as if he had come into an inheritance. Here he was fiddling away in his beloved operas, and it
was thirty years since he had last done so. These long thirty years
he explained to me in an interval, he had been rehearsing them in
his untidy lodgings in a back street, and more than that, he had
been thinking them out, phrase by phrase, " walking in the mists
upon these rain-soaked hills "—I give his very words. As he
spoke he swept his hand in a half-circle as if even there in the
theatre he could still behold them, the dreary hills that surround
Clonmoyle on every side and overlay it, as it were, with a sort of
perpetual gloom. And then he added: " Behind music is the
breath of life." A curious man, surely; I watched his face. It
was glowing, glowing, as long as the music held. And once when
in some happy passage the whole band was singing like one
" Bravo, Bravo! " I heard him whisper, and later on " Bravis-
simo! " and he ceased playing, ceased, until I thought of nudging
him with my elbow. And so, little by little, I came to forgive him
his flat playing and his awkward bowing.

Our conductor, a brute of a man, his body twisted into a knot
by rheumatism, was now constantly looking in our direction; but
whenever I saw him doing so I would make my violin sing for all
it was worth; were we not brothers in the same craft, this old man
and I? At rehearsal the second day my efforts to cover his
wretched playing failed; the conductor left his place, tied up and
all as he was in that knot of pain, shuffled over to where we sat
and stood between us! That settled for him which of us two was
playing flat. He scowled at the old resurrected musician, hissed
out a fierce, wicked word under his breath, and hobbled back to his
place. That night, just to make matters worse, I suppose, old
Byrne played altogether vilely! He had scarce a phrase in tune.
When the curtain fell he had to face a little tragic opera of his own
—the tragedy of old age and failing powers. He took it all without
a word. " The breath of life is behind music," he whispered to
me as he came from the interview; then he bent down, carefully
wrapped his fiddle in a piece of baize cloth, put it in his case and
made off.

The final explosion came at the rehearsal next day. He and I
were the first to arrive. The score of last night's opera, it was the
" Marriage of Figaro," still lay on the conductor's stand. He
turned the pages. They were pencilled all over with directions as
to the tempos of the various movements. Along these pencillings
old Byrne ran his finger. I could see he was having his revenge.
I could see him lift his brows—just a little—as if he were amused

partly astonished. But no word escaped him. Soon the conductor came in and we began. We had not got far when we heard " Get out! " roared in a terrible voice, the voice of one who had not slept for several nights. The old man rose up, wrapped his baize cloth around his instrument, and moved between the chairs. As he went how still the house was, only a chair moving, and his own almost silent feet! And how we watched him! But when he got as far as the conductor's chair he paused, glanced once more at the open score, once again ran his finger along the pencillings, and laughed a tiny little laugh!

I felt his going more than I should care to tell. Will you believe me? I had told that old musician, that stranger, the whole story of the sorrows of my life. Yes, I told him things I had hardly ever made clear even to myself! And he replied: " Is it not behind music, the breath of life? " as if sorrow was there for the one purpose of being transmuted into sweet sound! I recalled his words as I went to my task that night.

And that night the extraordinary thing happened; our conductor failed to make an appearance: his rheumatism had conquered. There was then a call for our leader. He was found. Alas, he was not in a condition to conduct anything. He could scarcely stand. And he became quite cross about it; we had to leave him there in his corner, resining his bow like anything and scowling like mad. What between principals, chorus, and band, all thinking they stood a chance of losing a night's pay, and the manager flustering about like a whirlwind, our little den beneath the stage was deafening; I slipped quietly out into the house. There outside the rail was old Byrne! " What's the matter? " he whispered. As I told him, up came the manager.

" Mr. Melton," he said to me, " will you please take the baton to-night? "

A very flattering compliment, indeed, and I should have taken that baton, if our band did not happen to be the scraggiest ever scraped together from the ends of the earth; our leader was in the condition I have mentioned. As we spoke I saw the players getting into their places, a tempting sight, yet still I hesitated, foreseeing collapse and ignominy.

" It is not possible," I began, but over the rail old Byrne was climbing like a boy. He had clutched the baton from the manager's hand. He had leaped into the conductor's chair. He gave but one glance to the right, to the left. " Now, boys," he said, and at the words we swam, sank, buried ourselves in the rich, broad, gentle strains of the overture to " Faust." Some wide gesture he had used, some thrill in his tone had bidden us to do so—to lose ourselves in the soul of the music. At the first chord we had got within the skin of it, as the saying is. And never was the mood broken; every progression told, and not a colour tone was faulty or blurred. That memorable waltz, which use has almost spoiled, he made a new thing of it—we were all spirits in thin air, so lightly it went. But our triumph was the tremendous trio at the close. The old man stood up to it, hiding the stage from a large sector of the house. What did he care! We felt his huge shabby figure above us as a darkness, a vastness of great potency. It commanded stage, orchestra, house, with a strong yet benign power. The voices, tenor, soprano, bass—all the instruments, strings, brass, wood, drums, the very shell of the old house itself, became as one instrument and sang the great strain with such strength and perfection that some of us trembled lest we should fall down with excitement and spoil everything.

" Oh! " we all sighed when it was over. For such moments does the artist live. I was so glad I had told him the story of my sorrows!

Now, sir, around Clonmoyle, as I have said, is a rampart of dark hills, bleak and rain-sodden, treeless and desolate. Why do I again mention them? " Wherever did you learn to conduct? " I asked him, as we made for our lodgings.

" There! " he answered, and his outstretched hand gestured around the deserted hills, " behind music we must get at the breath of life." Bare, wind-swept hills!—curious place to find out the secrets of life! Or what did he mean by " Life "? It cannot be that the breath of life that is behind all great music is the sigh of loneliness?

" And you took him with the company? "

" No, sir; an opera company, like any other company, must pay its way."

# THE CHILD SAINT

## Daniel Corkery

The people in the same lodging-house sometimes spoke of him as The Child: at other times they called him The Saint. One name was as apt as the other; in spite of the squalid environment in which he lived, he was a saint; in spite of his age, a child. His hair was scanty, wispy, tow-like, and the scalp, not too clean, showed through it. His knees were bent. He walked with his back almost parallel with the ground, his spine long since having suffered injury. From that awkward posture his eyes stared up at you, full of light, smiling, brave with innocence. In spite of his hand's heavy clutch

on its knob his stick was always trembling; the fact reminded you
of his age when his brave eyes would have deceived you.

His room was filled with objects of devotion; of other furniture
there was little or none. He had several pictures of the Blessed
Virgin, a few of the Holy Family, many of the better-known saints
—St. Patrick, St. Joseph, St. Anthony. He had several statues,
besides a bottle of Lourdes water, and of Holy Water he kept a
small supply in a little chinaware font which a chinaware angel,
kneeling, upheld. Among these, his treasures, he lived alone in
quiet ecstasy, speaking much to himself—perhaps to them, too, on
occasions.

He knew that the Phelan family, they lived on a lower landing,
were in trouble. His hand catching his door, he listened to the
rent-collector's voice growing louder, angrier; then he heard him
begin to pound his stick on the stairs; so sure as he did that a
notice-to-quit would follow. The Child began to scramble down
the stairs to the rescue. "My," "My," "My," he repeated as
he made from step to step.

"Give her till to-morrow, give her till to-morrow," he cried,
when he had come into view of the little group; and as he flopped
down he continued to call out, "Give her till to-morrow."

"'Tis too long I'm after giving her, I'm pestered with
her."

"Give her wan last chance, 'twill be paid to-morrow."

"At this time to-morrow?"

"Yes, at this time to-morrow; or say in the evening, at seven;
give us the whole day?"

The agent put his book in his breast-pocket, stooped his head,
and piloted himself down the crazy, box-like stairs. He trusted
The Child to come at the rent for Mrs. Phelan, it didn't matter to
him how, so long as he got it.

Meanwhile The Child refused to tell Mrs. Phelan how he meant
to relieve her; no, he wouldn't tell her, but she need have no fear,
he'd be there to-morrow to meet the Man, as they called the rent-
collector. With this she had to be satisfied. She tightened her
shawl about the white-faced babe on her arm, and was soon in the
midst of the traffic spiritlessly singing, "The Rocks of Bawn." A
hardened beggar-woman, who would believe her story of the notice-
to-quit? She didn't bother telling it.

When she had started on her rounds, The Child took up his chinaware angel, and having emptied the Holy Water into a bottle,
dusted the figure and put it into his beggarman's bag; the shining
head of golden curls looked out over the edge. Then he mounted
up on his rickety bed and took down one of his loveliest pictures.
In it the Blessed Virgin was seated on a Renaissance throne, behind
her an Italian-blue sky and hosts of golden stars. He cleaned off
the dust and laid the picture flat on the bed. Into the great tail-

pocket of his coat he put a small painted plaster statue of St. Anthony. Then he came back to his picture on the bed, looked at it, gave it a last rub, caught it up, and with great difficulty made down the narrow stairs. His beggar's bag he had also with him, the shining angel peeping from it.

Earnestly he shuffled his way to where Mrs. McCarthy was selling bedsteads, stools, and " altars " on the Coal Quay—the open-air market-place in that city. She undertook to sell his wares, he sitting by on one of her stools, his two hands on the knob of his stick. He knew she would make more on them than he would get in any pawn-office.

The china angel was the first to go. In the bartering the old man took no part, but just as the purchaser—a hale, soft-featured woman—was moving off, he said:

" Pardon me for making so bold, ma'am; but might you be living in Blarney Lane? "

He thought she looked like a woman from Blarney Lane.

" No, then," she answered, " I'm from the South Side."

" Ah," he murmured, " Evergreen, maybe? "

" No, Gunpowder Lane, if you know where that is? "

" I do then—Gunpowder Lane—well, well."

The purchaser went off, her bargain under her shawl. The picture being large, and judging by its look, expensive, took a lot of selling. A half-crown is big money on the Coal Quay, yet this Mrs. McCarthy fixed as the price. Several people examined it, and at each chance Mrs. McCarthy would take it up on her lap, stand it on an angle, wipe it with her apron, and call it a handsome piece. She succeeded in selling it to a young mother.

" I can't afford it," she said, " and I can't leave it after me— that's how it is."

" 'Tis a blessing you're taking into your house," said Mrs. McCarthy. Then the old man raised his eyes:

" If I'm not making too bold, are you the young woman that keeps the shop in Windmill Road? "

" I never had a shop, sir," she answered.

" Do you live in Windmill Road? "

" No."

" Nor in Gunpowder Lane? "

" No." She was looking at him with large, shining eyes.

" Do you live in the South Side at all? "

" No—'tis on the Rock Steps I live."

" The Rock Steps—well, well—that's not too far—well, well, look at that, and I thinking you were from the South Side."

Going from them she looked questioningly at Mrs. McCarthy; perhaps she had doubts of the old man's sanity.

It was just six o'clock when a very old woman bought the St. Anthony. As she was bargaining for it, the Angelus rang, and this, perhaps, made her give the full penny asked. She lived in Pouladuff.

" My, my," said The Child, " what a long way off, what a long way off."

He rose from his stool.

" What do you want to know where the people live for? " Mrs. McCarthy questioned him.

" Wouldn't I like to be thinking of where they are? Hadn't I that picture before my eyes for the last forty years? Will it be easy for me to live without thinking of it? "

Hobbling homewards, he repeated his lesson over and over again: The Angel in Gunpowder Lane, Holy Mother in a house on the Rock Steps, St. Anthony in Pouladuff.

The next day, he paid the rent for Mrs. Phelan. Straightway then he began to save up his odd pence and halfpence to buy back his treasures. There was a vacant space on his mantelpiece, another on his window-sill (how lovely the painted statue used to look there among the green-leaved geraniums when the sun shone in!); the worst gap of all, however, was the huge space of clean wall-paper where the picture had hung. Because of these blank spaces, the room looked upset, unfurnished. But he was a saint as well as a child; somehow his savings, pinch as he would, refused to mount up. The fact is, money would burn a hole in his pocket. How could he keep a grip on it if he saw a blind man's hand stretched out to the callous passers-by, or a hungry-looking boy staring in at a shop window?

Again and again he had to begin anew. One night in bed he reckoned up with some excitement that twelve months would soon have gone by. And, as luck had it, a few days afterwards he chanced to hear a powerful sermon on the precious cintment that Magdalen had poured upon our Lord's feet, " wasting money that might be devoted to charity," as the preacher said, throwing great scorn on the wisdom of the world into his enunciation of these words. Yes, the old man felt all that sermon come home to him, every phrase. Cost what it would, the end of the twelve months would see him with all his treasures gathered and housed once more within his attic under the slates.

On the anniversary of the sale he rose quite early, heard Mass, and set off in much uncertainty to gather his treasures. He almost fell down when it suddenly struck him that they might have frequently changed owners since his parting with them, and that he might after all never gather them together again.

He came in and went up the stairs at one o'clock in the day.

" Mrs. Mehigan! " he called, as he passed her door (she was an old bed-ridden woman).

" Yes, what is it? "

" I have wan of them—the angel."

At five o'clock he passed up again.

" Mrs. Mehigan! Mrs. Mehigan! "

" Yes."

" I've another—St. Anthony."

He passed up a third time; it was now about eight o'clock. He didn't speak. Mrs. Mehigan listened to his steps, how tired he seemed, going up to his room! She called out:

" Have you the last wan? "

" No." She thought 'twas a gasp; by way of sympathy she said: " Oh, dear."

" But I'm on the track of it," he answered quite brightly. He went out again.

The whole house was dark, its many inhabitants snoring when he was heard struggling up the stairs once more, almost as a drunken man would, falling from side to side, and missing his steps, it seemed.

The next morning Mrs. Phelan came into Mrs. Mehigan's room. She believed, she said, the Saint hadn't got the last one after all. Mrs. Mehigan answered that God was good. " Go up and see," she said. Mrs. Phelan went up, knocked, and got no reply. She came back to Mrs. Mehigan.

" He's fast asleep; I didn't knock very loud, I only tapped at the door; 'tis how he's exhausted entirely."

" I'm sure he had something in his arms, he nearly fell against that door as he went up."

After some time Mrs. Phelan was sent up again. Mrs. Mehigan heard her knocking once, twice, thrice. Then she came down, as white as a sheet.

" Go out for Father Maher, child," said Mrs. Mehigan.

They found the Saint sitting on the floor, an unfinished bowl of bread and milk between his legs; opposite his now-cold eyes was his Renaissance Madonna, it stood propped against the edge of the bed; guarding it on the right was St. Anthony, on the left the chinaware angel, its font full of holy water. The candle that had lighted his treasures for him had burnt out. Mrs. Phelan says when first she entered the room there was the smell of lovely flowers. Mrs. Mehigan says she heard far-away singing in the dead of night. In any case it is pleasant to think how sweet the old man's thoughts must have been as his eyes began to close for ever. Not far-away music nor newly-gathered flowers would be so sweet.

## LORD DUNSANY

B. 1878

# THE CITY ON MALLINGTON MOOR

BESIDES the old shepherd at Langside, whose habits render him
unreliable, I am probably the only person that has ever seen the city
on Mallington Moor.

I had decided one year to do no London season, partly because
of the ugliness of the things in the shops, partly because of the
unresisted invasion of German bands, partly perhaps because some
pet parrots in the oblong where I lived had learned to imitate cab-
whistles, but chiefly because of late there had seized me in London
a quite unreasonable longing for large woods and waste spaces,
while the very thought of little valleys underneath copses full of
bracken and fox-gloves was a torment to me, and every summer in
London the longing grew worse till the thing was becoming intolerable. So I took a stick and a knapsack and began walking north-
wards, starting at Tetherington and sleeping at inns, where one
could get real salt and the waiter spoke English, and where one had
a name instead of a number; and though the tablecloth might be
dirty, the windows opened so that the air was clean; where one had
the excellent company of farmers and men of the world, who could
not be thoroughly vulgar because they had not the money to be so
even if they had wished it. At first the novelty was delightful, and
then one day in a queer old inn up Uthering way beyond Langside
I heard for the first time the rumour of the city said to be on Mallington Moor. They spoke of it quite casually over their glasses of beer,
two farmers at the inn. " They say the queer folk be at Mallington
with their city," one farmer said. " Travelling they seem to be,"
said the other. And more came in then and the rumour spread.
And then, such are the contradictions of our little likes and dislikes
and all the whims that drive us, that I who had come so far to
avoid cities had a great longing all of a sudden for throngs again
and the great hives of Man, and then and there determined on that
bright Sunday morning to come to Mallington and there search for
the city that rumour spoke of so strangely.

Mallington Moor from all that they said of it was hardly a likely place to find a thing by searching. It was a huge high moor, very bleak and desolate, and altogether trackless. It seemed a lonely place from what they said. The Normans when they came had called it Mal Lieu, and afterwards Mallieutown, and so it changed to Mallington. Though what a town can ever have to do with a place so utterly desolate I do not know. And before that some say that the Saxons called it Baplas, which I believe to be a corruption of Bad Place.

And beyond the mere rumour of a beautiful city all of white marble and with a foreign look up on Mallington Moor, beyond this I could not get. None of them had seen it themselves, " only heard of it like," and my questions, rather than stimulating conversation, would always stop it abruptly. I was no more fortunate on the road to Mallington, until the Tuesday when I was quite near it; I had been walking two days from the inn where I had heard the rumour and could see the great hill, steep as a headland, on which Mallington lay, standing up on the skyline; the hill was covered with grass, where anything grew at all, but Mallington Moor is all heather; it is just marked Moor on the map; nobody goes there and they do not trouble to name it. It was there where the gaunt hill first came into sight, by the roadside as I inquired for the marble city of some labourers by the way, that I was directed, partly, I think, in derision, to the old shepherd of Langside. It appeared that he following sometimes sheep that had strayed, and wandering far from Langside, came sometimes up to the edge of Mallington Moor, and that he would come back from these excursions and shout through the villages, raving of a city of white marble and gold-tipped minarets. And hearing me asking questions of this city they had laughed and directed me to the shepherd at Langside. One well-meant warning they gave me as I went—the old man was not reliable.

And late that evening I saw the thatches of Langside sheltering under the edge of that huge hill that Atlas-like held up those miles of moor to the great winds and heaven.

They knew less of the city in Langside than elsewhere, but they knew the whereabouts of the man I wanted, though they seemed a little ashamed of him. There was an inn in Langside that gave me shelter, whence in the morning, equipped with purchases, I set out to find their shepherd. And there he was on the edge of Mallington Moor standing motionless, gazing stupidly at his sheep; his hands trembled continually and his eyes had a blear look, but he was quite sober, wherein all Langside had wronged him.

And then and there I asked him of the city, and he said he had never heard tell of any such place. And I said, " Come, come, you must pull yourself together." And he looked angrily at me; but when he saw me draw from amongst my purchases a full bottle of whisky and a big glass he became more friendly. As I poured out the whisky I asked him again about the marble city on Mallington Moor, but he seemed quite honestly to know nothing about it. The amount of whisky he drank was quite incredible, but I seldom express surprise, and once more I asked him the way to the wonderful city. His hand was steadier now and his eyes more intelligent, and he said that he had heard something of some such city, but his memory was evidently blurred and he was still unable to give me useful directions. I consequently gave him another tumbler, which he drank off like the first without any water, and almost at once he was a different man. The trembling in his hands stopped altogether, his eye became as quick as a younger man's, he answered my questions readily and frankly, and, what was more important to me still, his old memory became alert and clear for even minutest details. His gratitude to myself I need not mention, for I make no pretence that I bought the bottle of whisky that the old shepherd enjoyed so much, without at least some thought of my own advantage. Yet it was pleasant to reflect that it was due to me that he pulled himself together and steadied his shaking hand and cleared his mind, recovered his memory and his self-respect. He spoke to me quite clearly, no longer slurring his words; he had seen the city first one moonlight night when he was lost in the mist on the big moor; he had wandered far in the mist, and when it lifted he saw the city by moonlight. He had no food, but luckily had his flask. There never was such a city, not even in books. Travellers talked sometimes of Venice seen from the sea; there might be such a place or there might not, but, whether or no, it was nothing to the city on Mallington Moor. Men who read books and talked to him in his time, hundreds of books, but they never could tell of any city like this. Why the place was all of marble, roads, walls, and palaces, all pure white marble, and the tops of the tall thin spires were entirely of gold. And they were queer folk in the city, even for foreigners. And there were camels —but I cut him short, for I thought I could judge for myself, if there was such a place, and, if not, I was wasting my time as well as a pint of good whisky. So I got him to speak of the way, and after more circumlocution than I needed and more talk of the city he pointed to a tiny track on the black earth just beside us, a little twisty way you could hardly see.

I said the moor was trackless; untrodden of man or dog it certainly was and seemed to have less to do with the ways of man than any waste I have seen, but the track the old shepherd showed me, if track it was, was no more than the track of a hare—an elf-path the old man called it, Heaven knows what he meant.

And then before I left him he insisted on giving me his flask with the queer strong rum it contained. Whisky brings out in some men melancholy, in some rejoicing, with him it was clearly generosity, and he insisted until I took his rum though I did not mean to drink it. It was lonely up there, he said, and bitter cold, and the city hard to find, being set in a hollow, and I should need the rum, and he had never seen the marble city except on days when he had had his flask. He seemed to regard that rusted iron flask as a sort of mascot, and in the end I took it.

I followed that odd, faint track on the black earth under the heather till I came to the big grey stone beyond the horizon where the track divides into two, and I took the one to the left as the old man told me. I knew by another stone that I saw far off that I had not lost my way nor the old man lied.

And just as I hoped to see the city's ramparts before the gloaming fell on that desolate place I suddenly saw a long high wall of whiteness with pinnacles here and there thrown up above it, floating towards me silent and grim as a secret, and knew it for that evil thing the mist. The sun, though low, was shining on every sprig of heather, the green and scarlet mosses were shining with it too; it seemed incredible that in three minutes' time all those colours would be gone and nothing left all round but a grey darkness. I gave up hope of finding the city that day, a broader path than mine could have been easily lost. I hastily chose for my bed a thick patch of heather, wrapped myself in a waterproof cloak, and lay down and made myself comfortable. And then the mist came. It came like the careful pulling of lace curtains, then like the drawing of grey blinds; it shut out the horizon to the north, then to the east and west; it turned the whole sky white and hid the moor; it came down on it like a metropolis, only utterly silent, silent and white as tombstones.

And then I was glad of that strange strong rum, or whatever it was in the flask that the shepherd gave me: for I did not think that the mist would clear till night, and I feared the night would be cold. So I nearly emptied the flask; and sooner than I expected I fell asleep, for the first night out as a rule one does not sleep at once but is kept awake some while by the little winds and the unfamiliar sound of the things that wander at night and that cry to one another far off with their queer faint voices; one misses them afterwards when one gets to houses again. But I heard none of these sounds in the mist that evening.

And then I woke and found that the mist was gone and the sun was just disappearing under the moon, and I knew that I had not slept for as long as I thought. And I decided to go on while I could, for I thought that I was not very far from the city.

I went on and on along the twisty track, bits of the mist came down and filled the hollows but lifted again at once so that I saw my way. The twilight faded as I went, a star appeared, and I was able to see the track no longer. I could go no farther that night, yet before I lay down to sleep I decided to go and look over the edge of a wide depression in the moor that I saw a little way off. So I left the track and walked a few hundred yards, and when I got to the edge the hollow was full of mist all white underneath me. Another star appeared and a cold wind arose, and with the wind the mist flapped away like a curtain. And there was the city.

Nothing the shepherd had said was the least untrue or even exaggerated. The poor old man had told the simple truth, there is not a city like it in the world. What he had called thin spires were minarets, but the little domes on the top were clearly pure gold, as he said. There were the marble terraces he described, and the pure white palaces covered with carving, and hundreds of minarets. The city was obviously of the East, and yet where there should have been crescents on the domes of the minarets there were golden suns with rays, and wherever one looked one saw things that obscured its origin. I walked down to it and, passing through a wicket gate of gold in a low wall of white marble, I entered the city. The heather went right up to the city's edge and beat against the marble wall whenever the wind blew it. Lights began to twinkle from high windows of blue glass; as I walked up the white street, beautiful copper lanterns were lit up and let down from balconies by silver chains; from doors ajar came the sound of voices singing, and then I saw the men. Their faces were rather grey than black, and they wore beautiful robes of coloured silk with hems embroidered with gold and some with copper. And sometimes pacing down the marble ways with golden baskets hung on each side of them I saw the camels of which the old shepherd spoke.

The people had kindly faces, but though they were evidently friendly to strangers I could not speak with them, being ignorant of their language, nor were the sounds of the syllables they used like any language I had ever heard, they sounded more like grouse.

When I tried to ask them by signs whence they had come with their city they would only point to the moon, which was bright and full and was shining fiercely on those marble ways till the city danced in light. And now there began appearing one by one, stepping softly out through the windows, men with stringed instruments in the balconies. They were strange instruments with huge bulbs of wood and they played softly on them and very beautifully, and their queer voices softly sang to the music weird dirges of the griefs of their native land wherever that may be. And far off in the heart of the city others were singing too; the sounds of it came to me wherever I roamed, not loud enough to disturb my thoughts, but gently turning the mind to pleasant things. Slender carved arches of marble as delicate almost as lace crossed and re-crossed the ways wherever I went. There was none of that hurry of which foolish cities boast, nothing ugly or sordid so far as I could see. I saw that it was a city of beauty and song. I wondered how they had travelled with all that marble, how they had laid it down on

Mallington Moor, whence they had come and what their resources were, and determined to investigate closely next morning, for the old shepherd had not troubled his head to think how the city came, he had only noted that the city was there (and of course no one believed him, though that is partly his fault for his dissolute ways). But at night one can see little and I had walked all day, so I determined to find a place to rest in. And just as I was wondering whether to ask for shelter of those silk-robed men by signs, or whether to sleep outside the walls and enter again in the morning, I came to a great archway in one of the marble houses with two black curtains, embroidered below with gold, hanging across it. Over the archway were carved apparently in many tongues the words: " Here strangers rest.'' In Greek, Latin, and Spanish the sentence was repeated, and there was writing also in the language that you see on the walls of the great temples of Egypt, and Arabic, and what I took to be early Assyrian, and one or two languages I had never seen. I entered through the curtains, and found a tessellated marble court with golden braziers burning sleepy incense swinging by chains from the roof; all round the walls were comfortable mattresses lying upon the floor, covered with cloths and silks. It must have been ten o'clock and I was tired. Outside the music still softly filled the streets, a man had set a lantern down on the marble way, five or six sat down round him and he was sonorously telling them a story. Inside there were some already asleep on the beds; in the middle of the wide court under the braziers a woman dressed in blue was singing very gently; she did not move, but sung on and on, I never heard a song that was so soothing. I lay down on one of the mattresses by the wall, which was all inlaid with mosaics, and pulled over me some of the clothes with their beautiful alien work, and almost immediately my thoughts seemed part of the song that the woman was singing in the midst of the court under the golden braziers that hung from the high roof, and the song turned them to dreams and so I fell asleep.

A small wind having arisen I was awakened by a sprig of heather that beat continually against my face. It was morning on Mallington Moor and the city was quite gone.

# CORONATION OF MR. THOMAS SHAP

LORD DUNSANY

IT was the occupation of Mr. Thomas Shap to persuade customers that the goods were genuine and of an excellent quality, and that as regards the price their unspoken will was consulted. And in order to carry on this occupation he went by train very early every morning to the city from the suburb in which he slept. This was the use to which he put his life.

From the moment when he first perceived (not as one reads a thing in a book, but as truths are revealed to one's instinct) the very beastliness of his occupation, and of the house that he slept in, its shape, make and pretensions, and of even the clothes that he wore; from that moment he withdrew his dreams from it, his fancies, his ambitions, everything in fact except that ponderable Mr. Shap that dressed in a frock-coat, bought tickets and handled money and could in turn be handled by the statistician. The priest's share in Mr. Shap, the share of the poet, never caught the early train to the city at all.

He used to take little flights with his fancy at first, dwelt all day in his dreamy way on fields and rivers lying in the sunlight where it strikes the world more brilliantly farther south. And then he began to imagine butterflies there; after that, silken people and the temples they built to their gods.

They noticed that he was silent, and even absent at times, but they found no fault with his behaviour with customers, to whom he remained as plausible as of old. So he dreamed for a year, and his fancy gained strength as he dreamed.

He still read halfpenny papers, in the train, still discussed the passing day's ephemeral topic, still voted at elections, though he no longer did these things with the whole Shap—his soul was no longer in them.

He had had a pleasant year; his imagination was all new to him still, and it had often discovered beautiful things away where it went, south-east at the edge of the twilight. And he had a matter-of-fact and logical mind, so that he often said, " Why should I pay my twopence at the electric theatre when I can see all sorts of things quite easily without? " Whatever he did was logical before anything else, and those that knew him always spoke of Shap as "a sound, sane, level-headed man."

On far the most important day of his life he went as usual to town by the early train to sell plausible articles to customers, while the spiritual Shap roamed off to fanciful lands. As he walked from the station, dreamy but wide awake, it suddenly struck him that the real Shap was not the one walking to Business in black and ugly clothes, but he who roamed along a jungle's edge near the ramparts of an old and Eastern city that rose up sheer from the sand, and against which the desert lapped with one eternal wave. He used to fancy the name of that city was Larkar.

"After all, the fancy is as real as the body," he said, with perfect logic. It was a dangerous theory.

For that other life that he led he realised, as in Business, the importance and value of method. He did not let his fancy roam too far, until it perfectly knew its first surroundings. Particularly he avoided the jungle—he was not afraid to meet a tiger there (after all it was not real), but stranger things might crouch there.

Slowly he built up Larkar: rampart by rampart, towers for archers, gateway of brass, and all. And then one day he argued, and quite rightly, that all the silk-clad people in its streets, their camels, their wares that came from Inkustahn, the city itself, were all the things of his will—and then he made himself King.

He smiled after that when people did not raise their hats to him in the street, as he walked from the station to Business; but he was sufficiently practical to recognise that it was better not to talk of this to those that only knew him as Mr. Shap.

Now that he was King in the city of Larkar and in all the desert that lay to the east and north, he sent his fancy to wander farther afield. He took the regiments of his camel-guard and went jingling out of Larkar, with little silver bells under the camels' chins, and came to other cities far-off on the yellow sand, with clear white walls and towers, uplifting themselves in the sun. Through their gates he passed with his three silken regiments, the light-blue regiment of the camel-guard being upon his right and the green regiment riding at his left, the lilac regiment going on before. When he had gone through the streets of any city and observed the ways of its people, and had seen the way that the sunlight struck its towers, he would proclaim himself King there, and then ride on in fancy. So he passed from city to city and from land to land.

Clear-sighted though Mr. Shap was, I think he overlooked the lust of aggrandisement to which the kings have so often been victims: and so it was that when the first few cities had opened their gleaming gates and he saw peoples prostrate before his camel, and spear-men cheering along countless balconies, and priests come out to do him reverence, he that had never had even the lowliest authority in the familiar world became unwisely insatiate. He let his fancy ride at inordinate speed; he forsook method; scarce was he king of a land but he yearned to extend his borders; so he journeyed deeper and deeper into the wholly unknown.

The concentration that he gave to this inordinate progress through countries of which history is ignorant and cities so fantastic in their bulwarks that, though their inhabitants were human, yet the foe that they feared seemed something less or more; the amazement with which he beheld gates and towers unknown even to art, and furtive people thronging intricate ways to acclaim him as their sovereign: all these things began to affect his capacity for Business. He knew as well as any that his fancy could not rule these beautiful lands unless that other Shap, however unimportant, were sheltered and fed: and shelter and food meant money, and money, Business. His was more like the mistake of some gambler with cunning schemes who overlooks human greed.

One day his fancy, riding in the morning, came to a city gorgeous as the sunrise, in whose opalescent wall were gates of gold, so huge that a river poured between the bars, floating in, when the gates were opened, large galleons under sail. Thence there came dancing out a company with instruments, and made a melody all round the wall; that morning Mr. Shap, the bodily Shap in London, forgot the train to town. Until a year ago he had never imagined at all; it is not to be wondered at that all these things now newly seen by his fancy should play tricks at first with the memory of even so sane a man. He gave up reading the papers altogether, he lost all interest in politics, he cared less and less for things that were going on around him.

This unfortunate missing of the morning train even occurred again, and the firm spoke to him severely about it. But he had his consolation. Were not Arâthrion and Argun Zeerith and all the level coasts of Oora his? And even as the firm found fault with him, his fancy watched the yaks on weary journeys, slow specks against the snow-fields, bringing tribute; and saw the green eyes of the mountain men who had looked at him strangely in the city of Nith when he had entered it by the desert door.

Yet his logic did not forsake him; he knew well that his strange subjects did not exist, but he was prouder of having created them with his brain, than merely of ruling them only; thus in his pride he felt himself something more great than a king, he did not dare to think what! He went into the temple of the city of Zorra and stood some time there, alone: all the priests kneeled to him when he came away.

He cared less and less for the things we care about, for the affairs of Shap, a business-man in London. He began to despise the man with a royal contempt. One day when he sat in Sowla, the city of the Thuls, throned on one amethyst, he decided, and it was pro-

claimed on the moment by silver trumpets all along the land, that
he would be crowned as king over all the lands of Wonder.

By that old temple where the Thuls were worshipped, year in,
year out, for over a thousand years, they pitched pavilions in the
open air. The trees that blew there threw out radiant scents unknown in any countries that know the map; the stars blazed fiercely
for that famous occasion. A fountain hurled up, clattering, ceaselessly into the air armfuls on armfuls of diamonds; a deep hush
waited for the golden trumpets; the holy coronation night was
come.

At the top of those old, worn steps, going down we know not
whither, stood the king in the emerald-and-amethyst cloak, the
ancient garb of the Thuls; beside him lay that Sphinx that for the
last few weeks had advised him in his affairs. Slowly, with music
when the trumpets sounded, came up towards him from we know
not where, one-hundred-and-twenty archbishops, twenty angels and
two archangels, with that terrific crown, the diadem of the Thuls.
They knew as they came up to him that promotion awaited them
all because of this night's work. Silent, majestic, the king awaited
them.

.        .        .        .        .        .        .

The doctors downstairs were sitting over their supper, the warders
softly slipped from room to room, and when in that cosy dormitory
of Hanwell they saw the king still standing erect and royal, his
face resolute, they came up to him and addressed him: " Go to
bed," they said—" pretty bed."

So he lay down and soon was fast asleep: the great day was
over.

# THE SWORD AND THE IDOL

### LORD DUNSANY

It was a cold winter's evening late in the Stone Age, the sun had
gone down blazing over the plains of Thold; there were no clouds,
only the chill blue sky and the imminence of stars; and the surface
of the sleeping Earth began to harden against the cold of the night.
Presently from their lairs arose, and shook themselves and went
stealthily forth, those of Earth's children to whom it is the law to
prowl abroad as soon as the dusk has fallen. And they went pattering softly over the plain, and their eyes shone in the dark, and

crossed and recrossed one another on their courses.  Suddenly there became manifest in the midst of the plain that fearful portent of the presence of Man—a little flickering fire.  And the children of Earth who prowl abroad by night looked sideways at it and snarled and edged away; all but the wolves, who came a little nearer, for it was winter and the wolves were hungry, and they had come in thousands from the mountains, and they said in their hearts, " We are strong."  Around the fire a little tribe was encamped.  They, too, had come from the mountains, and from lands beyond them, but it was in the mountains that the wolves first winded them; they picked up bones at first that the tribe had dropped, but they were closer now on all sides.  It was Loz who had lit the fire.  He had killed a small furry beast, hurling his stone axe at it, and had gathered a quantity of reddish brown stones, and had laid them in a long row, and placed bits of the small beast all along it; then he lit a fire on each side, and the stones heated, and the bits began to cook.  It was at this time that the tribe noticed that the wolves who had followed them so far were no longer content with the scraps of deserted encampments.  A line of yellow eyes surrounded them, and when it moved it was to come nearer.  So the men of the tribe hastily tore up brushwood, and felled a small tree with their flint axes, and heaped it all over the fire that Loz had  made, and for a while the great heap hid the flame, and the wolves came trotting in and sat down again on their haunches much closer than before; and the fierce and valiant dogs that belonged to the tribe believed that their end was about to come while fighting, as they had long since prophesied it would.  Then the flame caught the lofty stack of brushwood, and rushed out of it, and ran up the side of it, and stood up haughtily far over the top, and the wolves seeing this terrible ally of Man revelling there in his strength, and knowing nothing of his frequent treachery to his masters, went slowly away as though they had other purposes.  And for the rest of that night the dogs of the encampment cried out to them and besought them to come back.  But the tribe lay down all round the fire under thick furs and slept.  And a great wind arose and blew into the roaring heart of the fire till it was red no longer, but all pallid with heat.  With the dawn the tribe awoke.

Loz might have known that after such a mighty conflagration nothing could remain of his small furry beast, but there was hunger in him and little reason as he searched among the ashes.  What he found there amazed him beyond measure; there was no meat, there was not even his row of reddish brown stones, but something longer than a man's leg and narrower than his hand was lying there like a great flattened snake.  When Loz looked at its thin edges and saw that it ran to a point, he picked up stones to chip it and make it sharp.  It was the instinct of Loz to sharpen things.  When he found that it could not be chipped his wonderment increased.

It was many hours before he discovered that he could sharpen the edges by rubbing them with a stone; but at last the point was sharp, and all one side of it except near the end, where Loz held it in his hand. And Loz lifted it and brandished it, and the Stone Age was over. That afternoon in the little encampment, just as the tribe moved on, the Stone Age passed away, which, for perhaps thirty or forty thousand years, had slowly lifted Man from among the beasts and left him with his supremacy beyond all hope of reconquest.

It was not for many days that any other man tried to make for himself an iron sword by cooking the same kind of small furry beast that Loz had tried to cook. It was not for many years that any thought to lay the meat along stones as Loz had done; and when they did, being no longer on the plains of Thold, they used flints or chalk. It was not for many generations that another piece of iron ore was melted and the secret slowly guessed. Nevertheless one of Earth's many veils was torn aside by Loz to give us ultimately the steel sword and the plough machinery and factories; let us not blame Loz if we think that he did wrong, for he did all in ignorance. The tribe moved on until it came to water, and there it settled down under a hill, and they built their huts there. Very soon they had to fight with another tribe, a tribe that was stronger than them; but the sword of Loz was terrible and his tribe slew their foes. You might make one blow at Loz, but then would come one thrust from that iron sword, and there was no way of surviving it. No one could fight with Loz. And he became the ruler of the tribe in the place of Iz, who hitherto had ruled it with his sharp axe, as his father had before him.

Now Loz begat Lo, and in his old age gave his sword to him, and Lo ruled the tribe with it. And Lo called the name of the sword Death, because it was so swift and terrible.

And Iz begat Ird, who was of no account. And Ird hated Lo because he was of no account by reason of the iron sword of Lo.

One night Ird stole down to the hut of Lo, carrying his sharp axe, and he went very softly, but Lo's dog, Warner, heard him coming, and he growled softly by his master's door. When Ird came to the hut he heard Lo talking gently to his sword. And Lo was saying, " Lie still, Death. Rest, rest, old sword," and then, " What, again, Death? Be still. Be still."

And then again: " What, art thou hungry, Death? Or thirsty, poor old sword? Soon, Death, soon. Be still only a little."

But Ird fled, for he did not like the gentle tone of Lo as he spoke to his sword.

And Lo begat Lod. And when Lo died, Lod took the iron sword and ruled the tribe.

And Ird begat Ith, who was of no account, like his father.

Now when Lod had smitten a man or killed a terrible beast, Ith would go away for a while into the forest rather than hear the praises that would be given to Lod.

And once, as Ith sat in the forest waiting for the day to pass, he suddenly thought he saw a tree trunk looking at him as with a face. And Ith was afraid, for trees should not look at men. But soon Ith saw that it was only a tree and not a man, though it was like a man. Ith used to speak to this tree, and tell it about Lod, for he dared not speak to any one else about him. And Ith found comfort in talking about Lod.

One day Ith went with his stone axe into the forest, and stayed there many days.

He came back by night, and the next morning when the tribe awoke they saw something that was like a man and yet was not a man. And it sat on the hill with its elbows pointing outwards and was quite still. And Ith was crouching before it, and hurriedly placing before it fruits and flesh, and then leaping away from it and looking frightened. Presently all the tribe came out to see, but dared not come quite close because of the fear that they saw on the face of Ith. And Ith went to his hut, and came back again with a hunting spear-head and valuable small stone knives, and reached out and laid them before the thing that was like a man, and then sprang away from it.

And some of the tribe questioned Ith about the still thing that was like a man, and Ith said, " This is Ged." Then they asked, " Who is Ged? " and Ith said, " Ged sends the crops and the rain; and the sun and the moon are Ged's."

Then the tribe went back to their huts, but later in the day some came again, and they said to Ith, " Ged is only as we are, having hands and feet." And Ith pointed to the right hand of Ged, which was not as his left, but was shaped like the paw of a beast, and Ith said, " By this ye may know that he is not as any man."

Then they said, " He is indeed Ged." But Lod said, " He speaketh not, nor doth he eat," and Ith answered, " The thunder is his voice and the famine is his eating."

After this the tribe copied Ith, and brought little gifts of meat to Ged; and Ith cooked them before him that Ged might smell the cooking.

One day a great thunderstorm came trampling up from the distance and raged among the hills, and the tribe all hid away from it in their huts. And Ith appeared among the huts looking unafraid. And Ith said little, but the tribe thought that he had expected the terrible storm because the meat that they had laid before Ged had been tough meat, and not the best parts of the beasts they slew.

And Ged grew to have more honour among the tribe than Lod. And Lod was vexed.

One night Lod arose when all were asleep, and quieted his dog, and took his iron sword and went away to the hill. And he came on Ged in the starlight, sitting still, with his elbows pointing outwards, and his beast's paw, and the mark of the fire on the ground where his food had been cooked.

And Lod stood there for a while in great fear, trying to keep to his purpose. Suddenly he stepped up close to Ged and lifted his iron sword, and Ged neither hit nor shrank. Then the thought came into Lod's mind, " Ged does not hit. What will Ged do instead? "

And Lod lowered his sword and struck not, and his imagination began to work on that, " What will Ged do instead? "

And the more Lod thought, the worse was his fear of Ged.

And Lod ran away and left him.

Lod still ruled the tribe in battle or in the hunt, but the chiefest spoils of battle were given to Ged, and the beasts that they slew were Ged's; and all questions that concerned war or peace, and questions of law and disputes, were always brought to him, and Ith gave the answers after speaking to Ged by night.

At last Ith said, the day after an eclipse, that the gifts which they brought to Ged were not enough, that some far greater sacrifice was needed, that Ged was very angry even now, and not to be appeased by any ordinary sacrifice.

And Ith said that to save the tribe from the anger of Ged he would speak to Ged that night, and ask him what new sacrifice he needed.

Deep in his heart Lod shuddered, for his instinct told him that Ged wanted Lod's only son, who should hold the iron sword when Lod was gone.

No one would dare touch Lod because of the iron sword, but his instinct said in his slow mind again and again, " Ged loves Ith. Ith has said so. Ith hates the sword-holders."

" Ith hates the sword-holders. Ged loves Ith."

Evening fell and the night came when Ith should speak with Ged, and Lod became ever surer of the doom of his race.

He lay down but could not sleep.

Midnight had barely come when Lod arose and went with his iron sword again to the hill.

And there sat Ged. Had Ith been to him yet? Ith whom Ged loved, who hated the sword-holders.

And Lod looked long at the old sword of iron that had come to his grandfather on the plains of Thold.

Good-bye, old sword! And Lod laid it on the knees of Ged, then went away.

And when Ith came, a little before dawn, the sacrifice was found acceptable unto Ged.

# THE HEN

## Lord Dunsany

ALL along the farmyard gables the swallows sat a-row, twittering uneasily to one another, telling of many things, but thinking only of Summer and the South, for Autumn was afoot and the North wind waiting.

And suddenly one day they were all quite gone. And every one spoke of the swallows and the South.

" I think I shall go South myself next year," said a hen.

And the year wore on and the swallows came again, and the year wore on and they sat again in the gables, and all the poultry discussed the departure of the hen.

And very early one morning, the wind being from the North, the swallows all soared suddenly and felt the wind on their wings; and a strength came upon them and a strange old knowledge and a more than human faith, and flying high they left the smoke of our cities and small remembered eaves, and saw at last the huge and homeless sea, and steering by grey sea-currents went south-ward with the wind. And going South they went by glittering fog-banks and saw old islands lifting their heads above them; they saw the slow quests of the wandering ships, and divers seeking pearls, and lands at war, till there came in view the mountains that they sought and the sight of the peaks they knew; and they descended into an austral valley, and saw Summer sometimes sleeping and sometimes singing song.

" I think the wind is about right," said the hen; and she spread her wings and ran out of the poultry-yard. And she ran fluttering out on to the road and some way down it until she came to a garden.

At evening she came back panting.

And in the poultry-yard she told the poultry how she had gone South as far as the high road, and saw the great world's traffic going by, and came to lands where the potato grew, and saw the stubble upon which men live, and at the end of the road had found a garden, and there were roses in it—beautiful roses!—and the gardener himself was there with his braces on.

" How extremely interesting," the poultry said, " and what a really beautiful description! "

And the Winter wore away, and the bitter months went by, and the Spring of the year appeared, and the swallows came again.

" We have been to the South," they said, " and the valleys beyond the sea."

But the poultry would not agree that there was a sea in the South: " You should hear our hen," they said.

# THE ASSIGNATION

### Lord Dunsany

Fame singing in the highways, and trifling as she sang, with sordid adventurers, passed the poet by.

And still the poet made for her little chaplets of song to deck her forehead in the courts of Time; and still she wore instead the worthless garlands, that boisterous citizens flung to her in the ways, made out of perishable things.

And after a while whenever these garlands died the poet come to her with his chaplets of song; and still she laughed at him and wore the worthless wreaths, though they always died at evening.

And one day in his bitterness the poet rebuked her, and said to her: " Lovely Fame, even in the highways and the byways you have not forborne to laugh and shout and jest with worthless men, and I have toiled for you and dreamed of you and you mock me and pass me by."

And Fame turned her back on him and walked away, but in departing she looked over her shoulder and smiled at him as she had not smiled before, and, almost speaking in a whisper, said:

" I will meet you in the graveyard at the back of the Workhouse in a hundred years."

# STORY-TELLERS OF THE OVERSEAS

## Canada—South Africa—Australia

IN these stories by Britons of the overseas the humour of the earlier writers, with its own simplicity and directness, makes less appeal in our day than the finer note struck by the later. Courageous daring, tender pity, the tragedy and pathos in the high romance of human life are conspicuous to the observer in the far-off places of the earth and so figure largely in his stories. Judge Haliburton, Nova Scotian lawyer (and in after years an English M.P.), with a fund of rollicking good spirits and shrewd common-sense, was endeared to a past generation as " Sam Slick." Little more than a practical joke is the point of " Sister Sall's Courtship," yet it is thoroughly characteristic of the author's style and humour.

### LOUIS BECKE

Australia of the bushranging period is the scene of William S. Walker's " Midnight," and the element of comedy plays round the yarn of the police-inspector until the crack of pistol brings death to end the tale. With " Rodman the Boat-steerer " we have the best of all the short stories of the southern seas, written by Louis Becke, the Australian. The motive is fraternal love, and though for Rodman no happiness is born of the care lavished on the younger brother and sister, strength and steadiness remain, and sympathy and understanding. Clara Morris, the Canadian, once a famous actress in America, has a very different tale to tell. " The Wild Horse of Tartary " is just a reminiscence of circus life set down in admirable form.    The fun of the amiable old horse turned on at a moment's notice to play the fiery untamed steed is irresistible, and the quick change from grave to gay makes the mirth more brilliant.    " George Egerton," Australian born, widely travelled and an artist, belongs rather to England and the London of the 'nineties, when the vogue was to end an episode on a note of interrogation.    So does " A Little Grey Glove " end.    The delicate touch, the atmosphere of doubt and uncertainty, the mingling of hope and sorrow, the introspection revealing the heart of youth, all these are characteristic of their time.    The treatment rather than the subject treated is the thing to be noted in the work of " George Egerton."

## CHARLES G. D. ROBERTS

C. G. D. Roberts, the New Brunswick professor, is more than a writer of novels.    He is a poet and a naturalist.    And both the poet and naturalist are manifest in the story of the "Freedom of the Black-faced Ram." It is a finely-wrought study in animal life, it is a poem, and it is in its way a parable.    Withal there is a story in it, a story that the reader must needs follow in expectation of the end.    Ralph Connor is well known for his tales of the vast wild regions of the north-west of Canada, and his "The Pilot at Swan Creek" displays completely in a small compass those redeeming qualities of pity and courage that turn a preacher into a saint.

## GILBERT PARKER

Sir Gilbert Parker (1861–1932), who was one of the foremost of British novelists, was Canadian by origin, hence his appearance in this group with three brilliant illustrations of his art.    " The Crimson Flag " is a masterpiece of passionate tragedy, showing the doom that comes swiftly and unexpectedly when life is mishandled.    " The Absurd Romance of P'tite Louison " contains no absurdity, but its pathos has a singular charm.    Pathos is the note, too, of " The Singing of the Bees "—a fragment of life beautiful in its simplicity.    Olive Schreiner (1862–1920) on the South African veld set down her dreams.    But her allegories, product of high imaginative powers, are not directly concerned with South Africa, and these two short studies, allegories both, " In a Far-off World " and " The Artist's Secret," belong to the universal order, and tell faithfully of the meaning of certain human experiences.

## H. B. MARRIOTT WATSON

Marriott Watson (1863–1921), who was born in Australia and spent his youth in New Zealand, was for many years a successful novelist and writer in England.    His work is not coloured by the atmosphere of new conditions and civilization in the making.    Yet a man must have travelled far overseas for the perfect tone of " Quarantine." It is a great story, a model of the short story, related with no waste of words and without a word misplaced. Admirable in its characterization it presents a problem of conduct and leaves the answer to the reader. Henry Lawson (1867–1922) was the real Australian. "When the Sun went Down" and "That there Dog o' Mine" are incidents described with a simple directness that makes them vital. Their sentiment touches the heroic and demands our sympathy—the miner dying for his brother at the pit, and the disreputable old shearer who won't be operated on at the hospital unless his dog is tended as well.

Mary Gaunt is also from Australia, but she has explored the remoteness of West Africa, and the mysteries of the unknown, and has lived long in London. " The Doctor's Drive " is not a story of man's dealing with man, but of man threatened by nature and well-nigh overcome. Yet by sheer force of will in man and beast nature is beaten, for " the mails have got to go through," and the doctor on duty was no less bound to get through : a fine finish to these tales of the overseas where man is up against pitiless nature all the time and must prevail or perish.

J. C.

# THOMAS CHANDLER HALIBURTON
1796–1865

# SISTER SALL'S COURTSHIP

" There goes one of them are everlastin rottin poles in that bridge; they are no better than a trap for a critter's legs," said the Clockmaker. " They remind me of a trap Jim Munroe put his foot in one night, that near about made one leg half a yard longer than t'other. I believe I told you of him, what a desperate idle feller he was—he came from Onion County in Connecticut. Well, he was courtin Sister Sall—she was a rael handsum-looking gall; you scarce ever seed a more out and out complete critter than she was—a fine figur-head, and a beautiful model of a craft as any in the state; a real clipper, and as full of fun and frolic as a kitten. Well, he fairly turned Sall's head; the more we wanted her to give him up, the more she wouldn't, and we got plaguy oneasy about it, for his character was none of the best. He was a universal favourite with the galls, and tho' he didn't behave very pretty neither, forgetting to marry where he promised, and where he hadn't ought to have forgot too; yet so it was, he had such an uncommon winnin way with him, he could talk them over in no time—Sall was fairly bewitched.

" At last, father said to him one evenin when he came a courtin, ' Jim,' says he, ' you'll never come to no good, if you act like old Scratch as you do; you ain't fit to come into no decent man's house, at all, and your absence would be ten times more agreeable than your company, I tell you. I won't consent to Sall's goin to them are huskin parties and quiltin frolics along with you no more, on no account, for you know how Polly Brown and Nancy White——'

" ' Now don't,' says he, ' now don't, Uncle Sam; say no more about that; if you know'd all, you wouldn't say it was my fault; and, besides, I have turned right about, I am on t'other tack now, and the long leg, too; I am as steady as a pump bolt, now. I intend to settle myself and take a farm.'

" ' Yes, yes, and you could stock it too by all accounts, pretty well, unless you are much misreported,' says father, ' but it won't do. I knowd your father, he was our sargeant, a proper clever and brave man he was, too; he was one of the heroes of our glorious

315

revolution. I had a great respect for him, and I am sorry, for his sake, you will act as you do; but I tell you once for all, you must give up all thoughts of Sall, now and for everlastin.'

" When Sall heerd this, she began to nit away like mad in a desperate hurry—she looked foolish enough, that's a fact. First she tried to bite in her breath, and look if there was nothin partikilar in the wind, then she blushed all over like scarlet fever, but she recovered that pretty soon, and then her colour went and came, and came and went, till at last she grew as white as chalk, and down she fell slap off her seat on the floor, in a faintin fit.

" ' I see,' says father, ' I see it now, you etarnal villain,' and he made a pull at the old-fashioned sword, that always hung over the fireplace (we used to call it old Bunker, for his stories always begun, ' When I was at Bunker's Hill,') and drawin it out he made a clip at him as wicked as if he was stabbin a rat with a hay-fork; but, Jim, he outs of the door like a shot, and draws it to arter him, and father sends old Bunker right through the panel.

" ' I'll chop you up as fine as mince-meat, you villain,' said he, ' if ever I catch you inside my door again; mind what I tell you, *you'll swing for it yet.*'

" Well, he made himself considerable scarce arter that, he never sot foot inside the door agin, and I thought he had ginn up all hopes of Sall, and she of him; when one night, a most particular oncommon dark night, as I was a comin home from neighbour Dearborne's, I heerd some one a talkin under Sall's window. Well, I stops and listens, and who should be near the ash saplin, but Jim Munroe, a tryin to persuade Sall to run off with him to Rhode Island to be married. It was all settled, he should come with a horse and shay to the gate, and then help her out of the window, jist at nine o'clock, about the time she commonly went to bed. Then he axes her to reach down her hand for him to kiss (for he was proper clever at soft sawder), and she stretches it down and he kisses it; and says he, ' I believe I must have the whole of you arter all,' and gives her a jirk that kinder startled her; it came so sudden like, it made her scream; so off he sot hot-foot, and over the gate in no time.

" Well, I cyphered over this all night, a calculatin how I should reciprocate that trick with him, and at last I hit on a scheme. I recollected father's words at partin, ' *mind what I tell you, you'll swing for it yet,*' and thinks I, Friend Jim, I'll make the prophecy come true yet, I guess. So the next night, jist at dark, I gives January Snow, the old nigger, a nidge woth my elbow, and as soon as he looks up, I winks and walks out and he arter me—says I, ' January, can you keep your tongue within your teeth, you old nigger you? '

" ' Why, massa, why you ax that are question? my Gor Ormity, you tink old Snow he don't know that are yet; my tongue he got plenty room now, debil a tooth left, he can stretch out ever so far, like a little leg in a big bed, he lay quiet enough, massa, neber fear.'

" ' Well, then,' says I, ' bend down that are ash saplin softly, you old Snowball, and make no noise.'

" The saplin was no sooner bent than secured to the ground by a notched peg and a noose, and a slip knot was suspended from the tree, jist over the track that led from the pathway to the house.

" ' Why, my Gor, massa, that's a——'

" ' Hold your mug, you old nigger,' says I, ' or I'll send your tongue a sarchin arter your teeth; keep quiet, and follow me in presently.'

" Well, jist as it struck nine o'clock, says I, ' Sally, hold this here hank of twine for a minute, till I wind a trifle on it off; that's a dear critter.'

" She sot down her candle, and I put the twine on her hands, and then I begins to wind and wind away ever so slow, and drops the ball every now and then, so as to keep her down-stairs.

" ' Sam,' says she, ' I do believe you won't wind that are twine off all night, do give it to January, I won't stay no longer, I'm een almost dead asleep.'

" ' The old feller's arm is so plaguy onsteady,' says I, ' it won't do; but hark, what's that? I'm sure I heerd something in the ash saplin, didn't you, Sall? '

" ' I heerd the geese there, that's all,' says she; ' they always come onder the windows at night '; but she looked scared enough, and says she, ' I vow I'm tired a holdin out of arms this way, and I won't do it no longer '; and down she throw'd the hank on the floor.

" ' Well,' says I, ' stop one minit, dear, till I send old January out to see if anybody is there; perhaps some o' neighbour Dear- borne's cattle have broke into the scarce garden.'

" January went out, tho' Sall say'd it was no use, for she knew the noise of the geese, they always kept close to the house at night, for fear of the varmin. Presently in runs old Snow, with his hair standin up an eend, and the whites of his eyes lookin as big as the rims of a soup plate; ' Oh! Gor Ormity,' says he, ' oh massa, oh Miss Sally, oh!! '

" ' What on airth is the matter with you? ' said Sally, ' how you do frighten me, I vow I believe you're mad.'

" ' Oh, my Gor,' said he, ' oh! massa, Jim Munroe he hang him- self, on the ash saplin under Miss Sally's window—oh my Gor!!! '

" That shot was a settler, it struck poor Sall right atwixt wind and water: she gave a lurch ahead, then heeled over and sunk right down in another faintin fit; and Juno, old Snow's wife, carried her off and laid down on the bed—poor thing, she felt ugly enough, I do suppose.

"Well, father, I thought he'd a fainted too, he was so struck up all of a heap, he was completely bung fungered.

"'Dear, dear,' said he, 'I didn't think it would come to pass so soon, but I knew it would come; I foretold it; says I, the last time I seed him, Jim, says I, mind what you say, *you'll swing for it yet.* Give me the sword I wore when I was at Bunker's Hill, may be there is life yet, I'll cut him down.'

"The lantern was soon made ready, and out we went to the ash saplin.

"'Cut me down, Sam, that's a good feller,' said Jim, 'all the blood in my body was swashed into my head, and's a runnin out o' my nose, I'm een amost smothered—be quick, for heaven's sake.'

"'The Lord be praised,' said father, 'the poor sinner is not quite dead yet. Why, as I'm alive—well if that don't beat all natur, why he has hanged himself by one leg, and's a swingin like a rabbit upside down, that's a fact. Why, if he aint snared, Sam, he is properly wired I declare—I vow this is some of your doings, Sam—well, it was a clever scheme, too, but a little grain too dangerous, I guess.'

"'Don't stand starin and jawin there all night,' said Jim, 'cut me down, I tell you—or cut my throat and be damned to you, for I am choking with blood.'

"'Roll over that are hogshead, old Snow,' said I, 'till I get a top on it and cut him down'; so I soon released him, but he couldn't walk a bit. His ankle was swelled and sprained like vengeance, and he swore one leg was near about six inches longer than t'other.

"'Jim Munroe,' says father, 'little did I think I should ever see you inside my door agin, but I bid you enter now, we owe you that kindness anyhow.'

"Well, to make a long story short, Jim was so chapfallen, and so down in the mouth, he begged for heaven's sake it might be kept a secret; he said he would *run* the state, if ever it got wind, he was sure he couldn't *stand it.*

"'It will be one while, I guess,' said father, 'afore you are able to run or stand either; but if you will give me your hand, Jim, and promise to give over your evil ways, I will not only keep it a secret, but you shall be a welcome guest at old Sam Slick's once more, for the sake of your father—he was a brave man, one of the heroes of Bunker's Hill, he was our sergeant and——'

"'He promises,' says I, 'father (for the old man had stuck his right foot out, the way he always stood when he told about the old war; and as Jim couldn't stir a peg, it was a grand chance, and he was a goin to give him the whole revolution from General Gage up to Independence)—'he promises,' says I, 'father.'

"'Well it was all settled, and things soon grew as calm as a pan of milk two days old; and afore a year was over, Jim was as steady agoin a man as Minister Joshua Hopewell, and was married to our Sall.   Nothin was ever said about the snare till arter the weddin.   When the minister had finished axin a blessin, father goes up to Jim, and says he:

" ' Jim Munroe, my boy,' givin him a rousin slap on the shoulder that sot him a coughin for the matter of five minutes (for he was a mortal powerful man was father); ' Jim Munroe, my boy,' says he, ' you've got the snare round your neck I guess now, instead of your leg; the saplin has been a father to you, may you be a father of many saplins.'

# WILLIAM S. WALKER
("COO-EE")
1846–1926

# "MIDNIGHT"

"What? Did you never hear the yarn about ' Midnight '? " queried the Inspector, as he drew his chair nearer to the fire. " Well, I'll tell you."

" Twenty years or more have gone by, and that's a lifetime for some of us, but about that time, Lord, it was pretty well all ' Midnight ' and his doings.

" Ben Hall and *his* gang had been broken up. Some had been shot red-handed, and the others had paid the penalty of their crimes in various ways.

" There had been a cessation of ' sticking-up ' mail-coaches, robbing banks, and scaring station owners and bank managers out of their wits; when, all of a sudden this desperado took up the running.

" You never could tell for certain where he would turn up—one day the mail-coach would be stuck up in New South Wales. At the end perhaps of a week, an equally audacious case would be reported from Queensland, and the telegraph wires would be cut.

" Anon, the Victorian papers would be teeming with sensational paragraphs. He was a proper cunning scoundrel, and nobody seemed to be able to swear to him. Sometimes he would be described as mounted, sometimes not. But he was generally described as a tall, dark man, some people said *black*, always completely masked, and well armed.

" At that time I was serving in the New South Wales mounted police. I was fond of active service, possessed a little influence at headquarters, and was always ready for a little more than mere duty, with a view to ultimate promotion.

" I was quartered at ' Morabinda,' a somewhat dreary little township on the border.

" The place was only kept alive by the traffic of wool-waggons and bullock drays to and from Collinsville and the neighbouring stations.

" Of course the shearers and station-hands at the latter used to come in and knock down their cheques, but there wasn't much

' running-in ' in those days, so they got ' boozed ' as much as they liked. In fact, it was a point of honour with most of them to get as well ' boozed ' as possible, and they did little damage except to themselves. Also there would be an outbreak of festivity during the local races, but nine days out of ten during the year were monotonous and dull.

" I had got my sergeant's stripes, and worked under orders from Inspector Lysaght at Collinsville, and our biggest town on that far-away border of New South Wales.

" The Queensland black troopers kept their inside district on the ' Warrigal ' and ' Narrabine ' clear from any trouble arising from the blacks, and occasionally arrested a white man for horse-stealing, or petty larceny, and Captain Garforth, the Inspector, was a great favourite with the squatters.

" Now, if ' Midnight ' had an enemy, a relentless uncompromising enemy, Captain Garforth was the man.

" Morn, noon, and night had he sworn to take him, alive or dead, the more especially as ' Midnight ' had outwitted him on two or three occasions, and the Captain was of opinion that these unsuccessful quests told seriously against him with the Queensland Government.

" Never was there a more painstaking man than he had proved himself to be, and never a greater victim to bad luck.

" He generally was quickly enough on the spot if one of ' Midnight's ' depredations occurred in his district, but he had never as yet even managed to catch a sight of him.

" It was not long after his accession to the post of Sub-Inspector at the Browar Barracks that ' Midnight ' commenced his little games, and the Inspector felt intensely annoyed at not being able to put a sudden stop to them. ' Midnight's ' last exploit in Garforth's district had been the robbery of a public-house and store, in a little bit of a township on the Warrigal, and since then nothing had been heard of the vagabond. People began to say that he had cleared out with his ill-gotten gains.

" Now Captain Garforth was especially tender about the last escapade. He and his troopers had come best pace down the river, only missing him by a couple of hours, but though they levied taxes on all the squatters for fresh horses, and followed him right on to New South Wales, they lost all trace of him!

It was rumoured too that it would be well-nigh impossible to catch ' Midnight,' because he had so many friends. ' Sly-shanty ' keepers, shepherds, ' old-hands '—even blacks, all seemed to act as ' bush-telegraphs ' for him. Leastways once he had started, and the policemen after him, he didn't seem like a common bushranger. Some people said he was the devil. One thing struck me at the time as being rather curious. ' Midnight ' never seemed to *steal* a horse, but was generally reported as being mounted on a very powerful coal-black animal. All three Governments, New South Wales, Queensland, and Victoria, now outlawed him, and set a price upon his head, and the sum total represented a prize worth winning.

" I had given a great deal of thought to the case. Many and many a night had it kept me from sleeping, and I was not the only anxious man in the force either.

" There were two things which no doubt added greatly to ' Midnight's ' popularity with the rough bush element.

" He never robbed a poor man, and had never attempted to kill any one, but it was generally understood that it would be terribly dangerous to meddle with or provoke him. Those few who had been let off lightly, especially some who had actually been presented with money by the bushranger, poor swagmen, were never tired of saying that he was a very powerful, athletic man.

" I believe it was partly the knowledge of this which piqued Garforth so much, as he himself had the reputation of being the best shot, rider, and boxer in Queensland, and was also very powerful and muscular.

" One of ' Midnight's ' idiosyncrasies, if remonstrated with or resisted in the slightest degree, was the tying of his victim to a tree, leaving him there to be found by the first passer-by. Well, eight months had passed in positive tranquillity, when, like a thunderbolt, came the news that the bank in Collinsville had been robbed after dark, the manager picked up senseless in the strong room, and about £8000 in notes and gold coin missing. The manager in this instance had been stunned by a heavy blow behind the ear, and on coming to his senses was completely ignorant as to how it was done or who did it.

" Of course gossip alleged that it must have been ' Midnight ' again; none but he had either the talent or daring to accomplish such a deed.

" Fate seemed, indeed, to have dealt hardly with Captain Garforth. Not only did he happen to be in the town at that identical time, but he had actually called at the Bank that very day and deposited a sum of fifty pounds with the manager, who was a personal friend of his.

" You would have thought the Captain was mad. ' I shall lose my commission through this,' said he.

" ' To think that out of the few times I come here, once or twice a year perhaps, that devil should have chosen one of them to rob the bank under my very nose. I believe he *is* the devil and no mortal man.'

" Well, it was boot and saddle for the police, white as well as black, you bet. Of course we were only too glad to get the valuable assistance and advice of Captain Garforth's famous ' tracker ' and orderly ' Joe.'

"Beyond the town he at once picked the hoof-marks of a horse, sometimes on and sometimes off the road. We followed them twenty miles, and arrested a quiet-looking fellow who looked as if he couldn't say ' bo ' to a goose, and who was riding a sorry-looking horse.

"There wasn't the smallest particle of evidence against him at the trial, and though we scoured the district far and near we did no good.

"Captain Garforth left for Queensland in a perfect fury, stating that he should send in his resignation.

"Luck was dead against him, and it was more than a fellow could stand.

"With all his ' swagger ' he was downcast and sullen, and there was a restless fire in his eyes, which seemed to show that he had been aggravated beyond endurance.

"I was at Morabinda when Garforth returned, and he blustered greatly as to what he would do with ' Midnight ' when he captured him. ' For,' said he, ' if they accept my resignation, I will hunt him down myself! '

"Well, I had been piecing my puzzle together bit by bit, week by week, month by month, and as Garforth, with all his advantages, did not seem to be able to act as thief-taker, or to solve the mystery, I made application to headquarters to be allowed to carry out a scheme of my own, and that was to put myself in such a position as to be ' stuck-up ' by ' Midnight,' either venturing upon his seizure then, if I got a show, or to mark his face and figure for further identification; so that I might have something tangible to go upon, better than this fleeting, uncertain individuality which had hitherto so successfully evaded the clutches of the law.

"Garforth went over to the barracks, and it was some time before he came back.

" ' Midnight ' had ceased to give further trouble; but a horse-stealing case at Fulliver's attracted the Captain's attention, and he was down on this new offender like lightning, bringing his prisoner into Morabinda, as it was proved he came from there. As luck would have it, I was away at the time on urgent business, but Captain Garforth and his faithful orderly ' Joe ' rode into the township, and having consigned the prisoner to the lock-up, went to the principal hotel, the ' Criterion.' (I daresay you have noticed that the smaller the town the more imposing is the name of the principal hotel.)

"Well, they walked into the bar, the Captain treating the orderly and calling for something stiff himself.

"There was an old shepherd there from the ' back-blocks,' spending his cheque liberally, a grizzled old fellow, with that half-shrewd, half-childish look generally stamped upon those accustomed to solitude. The old man was pretty ' well on,' and said he:

" ' Captain Garforth, you're a good hand at keeping down the blacks and catching horse-thieves, but I can't see why " Midnight " should be too much for you. You're a big, strong man, as big as " Midnight " himself, they say.'

" ' Who says so? ' asked the Captain.

" ' Well, nigh every one, I think,' said the old fellow, ' least-ways, every one I've spoken to about it.'

" ' Confound you! ' roared the Captain. ' You mind your own business, and let ' Midnight ' be. I've had enough of him. If I could only get at him, I'd stop this talk.'

" ' What would you do, Captain? What would you do? ' asked the shepherd pertinaciously.

" ' Do? ' said the Captain, ' I'll tell you what I'd do. I'd strip him and tie him to a tree, single-handed, in the way he is said to treat those who resist him, leaving him to boast of his deeds to the next passer-by, but I'd take care to be handy, and when he was released it would but be to be tied and handcuffed alongside of my saddle on his way to goal.'

" ' No! would you though? ' said the shepherd with a face as long as his arm.

" Then he asked the Captain to take drink with him, and the Captain knowing that nothing really offended an ' old-hand ' so much as a refusal to a special invitation in this form, acquiesced, ' shouting ' another for him afterwards.

" The old fellow was getting very well ' on ' when who should come in but young Hammersley from ' Yunta,' a cattle-station near by, and nothing would do but that the Captain must come to tea with him.

" ' I will come later on,' said the Captain. ' Can't come just yet,' and soon after that young Hammersley jumped upon his horse and rode away.

" Captain Garforth talked to the landlord a bit, and then went up to the store. When he came back it was near sundown, so telling ' Joe ' to ' saddle-up ' he remarked that ' Joe ' was to stay in the township that night to help to keep guard on the prisoner, ' but I shall take him (' Joe ') as far as the crossing-place, as I have instructions to give him. I must return the first thing in the morning myself, as I have to give evidence.'

" Just after dark, ' Joe ' came back saying that the Captain had gone on to Yunta, and that he had left him about two miles this side of the station.

" That night at about ten o'clock, as the down-river mailman got into the big timber near the crossing-place, his horse shied so suddenly as nearly to unseat him, and that was not easily done as a rule, for Jem Donelly was a smart lad in the saddle.

" There was Captain Garforth tied up to a tree, and his horse hitched up to another a little farther on.

" He was pretty stiff when Jem helped him to mount.

" He had been ' stuck-up ' and robbed by a tall man on a black horse; had tried to fight him, but found his pistol-holster empty; would have sworn it was there before he left the hotel.

" Well, when he got back to the township, ' Joe ' and he left at once to get the ' tracks,' but here again fortune was against them.

" They got the tracks at the river where the tussle had been, for the road crossed it twice on the way to Yunta, but a downpour of rain occurred, which obliterated everything, especially on the hard ground near the river. Once clear of the road there was no sign.

" The prisoner was to be tried, and they could not accomplish impossibilities, so they returned after daylight.

" I had got back, and by a curious coincidence, Colonel Lysaght, and Sergeant Major Tuke, with two constables, had arrived in time to take part in the proceedings. You should have seen poor old Magistrate Browning's face, when I walked across the Court just as Captain Garforth was going to question his prisoner, and laying my hand on his shoulder, said: ' Captain Garforth, alias " Midnight," I arrest you in the Queen's name for highway robbery generally, and assault and robbery at the bank in Collinsville in particular.'

" He fought like a wild cat.

" It was as much as four of us could do to hold him.

" But we got the bracelets on him, though I got that," said the Inspector, touching a deep scar of old standing under the right eye. " For some time, I believe, the bench and spectators thought we had gone mad, but Lysaght, Tuke, and I knew what we were about.

" ' Dick the Devil,' the man arrested for horse-stealing, was in our employ and had got arrested on purpose. He had been prowling about the barracks for some time before this, found that the Captain and Joe worked together, and gathered quite enough evidence to piece my puzzle together, though the two were very ' fly.'

" I had many proofs, quite unnecessary to go into now, but one of the best I had I consider I possessed when I personated the old ' back-block ' shepherd ' on the spree.'

" When I launched that shaft about the Captain's strength and size being identical with that of ' Midnight's ' he had turned deadly pale, but I played my part too well for him to suspect that I was in the secret.

" That ruse of getting ' Joe ' to tie him up to a tree near the Yunta crossing-place was a clever move and his trump card to allay suspicion, but the finding of the revolver in the river, alleged to be stolen by ' Midnight,' was only dead weight against him.

" Well, he confessed.

" It was as Captain Garforth he had assaulted the manager and robbed the bank. It will be remembered that earlier in the day he paid a visit there to pay in a sum of money. Returning after office hours to take further stock of the premises, he came suddenly upon the manager locking the safe in the strong room, and the opportunity was too much for a man of his propensities. That was to have been the end of it all, and the robbery was to have been accomplished at night, under the personality of ' Midnight,' after he himself, as Captain Garforth, had left.

" He never divulged where the money was hidden, probably in some remote corner, known only to him and ' Joe.' The latter vanished the instant he saw trouble brewing, taking his carbine, but leaving his horse and trappings.

" It was no use our trying to find an agile, bare-footed black fellow skilled in bush art then. Besides, our hands were completely filled with our prisoner, who was both game and desperate.

" A peculiar smile lit up his features when he heard that ' Joe ' had eluded us.

" As we wound along the up-river track *en route* for the Queensland capital with our prisoner strongly guarded in our midst, on the evening of our third day's journey from Morabinda, just where a beautiful pine ridge juts in on the river, I heard a sharp, ringing crack, saw Garforth fall lifeless from his saddle, and was conscious of seeing two of our men charge up the bank into the timber.

" There was another report. They found ' Joe ' in that ridge, but Death had got hold of him as well as Garforth, and Law was out of it. That's the story, gentlemen."

# LOUIS BECKE
1848–1913

# RODMAN THE BOATSTEERER

## I

WITH her white cotton canvas swelling gently out and then softly
drooping flat against her cordage, the *Shawnee,* sperm whaler of
New Bedford, with the dying breath of the south-east trade, was
sailing lazily over a sea whose waters were as calm as those of a
mountain lake.  Twenty miles astern the lofty peaks of Tutuila, one
of the islands of the Samoan group, stood out clearly in the dazzling
sunshine, and, almost ahead, what at dawn had been the purple
loom of Upolu was changing to a cloud-capped dome of vivid green
as the ship closed with the land.

The *Shawnee* was " a five-boat ship," and, judging from the
appearance of her decks, which were very clean, an unlucky one.
She had been out for over a year, and three months had passed
since the last fish had been killed.  That was off the coast of Chile,
and she was now cruising westward and northward towards the
eastern coast of New Guinea where Captain Harvey Lucy, the
master, expected to make up for the persistent ill-luck that had
attended him so far.  Naturally a man of most violent and ungovernable temper, his behaviour to his men on the present voyage
had led to disastrous consequences, and the crew, much as they
admired their captain as one of the most skilful whalemen who had
ever trod a deck, were now worked up into a state of exasperation
bordering on mutiny.  Shortly before the Samoan Islands were
sighted, the ship's cooper, a man who took the cue for his conduct
to the hands from the example set by the captain, had had a fierce
quarrel with a young boatsteerer, named Gerald Rodman, who,
in a moment of passion, struck the cooper such a terrific blow that
the man lay between life and death for some hours.  An attempt to
put Rodman in irons was fiercely resisted by a number of his shipmates, who were led by his younger brother.  But the after-guard
were too strong for the men, and after a savage conflict the two
Rodmans and three other seamen were overpowered by Captain
Lucy, his four mates and the carpenter and stewards.  As was
common enough in those days on American whaleships, nearly all

the officers were relatives or connections by marriage, and were always ready to stand by the captain; in this instance the cooper was a brother of the second mate. Six days had passed since this affair had occurred, and when Upolu was sighted the five men were still in irons and confined in the hot stifling atmosphere of the sail-locker, having been given only just enough food and water to keep body and soul together.

Four bells struck, and Captain Lucy made his appearance from below. The watch on deck, who had hitherto been talking among themselves as they went about their work, at once became silent, and muttered curses escaped from their lips as they eyed the tall figure of the captain standing at the break of the poop. For some minutes he apparently took no notice of any one about him; then he turned to the mate, who stood near him, and said:

" Have you had a look at those fellows this morning, Brant? "

" Yes," answered the officer. " They want to know if you're going to let them have a smoke."

A savage oath preceded Captain Lucy's reply:

" They can lie there till they die before any one of them shall put a pipe in his mouth."

" Just as you please, captain," said the mate, nonchalantly. " I guess you know best what you're doing. But there's going to be more trouble aboard this ship if you don't ease up a bit on those five men; and if I were you I wouldn't go too far. One of 'em —that youngest Rodman boy—can't stand much more of that sail locker in such weather as this. And I guess I don't want to go before a grand jury if he or any of 'em dies."

" I tell you, Brant, that rather than ease up on those fellows, I'd lose the ship. I'm going to keep them there till we strike another fish, and then I'll haze what life is left in them clean out of them."

Rough and harsh as he was with the crew of the Shawnee, Brant was no vindictive tyrant, and was about to again remonstrate with the savage Lucy, when, suddenly, the thrilling cry of " There she blows! " came from the look-out in the crow's nest; and in a few minutes the barque's decks were bustling with excitement. A small " pod " or school of sperm whales were in sight. Four boats were at once lowered and started in pursuit.

When first sighted from the ship the whales were not more than two miles distant, and moving towards her. The mate's boat was first away, and in a very short time fastened to the leader of the " pod "—a huge bull over sixty feet in length. In less than five seconds after the keen-edged harpoon had plunged deep into his body, the mighty fish " sounded " (dived) at a terrific speed; the other whales at once disappeared and Brant's boat shot away from the other three. The remaining boats were those of the captain and the second and third mates. For some ten or fifteen minutes their crews lay upon their oars watching the swift progress of the mate's boat, and scanning the sea from every point around them, to discern where the vanished and unstricken whales would rise to breathe again. At last they saw the great bull, to which the mate's boat was fast, burst out upon the surface of the water, two miles away. For a minute the mighty creature lay exposed to view, beating the sea into a white seeth of foam as he struck the water tremendous blows with his tail, and sought to free himself from the cruel steel in his body. As he thrashed from side to side, two of his convoys rose suddenly near him as if in sympathy with their wounded leader. Then, in an instant, they all disappeared together, the stricken whale still dragging the mate's boat after him at an incredible speed.

Knowing that in all probability the two whales which had just appeared would accompany the great bull to the last—when he would receive the stroke of the death-dealing lance from Brant— the captain of the *Shawnee* at once started off in pursuit, accompanied by the second and third mates' boats. The crews bent to their tough ash oars with strength and determination. There was no need for the dreadful oaths and blasphemies with which Captain Lucy and his officers assailed their ears, or his threats of punishment should they fail to catch up the mate's boat and miss killing the two " loose " whales; the prospect of such a prize was all the incentive the seamen needed. With set teeth and panting bosoms they urged the boats along, and presently they were encouraged by a cry from the third mate, who called out to the captain and second mate that the wounded whale was slackening his speed, and Mr. Brant was " hauling up alongside to give him the lance." In another fifty strokes the captain and the two officers saw the great head of the creature that was dragging the mate's boat along again appear on the surface, and on each side were his devoted cetacean companions, who were almost of as monstrous a size as the bull himself.

With savage oaths the captain urged his crew to fresh exertions, for just then he saw the mate go for'ard in his boat and plunge his keen lance of shining steel into his prize, then back his boat off as the agonised whale again sounded into the blue depths below, with his life-blood pouring from him in a bubbling stream.

## II

On board the *Shawnee* the progress of the boats was watched amid the most intense excitement; and even the imprisoned seamen, in their foul and horrible prison, stretched their wearied and manacled limbs and sought to learn by the sounds on deck whether any or all of the boats were " fast "—that is, had harpooned a whale. Broken-spirited and exhausted as they were by long days of cruel and undeserved punishment, they would have forgotten their miseries in an instant had the fourth mate ordered them on deck to lower his boat—the only one remaining on board—and join their shipmates in the other boats in the chase. But of this they knew there was little prospect, for this remaining boat had been seriously injured by a heavy sea, which had washed her inboard a few days before the fight between the officers and crew. Presently, however, they heard the hurried stamping of feet on deck, and then the voices of the fourth mate and cooper giving orders to take in sail.

" Jerry," said a young English lad named Wray, to the elder Rodman, " do you hear that? One of the boats must have got ' fast ' and killed. We'll be out of this in another half-hour, cutting-in. The captain won't let us lie here when there is work to be done on deck; he's too mean a Yankee to satisfy his revenge at the expense of his pocket."

But their pleasant belief that a whale had been killed, and that the ship was shortening sail while the carcass was being cut-in, was rudely disturbed a few minutes later, when the *Shawnee* took a sudden list over to port, and they were all pitched to the lee side of the sail locker in a heap. A squall had struck the barque.

Bruised and lacerated by the force with which they had been hurled together, the five prisoners sat up, and were soon enlightened as to the condition of affairs by the carpenter making his appearance, taking off their galling irons, and ordering them on deck.

The squall was a very heavy one, accompanied by savage gusts of stinging rain, and the old ship, with her canvas in great disorder, was every now and then thrown almost on her beam ends with its fury. After considerable trouble the officers and crew succeeded in saving her canvas from being blown to ribbons, and got the barque snug again. A quarter of an hour later the squall began to lose its force, but the rain descended in torrents, and obscured the view of the now agitated ocean to such an extent that the look-outs from aloft could not discern its surface a cable length away. All those on board the barque felt intense anxiety as to whether the mate had succeeded in killing his whale before the squall burst upon him, for they knew that had he not done so he would have been compelled to cut the line and let his prize escape; no boat could live in such a sea as had arisen when " fast " to a sperm whale which was travelling at such a speed, even though fatally wounded and weak from loss of blood.

An hour passed, and then, to the joy of all on board, the rain ceased, a faint air came from the westward and blew away the thick clouds of tropic mist which enveloped the ship. Ten miles distant the verdant hills and valleys of Upolu glistened in the sunshine, and then one of the look-outs hailed the deck:

" I can see a boat, Mr. Newman—it is Mr. Brant's. He has killed his whale, sir."

In an instant the fourth mate was running aloft, but before he had ascended to the fore-top the look-out cried:

"I can see the other three boats now, sir, and they are all 'fast,' too."

A cheer broke from the *Shawnee's* hands, and, disregarding for the time all discipline, they sprang aloft one after another to gaze upon the thrilling scene. Three miles away, and plainly discernible in the now clear atmosphere, was the mate's boat lying alongside the big bull, which had just been killed, and at about the same distance were the boats of the captain and second and third mates, all "fast" to whales, and racing swiftly to windward toward the horizon.

The fourth mate at once came down from aloft and held a hurried consultation with the cooper—an old and experienced whaler. It was evident to them that the three boats had only just succeeded in getting "fast," and that, as darkness was so near, the officers in them would have great difficulty in killing the whales to which they were "fast," as the sea was still very lumpy from the violence of the squall. None of the boats were provided with bomb-guns, the use of which would have killed the whales in a very short time; and the wind having again died away it was impossible for the ship to work up to them. Nothing, it was evident, could be done to assist the three boats, but it was decided to send the one remaining on board the barque to help the mate to tow his whale to the ship before the hordes of sharks, which would be attracted to the carcass by the smell of blood, began to devour it.

The carpenter was at once set to work to make her temporarily water-tight. By this time the sun had set, and only the position of the mate's boat was made known to the ship by a light displayed by Mr. Brant.

Standing on the port side of the poop, Martin Newman, the fourth mate, was gazing anxiously out into the darkness, hoping to see the other three boats show lights to denote that they had succeeded in killing their fish, and were waiting for a breeze to spring up to enable the barque to sail towards them. Although Newman was the youngest officer on board, he was an experienced one, and the fact that his boat had not been fit to lower with the other four had filled him with sullen rage; for he was of an intensely jealous nature, and would rather have seen the boats return unsuccessful from the chase than that he alone should have missed his chance of killing a fish.

Presently the younger of the two Rodmans, who was his (Newman's) own boatsteerer, ventured, in the fulness of his anxiety for his shipmates, to step up to the officer and speak:

"Do you think, sir, that the captain and Mr. Ford and Mr. Manning have had to cut their lines?"

The officer made no reply; and could the young boatsteerer have seen the dark, forbidding scowl upon his face, he would never have addressed him at such an unpropitious moment. But imagining that his question had not been heard, the youth repeated it.

Newman turned, and seeing the lad standing in an attitude of expectancy, asked him in savage tones what he was doing there.

" Nothing, sir; I only——"

" I'll teach you that a man doing nothing doesn't suit me when I'm in charge of the deck of this ship! " and he struck the boat-steerer a terrific blow in the mouth, which knocked him off the poop on to the main deck.

When Ned Rodman came to, he found his head supported by his brother and young Wray, and the rest of the hands on deck standing around him in sympathetic silence. Newman was the most liked of all the officers, and the lad whom he had struck down had been rather a favourite of his, principally, it was supposed, because the two Rodmans came from the same town as himself; and when the disturbance had arisen with the cooper, and the two brothers had been put in irons, Newman had several times expressed his sorrow to them when he had visited them in their prison. His sudden outburst of violence to Ned Rodman was therefore a surprise to the men generally; and several of them glanced threateningly at the figure of the fourth mate, who was now striding to and fro on the poop, occasionally hailing the look-outs in angry tones, and asking if any more boat-lights were visible.

Gerald Rodman, though no words escaped his lips as he wiped away the blood which welled from a terrible cut on his brother's temple, had in his eyes a red light of passion that boded ill for the fourth mate when the time came. He was five years older than his brother, and, although both were boatsteerers, and had made many cruises in the Pacific, this was the first time they had been shipmates. Unlike Ned, he was a man of passionate and revengeful nature, and the second mate, to whose boat he belonged, had warned the cooper of the *Shawnee* never to meet Gerald Rodman ashore alone.

" He is a man who will never forgive an injury, and I would not care to be in your shoes if he gets you by yourself one day." And, as a matter of fact, Gerald Rodman had sworn to himself, when he lay in irons, in the sail-locker, to have his revenge upon both the cooper and Captain Lucy, should he ever meet either of them ashore at any of the islands the barque was likely to touch at during her cruise. He was a man of great physical strength, and, for his position, fairly well educated. Both his parents were dead, and he and his brother Ned, and a delicate sister of nineteen, were the sole survivors of a once numerous family. The care of this sister was the one motive that animated the elder brother in his adventurous career; and while his reserved and morose nature seemed incapable of yielding to any tender sentiment or emotion, it yet concealed a wealth of the deepest affection for his weakly sister, of which the younger one had no conception. And yet, strangely enough, it was to Ned that Nellie Rodman was most attached; it was to *his* return that she most looked forward, never knowing that it was Gerald's money alone that maintained the old family home in the quiet little New England village in which her simple life was spent. Little did she think that when money was sent to her by Gerald, saying it came " from Ned and myself," that Ned had never had a dollar to send. For he was too careless and too fond of his own pleasure to ever think of sending her money. " Jerry," he thought, " was a mighty stingy fellow, and never spent a cent on himself—and could easily send Nell all she wanted." And yet Gerald Rodman, knowing his brother's weak and mercurial nature, and knowing that he took no care in the welfare of any living soul but himself, would have laid his life down for him, because happy, careless Ned had Nellie's eyes and Nellie's mouth, and in the tones of his voice he heard hers. So as he sat on the deck, with his brother's head upon his knees, he swore to " get even " with Martin Newman, as well as with Captain Lucy and cooper Burr, for as he watched the pale face of the lad it seemed to him to grow strangely like that of his far-off sister.

He had just completed sewing up the gaping wound in his brother's temple, when the cooper came up to the group:

" Here, lay along, you fellows; the carpenter has finished Mr. Newman's boat, and some of you loafing ' soldiers ' have to man her and help Mr. Brant to tow his whale alongside. Leave that man there, and look spry, or you'll feel mighty sorry."

### III

As the cooper turned away the younger Rodman, assisted by his brother, staggered to his feet. The fall from the poop had, in addition to the cut in his temple, severely injured his right knee, and he begged his brother to let him lie down again.

" Yes, yes," whispered Gerald Rodman, hurriedly; " lie down, Ned," and then the lad heard him speaking to Wray in eager, excited tones.

" I'm with you, Jerry," said the young Englishman, quickly, in answer to something that Rodman had said; " where is he now? "

" In the cabin, getting some Bourbon for Mr. Brant's boat. There is only the Dago steward with him, and if Porter and Tom Harrod will join us we shall manage the thing right enough."

" What is the matter, Jerry—what are you talking about? " asked Ned from where he lay.

" Keep still, Ned, and ask us nothing just now; there's a chance of our getting clear of this floating hell. I needn't ask *you* if you'll join us. Come on, Wray."

The fourth mate and the Portuguese steward were in the main cabin filling some bottles from a large jar of Bourbon whisky. Their backs were turned to the door, and both were so intent upon their task that they neither heard nor saw the four figures steal softly upon them. Suddenly they were seized from behind by Wray and Gerald Rodman, and then quickly gagged by Harrod and Porter before either had time to utter a cry. In a few minutes the four men had armed themselves with cutlasses from the rack around the mizzen-mast, which came through the cabin at the for'ard end of the table, Rodman also taking the captain's and chief mate's loaded revolvers out of their berths.

The fourth mate and steward were then carried into the captain's cabin, and Gerald Rodman spoke:

" Newman," he said, " we are going to take charge of this ship for awhile. If you make an attempt to give an alarm you are a dead man. Wray, stand here and run them both through if they make the ghost of a sound."

Again entering the captain's cabin, he returned with two or three charts, a sextant and the ship's chronometer, which he placed on the table just as a heavy footfall sounded on the companion steps. It was the cooper.

" The boat is all ready, Newman," he said, as he entered the somewhat darkened cabin; " who is going in her? "

" We are," said Rodman, dealing him a blow with the butt of his pistol and felling him. " Leave him there, Wray—he'll give us no trouble. Now take every one of those rifles out of the rack and put them on the table. There's two kegs of powder and a bag of bullets in Mr. Brant's cabin—get those as well."

This was quickly done, and, calling to the others to follow him, Rodman sprang up the companion. No one but the man at the wheel was on the poop, and the leader of the mutineers, looking over the rail, saw that the boat was alongside with only one hand in her. Besides this man there were but eight other persons as well as the mutineers on the ship, including the fourth mate, cooper, steward, and carpenter.

Calling the carpenter to him, Rodman covered him with his pistol, and told him and the rest of the startled men to keep quiet or it would be worse for them.

" Two of you help my brother into the boat," he ordered. He was at once obeyed, and Ned Rodman was passed over the side into the hands of the man in the boat.

" Put out every light on deck and aloft," was his next command, and this was done by the watch without delay; for there was in Rodman's face such a look of savage determination that they dared not think of refusing. Then he ordered them into the sail-locker.

" Now, Mr. Waller," he said, addressing the carpenter, " we

don't want to hurt you and these three men with you. But we are desperate, and bent on a desperate course. Still, if you don't want to get shot, do as I tell you. Get into that sail-locker and lie low. Mr. Newman and the cooper and the steward are already disposed of. And I'm going to put it out of the power of Captain ' Brute ' Lucy to get me and those with me into his hands again."

" You won't shut us up in the sail-locker and scuttle the ship and let us drown, will you? " asked the carpenter.

" No; I'm no murderer, unless you make me one. If there is any one I have a grudge against it is Mr. Newman and the cooper; but I won't do more to the cooper than I have already done. Still I'm not going to leave the ship in your hands until I have messed her up a bit. So away with you into the locker, and let us get to work."

Then, with the man from the boat, the carpenter and his companions were pushed into the sail-locker and the door securely fastened. Looking down from the skylight into the cabin Rodman saw that the cooper had not yet come to, and therefore no danger need be apprehended from him. Sending Wray below, the rifles, ammunition, and nautical instruments were passed up on deck and handed down into the boat. Then, leaving Porter on guard to watch the cooper, Rodman and the others went for'ard with a couple of axes and slashed away at the standing fore-rigging on both sides; they then cut half-way through the foremast, so that the slightest puff of wind, when it came, would send it over the side. Then, going for'ard, they cut through the head stays.

" That will do," said the boatsteerer, flinging down his axe; and then walking to the waist he hailed the boat:

" Are you all right, Ned? "

" Yes," answered the youth, " but hurry up, Jerry, I think a breeze is coming."

Running aft, the elder brother sprang up the poop ladder and looked down through the skylight into the cabin. " Cut Mr. Newman and the steward adrift," he said to Wray.

Wray disappeared into Captain Lucy's cabin, and at once liberated the two men, who followed him out into the main cabin.

" Martin Newman," said Rodman, bending down, " just a word with you. You, I thought, were a shade better than the rest of the bullying scoundrels who officer this ship. But now, I find, you are no better than Bully Lucy and the others. If I did justice to my brother, and *another person*, I would shoot you, like the cowardly dog you are. But stand up on that table—and I'll tell you why I don't."

The dark features of the fourth mate blanched to a deathly white, but not with fear. Standing upon the table he grasped the edge of the skylight, under the flap of which Gerald Rodman bent his head and whispered to him:

" Do you know why I don't want to hurt you, Martin Newman?
When I came home last year I found out my sister's love for you;
I found your letters to her, and saw her eating her heart out for
you day by day, and waiting for your return. And because I
know that she is a dying woman, and will die happy in the belief
that you love her, I said nothing. What I have now done will
prevent my ever seeing her again, though I would lay my life
down for her. But listen to me. Ned will, must, return to her,
and beware, if ever you accuse him of having taken a hand in
this mutiny——"

The hands of the fourth mate gripped the skylight ledge convulsively, and his black eyes shone luridly with passion. Then
his better nature asserted itself, and he spoke quietly:

" Jerry, I did not know it was Ned whom I struck to-night. I
was not myself. . . . I never meant to harm *him*. And for Nell's
sake, and yours and Ned's, give up this madness."

" Too late, too late, Newman. I would rather die to-night than
spend another hour on board this ship. But at least, for Nell's
sake, you and I must part in peace," and the mutineer held out
his hand. It was grasped warmly, and then with a simple " good-
bye " Rodman turned away, walked to the poop ladder and called
out:

" Into the boat, men! "

Five minutes later they shoved off from the *Shawnee*, whose
lofty spars and drooping canvas towered darkly up in the starless
night. At the last moment Gerald Rodman had hoisted a light
on the mizzen-rigging as a guide to the four absent boats. As the
mutineers pulled quickly away its rays shone dimly over the
barque's deserted decks.

When daylight came the *Shawnee* was still drifting about on a
sea as smooth as glass, and the four boats reached her just before
the dawn. The boat with the mutineers could not be discerned
even from aloft, and Captain Harvey Lucy, in a state of mind
bordering on frenzy, looked first at his tottering foremast and then
at the four whales which had been towed alongside, waiting to be
cut-in. With the rising sun came another rain-squall, and the
foremast went over the side, although Martin Newman with his
men had done their best to save it. But Lucy, being a man of
energy, soon rigged a jury-mast out of its wreck, and set to work
to cut-in his whales. Three days later the *Shawnee* stood away for
Apia Harbour in Samoa.

" Those fellows have gone to Apia," he said to mate Brant,
" and I'll go there and get them if it takes me a month of
Sundays."

But when the *Shawnee* dropped anchor in the reef-bound harbour, Captain Lucy found that he had come on a vain quest—the
mutineers' boat had not been seen.

For seven years nothing was ever heard of the missing boat, till one day a tall, muscular-looking man, in the uniform of a sergeant of the New South Wales Artillery, came on board the American whaleship *Heloise*, as she lay in Sydney harbour, refitting. He asked for Captain Newman, and was shown into the cabin.

The captain of the *Heloise* was sitting at the cabin table reading a book, and rose to meet his visitor.

" What can I do for you, sir? Good God! is it you, Gerald Rodman! "

The soldier put out his hand. " Is my sister alive, Newman? "

" She died three years ago in my arms, hoping and praying to the last that she might see you and Ned before she died. And Ned? "

" Dead, Newman; he and Wray and Porter died of thirst. Harrod and I alone survived that awful voyage, and reached New Zealand at last. Was Nell buried with the old folks, Martin? "

" Yes," answered the captain of the *Heloise*, passing his hand quickly over his eyes, " it was her wish to lie with them. We had only been married two years."

The sergeant rose, and took Newman's hand in his, " Goodbye, Martin. Some day I may stand with you beside her grave."

And then, ere the captain of the whaleship could stay him, he went on deck, descended the gangway, and was rowed ashore to the glittering lights of the southern city.

# CLARA MORRIS

B. 1849

# THE WILD HORSE OF TARTARY

BUT there! Just as I start to speak of my third season, I seem to look into a pair of big, mild eyes that say, " Can it be that you mean to pass *me* by? Do you forget that 'twas I who turned the great sensation scene of a play into a side-splitting farce? " —and I shake my head and answer truthfully, " I cannot forget. I shall never forget your work that night in Columbus, when you appeared as the ' fiery untamed steed ' (may Heaven forgive you!) in ' Mazeppa '! "

Mr. Robert E. J. Miles—or " All-the-Alphabet Miles," as he was frequently called—was starring at that time in the " horse " drama, doing such plays as " The Cataract of the Ganges," " Mazeppa," " Sixteen-String Jack," etc. " Mazeppa " was the favourite in Columbus, and both the star and the manager regretted that they had billed the other plays in advance, as there would have been more money in " Mazeppa " alone. Mr. Miles carried with him two horses; one, for " The Wild Horse of Tartary," was an exquisitely formed, satin-coated creature, who looked wickedly at you from the corner of her blazing eye: who bared her teeth savagely, and struck out with her forefeet, as well as with her hind ones. When she came rearing, plunging, biting, snapping, whirling, and kicking her way on to the stage, the scarlet lining of her dilating nostrils and the foam flying from her mouth made our screams very natural ones, and the women in front used to huddle close together, or even cover their faces.

One creature only did this beautiful vixen love—R. E. J. Miles. She fawned upon him like a dog, and did tricks for him like a dog, but she was a terror to the rest of mankind. It was really a thrilling scene when Mazeppa was bound, his head tailward, his feet maneward, to the back of that maddened beast. She seemed to bite and tear at him, and when set free, she stood straight up for a dreadful moment, in which she really endangered his life; then, with a wild neigh, she tore off up the " runs " as if fiends pursued her, with the man stretched helplessly along her inky back. The curtain used to go up again and again, it was so very effective.

The other horse who travelled with Mr. Miles was an entirely different sort. He would have been described—according to the State where he happened to be—as a piebald, a skewbald, a pinto, or a calico horse. He was very large, mostly of a satiny white colour, with big absurdly-shaped markings of bright bay. He was one of that breed of horses which in livery stables are always known as "Doctor" or "Judge." Benevolence beamed from his large, clear eyes, and he looked so mildly wise one half expected to see him put on spectacles. The boy at the stable said one day as he fed him, "I wouldn't wonder if this ol' parson of a hoss asked a blessin' on them there oats—I wouldn't!"

I don't know whether Old Bob, as he was called, had any speed or not, but if he had it was useless to him; for alas! he was never allowed to reach the goal under any circumstances. He was always ridden by the villain, and therefore had to be overtaken. Besides that he generally had to carry double, as the desperado usually fled holding the fainting heroine before him, and though Old Bob successfully leaped chasms thus heavily handicapped—for truly he was a mighty jumper—nevertheless he was compelled to accept defeat. Mr. Miles always came rushing up to the rescue on the black horse, when Bob was very lucky, indeed, if he didn't have to roll about and die; and he was a very impatient dead horse, often amusing the audience by lifting his head to see if the curtain was not down, and then dropping dead again, with a sigh the whole house could hear.

Anyway, being continually pushed back into second place, and compelled to listen to the unearned applause bestowed upon the beautiful black, Old Bob lost all ambition professionally, and he simply became a gourmet and a glutton. He lived to eat. A woman in his eyes was a sort of perambulating storehouse of cake, crackers, apples, sugar, etc.; only his love for children was disinterested. The moment he was loose he went off on a search for children, no matter whose so long as he found some; then down he would go on his knees, and wait to be pulled and patted. His habit of gathering very small people up by their back breadths, and carrying them a little way before dropping them, always filled the air with wild shrieks of laughter. In the theatre he walked sedately about before rehearsal began, and though we knew his attentions were entirely selfish, he was so urbane, so complaisant in his manner of going through us, that we could not resist his advances, and each day and night we packed our pockets and our muffs with such provender as women seldom carry about in their clothes. All our gloves smelled as though we worked at a cider mill. While the play was going on, Old Bob spent a great part of his time standing on the first of the screen platforms connecting the runs, and as every one of us had to pass him on our way to dress, he demanded toll of all. Fruits, domestic or foreign, he received with gentle eagerness. Cake, crackers, and sugar—the velvety nose snuffed at them approvingly, and if a girl, believing herself late, tried to pass him swiftly by, his look of amazement was comical to behold, and in an instant his iron-shod foot was playing a veritable devil's tattoo on the resounding board platform. If that failed to win attention, following her with his eyes, he lifted up his voice in a full-chested "Neigh—hay—hay—*haay!*" that brought her back in a hurry with her toll of sugar. And that piebald hypocrite would scrunch it with such a piteously ravenous air that the girl quite forgot the satirical words her landlady had directed against her recently-acquired sweet tooth.

The dreadful night of disaster came late in the week. I don't recall the name of the play, but in that one piece the beautiful, high-spirited black mare had to carry double up the runs. John Carroll and Miss Lucy Cutler were the riders. Mr. Carroll claimed that he could ride a little, and though he was afraid, he was ashamed to own it. Mr. Miles said in the morning: "Now if you are the least bit timid, Mr. Carroll, say so, and I will fasten the bridle reins to the saddle pommel, and Queen will carry you up of her own accord as true as a die and as safe as a rock; but if you are going to hold the bridle, for God's sake be careful! If it was Old Bob, you could saw him as much as you liked and he would pay no attention, but Queen, who has a tender mouth, is half-mad with excitement at night, and a very slight pressure on the wrong rein will mean a forty or fifty-foot fall for you all!" Miss Cutler expressed great fear, when Mr. Miles surprisedly said: "Why, you have ridden with me twice this week without a sign of fear?"

"Oh, yes," she answered, "but *you* know what you are doing—*you* are a horseman!"

It was an unfortunate speech, and in the face of it Mr. Carroll's vanity would not allow him to admit his anxiety. "He could ride well enough and he would handle the reins himself," he declared.

During the day his fears grew upon him. Foolishly and wickedly he resorted to spirits to try to build up some Dutch courage. Then when the scene came on, half-blind with fear and the liquor—which he was not used to—as he felt the fierce creature beneath him rushing furiously up the steep incline, a sort of madness came upon him. Without rhyme or reason he pulled desperately at the nigh rein, and in the same breath their three bodies were hurling downward like thunderbolts. It was an awful sight! I looked at them as they descended, and for the fraction of a second they seemed to be suspended in the air. They were all upside down. All, without turning or twisting, fell straight as plummets —the horse, the same as the man and woman, had its feet straight in the air. Ugh! the striking. Ugh! never mind details. The curtain was rushed down. Miss Cutler was picked up dazed, stunned, but without a mark. Mr. Carroll crept away unaided amid the confusion, the sorrow, and the tears, for splendid Queen was doomed. Though Mr. Miles had risked his own life in an awful leap to save her from falling through a trap, he could not save her life, and the almost human groan with which she dropped her lovely head upon her master's shoulders, and his streaming eyes as he tenderly wiped the blood from her velvety nostrils, made even the scene-shifters rub their eyes upon the backs of their hands. While Queen was half-carried to the fire-engine house next door (her stable was too far away), some one went before the curtain and assured the audience that the accident was very slight, and that the lady and gentleman would both appear presently. The audience applauded in a rather doubtful manner, for several ladies had fainted, and the carrying out of a helpless person in a place of amusement always has a depressing effect upon the lookers-on. Meantime Mr. Carroll was getting his wrist bandaged and a cut on his face patched up, while a basket of sawdust was hurriedly procured that certain cruel stains might be concealed. The orchestra played briskly, and the play went on. That's the one thing we can be sure of in this world—that the play will go on. Late that night, beautiful Queen died, with her head resting on her master's knee.

Now " Mazeppa " was billed for the next night, and there were many consultations held in the office and on the stage. " The Wild Horse of Tartary " was gone. It was impossible to find a new horse in one day. " Change the bill! " said Mr. Miles. " And have an empty house," answered Mr. Ellsler.

" But what can I do for a horse? " asked Mr. Miles.

" Use Old Bob," answered Mr. Ellsler.

" Good Lord! " groaned Bob's master. They argued long, but neither wanted to lose the good house, so the bill was allowed to stand and " Mazeppa " was performed with Old Bob as " The Wild Horse of Tartary." Think of it—that ingratiating Old Bob, that follower of women and playmate of children! Why, even the great bay blotches on his white old hide made one think of the circus, of paper hoops, and of *training*, rather than of wildness. With the hope of making him at least impatient and restless, he had been deprived of his supper, and the result was a settled gloom, an air of melancholy that made Mr. Miles swear under his breath every time he looked at him.

The play moved along nicely, the house was large, and seemed pleased. Mazeppa fell into his enemy's hands, the sentence was pronounced, and the order followed, " Bring forth the fiery, untamed steed! " The women of the audience began to draw close to their escorts. Many of them remembered the biting, kicking entrance of the black, and were frightened beforehand. The orchestra responded with incidental, creepy music, but that was all. Over in the entrance, Old Bob, surrounded by the four men who were supposed to restrain him, stood quietly. But those who sat in the left box heard " get-ups! " and " go-ons! " and the cluckings of many tongues. The mighty Khan of Tartary (who could not see that entrance) thought he had not been heard, and he roared again, " Bring forth the fiery, untamed steed! " Another pause; the house tittered; then some one hit Old Bob a crack across the rump with a whip, at which he gave a switch of his tail, and gently ambled on to the stage. He stopped of his own accord at the centre, and, lowering his head, stretched out his neck and sniffed at the leader of the orchestra, precisely as a dog sniffs at a stranger. It was deliciously ridiculous. We girls were supposed to scream with fear of the " wild horse," and alas! we were only too obedient; crowding down at the right, clinging together in attitudes of extremest fright, we shrieked and screeched until Old Bob pricked up his ears, and looked so astonished at our conduct that the audience simply rocked back and forth with laughter. And all the time Mazeppa was saying things that did not seem at all like prayers. Finally he gave orders for the men to surround Bob, which they did, and then a sharp little spike was used—that was to make him dance about pretty lively. It pricked him on the shoulder, and the " wild horse " stood and switched his tail. It pricked him again; he switched his tail again. The men had by this time grown careless, and when the spike was finally used at his mane, he suddenly kicked one of them clear of the stage, and then resumed his unruffled calm. The public thought it was having fun all this time, but pretty soon it knew it. Nothing under heaven could disturb the gentle serenity of that doglike old horse. When Mazeppa was brought forward to be bound upon Old Bob's back, instead of pulling away, and rearing and fighting against the burden, his one and only quick movement was his violent effort to break away from his tormentors and welcome his master joyously.

" Oh! " groaned Miles, " kill him, somebody, before he kills me! "

While Mazeppa was being bound on the " wild horse's " back our instructions were to scream; therefore we screamed as before, and, being on the verge of insanity, Miles lifted his head from the horse's back, and said, " Oh, shut up, do! " The audience heard, and—well, it laughed some more, and then it discovered, when the men sprang away and left the horse free to dash madly up the mountain, that Mazeppa had kept one foot unbound to kick Old Bob with; and truly it did seem that the audience was going into convulsions—such laughter, pierced every now and then by the shrill scream of hysterics. Old Bob ambled up the first run all right, but, alas! for poor Mazeppa, as the "wild horse" reached the first platform, a woman passed on the way to her room, and hungry Bob instantly stopped to negotiate a loan in sugar. Oh, it was dreadful—the wait—and when finally he reappeared, trotting —yes, trotting up the next run—Mr. Miles's foot could be plainly seen kicking with the regularity of a piston-rod, while his remarks were—well, they were irregular in the extreme!

Of course the play was hopelessly ruined. The audience laughed at the slightest mention of the "wild horse," and when the shepherds found horse and man, lying at the foot of the mountain, worn out and exhausted, the building seemed to shake with the laughter.

When the play was over at last, Old Bob walked up to his master and mumbled his hand. Mr. Miles pushed him away with pretended anger, crying: "You infernal old idiot, I'd sell you for a three-cent stamp with gum on it!"

Bob looked hard at him a moment; then he calmly crossed behind him and mumbled his other hand, and Mr. Miles pulled his ears, and said that he, himself, was the idiot for expecting an untrained, unrehearsed horse to play such a part, and Old Bob agreeing with him perfectly, they were, as always, at peace with each other.

# GEORGE EGERTON
# (MRS. GOLDING BRIGHT)
B. 1860

# A LITTLE GREY GLOVE

*" The book of life begins with a man and woman in a garden and ends—with Revelations."*—OSCAR WILDE.

YES, most fellows' book of life may be said to begin at the chapter where woman comes in; mine did. She came in years ago, when I was a raw undergraduate. With the sober thought of retro-spective analysis, I may say she was not all my fancy painted her; indeed, now that I come to think of it there was no fancy about the vermeil of her cheeks, rather an artificial reality; she had her bower in the bar of the Golden Boar, and I was madly in love with her, seriously intent on lawful wedlock. Luckily for me she threw me over for a neighbouring pork butcher, but at the time I took it hardly, and it made me sex-shy. I was a very poor man in those days. One feel one's grief more keenly then, one hasn't the wherewithal to buy distraction. Besides, ladies snubbed me rather, on the rare occasions I met them. Later I fell in for a legacy, the forerunner of several; indeed, I may say I am beastly rich. My tastes are simple too, and I haven't any poor relations. I believe they are of great assistance in getting rid of superfluous capital—wish I had some! It was after the legacy that women discovered my attractions. They found that there was something superb in my plainness (before, they said ugliness), something after the style of the late Victor Emanuel, something infinitely more striking than mere ordinary beauty. At least so Harding told me his sister said, and she had the reputation of being a clever girl. Being an only child, I never had the opportunity other fellows had of studying the undress side of women through familiar intercourse, say with sisters. Their most ordinary belongings were sacred to me. I had, I used to be told, ridiculous high-flown notions about them (by the way I modified those considerably on closer acquaint-ance). I ought to study them; nothing like a woman for developing a fellow. So I laid in a stock of books in different languages, mostly novels, in which women played title-rôles, in order to get up some

344

definite data before venturing amongst them. I can't say I derived much benefit from this course. There seemed to be as great a diversity of opinion about the female species as, let us say, about the salmonidae.

My friend Ponsonby Smith, who is one of the oldest fly-fishers in the three kingdoms, said to me once: " Take my word for it, there are only four true salmo; the salar, the trutta, the fario, the ferox; all the rest are just varieties, subgenuses of the above; stick to that. Some writing fellow divided all the women into good-uns and bad-uns. But as a conscientious stickler for truth, I must say that both in trout as in women, I have found myself faced with most puzzling varieties, that were a tantalising blending of several qualities." I then resolved to study them on my own account. I pursued the Eternal Feminine in a spirit of purely scientific investigation. I knew you'd laugh sceptically at that, but it's a fact. I was impartial in my selection of subjects for observation— French, German, Spanish, as well as the home product. Nothing in petticoats escaped me. I devoted myself to the freshest *ingénue* as well as the experienced widow of three departed; and I may as well confess that the more I saw of her, the less I understood her. But I think they understood me. They refused to take me *au sérieux*. When they weren't fleecing me, they were interested in the state of my soul (I preferred the former), but all humbugged me equally, so I gave them up. I took to rod and gun instead, *pro salute animae;* it's decidedly safer. I have scoured every country in the globe; indeed, I can say that I have shot and fished in woods and waters where no other white man, perhaps, ever dropped a beast or played a fish before. There is no life like the life of a free wanderer, and no lore like the lore one gleans in the great book of nature. But one must have freed one's spirit from the taint of the town before one can even read the alphabet of its mystic meaning.

What has this to do with the glove? True, not much, and yet it has a connection—it accounts for me.

Well, for twelve years I have followed the impulses of the wandering spirit that dwells in me. I have seen the sun rise in Finland and gild the Devil's Knuckles as he sank behind the Drachensberg. I have caught the barba and the gamer yellow fish in the Vaal river, taken muskelunge and black-bass in Canada, thrown a fly over *guapote* and *cavallo* in Central American lakes, and choked the monster eels of the Mauritius with a cunningly faked-up duckling. But I have been shy as a chub at the shadow of a woman.

Well, it happened last year I came back on business—another confounded legacy; end of June too, just as I was off to Finland. But Messrs. Thimble and Rigg, the highly respectable firm who look after my affairs, represented that I owed it to others, whom I kept out of their share of the legacy, to stay near town till affairs were wound up. They told me, with a view to reconcile me perhaps, of a trout stream with a decent inn near it; an unknown stream in Kent. It seems a junior member of the firm is an angler, at least he sometimes catches pike or perch in the Medway some way from the stream where the trout rise in audacious security from artificial lures. I stipulated for a clerk to come down with any papers to be signed, and started at once for Victoria. I decline to tell the name of my find, firstly because the trout are the gamest little fish that ever rose to fly and run to a good two pounds. Secondly I have paid for all the rooms in the inn for the next year, and I want it to myself. The glove is lying on the table next me as I write. If it isn't in my breast-pocket or under my pillow, it is in some place where I can see it. It has a delicate grey body (Suède, I think they call it) with a whipping of silver round the top, and a darker grey silk tag to fasten it. It is marked 5¾ inside, and has a delicious scent about it, to keep off moths, I suppose; naphthaline is better. It reminds me of a " silver-sedge " tied on a ten hook. I startled the good landlady of the little inn (there is no village fortunately) when I arrived with the only porter of the tiny station laden with traps. She hesitated about a private sitting-room, but eventually we compromised matters, as I was willing to share it with the other visitor. I got into knickerbockers at once, collared a boy to get me worms and minnow for the morrow, and as I felt too lazy to unpack tackle, just sat in the shiny arm-chair (made comfortable by the successive sitting of former occupants) at the open window and looked out. The river, not the trout stream, winds to the right, and the trees cast trembling shadows into its clear depths. The red tiles of a farm roof show between the beeches, and break the monotony of blue sky background. A dusty waggoner is slaking his thirst with a tankard of ale. I am conscious of the strange lonely feeling that a visit to England always gives me. Away in strange lands, even in solitary places, one doesn't feel it somehow. One is filled with the hunter's lust, bent on a " kill "; but at home in the quiet country, with the smoke curling up from some fireside, the mowers busy laying the hay in swaths, the children tumbling under the trees in the orchards, and a girl singing as she spreads the clothes on the sweetbrier hedge, amidst a scene quick with home sights and sounds, a strange lack creeps in and makes itself felt in a dull, aching way. Oddly enough, too, I had a sense of uneasiness, a " something going to happen." I had often experienced it when out alone in a great forest, or on an unknown lake, and it always meant " 'ware danger " of some kind. But why should I feel it here? Yet I did, and I couldn't shake it off. I took to examining the room. It was a common-place one of the usual type. But there was a work-basket on the table, a dainty thing, lined with blue satin. There was a bit of lace stretched over shiny blue linen, with the needle sticking in it; such fairy work, like cobwebs seen from below, spun from a branch against a background of sky. A gold thimble, too, with initials, not the landlady's I know. What pretty things, too, in the basket! A scissors, a capital shape for fly-making; a little file and some floss silk and tinsel, the identical colour I want for a new fly I have in my head, one that will be a demon to kill. The northern devil I mean to call him. Some one looks in behind me, and a light step passes up-stairs. I drop the basket; I don't know why. There are some reviews near it. I take up one, and am soon buried in an article on Tasmanian fauna. It is strange, but whenever I do know anything about a subject, I always find these writing fellows either entirely ignorant or damned wrong.

After supper I took a stroll to see the river. It was a silver grey evening, with just the last lemon and pink streaks of the sunset staining the sky. There had been a shower, and somehow the smell of the dust after rain mingled with the mignonette in the garden brought back vanished scenes of small-boyhood, when I caught minnows in a bottle, and dreamt of a shilling rod as happiness unattainable. I turned aside from the road in accordance with directions, and walked towards the stream. Holloa! some one before me, what a bore! The angler is hidden by an elder-bush, but I can see the fly drop delicately, artistically on the water. Fishing up-stream, too! There is a bit of broken water there, and the midges dance in myriads; a silver gleam, and the line spins out, and the fly falls just in the right place. It is growing dusk, but the fellow is an adept at quick, fine casting—I wonder what fly he has on—why, he's going to try down-stream now! I hurry forward, and as I near him, I swerve to the left out of the way. S-s-s-s! a sudden sting in the lobe of my ear. Hey! I cry as I find I am caught; the tail fly is fast in it. A slight, grey-clad woman holding the rod lays it carefully down and comes towards me through the gathering dusk. My first impulse is to snap the gut and take to my heels, but I am held by something less tangible but far more powerful than the grip of the Limerick hook in my ear.

" I am very sorry! " she says in a voice that matched the evening, it was so quiet and soft; " but it was exceedingly stupid of you to come behind like that."

" I didn't think you threw such a long line; I thought I was safe," I stammered.

" Hold this," she says, giving me a diminutive fly-book, out of which she has taken a scissors. I obey meekly. She snips the gut.

" Have you a sharp knife? If I strip the hook you can push it through; it is lucky it isn't in the cartilage."

I suppose I am an awful idiot, but I only handed her the knife, and she proceeded as calmly as if stripping a hook in a man's ear were an everyday occurrence. Her gown is of some soft grey stuff, and her grey leather belt is silver clasped. Her hands are soft and cool and steady, but there is a rarely disturbing thrill in their gentle touch. The thought flashed through my mind that I had just missed that, a woman's voluntary tender touch, not a paid caress, all my life.

" Now you can push it through yourself. I hope it won't hurt much." Taking the hook, I push it through, and a drop of blood follows it. " Oh! " she cries, but I assure her it is nothing, and stick the hook surreptitiously in my coat sleeve. Then we both laugh, and I look at her for the first time. She has a very white forehead, with little tendrils of hair blowing round it under her grey cap, her eyes are grey. I didn't see that then, I only saw they were steady, smiling eyes that matched her mouth. Such a mouth, the most maddening mouth a man ever longed to kiss, above a too pointed chin, soft as a child's; indeed, the whole face looks soft in the misty light.

" I am sorry I spoilt your sport! " I say.

" Oh, that don't matter, it's time to stop. I got two brace, one a beauty."

She is winding in her line, and I look in her basket; they *are* beauties, one two-pounder, the rest running from a half to a pound.

" What fly? "

" Yellow dun took that one, but your assailant was a partridge spider."

I sling her basket over my shoulder; she takes it as a matter of course, and we retrace our steps. I feel curiously happy as we walk towards the road; there is a novel delight in her nearness; the feel of woman works subtly and strangely in me; the rustle of her skirt as it brushes the black-heads in the meadow-grass, and the delicate perfume, partly violets, partly herself, that comes to me with each of her movements is a rare pleasure. I am hardly surprised when she turns into the garden of the inn, I think I knew from the first that she would.

" Better bathe that ear of yours, and put a few drops of carbolic in the water." She takes the basket as she says it, and goes into the kitchen. I hurry over this and go into the little sitting-room. There is a tray with a glass of milk and some oaten cakes upon the table. I am too disturbed to sit down; I stand at the window and watch the bats flitter in the gathering moonlight, and listen with quivering nerves for her step—perhaps she will send for the tray, and not come after all. What a fool I am to be disturbed by a grey-clad witch with a tantalising mouth! That comes of loafing about doing nothing. I mentally darn the old fool who saved her money instead of spending it. Why the devil should I be bothered? I don't want it anyhow. She comes in as I fume, and I forget everything at her entrance. I push the arm-chair towards the table, and she sinks quietly into it, pulling the tray nearer.

She has a wedding ring on, but somehow it never strikes me to wonder if she is married or a widow or who she may be. I am content to watch her break her biscuits. She has the prettiest hands, and a trick of separating her last fingers when she takes hold of anything. They remind me of white orchids I saw somewhere. She led me to talk; about Africa, I think. I liked to watch her eyes glow deeply in the shadow and then catch light as she bent forward to say something in her quick responsive way.

"Long ago when I was a girl," she said once.

"Long ago?" I echo incredulously, "surely not?"

"Ah, but yes, you haven't seen me in the daylight," with a soft little laugh. "Do you know what the gipsies say? ' Never judge a woman or a ribbon by candle-light.' They might have said moonlight equally well."

She rises as she speaks, and I feel an overpowering wish to have her put out her hand. But she does not, she only takes the work-basket and a book, and says good-night with an inclination of her little head.

I go over and stand next her chair; I don't like to sit in it, but I like to put my hand where her head leant, and fancy, if she were there, how she would look up.

I woke next morning with a curious sense of pleasurable excite-ment. I whistled from very lightness of heart as I dressed. When I got down I found the landlady clearing away her breakfast things. I felt disappointed and resolved to be down earlier in future. I didn't feel inclined to try the minnow. I put them in a tub in the yard, and tried to read and listen for her step. I dined alone. The day dragged terribly. I did not like to ask about her, I had a notion she might not like it. I spent the evening on the river. I might have filled a good basket, but I let the beggars rest. After all, I had caught fish enough to stock all the rivers in Great Britain. There are other things than trout in the world. I sit and smoke a pipe where she caught me last night. If I half close my eyes I can see hers, and her mouth in the smoke. That is one of the curious charms of baccy, it helps to reproduce brain pictures. After a bit I think " perhaps she has left." I get quite feverish at the thought and hasten back. I must ask. I look up at the window as I pass; there is surely a gleam of white. I throw down my traps and hasten up. She is leaning with her arms on the window-ledge staring out into the gloom. I could swear I caught a suppressed sob as I entered. I cough, and she turns quickly and bows slightly. A bonnet and gloves and lace affair and a lot of papers are lying on the table. I am awfully afraid she is going. I say:

"Please don't let me drive you away, it is so early yet. I half expected to see you on the river."

"Nothing so pleasant; I have been up in town (the tears have certainly got into her voice) all day; it was so hot and dusty, I am tired out.''

The little servant brings in the lamp and a tray with a bottle of lemonade.

'' Mistress hasn't any lemons, 'm, will this do? ''

'' Yes,'' she says wearily, she is shading her eyes with her hands; '' anything, I am fearfully thirsty.''

'' Let me concoct you a drink instead. I have lemons and ice and things. My man sent me down supplies to-day; I leave him in town. I am rather a dab at drinks; learnt it from the Yankees; about the only thing I did learn from them I care to remember. Susan! '' The little maid helps me to get the materials, and *she* watches me quietly. When I give it to her she takes it with a smile (she *has* been crying). That is an ample thank-you. She looks quite old. Something more than tiredness called up those lines in her face.

.　　　.　　　.　　　.　　　.　　　.

Well, ten days passed, sometimes we met at breakfast, sometimes at supper, sometimes we fished together or sat in the straggling orchard and talked; she neither avoided me nor sought me. She is the most charming mixture of child and woman I ever met. She is a dual creature. Now I never met that in a man. When she is here without getting a letter in the morning or going to town, she seems like a girl. She runs about in her grey gown and little cap, and laughs and seems to throw off all thought like an irresponsible child. She is eager to fish, or pick gooseberries and eat them daintily, or sit under the trees and talk. But when she goes to town—I notice she always goes when she gets a lawyer's letter, there is no mistaking the envelope—she comes home tired and haggard-looking, an old woman of thirty-five. I wonder why. It takes her, even with her elasticity of temperament, nearly a day to get young again. I hate her to go to town; it is extraordinary how I miss her; I can't recall, when she is absent, her saying anything very wonderful, but she converses all the time. She has a gracious way of filling the place with herself, there is an entertaining quality in her very presence. We had one rainy afternoon; she tied me some flies (I shan't use any of them); I watched the lights in her hair as she moved, it is quite golden in some places, and she has a tiny mole near her left ear and another on her left wrist. On the eleventh day she got a letter but she didn't go to town, she stayed up in her room all day; twenty times I felt inclined to send her a line, but I had no excuse. I heard the landlady say as I passed the kitchen window: '' Poor dear! I'm sorry to lose her! '' Lose her? I should think not. It has come to this with me that I don't care to face any future without her; and yet I know nothing about her, not even if she is a free woman. I shall find that out the next time I see her. In the evening I catch a glimpse of her gown in the orchard and I follow her. We sit down near the river. Her left hand is lying gloveless next me in the grass.

"Do you think from what you have seen of me, that I would ask a question out of any mere impertinent curiosity?"

She starts—"No, I do not."

I take up her hand and touch the ring. "Tell me, does this bind you to any one?"

I am conscious of a buzzing in my ears and a dancing blurr of water and sky and trees as I wait (it seems to me an hour) for her reply. I felt the same sensation once before, when I got drawn into some rapids and had an awfully narrow shave, but of that another time.

The voice is shaking.

"I am not legally bound to any one, at least; but why do you ask?" She looks me square in the face as she speaks, with a touch of haughtiness I never saw in her before.

Perhaps the great relief I feel, the sense of joy at knowing she is free, speaks out of my face, for hers flushes and she drops her eyes, her lips tremble. I don't look at her again, but I can see her all the same. After a while she says:

"I half intended to tell you something about myself this evening, now I *must*. Let us go in. I shall come down to the sitting-room after your supper." She takes a long look at the river and the inn, as if fixing the place in her memory; it strikes me with a chill that there is a good-bye in her gaze. Her eyes rest on me a moment as they come back, there is a sad look in their grey clearness. She swings her little grey gloves in her hand as we walk back. I can hear her walking up and down overhead; how tired she will be, and how slowly the time goes. I am standing at one side of the window when she enters; she stands at the other, leaning her head against the shutter with her hands clasped before her. I can hear my own heart beating, and, I fancy, hers through the stillness. The suspense is fearful. At length she says:

"You have been a long time out of England; you don't read the papers?"

"No." A pause. I believe my heart is beating inside my head.

"You asked me if I was a free woman. I don't pretend to misunderstand why you asked me. I am not a beautiful woman, I never was. But there must be something about me, there is in some women, 'essential femininity' perhaps, that appeals to all men. What I read in your eyes I have seen in many men's before, but, before God, I never tried to rouse it. To-day (with a sob) I can say I am free, yesterday morning I could not. Yesterday my husband gained his case and divorced me!" She closes her eyes and draws in her under-lip to stop its quivering. I want to take her in my arms, but I am afraid to.

" I did not ask you any more than if you were free! "

" No, but I am afraid you don't quite take in the meaning. I did not divorce my husband, he divorced *me*, he got a decree *nisi*; do you understand now? (she is speaking with difficulty) do you know what that implies? "

I can't stand her face any longer. I take her hands, they are icy cold, and hold them tightly.

" Yes, I know what it implies, that is, I know the legal and social conclusion to be drawn from it—if that is what you mean. But I never asked you for that information. I have nothing to do with your past. You did not exist for me before the day we met on the river. I take you from that day and I ask you to marry me."

I feel her tremble and her hands get suddenly warm. She turns her head and looks at me long and searchingly, then she says:

" Sit down, I want to say something! "

I obey, and she comes and stands next the chair. I can't help it, I reach up my arm, but she puts it gently down.

" No, you must listen without touching me, I shall go back to the window. I don't want to influence you a bit by any personal magnetism I possess. I want you to listen—I have told you he divorced me; the co-respondent was an old friend, a friend of my childhood, of my girlhood. He died just after the first application was made, luckily for me. He would have considered my honour before my happiness. *I* did not defend the case, it wasn't likely— ah, if you knew all? He proved his case; given clever counsel, willing witnesses to whom you make it worth while, and no defence, divorce is always attainable even in England. But re- member: I figure as an adulteress in every English-speaking paper. If you buy last week's evening papers—do you remember the day I was in town? "—I nod—" you will see a sketch of me in that day's; some one, perhaps he, must have given it; it was from an old photograph. I bought one at Victoria as I came out; it is funny (with an hysterical laugh) to buy a caricature of one's own poor face at a news-stall. Yet in spite of that I have felt glad. The point for you is that I made no defence to the world, and (with a lifting of her head) I will make no apology, no explanation, no denial to you, now or ever. I am very desolate and your attention came very warm to me, but I don't love you. Perhaps I could learn to (with a rush of colour), for what you have said to-night, and it is because of that I tell you to weigh what this means. Later, when your care for me will grow into habit, you may chafe at my past. It is from that I would save you."

I hold out my hands, and she comes and puts them aside and takes me by the beard and turns up my face and scans it earnestly. She must have been deceived a good deal. I let her do as she pleases, it is the wisest way with women, and it is good to have

her touch me in that way. She seems satisfied. She stands leaning against the arm of the chair and says:

"I must learn first to think of myself as a free woman again;
it almost seems wrong to-day to talk like this; can you understand
that feeling?"

I nod assent.

"Next time I must be sure, and you must be sure." She lays
her fingers on my mouth as I am about to protest. "S-sh! You
shall have a year to think. If you repeat then what you have said
to-day, I shall give you your answer. You must not try to find
me. I have money. If I am living, I will come here to you. If
I am dead you will be told of it. In the year between I shall look
upon myself as belonging to you, and render an account if you wish
of every hour. You will not be influenced by me in any way,
and you will be able to reason it out calmly. If you think better
of it, don't come."

I feel there would be no use trying to move her, I simply kiss
her hands and say:

"As you will, dear woman, I shall be here."

We don't say any more; she sits down on a footstool with her
head against my knee, and I just smooth it. When the clocks
strike ten through the house, she rises and I stand up. I see that
she has been crying quietly, poor lonely little soul. I lift her off
her feet and kiss her, and stammer out my sorrow at losing her,
and she is gone. Next morning the little maid brought me an
envelope from the lady, who left by the first train. It held a little
grey glove; that is why I carry it always, and why I haunt the inn
and never leave it for longer than a week; why I sit and dream in
the old chair that has a ghost of her presence always; dream of
the spring to come with the Mayfly on the wing, and the young
summer when midges dance, and the trout are growing fastidious;
when she will come to me across the meadow grass, through the
silver haze, as she did before; come with her grey eyes shining to
exchange herself for her little grey glove.

# CHARLES G. D. ROBERTS

B. 1860

# THE FREEDOM OF THE BLACK-FACED RAM

ON the top of Ringwaak Hill the black-faced ram stood motionless, looking off with mild, yellow eyes across the wooded level, across the scattered farmsteads of the settlement, and across the bright, retreating spirals of the distant river, to that streak of scarlet light on the horizon which indicated the beginning of sunrise. A few paces below him, half-hidden by a grey stump, a green juniper bush, and a mossy brown hillock, lay a white ewe with a lamb at her side. The ewe's jaws moved leisurely, as she chewed her cud and gazed up with comfortable confidence at the sturdy figure of the ram silhouetted against the brightening sky.

This sunrise was the breaking of the black-faced ram's first day in the wilderness. Never before had he stood on an open hill-top and watched the light spread magically over a wide, wild land-scape. Up to the morning of the previous day, his three years of life had been passed in protected, green-hedged valley pastures, amid tilled fields and well-stocked barns, beside a lilied water. This rugged, lonely, wide-visioned world into which fortune had so unexpectedly projected him, filled him with wonder. Yet he felt strangely at ease therein. The hedged pastures had never quite suited him; but here, at length, in the great spaces, he felt at home. The fact was that, alike in character and in outward appearance, he was a reversion to far-off ancestors. He was the product of a freak of heredity.

In the fat-soiled valley-lands, some fifteen miles back of Ring-waak Hill, the farmers had a heavy, long-woolled, hornless strain of sheep, mainly of the Leicester breed, which had been crossed, years back, by an imported Scotch ram of one of the horned, courageous, upland, black-faced varieties. The effect of this hardy cross had apparently all been bred out, save for an added stamina in the resulting stock, which was uniformly white and hornless. When, therefore, a lamb was born with a black face and blackish-grey legs, it was cherished as a curiosity; and when, in time, it

354

developed a splendid pair of horns, it became the handsomest ram in all the valley, and a source of great pride to its owner. But when black-faced lambs began to grow common in the hornless and immaculate flocks, the feelings of the valley folks changed, and word went round that the strain of the white-faced must be kept pure. Then it was decreed that the great horned ram should no longer sire the flocks, but be hurried to the doom of his kind and go to the shambles.

Just at this time, however, a young farmer from the backwoods settlement over behind Ringwaak chanced to visit the valley. The sheep of his settlement were not only hornless, but small and light-woolled as well, and the splendid, horned ram took his fancy. Here was a chance to improve his breed. He bought the ram for what he was worth to the butcher, and proudly led him away, over the hills and through the great woods, toward the settlement on the other side of Ringwaak.

The backwoodsman knew right well that a flock of sheep may be driven, but that a single sheep must be led; so he held his new possession securely by a piece of stout rope about ten feet long. For an hour or two the ram followed with an exemplary docility quite foreign to his independent spirit. He was subdued by the novelty of his surroundings—the hillocky, sloping pastures, and the shadowy solemnity of the forest. Moreover, he perceived, in his dim way, a kind of mastery in this heavy-booted, homespun-clad, tobacco-chewing, grave-eyed man from the backwoods, and for a long time he felt none of his usual pugnacity. But by and by the craving for freedom began to stir in his breast, and the blood of his hill-roving ancestors thrilled toward the wild pastures. The glances which, from time to time, he cast upon the backwoods-man at the other end of the rope became wary, calculating, and hostile. This stalwart form, striding before him, was the one barrier between himself and freedom. Freedom was a thing of which he knew, indeed, nothing—a thing which, to most of his kind, would have seemed terrifying rather than alluring. But to him, with that inherited wildness stirring in his blood, it seemed the thing to be craved before all else.

Presently they came to a little cold spring, bubbling up beside the road and tinkling over the steep bank. The road at this point ran along a hillside, and the slope below the road was clothed with blueberry and other dense shrubs. The backwoodsman was hot and thirsty. Flinging aside his battered hat, he dropped down on his hands and knees beside the spring and touched his lips to the water.

In this position, still holding the rope in a firm grasp, he had his back to the ram. Moreover, he no longer looked either formid-able or commanding. The ram saw his chance. A curious change came over his mild, yellow eyes. They remained yellow, indeed, but became cold, sinister, and almost cruel in their expression.

The backwoodsman, as he drank, held a tight grip on the rope. The ram settled back slightly, till the rope was almost taut. Then he launched himself forward. His movement was straight and swift, as if he had been propelled by a gigantic spring. His massive, broad-horned forehead struck the stooping man with terrific force.

With a grunt of pain and amazement, the man shot sprawling over the bank, and landed, half-stunned, in a clump of blueberry bushes. Dazed and furious, he picked himself up, passed a heavy hand across his scratched, smarting face, and turned to see the ram disappearing among the thickets above the road. His disappointment so overcame his wrath that he forgot to exercise his vigorous backwoods vocabulary, and resumed his homeward way with his head full of plans for the recapture of his prize.

The ram, meanwhile, trailing the length of rope behind him, was galloping madly through the woods. He was intoxicated with his freedom. These rough, wild, lonely places seemed to him his home. With all his love for the wilderness, the instinct which had led him to it was altogether faulty and incomplete. It supplied him with none of the needful forest lore. He had no idea of caution. He had no inkling of fear. He had no conception of the enemies that might lurk in thicket or hollow. He went crashing ahead as if the green world belonged to him, and cared not who might hear the brave sound of his going. Now and then he stepped on the rope, and stumbled; but that was a small matter.

Through dark strips of forest, over rocky, tangled spaces, across slopes burnt barren, his progress was always upward, until, having traversed several swampy vales and shadowy ravines, toward evening he came out upon the empty summit of Ringwaak. On the topmost hillock he took his stand proudly, his massive head and broad, curled horns in splendid relief against the amber sky.

As he stood, surveying his new realm, a low bleat came to him from a sheltered hollow close by, and, looking down, he saw a small white ewe with a new-born lamb nursing under her flank. Here was his new realm peopled at once. Here were followers of his own kind. He stepped briskly down from his hillock and graciously accepted the homage of the ewe, who snuggled up against him as if afraid at the loneliness and the coming on of night. All night he slept beside the mother and her young, in the sheltered hollow, and kept no watch because he feared no foe. But the ewe kept watch, knowing well what perils might steal upon them in the dark.

As it chanced, however, no midnight prowler visited the summit of Ringwaak Hill, and the first of dawn found the great ram again at his post of observation. It is possible that he had another motive besides his interest in his new, wonderful world. He may have expected the woodsman to follow and attempt his recapture, and resolved not to be taken unawares.  Whatever his motive, he kept his post till the sun was high above the horizon, and the dew-wet woods gleamed as if sown with jewels.  Then he came down and began to feed with the ewe, cropping the short, thin grass with quick bites and finding it far more sweet than the heavy growths of his old pasture.

Late in the morning, when pasturing was over for the time, the ram and the little ewe lay down in the shade of a steep rock, comfortably chewing their cud, while the lamb slept at its mother's side.  The ram, deeply contented, did not observe two grey-brown, stealthy forms creeping along the slope, from bush to rock, and from stump to hillock.  But the ewe, ever on the watch, presently caught sight of them, and sprang to her feet with a snort of terror.  She knew well enough what a lynx was.  Yet for all her terror she had no thought of flight.  Her lamb was too young to flee, and she would stay by it in face of any fate.

The ram got up more slowly, turned his head, and eyed the stealthy strangers with grave curiosity.  Curiosity, however changed into hostility as he saw the ewe's perturbation that the strangers were foes; and a sinister glitter came into the great gold eyes which shone so brilliantly from his black face.

Seeing themselves discovered, the two lynxes threw aside their cunning and rushed ravenously upon what they counted easy prey.  They knew something of the timorous hearts of sheep, and had little expectation of resistance.  But being, first of all, hungry rather than angry, they preferred what seemed easiest to get.  It was upon the lamb and the ewe that they sprang, ignoring the ram contemptuously.

One thing which they had not reckoned with, however, was the temper of the ewe.  Before one fierce claw could reach her lamb, she had butted the assailant so fiercely in the flank that he forgot his purpose and turned with a snarl of rage to rend her.  Meanwhile the other lynx, springing for her neck, had experienced the unexpected.  He had been met by the lightning charge of the ram, fair in the ribs, and hurled sprawling into a brittle, pointed tangle of dead limbs sticking up from the trunk of a fallen tree.

Having delivered this most effective blow, the ram stepped back a pace or two, mincing on his slender feet, and prepared to repeat it.  The lynx was struggling frantically among the branches, which stuck into him and tore his fine fur.  Just in time to escape the second assault he got free—but free not for fight but for flight.  One tremendous, wildly contorted leap landed him on the other side of the dead tree; and, thoroughly cowed, he scurried away down the hill-side.

The ram at once turned his attention to the ewe and her antagonist.  But the second lynx, who had not found his task so simple as he had expected it to be, had no stomach left for one more difficult. The ewe was bleeding about the head, and would, of course, if she had been left to fight it out, have been worsted in a very short time. But the enemy felt the weight of her blows upon his ribs, and had learned his lesson. For just a fraction of a second he turned, and defied the ram with a screeching snarl. But when that horned, black, battering head pitched forward at him he bounded aside like a furry grey ball and clambered to the top of the rock. Here he crouched for some moments, snarling viciously, his tufted ears set back against his neck, and his stump of a tail twitching with rage, while the ram minced to and fro beneath him, stamping defiance with his dainty hoofs. All at once the big cat doubled upon itself, slipped down the other side of the rock, and went gliding away through the stumps and hillocks like a grey shadow; and the ram, perhaps to conceal his elation, fell to grazing as if nothing out of the ordinary had happened. The ewe, on the other hand, seeing the danger so well past, took no thought of her torn face, but set herself to comfort and reassure the trembling lamb.

After this, through the slow, bright hours while the sun swung hotly over Ringwaak, the ram and his little family were undisturbed. An eagle, wheeling, wheeling, wheeling in the depths of the blue, looked down and noted the lamb. But he had no thought of attacking so well guarded a prey. The eagle had a wider outlook than others of the wild kindred, and he knew from of old many matters which the lynxes of Ringwaak had never learned till that day.

There were other visitors that came and glanced at the little family during the quiet content of their cud-chewing. A weasel ran restlessly over a hillock and peered down upon them with hard, bright eyes. The big ram, with his black face and huge, curling horns, was a novel phenomenon, and the weasel disappeared behind the hillock, only to appear again much nearer, around a clump of weeds. His curiosity was mingled with malicious contempt, till the ram chanced to rise and shake his head. Then the weasel saw the rope that wriggled from the ram's neck. Was it some new and terrible kind of snake? The weasel respected snakes when they were large and active; so he forgot his curiosity and slipped away from the dangerous neighbourhood.

The alarm of the weasel, however, was nothing to that of the wood-mice. While the ram was lying down they came out of their secret holes and played about securely, seeming to realise that the big animal's presence was a safeguard to them. But when he moved, and they saw the rope trail sinuously behind him through the scanty grass, they were almost paralysed with panic. Such a snake as that would require all the wood-mice on Ringwaak to assuage his appetite. They fairly fell backward into their burrows, where they crouched quivering in the darkest recesses, not daring to show their noses again for hours.

Neither weasel nor wood-mice, nor the chickadees which came to eye him saucily, seemed to the big ram worth a moment's attention. But when a porcupine, his quills rattling and bristling till he looked as big around as a half-bushel basket, strolled aimlessly by, the ram was interested and rose to his feet. The little, deep-set eyes of the porcupine passed over him with supremest indifference, and their owner began to gnaw at the bark of a hemlock sapling which grew at one side of the rock. To this gnawing he devoted his whole attention, with an eagerness that would have led one to think he was hungry—as, indeed, he was, not having had a full meal for nearly half an hour. The porcupine, of all nature's children, is the best provided for, having the food he loves lying about him at all seasons. Yet he is for ever eating, as if famine were in ambush for him just over the next hillock.

Seeing the high indifference of this small, bristling stranger, the ram stepped up and was just about to sniff at him inquiringly. Had he done so, the result would have been disastrous. He would have got a slap in the face from the porcupine's active and armed tail; and his face would have straightway been transformed into a sort of anguished pincushion, stuck full of piercing, finely barbed quills. He would have paid dear for his ignorance of woodcraft—perhaps with the loss of an eye, or even with starvation from a quill working through into his gullet. But fortunately for him the ewe understood the peculiarities of porcupines. Just in time she noted his danger, and rudely butted him aside. He turned upon her in a fume of amazed indignation; but in some way she made him understand that the porcupine was above all law, and not to be trifled with even by the lords of the wilderness. Very sulkily he lay down again, and the porcupine went on chiselling hemlock bark, serenely unconscious of the anger in the inscrutable yellow eyes that watched him from the ram's black face.

When the shadows grew long and luminous, toward evening, the ram, following some unexplained instinct, again mounted the topmost point of Ringwaak, and stood like a statue gazing over the vast, warm-coloured solitude of his new domain. His yellow eyes were placid with a great content. A little below him, the white lamb wobbling on weak legs at her side, the ewe pastured confidently, secure in the proved prowess of her protector. As the sun dropped below the far-off western rim of the forest, it seemed as if one wide wave of lucent rose-violet on a sudden flooded the world. Everything on Ringwaak—the ram's white fleece, the grey, bleached stumps, the brown hillocks, the green hollows and juniper clumps and poplar saplings—took on a palpitating aerial stain. Here and there in the distance the coils of the river gleamed clear gold; and overhead, in the hollow amber-and-lilac arch of sky, the high-wandering night-hawks swooped with the sweet twang of smitten strings.

Down at the foot of the northern slope of Ringwaak lay a dense cedar swamp. Presently, out from the green fringe of the cedars, a bear thrust his head and cast a crafty glance about the open. Seeing the ram on the hill-top and the ewe with her lamb feeding near by, he sank back noiselessly into the cover of the cedars, and stole around toward the darkening eastern slope, where a succession of shrubby copses ran nearly to the top of the hill.

The bear was rank, rusty-coated, old, and hungry; and he loved sheep. He was an adept in stalking this sweet-fleshed, timorous quarry, and breaking its neck with a well-directed blow as it dashed past him in a panic. Emerging from the swamp, he crept up the hill, taking cunning advantage of every bush, stump, and boulder. For all his awkward-looking bulk, he moved as lightly as a cat, making himself small, and twisting and flattening and effacing himself; and never a twig was allowed to snap, or a stone to clatter, under his broad unerring feet.

About this time it chanced that the backwoodsman, who had been out nearly all day hunting for his lost prize, approached the edge of the forest at the other side of Ringwaak—and saw the figure of the ram against the sky. Then, seeing also the ewe with the lamb beside her, he knew that the game was his.

Below the top of the hill there was not a scrap of cover for a distance of perhaps twenty paces. The bear crept to the very last bush, the ram being occupied with the world at a distance, and the ewe busy at her pasturing. Behind the bush—a thick, spreading juniper—the bear crouched motionless for some seconds, his little red eyes aglow, and his jaws beginning to slaver with eagerness. Then selecting the unconscious ewe, because he knew she was not likely to desert the lamb, he rushed upon his intended victim.

The ewe, as it chanced, was about thirty-five or forty feet distant from the enemy, as he lunged out, black and appalling, from behind the juniper. At the same time the ram was not more than twenty or twenty-five feet distant, straight above the lamb, in a direction at right angles to the path of the bear. The ewe looked up with a startled bleat, wheeled, sprang nimbly before the lamb, and faced her doom dauntlessly, with lowered head.

The ram's mild gaze changed in a flash to one of cold, yellow savagery at the sight of the great black beast invading his kingdom. Down went his conquering head. For just a fraction of a second his sturdy body sagged back, as if he were about to sit down. This, so to speak, was the bending of the bow. Then he launched himself straight down the slope, all his strength, his weight, and the force of gravity combining to drive home that mighty stroke.

The bear had never, in all his experience with sheep, encountered one whose resistance was worth taking into account. The defiance of the ewe was less than nothing to him. But as he saw, from the corner of his eye, the huge bulk plunging down upon him, he hesitated, and half turned, with great paw upraised for a finishing blow.

He turned not quite in time, however, and his defence was not quite strenuous enough for the emergency. He struck like lightning, as a bear always can, but just before the stroke could find its mark the ram's armed forehead crashed into his ribs. The blow, catching him as it did, was irresistible. His claws tore off a patch of wool and skin, and ploughed red furrows across the ram's shoulder— but the next instant he was sprawling, his breath jarred from his lungs, against a stump some ten feet down the slope.

As the bear struggled to his feet, furious but half-daunted with amazement, the ram danced backward a pace or two on his nimble feet, as if showing off, and then delivered his second charge. The bewildered bear was again caught unready, irresolute as to whether he should fight or flee; and again he was knocked headlong, a yard or two further down the slope. His was not the dauntless spirit that most of his kindred would have shown in such a case, and he would willingly have made his escape at once if he had seen his way quite clear to do so. But at this moment, while he hesitated, he heard a man's voice shouting loudly, and saw the tall backwoodsman running toward him up the hill. This sight turned his alarm into a blind panic. His feet seemed to acquire wings as he tore madly away among the thickets. When he was hidden by the leafage, his path could still be followed by the crashing of dry branches and the clattering of loosened stones.

The woodsman had seen the whole incident, and was wild with enthusiasm over the prowess of his prize. Bears had been the most dreaded scourge of the settlement sheep-farmers, but now, as he proudly said to himself, he had a ram that could " lick a b'ar silly! " He bore no grudge on account of his discomfiture that morning beside the spring, but rather thought of it with appreciation as a further evidence of his favourite's cunning and prowess; and he foresaw, with a chuckle, that there were painful surprises in store for the bears of the Ringwaak range. He had made a wise purchase indeed when he saved that splendid beast from the butcher.

Hearing the man's voice, the ram had halted in dismay just when he was about to charge the bear a third time. He had no mind to go again into captivity. But, on the other hand, for all his lordliness of spirit, he felt that the man was his master. At first he lowered his head threateningly, as if about to attack; but when the backwoodsman shouted at him there was an authority in those tones which he could not withstand, and he sullenly drew aside. With a good-natured laugh, the man picked the lamb up in his arms, whereupon the mother stepped timidly to his side, evidently having no fear. The man rubbed her nose kindly, and stroked her ears, and gave her something from his pocket which she ate

132*

greedily; and, as the ram looked on, the anger gradually faded out from his yellow eyes.  At length the man turned and walked slowly down the hill, carrying the lamb.  The ewe followed, crowding as close to him as she could, and stumbling as she went because her eyes were fixed upon her little one.

The ram hesitated.  He looked at the hillside, the woods, and the sky beginning to grow chill with the onrush of twilight.  Then he looked at the retreating figures.  Suddenly he saw his world growing empty and desolate.  With an anxious bleat he trotted after the ewe, and took his docile place a few feet behind the man's heels. The man glanced over his shoulders, and a smile of pleasure softened his rugged face.  In a few moments the little procession disappeared in the woods, moving toward the settlement, and Ringwaak Hill was left solitary in the dusk, with the lonely notes of the night-hawks twanging over it.

# RALPH CONNOR

B. 1860

# THE PILOT AT SWAN CREEK

CATTLEMEN of the Swan Creek country still speak of the winter of the big blizzard. For three days it raged over the hills and down the coolies, sweeping clean before it cattle and horses by the hundred to destruction. It was that blizzard that piled up more than a hundred and fifty of the XL cattle over the cut bank at the bend of the Little Porcupine; and there they were found a ghastly mass, after the first Chinook had licked up the snow banks. Not for the loss of cattle do I remember it, but for a loss that cut deep into my heart.

How well I remember the springlike airs of that bright December morning. A warm Chinook blew gently down through the hazy hills from the purple mountains at the horizon, and over all the sky arched a cloudless blue. We were sitting, the Pilot and I, with the door of our shack wide open to the sunny air, when Bill rode up.

" Fine spring day," said the Pilot.

" Too spring for me," answered Bill, with an ominous glance at the sky.

" You're pretty hard to please, Bill," said the Pilot, " I could stand about six weeks of this."

" Wall, you won't get six hours of it."

" Six hours? Why not? "

" Wall, if I kin read signs, there's the tallest kind of blizzard followin' up this blasted Chinook," answered Bill.

" How do you know? " said the Pilot doubtfully.

" Everyhow," replied Bill, before whose experienced eye the earth and sky lay like an open book. " Why, look at them hills; look at that mist."

" You don't call that mist," broke in the Pilot—" that's a lovely haze."

" Haze, is it? " drawled Bill; " wall, 'taint the kind of haze I aspire to this time o' year." Then he went on, " No! before you're six hours older you'll see a blizzard that'll blow till you can't see your feet. Coming past the cañon trail—by the way, the old man

363

up there is laid up rather—just along by the upper trail there, you know, I seen some deer makin' fer the bluffs. The cattle are dreadful oneasy, bunchin' and sniffin'. Oh, you just bet your gold dust there ain't no slouch of a blizzard a-hustlin' on the back of that there lovely haze."

" Where are you going? " I asked.

" Well, I'm goin' to run a bunch of cattle off the open into a coolie, where they won't be drove into next week, and where we kin find them without diggin'."

" Is the Old Timer in bed? " asked the Pilot.

" Oh, jest layin' round, you know. Nothin' too serious, I guess," replied Bill.

" Wall, I'm off," he continued, wheeling his broncho, " better make this your day at home. So long! " and off he went at a lope.

" Good-bye, Bill; come back for supper," sang out the Pilot after him.

" You watch me," he called back over his shoulder.

As the morning wore on, the haze deepened over the hills, and the sun lost its kindly, genial look and glared at the world with an angry, bloodshot eye. The Chinook wind fell into a dead calm. It may have been that Bill's ominous words impressed me, but it seemed that nature was gradually steadying herself for some tremendous shock. The Pilot could not settle to his work. He wandered about the room, looking out now at the glaring sun, and again at the distant purple mountains.

" I don't like it," he said uneasily, " and Gwen is alone up there with her sick father."

" Oh, he is not very ill," I said, rather more carelessly than I felt, and I saw that he detected the false tone in my voice.

After another restless half-hour I said, " I shall run across to the Muirs'. I promised to take dinner with them to-day. I'll be back right after." He nodded his head, still looking anxiously at the sky, which was beginning to take on a crimson tint.

I could not explain my own feeling of anxiety during the next hour, and as soon as I could decently leave I hurried back to my shack. I found the Pilot gone. On the table this note lay:—

" MY DEAR CONNOR—I can't rest here; Gwen may need help, and I have determined to ride up before the storm breaks to the Old Timer's ranch. Get Bill a bung-up supper. He will be tired and hungry.—Yours,    THE PILOT."

I looked out of the window. Large, soft flakes were falling out of a liver-coloured sky, and the wind was rising. I hurried down to the Stopping Place stable, and found old Latour at the door looking anxiously up at the sky.

" He's near half-way dere," he said.

" Who? "

" De Pilot. I tell heem he's fool for go, but he say he's better be fool nor coward." Old Latour was quite excited. " Dat leel gurl, he's fader go seeck. De Pilot say, ' he go up to see heem.' I say, ' he no good see heem. Dis awful beeg bleezard he's not get trou.' ' How long he las'? ' he say. ' Free day, mebbe,' I say. By Jeorje, he's mad for go den. ' Tree day, all alone. Not moush,' he say, and pull down hees saddle. I mak heem tak Louis. Das good pony for keep de trail. He's put hees nose into de storm. Noder feller he's put hees tail. Oh dat fine pony, Louis."

It seemed to comfort the old man a good deal to feel that the Pilot was riding a pony that could put his nose into the storm and overcome the tendency of the native cayuse to turn tail to it. I was very anxious, in spite of old Latour's confidence in his pony.

" How long has he been gone? " I asked.

" 'Bout half an hour, yes, more," he said.

I looked at my watch; it was three o'clock. The snow was now coming down in long, slanting lines, and beginning to bite. The sky was almost hidden, and had lost all light and colour.

" He ought to be about the cañon now," I said, " and then he'll be all right."

" Yes," said the old man, " he's all right nuff, when he's pass de upper trail. Das bad spot dere."

I knew the place well. The highest point on the whole way, where the trail to the Meredith ranch leaves the main Porcupine trail.

" He'll be der now, sure nuff," continued he, pulling out his big silver watch from his waistband.

" I hope so," I said with all my heart, for even as I spoke I heard a strange sound, such as had never come to my ears before. It was not a roar, it was too soft for that. There was a hissing, beating sound, as if unseen wings, great and innumerable, were sweeping down upon us; an awesome heart-smiting sound. A moment more and the blizzard had struck. I had to fight my way step by step to my shack, and by the time I had gained my door the world had vanished from my sight behind this whirling, shimmering curtain of choking, blinding snow. I had hardly got my fire going when the door was pushed open and in came Bill.

" Wall! " he called out, " how d'ye fancy your lovely haze now? Ain't this a sneezer? " He looked round the room, then stared at me and said, " Whar's the Pilot? "

I handed him the note, saying, " I was down at Muir's, and found this when I came back."

He heard it through slowly, and then asked, " When did he start? "

" About half-past two, old Latour said."

He said no more, but took up his leather coat which he had just laid off.

" What are you going to do? " I asked.

" I ain't goin' to sit here if I know myself, with the Pilot somewheres into this blizzard," he answered almost savagely. " Got any brandy? "

" A flask full."

" Roll up a pair o' blankets, and git me half-a-dozen biscuits. I'm goin' down to the stable. Kin you find your way down there? Bring 'em down."

I felt the bitterness in his voice, and I knew he was blaming me for not following the Pilot at once.

In ten minutes I was at the stable with the blankets done up in two rolls and the biscuits and brandy in my pocket. I found Bill saddling the Duke's black broncho, Jingo, who, having been in the stable for two weeks, was like to knock things to pieces. Bill, however, paid no attention to the antics, but stood up close to him while he cinched the saddle and lashed on the one blanket behind it. The black brute squealed and began to plunge, but Bill kept close to him, tying his tongs as regardless of his antics as if he were a lamb. When all was snug and taut he jerked the tie-line loose, flung the long bridle reins over the head of the rearing animal, then with a fierce grip he seized with both hands the rings of the bit, ran the horse back out of his stall, and, with a mighty wrench, hurled him clear off his feet on to his side.

" Git up! " he yelled, and Jingo sprang to his feet, more surprised and humbled than he had ever been in his whole previous history. " Stand thar, will you! " said Bill in a terrible voice; and Jingo stood quite still.

" What are you going to do? " asked Bill, seeing me with my horse saddled and all ready.

" Going to follow you," I said shortly, for his words and manner had so stung me that I had resolved to follow him till I dropped.

He looked at me a moment in silence, then suddenly stretching out his hand, he said in a husky voice:

" Ye're all right, pard; I take it all back," and without a word he swung himself on to his saddle and rode out into the blizzard.

The air was thick with whirling snow, the wind seemed to be blowing from every quarter at once. Every vestige of earth and sky was shut out from sight by the snow-cloud that seemed to wrap one's head about, filling eyes and throat and shutting off the breath. By what means he found and kept the trail I know not, but not once did Bill falter. On he pressed against and through that wall of blinding, choking snow. After the first quarter of a mile, during which it was difficult to keep him in sight, Jingo settled down into a long, easy, steady lope, as if he knew that serious business was in hand. Occasionally he dropped the beaten track, but a plunge or two and he was on the trail again. Keeping his black tail just before my pony's nose, I had no serious trouble in fighting my way through the blizzard. It is not the cold, nor the depth of the snow, nor the stress of the driving storm that makes the blizzard dangerous. It is its power to shut out the world and to utterly bewilder that strikes terror to the heart. Some men and some horses can make their way, however, without hesitation. Such a man was Bill, and such a horse Jingo.

For an hour we fought along, now slowly feeling our way and then breaking into a lope where the lie of the ground made the trail easier to keep. Suddenly Bill pulled up, and, dismounting, faced Jingo about and gave me his reins to hold.

" Keep 'em just as they are," he said. " I rather think the trail breaks off about here into the cañon. Mind you keep 'em just so. I don't want to lose my direction."

Even as he spoke he passed out of sight, but in a moment or two he reappeared and said:

" It's pretty tough keepin' your bearin's when you're tryin' to find a trail. I want you to count ten and then holler and keep on till I come back."

In a few minutes—they seemed hours—he came back and took his horse.

" You stay here till you hear me holler," he said, and disappeared again.

Soon his call came, and in a short time we were following the trail down into the cañon. Here the track was easier to find, and before long we were at the Old Timer's door.

" I guess I'll just peek in," said Bill in a low voice; " there ain't no occasion to make no row, case he ain't there."

He opened the door gently and passed in, but came out almost immediately.

" The good Lord help us, he ain't been there," he said with a kind of gasp.

" You didn't see Gwen? " I asked.

" No. Saw Joe. Look here, I'm goin' back to that upper trail," he added. " I think p'r'aps I'd be better alone."

" You go to thunder! " I replied; " don't lie to me. Anyway, I'm going with you."

He came close up to me.

" You're a white man," he said earnestly, " but I ain't comin' back till I find him, and there ain't no need for you——" He paused.

For an answer I turned my horse towards the gate. Bill swung himself up into his saddle, and in a few strides Jingo was leading me once more.

"Blamed if you ain't white—clear to the bone," he said, turning in his saddle towards me, and somehow his words gave me a great thrill of joy and put new courage into my heart.

Back through the cañon we rode and up to the open again. Once more Bill found the upper trail and came hurrying back to me.

"We ain't got half a minute to spare," he said anxiously. "It'll be dark in half an hour, and then God Almighty help us."

We went along at what seemed to me a reckless pace. But the black horse never swerved from his long, steady lope. After we had gone about half a mile Jingo suddenly stopped short. Before I could ask the cause, Bill was off and down in the snow exploring.

"Guess we've struck the scent," he called out. "Come here."

There, half covered by the drifting snow, lay a sleigh overturned, with its load strewn about. "Whar's the team? Whar's the driver?" Bill shouted to me. "Thar's where the Pilot is. You bet he's monkeyin' round pullin' some fool out o' the snow."

He dropped on his hands and knees, feeling all about, and finally vanishing into the darkening mist of blinding snow.

"Come on!" I heard him call; and on coming up I found him with a wisp of hay in his hand. "They've gone down the coolie, I do believe. Come on!" he cried. He was excited as I had never seen him before. He flung himself into his saddle and shouted to Jingo, who plunged headlong down the coolie. I followed as best I could, and after a few minutes' hard work came upon Bill standing at his horse's head, in the shelter of a poplar bluff. "Listen!" he said, holding up his hand, and we stood listening for our lives. But only the hissing boom of the blizzard beat upon our ears.

"I swear I heard something just as I—there——" He put up his hand again, and through the storm came the sound of a voice singing:

> God in the midst of her doth dwell,
> Nothing shall her remove.

Bill dropped on his knees, and taking off his cap he sobbed out: "Thank the good God! That's him. It's the Pilot." Then he sprang to his feet and yelled: "Hello! You dod-gasted fool-hunter, where in thunder an' lightnin' air you, anyway?"

"Hello, Bill! Here you are, old boy." In the bluff we found them; the Pilot livid with cold and near the last stage of exhaustion, holding up a stranger as they tramped wearily the path they had beaten around the horses to keep themselves from freezing to death.

"Oh, Bill," cried the Pilot, making a brave attempt at a smile, "you're a great man!"

Bill held him at arm's length a moment, and then said solemnly:

"Wall! I've come into contack with some fools, idjits, blanked idjits"—Bill had lost his grip of himself for a moment—"in my life, but such a blanked, conglomerated idjit it hasn't been my pleasure to mix with up to this point in my career."

The Pilot by this time was in fits of hysterical laughter. " And," continued Bill, with increased solemnity, " I cherish the conviction——"

" Oh, Bill," shrieked the Pilot, " for Heaven's sake, stop! You'll kill me if you say another word." Then Bill paused, looked anxiously into the Pilot's face, and saying, " Here! Let's get home," rolled a blanket round him and set him on Louis.

" You won't need your hands; he'll follow all right," he said as he mounted Jingo. " Come on."

" Wait, Bill! " cried the Pilot. " What about this man? He's almost played out."

" Played out, is he? " snorted Bill contemptuously. " If he's as strong as he smells he ought to get through. Any man that don't know when to leave whisky alone shouldn't travel without his keeper."

" But we can't leave him here! " pleaded the Pilot.

" Can't, eh! You watch my smoke," said Bill. " If he can't follow with two horses he can't with three."

" Oh, I say, Bill! take him along," said the Pilot earnestly.

" Look here! " cried Bill impatiently, " do you think I'm a blasted snow-plough? Come on! Every second counts. He'll follow all right." And so he did, and fighting our way through the storm, and dark, and cold now grown intense, we made the cañon, and soon after the Old Timer's door.

Bill carried the Pilot in and laid him on a pile of skins before the fire. He was not badly frozen, but he was utterly exhausted. During the three days of the blizzard he lay weak and faint, nursed by Bill day and night. With all a mother's tenderness in touch and tone, Bill waited on his every wish, breaking forth now and then in loving wrath upon his folly for going after the stranger.

" But he would have been lost, Bill," said the Pilot gently, after one of Bill's outbursts.

" Wall, let him," growled Bill.

" Bill," answered the Pilot softly, " we were lost once, you know."

And Bill turned and looked away and said not a word, remembering, I have no doubt, Him who came to seek the lost. The Pilot never was the same again, but long after, when the first bitterness of his going from us was over, Bill said one day to me : " That's how he got his death, seekin' after that lost idjit. It was all blamed foolishness, but I guess p'r'aps that's the best after all."

# SIR GILBERT PARKER, Bart.

1861–1932

# THE CRIMSON FLAG

TALK and think as one would, The Woman was striking to see;
with marvellous flaxen hair and a joyous violet eye. She was all
pulse and dash; but she was as much less beautiful than the
manager's wife as Tom Liffey was as nothing beside the manager
himself; and one would care little to name the two women in the
same breath if the end had been different. When The Woman
came to Little Goshen there were others of her class there, but they
were of a commoner sort and degree. She was the queen of a
lawless court, though she never, from first to last, spoke to one of
those others who were her people; neither did she hold commerce
with any of the ordinary miners, save Pretty Pierre—but he was
more gambler than miner—and he went, when the matter was all
over, and told her some things that stripped her soul naked before
her eyes. Pierre had a wonderful tongue. It was only the gentle-
men-diggers—and there were many of them at Little Goshen—who
called upon her when the lights were low; and then there was a
good deal of muffled mirth in the white house among the pines.
The rougher miners made no quarrel with this, for the gentlemen-
diggers were popular enough; they were merely sarcastic and
humorous, and said things which, coming to The Woman's ears,
made her very merry; for she herself had an abundant wit, and
had spent wild hours with clever men.

She did not resent the playful insolence that sent a dozen miners
to her house in the dead of night with a crimson flag, which they
quietly screwed to her roof, and paint, with which they deftly put
a wide stripe of scarlet round the cornice, and another round the
basement. In the morning, when she saw what had been done,
she would not have the paint removed nor the flag taken down;
for, she said, the stripes looked very well, and the other would show
that she was always at home.

Now, the notable thing was that Heldon, the manager, was in
The Woman's house on the night this was done. Tom Liffey, the
lumpish guide and trapper, saw him go in; and, days afterwards,
he said to Pierre: " Divils me own! but this is a bad hour for

370

Heldon's wife—she with a face like a princess and eyes like the fear o' God. Nivir a wan did I see like her, since I came out of Erin with a clatter of hoofs behind me and a squall on the sea before. There's wimmin there wid cheeks like roses and buther-milk, and a touch that'd make y'r heart pound on y'r ribs; but none that's grander than Heldon's wife. To lave her for that other, standin' hip-high in her shame, is temptin' the fires of Heaven, say I, that basted the sinners o' Sodom.''

Pierre, pausing between the whiffs of a cigarette, said: '' So? But you know more of catching foxes in winter, and climbing mountains in summer, and the grip of the arm of an Injun girl, than of these things. You are young, quite young in the world, Tom Liffey.''

'' Young I may be, with a glint o' grey at me temples from a night o' trouble beyand in the hills; but I'm the man, an' the only man, that's climbed to the glacier-top—God's Playground, as they call it; and nivir a dirty trick have I done to Injin girl or any other; and be damned to you there! say I.''

'' Sometimes I think you are as foolish as Shon M'Gann,'' compassionately replied the half-breed. '' You have almighty virtue, and you did that brave trick of the glacier; but great men have fallen. You are not dead yet. Still, as you say, Heldon's wife is noble to see. She is grave and cold, and speaks little; but there is something in her which is not of the meek of the earth. Some women say nothing, and suffer and forgive, and take such as Heldon back to their bosoms; but there are others—— I remember a woman—well, it is no matter, it was long ago; but they two are as if born of one another; and what comes of this will be mad play—mad play.''

'' Ov coorse his wife may not get to know of it, and——''

'' Not get to know it! 'Tsh, you are a child——''

'' Faith, I'll say what I think, and that in y'r face! Maybe he'll tire of the handsome rip—for handsome she is, like a yellow lily growin' out o' mud—and go back to his lawful wife, that believes he's at the mines when he's drinkin' and colloguin' wid a fly-away.''

Pierre slowly wheeled till he had the Irishman straight in his eye. Then he said in a low, cutting tone: '' I suppose your heart aches for the beautiful lady, eh? '' Here he screwed his slight fore-finger into Tom's breast; then he added sharply: '' By the holy Heaven, but you make me angry! You talk too much. Such men get into trouble. And keep down the riot of that sympathy of yours, Tom Liffey, or you'll walk on the edge of knives one day. And now take an inch of whisky and ease your anxious soul. Voilà! '' After a moment he added: '' Women work these things out for themselves.''

Then the two left the hut, and amiably strolled together to the centre of the village, where they parted.

It was as Pierre had said: the woman would work the thing out for herself.  Later that evening Heldon's wife stood cloaked and veiled in the shadows of the pines, facing the house with The Crimson Flag.  Her eyes shifted ever from the door to the flag, which was stirred by the light breeze.  Once or twice she shivered as with cold, but instantly she stilled again, and watched.  It was midnight.  Here and there beyond in the village a light showed, and straggling voices floated faintly towards her.  For a long time no sound came from the house.  But at last she heard a laugh.  At that she drew something from her pocket, and held it firmly in her hand.  Once she turned and looked at another house far up on the hill where lights were burning.  It was Heldon's house—her home.  A sharp sound as of anguish and anger escaped her; then she fastened her eyes on the door in front of her.

At that moment Tom Liffey was standing with his hands on his hips looking at Heldon's home on the hill; and he said some rumbling words, then strode down on the road, and suddenly paused near the wife.  He did not see her.  He faced the door at which she was looking, and shook his fist at it.

" A murrain on y'r sowl! " said he, " as there's plague in y'r body, and hell in the slide of y'r feet, like the trail of the red spider.  And out o' that come ye, Heldon, for I know y're there.  Out of that, ye beast! . . .  But how *can* ye go back—you that's rolled in *that* sewer—to the loveliest woman that ever trod the neck o' the world!  Damned y' are in every joint o' y'r frame, and damned is y'r soul, say I, for bringing sorrow to her; and I hate you as much for that, as I could worship her was she not your wife and a lady o' blood, God save her! "

Then shaking his fist once more, he swung away slowly down the road.  During this the wife's teeth held together as though they were of a piece.  She looked after Tom Liffey and smiled; but it was a dreadful smile.

" He worships me, that common man—worships me! " she said.  " This man who was my husband has shamed me, left me.  Well——"

The door of the house opened; a man came out.  His wife leaned a little forward, and something clicked ominously in her hand.  But a voice came up the road towards them through the clear air— the voice of Tom Liffey.  The husband paused to listen; the wife mechanically did the same.  The husband remembered this afterwards; it was the key to, and the beginning of, a tragedy.  These are the words the Irishman sang:

> She was a queen, she stood up there before me,
>   My blood went roarin' when she touched my hand;
> She kissed me on the lips, and then she swore me
>   To die for her—and happy was the land!

A new and singular look came into her face. It transformed her. " That," she said in a whisper to herself—" that! He knows the way."

As her husband turned towards his home, she turned also. He heard the rustle of garments, and he could just discern the cloaked figure in the shadows. He hurried on; the figure flitted ahead of him. A fear possessed him in spite of his will. He turned back. The figure stood still for a moment, then followed him. He braced himself, faced about, and walked towards it; it stopped and waited. He had not the courage. He went back again swiftly towards the house he had left. Again he looked behind him. The figure was standing, not far, in the pines. He wheeled suddenly towards the house, turned a key in the door, and entered.

Then the wife went to that which had been her home. Heldon did not go thither until the first flush of morning. Pierre, returning from an all-night sitting at cards, met him, and saw the careworn look on his face. The half-breed smiled. He knew that the event was doubling on the man. When Heldon reached his house, he went to his wife's room. It was locked. Then he walked down to his mines with a miserable shame and anger at his heart. He did not pass The Crimson Flag. He went by another way.

That evening, in the dusk, a woman knocked at Tom Liffey's door. He opened it.

" Are you alone? " she said.

" I am alone, lady."

" I will come in," she added.

" You will—come in? " he faltered.

She drew near him, and reached out and gently caught his hand.

" Ah! " he said, with a sound almost like a sob in its intensity, and the blood flushed to his hair.

He stepped aside, and she entered. In the light of the candle her eye burned into his, but her face wore a shining coldness. She leaned towards him.

" You said you could worship me," she whispered, " and you cursed *him*. Well—worship me—altogether—and that will curse him, as he has killed me."

" Dear lady! " he said, in an awed, overwhelmed murmur; and he fell back to the wall.

She came towards him. " Am I not beautiful? " she urged. She took his hand. His eyes swam with hers. But his look was different from hers, though he could not know that. His was the madness of a man in a dream; hers was a painful thing. The Furies dwelt in her. She softly lifted his hand above his head, and whispered: " Swear." And she kissed him. Her lips were icy, though he did not think so. The blood tossed in his veins. He swore; but, doing so, he could not conceive *all* that would be required of him. He was hers, body and soul, and she had resolved on a grim thing. . . . In the darkness, they left the hut and passed into the woods, and slowly up through the hills.

Heldon returned to his home that night to find it empty. There were no servants. There was no wife. Her cat and dog lay dead upon the hearth-rug. Her clothing was cut into strips. Her wedding-dress was a charred heap on the fireplace. Her jewellery lay molten with it. Her portrait had been torn from its frame.

An intolerable fear possessed him. Drops of sweat hung on his forehead and his hands. He fled towards the town. He bit his finger-nails till they bled as he passed the house in the pines. He lifted his arm as if the flappings of The Crimson Flag were blows in his face.

At last he passed Tom Liffey's hut. He saw Pierre coming from it. The look on the gambler's face was one of gloomy wonder. His fingers trembled as he lighted a cigarette, and that was an unusual thing. The form of Heldon edged within the light. Pierre dropped the match and said to him: " You are looking for your wife? "

Heldon bowed his head. The other threw open the door of the hut. " Come in here," he said. They entered. Pierre pointed to a woman's hat on the table. " Do you know that? " he asked, huskily, for he was moved. But Heldon only nodded dazedly.

Pierre continued: " I was to have met Tom Liffey here to-night. He is not here. You hoped—I suppose—to see your wife in your —home. She is not there. He left a word on paper for me. I have torn it up. Writing is the enemy of man. But I know where he is gone. I know also where your wife has gone."

Heldon's face was of a hateful paleness. . . . They passed out into the night.

" Where are you going? " Heldon said.

" To God's Playground, if we can get there."

" To God's Playground? To the glacier-top? You are mad."

" No, but *he* and *she* were mad. Come on." Then he whispered something, and Heldon gave a great cry, and they plunged into the woods.

In the morning the people of Little Goshen, looking towards the glacier, saw a flag (they knew afterwards that it was crimson) flying on it. Near it were two human figures. A miner, looking through a field-glass, said that one figure was crouching by the flagstaff, and that it was a woman. The other figure near was a man. As the morning wore on, they saw upon a crag of ice below the sloping glacier two men looking upwards towards the flag. One of them seemed to shriek out, and threw up his hands, and made as if to rush forward; but the other drew him back.

Heldon knew what revenge and disgrace may be at their worst. In vain he tried to reach God's Playground. Only one man knew the way, and he was dead upon it—with Heldon's wife: two shame-

less suicides. . . . When he came down from the mountain the
hair upon his face was white, though that upon his head remained
black as it had always been. And those frozen figures stayed there
like statues with that other crimson flag; until, one day, a great-
bodied wind swept out of the north, and, in pity, carried them
down a bottomless fissure.

But long before this happened, The Woman had fled from Little
Goshen in the night, and her house was burned to the ground.

# THE ABSURD ROMANCE
# OF P'TITE LOUISON

### Sir GILBERT PARKER

THE five brothers lived with Louison, three miles from Pontiac,
and Medallion came to know them first through having sold them,
at an auction, a slice of an adjoining farm. He had been invited
to their home, intimacy had grown, and afterwards, stricken with
a severe illness, he had been taken into the household and kept
there till he was well again. The night of his arrival, Louison,
the sister, stood with a brother on either hand—Octave and Florian
—and received him with a courtesy more stately than usual, an
expression of the reserve and modesty of her single state. This
maidenly dignity was at all times shielded by the five brothers,
who treated her with a constant and reverential courtesy. There
was something signally suggestive in their homage, and Medallion
concluded at last that it was paid not only to the sister, but to
something that gave her great importance in their eyes.

He puzzled long, and finally decided that Louison had a romance.
There was something which suggested it in the way they said
" P'tite Louison "; in the manner they avoided all gossip regarding
marriages and marriage-feasting; in the way they deferred to her
on questions of etiquette (as, for instance, Should the eldest child
be given the family name of the wife or a Christian name from
her husband's family?). And P'tite Louison's opinion was
accepted instantly as final, with satisfied nods on the part of all the
brothers, and with whispers of " How clever! how adorable! such
beauty! "

P'tite Louison affected never to hear these remarks, but looked
complacently straight before her, stirring the spoon in her cup, or
benignly passing the bread and butter. She was quite aware of the

homage paid to her, and she gracefully accepted the fact that she was an object of interest.

Medallion had not the heart to laugh at the adoration of the brothers or at the outlandish sister, for, though she was angular, and sallow and thin, and her hands were large and red, there was a something deep in her eyes, a curious quality in her carriage commanding respect. She had ruled these brothers, had been worshipped by them, for near half a century, and the romance they had kept alive had produced a grotesque sort of truth and beauty in the admiring " P'tite Louison "—an affectionate name for her greatness, like " The Little Corporal " for Napoleon. She was not little, either, but above the middle height, and her hair was well streaked with grey.

Her manner toward Medallion was not marked by any affectation. She was friendly in a kind, impersonal way, much as a nurse cares for a patient, and she never relaxed a sort of old-fashioned courtesy, which might have been trying in such close quarters, were it not for the real simplicity of the life, and the spirit and lightness of their race. One night Florian—there were Florian and Octave and Felix and Isidore and Emile—the eldest, drew Medallion aside from the others, and they walked together by the river. Florian's air suggested confidence and mystery, and soon, with a voice of hushed suggestion, he told Medallion the romance of P'tite Louison. And each of the brothers at different times during the next fortnight did the same, differing scarcely at all in details, or choice of phrase or meaning, and not at all in general facts and essentials. But each, as he ended, made a different exclamation.

" *Voilà!* so sad, so wonderful! She keeps the ring—dear P'tite Louison," said Florian, the eldest.

" *Alors!* she gives him a legacy in her will! Sweet P'tite Louison," said Octave.

" *Mais!* the governor and the archbishop admire her—P'tite Louison," said Felix, nodding confidently at Medallion.

" *Bien!* you should see the linen and the petticoats! " said Isidore, the humorous one of the family. " He was great—she was an angel—P'tite Louison! "

" *Attends!* what love! what history! what passion!—the perfect P'tite Louison! " cried Emile, the youngest, the most sentimental. " Ah, Molière! " he added, as if calling on the master to rise and sing the glories of this daughter of romance.

Isidore's tale was after this fashion:

" I ver' well remember the first of it; and the last of it—who can tell? He was an actor—oh, so droll, that! Tall, ver' smart, and he play in theatre at Montreal. It is in the winter. P'tite Louison visit Montreal. She walk past the theatre and, as she go by, she slip on the snow and fall. Out from a door with a jomp come M'sieu' Hadrian, and pick her up. And when he see the purty

face of P'tite Louison, his eyes go all fire, and he clasp her hand
to his breast.

" ' Ma'm'selle! Ma'm'selle! ' he say, ' we must meet again! '

" She thank him and hurry away quick. Next day we are on
the river, and P'tite Louison try to do the Dance of the Blue Fox
on the ice. While she do it, some one come up swift and catch
her hand and say, ' Ma'm'selle, let's do it together '—like that!
It take her breath away. It is M'sieu' Hadrian. He not seem
like the other men she know, but he have a sharp look, he is smooth
in the face, and he smile kind like a woman. P'tite Louison, she
give him her hand, and they run away, and every one stop to look.
It is a gran' sight! M'sieu' Hadrian laugh, and his teeth shine,
and the ladies say things of him, and he tell P'tite Louison that she
look ver' fine, and walk like a queen. I am there that day, and
I see all, and I think it dam good. I say, ' That P'tite Louison,
she beat them all '—I am only twelve year old then. When
M'sieu' Hadrian leave he give her two seats for the theatre, and
we go. Bagosh! that is grand thing that play, and M'sieu'
Hadrian, he is a prince; and when he say to his minister, ' But no,
my lord, I will marry out of my star, and where my heart go,
not as the State wills,' he look down at P'tite Louison, and she go
all red, and some of the women look at her, and there is a whisper
all roun'.

Nex' day he come to the house where we stay, but the Curé
come also pretty soon and tell her she must go home—he say an
actor is not good company. Never mind. And so we come out
home. Well, what you think? Nex' day M'sieu' Hadrian come
too, and we have dam good time—Florian, Octave, Felix, Emile,
they all sit and say bully-good to him all the time. Holy, what
fine stories he tell! And he talk about P'tite Louison, and his eyes
get wet, and Emile he say his prayers to him—bagosh! yes, I
think. Well, at last, what you guess? M'sieu' he come and
come, and at last one day, he say that he leave Montreal and go
to New York, where he get a good place in a big theatre—his time
in Montreal is finish. So he speak to Florian and say he want to
marry P'tite Louison, and he say, of course, that he is not marry
and he have money. But he is a Protestan', and the Curé at first
ver' mad, bagosh!

" But at last when he give a hunder' dollars to the Church, the
Curé say yes. All happy that way for while. P'tite Louison, she
get ready quick—*sapré*, what fine things had she! and it is all to
be done in a week, while the theatre in New York wait for M'sieu'.
He sit there with us, and play on the fiddle, and sing songs, and
act plays, and help Florian in the barn, and Octave to mend the
fence, and the Curé to fix the grape-vines on the wall. He show
me and Emile how to play sword-sticks; and he pick flowers and
fetch them to P'tite Louison, and teach her how to make an

omelette and a salad like the *chef* of the Louis Quinze Hotel, so he say. Bagosh, what a good time we have! But first one, then another, he get a choke-throat when he think that P'tite Louison go to leave us, and the more we try the more we are bagosh fools. And that P'tite Louison, she kiss us hevery one, and say to M'sieu' Hadrian, ' Charles, I love you, but I cannot go! ' He laugh at her, and say, ' *Voilà!* we will take them all with us,' and P'tite Louison she laugh. That night a thing happen. The Curé come, and he look ver' mad, and he frown and he say to M'sieu' Hadrian before us all, ' M'sieu', you are married! '

" *Sapré!* that P'tite Louison get pale like snow, and we all stan' roun' her close and say to her quick, ' Courage, P'tite Louison! ' M'sieu' Hadrian then look at the priest and say, ' No, M'sieu', I was married ten years ago; my wife drink and go wrong, and I get divorce. I am free like the wind.'

" ' You are not free,' the Curé say quick. ' Once married, married till death. The Church cannot marry you again, and I command Louison to give you up.'

" P'tite Louison stand like stone. M'sieu' turn to her. ' What shall it be, Louison? ' he say. ' You will come with me? '

" ' Kiss me, Charles,' she say, ' and tell me good-bye till—till you are free.'

" He look like a madman. ' Kiss me once, Charles,' she say, ' and let me go.'

" And he come to her and kiss her on the lips once, and he say, ' Louison, come with me. I will never give you up.'

" She draw back to Florian. ' Good-bye, Charles! ' she say. ' I will wait as long as you will. Mother of God! how hard it is to do right! ' she say, and then she turn and leave the room.

" M'sieu' Hadrian, he give a long sigh. ' It was my one chance,' he say. ' Now the devil take it all! ' Then he nod and say to the Curé, ' We'll thrash this out at Judgment Day, M'sieu'. I'll meet you there—you and that other woman that spoiled me.'

" He turn to Florian and the rest of us, and shake hands, and say, ' Take care of Louison. Thank you. Good-bye! ' Then he start toward the door, but stumble, for he look sick. ' Give me a drink,' he say, and begin to cough a little—a queer sort of rattle. Florian give him big drink, and he toss it off—whiff! ' Thank you,' he say, and start again, and we see him walk away over the hill ver' slow—an' he never come back! But every year there come from New York a box of flowers, and every year P'tite Louison send him a ' *Merci, Charles, mille fois. Dieu te garde.*' It is so every year for twenty-five year."

" Where is he now? " asked Medallion.

Isidore shook his head, then lifted his eyes religiously. " Waiting for Judgment Day and P'tite Louison," he answered.

" Dead! " cried Medallion.   " How long? "

" Twenty year."

" But the flowers—the flowers? "

" He left word for them to be sent just the same, and the money for it."

Medallion turned and took off his hat reverently, as if a soul were passing from the world, but it was only P'tite Louison going out into the garden.

" She thinks him living? " he asked gently, as he watched Louison.

" Yes; we have no heart to tell her.   And then he wish it so. And the flowers kep' coming."

" Why did he wish it so? "

Isidore mused a while.

" Who can tell?   Perhaps a whim.   He was a great actor— ah, yes, sublime! " he said.

Medallion did not reply, but walked slowly down to where P'tite Louison was picking berries.   His hat was still off.

" Let me help you, Mademoiselle," he said softly.   And henceforth he was as foolish as her brothers.

# THE SINGING OF THE BEES

## Sir Gilbert Parker

" MOTHER, didst thou not say thy prayers last night? "

" Twice, my child."

" Once before the little shrine, and once beside my bed—is it not so? "

" It is so, my Fanchon.   What hast thou in thy mind? "

" Thou didst pray that the storm die in the hills, and the flood cease, and that my father come before it was again the hour of prayer.   It is now the hour.   Canst thou not hear the storm and the wash of the flood?   And my father does not come! "

" My Fanchon, God is good."

" When thou wast asleep I rose from my bed, and in the dark I kissed the feet of—Him—on the little Calvary, and I did not speak, but in my heart I called."

" What didst thou call, my child? "

" I called to my father: ' Come back! come back! ' "

" Thou shouldst have called to God, my Fanchon."

" I loved my father, and I called to him."

" Thou shouldst love God."

" I knew my father first. If God loved thee, He would answer thy prayer. Dost thou not hear the cracking of the cedar trees and the cry of the wolves?—they are afraid. All day and all night the rain and wind come down, and the birds and wild fowl have no peace. I kissed His feet, and my throat was full of tears, but I called in my heart. Yet the storm and the dark stay, and my father does not come."

" Let us be patient, my Fanchon."

" He went to guide the priest across the hills. Why does not God guide him back? "

" My Fanchon, let us be patient."

" The priest was young, and my father has grey hair."

" Wilt thou not be patient, my child! "

" He filled the knapsack of the priest with food better than his own, and—thou didst not see it—put money in his hand."

" My own, the storm may pass."

" He told the priest to think upon our home as a little nest God set up here for such as he."

" There are places of shelter in the hills for thy father, my Fanchon."

" And when the priest prayed, ' That Thou mayst bring us safely to this place where we would go,' my father said so softly, ' *We beseech Thee to hear us, good Lord!* ' "

" My Fanchon, thy father hath gone this trail many times."

" The prayer was for the out-trail, not the in-trail, my mother."

" Nay, I do not understand thee."

" A swarm of bees came singing through the room last night, my mother. It was dark and I could not see, but there was a sweet smell, and I heard the voices."

" My child, thou art tired with watching, and thy mind is full of fancies. Thou must sleep."

" I am tired of watching. Through the singing of the bees as they passed over my bed I heard my father's voice. I could not hear the words, they seemed so far away, like the voice of the bees; and I did not cry out, for the tears were in my throat. After a moment the room was so still that it made my heart ache."

" Oh, my Fanchon, my child, thou dost break my heart! Dost thou not know the holy words?—

" ' *And their souls do pass like singing bees, where no man may follow. These are they whom God gathereth out of the whirlwind and the desert, and bringeth home in a goodly swarm.* ' "

Night drew close to the earth, and as suddenly as a sluice-gate drops and holds back a flood the storm ceased. Along the crest of the hills there slowly grew a line of light, and then the serene moon came up and on, persistent to give the earth love where it had had punishment. Divers flocks of clouds, camp-followers of the

storm, could not abash her. But once she drew shrinking back
behind a slow troop of them, for down at the bottom of a gorge
lay a mountaineer, face upward and unmoving, as he had lain since
a rock loosened beneath him, and the depths swallowed him. If
he had had ears to hear, he would have answered the soft, bitter
cries which rose from a hut on the Voshti Hills above him:
" Michel, Michel, art thou gone? "

" Come back; oh, my father, come back! "

But perhaps it did avail that there were lighted candles before a
little shrine, and that a mother, in her darkness, kissed the feet
of One on a Calvary.

# OLIVE SCHREINER
1862–1920

# IN A FAR-OFF WORLD

THERE is a world in one of the far-off stars, and things do not happen here as they happen there.

In that world were a man and woman; they had one work, and they walked together side by side on many days, and were friends —and that is a thing that happens now and then in this world also.

But there was something in that star-world that there is not here. There was a thick wood; where the trees grew closest, and the stems were interlocked, and the summer sun never shone, there stood a shrine. In the day all was quiet, but at night, when the stars shone or the moon glinted on the tree-tops, and all was quiet below, if one crept here quite alone and knelt on the steps of the stone altar, and uncovering one's breast, so wounded it that the blood fell down on the altar steps, then whatever he who knelt there wished for was granted him. And all this happens, as I said, because it is a far-off world, and things often happen there as they do not happen here.

Now, the man and woman walked together; and the woman wished well to the man. One night when the moon was shining so that the leaves of all the trees glinted, and the waves of the sea were silvery, the woman walked alone to the forest. It was dark there; the moonlight fell only in little flecks on the dead leaves under her feet, and the branches were knotted tight overhead. Farther in it got darker; not even a fleck of moonlight shone. Then she came to the shrine: she knelt down before it and prayed; there came no answer. Then she uncovered her breast; with a sharp two-edged stone that lay there she wounded it. The drops dripped slowly down on to the stone, and a voice cried, "What do you seek?"

She answered, "There is a man; I hold him nearer than anything. I would give him the best of all blessings."

The voice said, "What is it?"

The girl said, "I know not, but that which is most good for him I wish him to have."

The voice said, "Your prayer is answered; he shall have it."

382

Then she stood up. She covered her breast and held the garment tight upon it with her hand, and ran out of the forest, and the dead leaves fluttered under her feet. Out in the moonlight the soft air was blowing, and the sand glittered on the beach. She ran along the smooth shore, then suddenly she stood still. Out across the water there was something moving. She shaded her eyes and looked. It was a boat; it was sliding swiftly over the moonlit water out to sea. One stood upright in it; the face the moonlight did not show, but the figure she knew. It was passing swiftly; it seemed as if no one propelled it; the moonlight's shimmer did not let her see clearly, and the boat was far from shore, but it seemed almost as if there was another figure sitting in the stern. Faster and faster it glided over the water, away, away. She ran along the shore; she came no nearer it. The garment she held closed fluttered open; she stretched out her arms, and the moonlight shone on her long loose hair.

Then a voice beside her whispered, " What is it? "

She cried, " With my blood I bought the best of all gifts for him. I have come to bring it him! He is going from me! "

The voice whispered softly, " Your prayer was answered. It has been given him."

She cried, " What is it? "

The voice answered, " It is that he might leave you."

The girl stood still.

Far out at sea the boat was lost to sight beyond the moonlight sheen.

The voice spoke softly, " Art thou contented? "

She said, " I am contented."

At her feet the waves broke in long ripples softly on the shore.

# THE ARTIST'S SECRET

### Olive Schreiner

There was an artist once, and he painted a picture. Other artists had colours richer and rarer, and painted more notable pictures. He painted his with one colour; there was a wonderful red glow on it; and the people went up and down, saying, " We like the picture; we like the glow."

The other artists came and said, " Where does he get his colour from? " They asked him, and he smiled and said, " I cannot tell you "; and worked on with his head bent low.

And one went to the Far East and bought costly pigments, and made a rare colour and painted, but after a time the picture faded. Another read in the old books, and made a colour rich and rare, but when he had put it on the picture it was dead.

But the artist painted on. Always the work got redder and redder, and the artist grew whiter and whiter. At last one day they found him dead before his picture, and they took him up to bury him. The other men looked about in all the pots and crucibles, but they found nothing they had not.

And when they undressed him to put his grave-clothes on him, they found above his left breast the mark of a wound—it was an old, old wound, that must have been there all his life, for the edges were old and hardened; but Death, who seals all things, had drawn the edges together, and closed it up.

And they buried him. And still the people went about saying, " Where did he find his colour from? "

And it came to pass that after a while the artist was forgotten— but the work lived.

# H. B. MARRIOTT WATSON

1863–1921

# QUARANTINE

THE Doctor took the pipe from his mouth and glanced about the room.

You have been talking a lot about right and wrong (said he), and I've listened carefully. But it doesn't seem to me that it is always as easy as some of you think. There is a case in my memory illustrative. It swims to the surface of the undredged pool after nearly thirty years. You know me now as a staid and contented old fogey with a quiet practice. In those days I was a rover, and at the time I speak of I was surgeon on the corvette *Seagull*. The very name is antediluvian. Where are they now, the sloops, corvettes, frigates? . . . The *Seagull* was on the Australian station, and we popped in and out of Australasian harbours, were merrily and hospitably entertained, and enjoyed ourselves to the full. It was as good a station as any in the seven seas in my time. There was junketing, there were picnics, there were parties . . . and there were pleasant cruises in the South Seas, policing the islands, and meeting new races and seeing strange sights all the time. Well, at the time I'm talking of we were in the neighbourhood of the Solomon Islands, and it was late spring. I believe we were steaming south patrolling the Melanesian belt. Anyway, it was a beautiful still night with a moon full on the quiet sea, and I was below looking after some personal matter. Suddenly a steward knocked and entered abruptly, with an urgent message from the Captain, and I was conscious at the same time that the *Seagull* had slowed down. Up I skipped in excitement, for nothing had broken the monotony of the voyage for days, and I guessed that something was forward. On deck I found the Captain and other officers leaning over the side and looking down into a boat which the sailors were handling.

" What is it? " I asked.

" Castaway," said the second officer.

We watched the sailors bring something aboard in the moonlight, and there my work came in. It was a bad case, and the poor devil had suffered cruelly. When I got him down below I made an examination. He was a man of about thirty, I should guess, and with a queer suggestion of clerical attire by means of a white bow in what was otherwise the usual island rig for white men. He was unconscious when we picked him up, and his face and body were much emaciated. I saw what it all meant—privation, exhaustion, shock. From beginning to end it looked a bad case, and it proved so. I did what I could for him, and he revived, and flickered up a bit; but the drain on his vitality had been too great, and he sank and died on the fourth day. But he was able and anxious to talk at intervals during the few days that he lingered, and was particularly urgent that we should put the corvette about for an island called Manira. I got the whole story in pieces, and I put it together in my mind when he was dead and buried; and the thing emerges just now from my memories as vivid as if it were yesterday. . . .

His name was McCulloch, the Rev. Gavin McCulloch, and he belonged to a Methodist persuasion in Vermont or somewhere there. He had been educated at a Methodist college, and filled with Christian fervour, ideas of humanity, brotherhood, and sacrifice. You know how ardently that flame may burn in youth. It often takes a missionary direction, and that's what it took with him. He yearned to devote himself and his life to the services of barbarous savages somewhere, China or Timbuctoo—anywhere. And fate, providence, chance, what you will, sent him out to a lonely island in the Pacific black belt.

Manira is an isolated isle, outlying a scattered group, and inhabited by a Melanesian people. Altogether it seems Manira had a population of three or four hundred, and of these all were of the usual colour save a handful of white settlers on the west side. The island was of coral origin, and was no more than six or seven miles from end to end. McCulloch settled on the east end, where the bulk of the natives were, and began his work. He worked with a zeal worthy of the apostolic times, and the easy-going, simple natives respected him, got to trust him, and went to him for advice and assistance in trouble. They were adaptable in faith, and he roped in converts wholesale. On the west end was the white station, where a small partnership of four men from Sydney grew palm oil, collected bêche-de-mer and copra, and prospected around generally. They had arrived a few years before McCulloch, and had engaged some fifty natives in their commercial operations. McCulloch confessed that they treated their employés very fairly, though the system amounted to a kind of corvée, for they pressed the Kanakas into their service willy-nilly. Yet they fed them well, and used them with some kindness. McCulloch got on pretty well with the whites, though, of course, they were not much of the same way of thinking in many matters, particularly religion. He walked over, or was pulled round in a boat, occasionally, and looked after the spiritual welfare of the plantation natives. He regarded himself as pastor of a parish which was the whole island. I fancy he tried to convert the whites, but he probably got discouraged; anyway, the Kanakas were his flock, and he preached and tended, and gave advice, and no one objected, so long as he didn't interfere with the work of the station. I gathered that in a sort of contemptuous way they had a liking for the sky-pilot, though they chaffed him a good deal. He didn't drink or smoke or play cards, and that was about all they had to do for recreation; but he talked and he listened, and he prayed in his heart, I have no doubt. He was a man of prayer. Naturally they hadn't much in common, but they were all whites together. McCulloch looked after the body as well as the spirit, and he had a medicine case, about which he knew something. Wilson gave him brandy when he wanted it for a case of dysentery, and loaned him drugs which he lacked. Oh yes, they got on well enough together.

Manira lies pretty much in the desert of waters, so to speak, and ships mainly drift there by chance. Wilson and Co. had made arrangements in Sydney by which a boat called once in six months with stores and news, and took off their produce. This steamer had made three trips during McCulloch's residence, and was due for a fourth visit when another visitor blew in. This was a schooner that put into the little cove where the missionary's village lay, and sent a boat ashore. It was a tramp, worn and battered with years, and was homing at last. A mate came ashore on the boat, and explained his dilemma to McCulloch. They'd got a sick man aboard, and had no means of looking after him, neither medicines nor knowledge. He asked McCulloch to receive the man and do his best for him; and McCulloch, who thought he was placed in the world to follow his Master and do good, willingly consented. The man, a Kanaka, one of the crew, was landed, and the schooner set sail. Now McCulloch was puzzled about this sickness. The mate said that no one knew what was the matter with the Kanaka, and urged that the poor devil ought to have a chance. This went right home to McCulloch, but he hung about the man, wondering what was wrong. He suspected one thing and then another, and hunted through his medical book. He had had no training in medicine, but had a smattering of picked-up knowledge. And he hunted through the pages. By and by some spots appeared, and he turned up measles; but it did not seem to be measles. He fed the man and tended him, and observed him and studied his books for some days, and then he got an idea, and it worried him.

It was two days after that Wilson went over to the missionary village. The steamer had paid its expected visit, landed stores, loaded up, and departed, and Wilson, pretty well pleased with the results, walked over in the cool of the evening with some papers

and books for McCulloch.  The steamer brought these literary supplies to keep up connection with the outside world, and furnish
occupation for the leisure of the settlement.  Wilson strode into
McCulloch's shanty, a big gaunt cornstalk of six feet three, and
chucked the papers on the table.

" We might have been at war with Russia for all we knew," he
said, with a laugh.  " There's been a row over a place called
Penjdeh or something.  But that don't interest you under the
Stars and Stripes."

McCulloch was looking worried, but he politely said that he
hoped he was interested in the welfare of all men.  Wilson noted
his looks and commented on them.

McCulloch, if I'm any judge of men, was the honestest soul
alive.  He was simple to boot, and he had a touching confidence in
the real goodness of human nature.

" Yes," said he, " I'm troubled.  I had a case of illness entrusted to me from a schooner a week ago.  The man's bad."

" Humph! " says Wilson.  " Kanaka, I suppose?  They've no
real stamina."

" It's not that," said McCulloch.  " It's the disease I'm afraid
of.  It puzzled me for a long time.  But I'm pretty sure now, and
it makes me very anxious.  I'm afraid the man will die."

" What's he got? " asked Wilson indifferently.

" I very much fear it's smallpox," said McCulloch.  Now you
here, I and all of us in old countries with the evils and travails of
worn centuries upon them (said the doctor), don't take much
account of smallpox.  We may even live cheek by jowl with smallpox isolation hospitals.  Anyway, it's endemic among us.  But that
is not how they regard the malady south of the line, and particularly in Australia and New Zealand.  I remember being in Port
Lyttelton once when there was a scare of smallpox raised, not, mind
you, in New Zealand, but in Sydney, five days' steam away.  A
case had occurred on an emigrant ship, and was promptly quaran-
tined, but from the scareheads of the papers, and the cablegrams
flashed in all directions and thousands of miles, you would have
thought the end of the world had come.  Well, when Wilson heard
the word he answered to it as any other colonial would have done.
He rose from his seat.

" H——! " he said, and stared at the missionary with his hard
grey eyes.  " Where is he? " he demanded, and when he learned
that the sick-room was in the next shanty he backed to the
door.

" Look here, McCulloch," he said.  " This won't do.  I'm vacci-
nated, but I don't take unnecessary risks.  I guess you're in quarantine, and don't you forget it.  Man, you were a damn fool to take
that sick man, but you're going to die a damn fool.  Anyway, keep
clear of us.  I'm sorry for you, but we've got ourselves and our

men to look after. This is Quarantine Island, and don't you forget it."

Wilson was a bluff, deliberate fellow of few fears and scruples, as I could see when I came upon him later. But the others in his company were different. O'Reilly had the temper of a savage, and Wilks was a nervous, irritable man. There was also a boy of twenty, fresh from his mother, with a lion's heart, and a fresh zest for life. He was full of cheer and sang comic songs. His companions were fond of him. Wilson's report brought the alarm to them, and they had a bad scare, and watched out for some days. At the end of that time no news had come from McCulloch, and the party began to fidget, so it ended in Wilson's rowing round with the boy, and hailing the parson from the cove. After some minutes McCulloch came down to the beach in his ducks, and told them that the Kanaka was dead. He had died the day after Wilson had paid his visit. I have said McCulloch was an incredibly honest man, and so he went on to say, " I regret there's another case developed."

Wilson's face tightened, and an ugly look seized it. " You know what quarantine is, McCulloch," he said. " You've got to keep it, by——"

McCulloch said he would do all that was possible to maintain isolation. " I'm short of some medicine," he said, and Wilson struck in:

" I'll send over what you want. We'll land 'em here, if you tell me what." And when that was over the boat paddled out, and Wilson shouted back, " I'm sorry, McCulloch, but you've got to keep the laws," and the boy, who was fresh and full-hearted, waved his hand. " So long, old man! " he called.

The boy carried the medicines and some stores round in the boat next day, and left them on the beach, having signalled to McCulloch. " What's the news? " he cried from the boat, and McCulloch, looking grave and quiet, answered, " There are two more cases."

" Hard luck! " said the youngster. But he did not know what more to say or do, and after a silence shouted good-bye and rowed off. McCulloch had his hands full during the next few days.

There was a native called Tommy who had picked up civilised white ways pretty quickly, and whom McCulloch employed more familiarly about him than others. Tommy rang the bell for church service, and Tommy officiated as body-servant, and interpreted between the pastor and his flock generally. McCulloch had the lingo himself pretty well. Well, Tommy, who was young and smart, had a sweetheart at the other end of the island, and, quarantine regulations being nothing to him, he paid her a visit one night when he was quit of his duties. He was seen in the vicinity of the settlement, and Wilson came over the following day. and hailed McCulloch.

" Understand, McCulloch," he said, " we can't have any monkeying about this business. I don't mind a risk, but this is a dead certainty. You've got to keep your people in quarantine bounds."

There was a stream wandering out of some hills about half-way across the island, and the hills and the stream divided the island; so Wilson made these the boundaries, and he let McCulloch know that they must be kept.

" If that Tommy of yours or any other comes over the line," he said, " we'll deal with him."

McCulloch promised he would observe the boundaries, and the deputation returned. But the poor wretch was all alone in a nest of ignorant savages. He wanted a guard of sentinels to help him, and Tommy was a childlike native with the instinct to obey when his master's eye was on him, and the child's instinct to follow his own bent when the eye wasn't there. So Tommy, though warned and put on his honour, went over again to see his young lady. Wilson and Co. were now more on the alert, realising the danger, and Tommy was chased and all but caught in the thickets. Then came the ultimatum. Wilson and O'Reilly went to the cove, and gave warning.

" If you can't control your natives, we'll not be responsible," they told him. " And we give you fair and square notice that we won't have the plague brought over on us. So if we catch Tommy he'll be shot."

McCulloch begged them earnestly to reconsider this threat of warfare. He appealed to them as Christians, but got no response. They went back sullenly resolute to protect themselves, and McCulloch went to his house and prayed for hours on end. Things were beginning to look ugly. He talked to Tommy very gravely, and Tommy gave glib promises, and kept to them for ten days or so. There were some more cases of the disease, and McCulloch worked night and day. Meanwhile Tommy got restive, heard the call of romance, and gave him the slip. McCulloch had gone to rest for an hour, exhausted by his labours, and Tommy had been instructed to wake him. He was not called, and slept heavily, till at last he woke with a start, and looking at his watch found it was midnight. Tommy was nowhere to be found, and one of the natives who helped to nurse the sick men pointed to the hills and the darkness. McCulloch had misgivings, and he went off in the direction of the quarantine boundaries. There was a track which the natives had been accustomed to use in going to and fro, and this crossed the stream and went up the hills into the jungle, and so down to the plantations of Wilson and Co., on the farther side. McCulloch spoke with the natives in a little hamlet on his own frontier and had news of Tommy. There was no doubt that Tommy had broken parole and bounds too. McCulloch waited anxiously.

It came just before dawn. In that region there is practically no night, but a benevolent moving twilight, and the trees and scrub of the jungle were visible all through his watch. First there came a noise, faint but persistent, and it grew in intensity, till he began to recognise it as the sound of some one breaking through the jungle at a tearing pace. McCulloch in alarm ran across the dividing stream, and towards the hill. He could see no one, but he knew that some one was flying from a pursuer. And then a figure ran out of the scrub into the open flat, and came fast towards him. McCulloch heard sounds in the jungle higher up the hill. As he stood, wondering, fearing, and indecisive, a report rang out, and the man running towards him plunged heavily to the earth. McCulloch dashed forward and reached the prostrate man. It was Tommy, shot dead through the back. McCulloch straightened himself and looked towards the hill, where a black figure stood clearly visible.

" Damn you, I'll shoot you too, if you don't keep bounds, Parson," shouted a voice he recognised. It was O'Reilly's, passionate and flamboyantly Irish. McCulloch shouted back :

" It's murder! It's murder. God will avenge. It's cold-blooded murder! "

O'Reilly turned his back on him and walked off, and McCulloch stumbled across the stream with his burden. After that there was no Tommy to cause any trouble, and things were quiet for a week. That is to say, McCulloch heard nothing and saw nothing of the plantation people. But work crowded on his hands; there were more cases of smallpox, and his medicine chest and stores began to give out. He found himself obliged to apply to Wilson against his will, and with two natives rowed round the island to the landing-stage. He was warned off by Wilks, who was the first to espy them, and presently three of the company were gathered together in consultation—Wilson, Wilks, and the boy.

McCulloch shouted out what he wanted, and they consulted again. The boy ran up the beach to the huts, and Wilson and Wilks kept guard.

" I can give you brandy and some other things," shouted Wilson. " But you'd a damn sight better shoot your cases, McCulloch."

McCulloch naturally didn't answer that, and he was told he could come ashore and pick up the medicines at a distance. He was glad to get them, and returned grateful thanks.

" I know your heart's in the right place, Mr. Wilson," he said. " But you have an evil associate."

Wilson grinned very grimly. O'Reilly wasn't there.

McCulloch had trained some of his flock into nursing ways, but they must have made an odd show. They were docile folk, I gathered, but stupid, vacant, and very animal. So far they had not taken alarm at the epidemic; I suppose they were more or less used to unexpected death, if I may put it that way. Within the quarantine bounds there were about two hundred Kanakas all told, men, women, and children, and on the farther side of the dividing stream and hills somewhere about the same. Wilson and Co. employed fifty or sixty hands, and they treated them decently, as I have said. They had even gone the length of putting up a model village. That is to say, they had drafted the families out of their dirty hovels into a convenient place, established them on a sort of system, and supervised them. It paid them to do so, for they got better work out of the men, and they had them always under authority. Wilson was no fool.

A little after the missionary's visit for supplies Wilson paid him a return visit, Wilson and the boy; and they had a passenger.

Wilson landed, and they landed the passenger on the beach, and Wilson's face was terrific. It awed even poor overworked, exhausted, and obdurate McCulloch. This was the first case of smallpox in the plantation and they had brought it round. It pointed the finger of doom, and Wilson pointed the clenched fist of menace. His language must have been appalling. The parson did not repeat it to me.

" This is war, McCulloch," said that six foot and a half of cornstalk. " This is deadly like open declaration. You have been warned before; but there's more behind and worse. Better die by bullet than this way," and he made a gesture at the dying native. He left the body there, and rowed away cursing, and the boy said nothing, but stared at the shore as he pulled. McCulloch saw him staring.

It was inevitable that the natives should take fright in the end. The death-roll was so long and grew so fast. They must have died like flies. . . . And then the second act of the tragedy opened. The Kanakas left their homes and fled to the hills to escape the contagion. They looked upon it as the invasion of a personal and malignant devil. They took to the hills and hid in the jungle, and so some of them reached the plantation village. Wilson and his men drove them in under guns to the quarantine bounds, and there among a few huts across the stream they saw McCulloch on his knees with the sun on his hair, praying for mercy, praying for help. The plague had broken out there, and children had died of it. He prayed in the centre of the stricken place and saw and heard no one. Somehow the sight, and what it all meant in pathos, went to Wilson's heart, and what he was going to do he didn't do, as he told me afterwards.

McCulloch rose and saw the enemy, and Wilson explained suddenly what had happened. McCulloch was haggard and thin, and showed all the marks of the strain to which he had been subjected, and he stuttered out brokenly his apologies and said that he would do all he could to confine his natives to the Quarantine. Then, I take it, Wilson was moved to a certain rude sympathy.

" Look here, McCulloch," he said with bluff friendliness, " you know you're fighting a lost battle. You can't stop it; you can only prevent the ravages from spreading further, as we're trying to do. I'll tell you what. Here's an offer. Give it up and come out of that, where you're only killing yourself. Give yourself a chance. Come out, and we'll establish you in an isolation hut near the plantation, and after the usual time you can get *pratique*, or whatever they call it, and join us, if you're free from the disease. As for these wretches, well, *Kismet!* You've done all you can."

It was well meant, as I say, but it had about as much chance with McCulloch as a proposal from his satanic majesty. I gathered that he quoted scripture and garnished his refusal in that way; at which the cornstalk lost patience.

" Oh, go to hell your own way," he said as he strode off, and shouted back, " Remember, we're fighting for lives as much as you, and we'll shoot."

The immediate result of the encounter was that Wilson took precautions, as it were, against a declared enemy. He armed sentinels whom he could trust, and stationed them along the boundaries. He drew a cordon, in fact, across the hostile territory. There could be only one issue to that in the conditions prevailing. The Kanakas got more panicky, and McCulloch was helpless, though he prayed and preached day after day. Death was among them in their huts, and they broke the cordon and climbed the hills, and then they found death in the jungles—an easier death, maybe.

The armed natives, pleased with their toys, the rifles, and also with their prowess, shot whenever a chance offered, and there were a dozen dead men on the hills within the week. McCulloch, saddened and embittered, and worn to the bone, worked on. I don't know if you will call it fanaticism; at any rate, it was nobility; it was sheer self-sacrifice. It was suicide. I am getting near the climax now, and it's ugly—it's ugly even as I look back at it over a quarter of a century. It is a fatal mistake to extend to an inferior civilisation the instruments and equipments of a superior. I know that's putting it grandiosely. I'll put it tersely and bluntly. " Don't trust niggers with guns." Wilson did. The Kanakas in the missionary settlement got more scared, and made attempts to bolt. One family from the huts near the stream made a rush for it, and were shot down. There were two children. . . . Then McCulloch saw red. He was not a man of war, but then he came so near to it as to be a prophet of wrath, like a Hebrew of old, ingeminating hell. He visited the plantation, and was thrust back

133*

into the sea at the end of bayonets.

"God will smite you!" he cried. "God takes His vengeance. Vengeance is His, not man's. God shall smite you, you whited wall!"

O'Reilly laughed, Wilson swore, and the boy stared shamefacedly. Was there a curse on the settlement?

Anyway, two cases broke out next day in the plantation village, and Wilks was in desperate terror. He was a coward, was Wilks, I fancy. Wilson got panicky too; the dread thing was coming very close. They talked it over, and isolated the cases; but they had as little guarantee that the quarantine would be kept as had poor McCulloch. So in the end they rowed the patients round to McCulloch, and dumped them on him. Wilson must have felt he was doing a mean thing. McCulloch stared at him with hot, red eyes, a gaunt figure, and said no word. Wilson promised supplies, offered medicines and other necessaries.

"We reckon this is hospital," he said grimly, and then O'Reilly touched him on the arm, and they spoke together in low tones so that the boy heard nothing.

"See here," said Wilson, raising his voice, "we'll leave supplies to-morrow evening at the Palm Cove yonder, and you can come for them. They'll be there by dusk."

McCulloch still answered nothing, but stooped over the stricken natives on the beach wearifully. The fact is that there and then Wilson and O'Reilly made up their minds to whole measures. They were badly frightened, and they couldn't see any way out. There was more talk at night in their quarters, and next day McCulloch was astonished to see the boy walking out of a palm tree grove towards his house. He had come across the island, and his visit was unknown to his companions. I never learnt that boy's name, or I should like to have put it on record. He was young and new to desperate deeds, and he had heard things that shocked him. But McCulloch, who thought that maybe he had brought some of the supplies with him, warned him off.

"You'd better stay where you are," he called out, "and come no nearer. We're rank bad here. Put what you've got down, and I'll fetch it."

"I haven't got anything," said the boy nervously. "I've just come to see you."

"Well, you must do no more than that," said McCulloch, and added bitterly, "You can go back and say you've seen one man trying to do his duty."

"And by ——!" broke out the boy, "you've done it."

McCulloch softened. "Sit down on that rock," said he, "and we can talk."

"What's that building there?" asked the boy. "Is that your chapel?"

" It is the chapel, and it's the hospital," said McCulloch. " The dead and the dying are there."

" It's a blooming mortuary! " said the boy, shuddering.

McCulloch pointed to the huts. This one had two dead in it; another was full of sick; three children and a mother lay dying in a third. . . . The boy swore.

" Cut it, McCulloch," he said. " Come over to us, as Wilson suggested. You've done more than enough."

" I have put my hand to the plough, and I dare not look back," said McCulloch simply.

The boy swore again, swore no doubt to cover his feelings. He stood up.

" There's something, anyway, I want to tell you, and it's what I came for," he said. " It seems a bit absurd after what I've advised. Anyway, here goes. No one knows I'm here. To-night don't go for that medicine and the stores. Take it from me, and stay away. So long! " he shouted, and stepped away briskly without looking back. Perhaps he was ashamed of his feelings.

McCulloch had practically run out of all necessaries, and if he was to carry on at all he must have fresh supplies. God alone knows how he did manage through those terrible days, tending the sick, ministering, praying, encouraging, exhorting, and burying. It makes one wince to think of it. McCulloch could not afford to be without the stores; if he lacked these he must give up. He told me that he paid little heed to the boy's cryptic warning, but it was in his mind vaguely as he made his way to the cove that he might be shot down like the poor creatures who had crossed the cordon. His brain was dulled and his imagination a blur. He did not care what became of him, but realised merely that he had got to struggle on for his sick, as long as his life lasted. He got down to the cove through the scrub at dusk, and could see no one. He was a conspicuous figure for a marksman as he descended to the beach, but no one fired at him. Wilson had been as good as his word, and there were the stores and the medicine in a small cache. McCulloch rolled the stones away, and was pocketing the drugs, when suddenly he was seized from behind, and ere he could turn, his elbows drawn back.

" Damn you, don't make it worse for yourself! " said a voice he recognised as O'Reilly's.

He struggled for all that, but a cord was inserted under his arms, and they were tied back. He was as helpless as a trussed fowl.

Now he recognised Wilson, who came up from the covert of some bushes. McCulloch protested, and demanded to know what they intended. They made no reply, but he was forced forward, arms raised behind, head down in front—the most hopeless physical attitude for any man. He perceived that they were nearing the water, and then he saw a boat. Into this he was thrown by

O'Reilly, and Wilson pushed the boat off with a powerful shove. The tide was making outwards, and the boat was soon a score of yards from shore.

"You can work your arms free, McCulloch," yelled Wilson. "There's a fortnight's supplies in the boat, and no oars. And now make the best of it. You're too damn dangerous. It's our lives against a lot of niggers. Good luck to you!"

The ebb was flowing fast; McCulloch was helpless; and the boat passed swiftly out to sea and away from Manira. McCulloch never saw the island again. It was sixteen days afterwards that we picked him up.

The Doctor paused for quite a long time.

"And that was all?" asked one of the company.

No (he replied slowly), not quite; nearly. McCulloch died, as I told you. We finished the patrolling south, and the *Seagull* went north again. The captain decided to put into Manira, and did so. It was a pretty island, set in a prettily foaming sea, and under a sky of infinite blueness. I went ashore to inspect, and found the settlement deserted. There was nothing there but wreck, debris, and—well, you know what else. There was only one course of action, and after sending word to the captain I took it. The huts and all that they signified and held went up in one conflagration; the flames mounted to heaven, and drew down from the hills and the jungle some frightened people. These were the remnants of the population, who had taken refuge from the plague, and were ill-fed, unclothed, and demoralised. I knew nothing of their language, and could learn nothing. But we did what was possible, and put out stores and left them seeds to carry on. Later a relief ship was sent from Auckland.

Then I went round to the plantation. Fire had been busy there in patches. The village was practically wiped out, and as I landed I saw a white man's work and judgment in that. In the house there were two live men, and one was dying. This was Wilson, emaciated and motionless upon his pallet, and the live man was a native, one of those faithful hearts which we whites find now and then everywhere among inferior races, a dumb, devoted animal, tending his stricken master.

Wilson was far gone, but on seeing me he rallied, and brightened.

"Where do you spring from?" he asked with difficulty.

I told him, and spoke of McCulloch.

"Dead?" he asked, and when I assented, went on weakly, "They all died. They all began to go. I burnt the cottages. Wilks went first, and then O'Reilly. I buried the boy last of all" . . . and he sank into silence.

I did everything possible, but it was hopeless. Just before the end he lifted his head.

" McCulloch! " he exclaimed, and fixed me with his eye. " Was I right? "

I did not answer, and he repeated the question almost vehemently, " Was I right? " and then ere I could answer fell back. " Anyway, it's done," he murmured.

He never spoke again.

Well, it's easy to lay down ethical principles in the drawing-room, the study, or the church. But on the battlefield—I don't know. I have often wondered, and put that last unanswered question to myself. Which was right, Wilson or McCulloch?

# HENRY LAWSON

1867–1922

# WHEN THE SUN WENT DOWN

JACK DREW sat on the edge of the shaft, with his foot in the loop and one hand on the rope, ready to descend. His elder brother, Tom, stood at one end of the windlass and the third mate at the other. Jack paused before swinging off, looked up at his brother, and impulsively held out his hand:

" You ain't going to let the sun go down, are you, Tom? "

But Tom kept both hands on the windlass-handle and said nothing.

" Lower away! "

They lowered him to the bottom, and Tom shouldered his pick in silence and walked off to the tent. He found the tin-plate, pint-pot, and things set ready for him on the rough slab table under the bush shed. The tea was made, the cabbage and potatoes strained and placed in a billy near the fire. He found the fried bacon and steak between two plates in the camp-oven. He sat down to the table but he could not eat. He felt mean. The inexperience and hasty temper of his brother had caused the quarrel between them that morning; but then Jack admitted that, and apologised when he first tried to make it up.

Tom moved round uneasily and tried to smoke; he could not get Jack's last appeal out of his ears—" You ain't going to let the sun go down, Tom? "

Tom found himself glancing at the sun. It was less than two hours from sunset. He thought of the words of the old Hebrew—or Chinese—poet; he wasn't religious, and the authorship didn't matter. The old poet's words began to haunt him: " Let not the sun go down upon your wrath. Let not the sun go down upon your wrath."

The line contains good, sound advice; for quick-tempered men are often the most sensitive, and when they let the sun go down on the aforesaid wrath that quality is likely to get *them* down and worry them during the night.

Tom started to go to the claim, but checked himself, and sat down and tried to draw comfort from his pipe. He understood his brother thoroughly, but his brother never understood him—that was where the trouble was. Presently he got thinking how Jack

398

would worry about the quarrel and have no heart for his work. Perhaps he was fretting over it now, all alone by himself, down at the end of the damp dark drive. Tom had a lot of the old woman about him, in spite of his unsociable ways and brooding temper.

He had almost made up his mind to go below again, on some excuse, when his mate shouted from the top of the shaft:

" Tom! Tom! For Christ's sake come here! "

Tom's heart gave a great thump, and he ran like a kangaroo to the shaft. All the diggers within hearing were soon on the spot. They saw at a glance what had happened. It was madness to sink without timber in such treacherous ground. *The sides of the shaft were closing in.*

Tom sprang forward and shouted through the crevice:

" To the face, Jack! To the face, for your life."

" The old workings! " he cried, turning to the diggers. " Bring a fan and tools. We'll dig him out."

A few minutes later a fan was rigged over a deserted shaft close by, where fortunately the windlass had been left for bailing purposes, and men were down in the old drive. Tom knew that he and his mates had driven very close to the old workings.

He knelt in the damp clay before the face and worked like a madman; he refused to take turn about, and only dropped the pick to seize a shovel in his strong hands, and snatch back the loose clay from under his feet; he reckoned that he had six, or, perhaps, eight feet to drive, and he knew that the air could not last long in the new drive—even if that had not already fallen in and crushed his brother. Great drops of perspiration stood out on Tom's forehead, and his breath began to come in choking sobs, but he still struck strong, savage blows into the clay before him, and the drive lengthened quickly. Once he paused a moment to listen, and then distinctly heard a sound as of a tool or stone being struck against the edge of the new drive. Jack was safe!

Tom dug on until the clay suddenly fell away from his pick and left a hole, about the size of a plate, in the " face " before him. " Thank God! " said a hoarse strained voice at the other side.

" All right, Jack? "

" Yes, old man; you are just in time; I've hardly got room to stand in, and I'm nearly smothered." He was crouching against the " face " of the new drive.

Tom dropped his pick and fell back against the man behind him. " Oh, God! my back! " he cried.

Suddenly he struggled to his knees, and then fell forward on his hand and dragged himself close to the hole in the end of the drive.

" Jack! " he gasped, " Jack! "

" Right, old man; what's the matter? "

" I've hurt my heart, Jack! Put your hand—quick! . . . The sun's going down."

Jack's hand came out through the hole, Tom gripped it, and then fell with his face in the damp clay.

They half carried, half dragged him from the drive, for the roof was low and they were obliged to stoop. They took him to the shaft and sent him up, lashed to the rope.

A few blows of the pick, and Jack scrambled from his prison and went to the surface, and knelt on the grass by the body of his brother. The diggers gathered round and took off their hats. And the sun went down.

# THAT THERE DOG O' MINE

## HENRY LAWSON

MACQUARIE the shearer had met with an accident. To tell the truth, he had been in a drunken row at a wayside shanty, from which he had escaped with three fractured ribs, a cracked head, and various minor abrasions. His dog, Tally, had been a sober but savage participator in the drunken row, and had escaped with a broken leg. Macquarie afterwards shouldered his swag and staggered and struggled along the track ten miles to the Union Town Hospital. Lord knows how he did it. He didn't exactly know himself. Tally limped behind all the way, on three legs.

The doctors examined the man's injuries and were surprised at his endurance. Of course they would take him in, but they objected to Tally. Dogs were not allowed on the premises.

" You will have to turn that dog out," they said to the shearer, as he sat on the edge of a bed. Macquarie said nothing.

" We cannot allow dogs about the place, my man," said the doctor in a louder tone, thinking the man was deaf.

" Tie him up in the yard then."

" No. He must go out. Dogs are not permitted on the grounds."

Macquarie rose slowly to his feet, shut his agony behind his set teeth, painfully buttoned his shirt over his hairy chest, took up his waistcoat, and staggered to the corner where the swag lay.

" What are you going to do? " they asked.

" You ain't going to let my dog stop? "

" No. It's against the rules. There are no dogs allowed on the premises." He stooped and lifted his swag, but the pain was too great, and he leaned back against the wall.

" Come, come now! man alive! " exclaimed the doctor, impatiently. " You must be mad. You know you are not in a fit state to go out. Let the wardsman help you to undress."

" No! " said Macquarie. " No. If you won't take my dog in

you don't take me. He's got a broken leg and wants fixing up just—just as much as—as I do. If I'm good enough to come in, he's good enough—and—and better.'' He paused awhile, breathing painfully, and then went on. '' That—that there old dog of mine has follered me faithful and true these twelve long hard and hungry years. He's about—about the only thing that ever cared whether I lived or fell and rotted on the cursed track.''

He rested again; then he continued: '' That—that there dog was pupped on the track,'' he said, with a sad sort of a smile. '' I carried him for months in a billy-can, and afterwards on my swag when he knocked up. . . . And the old slut—his mother—she'd foller along quite contented—and sniff the billy now and again—just to see if he was all right. . . . She follered me for God knows how many years. She follered me till she was blind—and for a year after. She follered me till she could crawl along through the dust no longer, and—and then I killed her, because I couldn't leave her behind alive! ''

He rested again.

'' And this here old dog,'' he continued, touching Tally's up-turned nose with his knotted fingers, '' this here old dog has follered me for—for ten years; through floods and droughts, through fair times and—and hard—mostly hard; and kept me from going mad when I had no mate nor money on the lonely track; and watched over me for weeks when I was drunk—drugged and poisoned at the cursed shanties; and saved my life more'n once, and got kicks and curses very often for thanks; and forgave me for it all; and—and fought for me. He was the only living thing that stood up for me against that crawling push of curs when they set onter me at the shanty back yonder—and he left his mark on some of 'em too; and—so did I.'' He took another spell. Then he drew in his breath, shut his teeth hard, shouldered his swag, stepped into the doorway, and faced round again.

The dog limped out of the corner and looked up anxiously.

'' That there dog,'' said Macquarie to the Hospital staff in general, '' is a better dog than I'm a man—or you too, it seems—and a better Christian. He's been a better mate to me than I ever was to any man—or any man to me. He's watched over me; kep' me from getting robbed many a time; fought for me; saved my life and took my drunken kicks and curses for thanks—and forgave me. He's been a true, straight, honest, and faithful mate to me—and I ain't going to desert him now. I ain't going to kick him out in the road with a broken leg. I—Oh, my God! my back! '' He groaned and lurched forward, but they caught him, slipped off the swag, and laid him on a bed.

Half an hour later the shearer was comfortably fixed up. '' Where's my dog? '' he asked, when he came to himself.

'' Oh, the dog's all right,'' said the nurse, rather impatiently. '' Don't bother. The doctor's setting his leg out in the yard.''

# MARY GAUNT

B. 1894

# THE DOCTOR'S DRIVE

" THE Mails has got to go through."

Peter Miles was store-keeper and postmaster at Bilsin's, and had been store-keeper there ever since Bilson's was any place at all, and postmaster ever since the Government had seen fit to open a post-office. His motto was, and he stuck to it, " The mails has got to go through." Rain or sunshine, flood or drought, snow or fire, " the mails has got to go through." And this January day the wind was howling like a demon possessed. Down through the narrow gully it tore, a veritable blast from a fiery furnace—the green things shrivelled up before its breath, the tall trees, their great branches tossed hither and thither like twigs, bent and snapped, and every now and then one was rent up by the roots and falling, crashed among its fellows, and with its wide-spreading roots, which left mother earth so reluctantly, brought away part of the hillside; even above the howling of the wind could be heard the slow slipping and sliding of the loosened earth as it fell towards the roadway. No sunshine to-day, no scrap of blue sky, the heavy clouds hung low, clouds of smoke they were, and the strong smell of that smoke and the aromatic scent of burning gum leaves was heavy in the air.

Just in front of the little store stood the mail-coach, and the horses were being yoked up—only a small coach to-day, but there were four horses—four horses that were laying back their ears and kicking and plunging as if they did not like the job before them. The driver, a tall, lithe young fellow of five-and-twenty, with a slouch hat drawn down over his eyes and fastened with a leather thong under his chin, stood watching the final touches being put to the harness and the mail bags being brought out and flung into the boot and put on top of the coach. There were a good many mail bags to-day; usually the big coach would have taken them through, but the weather was so threatening that Miles on his own responsibility had decided to send them along in the little coach he kept for emergencies. " The mails has got to go through," and the sooner they get through the better on a day like this.

" No passengers? " asked the driver laconically. " You'd better send a man along to help then, case of trouble."

Peter Miles looked thoughtfully down the road and rubbed his bald forehead hard.

" I was thinking——" he began, and then hesitated, and one of the stable helps, with his hair coming through the broken crown of his straw hat, laughed ironically.

" Sweet day for a *passear*," he said; " the hills'll be in a blaze long before you reach Bethambia."

" Lucky if we reach Bethambia unsinged, eh, old man? " said the coach-driver grimly, as he gathered up the reins and prepared to mount the box.  " Now which of you fellows is coming along? "

Still Peter Miles shaded his eyes and looked along the road.  The howling of the wind deadened all other sounds, and the thick smoke and haze made it impossible to see very far; still he looked out expectantly and delayed the coach yet another five minutes.  The secrets of the telegraph were his, and he could not betray them; but he knew well enough the contents of that urgent telegram he had sent along to the doctor an hour ago.  There was still time for him to catch the coach, and he hesitated to let it go without him.

The horses grew more impatient, and so did the driver.

" Come, old man," he said, " give the word.  You're risking our lives."

" Hold on one minute.  Here he is!  Here he is! "

Through the haze and smoke dashed a man on horseback.

" Here, I say, hold on a minute; I'm coming too."

" Better not, doctor," said the lean coachman, " we're going to have a hell of a time."

" Must," said Dr. Smith, dropping from his horse and throwing his bag inside the coach.  " Now shall I come up in front? "

The driver nodded.

" Look after my horse, Miles," cried the doctor, scrambling to the box-seat and settling himself there.

It was lucky he was young and active, for the horses were more impatient than ever now, and the driver, with a quite unnecessary crack of his whip, gave them their heads.

" It'll be hell for leather, Mat," cried he of the straw hat, as the stable helpers jumped aside to let the swaying coach pass, and Mat nodded his head.

Up the road, straight up the hill, swept the horses right in the teeth of the wind, and Bilson's was left behind in the gathering haze.

" Where 're you goin' to, doctor? " asked Mat as they steadied down to a trot, for the hill was steep and the wind strong.

" To Coulson's—just this side of Bethambia, isn't it? "

A faint smile stole over Mat Jackson's impassive face.

" Eh, I thought they'd be wantin' you there.  It's her first, you see, and Jim Coulson's mighty set on her.  But it's an uncommon awkward time she's chosen."

" They always do," murmured the other out of the depths of his experience. " Never mind, they'll take it more coolly next time."

" I'd have ridden through, if I was you," said the driver. " You'd have done it easier."

But the other shook his head.

" I've been riding all the morning," said he. " And I never got to bed at all last night. I reckoned on getting some sleep in the coach once we get through this smother."

" Lordy! we ain't goin' to get through this. All the ranges are on fire way back there. I reckon we'll be lucky if we get through at all. It's gettin' worse."

" Ye gods and little fishes! It can't be worse."

" Oh, can't it? Just you wait an' see."

" I'm bound to get through."

" So's the mails. And once we top this hill it'll be neck or nothing with us. Say the word, doctor; will you go back? " And the driver slightly checked his horses.

" Can't we get through? "

He raised his head. The smoke made his eyes smart, and he pulled his hat over them, but it was little good, it was all round them, heavy and dense. On either hand the tree-tops were shut out as by a pall, and even the leaders were only visible to the men on the box as through a dense grey haze.

Mat, the driver, took a long breath, then pushed back the flapping brim of his hat, and, standing up, took a long look round.

Nothing but dense grey smoke and trees swaying and tossing in the wind seen dimly through it.

" Well, we mout get through. I've seen it worse—only the farther we go, the less chance of getting back if it's too bad to go on. And it ain't pleasant, let me tell you, to be roasted alive without any preliminary preparation. And it's kinder anticipatin'."

The doctor smiled grimly.

" As bad as that? " he said.

" Well," drawled the driver, " it mout be, and it mout not. The wind mout drop, you know, or it mout shift, or it mout rain, or it moutn't be as bad as I think. There's a hundred chances agin things goin' wrong. But if we meet the fire two or three miles on ahead there, I tell you, doctor, it isn't much I'd give for your chance of seein' Jim Coulson's wife through her trouble. But then again, we moutn't meet the fire; but I'm telling you the truth, if I hadn't the mails behind me, it's on the back track I'd be at this minute."

" And if the mails can get through, I can," said the doctor. " I reckon we'll go on, Mat."

" Right you are, boss," and he leaned over and touched the off leader, who was fretting herself into a foam over the smoke, with his long whip.

Then the doctor pulled down his straw hat over his eyes again, and in spite of the discomfort of his seat and his doubts as to the safety of his situation, fell into an uneasy doze. The heat was overpowering, the smoke grew denser than ever, and every now and then he was dreamily aware that his companion was exhorting him to keep awake, to hold up and look out that he did not fall off. He was rather afraid of this last accident himself, and grasped the iron rail of the box-seat with a firm hand, and then kept starting wide awake, thinking he had lost it. If he could only have wakened himself up thoroughly, he would have made an effort and gone inside as safer, but dead beat as he was the smoke and the heat made him drowsier than ever, and he kept putting it off and putting it off till of a sudden the horses were pulled to a standstill with a jerk that threw them on to their haunches.

" God Almighty! " he heard Mat's voice in horror and dread. " We're dead men! "

Then he sat upright in a moment, and rubbed his eyes.

It was darker now, much darker, though it was but two o'clock in the afternoon, the wind was wilder than ever as it tore shrieking through the trees, and the smoke denser and more choking; but that was not the worst, for right ahead, directly in their paths, was a lurid glare thrown right on the heavy smoke banks.

The doctor sat up and rubbed his eyes sleepily, for the moment hardly grasping the gravity of the situation.

" What's the matter, Mat? "

The coach-driver pointed with his whip.

" The fire, right ahead," he said. " Both sides of the track, too. The scrub's thick and the track's narrow. We're dead men, doctor."

The doctor stood up and looked back; but the driver anticipated his thought.

" No good, doctor, we can't go back. The fire'd be on us before you could say Jack Robinson. And it would stop with us all the way. It's due south is Bilson's, and the wind's dead from the north."

The solitary passenger looked to the right and left, but the scrub was close and thick; the country was poor enough, but the messmate grew up thick and bushy, and in between was tea-tree and bracken and twining creepers and prickly shrubs of which he did not know the names. But it was close enough; there was no escape that way either for man or beast.

" It's sorter different when it comes to the point, doctor, isn't it? " said the driver. " All very well to talk o' gettin' the mails through, neck or nothing, till you have to do it; but to drive into that muck of smoke an' fire—the Lord ha' mercy upon us."

" Is it the only way? "

" The only way. We're not above three miles from Bethambia."
And he brought down the whip heavily across the horses' backs.
" Now then, fellows, for all you're worth."

The doctor put his hand down and gripped firmly the rail as the
coach plunged forward and rocked from side to side; but he said
nothing. There was nothing left for him to say.

" Let's get it over, in God's name," cried the driver, and he
lashed the horses to a hard gallop. They kicked and plunged and
snorted in terror, for the breath of the fire was upon them now, but
the hand that held them was firm and strong, and the cruel whip
came down on their backs unerringly. There was no turning back
for them either.

The hot wind was hotter than ever now; the mouth of the furnace
was open, and it was pouring forth smoke and flame. The reek of
it was in their nostrils, and the doctor pulled his hat down closely
over his face.

" Look out you don't choke and fall off," said the driver grimly.
" I couldn't stop if I wanted to."

" All right," said his companion, and looking out again he noted
that the air was full of burning gum leaves. They fell on the
frightened horses and on the mail bags, and his own coat was
already smouldering in one or two places, and right ahead was the
fire. On either side scrub and bracken and tall trees were all one
mass of flame, and momentarily it came nearer, borne on the fierce
wind.

The horses saw it too and stopped dead, plunging and fighting to
be free, and though Mat stood up in his seat and lashed them with
a hand made desperate by stern necessity, they were desperate
too, and they swerved aside and turned from the track to the right,
bringing the coach sharply against a tree-trunk.

" Good Lord! " cried Mat in desperation. " Rats in a hole! "

" We'll have to blindfold them," said the doctor. " Give me
that necktie of yours, they'll never face it as it is—and your handkerchief. Now, don't leave me behind."

It is hardly an easy matter to blindfold a horse at any time, but
never surely did it take so long as that day, when the minutes were
so precious. Young Willie Smith cursed the fate that had sent him
out from civilisation many times, as he struggled for that plunging
off leader's head, but it was done at last—all four horses were blind-
folded, and he scrambled up to the box again as the driver lashed
them to a gallop.

He wondered if it would be a good move. How could those
terrified horses take the coach along that rough track, now scattered
over with living coals as the burning branches and twigs fell upon
it? But it was their only chance. Mat's hands were firm and
strong, and the horses answered to the guiding rein. The fire was

on either hand now, their faces were blistering under the heat, every piece of wood and ironwork was too hot to touch, and the horses stumbled every now and then where a fall would mean certain death. He bowed his head in his hands. This was the end then. All his hopes, all his ambition, and his little sweetheart waiting for him so patiently till he could make a home for her up here among the mountains. All, all was lost; this was the end. How long now, how long? Then the driver's voice broke in on his reverie.

" The mails are afire, doctor. Couldn't you put them out? Take this waterproof apron."

The waterproof apron had been pulled up to shield their own legs; but no matter—if Mat were so faithful to his trust, he could not be less so, and with his pocket-knife he ripped it up, and turning round threw it across the mail bags. It didn't half cover them, and he had to crawl half over them and put out the blaze with his fingers. Sometimes he managed to get the waterproof in between his bare hand and the fire, but always that was not practicable, and the mails were such inflammable material, before he got one place out another would be alight. His hands grew sore and painful but he hardly noticed it, only the smoke was so choking and the heat so fierce he could only wonder they held on so long.

First one horse stumbled, then another, but the practised hand of the driver drew them to their feet again. The off leader was down on her knees once, and the coach gave such a lurch he gave up all for lost, while he mechanically laid his arm across the corner of the woodwork that burst into flame.

" Do that again," said Mat between his teeth, " and it's all up with us." But the mare, helped by his guiding hand, struggled to her feet again.

A burning branch fell right across the top of the coach, miraculously sparing the two men on the box-seat, and the doctor, with a great effort, flung it off. Another fell right in front of the horses, but the track luckily was wider here, and Mat managed to draw horses and coach a little aside. It was only clever hands that did it at that headlong pace, but it was done, and they were a little nearer the end.

How long? How long?

Eyebrows, eyelashes, hair were all singed by the flames; the curtains in the coach windows were on fire, and the horses—their scanty harness was red-hot, and the white handkerchief he had tied round the eyes of one of the leaders was already smouldering. The end *must* come soon now, things could not go on like this any longer.

" Woa, there. Steady, good mare. Hold up, will you? " And the whip came down with a heavy crack across the backs of the stumbling horses.

Crash! And a tall tree fell close alongside them, and men and coach and horses received the burst of sparks that flew around them.

" It *is* the end," cried the doctor, his lips cracked and swollen and his mouth dry and parched, yet still making one last effort to put out with his bare, burnt hands the fire that was kindling afresh among the mails.

" By the living God! no," shouted the driver. " We're through! My God! we're through! "

Then the other man turned his head and looked through the dense haze with red-rimmed, smoke-weary eyes, and he saw that his companion spoke the truth. Behind them was the fire, behind them the flames dancing yellow and red and blue in the heavy smoke, and here—here was only the path of the fire, hot wind, heavy smoke, dense and thick as ever. The breath of the fire had passed, and every living thing was dead. The tall trees were blackened, smoking skeletons, in which the red fire still smouldered, and the air was full of the soft, white, powdery ash that had once been bark and green leaves. But they were safe, safe! and in a few more yards Mat drew up the horses, and they put out the last remnants of the fire that had clung to the coach.

Then they were off again, and in another five minutes were clattering down the road into the township of Bethambia.

The township had fought for its life, and at the first roadside cottage they came across a little knot of men armed with branches and sacks, and looking scarcely less dishevelled than the newcomers themselves. These had been beating back the fire from the township.

" And it was a mighty close shave," said one of them, stepping forward. " But, lordy! Mat, whatever brought ye through on a day like this? "

" The mails, Jim Coulson," said Mat, drawing himself up with dignity, " has got to go through, an' they're through. An' here's the doctor for your missus."

Then a woman made her appearance in the doorway, winding up her hands in her long white apron.

" Is it the doctor? " she asked. " Oh, doctor, I'm that sorry, but the baby was born more than half an hour ago. Just as fine a child as ever you set eyes on, bless him! "

# ACKNOWLEDGMENTS

To the living authors whose work is included in this volume, the thanks of the editor are hereby tendered for their courtesy in permitting the reprinting of their copyright stories, and thanks are likewise recorded to the various publishers who have also given their consent. These items are individually acknowledged in the following list :

" A Thorough Gentleman," from *A Spoiled Priest*, by Canon P. A. Sheehan. Messrs. BURNS & OATES, LTD., 28 Orchard Street, London, W.

" The Comedy of the Old Love," from *Nell Gwyn, Comedian*, by F. Frankfort Moore. Messrs. C. ARTHUR PEARSON, LTD., 17 Henrietta Street, London, W.C.

" The Birthday of the Infanta," from *The House of Pomegranates*, by Oscar Wilde. Messrs. METHUEN & Co., LTD., 36 Essex Street, London, W.C.

" Maureen's Fairing," from *Maureen's Fairing*, by Jane Barlow. Messrs. J. M. DENT & SONS, LTD., 10 Bedford Street, London, W.C.

" At the Spotted Lamb," and " The Meeting in the Library," from *The Yellow Domino*, by Katherine Tynan.

" A Nursery Tea," from *Earth to Earth*, by Richard Dehan. Mr. WM. HEINEMANN, 21 Bedford Street, London, W.C.

" They that Mourn," and " Th' Ould Boy," from *Ring o' Rushes*, by Shan F. Bullock. Messrs. WARD, LOCK & Co., LTD., Salisbury Square, London, E.C.

" The Rev. Peter Flannery," and " A Connemara Miracle," from *At the Rising of the Moon*, by Frank Mathew.

" The Twisting of the Rope," from *Stories of Red Hanrahan*, by W. B. Yeats. DUN EMER PRESS, Dundrum, Ireland.

" Rosanna," from *Chance the Piper*, by Agnes Castle. Mr. JOHN MURRAY, Albemarle Street, London, W.

" The Bewitched Fiddle," from *The Bewitched Fiddle*, and " The Resurrection of Dinny O'Dowd," from *Irish Nights*, by Seumas MacManus.

" Priscilla," from *The Father Confessor and Other Stories*, by Dora Sigerson Shorter. By permission of Mr. C. K. SHORTER.

" The House of Fahy," from *Some Experiences of an Irish R.M.*, by E. Œ. Somerville and Martin Ross. Messrs. LONGMANS, GREEN & CO., 39 Paternoster Row, London.

" The Breath of Life," and " The Child Saint," from *A Munster Twilight*, by Daniel Corkery. TALBOT PRESS, Dublin.

" The City on Mallington Moor, from *Tales of Wonder*. " The Assignation," and " The Hen," from *Fifty-One Tales*, by Lord Dunsany. Mr. ELKIN MATHEWS, 4A Cork Street, London, W. " Coronation of Mr. Thomas Shap," from *Book of Wonder*, by Lord Dunsany. Mr. WILLIAM HEINEMNAN, 21 Bedford Street, London, W.C. " The Sword and the Idol," from *A Dreamer's Tales*, by Lord Dunsany. Messrs. GEORGE ALLEN & UNWIN, LTD., 40 Museum Street, London, W.C.

" Rodman the Boatsteerer," from *Rodman the Boatsteerer*, by Louis Becke. Mr. T. FISHER UNWIN, 1 Adelphi Terrace, London, W.C.

" A Little Grey Glove," from *Keynotes*, by George Egerton. Mr. JOHN LANE, Vigo Street, London, W.

" The Freedom of the Black-Faced Ram," from *Watchers of the Trail*, by C. G. D. Roberts. Messrs. DUCKWORTH & CO., 3 Henrietta Street, London, W.C.

" The Pilot at Swan Creek," from *The Pilot at Swan Creek*, by Ralph Connor. Messrs. HODDER & STOUGHTON, 20 Warwick Square, London, E.C.

" The Crimson Flag," from *Pierre and his People*, by Sir Gilbert Parker. Messrs. METHUEN & CO., LTD. " The Absurd Romance of P'tite Louison," and " The Singing of the Bees," from *The Lane that had no Turning*, by Sir Gilbert Parker, Bart. Mr. WILLIAM HEINEMANN, 21 Bedford Street, London, W.C.

" In a Far-Off World," and " An Artist's Secret," from *Dreams*, by Olive Schreiner. Mr. T. FISHER UNWIN, 1 Adelphi Terrace, London, W.C.

" Quarantine," from *Chapman's Wares*, by H. B. Marriott Watson. Messrs. MILLS & BOON, LTD., 49 Rupert Street, London, W.

" The Doctor's Drive," from *The Ends of the Earth*, by Mary Gaunt. Messrs. T. WERNER LAURIE, LTD., 30 New Bridge Street, London, E.C.

# XII
# RUSSIAN

# THE
# Masterpiece Library
# of Short Stories

*The Thousand Best Complete
Tales of all Times and
all Countries*

Selected by

## AN INTERNATIONAL BOARD
## OF EMINENT CRITICS

Sir William Robertson Nicoll, LL.D.
Sir Arthur Quiller-Couch   Sir Frederick Wedmore
Clement Shorter   Sir Edmund Gosse, C.B., LL.D.
George Saintsbury, LL.D.   W. P. Trent, LL.D.
Richard le Gallienne   Carl Van Doren
Brander Matthews, Litt.D.   Thomas Seccombe

Edited by
Sir J. A. Hammerton

# XII. RUSSIAN

LONDON
THE EDUCATIONAL BOOK COMPANY LIMITED

# Contents of Volume XII

# CONTENTS

416

# THE RUSSIAN STORY-
TELLERS

## From Pushkin to Sologub

RUSSIAN literature was revealed to the Western reader through the works of Russia's greatest masters—Turgeniev, Tolstoy, and Dostoyevsky—whose novels, true epics of Russian life and thought, are vast in bulk and purpose. Their extensive proportions seem, in a way, an essential element of Russian art in its variety of observation and deep search after truth and the aims of existence.

Russia is a vast country. It includes a greater divergency of human types and modes of consciousness than any other State in Europe. Russia is comparatively young, too. She began cultured life at a much later period than the rest of Europe, and from a certain point in her history made gigantic strides to overtake the level of Western culture. In some respects she is ahead of it, though many remnants of an uncultured past are latent in the steady and sometimes feverishly hasty growth of her inner development.

Russian life seems to extend over a simultaneous range of several centuries, to contain conditions and conceptions which are almost mediæval, while the psychology and idealism of Russian intellectuals as well as the spontaneous spirituality of the Russian masses are in many cases in advance of the normal and gradual progress of Western Europe. This accounts for the complexity of Russian problems, both individual and social. Until the consummation of its wonderful revolution, the nation's creative power had not had sufficient opportunities to apply itself to active and constructive work in the way of social progress. Until then, by a sort of instinct, and for historic reasons, too, it had been centred on inner development. It is too early yet to discern how Russia's new political freedom may react on her intellectual progress. The spirit of the nation had already achieved higher standards than those manifested in pre-Revolution realities. The outstanding, all-embracing problem is how to fulfil in the actual conditions of life all that the Russian spirit has gained in its long trials and through its endurance.

This problem is at the bottom of all Russian literature, and accounts for the high idealism of Russian writers, combined with a strong realistic vein and an all-pervading spirit of humanity. It forms that peculiar atmosphere of tense inner life, longing to assert itself in action, which is so characteristic of Russian novels, and makes them so fascinating to the Western reader.

The same atmosphere, the same problems are characteristic of the Russian short story. As a distinct type of literature the short story made its first appearance in Russia towards the end of the nineteenth century with Garshin and Chekhov, who excelled in the art of story-telling and specialised in it. From the very beginning of the nineteenth century, however, at the outset of Russia's literary life, and all through the succeeding periods of its further development, all the best Russian novelists, as well as Russia's greatest poets, wrote short stories in the same spirit, many of which possessed the same literary value as their works of a much wider scope. A series of representative short Russian stories such as those contained in this volume affords in consequence a general view of Russian literature with its successive tendencies, pervaded with the one and same spirit peculiar to Russian art.

## PUSHKIN

Alexander Pushkin (1799–1837), the greatest Russian poet, the founder of both Russian prose and poetry in its classic form, is the first link between Russian and Western literature. His deepest inspiration came from the very heart of Russia—from Russian folk-lore. He was the first to reveal the imaginative power and intuitive moral force of the Russian peasant. In the mainsprings, however, his genius was akin to Western culture and influenced to a large extent by the romantic school of his time. He was under the spell of Byronic " Titanism," which took a markedly Russian form in his works. His story " The Pistol-Shot " is very representative in this respect. The Western romantic spirit of it blends originally and naturally with the Russian motive of pity, which solves, by a sort of inner revelation, the most complex problems. The hero of the story is distinctly " Byronic " in his cool aloofness, in his gambling with fate, but in the supreme moment, when his " Satanic " disposition is brought to a test, the instinct of humanity and pity triumphs over his romantic intellectuality.

The best of Pushkin's stories—a gem of romantic literature—is " The Queen of Spades," perfect in its artistic finish. It is a fantastic ghost story, told with an entrancing power of imagination, yet with sufficient psychological motives to make it real. Its background is strongly realistic. It gives a true picture of high society life under Alexander I, with significant details of the home of the period. The old countess is a curious remnant of eighteenth-century grandeur, a court beauty, Russian to the core despite her adventurous Parisian past, despotic, yet generous by impulse. It is an afterthought of compassion for the victim of betrayed love that moves her soul to disclose the fatal secret to the unfortunate gambler. Lisa, the young lady-companion, is a type created of social conditions, a poor victim of self-indulgent, idle sur- roundings, dragged into a luxurious life in which she remains a lonely stranger, half-lady, half-servant, fed on romantic dreams which lead her fatally to ruin—crushed in her human dignity as a plaything of the idle rich. There is a great human truth in this type, the more remarkable as revealed by a romantic poet.

## LERMONTOFF

Michail Lermontoff (1814–1841) was Pushkin's younger contemporary, and ranks next to him as Russia's second great poet. Lermontoff's short stories are purely romantic. Many of them show a Byronic vein like those of Pushkin. He dwells in preference on characters of wild beauty, of irresistible personality, cruel, yet justified by their inner tragedy and their defiant attitude to life. The Russian element in them consists in the passionate instinct of inner freedom, that justifies even the outlaws, as we see in the picturesque Cossack story, " A Fair Smuggler." The heroine and her associates are desperate characters, yet the victim of their conspiracy is ready to forgive his loss and the fair lady's deception on account of the beautiful instincts of freedom he observes in the gang. The " Fair Smuggler " cheats him un- scrupulously, but remains true to her freely chosen lover. The woman and her lover, as well as the boy who pretends to be blind, have their own moral standards and are true to them. The atmosphere of inner freedom in this story has a psychological value and is representative of the Russian mind.

## GOGOL

Realism, that great force of Russian art, makes its appearance in Russian literature with Nicolai Gogol (1809–1852). His genius of observation and true representation of life was united to the romantic soul of the Ukranian. He became the poet of Russian reality. Abso- lute truth to life is combined in Gogol's works with the utmost simplicity of invention. He never flatters life, nor does he slander it. He is happy to show all that is beautiful and humane in it, but does not hide its ugly sides. His novels and stories contain a gallery of immortal types of Russian officials demoralised by the arbitrary power they possess, monstrous in their pettiness and inhumanity; of idle, self-indulgent, narrow-minded land- and serf-owners before the emancipation, and of all the social deformities created by excess of power on the one hand and total defencelessness on the other. With a grim humour does he paint these portraits of depravity, but alongside he gives us a world of beauty, poetry, light and colour in his masterful stories of peasant life, of pure innocent souls, as well as in his broad emotional pictures of Russian scenery—the steppes, the rivers and the woods.

The peculiar atmosphere of peasant life appears in the story "The Eve of St. John," with its tale of superstitions influencing the life and psychology of the simple souls. The minute rendering of the village types, the happy tone of a fairy tale that makes the fantastic appear real, the genuine, deep emotions running through it form the beauty of the story. The plot of "The Carriage" is of the simplest—a mere incident of daily life—yet Gogol's humour mirrors in it a wonderful picture of petty life with its lack of activity, idle rivalries and amusements.

## TURGENIEV

Ivan Turgeniev (1818–1883), the great master of Russian prose, gives a vast picture of Russian conditions in his novels. He was the first to reveal the new social types created by the transitionary period of the abolition of serfdom, which transformed the old Russia, as she used to live and to feel and to reason before the great reform of Alexander II. His short stories, especially those included in "Memoirs of a Sportsman," rank among his masterpieces, both as perfect works of art and as the expression of his higher humanitarian ideals. Turgeniev revealed in them the poetic beauty of the Russian landscape, and, above all, the soul of the Russian serfs, the peasants with their reserved but deep emotions, and the spiritual treasures hidden in their simple hearts.

There is nothing sentimental or artificial about Turgeniev's peasants. He does not idealise them for the purposes of mere social propaganda. He gives them to us with all their peculiarities and limitations resulting from their uncultured state, the more striking because of the revelation of their rich and deep emotions in the sober, simple pictures of their lives. "The Singers" is one of Turgeniev's particularly interesting tales. In it he reveals the artistic temperament of the Russian peasant, his delight in music, showing what a world of passion, of harmony with the universe is concealed in his soul. He pours out his inmost self in the weird strains of Russian songs, then resumes his humble existence and works like a slave, or gets drunk, as he does in the end of the story. "The Rendezvous" is a pathetic story of disappointed love, deeply humane, showing the genuine emotions of a simple peasant girl and the demoralising effect of half-cultured town life on her lover. " Visions " discloses a mystic side in Turgeniev, to be met with in other stories of his. Others of his tales might well have found places in this collection, but with few exceptions they exceed the average length of story admitted in this compilation, while others, again, of the desired length are less stories than sketches.

## DOSTOYEVSKY

Fiodor Dostoyevsky (1822–1881) is Russia's great mystic, whose vision of the world is that of a contest between the questioning and often rebellious human mind and the mystery of divine omnipresence revealed to the enlightened in the very midst of life's bitterest wrongs and agony. The outcome of Dostoyevsky's mystic teaching is his message of pity, manifested in all his work. " The Honest Thief " is one of this author's tales of pity, in which he reveals that compassionate sympathy of the Russian mind for all suffering. All human relations in Dostoyevsky's story are based on intuitive pity, which discovers a pure and wide-awakened conscience in the fallen man. Pity as revealed in this story is active, and brings spiritual beauty and light into what would have seemed abject and ugly seen without that compassionate love for humanity.

## SCHEDRIN

Along with those great masters, prophets of religious and spiritual truth, Russia possesses story-tellers chiefly concerned with social ideals and struggles. Nicolai Schedrin, the *nom de plume* of Michail T. Saltickov (1826–1889), is the greatest of them. A satirist of remarkable force and rich invention, Schedrin lashes with his inexhaustible wit the self-complacency, self-indulgence and cruelty of the higher administrative power. He has a particular genius in drawing portraits of the bureaucratic caste which covers it with contempt and ridicule. These portraits have to a large extent revealed the psychology of the Russian bureaucratic mind, and the names of many of Schedrin's ridiculed heroes have become the nicknames of certain types of officials. The pathetic tale, " Two Little Moujiks," shows the grim side of Schedrin's talent in the story of the two children who are animated with the desperate desire to avenge their humiliation, to assert their human dignity against despotic cruelty. Their only means to that end is suicide—a grim symbol of social wrongs. Schedrin's sarcasm, however, does not spare those who are too weak to oppose evil, as we see in the delightful story " The Self-Sacrificing Rabbit."

## TOLSTOY

Leo Tolstoy (1828–1910), the genius of world-wide fame, needs little introduction to the Western reader.   His short stories were a part of his life-work from the very outset of his literary career and all through the first half of his life, when his moral teaching, though asserting itself strongly in his vast psychological and artistic conceptions, had not yet crystallised into a positive message.   From 1881, when his religious crisis resolved itself into active moral teaching, Tolstoy made the short story a means to convey his ideas to simple minds.   He put all his artistic power and inspiration into the tales written for the peasants, but read by the whole cultured world.   " How Much Land does a Man Need ? " is simple in its teaching, and convincing as a true and symbolic picture of unreasoned and instinctive greed.   " The Three Hermits " contrasts journalistic dogmatism with genuine faith and the moral force it brings—a favourite subject of Tolstoy's.   The remaining stories in the present volume are typical of his peculiar vein of story-telling—clear and strong in their purpose, simple and full of artistic details, so characteristic of Tolstoy's work as a whole.

## LESKOV

Of a different type from any of the preceding writers in this volume is Nicolai S. Leskov (1831–1895).   A strong enemy of the revolutionary movement of the 'sixties, his early work was chiefly concerned in attacking it.   It was only towards the latter half of his career that he left the bitterness of politics behind him and began to devote himself to pure literature.   He has given us numerous stories, unique in both style and conception.   His subjects were largely the clergy, the church, the beliefs —dogmatic and otherwise—of the people, and their superstitions. Rich in invention, his language full of colour, he could give us in five or six pages the content of a whole volume.   He had a wonderful way of creating an atmosphere, so admirably illustrated in " The Ghost of the Engineers' Castle."

## USPENSKY

Nicolai Uspensky (1837–1889), one of the minor Russian writers, could tell a good realistic story without any deep psychological problems.   He began life as a schoolmaster, then developed a taste for literature, which paid him so badly at first that, owing to his extreme poverty, he was forced to live in common doss-houses—an experience that stood him in good stead afterwards, and afforded him many types for his stories.

## MAMIN-SIBIRIAK

Dmitri Mamin-Sibiriak (b. 1852) was born in the Urals—the background of many of his novels and stories. Mining, greed, the severity of the military authorities formed the principal subjects of his plots. The story " In the Heart of the Urals " shows us what an immense amount of love and sympathy he felt for the simple people—primitive and unspoiled by civilisation—whose lives were disturbed by the first shriek of a train that broke the stillness of their forests, to the wonder of the boy Pimka, the disgust of old grandfather Tit, and the delight of the soldier. We see Mamin-Sibiriak in a different vein in the story " There is no Reply," with its atmosphere of tragedy.

## KOROLÉNKO

Vladimir Korolénko (1853–1921) was a Little Russian, whose work was coloured by Polish romanticism and Ukranian poetry and sadness. His prose is like music, singing now of nature, now of human emotions. Even in moments of greatest tragedy he was utterly devoid of bitterness, as we see in the story " Easter Eve," and in the quieter story of " The Old Verger " called to his eternal rest.

## GARSHIN

Vsevolod Garshin (1855–1888) did not live long enough to write more than about ten stories, but they rank him as one of the greatest masters of Russian prose. Every line was wrung out of him from his deep inner experience. We see the spiritual nature of the man in the wonderful realistic story, depicting the horrors of war, " Four Days," and in the powerful story " The Red Flower," a tale that was largely biographical ; for Garshin used to suffer from fits of madness (the cause of his tragic death), during which he dreamt of destroying all evil in the world at one fell swoop. His melancholy nature, however, had little faith in the force of good, or in the destruction of evil, and still less belief had he in that the attainment of his dreams could bring him either peace or happiness. " Is this all ? " asks the palm, in the charming, poetic story " Attalea Princeps," when after all her tremendous efforts she emerges into freedom, the goal of her desires.

## POTAPENKO

Ignati Potapenko (b. 1856) had the curious career of being first a Uhlan officer and then a priest. Some of his best stories are about the rural clergy. He has a wonderful power of observation and a ready style.  In the story " Bigger than Yourself " we have an ordinary, average young man who lets his present opportunities of action and happiness slip by for some illusory ideas of greatness.

## CHEKHOV

Anton Chekhov (1860–1904), the chronicler of the Russian period of depression and pessimism, was the leader of the realistic school of the Russian short story.  Many writers have compared him to Guy de Maupassant in his masterful manner of creating an atmosphere and reaching a climax.  He seizes a given moment in his heroes' lives and reveals their souls in two or three pages.  Mediocrity, the tragedy of pettiness, commonplaceness, the emptiness and meaninglessness of everyday life form the principal themes of his stories.  He reveals the rottenness of the social structure, yet, unlike most great Russian writers, has no doctrine to teach.  The few stories of his given in this volume are remarkably characteristic of his work.  " The Avenger," " The Chameleon," " A Work of Art," " The Slanderer," show him to us as a humorist, the rest show him in his more artistic vein.

## SOLOGUB

Feódor Sologub (1863–1927), mystic and realist, was a writer of long novels in the Dostoyevsky school, and many short stories, of which those included in this volume are very representative.  A favourite theme of his was reincarnation, which he used very powerfully in the three stories, " The White Mother," " The Invoker of the Beast," and "A Soothing Dream."                                      R. S. T.

# ALEXANDER S. PUSHKIN

1799–1837

# THE PISTOL-SHOT

WE were in camp in a small Russian village. Every one knows the life of an officer of the line: in the morning, drill and horseback exercise; then comes dinner with the colonel of the regiment, or else at the Jewish restaurant; and at night, drinks and cards. At this place, however, there were no entertainments of any kind, for no one had a marriageable daughter to bring out. We spent our time in one another's quarters, and at our evening gatherings there were uniforms only.

However, there was one man in our set who was not a soldier. He must have been about thirty-five, and, consequently, we looked upon him as quite old. His experience had great weight with us; and besides, his reserve, his grand air, and his sarcastic manner made a deep impression on us young men. There seemed to be something mysterious about his life. He looked like a Russian, though he bore a foreign name. In days gone by he had been in a regiment of hussars, where he was quite prominent at one time; but suddenly he had sent in his resignation, no one knew why, and had retired to this poor, out-of-the-way village, where he fared very badly, while at the same time he spent much money. He always wore a shabby overcoat, and still he kept open house, where every officer was made welcome. To tell the truth his dinners generally consisted of two or three simple dishes prepared by his servant, an old discharged soldier, but the champagne always flowed. No one knew anything of his affairs or his means, and no one dared ask him any questions on the subject. There were plenty of books in his house—mostly military—among them a few novels. He lent them willingly and never asked for them again.

On the other hand, he never returned those he borrowed. His one pastime was pistol-shooting. The walls of his room were riddled with bullets, giving it the appearance of a honeycomb. A rich collection of pistols was the only luxury to be seen in the miserable house which he occupied. The accuracy of his aim was remarkable, and if he had taken a bet that he could shoot the pompom on a helmet, not one of us would have hesitated to put the helmet on. Sometimes we talked of duelling, but Silvio (I will give him that name) never opened his lips on the subject. If some one asked him if he had ever fought a duel, he answered shortly that he had, and that was all. He never entered into any particulars, and it was evident that he disliked being asked such questions. We surmised that the death of one of his victims had left a blight on his life. Never for a minute would any of us have thought that he could have been guilty of faint-heartedness. There are some people whose very appearance precludes such an idea.

One day eight or ten of our officers were dining at Silvio's. We drank as much as usual—that is, excessively. When dinner was over we begged of our host to take the bank in a game of faro. After refusing to do so, for he seldom played, he finally called for cards, and laying fifty ducats on the table before him, he sat down and shuffled. We formed in a circle about him and the game began. When playing Silvio never uttered a word, neither objecting nor explaining. If a player made a mistake he paid out exactly the amount due to him or else credited it to himself. We were all familiar with his manner of playing, and always let him have his own way. But on the day I speak of there was with us an officer newly arrived who, through absent-mindedness, doubled his stakes on a certain card. Silvio took the chalk and marked down what was due to him. The officer, convinced that there was a mistake, made some objections. Silvio, still mute, went on dealing as if he had not heard. The officer, out of patience by that time, took the brush and wiped off the figures. Silvio picked up the chalk and wrote them down again. At this the officer, excited by the wine, by the play, and by the laughter of his comrades, and thinking he had been insulted, took up a brass candlestick and hurled it at Silvio, who by bending aside averted the blow. Great was the uproar! Silvio rose, pale with rage, and with eyes blazing.

" My dear sir," he said, " you will please leave this room, and be thankful that this has happened in my house."

Not one of us doubted the outcome of this affair, and we all looked upon our new comrade as a dead man. The officer went out, saying he was ready to meet the banker just as soon as it was convenient. The game proceeded a few minutes longer, but it was evident that the master of the house was not paying much attention to what was going on. We all left, one by one, and returned to our quarters, discussing the while the vacancy in our ranks which was sure to take place.

Next morning, while at riding exercise, we all wondered if the poor lieutenant were dead or alive, when, to our surprise, he appeared among us. We plied him with questions, and he answered that he had had no challenge from Silvio, which caused us all much surprise. We called on Silvio and found him in his yard, firing bullet after bullet at an ace nailed to the door. He received us in his usual manner, never mentioning the scene of the night before. Three days went by and the lieutenant was still alive. We kept saying to each other, " Will Silvio not fight? " amazed at such a thing. But Silvio did not fight. He simply gave a very lame explanation, and that was all that was said about the matter.

This forbearance on his part did him much harm among us young men. Youth never quite forgives a want of courage, for to youth fearlessness is the greatest quality one can possess, and it excuses many faults. Still, after a while all this was forgotten, and by degrees Silvio regained his old ascendancy over us.

I alone could never feel the same toward him. Being of a romantic turn of mind I had loved this man whose life was an enigma to us all more than any one else, and I had made him, in my thoughts, the hero of some mysterious drama; and he liked me—of this I felt sure. For when we were alone, dropping his sharp and sarcastic speeches, he would converse on all sorts of subjects and unbend to me in a fascinating manner. Ever since that unlucky evening of which I have spoken, the fact that he had been insulted and had not wiped out the offence in blood worried me to such an extent that I never could feel at ease with him as in the days gone by. I even avoided looking at him, and Silvio was too clever and quick not to notice it and to guess at the reason. He seemed to me to feel it deeply. On two occasions I thought I had detected a wish on his part to explain matters, but I avoided him, and he did not pursue me.

Those happy mortals who live in cities, where there is so much to see and to do, can never imagine how important certain small happenings can become in an out-of-the-way village or town. One of these is the arrival of the mail. On Tuesdays and Fridays the offices of our regiment were besieged with men; one expected money, another a letter, and again others looked for newspapers. As a rule everything was opened and read on the spot. News was given, and the improvised post-office was full of animation. Silvio's letters were addressed to the care of our regiment, and he called for them with us. One day a letter was handed to him, the seal of which he broke hurriedly. While reading it his eyes flashed with suppressed excitement. None of the officers except myself noticed this, as they were all busy reading their own letters.

" Gentlemen," said Silvio, " business compels me to leave town immediately. I must go to-night. I hope none of you will refuse to dine with me for the last time. I shall expect you," said he, turning to me pointedly. " I hope you will not disappoint me."

After saying this he went away in great haste, and we all retired to our own quarters, agreeing to meet at his house later.

I arrived at Silvio's at the hour he had named, and found almost the whole regiment there. Everything he possessed was packed, and the bare walls, riddled with bullets, stared back at us. We

sat down to dinner, and our host was in such a jovial mood that
before long we were all in the greatest of spirits. Corks flew about,
the froth rose in our glasses, which we refilled as rapidly as they
were emptied. We all felt great affection for our host, and wished
him a pleasant journey, with joy and prosperity at the end of it.
It was very late when we got up from the table, and while we were
all picking out our caps in the hall, Silvio took me by the hand and
detained me as I was about to leave.

" I must speak to you," he said in a low tone.

So I remained after the others went away; and, seated facing
each other, we smoked our pipes for a while in silence. Silvio
seemed worried, and there was no trace of the feverish gaiety he
had displayed in the earlier part of the evening. His dreadful
pallor, the brilliancy of his eyes, and the long puffs of smoke he
blew from his mouth gave him the appearance of a fiend. After
a few moments he broke the silence.

" It may be," he said, " that we shall never see each other
again. Before we part I wish to explain certain things to you.
You have noticed, perhaps, that I attach very little importance to
the average man's opinion; but I like you, and I feel that I cannot
leave without having you think better of me than you do."

He stopped to shake the ashes out of his pipe. I remained
silent and avoided looking at him.

" It may have seemed strange to you," he continued, " that I
did not ask any satisfaction from that drunkard—that young fool
Rassinoff. You will admit that, I having the choice of weapons,
he was at my mercy, and that there was not much chance of his
killing me. I might call it generosity on my part, but I will not
lie about it. If I could have given Rassinoff a good lesson without
in any way risking my life, he would not have been rid of me so
easily."

I looked at Silvio in the greatest surprise. Such an admission
from him was astounding. He went on :

" As it is, unhappily, I have no right to risk my life. Six years
ago I received a blow, and the man who struck me is still alive."
This excited my curiosity to an unusual degree.

" You did not meet him? " I asked. " Surely some extraordinary circumstance must have prevented your doing so? "

" I did meet him," answered Silvio, " and here you see the
result of our encounter."

He rose and drew from a box near him a cap of red cloth with a
gilt braid and tassel, such as Frenchmen call *bonnet de police*.[1]
He put it on his head, and I saw that a bullet had pierced it about
an inch above the forehead.

" You know," said Silvio, " that I was in the Imperial Hussars,
and you also know what kind of a disposition I have. I like to

[1] A *bonnet de police* is a small cloth cap worn with undress uniform.

rule every one. Well, in my youth it was positively a passion with me. In my day brawlers were in fashion, and I was the foremost brawler of the regiment. To get drunk was then considered a thing to be proud of. I could outdrink the famous B——, celebrated in song by Davidoff. Every day brought its duel, and every day saw me either the principal actor in them or else taking the part of a second. My comrades looked up to me; and our superior officers, who were constantly being transferred, considered me a plague of which they could not be rid.

" As for me I kept on quietly—or, rather, riotously—in my glorious career, when one day a young fellow who was very wealthy and of good family was transferred to our regiment. I will not give you his name, but never have I met a fellow with such unheard-of luck. Imagine having youth, a fine figure, no end of spirits, a daring which is utterly indifferent to danger, a great name, and unlimited means to do with as one likes, and you may have a faint idea of the impression he created among us. My power was gone in an instant. At first, dazzled by my reputation, he tried to make friends with me, but I received his advances very coldly, seeing which he quietly dropped me without showing any annoyance whatever.

" I took such a dislike to him when I saw his popularity in the regiment, and his success with the ladies, that I was driven almost to despair. I tried to pick a quarrel with him, but to my sarcastic remarks he answered with caustic and unexpected wit that had the merit, besides, of being more cheerful than mine. He was always in jest, while I was in dead earnest. Finally, one night while at a ball in a Polish house, seeing how much the ladies admired him, especially our hostess, with whom I had been very friendly, I whispered in his ear some insulting remark, which I have long since forgotten. He turned around and struck me. We grasped our swords, some of the ladies fainted, and a few officers parted us. We went out immediately in order to fight it out right then and there.

" The three witnesses and myself reached the meeting-place, and I awaited the coming of my adversary with no ordinary impatience. The sun rose and its intense heat was being felt more and more every minute, when I finally saw him coming in the distance. He was on foot, and in his shirt-sleeves, carrying his uniform over his arm; he was attended by only one witness. I went forward to meet him, and I noticed that his cap, which he carried in his hand, was full of cherries. Our witnesses placed us twelve paces from each other. It was my privilege to shoot first, but with passion and hatred blinding me I feared my aim would be poor, and to gain time to steady my hand I offered to let him fire first. He refused to do so, and it was then agreed we should leave it to chance. Luck was, as usual, with this spoiled child of fortune. He fired and pierced my cap. It was then my turn, and I felt that he was at my mercy. I looked at him with eagerness, hoping to find him at least a little uneasy. Not at all, for there he stood within range of my pistol, coolly picking the ripest cherries out of his cap and blowing the pips in my direction, where they fell at my feet.

" ' What shall I gain,' thought I, ' by taking his life, when he thinks so little of it? '

" A diabolical thought crossed my mind. I unloaded a pistol.

" ' It seems,' I said, ' that you care very little whether you die or not at the present moment. You seem more anxious to breakfast instead. It shall be as you please. I have no wish to disturb you.'

" ' You will be kind enough to attend to your own business,' answered he, ' and please to fire; but, after all, you may do as you like. You can always fire your shot when and where you like. I shall always be at your call.'

" I went away with my witnesses, to whom I said that I did not care to shoot just then, and the thing ended there.

" I sent in my resignation, and retired to this out-of-the-way village. From that day to this I have thought of nothing but revenge. And now the time has come! "

Silvio drew from his pocket the letter received that morning. Some one, his lawyer, it seemed, had written from Moscow that the *person in question* was soon to be married to a young and pretty girl.

" You can guess, I have no doubt," said Silvio, " who is the *person in question*. I am leaving for Moscow, and we shall see if he will look at death in the midst of bridal festivities with as much coolness as he did when facing it with a pound of cherries in his cap! "

After saying these words he rose, and throwing his cap viciously on the floor, walked back and forth the length of the room like a caged tiger. I had listened to him without saying a word, stirred by very contradictory feelings.

A servant entered, saying the carriage was at the door. Silvio grasped my hand, which he shook with all his might. He entered a small open carriage in which were two boxes, one containing his pistols and the other his baggage. We said good-bye once more, and he was driven away.

## II

Years went by, and family matters compelled me to live in an obscure village in the district of Yerna. While looking after my interests I often sighed for the enjoyable life I had led until then. The long, solitary evenings of winter and spring were the hardest to bear. I could not become reconciled to their lonesomeness.

Until the dinner-hour I managed somehow to kill time by chatting with the landowner, visiting my workmen, and watching the new buildings being erected. But as soon as night came I was at a loss to know what to do. I knew by heart the few books I had found in the ancient bookcases and in the garret. All the stories known to my old housekeeper, Kirilovna, I had asked her to tell me over and over again, and the songs of the peasants saddened me. I drank everything at hand, until my head ached. I will even admit that at one time I thought I should become a drunkard from sheer desperation—the worst kind of drunkard—of which this district offered me a good many examples.

My nearest neighbours consisted of two or three of these confirmed inebriates, whose conversations were ever interspersed with sighs and hiccups, so that even complete solitude was to be preferred to their society. I finally got into the habit of dining as late as possible and retiring as early as I could afterward, and in that way I solved the problem of shortening the evenings and lengthening the days.

About four versts from my house was a beautiful estate belonging to the Countess Birovna. It was occupied by her steward, the countess herself never having lived in the place except for a month at one time, and that in the first year of her marriage.

One day, in the second year of this lonely existence of mine, I heard that the countess and her husband were to occupy their residence during the summer months. In the early part of June they arrived with all their household.

The coming of a rich neighbour is always an event in the life of country people. The owners of property, and their servants also, speak of it two months before they arrive, and it is still a topic of interest three years after they have left. For my part, the fact that a young and pretty woman would live so near upset me very much. I was dying to see her, and the first Sunday after they had settled I walked over, after dinner, to pay my respects to the lady and introduce myself as her nearest neighbour and devoted slave.

A footman led me to the count's library and left to announce me. This library was large and magnificently furnished. Against the walls were shelves filled with books, and on each one was a figure in bronze! above a marble mantelpiece stood a large mirror. The floor was covered with a green carpet, over which were thrown rich Persian rugs. Unused as I was in my hovel to any kind of luxury, it was so long since I had seen anything like this display of wealth that I actually felt timid and experienced inward tremblings while waiting for the count—such nervousness as a country solicitor might feel when asking an audience of a minister. The door opened and a young man about thirty-two years of age entered. He greeted me in a most cordial and charming manner. I tried to appear at ease, and was going to make the usual commonplace remarks about being delighted at having such neighbours, when he forestalled me by saying how welcome I was.

We sat down and his manner was so cordial that it soon dispelled my unusual timidity. I was just beginning to feel like myself again when the countess appeared in the doorway, and once more I grew desperately shy. She was a beauty. The count introduced me, and the more I tried to be natural and quite at ease, the more I looked awkward and embarrassed. My hosts, in order to give me time to recover from my bashfulness, chatted together as if to show that they already considered me an old acquaintance and one to be treated as such, so that while walking about the library I looked at the books and pictures. So far as pictures are concerned I am no connoisseur, but there was one there that attracted my attention. It represented a Swiss scene, and the beauty of the landscape did not attract me quite as much as did the fact that the canvas was pierced by two bullets, evidently fired one over the other.

" That is a pretty good shot! " I cried, turning to the count.

" Yes," said he, " and rather a peculiar one. Are you a pistol-shot? " he added.

" Why, yes, a fairly good one," I answered, delighted to have a chance to speak of something with which I was familiar. " I think I could hit a card at thirty paces—with my own pistols, of course."

" Really? " said the countess, seeming much interested. " And you, my dear "—this to her husband—" could you hit a card at thirty paces? "

" I don't know about that," answered the count, " but I was a pretty good shot in my day, though it must be four years now since I used a pistol."

" In that case, sir," I continued, " I'll bet you anything that even at twenty paces you could not hit a card; because to excel at pistol-shooting constant practice is necessary. I know this from experience. At home I was considered one of the best shots in the regiment, but it happened once that I was a month without using a pistol, mine being at the gunsmith's. We were called to the shooting-gallery one day, and what do you think happened to me, sir? I missed a bottle standing twenty-five paces away four times in succession. There was with us, at the time, a major of cavalry, a good fellow, who was for ever joking: ' Faith, my friend,' he said to me, ' this is too much moderation. You have too great a respect for the bottle.' Believe me, sir, one must practise all the time. Otherwise one gets rusty. The best marksman I ever knew practised every day, firing at least three shots before his dinner; he would have no more missed them than he would have omitted his cognac before eating."

Both the count and his wife seemed pleased to listen to me.

" And how did he shoot? " asked the count.

" How? Let me tell you. He would see a fly on the wall.

You laugh! Madame, I swear to you, this is true. ' Eh, Kouska! a pistol! ' Kouska would bring one loaded. Crack! there lay the fly flattened against the wall.''

" What consummate skill! " cried the count. " And what was this man's name? "

" Silvio, sir.''

" Silvio? " cried the count, starting to his feet. " You have known Silvio? "

" Have I known him? Well, rather. We were the greatest of friends; he was like one of us in the regiment. But it is now five years since I heard of him. And you, also, knew him? "

" Yes, I knew him well. Did he ever tell you a peculiar thing which happened to him once? "

" How he received a slap in the face one evening from a cad? "

" And did he tell you the name of this cad? "

" No, sir, he did not. Ah! " I cried, guessing at the truth. " Forgive me, sir, I did not know. Can it be you? "

" Yes, it was I," answered the count, in an embarrassed manner, " and that picture with a hole in it is the souvenir of our last interview.''

" For God's sake, my dear," said the countess, " don't speak of it. The thought of it terrifies me to this day.''

" No," said the count, " I feel I ought to tell this gentleman. He knows how I offended his friend, and it is only fair that he should learn how he revenged himself.''

The count drew up an armchair for me to sit in, and I listened with the greatest interest to the following story:

" Five years ago we were married. We spent the first month of our honeymoon here in this house, and to it clings the memory of the happiest days of my life, coupled with one of the most painful experiences I have ever had.

" One evening we had both gone out riding. My wife's horse became very restless, and she was so frightened that she begged me to lead him to the stables and she would walk back by herself. On reaching the house I found a travelling-coach at the door, and was told that a man was waiting in the library. He had refused to give his name, saying he wished to see me on business. I came into this room, and in the half-light I saw a man with a beard standing before the mantelpiece, still in his dusty travelling-clothes. I drew nearer to him, trying to place him in my memory.

" ' You do not remember me, count? ' said he, in a voice that shook.

" ' Silvio! ' I cried.

" And, to be candid with you, I felt as if my hair were standing on end.

" ' Exactly,' he continued, ' and it is my turn to shoot. I have come to fire. Are you ready? '

"I saw a pistol sticking out of his left pocket. I measured twelve paces, and stood there in that corner, begging him to be quick about it, as my wife would return in a few moments. He said he wanted a light first, and I rang for candles.

"I closed the door, after giving instructions not to admit any one, and once more I told him to proceed. He raised his pistol and took aim. I was counting the seconds. I was thinking of her. All this lasted a full minute, and suddenly Silvio lowered his weapon.

"'I am very sorry,' he said, ' but my pistol is not loaded with cherry-pips, and bullets are hard. After all, come to think of it, this does not look much like a duel. It is more like a murder. I am not in the habit of firing on an unarmed man. Let us begin all over again. Let us draw lots to see who will shoot first.'

"My head was in a whirl, and it turned out that I at first refused. Finally, we loaded our pistols, and put two pieces of paper in the very cap I had once perforated with a bullet. I took one of the pieces; and, as luck would have it, I drew number one.

"You are devilish lucky, count!' said he, with a smile I will never forget.

"I cannot to this day understand it, but he finally compelled me to fire, and my bullet hit that picture there."

The count pointed to the landscape with the hole in it. His face was crimson. There was the countess, as white as a sheet, and as for me, I barely suppressed a cry.

"I fired at him," continued the count, "and, thank God, I missed him."

"Then Silvio—at that moment he was positively hideous— stood back and took aim. Just then the door opened. My wife came in, and seeing us facing each other, threw herself in my arms. Her presence gave me back my courage.

"'My dear,' I said, ' do you not see we are only jesting? How frightened you are! Go, now, get a glass of water, and come back to us. I will then introduce my old friend and comrade to you.'

"But my wife knew better than to believe my words.

"'Tell me, is what my husband says true?' she asked the terrible Silvio. 'Is it true that this is only a jest?'

"'He is always jesting, madam,' replied Silvio. 'Once upon a time he gave me a slap in jest; again, in jest, he pierced my cap with a bullet; and a few minutes ago, still jesting, he just missed me. Now it is my turn to laugh a little.'

"Saying which, he took aim once more, with my wife looking on. She fell on her knees at his feet.

"'Get up, Macha,' I cried, enraged. 'Are you not ashamed of yourself? And you, sir, do you wish to drive this poor woman crazy? Will you please fire—yes or no?'

"'I will not,' answered Silvio. 'I am satisfied. I saw you falter. You were pale with fright, and that is all I hoped to see.

I compelled you to fire on me, and I know you will never forget me. I leave you to your conscience.'

" He walked toward the door; and, turning round, he glanced at the picture with the bullet-hole, and without aiming at all he fired and doubled my shot. Then he went out. My wife fainted—none of the servants dared stop him, and the doors opened before him in great haste. In the porch he called for his carriage; and he was already some distance away when I recovered from my bewilderment."

The count stopped.

It was thus I heard the end of a story, the beginning of which had interested me much. I never saw Silvio again. It was said that at the time of the insurrection of Alexander Ypsilanti he was at the head of a regiment of rebels, and that he was killed when the enemy was routed at Skouliani.

# THE SNOW-STORM

## Alexander S. Pushkin

Towards the end of 1811, at a memorable period for Russians, lived on his own domain of Nenaradova the kind-hearted Gavril R. He was celebrated in the whole district for his hospitality and his genial character. Neighbours constantly visited him to have something to eat and drink, and to play at five-copeck boston with his wife, Praskovia. Some, too, went to have a look at their daughter, Maria, a tall pale girl of seventeen. She was an heiress, and they desired her either for themselves or for their sons.

Maria had been brought up on French novels, and consequently was in love. The object of her affection was a poor ensign in the army, who was now at home in his small village on leave of absence. As a matter of course the young man reciprocated Maria's passion. But the parents of his beloved, noticing their mutual attachment, forbade their daughter even to think of him, while they received him worse than an ex-assize judge.

Our lovers corresponded and met alone daily in the pine wood or by the old roadway chapel. There they vowed everlasting love, inveighed against fate, and exchanged various suggestions. Writing and talking in this way, they quite naturally reached the following conclusion: —

If we cannot exist apart from each other, and if the tyranny of hard-hearted parents throws obstacles in the way of our happiness, then can we not manage without them?

Of course this happy idea originated in the mind of the young man; but it pleased immensely the romantic imagination of Maria.

Winter set in and put a stop to their meetings. But their correspondence became all the more active. Vladimir begged Maria in every letter to give herself up to him that they might get married secretly, hide for a while, and then throw themselves at the feet of their parents, who would of course in the end be touched by their heroic constancy and say to them, " Children, come to our arms! "

Maria hesitated a long while, and out of many different plans proposed, that of flight was for a time rejected. At last, however, she consented. On the appointed day she was to decline supper and retire to her room under the plea of a headache. She and her maid, who was in the secret, were then to go out into the garden by the back stairs, and beyond the garden they would find a sledge ready for them, would get into it and drive a distance of five miles from Nenaradova, to the village of Jadrino, straight to the church, where Vladimir would be waiting for them.

On the eve of the decisive day Maria did not sleep all night; she was packing and tying up linen and dresses. She wrote, moreover, a long letter to a friend of hers, a sentimental young lady; and another to her parents. Of the latter she took leave in the most touching terms. She excused the step she was taking by reason of the unconquerable power of love, and wound up by declaring that she should consider it the happiest moment of her life when she was allowed to throw herself at the feet of her dearest parents. Sealing both letters with a Toula seal, on which were engraven two flaming hearts with an appropriate inscription, she at last threw herself upon her bed before daybreak and dozed off, though even then she was awakened from one moment to another by terrible thoughts. First it seemed to her that at the moment of entering the sledge in order to go and get married her father stopped her, and with cruel rapidity dragged her over the snow and threw her into a dark bottomless cellar—down which she fell headlong with an indescribable sinking of the heart. Then she saw Vladimir, lying on the grass, pale and bleeding; with his dying breath he implored her to make haste and marry him. Other hideous and senseless visions floated before her one after another. Finally she rose paler than usual and with a real headache.

Both her father and her mother remarked Maria's indisposition. Their tender anxiety and constant inquiries, " What is the matter with you, Masha—are you ill? " cut her to the heart. She tried to pacify them and to appear cheerful; but she could not. Evening set in. The idea that she was passing the day for the last time in the midst of her family oppressed her. In her secret heart she took leave of everybody, of everything which surrounded her.

Supper was served; her heart beat violently. In a trembling

voice she declared that she did not want any supper, and wished her father and mother good-night. They kissed her, and as usual blessed her; and she nearly wept.

Reaching her own room she threw herself into an easy-chair and burst into tears. Her maid begged her to be calm and take courage. Everything was ready. In half an hour Maria would leave for ever her parents' house, her own room, her peaceful life as a young girl.

Out of doors the snow was falling, the wind howling. The shutters rattled and shook. In everything she seemed to recognise omens and threats.

Soon the whole home was quiet and asleep. Maria wrapped herself in a shawl, put on a warm cloak, and, with a box in her hand, passed out on to the back staircase. The maid carried two bundles after her. They descended into the garden. The snow-storm raged; a strong wind blew against them, as if trying to stop the young culprit. With difficulty they reached the end of the garden. In the road a sledge awaited them.

The horses, from cold, would not stand still. Vladimir's coachman was walking to and fro in front of them, trying to quiet them. He helped the young lady and her maid to their seats, and packing away the bundles and the dressing-case, took up the reins, and the horses flew forward into the darkness of the night.

Having entrusted the young lady to the care of fate and of Tereshka the coachman, let us return to the young lover.

Vladimir had spent the whole day in driving. In the morning he had called on the Jadrino priest, and, with difficulty, came to terms with him. Then he went to seek for witnesses from amongst the neighbouring gentry. The first on whom he called was a former cornet of horse, Dravin by name, a man in his forties, who consented at once. The adventure, he declared, reminded him of old times and of his larks when he was in the Hussars. He persuaded Vladimir to stop to dinner with him, assuring him that there would be no difficulty in getting the other two witnesses. Indeed, immediately after dinner in came the surveyor Schmidt, with a moustache and spurs, and the son of a captain-magistrate, a boy of sixteen, who had recently entered the Uhlans. They not only accepted Vladimir's proposal, but even swore that they were ready to sacrifice their lives for him. Vladimir embraced them with delight, and drove off to get everything ready.

It had long been dark. Vladimir despatched his trustworthy Tereshka to Nenaradova with his two-horsed sledge, and with appropriate instructions for the occasion. For himself he ordered the small sledge with one horse, and started alone without a coachman for Jadrino, where Maria ought to arrive in a couple of hours. He knew the road, and the drive would only occupy twenty minutes.

But Vladimir had scarcely passed from the enclosure into the open field when the wind rose, and soon there was a driving snowstorm so heavy and so severe that he could not see. In a moment the road was covered with snow. All landmarks disappeared in the murky yellow darkness, through which fell white flakes of snow. Sky and earth became merged into one. Vladimir, in the midst of the field, tried in vain to get to the road. The horse walked on at random, and every moment stepped either into deep snow or into a rut, so that the sledge was constantly upsetting. Vladimir tried at least not to lose the right direction; but it seemed to him that more than half an hour had passed, and he had not yet reached the Jadrino wood. Another ten minutes passed, and still the wood was invisible. Vladimir drove across fields intersected by deep ditches. The snow-storm did not abate, and the sky did not clear. The horse was getting tired and the perspiration rolled from him like hail, in spite of the fact that every moment his legs were disappearing in the snow.

At last Vladimir found that he was going in the wrong direction. He stopped; began to reflect, recollect, and consider; till at last he became convinced that he ought to have turned to the right. He did so now. His horse could scarcely drag along. But he had been more than an hour on the road, and Jadrino could not now be far. He drove and drove, but there was no getting out of the field. Still snow-drifts and ditches. Every moment the sledge was upset, and every moment Vladimir had to raise it up.

Time was slipping by; and Vladimir grew seriously anxious. At last in the distance some dark object could be seen.

Vladimir turned in its direction, and as he drew near found it was a wood.

" Thank Heaven," he thought, " I am now near the end."

He drove by the side of the wood, hoping to come at once upon the familiar road, or, if not, to pass round the wood. Jadrino was situated immediately behind it.

He soon found the road, and passed into the darkness of the wood, now stripped by the winter. The wind could not rage here; the road was smooth, the horse picked up courage, and Vladimir was comforted.

He drove and drove, but still Jadrino was not to be seen; there was no end to the wood. Then, to his horror, he discovered that he had got into a strange wood! He was in despair. He whipped his horse, and the poor animal started off at a trot. But it soon got tired, and in a quarter of an hour, in spite of all poor Vladimir's efforts, could only crawl.

Gradually the trees became thinner, and Vladimir drove out of the wood; but Jadrino was not to be seen. It must have been about midnight. Tears gushed from the young man's eyes. He drove on at random; and now the weather abated, the clouds dis-

persed, and before him was a wide stretch of plain covered with a
white billowy carpet. The night was comparatively clear, and he
could see a small village a short distance off, which consisted of
four or five cottages. Vladimir drove towards it. At the first door
he jumped out of the sledge, ran up to the window, and tapped.

After a few minutes a wooden shutter was raised, and an old
man stuck out his grey beard.

" What do you want? "

" How far is Jadrino? "

" How far is Jadrino? "

" Yes, yes! Is it far? "

" Not far; about ten miles."

At this answer Vladimir clutched hold of his hair, and stood
motionless, like a man condemned to death.

" Where do you come from? " added the man. Vladimir had
not the courage to reply.

" My man," he said, " can you procure me horses to Jadrino? "

" We have no horses," answered the peasant.

" Could I find a guide? I will pay him any sum he likes."

" Stop! " said the old man, dropping the shutter; " I will send
my son out to you; he will conduct you."

Vladimir waited. Scarcely a minute had passed when he again
knocked. The shutter was lifted, and a beard was seen.

" What do you want? "

" What about your son? "

" He'll come out directly: he is putting on his boots. Are you
cold? Come in and warm yourself."

" Thanks; send out your son quickly."

The gate creaked; a youth came out with a cudgel, and walked
on in front, at one time pointing out the road, at another looking
for it in a mass of drifted snow.

" What o'clock is it? " Vladimir asked him.

" It will soon be daylight," replied the young peasant. Vladimir
spoke not another word.

The cocks were crowing, and it was light when they reached
Jadrino. The church was closed. Vladimir paid the guide, and
drove into the yard of the priest's house. In the yard his two-
horsed sledge was not to be seen. What news awaited him!

But let us return to the kind proprietors of Nenaradova, and see
what is going on there.

Nothing.

The old people awoke, and went into the sitting-room, Gavril in
a night-cap and flannel jacket, Praskovia in a wadded dressing-
gown. The samovar was brought in, and Gavril sent the little
maid to ask Maria how she was and how she had slept. The little
maid returned, saying that her young lady had slept badly, but that

she was better now, and that she would come into the sitting-room in a moment. And indeed the door opened and Maria came in and wished her papa and mamma good morning.

" How is your headache, Masha? " (familiar to Mary) inquired Gavril.

" Better, papa," answered Masha.

" The fumes from the stoves must have given you your head-ache," remarked Praskovia.

" Perhaps so, mamma," replied Masha.

The day passed well enough, but in the night Masha was taken ill. A doctor was sent for from town. He came towards evening and found the patient delirious. Soon she was in a severe fever, and in a fortnight the poor patient was on the brink of the grave.

No member of the family knew anything of the flight from home. The letters written by Masha the evening before had been burnt; and the maid, fearing the wrath of the master and mistress, had not breathed a word. The priest, the ex-cornet, the big mous-tached surveyor, and the little lancer were equally discreet, and with good reason. Tereshka, the coachman, never said too much, not even in his drink. Thus the secret was kept better than it might have been by half a dozen conspirators.

But Maria herself, in the course of her long fever, let out her secret. Nevertheless, her words were so disconnected that her mother, who never left her bedside, could only make out from them that her daughter was desperately in love with Vladimir, and that probably love was the cause of her illness. She consulted her husband and some of her neighbours, and at last it was decided unanimously that the fate of Maria ought not to be interfered with, that a woman must not ride away from the man she is destined to marry, that poverty is no crime, that a woman has to live not with money but with a man, and so on. Moral proverbs are wonderfully useful on such occasions, when we can invent little or nothing in our own justification.

Meanwhile the young lady began to recover. Vladimir had not been seen for a long time in the house of Gavril, so frightened had he been by his previous reception. It was now resolved to send and announce to him the good news which he could scarcely expect; the consent of her parents to his marriage with Maria.

But what was the astonishment of the proprietors of Nenaradova when, in answer to their invitation, they received an insane reply. Vladimir informed them he could never set foot in their house, and begged them to forget an unhappy man whose only hope now was in death. A few days afterwards they heard that Vladimir had left the place and joined the army.

A long time passed before they ventured to tell Masha, who was now recovering. She never mentioned Vladimir. Some months later, however, finding his name in the list of those who had dis-

tinguished themselves and been severely wounded at Borodino, she
fainted, and it was feared that the fever might return.    But,
Heaven be thanked! the fainting fit had no bad results.

Maria experienced yet another sorrow.    Her father died, leaving
her the heiress of all his property.    But the inheritance could not
console her.    She shared sincerely the affliction of her mother, and
vowed she would never leave her.

Suitors clustered round the charming heiress; but she gave no
one the slightest hope.    Her mother sometimes tried to persuade
her to choose a companion in life; but Maria shook her head, and
grew pensive.

Vladimir no longer existed.    He had died at Moscow on the eve
of the arrival of the French.    His memory was held sacred by
Maria, and she treasured up everything that would remind her of
him : books he had read, drawings which he had made, songs he
had sung, and the pieces of poetry which he had copied out for her.

The neighbours, hearing all this, wondered at her fidelity, and
awaited with curiosity the arrival of the hero who must in the end
triumph over the melancholy constancy of this virgin Artemis.

Meanwhile the war had been brought to a glorious conclusion,
and our armies were returning from abroad.    The people ran to
meet them.    The music played by the regimental bands consisted
of war songs, " Vive Henri-Quatre," Tirolese waltzes and airs from
Joconde.    Nourished on the atmosphere of winter, officers who
had started on the campaign mere striplings, returned grown men,
and covered with decorations.    The soldiers conversed gaily among
themselves, mingling German and French words every moment in
their speech.    A time never to be forgotten—a time of glory and
delight!    How quickly beat the Russian heart at the words,
" Native land! "    How sweet the tears of meeting!    With what
unanimity did we combine feelings of national pride with love for
the Tsar!    And for him, what a moment!

The women—our Russian women—were splendid then.    Their
usual coldness disappeared.    Their delight was really intoxicating
when, meeting the conquerors, they cried, " Hurrah! "    And they
threw up their caps in the air.

Who of the officers of that period does not own that to the
Russian women he was indebted for his best and most valued
reward?    During this brilliant period Maria was living with her
mother in retirement, and neither of them saw how, in both the
capitals, the returning troops were welcomed.    But in the districts
and villages the general enthusiasm was, perhaps, even greater.
In these places the appearance of an officer became for him a
veritable triumph.    The accepted lover in plain clothes fared badly
by his side.

We have already said that, in spite of her coldness, Maria was still, as before, surrounded by suitors. But all had to fall in the rear when there arrived at his castle the wounded young captain of Hussars—Bourmin by name—with the order of St. George in his button-hole, and an interesting pallor on his face. He was about twenty-six. He had come home on leave to his estates, which were close to Maria's villa. Maria paid him such attention as none of the others received. In his presence her habitual gloom disappeared. It could not be said that she flirted with him. But a poet, observing her behaviour, might have asked, " S' amor non è, che dunque? "

Bourmin was really a very agreeable young man. He possessed just the kind of sense that pleased women: a sense of what is suitable and becoming. He had no affectation, and was carelessly satirical. His manner towards Maria was simple and easy. He seemed to be of a quiet and modest disposition; but rumour said that he had at one time been terribly wild. This, however, did not harm him in the opinion of Maria, who (like all young ladies) excused, with pleasure, vagaries which were the result of impulsiveness and daring.

But above all—more than his love-making, more than his pleasant talk, more than his interesting pallor, more even than his bandaged arm—the silence of the young Hussar excited her curiosity and her imagination. She could not help confessing to herself that he pleased her very much. Probably he too, with his acuteness and his experience, had seen that he interested her. How was it, then, that up to this moment she had not seen him at her feet; had not received from him any declaration whatever? And wherefore did she not encourage him with more attention, and, according to circumstances, even with tenderness? Had she a secret of her own which would account for her behaviour?

At last Bourmin fell into such deep meditation, and his black eyes rested with such fire upon Maria, that the decisive moment seemed very near. The neighbours spoke of the marriage as an accomplished fact, and kind Praskovia rejoiced that her daughter had at last found for herself a worthy mate. The lady was sitting alone once in the drawing-room, laying out grande-patience, when Bourmin entered the room, and at once inquired for Maria.

" She is in the garden," replied the old lady: " go to her, and I will wait for you here." Bourmin went, and the old lady made the sign of the cross and thought, " Perhaps the affair will be settled to-day! "

Bourmin found Maria in the ivy-bower beside the pond, with a book in her hands, and wearing a white dress—a veritable heroine of romance. After the first inquiries Maria purposely let the conversation drop; increasing by these means the mutual embarrassment, from which it was only possible to escape by means of a sudden and positive declaration. It happened thus. Bourmin, feeling the awkwardness of his position, informed Maria that he had long sought an opportunity of opening his heart to her, and that he begged for a moment's attention. Maria closed the book and lowered her eyes, as a sign that she was listening.

" I love you," said Bourmin, " I love you passionately! " Maria blushed and bent her head still lower.

" I have behaved imprudently, yielding as I have done to the seductive pleasure of seeing and hearing you daily." Maria recollected the first letter of St. Preux in *La Nouvelle Héloïse.* " It is too late now to resist my fate. The remembrance of you, your dear incomparable image, must from to-day be at once the torment and the consolation of my existence. I have now a terrible secret to disclose, which will place between us an insurmountable barrier."

" It has always existed! " interrupted Maria; " I could never have been your wife."

" I know," he replied quickly; " I know that you once loved. But death and three years of mourning may have worked some change. Dear, kind Maria, do not try to deprive me of my last consolation; the idea that you might have consented to make me happy if——. Don't speak, for God's sake don't speak—you torture me. Yes, I know, I feel that you could have been mine, but—I am the most miserable of beings—I am already married! "

Maria looked at him in astonishment.

" I am married," continued Bourmin; " I have been married more than three years, and do not know who my wife is, or where she is, or whether I shall ever see her again."

" What are you saying? " exclaimed Maria; " how strange! Pray continue."

" In the beginning of 1812," said Bourmin, " I was hurrying on to Wilna, where my regiment was stationed. Arriving one evening late at a station, I ordered the horses to be got ready quickly, when suddenly a fearful snow-storm broke out. Both stationmaster and drivers advised me to wait till it was over. I listened to their advice, but an unaccountable restlessness took possession of me, just as though some one was pushing me on. Meanwhile, the snow-storm did not abate. I could bear it no longer, and again ordered the horses, and started in the midst of the storm. The driver took it into his head to drive along the river, which would shorten the distance by three miles. The banks were covered with snowdrifts; the driver missed the turning which would have brought us out on to the road, and we turned up in an unknown place. The storm never ceased. I could discern a light, and told the driver to make for it. We entered a village, and found that the light proceeded from a wooden church. The church was open. Outside the railings stood several sledges, and people were passing in and out through the porch.

" ' Here! here! ' cried several voices. I told the coachman to drive up. ' Where have you dawdled? ' said some one to me. ' The bride has fainted; the priest does not know what to do; we were on the point of going back. Make haste and get out! '

" I got out of the sledge in silence, and stepped into the church, which was dimly lighted with two or three tapers. A girl was sitting in a dark corner on a bench; another girl was rubbing her temples. ' Thank God,' said the latter, ' you have come at last! You have nearly been the death of the young lady.'

" The old priest approached me, saying, ' Shall I begin? '

" ' Begin—begin, reverend father,' I replied, absently.

" The young lady was raised up. I thought her rather pretty. Oh, wild, unpardonable frivolity! I placed myself by her side at the altar. The priest hurried on. Three men and the maid supported the bride, and occupied themselves with her alone. We were married!

" ' Kiss your wife,' said the priest.

" My wife turned her pale face towards me. I was going to kiss her, when she exclaimed, ' Oh! it is not he—not he! ' and fell back insensible. The witnesses stared at me. I turned round and left the church without any attempt being made to stop me, threw myself into the sledge, and cried, ' Away! ' ' "

" What! " exclaimed Maria. " And you don't know what became of your unhappy wife? "

" I do not," replied Bourmin; " neither do I know the name of the village where I was married, nor that of the station from which I started. At that time I thought so little of my wicked joke that, on driving away from the church, I fell asleep, and never woke till early the next morning, after reaching the third station. The servant who was with me died during the campaign, so that I have now no hope of ever discovering the unhappy woman on whom I played such a cruel trick, and who is now so cruelly avenged."

" Great heavens! " cried Maria, seizing his hand. " Then it was you, and you do not recognise me? "

Bourmin turned pale—and threw himself at her feet.

# THE QUEEN OF SPADES

### Alexander S. Pushkin

I

There was a card party at the rooms of Naroumoff, a lieutenant in the Horse Guards. A long winter night had passed unnoticed, and it was five o'clock in the morning when supper was served. The winners sat down to table with an excellent appetite; the losers let their plates remain empty before them. Little by little, however, with the assistance of the champagne, the conversation became animated, and was shared by all.

" How did you get on this evening, Surin? " said the host to one of his friends.

" Oh, I lost, as usual. I really have no luck. I play *mirandole*. You know that I keep cool. Nothing moves me; I never change my play, and yet I always lose."

"Do you mean to say that all the evening you did not once back the red? Your firmness of character surprises me."

" What do you think of Hermann? " said one of the party, pointing to a young Engineer officer. " That fellow never made a bet or touched a card in his life, and yet he watches us playing until five in the morning."

" It interests me," said Hermann; " but I am not disposed to risk the necessary in view of the superfluous."

" Hermann is a German, and economical; that is the whole of the secret," cried Tomski. " But what is really astonishing is the Countess Anna Fedorovna! "

" How so? " asked several voices.

" Have you not remarked," said Tomski, " that she never plays? "

" Yes," said Naroumoff, " a woman of eighty, who never touches a card; that is indeed something extraordinary! "

" You do not know why? "

" No; is there a reason for it? "

" Just listen. My grandmother, you know, some sixty years ago, went to Paris, and became the rage there. People ran after her in the streets, and called her the ' Muscovite Venus.' Richelieu made love to her, and my grandmother makes out that, by her rigorous demeanour, she almost drove him to suicide. In those days women used to play at faro. One evening at the Court she lost, on *parole*, to the Duke of Orleans, a very considerable sum.

When she got home, my grandmother removed her beauty spots, took off her hoops, and in this tragic costume went to my grandfather, told him of her misfortune, and asked him for the money she had to pay. My grandfather, now no more, was, so to say, his wife's steward. He feared her like fire; but the sum she named made him leap into the air. He flew into a rage, made a brief calculation, and proved to my grandmother that in six months she had got through half a million roubles. He told her plainly that he had no villages to sell in Paris, his domains being situated in the neighbourhood of Moscow and of Saratoff; and finally refused point blank. You may imagine the fury of my grandmother. She boxed his ears, and passed the night in another room.

" The next day she returned to the charge. For the first time in her life, she condescended to arguments and explanations. In vain did she try to prove to her husband that there were debts and debts, and that she could not treat a Prince of the blood like her coachmaker.

" All this eloquence was lost. My grandfather was inflexible. My grandmother did not know where to turn. Happily she was acquainted with a man who was very celebrated at this time. You have heard of the Count of St. Germain, about whom so many marvellous stories were told. You know that he passed for a sort of Wandering Jew, and that he was said to possess an elixir of life and the philosopher's stone.

" Some people laughed at him as a charlatan. Casanova, in his memoirs, says that he was a spy. However that may be, in spite of the mystery of his life, St. Germain was much sought after in good society, and was really an agreeable man. Even to this day my grandmother has preserved a genuine affection for him, and she becomes quite angry when any one speaks of him with disrespect.

" It occurred to her that he might be able to advance the sum of which she was in need, and she wrote a note begging him to call. The old magician came at once, and found her plunged in the deepest despair. In two or three words she told him everything; related to him her misfortune and the cruelty of her husband, adding that she had no hope except in his friendship and his obliging disposition.

" ' Madam,' said St. Germain, after a few moments' reflection, ' I could easily advance you the money you want, but I am sure that you would have no rest until you had repaid me, and I do not want to get you out of one trouble in order to place you in another. There is another way of settling the matter. You must regain the money you have lost.'

" ' But, my dear friend,' answered my grandmother, ' I have already told you that I have nothing left.'

" ' That does not matter,' answered St. Germain. ' Listen to me, and I will explain.'

" He then communicated to her a secret which any of you would, I am sure, give a good deal to possess."

All the young officers gave their full attention. Tomski stopped to light his Turkish pipe, swallowed a mouthful of smoke, and then went on.

" That very evening my grandmother went to Versailles to play at the Queen's table. The Duke of Orleans held the bank. My grandmother invented a little story by way of excuse for not having paid her debt, and then sat down at the table, and began to stake. She took three cards. She won with the first; doubled her stake on the second, and won again; doubled on the third, and still won."

" Mere luck! " said one of the young officers.

" What a tale! " cried Hermann.

" Were the cards marked? " said a third.

" I don't think so," replied Tomski gravely.

" And you mean to say," exclaimed Naroumoff, " that you have a grandmother who knows the names of three winning cards, and you have never made her tell them to you? "

" That is the very deuce of it," answered Tomski. " She had three sons, of whom my father was one; all three were determined gamblers, and not one of them was able to extract her secret from her, though it would have been of immense advantage to them, and to me also. Listen to what my uncle told me about it, Count Ivan Ilitch, and he told me on his word of honour.

" Tchaplitzki—the one you remember who died in poverty after devouring millions—lost one day, when he was a young man, to Zoritch about three hundred thousand roubles. He was in despair. My grandmother, who had no mercy for the extravagance of young men, made an exception—I do not know why—in favour of Tchaplitzki. She gave him three cards, telling him to play them one after the other, and exacting from him at the same time his word of honour that he would never afterwards touch a card as long as he lived. Accordingly Tchaplitzki went to Zoritch and staked for his revenge. On the first card he staked fifty thousand roubles. He won, doubled the stake, and won again. Continuing his system he ended by gaining more than he had lost.

" But it is six o'clock! It is really time to go to bed."

Every one emptied his glass and the party broke up.

## II

The old Countess Anna Fedorovna was in her dressing-room, seated before her looking-glass. Three maids were in attendance. One held her pot of rouge, another a box of black pins, a third an enormous lace cap, with flaming ribbons. The Countess had no longer the slightest pretence to beauty, but she preserved all the habits of her youth. She dressed in the style of fifty years before, and gave as much time and attention to her toilet as a fashionable beauty of the last century. Her companion was working at a frame in a corner of the window.

"Good morning, grandmother," said the young officer, as he entered the dressing-room. "Good morning, Mademoiselle Lise. Grandmother, I have come to ask you a favour."

"What is it, Paul?"

"I want to introduce to you one of my friends, and to ask you to give him an invitation to your ball."

"Bring him to the ball and introduce him to me there. Did you go yesterday to the Princess's?"

"Certainly. It was delightful! We danced until five o'clock in the morning. Mademoiselle Eletzki was charming."

"My dear nephew, you are really not difficult to please. As to beauty, you should have seen her grandmother, the Princess Daria Petrovna. But she must be very old, the Princess Daria Petrovna!"

"How do you mean old?" cried Tomski thoughtlessly; "she died seven years ago."

The young lady who acted as companion raised her head and made a sign to the officer, who then remembered that it was an understood thing to conceal from the Princess the death of any of her contemporaries. He bit his lips. The Countess, however, was not in any way disturbed on hearing that her old friend was no longer in this world.

"Dead!" she said, "and I never knew it! We were maids of honour in the same year, and when we were presented, the Empress"—and the old Countess related for the hundredth time an anecdote of her young days. "Paul," she said, as she finished her story, "help me to get up. Lisabeta, where is my snuff-box?"

And, followed by the three maids, she went behind a great screen to finish her toilet. Tomski was now alone with the companion.

"Who is the gentleman you wish to introduce to madame?" asked Lisabeta.

"Naroumoff. Do you know him?"

"No. Is he in the army?"

"Yes."

"In the Engineers?"

"No, in the Horse Guards. Why did you think he was in the Engineers?"

The young lady smiled, but made no answer.

"Paul," cried the Countess from behind the screen, "send me a new novel; no matter what. Only see that it is not in the style of the present day."

"What style would you like, grandmother?"

"A novel in which the hero strangles neither his father nor his mother, and in which no one gets drowned. Nothing frightens me so much as the idea of getting drowned."

" But how is it possible to find you such a book? Do you want it in Russian? "

" Are there any novels in Russian? However, send me something or other. You won't forget? "

" I will not forget, grandmother. I am in a great hurry. Good-bye, Lisabeta. What made you fancy Naroumoff was in the Engineers? " and Tomski took his departure.

Lisabeta, left alone, took out her embroidery, and sat down close to the window. Immediately afterwards, in the street, at the corner of a neighbouring house, appeared a young officer. The sight of him made the companion blush to her ears. She lowered her head, and almost concealed it in the linen. At this moment the Countess returned, fully dressed.

" Lisabeta," she said, " have the horses put in; we will go out for a drive."

Lisabeta rose from her chair, and began to arrange her embroidery.

" Well, my dear child, are you deaf? Go and tell them to put the horses in at once."

" I am going," replied the young lady, as she went out into the ante-chamber.

A servant now came in, bringing some books from Prince Paul Alexandrovitch.

" Say I am much obliged to him. Lisabeta! Lisabeta! Where has she run off to? "

" I was going to dress."

" We have plenty of time, my dear. Sit down, take the first volume, and read to me."

The companion took the book and read a few lines.

" Louder," said the Countess. " What is the matter with you? Have you a cold? Wait a moment, bring me that stool. A little closer; that will do."

Lisabeta read two pages of the book.

" Throw that stupid book away," said the Countess. " What nonsense! Send it back to Prince Paul, and tell him I am much obliged to him; and the carriage, is it never coming? "

" Here it is," replied Lisabeta, going to the window.

" And now you are not dressed. Why do you always keep me waiting? It is intolerable! "

Lisabeta ran to her room. She had scarcely been there two minutes when the Countess rang with all her might. Her maids rushed in at one door and her valet at the other.

" You do not seem to hear me when I ring," she cried. " Go and tell Lisabeta that I am waiting for her."

At this moment Lisabeta entered, wearing a new walking dress and a fashionable bonnet.

" At last miss," cried the Countess. " But what is that you

have got on? and why? For whom are you dressing? What sort of weather is it? Quite stormy, I believe."

" No, your Excellency," said the valet; " it is exceedingly fine."

" What do you know about it? Open the ventilator. Just what I told you! A frightful wind, and as icy as can be. Unharness the horses. Lisabeta, my child, we will not go out to-day. It was scarcely worth while to dress so much."

" What an existence! " said the companion to herself.

Lisabeta Ivanovna was, in fact, a most unhappy creature. " The bread of the stranger is bitter," says Dante, " and his staircase hard to climb." But who can tell the torments of a poor little companion attached to an old lady of quality? The Countess had all the caprices of a woman spoilt by the world. She was avaricious and egotistical, and thought all the more of herself now that she had ceased to play an active part in society. She never missed a ball, and she dressed and painted in the style of a bygone age. She remained in a corner of the room, where she seemed to have been placed expressly to serve as a scarecrow. Every one on coming in went to her and made her a low bow, but this ceremony once at an end no one spoke a word to her. She received the whole city at her house, observing the strictest etiquette, and never failing to give to every one his or her proper name. Her innumerable servants, growing pale and fat in the ante-chamber, did absolutely as they liked, so that the house was pillaged as if its owner was really dead. Lisabeta passed her life in continual torture. If she made tea she was reproached with wasting the sugar. If she read a novel to the Countess she was held responsible for all the absurdities of the author. If she went out with the noble lady for a walk or drive, it was she who was to blame if the weather was bad or the pavement muddy. Her salary, more than modest, was never punctually paid, and she was expected to dress " like every one else "; that is to say, like very few people indeed. When she went into society her position was sad. Every one knew her; no one paid any attention. At a ball she sometimes danced; but only when a *vis-à-vis* was wanted. Women would come up to her, take her by the arm, and lead her out of the room if their dress required attending to. She had her portion of self-respect, and felt deeply the misery of her position. She looked with impatience for a liberator to break her chain. But the young men, prudent in the midst of their affected giddiness, took care not to honour her with their attentions, though Lisabeta Ivanovna was a hundred times prettier than the shameless or stupid girls whom they surrounded with their homage. More than once she slunk away from the splendour of the drawing-room to shut herself up alone in her little bedroom, furnished with an old screen and a pieced carpet, a chest of drawers, a small looking-glass, and a wooden bedstead. There she shed tears at her ease, by the light of a tallow candle in a tin candlestick.

One morning—it was two days after the party at Naroumoff's, and a week before the scene we have just sketched—Lisabeta was sitting at her embroidery before the window, when, looking carelessly into the street, she saw an officer, in the uniform of the Engineers, standing motionless with his eyes fixed upon her. She lowered her head, and applied herself to her work more attentively than ever. Five minutes afterwards she looked mechanically into the street, and the officer was still in the same place. Not being in the habit of exchanging glances with young men who passed by her window, she remained with her eyes fixed on her work for nearly two hours, until she was told that lunch was ready. She got up to put her embroidery away, and, while doing so, looked into the street, and saw the officer still in the same place. This seemed to her very strange. After lunch she went to the window with a certain emotion, but the officer of Engineers was no longer in the street.

She thought no more of him. But two days afterwards, just as she was getting into the carriage with the Countess, she saw him once more, standing straight before the door. His face was half concealed by a fur collar, but his black eyes sparkled beneath his helmet. Lisabeta was afraid, without knowing why, and she trembled as she took her seat in the carriage.

On returning home, she rushed with a beating heart towards the window. The officer was in his habitual place, with his eyes fixed ardently upon her. She at once withdrew, burning at the same time with curiosity, and moved by a strange feeling, which she now experienced for the first time.

No day now passed but the young officer showed himself beneath the window. Before long a dumb acquaintance was established between them. Sitting at her work she felt his presence, and when she raised her head she looked at him for a long time every day. The young man seemed full of gratitude for these innocent favours.

She observed, with the deep and rapid perceptions of youth, that a sudden redness covered the officer's pale cheeks as soon as their eyes met. After about a week she would smile at seeing him for the first time.

When Tomski asked his grandmother's permission to present one of his friends, the heart of the poor young girl beat strongly, and when she heard that it was Naroumoff, she bitterly repented having compromised her secret by letting it out to a giddy young man like Paul.

Hermann was the son of a German settled in Russia, from whom he had inherited a small sum of money. Firmly resolved to preserve his independence, he had made it a principle not to touch his private income. He lived on his pay, and did not allow himself the slightest luxury. He was not very communicative; and his reserve rendered it difficult for his comrades to amuse themselves at his expense.

Under an assumed calm he concealed strong passions and a highly-imaginative disposition. But he was always master of himself, and kept himself free from the ordinary faults of young men. Thus, a gambler by temperament, he never touched a card, feeling, as he himself said, that his position did not allow him to " risk the necessary in view of the superfluous." Yet he would pass entire nights before a card-table, watching with feverish anxiety the rapid changes of the game. The anecdote of Count St. Germain's three cards had struck his imagination, and he did nothing but think of it all that night.

" If," he said to himself next day as he was walking along the streets of St. Petersburg, " if she would only tell me her secret—if she would only name the three winning cards! I must get presented to her, that I may pay my court and gain her confidence. Yes! And she is eighty-seven! She may die this week—to-morrow perhaps. But after all, is there a word of truth in the story? No! Economy, Temperance, Work; these are my three winning cards. With them I can double my capital; increase it tenfold. They alone can ensure my independence and prosperity."

Dreaming in this way as he walked along, his attention was attracted by a house built in an antiquated style of architecture. The street was full of carriages, which passed one by one before the old house, now brilliantly illuminated. As the people stepped out of the carriages Hermann saw now the little feet of a young woman, now the military boot of a general. Then came a clocked stocking, then a diplomatic pump. Fur-lined cloaks and coats passed in procession before a gigantic porter.

Hermann stopped. " Who lives here? " he said to a watchman in his box.

" The Countess Anna Fedorovna." It was Tomski's grandmother.

Hermann started. The story of the three cards came once more upon his imagination. He walked to and fro before the house, thinking of the woman to whom it belonged, of her wealth and her mysterious power. At last he returned to his den. But for some time he could not get to sleep; and when at last sleep came upon him, he saw, dancing before his eyes, cards, a green table, and heaps of roubles and bank-notes. He saw himself doubling stake after stake, always winning, and then filling his pockets with piles of coin, and stuffing his pocket-book with countless bank-notes. When he awoke, he sighed to find that his treasures were but creations of a disordered fancy; and, to drive such thoughts from him, he went out for a walk. But he had not gone far when he found himself once more before the house of the Countess. He seemed to have been attracted there by some irresistible force. He stopped, and looked up at the windows. There he saw a girl's head with beautiful black hair, leaning gracefully over a book or an embroidery-frame. The head was lifted, and he saw a fresh complexion and black eyes.

This moment decided his fate.

## III

Lisabeta was just taking off her shawl and her bonnet when the Countess sent for her. She had had the horses put in again.

While two footmen were helping the old lady into the carriage, Lisabeta saw the young officer at her side. She felt him take her by the hand, lost her head, and found, when the young officer had walked away, that he had left a paper between her fingers. She hastily concealed it in her glove.

During the whole of the drive she neither saw nor heard. When they were in the carriage together the Countess was in the habit of questioning Lisabeta perpetually.

" Who is that man that bowed to us? What is the name of this bridge? What is there written on that signboard? "

Lisabeta now gave the most absurd answers, and was accordingly scolded by the Countess.

" What is the matter with you, my child? " she asked. " What are you thinking about? Or do you really not hear me? I speak distinctly enough, however, and I have not yet lost my head, have I? "

Lisabeta was not listening. When she got back to the house she ran to her room, locked the door, and took the scrap of paper from her glove. It was not sealed, and it was impossible, therefore, not to read it. The letter contained protestations of love. It was tender, respectful, and translated word for word from a German novel. But Lisabeta did not read German, and she was quite delighted. She was, however, much embarrassed. For the first time in her life she had a secret. Correspond with a young man! The idea of such a thing frightened her. How imprudent she had been! She had reproached herself, but knew not now what to do.

Cease to do her work at the window, and by persistent coldness try and disgust the young officer? Send him back his letter? Answer him in a firm, decided manner? What line of conduct was she to pursue? She had no friend, no one to advise her. She at last decided to send an answer. She sat down at her little table, took pen and paper, and began to think. More than once she wrote a sentence and then tore up the paper. What she had written seemed too stiff, or else it was wanting in reserve. At last, after much trouble, she succeeded in composing a few lines which seemed to meet the case. " I believe," she wrote, " that your intentions are those of an honourable man, and that you would not wish to offend me by any thoughtless conduct. But you must understand that our acquaintance cannot begin in this way. I return your letter, and trust that you will not give me cause to regret my imprudence.''

Next day as soon as Hermann made his appearance, Lisabeta left her embroidery, and went into the drawing-room, opened the ventilator, and threw her letter into the street, making sure that the young officer would pick it up.

Hermann, in fact, at once saw it, and, picking it up, entered a confectioner's shop in order to read it. Finding nothing discouraging in it, he went home sufficiently pleased with the first step in his love adventure.

Some days afterwards, a young person with lively eyes called to see Miss Lisabeta, on the part of a milliner. Lisabeta wondered what she could want, and suspected, as she received her, some secret intention. She was much surprised, however, when she recognised, on the letter that was now handed to her, the writing of Hermann.

'' You make a mistake,'' she said, '' this letter is not for me.''

'' I beg your pardon,'' said the milliner, with a slight smile; '' be kind enough to read it.''

Lisabeta glanced at it. Hermann was asking for an appointment.

'' Impossible! '' she cried, alarmed both at the boldness of the request and at the manner in which it was made. '' This letter is not for me,'' she repeated; and she tore it into a hundred pieces.

'' If the letter was not for you, why did you tear it up? You should have given it me back, that I might take it to the person it was meant for.''

'' True,'' said Lisabeta, quite disconcerted. '' But bring me no more letters, and tell the person who gave you this one that he ought to blush for his conduct.''

Hermann, however, was not a man to give up what he had once undertaken. Every day Lisabeta received a fresh letter from him,— sent now in one way, now in another. They were no longer translated from the German. Hermann wrote under the influence of a commanding passion, and in a language which was his own. Lisabeta could not hold out against such torrents of eloquence. She received the letters, kept them, and at last answered them. Every day her answers were longer and more affectionate, until at last she threw out of the window a letter couched as follows:—

'' This evening there is a ball at the Embassy. The Countess will be there. We shall remain until two in the morning. You may manage to see me alone. As soon as the Countess leaves home, that is to say towards eleven o'clock, the servants are sure to go out, and there will be no one left but the porter, who will be sure to be asleep in his box. Enter as soon as it strikes eleven, and go upstairs as fast as possible. If you find any one in the ante-chamber, ask whether the Countess is at home, and you will be told she is out, and, in that case, you must resign yourself, and go away. In all probability, however, you will meet no one. The

Countess's women are together in a distant room. When you are once in the ante-chamber, turn to the left, and walk straight on, until you reach the Countess's bedroom. There, behind a large screen, you will see two doors. The one on the right leads to a dark room. The one on the left leads to a corridor at the end of which is a little winding staircase, which leads to my parlour.''

At ten o'clock Hermann was already on duty before the Countess's door. It was a frightful night. The winds had been unloosed, and the snow was falling in large flakes; the lamps gave an uncertain light; the streets were deserted; from time to time passed a sleigh, drawn by a wretched hack, on the look-out for a fare. Covered by a thick overcoat, Hermann felt neither the wind nor the snow. At last the Countess's carriage drew up. He saw two huge footmen come forward and take beneath the arms a dilapidated spectre, and place it on the cushions, well wrapped up in an enormous fur cloak. Immediately afterwards, in a cloak of lighter make, her head crowned with natural flowers, came Lisabeta, who sprang into the carriage like a dart. The door was closed, and the carriage rolled on softly over the snow.

The porter closed the street door, and soon the windows of the first floor became dark. Silence reigned throughout the house. Hermann walked backwards and forwards; then coming to a lamp he looked at his watch. It was twenty minutes to eleven. Leaning against the lamp-post, his eyes fixed on the long hand of his watch, he counted impatiently the minutes which had yet to pass. At eleven o'clock precisely Hermann walked up the steps, pushed open the street door, and went into the vestibule, which was well lighted. As it happened the porter was not there. With a firm and rapid step he rushed up the staircase and reached the ante-chamber. There, before a lamp, a footman was sleeping, stretched out in a dirty greasy dressing-gown. Hermann passed quickly before him and crossed the dining-room and the drawing-room, where there was no light. But the lamp of the ante-chamber helped him to see. At last he reached the Countess's bedroom. Before a screen covered with old icons [sacred pictures] a golden lamp was burning. Gilt arm-chairs, sofas of faded colours, furnished with soft cushions, were arranged symmetrically along the walls, which were hung with China silk. He saw two large portraits, painted by Madame le Brun. One represented a man of forty, stout and full coloured, dressed in a light green coat, with a decoration on his breast. The second portrait was that of an elegant young woman, with an aquiline nose, powdered hair rolled back on the temples, and with a rose over her ear. Everywhere might be seen shepherds and shepherdesses in Dresden china, with vases of all shapes, clocks by Leroy, work-baskets, fans, and all the thousand playthings for the use of ladies of fashion, discovered at the time of Montgolfier's balloons and Mesmer's animal magnetism.

Hermann passed behind the screen, which concealed a little iron bedstead. He saw the two doors; the one on the right leading to the dark room, the one on the left to the corridor. He opened the latter, saw the staircase which led to the poor little companion's parlour, and then, closing this door, went into the dark room.

The time passed slowly. Everything was quiet in the house. The drawing-room clock struck midnight, and again there was silence. Hermann was standing up, leaning against the stove, in which there was no fire. He was calm; but his heart beat with quick pulsations, like that of a man determined to brave all dangers he might have to meet, because he knows them to be inevitable. He heard one o'clock strike; then two; and soon afterwards the distant roll of a carriage. He now, in spite of himself, experienced some emotion. The carriage approached rapidly and stopped. There was at once a great noise of servants running about the staircases, and a confusion of voices. Suddenly the rooms were all lit up, and the Countess's three antiquated maids came at once into the bedroom. At last appeared the Countess herself.

The walking mummy sank into a large Voltaire armchair. Hermann looked through the crack in the door; he saw Lisabeta pass close to him, and heard her hurried step as she went up the little winding staircase. For a moment he felt something like remorse; but it soon passed off, and his heart was once more of stone.

The Countess began to undress before a looking-glass. Her headdress of roses was taken off, and her powdered wigs separated from her own hair, which was very short and quite white. Pins fell in showers around her. At last she was in her dressing-gown and her night-cap, and in this costume, more suitable to her age, was less hideous than before.

Like most old people, the Countess was tormented by sleeplessness. She had her armchair rolled towards one of the windows, and told her maids to leave her. The lights were put out, and the room was lighted only by the lamp which burned before the holy images. The Countess, sallow and wrinkled, balanced herself gently from right to left. In her dull eyes could be read an utter absence of thought; and as she moved from side to side, one might have said that she did so not by any action of the will, but through some secret mechanism.

Suddenly this death's-head assumed a new expression; the lips ceased to tremble, and the eyes became alive. A strange man had appeared before the Countess!

It was Hermann.

" Do not be alarmed, madam," said Hermann, in a low voice, but very distinctly. " For the love of Heaven, do not be alarmed. I do not wish to do you the slightest harm; on the contrary, I come to implore a favour of you."

The old woman looked at him in silence, as if she did not understand. Thinking she was deaf, he leaned towards her ear and repeated what he had said; but the Countess still remained silent.

" You can ensure the happiness of my whole life, and without its costing you a farthing. I know that you can name to me three cards——"

The Countess now understood what he required.

" It was a joke," she interrupted. " I swear to you it was only a joke."

" No, madam," replied Hermann in an angry tone. " Remember Tchaplitzki, and how you enabled him to win."

The Countess was agitated. For a moment her features expressed strong emotion; but they soon resumed their former dulness.

" Cannot you name to me," said Hermann, " three winning cards? "

The Countess remained silent. " Why keep this secret for your great-grandchildren? " he continued. " They are rich enough without; they do not know the value of money. Of what profit would your three cards be to them? They are debauchees. The man who cannot keep his inheritance will die in want, though he had the science of demons at his command. I am a steady man. I know the value of money. Your three cards will not be lost upon me. Come! "

He stopped tremblingly, awaiting a reply. The Countess did not utter a word. Hermann went upon his knees.

" If your heart has ever known the passion of love; if you can remember its sweet ecstasies; if you have ever been touched by the cry of a new-born babe; if any human feeling has ever caused your heart to beat, I entreat you by the love of a husband, a lover, a mother, by all that is sacred in life, not to reject my prayer. Tell me your secret! Reflect! You are old; you have not long to live! Remember that the happiness of a man is in your hands; that not only myself, but my children and my grandchildren will bless your memory as a saint."

The old Countess answered not a word.

Hermann rose, and drew a pistol from his pocket.

" Hag! " he exclaimed, " I will make you speak."

At the sight of the pistol the Countess for the second time showed agitation. Her head shook violently; she stretched out her hands as if to put the weapon aside. Then suddenly she fell back motionless.

" Come, don't be childish! " said Hermann. " I adjure you for the last time; will you name the three cards? "

The Countess did not answer. Hermann saw that she was dead!

## IV

Lisabeta was sitting in her room, still in her ball dress, lost in the deepest meditation. On her return to the house, she had sent away her maid, and had gone upstairs to her room, trembling at the

135*

idea of finding Hermann there; desiring, indeed, *not* to find him.
One glance showed her that he was not there, and she gave thanks
to Providence that he had missed the appointment.  She sat down
pensively, without thinking of taking off her cloak, and allowed
to pass through her memory all the circumstances of the intrigue
which had begun such a short time back, and had already advanced
so far.  Scarcely three weeks had passed since she had first seen
the young officer from her window, and already she had written
to him, and he had succeeded in inducing her to make an appointment.  She knew his name, and that was all.  She had received
a quantity of letters from him, but he had never spoken to her;
she did not know the sound of his voice, and until that evening,
strangely enough, she had never heard him spoken of.

But that very evening Tomski, fancying he had noticed that the
young Princess Pauline, to whom he had been paying assiduous
court, was flirting, contrary to her custom, with another man, had
wished to revenge himself by making a show of indifference.  With
this noble object he had invited Lisabeta to take part in an inter-
minable mazurka; but he teased her immensely about her partiality
for Engineer officers, and pretending all the time to know much
more than he really did, hazarded purely in fun a few guesses
which were so happy that Lisabeta thought her secret must have
been discovered.

" But who tells you all this? " she said with a smile.

" A friend of the very officer you know, a most original man."

" And who is this man that is so original? "

" His name is Hermann."

She answered nothing, but her hands and feet seemed to be of ice.

" Hermann is a hero of romance," continued Tomski.  " He
has the profile of Napoleon, and the soul of Mephistopheles.  I
believe he has at least three crimes on his conscience. . . .  But
how pale you are! "

" I have a bad headache.  But what did this Mr. Hermann tell
you?  Is not that his name? "

" Hermann is very much displeased with his friend, with the
Engineer officer who has made your acquaintance.  He says that
in his place he would behave very differently.  But I am quite
sure that Hermann himself has designs upon you.  At least, he
seems to listen with remarkable interest to all that his friend tells
him about you."

" And where has he seen me? "

" Perhaps in church, perhaps in the street; heaven knows where."

At this moment three ladies came forward according to the
custom of the mazurka, and asked Tomski to choose between
" forgetfulness and regret."[1]

[1] The figures and fashions of the mazurka are reproduced in the cotillon
of Western Europe.—TRANSLATOR.

And the conversation which had so painfully excited the curiosity of Lisabeta came to an end.

The lady who, in virtue of the infidelities permitted by the mazurka, had just been chosen by Tomski, was the Princess Pauline. During the rapid evolutions which the figure obliged them to make, there was a grand explanation between them, until at last he conducted her to a chair, and returned to his partner.

But Tomski could now think no more, either of Hermann or Lisabeta, and he tried in vain to resume the conversation. But the mazurka was coming to an end, and immediately afterwards the old Countess rose to go.

Tomski's mysterious phrases were nothing more than the usual platitudes of the mazurka, but they had made a deep impression upon the heart of the poor little companion. The portrait sketched by Tomski had struck her as very exact; and with her romantic ideas, she saw in the rather ordinary countenance of her adorer something to fear and admire. She was now sitting down with her cloak off, with bare shoulders; her head, crowned with flowers, falling forward from fatigue, when suddenly the door opened and Hermann entered. She shuddered.

" Where were you? " she said, trembling all over.

" In the Countess's bedroom. I have just left her," replied Hermann. " She is dead."

" Great heavens! What are you saying? "

" I am afraid," he said, " that I am the cause of her death."

Lisabeta looked at him in consternation, and remembered Tomski's words: " He has at least three crimes on his conscience."

Hermann sat down by the window, and told everything. The young girl listened with terror.

So those letters so full of passion, those burning expressions, this daring obstinate pursuit—all this had been inspired by anything but love! Money alone had inflamed the man's soul. She, who had nothing but a heart to offer, how could she make him happy? Poor child! she had been the blind instrument of a robber, of the murderer of her old benefactress. She wept bitterly in the agony of her repentance. Hermann watched her in silence; but neither the tears of the unhappy girl, nor her beauty, rendered more touching by her grief, could move his heart of iron. He had no remorse in thinking of the Countess's death. One sole thought distressed him—the irreparable loss of the secret which was to have made his fortune.

" You are a monster! " said Lisabeta, after a long silence.

" I did not mean to kill her," replied Hermann coldly. " My pistol was not loaded."

They remained for some time without speaking, without looking at one another. The day was breaking, and Lisabeta put out her candle. She wiped her eyes, drowned in tears, and raised them towards Hermann. He was standing close to the window, his arms crossed, with a frown on his forehead. In this attitude he reminded her involuntarily of the portrait of Napoleon. The resemblance overwhelmed her.

" How am I to get you away? " she said at last. " I thought you might go out by the back stairs. But it would be necessary to go through the Countess's bedroom, and I am too frightened."

" Tell me how to get to the staircase, and I will go alone."

She went to a drawer, took out a key, which she handed to Hermann, and gave him the necessary instructions. Hermann took her icy hand, kissed her on the forehead and departed.

He went down the staircase and entered the Countess's bedroom. She was seated quite stiff in her armchair, but her features were in no way contracted. He stopped for a moment, and gazed into her face as if to make sure of the terrible reality. Then he entered the dark room, and, feeling behind the tapestry, found the little door which opened on to a staircase. As he went down it, strange ideas came into his head. " Going down this staircase," he said to himself, " some sixty years ago, at about this time, may have been seen some man in an embroidered coat with powdered wig, pressing to his breast a cocked hat: some gallant who has long been buried; and now the heart of his aged mistress has ceased to beat."

At the end of the staircase he found another door, which his key opened, and he found himself in the corridor which led to the street.

v

Three days after this fatal night, at nine o'clock in the morning, Hermann entered the convent where the last respects were to be paid to the mortal remains of the old Countess. He felt no remorse, though he could not deny to himself that he was the poor woman's assassin. Having no religion, he was, as usual in such cases, very superstitious; believing that the dead Countess might exercise a malignant influence on his life, he thought to appease her spirit by attending her funeral.

The church was full of people, and it was difficult to get in. The body had been placed on a rich catafalque, beneath a canopy of velvet. The Countess was reposing in an open coffin, her hands joined on her breast, with a dress of white satin, and head-dress of lace. Around the catafalque the family was assembled, the servants in black caftans with a knot of ribbons on the shoulder, exhibiting the colours of the Countess's coat-of-arms. Each of them held a wax candle in his hand. The relations, in deep mourning—children, grandchildren, and great-grandchildren—were all present; but none of them wept.

To have shed tears would have looked like affectation. The

Countess was so old that her death could have taken no one by surprise, and she had long been looked upon as already out of the world. The funeral sermon was delivered by a celebrated preacher. In a few simple, touching phrases he painted the final departure of the just, who had passed long years of contrite preparation for a Christian end. The service concluded in the midst of respectful silence. Then the relations went towards the defunct to take a last farewell. After them, in a long procession, all who had been invited to the ceremony bowed, for the last time, to her who for so many years had been a scarecrow at their entertainments. Finally came the Countess's household; among them was remarked an old governess, of the same age as the deceased, supported by two women. She had not strength enough to kneel down, but tears flowed from her eyes, as she kissed the hand of her old mistress.

In his turn Hermann advanced towards the coffin. He knelt down for a moment on the flagstones, which were strewed with branches of yew. Then he rose, as pale as death, and walked up the steps of the catafalque. He bowed his head. But suddenly the dead woman seemed to be staring at him; and with a mocking look she opened and shut one eye. Hermann by a sudden movement started and fell backwards. Several persons hurried towards him. At the same moment, close to the church door, Lisabeta fainted.

Throughout the day, Hermann suffered from a strange indisposition. In a quiet restaurant, where he took his meals, he, contrary to his habit, drank a great deal of wine, with the object of stupefying himself. But the wine had no effect but to excite his imagination, and give fresh activity to the ideas with which he was preoccupied.

He went home earlier than usual; lay down with his clothes on upon the bed, and fell into a leaden sleep. When he woke up it was night, and the room was lighted up by the rays of the moon. He looked at his watch; it was a quarter to three. He could sleep no more. He sat up on the bed and thought of the old Countess. At this moment some one in the street passed the window, looked into the room, and then went on. Hermann scarcely noticed it; but in another minute he heard the door of the ante-chamber open. He thought that his orderly, drunk as usual, was returning from some nocturnal excursion; but the step was one to which he was not accustomed. Somebody seemed to be softly walking over the floor in slippers.

The door opened, and a woman, dressed entirely in white, entered the bedroom. Hermann thought it must be his old nurse, and he asked himself what she could want at that time of night.

But the woman in white, crossing the room with a rapid step, was now at the foot of his bed, and Hermann recognised the Countess.

" I come to you against my wish," she said in a firm voice. " I am forced to grant your prayer. Three, seven, ace will win, if played one after the other; but you must not play more than one card in twenty-four hours, and afterwards as long as you live you must never touch a card again. I forgive you my death, on condition of your marrying my companion, Lisabeta Ivanovna."

With these words she walked towards the door, and gliding with her slippers over the floor, disappeared. Hermann heard the door of the ante-chamber open, and soon afterwards saw a white figure pass along the street. It stopped for a moment before his window, as if to look at him.

Hermann remained for some time astounded. Then he got up and went into the next room. His orderly, drunk as usual, was asleep on the floor. He had much difficulty in waking him, and then could not obtain from him the least explanation. The door of the ante-chamber was locked.

Hermann went back to his bedroom, and wrote down all the details of his vision.

## VI

Two fixed ideas can no more exist together in the moral world than in the physical two bodies can occupy the same place at the same time; and " three, seven, ace " soon drove away Hermann's recollection of the old Countess's last moments. " Three, seven, ace " were now in his head to the exclusion of everything else.

They followed him in his dreams, and appeared to him under strange forms. Threes seemed to be spread before him like magnolias, sevens took the form of Gothic doors, and aces became gigantic spiders.

His thoughts concentrated themselves on one single point. How was he to profit by the secret so dearly purchased? What if he applied for leave to travel? At Paris, he said to himself, he would find some gambling-house where, with his three cards, he could at once make his fortune.

Chance soon came to his assistance. There was at Moscow a society of rich gamblers, presided over by the celebrated Tchekalinski, who had passed all his life playing at cards, and had amassed millions. For while he lost silver only, he gained banknotes. His magnificent house, his excellent kitchen, his cordial manners had brought him numerous friends and secured for him general esteem.

When he came to St. Petersburg, the young men of the capital filled his rooms, forsaking balls for his card-parties, and preferring the emotions of gambling to the fascinations of flirting. Hermann was taken to Tchekalinski by Naroumoff. They passed through a long suite of rooms, full of the most attentive, obsequious servants. The place was crowded. Generals and high officials were playing at whist; young men were stretched out on the sofas, eating ices and smoking long pipes. In the principal room at the head of a long table, around which were assembled a score of players, the master of the house held a faro bank.

He was a man of about sixty, with a sweet and noble expression of face, and hair white as snow. On his full, florid countenance might be read good humour and benevolence. His eyes shone with a perpetual smile. Naroumoff introduced Hermann. Tchekalinski took him by the hand, told him that he was glad to see him, that no one stood on ceremony in his house; and then went on dealing. The deal occupied some time, and stakes were made on more than thirty cards. Tchekalinski waited patiently to allow the winners time to double their stakes, paid what he had lost, listened politely to all observations, and, more politely still, put straight the corners of cards, when in a fit of absence some one had taken the liberty of turning them down. At last when the game was at an end, Tchekalinski collected the cards, shuffled them again, had them cut, and then dealt anew.

" Will you allow me to take a card? " said Hermann, stretching out his arms above a fat man who occupied nearly the whole of one side of the table. Tchekalinski, with a gracious smile, bowed in consent. Naroumoff complimented Hermann, with a laugh, on the cessation of the austerity by which his conduct had hitherto been marked, and wished him all kinds of happiness on the occasion of his first appearance in the character of a gambler.

" There! " said Hermann, after writing some figures on the back of his card.

" How much? " asked the banker, half closing his eyes. " Excuse me, I cannot see."

" Forty-seven thousand roubles," said Hermann.

Every one's eyes were directed toward the new player.

" He has lost his head," thought Naroumoff.

" Allow me to point out to you," said Tchekalinski, with his eternal smile, " that you are playing rather high. We never put down here, as a first stake, more than a hundred and seventy-five roubles."

" Very well," said Hermann; " but do you accept my stake or not? "

Tchekalinski bowed in token of acceptance. " I only wish to point out to you," he said, " that although I am perfectly sure of my friends, I can only play against ready money. I am quite convinced that your word is as good as gold; but to keep up the rules of the game, and to facilitate calculations, I should be obliged to you if you would put the money on your card."

Hermann took a bank-note from his pocket and handed it to

Tchekalinski, who, after examining it with a glance, placed it on Hermann's card.

Then he began to deal. He turned up on the right a ten, and on the left a three.

"I win," said Hermann, exhibiting his three.

A murmur of astonishment ran through the assembly. The banker knitted his eyebrows, but speedily his face resumed its everlasting smile.

"Shall I settle at once?" he asked.

"If you will be kind enough to do so," said Hermann.

Tchekalinski took a bundle of bank-notes from his pocket-book and paid. Hermann pocketed his winnings and left the table.

Naroumoff was lost in astonishment. Hermann drank a glass of lemonade and went home.

The next evening he returned to the house. Tchekalinski again held the bank. Hermann went to the table, and this time the players hastened to make room for him. Tchekalinski received him with a most gracious bow. Hermann waited, took a card, and staked on it his forty-seven thousand roubles, together with the like sum which he had gained the evening before.

Tchekalinski began to deal. He turned up on the right a knave, and on the left a seven.

Hermann exhibited a seven.

There was a general exclamation. Tchekalinski was evidently ill at ease, but he counted out the ninety-four thousand roubles to Hermann, who took them in the calmest manner, rose from the table, and went away.

The next evening, at the accustomed hour, he again appeared. Every one was expecting him. Generals and high officials had left their whist to watch this extraordinary play. The young officers had quitted their sofas, and even the servants of the house pressed round the table.

When Herman took his seat, the other players ceased to stake, so impatient were they to see him have it out with the banker, who, still smiling, watched the approach of his antagonist and prepared to meet him. Each of them untied at the same time a pack of cards. Tchekalinski shuffled, and Hermann cut. Then the latter took up a card and covered it with a heap of bank-notes. It was like the preliminaries of a duel. A deep silence reigned through the room.

Tchekalinski took up the cards with trembling hands and dealt. On one side he put down a queen and on the other side an ace.

"Ace wins," said Hermann.

"No. Queen loses," said Tchekalinski.

Hermann looked. Instead of ace, he saw a queen of spades

before him. He could not trust his eyes! And now as he gazed in fascination on the fatal card, he fancied that he saw the queen of spades open and then close her eye, while at the same time she gave a mocking smile. He felt a thrill of nameless horror. The queen of spades resembled the dead Countess!

Hermann is now at the Aboukhoff Asylum, room No. 17—a hopeless madman! He answers no questions which we put to him. Only he mumbles to himself without cessation, " Three, seven, ace; three, seven, *queen*! "

# NICOLAI V. GOGOL
1809–1852

# THE EVE OF SAINT JOHN

ALL his life Thomas Grigorovitch refused to tell the same story twice. It was an odd fancy of his, but he was never known to depart from it. If you insisted on hearing a story a second time, it was certain to become a new one in the retelling; the old man's busy imagination would be ever inventing new facts and characters or transforming the originals until it was impossible to recognise them. One of his stories was once eagerly seized upon by a hungry journalist, on the prowl for scraps of any sort out of which to make fillings for the wretched little bundles of paper which these gentry are in the habit of giving out once a week or once a month. Thomas himself forgot all about the incident until one day the same young man, in his bright green cap, turned up again, this time bringing with him a small book which he opened and laid before us; and the old man, taking up his spectacles, prepared to examine the pages. But the spectacles were out of commission; they refused to stick upon his nose without the application of thread and wax which he was always forgetting to give them; so he passed the book over to me. I know something of the arts of reading and writing, and have good eyesight; so I started to read it to him.

" Wait! " he interrupted, before I had read more than three or four pages. " Tell me what it is all about."

" What it is about! " I exclaimed in amazement. " Why, it is your own story, Thomas! "

" Who says it is my story? " he demanded.

" Who says so? Well, look here. Here it is in black and white: *Related by the verger of Dikanka*."

" A plague on the man who said that," cried the old verger. " I never told him any of this stuff, the sneaking liar! Listen to me, now, and I'll tell you the real story."

With that he began the following history.

My grandfather—God rest his soul!—was a rare one to tell a story. Folks would sit and listen to him, and never move while he was talking, though it should take all day to tell. He was none of your modern romancers, spinning a yarn like a beggar on the door-step, till you get sick and tired of their lies. In those old days, before my mother died, we used to sit round the stove those dark nights in winter, she spinning and gently crooning a lullaby and rocking the cradle with her foot, while the frost glistened on the frozen window-panes and the little room was like an oven.

Grandfather was very very old; for years he had never left the stove side, where he sat all day and night crouched over the heat; and we children were never tired of sitting round him, huddled close together, while the spindle whirred and the lamp guttered and flared, and he told his wonderful stories. He had tales of all kinds, of heroes and adventures and battles, but those we loved best were his queer fairy tales, eerie stories of elves and witches and demons, which made our flesh creep and our hair stand on end. The fear-someness of these stories used at times to impress us so strongly that everything for days afterward would seem strange and haunted. I well remember the impression I used to have of un-earthly visitors slinking about the house, and how when I saw my own clothes hanging up I used to take them for the form of the foul fiend. Granddad's stories were indeed rather awful, but we always knew that every word of them was true.

The story which I am now going to tell you is one of the most extraordinary in his repertory. I know very well that many superior people would laugh at it; but, after all, do they not laugh at everything in heaven and earth, and call that wisdom? Thank God, I have lived long enough to have learned the folly of in-credulity. But let the old man speak for himself:

You would not have recognised this village if you had seen it as it was when I was a boy. It was then nothing more than a collec-tion of wretched hovels. The fields were unfenced and there were no barns or stables. Even the most prosperous lived in broken-down cottages, and the poor were glad of any kind of shelter. This was not altogether due to poverty, but at least in part came from nomadic instincts. The Cossack tradition of a wandering life was strong among us; there was little respect for property, and, by reason of the wandering hordes, no one felt much security. No one, therefore, took the trouble to build a comfortable house.

What a strange figure the man made! Was he, indeed, a man or devil? Whence did he come, and with what purpose? You might meet him at any time prowling about the neighbourhood, often half-drunk, and then suddenly he would have disappeared and left no trace behind. He was a fellow of infinite humour; all the Cossacks would crowd about him, and sing and laugh in merry carousal. He had ever a pleasant word for the girls and some pretty gaud to give them; they were often unwilling to take his gifts, being doubtful perhaps of their origin. An ancient aunt of mine, whose tavern was specially favoured by this diabolical Basavriuk (for that was his name), used to say that nothing would persuade her to accept one of these presents with which he was so free. Yet it was difficult to refuse. The man frowned in such an ugly and uncanny manner when any of us crossed his will that we found it best to fall in with his every mood. Yet his gifts had unpleasant consequences; a necklace of his beads round your neck would presently seem to strangle and burn your skin; one of his rings would seem to bite your finger, and his ribbons twined in your hair would pull like the very devil. Moreover these fatal gifts were not to be got rid of; you might throw them into the pond, but in some mysterious way they soon would be back with you again.

Next to the village church lived Father Athanasius, a man respected and beloved. He kept his eye on Basavriuk, and finding that this heathen neglected his Easter duties, reproved him boldly and laid penance upon him. The outlaw went near to murdering him. " You jolly well attend to your own business," he roared, " or I will do you in." What hope was there for this wretched fellow? The good priest gave out that none of his flock should speak to Basavriuk, on pain of being considered an enemy of Christ and of the human race.

Peter the orphan (so called because no one had memory of his mother or father) was a labourer in the employment of a small farmer by name of Korzh. Some said that they had died of plague when the boy was two years old; but old Aunt would not agree to this, and invented parents for him, though it is difficult to see what good that did to Peter. Her story was that his father had been taken prisoner by the Turks, had suffered incredible torments at their hands, and had at last escaped in disguise. The lads and girls of the village used to say that Peter would have made a fine figure if he had been well dressed. Unfortunately, however, he had nothing but an old grey suit full of holes as a Jew's pocket is of sovereigns. Now, Korzh had a daughter of incomparable beauty. Her cheeks were fresh as flowers of dawn, her eyebrows were like cords of black silk, her enticing little lips seemed suited to songs more beautiful than those of the nightingale, and her hair, soft as flax and raven-black, fell in the loveliest curls. Old as I am and worried by an aged wife, I would have given much to kiss her.

Then happened what always happens where youths and maidens are together. This pretty Pidorka and her Peter were ever whispering in twilight corners. Korzh, her father, was quite unsuspicious until one day he saw Peter kissing the girl with passionate fervour. The old man, who had just opened the door of his cottage, was astounded and horrified, as if he had received a blow on the head. As soon as he came to himself he took down his old hunting-crop from the wall, and was about to do justice upon Peter, when little Ivas, Pidorka's young brother, ran up and caught his father's knees, crying, " Oh, Daddy, don't hit Peter."

The old man relented and hung his whip again upon its nail, but, seizing Peter, threatened him with the direst punishment if he should be ever found about the cottage again. He concluded his address by striking the lad with his fists in the neck. The boy fled from his presence, and all their young love was blighted.

And now a report went about the village that a handsome soldier with splendid uniform and fierce moustache was a favoured visitor at the cottage where dwelled the pretty girl, and soon was talk of a marriage between the two. Pidorka, heartbroken, at last succeeded in sending a message to Peter by the hand of her little brother. " Beloved," she told him, " it is you alone whom I could have loved and worshipped all my life. To you only could I ever have belonged. But a cruel destiny has separated us for ever. Think not that I will be married to this soldier whom people name as my lover; they will carry me to my funeral instead of dancing at my wedding. Death, beloved, is now my choice, for I will never wed another man."

This message awoke Peter from the castle of dreams in which he had been building up a happy future for himself and Pidorka after successful adventures abroad should have made him rich. " Alas! " he cried, " an evil fate is upon us. There remains for me nothing but to die too. But who am I that I should complain of fate? Since it is the will of God to destroy me, I am content."

Early in the morning, when all the pious were at mass, my aunt was astonished to see Peter come into her tavern and order a great tankard of neat spirit, which he drank off at one gulp. But it was of no use; oblivion would not come to him. As he cast the tankard, in overwhelming gloom and despair, to the floor, he heard a deep voice behind him. It was Basavriuk, who thrust his hideous face with its fierce eyes and bristly hair close to his own. " Come, my friend, you have drunk deep enough of this bitter cup; is it not so? It is time for a new order of things. I can help you to what you desire; see, this is what you need, is it not? " and he rattled the coins in his huge leather purse with a cunning smile.

Peter looked at him, and a cold shudder ran suddenly down his back. The tempter shook out some of the coins into his hand and let the light gleam upon them. " Ha, ha," he laughed, " that is a fair sight; and a fair sound they make, too. A whole sack of this treasure shall be yours in return for one small condition."

" Done," cried Peter, recognising that this was indeed the devil himself. " They are mine. I will do anything you like." And the contract was sealed.

" Meet me at midnight in the glade of the Bear's Den. This is the Eve of Saint John Baptist, and the only night in the year when the fern blossoms. You are in the nick of time." And with that he was gone.

Peter waited with the utmost impatience for the end of the day, for sunset and the dark night. It was the longest day he had ever spent. At last the time came, and he made his way through the thick woods into the deep glade which bore the name of the Bear's Den. He found Basavriuk there waiting for him, who took him by the hand and led him through soft marshy ground where they had to walk carefully and with difficulty, clinging to the bushes, until they emerged upon a level stretch of open ground. The place was quite strange to Peter.

" See," said Basavriuk, pointing, " over there are three grassy mounds, and upon them myriad flowers of all kinds. You must not pick any of these flowers or evil will befall you; but the moment that you see the fern burst into bloom, pick its flower, and take no heed of anything that may be going on around you."

With the last words, Basavriuk disappeared, and Peter was alone. He walked across to the grassy mounds, but could see no flowers, only the rank gloomy steppe-grass growing everywhere. Then came a flash of lightning, and suddenly the ground before him was carpeted with a glowing mass of strange and beautiful flowers, and among them the plain green fern fronds. Peter stood staring at this marvellous wealth of beauty and colour, not quite certain that he was not dreaming. Then, as he was gazing at the homely fern-fronds, wondering whether Basavriuk had been laughing at him when he spoke of their blossoms, he observed upon the green a tiny crimson bud. It glowed and stirred as if alive, growing larger and larger every moment, and kindling as if with its own ardour. Then, radiant as a star, the swelling bud burst open, and the wonderful flower flamed in full glory, lighting up all around it. " This is the moment," Peter told himself, and stretched out his hand to pluck it. As he did so, he became aware of the sound of trampling feet all about him, and of hundreds of hoof-like hands trying to reach the flower. Remembering his instructions, he closed his eyes so as not to see them, and feverishly grasped at the fern stem. The flower was in his hand. Then everything was silent, and he saw nothing but Basavriuk, blue and ghastly as a spectre, seated upon a tree stump, and gazing open-mouthed and as if transfixed into the space before him. Suddenly through the gruesome stillness came a low whistle, freezing Peter's heart within him; and then the wood became alive with the silvery voices of the flowers and the whisperings of the trees and grasses.

The whistle had stirred Basavriuk also into life. His eyes lighted up, and the colour came back to his face. " The old witch has got back," he muttered to himself; and then to Peter, " Listen, Peter. In a few moments you will see before you a new kind of beauty. Take care to do whatever she tells you; otherwise you will be utterly lost." Then, taking a stick, he pushed aside the branches of a bush beside him; and there appeared a diminutive hut, which he hammered with his fist until it shook and shook again. Out of the hut

THE EVE OF SAINT JOHN

leaped a huge black dog, which immediately after had become a fierce cat, and sprang at Basavriuk's eyes. " Come, come, old hag," said Basavriuk, swearing vilely at it, " you have no need to be in a temper."

As he spoke, the cat was gone, and a little hunched-up old woman, with wrinkled face and nut-cracker jaw, and of the most devilish aspect, stood in its place. " This is indeed a new sort of beauty," thought Peter, but he shivered with horror as she came near him and snatched the flower out of his hand. Taking water, she muttered incantations over it, while her mouth gave out jets of fire. Then, returning it to Peter, " Cast it from you," she commanded. As he obeyed he was astounded to observe that it did not fall to the ground, but flew through the air, gliding gently away, until at last, at a great distance, it fell gradually and softly to earth. " There is the place," growled the old witch in a voice like a frog.

Basavriuk handed him a spade. " Go and dig there," he said, " and you will have riches beyond all that Korzh could ever imagine."

Peter took the tool and set to work in a businesslike manner. He had only turned up four spadefuls when the blade came in contact with something hard and resisting, and he could make out a little chest clamped with iron. He tried to lift it up, but it immediately sank deeper into the ground and out of his reach; and at the same time he heard a horrid hissing laugh at his ear. " Aha," said the old witch, " you must pay my price for the treasure. I must have human blood." She led up to him a young child, his face veiled in a white cloth, and signed to him to kill it. A mighty anger inflamed the heart of Peter, as he tore away the veil and discovered beneath it Pidorka's little brother Ivas; he grasped the knife she had given him, and sprang like a wild beast upon the old witch.

But Basavriuk was upon him, shouting, " You promised anything for your beautiful bride," and as the old witch stamped on the ground, flames shot forth all about him. He could see now all the treasure that lay buried in the earth. There, beneath his feet, reposed countless wealth, jewel-chests, and hoards of money, maddening stores beyond the power of man to count. He gazed on the intoxicating sight till his brain reeled, and suddenly seizing the knife in frenzy, he did the deed.

The horrible laughter of demons was all about him. The wood was full of gruesome and distorted forms. The old witch fell upon her victim. Peter fled headlong from the place, seeing red in everything, the trees, the sky, the air itself. At last he reached the wretched hut which served him as a dwelling, and, collapsing in a corner, fell into a heavy stupor of sleep.

When he awoke, three days later, all recollection of his adventure in the wood was obliterated from his memory. His foot touched something which jingled, and there beside him lay two great sacks of gold. A dim memory of having gone out to search for riches came back to him, and a vague sense of having been badly frightened; but for the rest, he remembered nothing at all.

The sacks of gold at once reached the heart of Korzh, and he discovered that Peter had always been to him as a beloved son, over whom he finally wept with emotion, and whom he welcomed with open arms as Pidorka's husband. The obnoxious soldier was sent about his business, and the wedding was arranged for an early day. Pidorka tried to tell her lover of the loss of her little brother, who had been stolen by gypsies, but so far did the devil's baneful influence extend, that Peter could not even remember the name or the features of little Ivas.

A wedding in those days was a grand affair. There was a great feast with music of all kinds, and then the young men and maidens, in their gorgeous attire, danced the old graceful and stately dances of the country. First the girls in their embroidered silk costumes, their high-heeled shoes, and their gaily-tied hair, danced their own graceful gliding dance; then the young men, in red and blue silk tunics and grotesque gold head-dress, each performed a dignified *pas seul*; and after this all the boys in their tall caps, light shirts, and gay silver belts, each with a short pipe stuck jauntily in his mouth, pranced about making everybody laugh by their pranks and jokes. Even Korzh himself felt the infection of youth in the light-hearted throng, and began to dance and sing with the rest. The fun became faster and more riotous; the young people took to dressing up as fairies and demons and all sorts of odd characters, getting ever less decorous and more hilarious. Even the old people could not remember a wedding so festive as this one.

After their marriage Pidorka and Peter lived in great style. Everything in their establishment was of the best, and there was enough and to spare of everything. There was a good deal of head-shaking over their way of living by the good folks of the neighbourhood. " No good ever yet came of ill-gotten wealth," they said to one another; " and how could Peter come honestly by so much money? It must have come from the Father of Evil himself." And in proof of their theory, they pointed out that Basavriuk had never been seen since the time of Peter's good fortune.

There was only too sad witness to the perspicuity of these good people. Before he had been married one month, you could hardly have known Peter for the same man. He had become altogether silent and morose, sitting all day without moving, and apparently deep in thought, perplexed by the continual effort to remember something which always eluded his mind. Occasionally Pidorka would manage to draw him into life for a few moments, when he would talk and perhaps smile, forgetting his preoccupation; but it was only a momentary relief; the sight of his riches would suddenly bring back his misery, and crying, " Wait, I forget; I must recollect," he would bury his face in his hands and sink once more into his gloomy reverie.

Pidorka tried every available remedy. She called in the help of a wise woman, and together they tried all sorts of spells for exorcising the source of the evil; but in vain. And in this state of misery for both, the summer wore away. The harvest was gathered in; and the flocks of wild ducks had sought their winter quarters in the home marshes; the steppes had grown red, and the logs and faggots for the winter firing were being collected fast; the ground was everywhere hardening, and touches of frost might be seen in the mornings. And the winter itself wore through, till the snow melted away and the frost disappeared; but there was no change in Peter, except that he grew always more gloomy and more sullen. All day long he sat there, the bags of gold lying at his feet, always intent on remembering—remembering no one knew what. He became wild and dreadful to behold, with long unkempt hair and the fierce frightened glare of a wild beast; and his anger grew to a mad rage because he could not remember.

It seemed that Peter was going mad. He would get up from his chair, and with fixedly staring eyes would make the wildest motions as of seizing something intangible, his lips moving rapidly all the time as if trying to form an unfamiliar word, but never making a sound. Then he would grow suddenly mad with rage, pulling out his hair and tearing at his hands and body like a maniac; until, the spasm past, he would fall again into silence and sit brooding upon the memory which always escaped him, until another spasm of madness seized him, to pass off eventually in the same manner.

Life had become unbearable to Pidorka. At first a poignant anguish, it had become a dull dead misery worse than any suffering. No one would have recognised the beauty of Dikanka in this pale thin shadow with eyes faded by tears, who never smiled, and from whose face all hope and joy and sense was utterly obliterated. At last some one, pitying her wretchedness, advised her to seek the aid of the witch of the Bear's Den, who was said to be so clever that she could cure every illness that had ever been known. Pidorka in desperation decided to follow the advice, and at last induced the witch to come to her. As it happened it was the Eve of Saint John. Peter, who had been lying, unseeing, on a couch, gradually aroused himself on her entrance and began to glare around him, trembling violently and in mortal terror. Suddenly he broke into an unearthly laugh, which smote Pidorka with a terrible fear. " Ha, ha," he shouted, " I remember now."

With that he seized a hatchet and giving it a great sweep round his head, flung it with tremendous force at the old witch. It missed its mark, but buried its head to the depth of four inches in the stout oaken door. The witch vanished, and in her place stood a child, its head veiled in a white cloth; and then, the cloth falling off, Pidorka recognised him. " Ivas! " she cried, and rushed to embrace him; but before she could reach him the child's figure became blood-red all over, glowing with a terrible light. Pidorka, terrified, rushed out of the room; and before she could recover sufficiently to return, the door was made fast behind her so that she could not enter. She called in neighbours to her help, and at last between them they succeeded in battering in the door. By this time the house was full of smoke; and in the middle of the room, at the spot where Peter had been standing, they found a little heap of ashes, still smouldering, and beside it, the fatal sacks. The people fell on the sacks and tore them open. They contained nothing but broken earthenware. There was no treasure to be seen.

After these happenings, Pidorka, gathering together what property her father had left her, set out on a pilgrimage; and before long, as is the usual way, she had become but a memory in the village. No one knew where she had gone. However, some years later, a soldier who came from Kief on a visit to Dikanka gave an account of a nun whom he had seen in a convent there, whom every one recognised as being certainly Pidorka. Her frame was worn to a shadow, and she spent her life in unceasing prayer, never speaking a word to any one. It was reported that she had come to the convent alone and on foot, and had brought with her a frame of precious stones for the holy picture of the Mother of God, of such marvellous worth and beauty that it dazzled all who looked at it.

# THE CARRIAGE

### Nicolai V. Gogol

THE little town of B—— became quite animated when the —— cavalry regiment came to be quartered there. Until then it had been horribly dull. When you happened to drive through it and looked out on the low greasy little houses that stared at the street in an incredibly sour manner, it was impossible to say what took place in your heart; a feeling of despair such as you experience when you have lost heavily at cards, or when you have made some stupid remark—in a word, a most unpleasant feeling. The rain had washed some of the clay from the walls, so that, instead of being white, they were piebald. The roofs were, for the most part, made of cane, as is usual in our southern towns. The little front gardens had long been abolished by order of the police. Not a soul was to be met in the street, unless perhaps a cock happened to cross the bridge that felt as soft as a pillow from the thick layer of dust on it. This dust would turn to mud at the slightest rainfall. Then the streets of B—— would be full of those fat animals that the local police called " Frenchmen." Putting out their snouts from their troughs they raised such a grunting as to cause any one driving through to whip up his horses. However, one seldom met with any one driving through the town of B——. It was but rarely that some landowner, possessing eleven serfs, would appear over the bridge, dressed in a nankeen coat, in a vehicle that was a cross between a trap and a cart, and would peep out from among numerous sacks of flour, and pull up the bay mare after whom trotted a foal. Even the market square had a rather depressing appearance; the tailor's house stood out cornerwise to the road in an absurd manner. On the opposite side of the road was some sort of two-storeyed building in stone that had been in the course of construction for fifteen years. Further on, there stood, quite by itself, a modern wooden fence painted grey but covered with dirt, which the chief of police had erected in keeping with the houses in his youth, before he had taken to sleeping after dinner, and drinking a concoction of dried gooseberries at night. In other places the fences were entirely of wattle. In the middle of the square were tiny little shops; in them could be seen bundles of cracknels, a heap of soap, bitter almonds, buckshot, mercerized goods, and so on, while there was always a peasant woman in a red kerchief, and two merchant's clerks who always were to be found playing cards. But no sooner was the cavalry regiment quartered in B—— than everything was changed. The streets shone with gay colours and grew lively—in a word, took on quite another appearance. The low little houses would often see a handsome stately beplumed officer pass by on his way to a comrade to discuss the possibility of promotion or the merits of various tobaccos; or sometimes he would be paying calls in what may be called the regimental carriage, since it was used only by the regiment. Thus, one day the major would be seen driving in it, the next day it would be in the lieutenant's stables, and a week later the major's orderly would be seen greasing it with tallow. The wattle fences between the houses were covered with soldiers' caps airing in the sun; a grey coat would protrude somewhere on a gate; in the little streets you would meet soldiers with moustaches as stiff as a boot-brush. These moustaches were seen everywhere; the women had only to gather in the market-place with their jugs, when over their shoulders these moustaches were sure to be seen. The officers were a great addition to society which, up to that time, had consisted of the judge, who lived in the same house with the deacon's wife and the chief of police, a worthy man who slept abso-

lutely the whole day—from dinner until the evening, and from the
evening until dinner.  Society grew larger and busier when the
brigadier-general came to live in the town.  The neighbouring landowners, whose existence one had barely suspected till then, came
into the county town to see the gentlemen and officers, and sometimes to play cards, that had turned their heads already, muddled
with their wives' commissions, the sowing and shooting.  It is a
pity I cannot remember what made the brigadier-general give his
big dinner.  The preparations for it were enormous; the sound of
the chef's knives in the general's kitchen could be heard at the end
of the town.  Everything in the town was used for the dinner; the
judge and his deaconess, for instance, could only eat buck-wheat
cakes and corn-flour fruit jelly.  The small courtyard belonging to
the general's house was full of cabs and carriages.  The company
consisted of the officers and several local landowners.  The most
remarkable of the latter was Pifogor Pifogorovitch Chertokutsky,
who had driven over in a smart carriage.  He was one of the principal gentry of the county of B——, and made most noise at elections.  He had once served in a cavalry regiment and was one of
those " important " ubiquitous officers.  He was always to be seen
at balls or reunions wherever his regiment happened to be stationed
—the girls of the Tambovsk and Simirsk governments could testify
to that.  It is highly probable that he would have covered himself
in glory—useful to himself—in other governments had he not been
compelled to resign owing to what is commonly called an " ugly
story "; either he had boxed the ears of some one older than himself, or that person had boxed his ears—I cannot remember which,
at any rate the upshot of it was that he was requested to resign.
However, this in no way made him lose his balance; he wore a
high-waisted frock-coat, cut in military style, had spurs on his boots,
and a moustache under his nose, since without this latter the gentry
might have thought that he had been in the infantry, for which he
had a profound contempt.  He went to all the crowded fairs where
the heart of Russia—consisting of mothers, daughters, children, and
portly landowners—came to make merry in traps, carriages, dog-
carts, and such vehicles as one has never seen even in dreams.  He
could scent from afar where a cavalry regiment was quartered and
would always come over to visit the officers, alighting nimbly
before them from his elegant carriage, and soon getting acquainted
with them.  At past elections he had given a dinner to the gentry,
at which he told them that if they elected him president he would
place them in the very best position.  Altogether, he conducted
himself in a " noble style," as they say in the provinces.  He
married a very pretty girl, with whom he got a dowry of two
hundred souls, besides several thousands in cash.  The money was
soon spent on a team of six horses—certainly excellent ones—gilt
locks for the doors, a tame monkey for the house, and a French

in common, what is his is as good as mine. I won it from him in a game of cards. Would you be good enough, Your Excellency, to do me the honour of dining with me to-morrow? You could see the calèche at the same time."

"I do not know what to say to that. Alone I . . . may I bring these gentlemen, my officers?"

"I shall be delighted. Gentlemen, I look upon it as a great honour to have the pleasure of seeing you in my house!"

The colonel, the major, and the other officers thanked him by a polite bow.

"It is my opinion, Your Excellency, that if you buy anything, it may as well be good, otherwise it is not worth while. When you do me the honour of coming to see me to-morrow, I will show you various implements I have introduced for agricultural purposes."

The general stared straight before him, sending out clouds of smoke.

Chertokutsky was very pleased that he had invited the officers; he began already to decide on the various pies and sauces he would have, and smiled amiably at the officers, who in their turn seemed to double their good disposition towards him, as could be seen in their eyes and their slight half-bows to him. Chertokutsky grew more at ease, and his voice was laden with pleasure.

"I shall have the pleasure, Your Excellency, of introducing you to the mistress of the house."

"It will give me great pleasure," the general said, stroking his moustache.

After this, Chertokutsky was anxious to go home quickly so as to prepare everything in good time for the next day's reception and dinner; he was about to take up his hat, but strangely enough, stayed on a little while longer. Meanwhile card-tables were placed about the room, and soon the whole company divided into fours and sat down to whist.

The candles were brought in. Chertokutsky could not, for a long time, decide whether to sit down and play or not. But as the officers began to press him, he felt it to be against the rules of convention to refuse, and sat down. Automatically a glass of punch appeared before him, which he drank off at once, unconsciously. After playing two rubbers he again found a glass of punch to hand which he again drank off unconsciously, saying beforehand:

"Gentlemen, it is time I was going home, quite time." But he sat down again to another rubber. Meanwhile the conversation in the various corners of the room was taking various directions. The whist players were rather silent, but those who did not play and sat on couches to one side, carried on conversations among themselves. In one corner the cavalry staff captain, with a cushion at his side and a pipe between his teeth, was talking about his love affairs in a free-and-easy way, completely holding the attention of those round him. One very portly squire, with short hands that looked like overgrown potatoes, listened with an unusually sweet expression, and only from time to time took the trouble to put one short hand behind his back to pull out his snuff-box. In another corner there was quite a heated discussion about squadron drill, and Chertokutsky, who at this time had twice played a knave instead of a queen, joined in the conversations and called out from his corner, " In what year? " or " What regiment? " without noticing that sometimes his questions had no connection with the matter under discussion. At last, a few minutes before supper, whist-playing was stopped, but continued in words, and it seemed that all heads were full of whist. Chertokutsky well recollected that he had won a great deal, but actually found nothing, and getting up from the table, stood for a long time like one who has lost a handkerchief. Meanwhile, supper was served. It goes without saying that there was no lack of wine, and Chertokutsky was almost compelled to fill his glass from time to time since there were bottles to the right and left of him.

The conversation at table became long and involved, but was conducted in a strange manner. A certain colonel who had served in the campaign of 1812 was telling them of a battle that had never taken place, and then, for some mysterious reason, he took the stopper from one of the decanters and stuck it in the fire. In a word, when the guests began to depart it was already three o'clock, and the coachmen had to carry some of them out in their arms like bundles of purchases, and Chertokutsky, notwithstanding his high birth, bowed so long and with such inflections of his head on taking his seat in the carriage that when he got home there were two burdocks in his moustache.

Every one in the house was asleep; the coachman could scarcely find the valet, who guided his master through the drawing-room and handed him over to the housemaid, after which Chertokutsky somehow or other got to his bedroom and lay down beside his pretty young wife, who was sleeping in a most graceful attitude clad in a nightdress as white as snow. Her husband's fall on the bed woke her. Stretching herself, she raised her lashes and blinking quickly three or four times, opened her eyes with a half-angry smile, but seeing that he took no notice of her, she turned over on the other side, and putting her soft cheek on her hand, went to sleep soon after he did.

It was at an hour that is not called *early* in the country when the young mistress awoke beside her snoring spouse. Recollecting that he had returned home at four in the morning, she did not want to wake him. She put on her bedroom slippers that her husband had ordered in St. Petersburg, and slipping on a white dressing-jacket that flowed round her like running water, she went into her dressing-room, washed in water as fresh as herself, and then walked up to the dressing-table. She found herself looking very pretty that day. This apparently important circumstance made her spend two extra hours before the mirror. At last she put on a pretty dress and went out into the garden for some fresh air. As though on purpose, the weather happened to be beautiful at the time, the kind of weather that only a southern summer day can boast of. The sun, almost at its zenith, poured down its burning rays, but it was cool walking under the thick shady avenues, and the flowers, warmed by the sun, trebled their scent. The pretty mistress quite forgot that it was twelve o'clock and that her husband was still asleep. Already there reached her the after-dinner snoring of the two coachmen asleep in the stables at the back of the garden. But she still sat on in the shady garden whence could be seen a view of the main road and gazed absently into the solitary plain, when suddenly her attention was attracted by distant clouds of dust. Looking hard, she soon distinguished several carriages. In front came an open, two-seated light calèche in which sat the general, his epaulettes sparkling in the sun, and beside him sat the colonel. Then followed another vehicle in which sat the general's aide and two other officers; behind that came the famous regimental carriage, that belonged for the moment to the portly major; behind the carriages came a four-seater bon voyage with four officers and a fifth on the box; behind that were seen three officers on beautiful bay horses amidst dark clouds.

"Are they coming to us, I wonder?" the mistress of the house thought. "Oh, heavens! they have turned at the bridge!" she cried, clapping her hands, and she ran over the flower-beds through the flowers, straight into her husband's bedroom. He was sleeping like a log.

"Get up, get up, get up quickly," she cried, pulling his hand.

"Yes," Chertokutsky said, stretching himself but not opening his eyes.

"Get up! do you hear! Guests are coming!"

"Guests? what guests?" Saying this, he made a noise like a calf when it seeks its mother's breast. "Mm . . ." he mumbled. "Come here, I want to kiss you, dear!"

"Get up, dear, for God's sake, get up quickly! The general and the officers are coming. Oh, heavens, you have burdocks in your moustache!"

"The general? Is he coming already? The devil! Why did no one wake me? And the dinner, what about the dinner? Is everything ready as it should be?"

"What dinner?"

"Didn't I tell you?"

"You? You came home at four in the morning, and in spite of all my questions would not tell me anything. I thought it a pity to wake you, dear, you had so little sleep. . . ." The last words were uttered in a soft, pleading voice.

Chertokutsky, rubbing his eyes, lay on the bed as though struck by lightning. At last he jumped out of bed.

" Oh, what an idiot I am! " he said, striking his forehead. " I invited them to dinner! What shall I do? Are they far away? "

" I don't know. . . . They should be here at any moment now."

" Darling . . . hide yourself! Who is there? You? What are you afraid of, you little fool? Some officers will be here in a moment, tell them that master is not at home, that he went away in the morning. . . . Do you hear? Tell the other servants too! Quickly! "

Saying this, he seized his dressing-gown and rushed away to hide himself in the coach-house, thinking that his position there would be without danger. But, standing in a corner, he realised that even here he could be seen. " That will be better," flashed through his head, and in a moment he stepped into the glittering calèche and shut the door behind him, and for greater safety put up the hood and sat huddled up in his dressing-gown and the rug.

Meanwhile the carriages arrived at the door. The general got out and shook himself, and after him came the colonel arranging the plumes on his hat with both hands. Then the portly major alighted, carrying his sword under his arm, then the slim lieutenants and the ensign alighted from the bon voyage, and finally the other officers got off their horses.

" Master is not at home," a footman announced, coming out of the porch.

" Not at home! Perhaps he will be home to dinner? "

" No, he went away for the day. He will be back about this hour to-morrow."

" Well! " the general exclaimed; " what does this mean? "

" I believe it is a joke," the colonel said with a laugh.

" But how could he? " the general continued with displeasure. " Confound it! If he could not receive us, why did he invite us? "

" I cannot understand, Your Excellency, how a man could behave like that," a young officer remarked.

" What? " the general said—he always made use of this interrogation when addressing a subaltern.

" I merely wondered, Your Excellency, how a man could behave like that! "

" Naturally. . . . If something had happened, he might have let us know, or not have asked us at all."

" There is nothing to do, Your Excellency, but to go back," the colonel said.

" Of course there is nothing else to be done. However, we can see his carriage without him. He probably did not take it with him. Hi! who is there! Come here! "

" What can I do for you, sir? "

" Are you a stable man? "

" Yes, Your Excellency."

" Show us the new carriage that your master acquired lately."

" Come into the coach-house, please."

The general and the officers went into the coach-house.

" Allow me, I will wheel it round; it is rather dark here."

The general and the officers walked round the carriage and carefully examined the wheels and springs.

" Well, there is nothing remarkable about it," the general said, " a most ordinary carriage."

" A most ordinary carriage," the major said. " There is nothing remarkable about it."

" I don't think, Your Excellency, that it was worth four thousand roubles," one of the young officers remarked.

" What? "

" I said, Your Excellency, that it was not worth four thousand roubles."

" Four thousand! It is not worth two! There is nothing to see in it, unless there is something extraordinary inside. Will you please open the flaps. . . ."

And before their eyes was Chertokutsky in his dressing-gown, huddled up in a most strange fashion. " Ah, you here! " the astonished general exclaimed. With these words he banged the carriage door on Chertokutsky and went away, followed by his officers.

# MICHAIL Y. LERMONTOFF

1814–1841

# A FAIR SMUGGLER

TAMAN is the most wretched of all our maritime towns. I almost died of hunger there, besides being nearly drowned.

I arrived very late at night in a wretched *telega*. The coachman stopped his tired horses close to a stone building, which stands by itself at the entrance to the town. A Black Sea Cossack, who was on guard, heard the bells of my carriage, and cried out, with the sharp accent of a person suddenly waked up, " Who goes there? "

Out came the sergeant and corporal. I told them I was an officer, travelling by order of the Crown, and that I wanted a billet somewhere.

The corporal took us into the town. All the houses we tried were already occupied. The weather was cold; I had been three nights without sleep. I was very tired, and our useless inquiries ended by irritating me.

" My friend," I said to the corporal, " take me to some place where I can at least lie down, no matter where it is."

" I know a hut in the neighbourhood," replied the corporal, " where you might sleep; but I am afraid it would scarcely suit your honour."

" Go on," I said, paying no attention to his observation.

After much walking through dirty little streets, we at last reached a sort of cabin on the edge of the sea.

The full moon cast its light on the thatched roof and the white walls of my proposed habitation. In the court, surrounded by a sort of palisade, I saw a hut, older and more broken down than the principal one. From this hut the ground sloped rapidly through the court down towards the sea, and I saw at my feet the foam of the troubled waters. The moon seemed to be contemplating the restless element, which was undergoing her influence. By the rays of the ruler of the night, I could make out, at a considerable distance from the shore, two ships, whose black sails stood out like spiders' webs against the dull tints of the sky. " This will do," I said to myself, " to-morrow morning I shall start for Ghelendchik."

A Cossack of the line was acting as my servant. I told him to take out my trunk and send away the postillion; after which I called the master of the house. I could get no answer. I knocked, but there was still no reply. What could it mean? I knocked again, and at last a boy of about fourteen showed himself.

" Where's the master of the house? "

" There is none," returned the child, in the dialect of Little Russia.

" No master! then where is the mistress? "

" Gone into the village."

" Who will open the door then? " I cried, at the same time kicking at it.

The door opened of itself, and out came a wave of damp steam. I struck a match, and saw by its light a blind boy, standing motionless before me.

I must here say that I am strongly prejudiced against the blind, the deaf, the lame, the hunch-backed; in short, against the deformed in general. I have remarked that there is always a singular correspondence between the physical formation of a man and his moral nature; as though by the loss of a member the individual lost certain faculties of the soul.

I examined the child's face; but what can one make of a physiognomy without eyes? I looked at him for some time, with a feeling of compassion, when suddenly I saw on his lips a cunning smile, which produced upon me a very disagreeable impression. " Could this blind boy be not so blind as he appeared? " I said to myself. Answering my own question I said that the boy was evidently suffering from cataract, and that the appearance of cataract cannot be simulated. Why, moreover, should he affect blindness? Yet in spite of my argument I still remained vaguely suspicious.

" Is the mistress of the cabin your mother? " I said to the boy.

" No."

" Who are you, then? "

" A poor orphan," he replied.

" Has the mistress any children? "

" She has one daughter, who has gone to sea with a Tartar."

" What Tartar? "

" How do I know? A Tartar of the Crimea, a boatman from Kertch."

I went into the hut. Two benches, a table, and a large wardrobe, placed near the stove, composed the whole of the furniture. No holy image against the wall—bad sign!

The sea-breeze came in through the broken panes of the window. I took a wax candle from my portmanteau, and after lighting it prepared to install myself. I placed on one side my sabre and my carbine, laid my pistols on the table, stretched myself out on a bench, and, wrapping myself up in my fur-lined coat, lay down.

My Cossack took possession of the other bench. Ten minutes afterwards he was fast asleep; I, moreover, was still awake, and could not drive from my mind the impression made upon me by the boy, with his two white eyes.

An hour passed. Through the window fell upon the floor the fantastic light of the moon.

Suddenly a shadow was cast, where before there had been bright light. I sprang up, and went to the window. A human figure passed once more, and then disappeared—heaven knows where. I could scarcely believe that it had escaped by the slope into the sea; yet there was no other issue.

Throwing on my overcoat, and taking my sabre, I went out of the cabin, and saw the blind boy before me. I concealed myself behind the wall, and he passed on confidently, but with a certain cautiousness. He was carrying something under his arm, and advanced slowly down the slope towards the sea. " This is the hour," I said to myself, " in which speech is restored to the dumb and sight to the blind."

I followed him at some distance, anxious not to lose sight of him.

During this time the moon became covered with clouds, and a black fog rose over the sea. It was just possible to distinguish in the darkness a lantern on the mast of a ship at anchor, close to the shore. The waves were rolling in, and threatened, if he continued to advance, to swallow up my blind adventurer. He was now so near the sea, that with another step he would be lost. But this was not the first of his nocturnal expeditions; so at least I concluded from the agility with which he now sprang from rock to rock, while the sea poured in beneath his feet. Suddenly he stopped as though he had heard some noise, sat down upon a rock, and placed his burden by his side. He was now joined by a white figure walking along the shore. I had concealed myself behind one of the rocks, and overheard the following conversation.

" The wind," said a woman's voice, " is very violent; Janko will not come."

" Janko," replied the blind boy, " Janko is not afraid of the wind."

" But the clouds get thicker and thicker."

" In the darkness it is easier to escape the coast-guard."

" And what if he gets drowned? "

" You will have no more bright ribbons to wear on Sunday."

As I listened to this colloquy, I remarked that the blind boy, who had spoken to me in the Little Russian dialect, talked quite correctly the true Russian language.

" You see," he continued, clapping his hands, " I was right. Janko fears neither the sea, nor the wind, nor the fog, nor the coast-guard. Listen! It is not the breaking of the waves I hear. No, it is the noise of his oars."

The woman got up, and, with an anxious look, tried to pierce the darkness. " You are wrong," she said, " I hear nothing."

I also tried to see whether there was not some sort of craft in the distance, but could distinguish nothing. A moment later, however, a black speck showed itself among the waves, now rising, now falling. At last I could make out the form of a boat dancing on the waters, and rapidly approaching the shore.

The man who was guiding it must have been a bold sailor to cross on such a night an arm of the sea some fourteen miles across, and must have had good reasons for braving so much danger. I watched the frail little craft which was now diving and plunging like a duck through the breakers. It seemed as though she must the next moment be dashed to pieces on the shore, when suddenly the skilful rower turned into a little bay, and there, in comparatively calm water, effected a landing.

The man was of middle height, and wore on his head a cap of black sheep-skin. He made a sign with his hand, when the two mysterious persons who had been talking together, joined him. Then the three united their forces to drag from the boat a burden which seemed to be so heavy, that I cannot even now understand how so slight a craft could have supported such a weight. They at last hoisted the cargo on their shoulders, then walked away and soon disappeared.

The best thing for me to do now was to return to my resting-place. But the strange scene I had witnessed had so struck me that I waited impatiently for daybreak.

My Cossack was much surprised when, on waking up, he found me fully dressed. I said nothing to him about my nocturnal excursion. I remained for some little time looking through the window with admiration at the blue sky, studded with little clouds, and the distant shore, the Crimea, stretched along the horizon like a streak of violet, ending in a rock, above which could be seen the tower of a lighthouse. Then I went out, and walked to the fort of Chanagora to ask the commandant when I could go to Ghelendchik.

Unfortunately the commandant could give me no positive answer; the only vessels in port were stationary ones, and trading ships which had not yet taken in their cargo. " Perhaps," he said, " in three or four days a mail packet will come in, and then something can be arranged."

I went back in a very bad humour to my lodging. At the door stood the Cossack, who, coming towards me with rather a scared look, said inquiringly:

" Bad news? "

" Yes," I answered. " Heaven knows when we shall get away from here."

At these words the anxiety of the soldier seemed to increase. He came close to me, and murmured, in a low voice:

488 MICHAIL Y. LERMONTOFF

" This is not a place to stop at. I met just now a Black Sea Cossack of my acquaintance—we were serving in the same detachment last year. When I told him where we had put up: ' Bad place,' he said, ' bad people.' And what do you think of that blind boy? Did any one ever before see a blind person running about from one place to another; going to the bazaar, bringing in bread and water? Here they seem to think nothing of it."

" Has the mistress of the place come in? "

" This morning, while you were out, an old woman came with her daughter."

" What daughter? Her daughter is away."

" I don't know who it is, then. But look, there is the old woman sitting down in the cabin."

I went in. A good fire was shining in the stove, and a breakfast was being prepared, which, for such poor people, seemed to me rather a luxurious one. When I spoke to the old woman, she told me that she was stone deaf.

It was impossible, then, to talk with her. I turned to the blind boy, and, taking him by the ear, said:

" I say, you little wizard, where were you going last night with that parcel under your arm? "

He at once began to moan and cry, and then sobbed out:

" Where was I going last night? I went nowhere. And with a parcel! What parcel? "

The old woman now proved that her ears, when she so desired it, were by no means closed.

" It is not true," she cried. " Why do you tease an unfortunate boy? What do you take him for? What harm has he done you? "

I could stand the noise no longer. So I went out, determined somehow or other to find the solution of this riddle.

Wrapped up in my overcoat, I sat down on a bench before the door. Before me broke the waves of the sea, still agitated by the tempest of the night. Their monotonous noise seemed to resemble the confused murmurs of a town. As I listened I thought of bygone years—of the years I had passed in the north, of our bright, fresh capital; and little by little I became absorbed in my recollections.

About an hour passed, perhaps more. Suddenly the cadences of a singing voice struck my ear. I listened, and heard a strange melody, now slow and sad, now rapid and lively. The sounds seemed to fall from the sky. I looked up, and on the roof of the cabin I saw a young girl, in a straight dress, with dishevelled hair, like a naiad. With one hand placed before her eyes to keep off the rays of the sun, she looked towards the distant horizon and still continued her song.

It seemed to me that this was the woman whose voice I had heard the night before on the seashore. I looked again towards the singer, but she had disappeared. A moment after she passed rapidly before me, singing another song and snapping her fingers. She went to the old woman and said something to her. The old woman seemed annoyed. The young girl burst into a laugh. Then, with a bound, she came close to me, suddenly stopped and looked at me fixedly, as though surprised to see me. Then turning away with an air of indifference, she walked quietly towards the shore.

But her manœuvres were not yet at an end. All the rest of the day I saw her at short intervals, always singing and dancing. Strange creature! There was nothing in her physiognomy to denote insanity. On the contrary, her eyes were intelligent and pene-trating. They exercised on me a certain magnetic influence, and seemed to expect a question. But whenever I was on the point of speaking she took to flight with a sly smile on her lips.

I had never seen such a woman before. She could scarcely be called beautiful; but I have my own ideas on the subject of beauty. There was a thoroughbred look about her, and with women as with horses, there is nothing like breed. It can be recognised in the walk and in the shape of the hands and feet. The nose is also an important feature. In Russia regular noses are more rare than little feet. My siren must have been about eighteen years of age.

What charmed me in her was the extraordinary suppleness of her figure, the singular movements of her head, and the long, fair hair, hanging down in waves of gold on her neck, and her nose, which was perfectly formed.

In her sidelong glance there was something dark and wild; as there was something fascinating in the pure lines of her nose. The light-hearted singer recalled to me the Mignon of Goethe, that fan-tastic creation of the German mind. Between these two personages there was indeed a striking resemblance. The same sudden transi-tions from restless agitation to perfect calm; the same enigmatic words and the same songs.

Towards the evening I stopped my Undine at the door of the hut, and said to her:

" Tell me, my pretty one, what you were doing to-day on the roof? "

" I was seeing in what direction the wind blew."

" How did that concern you? "

" Whence blows the wind, thence comes happiness."

" And your singing was to bring you good fortune? "

" Where singing is heard, there is joy."

" But what should you say if your singing caused unhappi-ness? "

" If unhappiness arrives it must be borne. And from grief to joy the distance is not great."

" Who taught you these songs? "

" No one; I dream and I sing; those who understand me listen to me, and those who do not listen to me cannot understand me."

" What is your name? "

" Ask those who baptized me."

" And who baptized you? "

" I do not know."

" Ah! you are very mysterious; but I know something about you."

There was no sign of emotion on her face; her lips did not move.

" Last night," I continued, " you were on the seashore." Then I told her the scene I had witnessed. I thought this would have caused her to evince some symptom of anxiety, but it had no such effect.

" You assisted at a curious interview," she said to me with a laugh, " but you do not know much, and what you do know you had better keep under lock and key, as you would keep some precious treasure."

" But if," I continued, with a grave and almost menacing air, " I were to relate what I saw to the commandant? "

At these words she darted away, singing, and disappeared like a frightened bird. I was wrong in addressing this threat to her. At the moment I did not understand all its gravity.

The night came. I told my Cossack to prepare the tea-urn, lighted a wax candle, and sat down at the table, smoking my long pipe. I was drinking my tea when the door opened, and I heard the rustling of a dress. I rose hastily and recognised my siren.

She sat down silently before me, and fixed me with a look which made me tremble; one of those magical looks which had troubled my life in earlier days. She seemed to expect me to speak to her, but some undefinable emotion deprived me of the faculty of speech. Her countenance was as pale as death. In this paleness I thought I could see the agitation of her heart. Her fingers struck mechanically on the table; her body seemed to shudder; her bosom rose violently and the moment afterwards seemed compressed.

This species of comedy tired me at last, and I was about to bring it to an end, in the most prosaic manner, by offering my fair visitor a cup of tea; when suddenly she rose, and taking my head in her hands, gazed at me with all the appearance of passionate tenderness.

A cloud covered my eyes, and I wished in my turn to kiss her, but she escaped like a snake, murmuring as she did so, " To-night, when everything is quiet, meet me on the shore." Then she disappeared, upsetting as she did so my tea-urn and my solitary light.

" She is the very mischief! " cried my Cossack, who had been looking out for his share of the tea.

He then lay down on his bench; and gradually my agitation subsided.

" Listen," I said to him. " If you hear a pistol-shot, hurry down as fast as you can to the shore."

He rubbed his eyes, and replied mechanically, " Yes, sir."

I placed my pistol in my belt, and went out. The siren was waiting for me at the top of the path leading down to the sea, lightly clad in a stuff which clung to her waist like a scarf.

" Follow me," she said, taking me by the hand.

We walked down the rocky path in such a manner that I cannot understand how I failed to break my neck. Then we turned sharply to the right, as the blind boy had done the night before. The moon was not yet up. Two little stars, like the fires of lighthouses, relieved the darkness. The agitated waves lifted and let fall in regular cadence a solitary boat close to the shore.

" Get in," she said. I hesitated, for I confess that I have not the least taste for sentimental excursions on the sea. But it was impossible to refuse. She leapt into the barque, I followed her, and off we went.

" What does all this mean? " I said, getting angry.

" It means," she replied, making me sit down on a bench, and putting her arms round my waist, " it means that I love you." Her burning cheek was close to mine, and I felt her hot breath on my face. Suddenly I heard something fall into the water. Instinctively my hand went to my belt. The pistol was no longer there!

A horrible suspicion seized me. The blood rushed to my brain. I looked at her. We were far from the shore and I could not swim. I tried to escape from her embrace, but she clung to me like a cat, and almost succeeded by a sudden jerk in throwing me out of the boat, which was already on one side. I contrived, however, to restore the equilibrium; and then began, between my perfidious companion and myself, a desperate struggle, in which I employed all my strength, while feeling that the abominable creature was overcoming me by her agility.

" What do you mean? " I said to her, squeezing her little hands so tightly that I heard her fingers crack; but whatever pain I may have caused her she did not utter a word. Her reptile nature could not thus be overcome.

" You saw us," she cried at last. " You want to denounce us." Then by a rapid and violent effort she threw me down. Her body and mine were now bending over the side of the frail craft, and her hair was in the water. The moment was a critical one. I got up on my knees, took her with one hand by the hair, with the other by the throat, and when I had at last compelled her to unclutch my clothes, I threw her into the sea.

Twice her head reappeared above the foaming waves. Then I saw her no more.

In the bottom of the boat I found an old oar, with which, after much labour, I succeeded in getting to the shore. As I walked back to the hut by the path leading to the sea, I looked towards the place where the night before the blind boy had been awaiting the arrival of the sailor. The moon at this moment was shining in the sky, and I fancied I could discern on the seashore a white figure. Filled with curiosity, I concealed myself behind a sort of promontory, from which I could remark what was going on around me. What was my surprise, and I almost say my joy, when I saw that the white figure was my naiad? She was wringing the water out of her long, fair locks, and her wet dress clung to her body. A boat, which I could just see in the distance, was coming towards us. Out of it sprang the same boatman whom I had seen the night before, with the same Tartar cap. I now saw that his hair was cut in the Cossack fashion, and that from his girdle hung a large knife.

" Janko," cried the young girl, " all is lost."

Then they began to talk, but in so low a voice that I could not hear them.

" Where is the blind boy? " said Janko at last, raising his voice.

" He will be here soon," was the answer.

At that very moment the blind boy appeared, carrying on his back a packet, which he placed in the barque.

" Listen," said Janko, " keep a good watch here; the things you know are valuable. Tell "—(here a name was uttered which I could not catch) " that I am no longer in his service. Things have taken a bad turn. He will see me no more. The situation is so dangerous that I must get something to do elsewhere. He will not find such another very easily. You may add that, if he had rewarded more liberally the dangerous services rendered to him, Janko would not have left him in the lurch. If he wants to know where to find me—where the wind howls, where the sea foams, that is where I am at home."

After a moment's silence, Janko went on: " Say she accompanies me. She cannot remain here. Tell the old woman that she has done her time, and that she ought to be satisfied. We shall not see her again."

" And I? " murmured the blind boy.

" I cannot be troubled about you."

The young girl leapt into the boat, and with her hand made a sign to her companion.

" Here," he said to the blind boy, " that will do to buy a ginger-bread."

" Nothing more? " replied the child.

" Yes, take this," and a piece of money fell upon the sands.

The blind boy did not pick it up.

Janko took his place in the boat. The blind boy remained sitting down on the seashore, and he seemed to be crying. Poor fellow! his grief afflicted me. Why had fate thrown me in the midst of this peaceful circle of smugglers? As a stone troubles the water, I had brought disorder into these lives, and like the stone, moreover, I had very nearly sunk.

When I got back to the cabin, my Cossack was so fast asleep that it would have been cruel to disturb him. I lighted the candle, and saw that my little box containing my valuables, my sabre with silver mountings, my Circassian dagger (given to me by a friend), had all been carried off. I now understood what the packet placed in the boat by the blind boy must have contained.

I woke up my Cossack with a blow, reproached him for his negligence, and fairly lost my temper. But my anger could not make me find what I had lost.

And how could I complain to the authorities? Should not I have been laughed at if I told them that I had been robbed by a blind boy, and almost drowned by a young girl?

# IVAN S. TURGENIEV

1818–1883

# THE SINGERS

THE small village of Kolotovka once belonged to a lady known in the neighbourhood by the nickname of Skin-flint, in allusion to her keen business habits (her real name is lost in oblivion), but has of late years been the property of a German from Petersburg. The village lies on the slope of a barren hill, which is cut in half from top to bottom by a tremendous ravine. It is a yawning chasm, with shelving sides hollowed out by the action of rain and snow, and it winds along the very centre of the village street; it separates the two sides of the unlucky hamlet far more than a river would do, for a river could, at least, be crossed by a bridge. A few gaunt willows creep timorously down its sandy sides; at the very bottom, which is dry and yellow as copper, lie huge slabs of argillaceous rock. A cheerless position, there's no denying, yet all the surrounding inhabitants know the road to Kolotovka well; they go there often, and are always glad to go.

At the very summit of the ravine, a few paces from the point where it starts as a narrow fissure in the earth, there stands a small square hut. It stands alone, apart from all the others. It is thatched, and has a chimney; one window keeps watch like a sharp eye over the ravine, and on winter evenings when it is lighted from within, it is seen far away in the dim frosty fog, and its twinkling light is the guiding star of many a peasant on his road. A blue board is nailed up above the door; this hut is a tavern, called the "Welcome Resort." Spirits are sold here probably no cheaper than the usual price, but it is far more frequented than any other establishment of the same sort in the neighbourhood. The explanation of this is to be found in the tavern-keeper, Nikolai Ivanitch.

Nikolai Ivanitch—once a slender, curly-headed and rosy-cheeked young fellow, now an excessively stout, grizzled man with a fat face, sly and good-natured little eyes, and a shiny forehead, with wrinkles like lines drawn all over it—has lived for more than twenty years in Kolotovka. Nikolai Ivanitch is a shrewd, acute fellow, like the majority of tavern-keepers. Though he makes no conspicuous effort to please or to talk to people, he has the art of

attracting and keeping customers, who find it particularly pleasant
to sit at his bar under the placid and genial, though alert eye, of
the phlegmatic host. He has a great deal of common sense; he
thoroughly understands the landowner's conditions of life, the
peasant's, and the tradesman's. He could give sensible advice on
difficult points, but, like a cautious man and an egoist, prefers to
stand aloof, and at most—and that only in the case of his favourite
customers—by remote hints, dropped, as it were, unintentionally,
to lead them into the true way. He is an authority on everything
that is of interest or importance to a Russian; on horses and cattle,
on timber, bricks, and crockery, on woollen stuffs and on leather,
on songs and dances. When he has no customers he is usually
sitting like a sack on the ground before the door of his hut, his thin
legs tucked under him, exchanging a friendly greeting with every
passer-by. He has seen a great deal in his time; many a score of
petty landowners, who used to come to him for spirits, he has seen
pass away before him; he knows everything that is done for eighty
miles round, and never gossips, never gives a sign of knowing what
is unsuspected by the most keen-sighted police-officer. He keeps
his own counsel, laughs, and makes his glasses ring. His neighbours respect him; the civilian general Shtcherpetenko, the landowner highest in rank in the district, gives him a condescending nod
whenever he drives past his little house. Nikolai Ivanitch is a man
of influence; he made a notorious horse-stealer return a horse he
had taken from the stable of one of his friends; he brought the
peasants of a neighbouring village to their senses when they refused
to accept a new overseer, and so on. It must not be imagined,
though, that he does this from love of justice, from devotion to his
neighbour—no! he simply tries to prevent anything that might, in
any way, interfere with his ease and comfort. Nikolai Ivanitch is
married, and has children. His wife, a smart, sharp-nosed, and
keen-eyed woman of the tradesman class, has grown somewhat
stout of late years, like her husband. He relies on her in everything, and she keeps the key of the cash-box. Drunken brawlers
are afraid of her; she does not like them; they bring little profit and
make a great deal of noise: those who are taciturn and surly in
their cups are more to her taste. Nikolai Ivanitch's children are
still small; the first four all died, but those that are left take after
their parents: it is a pleasure to look at their intelligent, healthy
little faces.

It was an insufferably hot day in July when, slowly dragging my
feet along, I went up alongside the Kolotovka ravine with my dog
towards the Welcome Resort. The sun blazed, as it were, fiercely
in the sky, baking the parched earth relentlessly; the air was thick
with stifling dust. Glossy crows and ravens with gaping beaks
looked plaintively at the passers-by, as though asking for sympathy;
only the sparrows did not droop, but, pluming their feathers,

twittered more vigorously than ever as they quarrelled among the hedges, or flew up all together from the dusty road, and hovered in grey clouds over the green hempfields. I was tormented by thirst. There was no water near: in Kolotovka, as in many other villages of the steppes, the peasants, having no spring or well, drink a sort of thin mud out of the pond. . . . For no one could call that repulsive beverage water. I wanted to ask for a glass of beer or kvas at Nikolai Ivanitch's.

It must be confessed that at no time of the year does Kolotovka present a very cheering spectacle; but it has a particularly depressing effect when the relentless rays of a dazzling July sun pour down full upon the brown, tumble-down roofs of the houses and the deep ravine, and the parched, dusty common over which the thin, long-legged hens are straying hopelessly, and the remains of the old manor-house, now a hollow, grey framework of aspenwood, with holes instead of windows, overgrown with nettles, wormwood, and rank grass, and the pond black, as though charred and covered with goose feathers, with its edge of half-dried mud, and its broken-down dyke, near which, on the finely trodden, ash-like earth, sheep, breathless and gasping with the heat, huddle dejectedly together, their heads drooping with weary patience, as though waiting for this insufferable heat to pass at last. With weary steps I drew near Nikolai Ivanitch's dwelling, arousing in the village children the usual wonder manifested in a concentrated, meaningless stare, and in the dogs an indignation expressed in such hoarse and furious barking that it seemed as if it were tearing their very entrails, and left them breathless and choking, when suddenly in the tavern doorway there appeared a tall peasant without a cap, in a frieze cloak, girt about below his waist with a blue handkerchief. He looked like a house-serf; thick grey hair stood up in disorder above his withered and wrinkled face. He was calling to some one hurriedly, waving his arms, which obviously were not quite under his control. It could be seen that he had been drinking already.

" Come, come along! " he stammered, raising his shaggy eyebrows with an effort. " Come, Blinkard, come along! Ah, brother, how you creep along, 'pon my word! It's too bad, brother. They're waiting for you within, and here you crawl along. . . . Come."

" Well, I'm coming, I'm coming! " called a jarring voice, and from behind a hut a little, short, fat, lame man came into sight. He wore a rather tidy cloth coat, pulled half on, and a high pointed cap right over his brows, which gave his round plump face a sly and comic expression. His little yellow eyes moved restlessly about, his thin lips wore a continual forced smile, while his sharp, long nose peered forward saucily in front like a rudder. " I'm coming, my dear fellow." He went hobbling towards the tavern. " What are you calling me for? . . . Who's waiting for me? "

" What am I calling you for? " repeated the man in the frieze
coat reproachfully. " You're a queer fish, Blinkard: we call you
to come to the tavern, and you ask what for? Here are honest
folks all waiting for you: Yashka the Turk, and the Wild Master,
and the booth-keeper from Zhizdry. Yashka's got a bet on with
the booth-keeper: the stake's a pot of beer—for the one that does
best, sings the best, I mean . . . do you see? "

" Is Yashka going to sing? " said the man addressed as
Blinkard, with lively interest. " But isn't it your humbug,
Gabbler? "

" I'm not humbugging," answered the Gabbler, with dignity;
" it's you are crazy. I should think he would sing since he's got a
bet on it, you precious innocent, you noodle, Blinkard! "

" Well, come in, simpleton! " retorted the Blinkard.

" Then give us a kiss at least, lovey," stammered the Gabbler,
opening wide his arms.

" Get out, you great softy! " responded the Blinkard contemptuously, giving him a poke with his elbow, and both, stooping, entered the low doorway.

The conversation I had overheard roused my curiosity exceedingly. More than once rumours had reached me of Yashka the
Turk as the best singer in the vicinity, and here was an opportunity
all at once of hearing him in competition with another master of
the art. I quickened my steps and went into the house.

Few of my readers have probably had an opportunity of getting
a good view of any village taverns, but we sportsmen go everywhere. They are constructed on an exceedingly simple plan.
They usually consist of a dark outer-shed, and an inner room with
a chimney, divided in two by a partition, behind which none of the
customers have a right to go. In this partition there is a wide
opening cut above a broad oak table. At this table or bar the
spirits are served. Sealed-up bottles of various sizes stand on the
shelves, right opposite the opening. In the front part of the room,
devoted to customers, there are benches, two or three empty barrels,
and a corner table. Village taverns are for the most part rather
dark, and you hardly ever see on their wainscoted walls any of
the glaring cheap prints which few huts are without.

When I went into the Welcome Resort, a fairly large party were
already assembled there.

In his usual place behind the bar, almost filling up the entire
opening in the partition, stood Nikolai Ivanitch in a striped print
shirt; with a lazy smile on his full face, he poured out with his
plump white hand two glasses of spirits for the Blinkard and the
Gabbler as they came in; behind him, in a corner near the window,
could be seen his sharp-eyed wife. In the middle of the room was
standing Yakov the Turk, a thin, graceful fellow of three-and-
twenty, dressed in a long skirted coat of blue nankin. He looked

a smart factory hand, and could not, to judge by his appearance, boast of very good health. His hollow cheeks, his large, restless grey eyes, his straight nose, with its delicate mobile nostrils, his pale brown curls brushed back over the sloping white brow, his full but beautiful, expressive lips, and his whole face betrayed a passionate and sensitive nature. He was in a state of great excitement; he blinked, his breathing was hurried, his hands shook, as though in fever, and he was really in a fever—that sudden fever of excitement which is so well known to all who have to speak and sing before an audience. Near him stood a man of about forty, with broad shoulders and broad jaws, with a low forehead, narrow Tartar eyes, a short flat nose, a square chin, and shining black hair coarse as bristles. The expression of his face—a swarthy face, with a sort of leaden hue in it—and especially of his pale lips, might almost have been called savage, if it had not been so still and dreamy. He hardly stirred a muscle; he only looked slowly about him like a bull under the yoke. He was dressed in a sort of surtout, not over new, with smooth brass buttons; an old black silk handkerchief was twisted round his immense neck. He was called the Wild Master. Right opposite him, on a bench under the holy pictures, was sitting Yashka's rival, the booth-keeper from Zhizdry; he was a short, stoutly-built man about thirty, pock-marked, and curly-headed, with a blunt, turn-up nose, lively brown eyes, and a scanty beard. He looked keenly about him, and, sitting with his hands under him, he kept carelessly swinging his legs and tapping with his feet, which were encased in stylish top-boots with a coloured edging. He wore a new thin coat of grey cloth, with a plush collar, in sharp contrast with the crimson shirt below, buttoned close across the chest. In the opposite corner, to the right of the door, a peasant sat at the table in a narrow, shabby smock-frock, with a huge rent on the shoulder. The sunlight fell in a narrow, yellowish streak through the dusty panes of the two small windows, but it seemed as if it struggled in vain with the habitual darkness of the room; all the objects in it were dimly, as it were patchily, lighted up. On the other hand, it was almost cool in the room, and the sense of stifling heat dropped off me like a weary load directly I crossed the threshold.

My entrance, I could see, was at first somewhat disconcerting to Nikolai Ivanitch's customers; but observing that he greeted me as a friend, they were reassured, and took no more notice of me. I asked for some beer and sat down in the corner, near the peasant in the ragged smock.

" Well, well," piped the Gabbler, suddenly draining a glass of spirits at one gulp, and accompanying his exclamation with the strange gesticulations, without which he seemed unable to utter a single word; " what are we waiting for? If we're going to begin, then begin. Hey, Yashka? " (familiar for Yakov).

" Begin, begin," chimed in Nikolai Ivanitch approvingly.

" Let's begin, by all means," observed the booth-keeper coolly, with a self-confident smile; " I'm ready."

" And I'm ready," Yakov pronounced in a voice thrilled with excitement.

" Well, begin, lads," whined the Blinkard. But, in spite of the unanimously expressed desire, neither began; the booth-keeper did not even get up from the bench—they all seemed to be waiting for something.

" Begin! " said the Wild Master sharply and sullenly. Yashka started. The booth-keeper pulled down his girdle and cleared his throat.

" But who's to begin? " he inquired in a slightly changed voice of the Wild Master, who still stood motionless in the middle of the room, his stalwart legs wide apart and his powerful arms thrust up to the elbow into his breeches pockets.

" You, you, booth-keeper," stammered the Gabbler; " you, to be sure, brother."

The Wild Master looked at him from under his brows. The Gabbler gave a faint squeak, in confusion looked away at the ceiling, twitched his shoulder, and said no more.

" Cast lots," the Wild Master pronounced emphatically; " and the pot on the table."

Nikolai Ivanitch bent down, and with a gasp picked up the pot of beer from the floor and set it on the table.

The Wild Master glanced at Yakov, and said " Come! "

Yakov fumbled in his pockets, took out a halfpenny, and marked it with his teeth. The booth-keeper pulled from under the skirts of his long coat a new leather purse, deliberately untied the string, and shaking out a quantity of small change into his hand, picked out a new halfpenny. The Gabbler held out his dirty cap, with its broken peak hanging loose; Yakov dropped his halfpenny in, and the booth-keeper his.

" You must pick out one," said the Wild Master, turning to the Blinkard.

The Blinkard smiled complacently, took the cap in both hands, and began shaking it.

For an instant a profound silence reigned; the halfpennies clinked faintly, jingling against each other. I looked round attentively; every face wore an expression of intense expectation; the Wild Master himself showed signs of uneasiness; my neighbour, even, the peasant in the tattered smock, craned his neck inquisitively. The Blinkard put his hand into the cap and took out the booth-keeper's halfpenny; every one drew a long breath. Yakov flushed, and the booth-keeper passed his hand over his hair.

" There, I said you'd begin," cried the Gabbler; " didn't I say so? "

"There, there, don't cluck," remarked the Wild Master contemptuously. "Begin," he went on, with a nod to the booth-keeper.

"What song am I to sing?" asked the booth-keeper, beginning to be nervous.

"What you choose," answered the Blinkard; "sing what you think best."

"What you choose, to be sure," Nikolai Ivanitch chimed in, slowly smoothing his hand on his breast, "you're quite at liberty about that. Sing what you like; only sing well; and we'll give a fair decision afterwards."

"A fair decision, of course," put in the Gabbler, licking the edge of his empty glass.

"Let me clear my throat a bit, mates," said the booth-keeper, fingering the collar of his coat.

"Come, come, no nonsense—begin!" protested the Wild Master, and he looked down.

The booth-keeper thought a minute, shook his head, and stepped forward. Yakov's eyes were riveted upon him.

But before I enter upon a description of the contest itself, I think it will not be amiss to say a few words about each of the personages taking part in my story. The lives of some of them were known to me already when I met them in the Welcome Resort; I collected some facts about the others later on.

Let us begin with the Gabbler. This man's real name was Evgraf Ivanovitch; but no one in the whole neighbourhood knew him as anything but the Gabbler, and he himself referred to himself by that nickname; so well did it fit him. Indeed, nothing could have been more appropriate to his insignificant, ever-restless features. He was a dissipated, unmarried house-serf, whose own masters had long ago got rid of him, and who, without any employment, without earning a halfpenny, found means to get drunk every day at other people's expense. He had a great number of acquaintances who treated him to drinks of spirits and tea, though they could not have said why they did so themselves; for, far from being entertaining in company, he bored every one with his meaningless chatter, his insufferable familiarity, his spasmodic gestures and incessant, unnatural laugh. He could neither sing nor dance; he had never said a clever, or even a sensible thing in his life; he chattered away, telling lies about everything—a regular Gabbler! And yet not a single drinking party for thirty miles around took place without his lank figure turning up among the guests; so that they were used to him by now, and put up with his presence as a necessary evil. They all, it is true, treated him with contempt; but the Wild Master was the only one who knew how to keep his foolish sallies in check.

The Blinkard was not in the least like the Gabbler. His nickname, too, suited him, though he was no more given to blinking than other people; it is a well-known fact, that the Russian peasants have a talent for finding good nicknames. In spite of my endeavours to get more detailed information about this man's past, many passages in his life have remained spots of darkness to me, and probably to many other people; episodes, buried, as the bookmen say, in the darkness of oblivion. I could only find out that he was once a coachman in the service of an old childless lady; that he had run away with three horses he was in charge of; had been lost for a whole year, and no doubt, convinced by experience of the drawbacks and hardships of a wandering life, he had gone back, a cripple, and flung himself at his mistress's feet. He succeeded in a few years in smoothing over his offence by his exemplary conduct, and, gradually getting higher in her favour, at last gained her complete confidence, was made a bailiff, and on his mistress's death, turned out—in what way was never known—to have received his freedom. He got admitted into the class of tradesmen; rented patches of market garden from the neighbours; grew rich, and now was living in ease and comfort. He was a man of experience, who knew on which side his bread was buttered; was more actuated by prudence than by either good or ill-nature; had knocked about, understood men, and knew how to turn them to his own advantage. He was cautious, and at the same time enterprising, like a fox; though he was as fond of gossip as an old woman, he never let out his own affairs, while he made every one else talk freely of theirs. He did not affect to be a simpleton, though, as so many crafty men of his sort do; indeed it would have been difficult for him to take any one in, in that way; I have never seen a sharper, keener pair of eyes than his tiny cunning little " peepers," as they call them in Orel. They were never simply looking about; they were always looking one up and down and through and through. The Blinkard would sometimes ponder for weeks together over some apparently simple undertaking, and again he would suddenly decide on a desperately bold line of action, which one would fancy would bring him to ruin. . . . But it would be sure to turn out all right; everything would go smoothly. He was lucky, and believed in his own luck, and believed in omens. He was exceedingly superstitious in general. He was not liked, because he would have nothing much to do with any one, but he was respected. His whole family consisted of one little son, whom he idolised, and who, brought up by such a father, is likely to get on in the world. " Little Blinkard'll be his father over again," is said of him already in undertones by the old men, as they sit on their mud walls gossiping on summer evenings, and every one knows what that means; there is no need to say more.

As to Yakov the Turk and the booth-keeper, there is no need to say much about them. Yakov, called the Turk because he actually was descended from a Turkish woman, a prisoner from the war, was by nature an artist in every sense of the word, and by calling, a ladler in a paper factory belonging to a merchant. As for the booth-keeper, his career, I must own, I know nothing of; he struck me as being a smart townsman of the tradesman class, ready to turn his hand to anything. But the Wild Master calls for a more detailed account.

The first impression the sight of this man produced on you was a sense of coarse, heavy, irresistible power. He was clumsily built, a " shambler," as they say about us, but there was an air of triumphant vigour about him, and—strange to say—his bear-like figure was not without a certain grace of its own, proceeding, perhaps, from his absolutely placid confidence in his own strength. It was hard to decide at first to what class this Hercules belonged: he did not look like a house-serf, nor a tradesman, nor an impoverished clerk out of work, nor a small ruined landowner, such as takes to being a huntsman or a fighting man; he was, in fact, quite individual. No one knew where he came from or what brought him into our district; it was said that he came of free peasant-proprietor stock, and had once been in the Government service somewhere, but nothing positive was known about this; and indeed there was no one from whom one could learn—certainly not from him; he was the most silent and morose of men. So much so that no one knew for certain what he lived on; he followed no trade, visited no one, associated with scarcely any one; yet he had money to spend; little enough, it is true, still he had some. In his behaviour he was not exactly retiring—retiring was not a word that could be applied to him: he lived as though he noticed no one about him, and cared for no one. The Wild Master (that was the nickname they had given him; his real name was Perevlyesov) enjoyed an immense influence in the whole district; he was obeyed with eager promptitude, though he had no kind of right to give orders to any one, and did not himself evince the slightest pretension to authority over the people with whom he came into casual contact. He spoke—they obeyed: strength always has an influence of its own. He scarcely drank at all, had nothing to do with women, and was passionately fond of singing. There was much that was mysterious about this man; it seemed as though vast forces sullenly reposed within him, knowing, as it were, that once roused, once bursting free, they were bound to crush him and everything they came in contact with; and I am greatly mistaken if, in this man's life, there had not been some such outbreak; if it was not owing to the lessons of experience, to a narrow escape from ruin, that he now kept himself so tightly in hand. What especially struck me in him was the combination of a sort of inborn natural ferocity, with an equally inborn generosity—a combination I have never met in any other man.

And so the booth-keeper stepped forward, and, half shutting his eyes, began singing in high falsetto. He had a fairly sweet and pleasant voice, though rather hoarse: he played with his voice like a woodlark, twisting and turning it in incessant roulades and trills up and down the scale, continually returning to the highest notes, which he held and prolonged with special care. Then he would break off, and again suddenly take up the first motive with a sort of go-ahead daring. His modulations were at times rather bold, at times rather comical; they would have given a connoisseur great satisfaction, and have made a German furiously indignant. He was a Russian *tenore di grazia, ténor léger.* He sang a song to a lively dance-tune, the words of which, all that I could catch through the endless maze of variations, ejaculations, and repetitions, were as follows:

> A tiny patch of land, young lass,
>   I'll plough for thee,
> And tiny crimson flowers, young lass,
>   I'll sow for thee.

He sang; all listened to him with great attention. He seemed to feel that he had to do with really musical people, and therefore was exerting himself to do his best. And they really are musical in our part of the country; the village of Sergievskoe on the Orel high road is deservedly noted throughout Russia for its harmonious chorus-singing. The booth-keeper sang for a long while without evoking much enthusiasm in his audience; he lacked the support of a chorus; but at last, after one particularly bold flourish, which set even the Wild Master smiling, the Gabbler could not refrain from a shout of delight. Every one was roused. The Gabbler and the Blinkard began joining in in an undertone, and exclaiming: " Bravely done! . . . Take it, you rogue! . . . Sing it out, you serpent! Hold it! That shake again, you dog you! . . . May Herod confound your soul! " and so on. Nikolai Ivanitch behind the bar was nodding his head from side to side approvingly. The Gabbler at last was swinging his legs, tapping with his feet and twitching his shoulder, while Yashka's eyes fairly glowed like coal, and he trembled all over like a leaf, and smiled nervously. The Wild Master alone did not change countenance, and stood motionless as before; but his eyes, fastened on the booth-keeper, looked somewhat softened, though the expression of his lips was still scornful. Emboldened by the signs of general approbation, the booth-keeper went off in a whirl of flourishes, and began to round off such trills, to turn such shakes off his tongue, and to make such furious play with his throat, that when at last, pale, exhausted, and bathed in hot perspiration, he uttered the last dying note, his whole body flung back, a general united shout greeted him in a violent outburst. The Gabbler threw himself on his neck and began strangling him in his long, bony arms; a flush came out on Nikolai Ivanitch's oily face, and he seemed to have grown younger; Yashka shouted like mad, " Capital, capital! "—even my neighbour, the peasant in the torn smock, could not restrain himself, and with a blow of his fist on the table he cried, " Aha! well done, bless my soul, well done! " And he spat on one side with an air of decision.

" Well, brother, you've given us a treat! " bawled the Gabbler, not releasing the exhausted booth-keeper from his embraces; " you've given us a treat, there's no denying! You've won, brother, you've won! I congratulate you—the quart's yours! Yashka's miles behind you . . . I tell you: miles . . . take my word for it." (And again he hugged the booth-keeper to his breast.)

" There, let him alone, let him alone; there's no being rid of you " . . . said the Blinkard with vexation; " let him sit down on the bench; he's tired, see . . . You're a ninny, brother, a perfect ninny! What are you sticking to him like a wet leaf for? . . ."

" Well, then, let him sit down, and I'll drink to his health," said the Gabbler, and he went up to the bar. " At your expense, brother," he added, addressing the booth-keeper.

The latter nodded, sat down on the bench, pulled a piece of cloth out of his cap, and began wiping his face, while the Gabbler, with greedy haste, emptied his glass, and, with a grunt, assumed, after the manner of confirmed drinkers, an expression of careworn melancholy.

" You sing beautifully, brother, beautifully," Nikolai Ivanitch observed caressingly. " And now it's your turn, Yashka; mind, now, don't be afraid. We shall see who's who; we shall see. The booth-keeper sings beautifully, though; 'pon my soul, he does."

" Very beautifully," observed Nikolai Ivanitch's wife, and she looked with a smile at Yakov.

" Beautifully, ha! " repeated my neighbour in an undertone.

" Ah, a wild man of the woods! " the Gabbler vociferated suddenly, and going up to the peasant with the rent on his shoulder, he pointed at him with his finger, while he pranced about and went off into an insulting guffaw. " Ha! ha! get along! wild man of the woods! Here's a ragamuffin from Woodland village! What brought you here? " he bawled amidst laughter.

The poor peasant was abashed, and was just about to get up and make off as fast as he could, when suddenly the Wild Master's iron voice was heard:

" What does the insufferable brute mean? " he articulated, grinding his teeth.

" I wasn't doing nothing," muttered the Gabbler. " I didn't . . . I only . . ."

" There, all right, shut up! " retorted the Wild Master. " Yakov, begin! "

Yakov took himself by his throat:

" Well, really, brothers, . . . something. . . . H'm, I don't know, on my word, what . . ."

" Come, that's enough; don't be timid. For shame! . . . why go back? . . . Sing the best you can, by God's gift."

And the Wild Master looked down expectant. Yakov was silent for a minute; he glanced round, and covered his face with his hand. All had their eyes simply fastened upon him, especially the booth-keeper, on whose face a faint, involuntary uneasiness could be seen through his habitual expression of self-confidence and the triumph of his success. He leant back against the wall, and again put both hands under him, but did not swing his legs as before. When at last Yakov uncovered his face it was pale as a dead man's; his eyes gleamed faintly under their drooping lashes. He gave a deep sigh, and began to sing. . . . The first sound of his voice was faint and unequal, and seemed not to come from his chest, but to be wafted from somewhere afar off, as though it had floated by chance into the room. A strange effect was produced on all of us by this trembling, resonant note; we glanced at one another, and Nikolai Ivanitch's wife seemed to draw herself up. This first note was followed by another, bolder and prolonged, but still obviously quivering, like a harp-string when suddenly struck by a stray finger it throbs in a last, swiftly-dying tremble; the second was followed by a third, and gradually gaining fire and breadth, the strains swelled into a pathetic melody. " Not one little path ran into the field," he sang, and sweet and mournful it was in our ears. I have seldom, I must confess, heard a voice like it; it was slightly hoarse, and not perfectly true; there was even something morbid about it at first; but it had genuine depth of passion, and youth and sweetness and a sort of fascinating, care-less, pathetic melancholy. A spirit of truth and fire, a Russian spirit, was sounding and breathing in that voice, and it seemed to go straight to your heart, to go straight to all that was Russian in it. The song swelled and flowed. Yakov was clearly carried away by enthusiasm; he was not timid now; he surrendered himself wholly to the rapture of his art; his voice no longer trembled; it quivered, but with the scarce perceptible inward quiver of passion, which pierces like an arrow to the very soul of the listeners; and he steadily gained strength and firmness and breath. I remember I once saw at sunset on a flat sandy shore, when the tide was low and the sea's roar came weighty and menacing from the distance, a great white sea-gull; it sat motionless, its silky bosom facing the crimson glow of the setting sun, and only now and then opening wide its great wings to greet the well-known sea, to greet the sinking lurid sun: I recalled it, as I heard Yakov. He sang, utterly forgetful of his rival and all of us; he seemed supported, as a bold swimmer by the waves, by our silent, passionate sympathy. He sang, and in every sound of his voice one seemed to feel something dear and akin to us, something of breadth and space, as though the familiar steppes were unfolding before our eyes and stretching away into endless distance. I felt the tears gathering in my bosom and rising to my eyes; suddenly I was struck by dull, smothered sobs. . . . I looked round—the inn-keeper's wife was weeping, her bosom pressed close to the window. Yakov threw a quick glance at her, and he sang more sweetly, more melodiously than ever; Nikolai Ivanitch looked down; the Blinkard turned away; the Gabbler, quite touched, stood, his gaping mouth stupidly open; the humble peasant was sobbing softly in the corner, and shaking his head with a plaintive murmur; and on the iron visage of the Wild Master, from under his overhanging brows there slowly rolled a heavy tear; the booth-keeper raised his clenched fist to his brow, and did not stir. . . . I don't know how the general emotion would have ended, if Yakov had not suddenly come to a full stop on a high, exceptionally shrill note—as though his voice had broken. No one called out, or even stirred; every one seemed to be waiting to see whether he was not going to sing more; but he opened his eyes as though wondering at our silence, looked round at all of us with a face of inquiry, and saw that the victory was his. . . .

" Yashka," said the Wild Master, laying his hand on his shoulder, and he could say no more.

We all stood, as it were, petrified. The booth-keeper softly rose and went up to Yakov.

" You . . . yours . . . you've won," he articulated at last with an effort, and rushed out of the room. His rapid, decided action, as it were, broke the spell; we all suddenly fell into noisy, delighted talk. The Gabbler bounded up and down, stammered and brandished his arms like mill-sails; the Blinkard limped up to Yakov and began kissing him; Nikolai Ivanitch got up and solemnly announced that he would add a second pot of beer from himself. The Wild Master laughed a sort of kind, simple laugh, which I should never have expected to see on his face; the humble peasant as he wiped his eyes, cheeks, nose, and beard on his sleeves, kept repeating in his corner, " Ah, beautiful it was, by God! blast me for the son of a dog, but it was fine! " while Nikolai Ivanitch's wife, her face red with weeping, got up quickly and went away. Yakov was enjoying his triumph like a child; his whole face was transformed, his eyes especially fairly glowed with happiness. They dragged him to the bar; he beckoned the weeping peasant up to it, and sent the innkeeper's little son to look after the booth-keeper, who was not found, however; and the festivities began. "You'll sing to us again; you're going to sing to us till evening," the Gabbler declared, flourishing his hands in the air.

I took one more look at Yakov and went out. I did not want to stay—I was afraid of spoiling the impression I had received. But the heat was as insupportable as before. It seemed hanging in a thick, heavy layer right over the earth; over the dark blue sky, tiny bright fires seemed whisking through the finest, almost black dust. Everything was still; and there was something hopeless and oppressive in this profound hush of exhausted nature. I made my way to a hay-loft, and lay down on the fresh-cut, but already almost dry grass. For a long while I could not go to sleep; for a long while Yakov's irresistible voice was ringing in my ears. . . . At last the heat and fatigue regained their sway, however, and I fell into a dead sleep. When I waked up, everything was in darkness; the hay scattered around smelt strong and was slightly damp; through the slender rafters of the half-open roof pale stars were faintly twinkling. I went out. The glow of sunset had long died away, and its last trace showed in a faint light on the horizon; but above the freshness of the night there was still a feeling of heat in the atmosphere, lately baked through by the sun, and the breast still craved for a draught of cool air. There was no wind, nor were there any clouds; the sky all round was clear, and transparently dark, softly glimmering with innumerable, but scarcely visible stars. There were lights twinkling about the village; from the flaring tavern close by rose a confused, discordant din, amid which I fancied I recognised the voice of Yakov. Violent laughter came from there in an outburst at times. I went up to the little window and pressed my face against the pane. I saw a cheerless, though varied and animated scene; all were drunk—all from Yakov upwards. With breast bared, he sat on a bench, and singing in a thick voice a street song to a dance-tune, he lazily fingered and strummed on the strings of a guitar. His moist hair hung in tufts over his fearfully pale face. In the middle of the room, the Gabbler, completely "screwed" and without his coat, was hopping about in a dance before the peasant in the grey smock; the peasant, on his side, was with difficulty stamping and scraping with his feet, and grinning meaninglessly over his dishevelled beard; he waved one hand from time to time, as much as to say, "Here goes!" Nothing could be more ludicrous than his face; however much he twitched up his eyebrows, his heavy lids would hardly rise, but seemed lying upon his scarcely visible, dim, and mawkish eyes. He was in that amiable frame of mind of a perfectly intoxicated man, when every passer-by, directly he looks him in the face, is sure to say, "Bless you, brother, bless you!" The Blinkard, as red as a lobster, and his nostrils dilated wide, was laughing malignantly in a corner; only Nikolai Ivanitch, as befits a good tavern-keeper, preserved his composure unchanged. The room was thronged with many new faces; but the Wild Master I did not see in it.

I turned away with rapid steps and began descending the hill on which Kolotovka lies. At the foot of this hill stretches a wide plain; plunged in the misty waves of the evening haze, it seemed more immense, and was, as it were, merged in the darkening sky. I walked with long strides along the road by the ravine, when all at once from somewhere far away in the plain came a boy's clear voice: " Antropka! Antropka-a-a! . . ." He shouted in obstinate and tearful desperation, with long, long drawing out of the last syllable.

He was silent for a few instants, and started shouting again. His voice rang out clear in the still, lightly slumbering air. Thirty times at least he had called the name, Antropka. When suddenly, from the farthest end of the plain, as though from another world, there floated a scarcely audible reply:

" Wha-a-t? "

The boy's voice shouted back at once with gleeful exasperation: " Come here, devil! woo-od imp! "

" What fo-or? " replied the other, after a long interval.

" Because dad wants to thrash you! " the first voice shouted back hurriedly.

The second voice did not call back again, and the boy fell to shouting Antropka once more. His cries, fainter and less and less frequent, still floated up to my ears, when it had grown completely dark, and I had turned the corner of the wood which skirts my village and lies over three miles from Kolotovka. . . . " Antropka-a-a! " was still audible in the air, filled with the shadows of night.

# VISIONS—A PHANTASY

### Ivan S. Turgeniev

For a long time I tried in vain to sleep, and kept tossing from side to side. " The devil take all this nonsense of tipping tables," I said to myself, " it certainly shakes the nerves." At length, however, drowsiness began to get the upper hand.

Suddenly it seemed to me that a harp-string twanged feebly in my chamber. I lifted my head. The moon was low in the sky and shone full in my face; its light lay like a chalk-mark on the carpet. The strange sound was distinctly repeated. I raised

myself on my elbow, my heart beat forcibly.  A minute passed so
—another—then in the distance a cock crowed and a second
answered him from yet further.

My head fell back on the pillow.  " It comes even to that," I
thought, " my ears are fairly ringing."

In a moment more I was asleep, or seemed to myself to be
sleeping.  I had a singular dream.  I thought that I was in my
chamber in my own bed, wide awake.  Suddenly I hear the noise
again.  I turn.  The moonbeam on the floor begins to waver, to
rise, to take shape, stands motionless before me like the white
figure of a woman, transparent as mist.

" Who are you? " I ask, trying to retain my composure.

A voice resembling the soughing of the wind among the tree-tops
answers me.  " It is I—I—I.  I am come for you."

" For me?  But who are you? "

" Come at nightfall to the old oak-tree at the edge of the wood.
I will be there."

I wish to see more closely the features of this mysterious being;
an involuntary cold shudder runs through me.  I find myself not
lying, but in a sitting posture on my bed, and where the appearance of the figure was there is a long pale moon-streak on the
floor.

I do not know how the next day passed.  I tried, I remember,
to read and to work a little, but could accomplish nothing.  Night
fell; my heart beat as if I had been expecting some one.  I went
to bed and turned my face to the wall.

" Why did you not come? "  The whisper was plainly audible
in the chamber.

Hastily I turned my head.

There was the form again, the mysterious being with fixed eyes
in its rigid countenance and an expression of woe.

" Come! " I heard faintly.

" I will come," I answered with uncontrollable terror.  The
shape wavered, sank into itself like a puff of smoke, and once more
it was only the wan moonlight that lay on the smooth floor.

I passed the day in excitement.  At tea I nearly emptied a bottle
of wine, and for a moment stood hesitating at the open door, but
almost immediately turned back and threw myself upon my couch.
The blood rushed at fever-speed through my veins.

Again I heard the tones.  I shrank, but would not look up.
Then suddenly I felt myself tightly clasped by something,
and a whisper in my very ear, " Come, come come! "
Trembling with fright I stammered, " I will come," and raised
myself upright.

The woman's form was bending over the head of my bed.  It
smiled slightly, and faded, but not before I had been able to distinguish the features.  It seemed to me that I had seen them

before; but where—when?  It was late when I rose, and I spent almost the whole day in the fresh air, went to the old oak-tree at the edge of the wood and regarded it thoroughly.  Toward evening I seated myself beside the open window in my study.  My housekeeper brought me a cup of tea, but I was unable to taste it.  All sorts of thoughts besieged me, and I asked myself seriously whether I was not on the road to madness.

It was just after sunset, and not only the sky but the whole atmosphere was suddenly suffused with a supernatural purple light; leaves and weeds, smooth as if freshly varnished, were alike motionless, there was something singular, almost mysterious, in this absolute quiet, this dazzling sharpness of outline, this combination of intense glow with the stillness of death itself.  A large grey bird flew noiselessly toward me and settled itself upon the balustrade of my balcony.  I looked at it and it looked at me, its head sideways, with its round, dusky eye.

" Are you sent to remind me? " I thought.

The bird spread its wings and flew away as silently as it had come.  I remained at the window for some time longer absorbed in thought.  I seemed to be under a spell, a gentle but irresistible power controlled me, as the boat is swept on by the current long before the cataract is in sight.

When I regained possession of myself the glow was gone from the sky, which had grown dark, and the enchanted stillness had ceased.  A light breeze had sprung up, the moon rode bright and brighter through the blue expanse, and in her cold light the trees shimmered, half dusk, half silver.  My old servant entered with a lamp, but the draught from the window extinguished the flame.  I waited no longer, thrust my hat on my head and hurried to the old oak-tree at the edge of the wood.

Years ago this oak had been struck by lightning; its top was shivered and entirely blasted, but the trunk had still vigour for coming centuries.  As I approached, a filmy cloud drew over the moon; blackest shadow lay under the broad branches.  At first I was not conscious of anything unusual, but as I glanced to one side my heart throbbed—a white form was standing motionless by a tall sapling between me and the tree.  My hair stood on end, but I plucked up courage and walked steadily on.

Yes, it was she, my nightly visitant.  As I drew near, the moon shone out in full splendour.  The figure seemed woven, as it were, out of a half-transparent milky cloud; through the face I could see a twig that stirred with the wind, only the hair and the eyes were of a somewhat darker colouring, and on one finger of the folded hands I saw the faint glimmer of a narrow ring.  I remained standing before it and attempted to speak to it, but my voice died in my throat; although I was not sensible of fear.  Its glance was full upon me, the expression was neither of grief nor of gladness, but a rigid, unlife-like attention. I waited to be addressed, but it kept immovable and silent, with its death-like stare fixed on me. Again I felt my self-possession failing.

" I am come," I said at last with a mighty effort. My voice was hollow and unnatural.

" I love you," returned a whisper.

" You love me? " I asked in amazement.

" Give yourself to me," was answered, still in the same tone.

" Give myself to you? You are only a ghost. You have no bodily existence." A peculiar excitement had taken possession of me. " What are you? Smoke—air—vapour? Give myself up to you? First answer me—who are you? Have you lived on earth? And whence do you now come? "

" Give yourself to me. I will do you no ill. Say but two words : ' Take me.' "

I looked at it attentively. " What is it talking about? " I thought. " What does it all mean? How can it take me? Shall I venture? "

" Very good," I answered so that it should hear, with unexpected loudness, indeed, as if some one had hit me from behind, " Take me! "

I had hardly pronounced the syllables when the form bent forward with a smile, so that the features trembled for a moment, and slowly extended its arms. I would fain have drawn back, but found it already out of my power. It twined about me, my body was caught up a yard from the ground, and gently, and not too rapidly, I floated over the still and dewy grass.

My head swam. Involuntarily I closed my eyes, only to open them, however, the next moment. We were still floating upward. But the wood was no longer to be seen. Under us lay a wide plain, flecked here and there with shadow. With horror I realised that we had gained a fearful height.

" I am lost. I am in the devil's clutches," was the thought that shot lightning-like through my brain. Till this moment the idea of demoniacal interference in my undertaking had not occurred to me. We were borne constantly farther, and took our flight higher and higher, as it appeared.

" Where are you taking me? " burst from me at length.

" Wherever you will," answered my guide. It clung closer and closer to me, its face almost touching my own. Yet I could not feel the contact.

" Take me back to the earth. This height makes me giddy."

" Good; only shut your eyes and hold your breath."

I followed this counsel and found myself sinking like a stone, the wind fairly whistling through my hair. When I recovered myself we were hovering just above the ground, so that we stirred the tops of the grass blades.

" Put me down," I said, " on my feet, I have had enough of flying. I am no bird."

" I believed it would be pleasant to you. We have no other power."

" We? Who are you, then? "

No answer.

" Can't you tell me anything? "

A woeful tone, like that which had wakened me the first night, trembled at my ear. All this while we had been moving almost imperceptibly through the damp night air.

" Set me down," I repeated. My guide moved quietly aside, and I stood upon my feet. It remained before me again with folded hands. I had regained my composure, and looked closely in its face. There was the same expression of melancholy not human.

" Where are we? " I inquired, for I did not recognise my surroundings.

You are not far from home, but in a moment you may be there."

" What? Must I trust myself to you again? "

" I have done you no harm and will let none come to you. We can fly till dawn, not later. I can take you wherever you may desire—to the ends of the earth. Resign yourself to me; say once more, ' Take me.' "

" Then—' take me.' "

Again she clasped me. I was lifted from the ground and we floated in air.

" Whither? " she asked me.

" On, straight on."

" But here are trees."

" Rise above them—only gingerly."

We soared upward, and took once more an onward course. Instead of grass, the tops of the trees waved under our feet. The wood, seen from above, presented a singular appearance, with its moon-lighted, prickly back. It was like some monstrous sleeping creature, and the low, steady rustling of the leaves, like measured breath, carried the resemblance yet farther. Now and then we passed above a little clearing, along whose edge a charmingly indented line of shadow lay. Occasionally we heard below us the plaintive cry of a hare, nearer, the hoot of owls rang dolefully; the air was full of wild and piny smells; on all sides the moonlight lay absolute and cold, and high above our heads shone the Pleiades.

Speedily we left the wood behind us, and debouched upon a plain through which some stream ran like a ribbon of mist. We flew along its banks over bushes that were still and heavy with dampness. Here the little waves swelled blue on the river, there they rose dark and threatening. Sometimes a fine faint fragrance rose in a wonderful fashion, as if the water were taking life and soul; it was where the water-lilies unfolded their white petals in a

maidenly splendour, conscious that no hand could reach them. The
whim seized me to gather one of these, and behold me already at
the surface of the stream. There was an unpleasant sensation of
moisture in my face as I broke the tough stem of a great flower.

We flew from shore to shore like the jack-o'-lanthorns which we
saw glittering about us, and which we seemed to chase. At times
we hit upon whole families of wild ducks squatting in a circle in a
hollow of the reeds, but they did not stir; it was a chance if one
or another would withdraw its head from its wing, look about it,
and hasten to bury its beak again in the soft down, or make a
cackling accompanied by a shake of the whole body. We roused
a heron; he emerged from a clump of willows, stretched his legs,
spread his clumsy wings, and flapped heavily away. Nowhere did
a fish leap in the water, apparently they also slept. I had by this
time become accustomed to the sensation of flying, and even began
to find it agreeable; every one who has dreamed of flying will understand this. I began to scrutinise the wonderful being who bore
me, and whom I had to thank for these incredible experiences.

It had the appearance of a woman with delicate, not Russian,
features. Greyish-white, nearly transparent, with scarcely perceptible shading, it reminded me of an alabaster vase, and once more
seemed suddenly, strangely familiar to me.

" May I talk to you? " I asked it.

" Speak."

" I see a ring on your finger. You have lived on earth, then,
have you been married? "

I stopped, but there was no answer.

" What is your name, or rather what was your name? "

" You may call me Ellis."

" Ellis! That is an English name. Are you an Englishwoman?
Have you known me before? "

" No."

" Why have you appeared to me then? "

" I love you."

" Well—does this satisfy you? "

" Yes; we are flying and circling together in pure space."

" Ellis! " I cried, " can it be that you are a lost soul? "

My companion's head sank. " I do not understand," she whispered.

" I conjure you in the name of God "—I began.

" What are you saying? " she asked, bewildered. And I fancied
that the arm that surrounded me like a chill girdle, trembled slightly.

" Do not fear, my beloved," Ellis said, " do not fear." Her
face turned to mine and approached it closely, and I felt a curious
sensation on my lips, like the prick of a fine needle.

I looked down. We had again ascended to a tremendous height,

137

and were flying over a large city unknown to me, which was built
on the side of a high hill.   Church spires rose here and there from
the dark mass of roofs and gardens, a bridge arched the river-bend,
everything lay in the deepest stillness, bound in sleep.   Domes and
crosses glimmered faintly in the peaceful light; a grey-white road ran
still and straight in the dim distance among the monotonous fields.
    " What is this city? " I asked.
    "——sow.
    "——sow is in the ——schen province, is it not? "
    " Yes."
    " Then we are a long way from home? "
    " For us distance is not."
    " Truly? "   A sudden recklessness awoke in me.   " Take me
to South America then."
    " To America—there I cannot.   There it is day."
    " So, we are birds o' night, then, both of us.   Well, wherever
you can, only let it be far—far."
    " Shut your eyes and hold your breath," was Ellis's response,
and we began to move with the swiftness of a hurricane.   With
stunning violence the wind rushed past my ears.
    We stopped, but the rushing sound did not cease.   On the con-
trary, it increased to a frightful roar, like a thunder peal.
    " Now you can open your eyes," Ellis said.
    I obeyed.   Good Heavens, where am I?
    Above, the heavy clouds are hurrying across the sky like a herd of
angry beasts, and below is another monster, the sea, in wildest rage.
White foam is spouting and seething madly, waves tower mountain-
high and dash themselves with hoarse fury against a gigantic, pitch-
black reef.   Everywhere the howling of the tempest, the icy breath
of the revolted elements, the hollow roar of the breakers, through
which at times I caught something like loud lamentations, distant
cannon and the peal of bells; ear-splitting grate and crunch of the
chalk cliffs, the sudden cry of an unseen gull, and against the grey
horizon the outline of a reeling vessel—everywhere confusion,
horror, and death.   My head swam, my heart stopped; I closed
my eyes anew.
    " What is that and where are we? "
    " Off the southerly coast of the Isle of Wight, before the Black-
gang Rock, where so many vessels are lost," replied Ellis, this time
with great distinctness of tone, and, as I fancied, a shade of joyous
excitement.
    " Take me away—away from here—home."
    I shrank into myself and pressed my hands over my eyes.   I
could feel that we were moving more swiftly than before; already
the wind ceased to howl and shriek, it blew evenly in my face, but
so strongly that I could hardly breathe.
    " Take your foothold," I heard Ellis say.

I made a mighty effort to regain my full consciousness and the mastery of myself. I felt the ground beneath my feet, but could hear no more than if everything about me lay dead; only on my own temples the veins throbbed violently, unevenly, and with a little inward ringing; I was still half fainting. But I stood up and opened my eyes.

We were on the bank of my own pond. Straight before me I could see through the slender willow leaves the glassy surface of the water, dappled here and there with mist. On the right was a rye-field in tremulous motion, on the left rose steady and dewy-wet the trees of my garden. The morning had already breathed on them. In the empty grey sky a pair of narrow clouds hung like smoke-wreaths; they were russet, the first faint hint of dawn had reached them, the eye could not distinguish as yet any spot on the wide horizon where the daylight should break. The stars were gone, there was no stir yet in the magical half-light, everything drew consciously to its awakening.

" Morning, morning is here! " Ellis murmured in my ear. " Farewell till to-morrow."

I turned to her. She rose, lightly swaying, from the ground, and lifted both arms above her head. Head, arms, and shoulders were suddenly suffused with a warm, rosy flesh tint, the fire of life glowed in the shadowy eyes, a smile of secret joy played over the scarlet lips, it was a charming woman all at once who stood before me. But almost instantly she sank back as if exhausted, and melted away like mist.

I stood motionless.

When things about me had reassumed the aspects of ordinary life, I looked round, and it seemed to me as if the rosy glow that had irradiated the form of my shadowy companion had not faded, but still permeated the air and surrounded me on every side. It was the Dawn. An irresistible languor crept over me, and I went to the house.

As I was passing the hennery my ear caught the first morning gabble of the young geese (of all winged creatures these are the earliest to stir), and I saw the jackdaws perched on the ridge-pole busily preening their feathers against the milky-coloured sky. From time to time they all flew off simultaneously, and after a short flight settled again silently in their old places. From the wood at hand sounded twice or thrice the shrill cry of the mountain cock that had alighted in the dewy grass to seek for berries there. With a slight chilliness in my limbs I reached my own bed and sank at once into a profound sleep.

On the following night as I neared the oak-tree, Ellis glided to meet me as toward a familiar friend. Nor did I experience the horror of yesterday in her presence, indeed I was almost glad to see her; I did not even speculate on what might happen, but only desired to be taken to some great distance and to some interesting places.

Ellis placed her arm about me and our flight began.

.    .    .    .    .    .    .    .

Our flight was less rapid than usual, and I could follow with my eye the unfamilar aspect of the familiar ground as it unrolled like an endless panorama before me. Woods, bushes, fields, ravines, streams, occasionally villages and churches; then fields, woods, bushes, and ravines again. I had a feeling of sadness and also of indifference, almost of ennui; but not in the least because it was Russia over which we were taking our flight. No; the earth in and for itself; this flat plain that spread beneath me, the whole planet with its short-lived, helpless races, oppressed with poverty, sickness, and care, chained to a clod of dust; this rough and brittle crust, this sediment upon our planet's fiery core on which a mould is grown that we call by the high-sounding title of the vegetable world; these men-flies, a hundred times less useful than the flies themselves, with their dwellings of clay and the fugitive trace of their little monotonous lives, their eternal strife against the inevitable and the immutable—how it shocked me!

My heart beat heavily in my bosom; the desire to contemplate any longer these unmeaning pictures had entirely left me. Yes, it was ennui that I felt, but something sharper than ennui as well. Not once did I feel pity for my fellow-men; every other thought was swallowed up in one that I hardly dare to name; it was loathing, and the profoundest, deepest loathing of all was—for myself.

" O cease," breathed Ellis, " cease your thoughts, else it would be impossible for me to carry you. You are too heavy."

" Home! " I cried to her with the tone in which I had summoned my driver once when at four o'clock in the morning I took leave of the friends at Moscow with whom I had been discussing Russia's future. " Home! " I repeated and closed my eyes.

It was not long till I opened them. Ellis began to nestle against me in a singular way; she nearly stifled me. I turned my eyes upon her and the blood curdled in my veins. Every one will understand me who has ever chanced to catch an expression of extreme terror on a stranger's face without any suspicion of its cause. A transport of horror drew and distorted Ellis's pallid, almost blotted-out features. Never had I seen the like on mortal face; here was a bodiless, nebulous ghost, a shadow, and such rigidity of fear!

" Ellis! What is the matter with you? " I asked at last.

" He! It is he! " With difficulty she brought the words forth.

" He? Who is he? "

" Do not name him, do not name him," Ellis stammered in haste. " We must seek some refuge, else it is all at an end, and for ever. Look! There! "

I turned my head to the side where her shuddering finger was pointing, and was conscious of Something—something that was indeed awful to look upon.

This something was the more frightful that it had no decided form. A clumsy, horrible, dark-yellow thing, spotted like a lizard's belly, neither cloud nor smoke, was crawling snake-like over the earth. Its motion was measured, broad-sweeping from above to below and from below to above, like the ill-omened flight of a bird of prey that seeks its booty; from time to time it swooped upon the earth in an indescribable, hideous way; so the spider pounces upon the entrapped fly.

Who or what art thou, gruesome Shape? Under its influence— I saw and felt this—everything shrivelled and grew rigid. A foul, pestilential chill spread upward. I felt myself fainting; my sight grew dim, my hair stood on end. It was a Power that was approaching; a power that knows no obstacle, that subjects everything to itself, that, blind and formless and senseless, sees everything, knows everything, controls everything; like a vulture selects its prey, like a snake crushes it and licks it with its deadly tongue.

" Ellis, Ellis," I shrieked like a madman, " That is Death! The very, living Death himself! "

The lamentable sound that I had heard before escaped Ellis's lips, only this time it was far more like a mortal cry of despair; and we flew on. Our flight was singularly and frightfully unsteady; Ellis turned over and over in the air, plunged first in one direction, then in the other, like a partridge that, wounded unto death, still endeavours to distract the dog from her brood. But in the meanwhile long feelers, like extended arms, had disengaged themselves from the lump, and were stretching out after us with groping movements. And then of a sudden it rose into the gigantic shape of a shrouded figure on a pale horse. It grew, filling the heavens themselves. More agitated, more desperate became Ellis's flight. " He has seen me—it is all over—I am lost," I caught in broken whispers. " O miserable that I am! The opportunity so close! Life within my grasp! and now—nothingness—nothingness! "

I could bear it no longer. Consciousness left me.

When I came to myself I was lying on my back in the grass, and I felt through my body a dull ache as if after a heavy fall. Morning flickered in the sky. I could clearly distinguish my surroundings. Not far off there was a willow-fringed road that ran beside a birch wood. The region seemed familiar. I began to recall what had happened to me, and could not repress a shudder as I remembered the last awful spectacle.

" But what can have terrified Ellis? " I thought. " Can she be subject to his power? Is she not immortal? How is it possible that she can be doomed to annihilation? "

A low moan sounded not far away. I hastily turned my head in that direction, and there, two paces from me, lay the motionless form of a young woman in a white garment, with thick, unbound hair, and shoulders bared. One arm was over her head, the other had fallen across her bosom, the eyelids were closed, and the tightly-compressed lips were stained slightly with a reddish froth.

Could it be Ellis? But Ellis was a ghost, and it was a real woman whom I saw. I crawled over to her and bent above her. " Ellis, is it you? " I cried. The eyelids quivered, slowly uplifted; dark, expressive eyes fixed themselves earnestly on my face, and in the next instant a warm, moist, fragrant mouth was pressed to mine, slender, strong arms clasped themselves round my neck, a hot breast swelled against my own. " Farewell! farewell! " the dying voice said, and everything disappeared.

I staggered to my feet like a drunken man, passed my hand across my forehead, and looked about me. I found myself on the ——schen road, two versts from my country-seat. Before I reached home the sun had risen.

For some nights following this I waited, let me confess it, not altogether without fear, for the return of my companion, but she came no more. One evening, indeed, I stationed myself at the old place, at the old hour, but nothing unusual occurred. After all, I could not regret the end of so singular an intimacy. I pondered much and earnestly upon this inexplicable, incomprehensible experience, and had to come to the conclusion that not only positive science is in no condition to handle it, but that it is out of the range of legends and fairy tales even. Indeed, what was Ellis? A ghost, a wandering soul, an evil spirit, a sylph, a vampire, finally? At times the fancy possessed me that Ellis was in truth a woman whom I had known; and I ransacked my memory to find where I might have seen her before. Hold! a moment more and I have it!

But it never came. Everything grew confused like a dream. Yes, I have thought much and, as is very often the case, have arrived at no conclusion. I could not bring myself to ask the advice or the opinion of others, for fear of being taken for a madman. At last I gave up all my gropings; to tell the truth, I had other things to think of. First, the emancipation of the serfs and the equal distribution of lands, etc., intervened; then the condition of my health, that has received a shock; I have a pain in my chest, cough much, and suffer from sleeplessness. I am visibly growing thin. I am as yellow as a mummy and suffer sleeplessness. The doctor assures me that I suffer from consumption of the blood, calls my complaint by a Greek name, " *anémie*," and declares that I must go to Gastein.

# THE RENDEZVOUS

Ivan S. Turgeniev

I was sitting in a birch grove in autumn, near the middle of September. It had been drizzling ever since morning; occasionally the sun shone warmly; the weather was changeable. Now the sky was overcast with watery white clouds; now it suddenly cleared up for an instant, and then the bright, soft azure, like a beautiful eye, appeared from beyond the dispersed clouds. I was sitting looking about me and listening. The leaves were slightly rustling over my head; and by their very rustle one could tell what season of the year it was. It was not the gay, laughing palpitation of spring; not a soft whispering, nor the lingering chatter of summer, nor the timid and cold lisping of late autumn, but a barely audible, drowsy prattle. A faint breeze was whisking over the tree-tops. The interior of the grove, moist from the rain, was ever changing, as the sun shone or hid beyond the clouds; now the wood was all illumined as if everything in it had burst into a smile; the trunks of the birch trees suddenly assumed the soft reflection of white silk; the small leaves which lay scattered on the ground all at once became variegated and flashed up like red gold; and the comely stalks of the tall, branchy ferns, already tinted to their autumn hue, resembling the colour of over-ripe grapes, appeared here and there tangling and crossing one another. Now again everything suddenly turned blue; the bright colours died out instantly, the birch trees stood all white, lustreless, like snow which has not yet been touched by the cold rays of the winter sun; and stealthily, furtively, a drizzling rain began to sprinkle and whisper over the forest. The leaves on the birches were almost all green yet, though they had turned somewhat pale; only here and there stood a solitary young little birch, all red or all golden, and you should have seen how brightly these birches flashed in the sun when its rays suddenly appeared, gliding and flashing through the dense net of the thin branches which had just been washed by the sparkling rain. Not a single bird was heard; all had found shelter, and were silent; only rarely the mocking voice of the robin sang out like a little steel bell.

Before stopping in this birch wood I passed with my dog through a poplar grove. I confess I am not very fond of the poplar tree with its pale lilac-coloured trunk and its greyish-green, metallic leaves, which it lifts high and spreads in the air like a trembling fan; I do not like the constant shaking of its round, untidy leaves, which are so awkwardly attached to long stems. The poplar is beautiful only on certain summer evenings, when, rising high amid the low copse, it stands against the red rays of the setting sun, shining and trembling, bathed from root to top in uniform yellowish purple; or when, on a clear windy day, it rocks noisily, waving against the blue sky, and each leaf seems eager to tear itself away, to fly and hurry off into the distance. But in general I do not like this tree, and, therefore, not stopping to rest in the poplar grove, I made my way to the birch wood, and seated myself under a tree whose branches started near the ground, and thus could protect me from the rain. Having admired the surrounding view, I fell asleep; I slept that tranquil, sweet sleep which is known only to sportsmen.

I cannot say how long I slept, but when I opened my eyes the entire hollow of the forest was filled with sunshine, and everywhere the bright blue sky was flashing through the cheerfully whispering leaves; the clouds disappeared, driven asunder by the wind which had begun to play; the weather was clear now, and one felt in the air that peculiar, dry freshness which, filling the heart with vigour, almost always predicts a quiet, clear night after a rainy day. I was about to rise and try my luck at shooting again, when my eyes suddenly fell on a motionless human figure. I gazed at it steadily; it was a young peasant girl. She was sitting some twenty feet away from me, her head bowed pensively and her hands dropped on her knees; in one hand, which was half open, lay a heavy bunch of field flowers, and every time she breathed the flowers were softly gliding over her checkered skirt. A clear white blouse, buttoned at the neck and the wrists, fell in short, soft folds about her waist; large yellow beads were hanging down from her neck on her breast in two rows. She was not at all bad-looking. Her heavy fair hair, of a beautiful brown, parted in two neatly combed half-circles from under a narrow, dark-red head-band, which came down almost to her ivory-white forehead; the rest of her face was slightly tanned, with the golden sunburn peculiar to a tender skin. I could not see her eyes, for she did not lift them; but I saw her thin, high eyebrows, her long lashes; these were moist, and on her cheek gleamed a tear-drop, which had stopped near her somewhat pale lips. Her little head was very charming; even her somewhat thick round nose did not spoil it. I liked especially the expression of her face; it was so simple and gentle, so sad, and so full of childish perplexity at her own sadness. She was apparently waiting for some one.

Something cracked faintly in the woods. Immediately she raised her head and looked round; her eyes flashed quickly before me in the transparent shade; they were large, bright, and shy like a deer's. She listened for a few seconds, not moving her wide-open eyes from the spot whence the faint sound had come; she heaved a sigh, turned her head slowly, bent down still lower and began to examine

the flowers. Her eyelids turned red, her lips quivered bitterly, and
a new tear-drop rolled down from under her heavy eyelashes,
stopping and sparkling on her cheek. Thus quite a long while
passed; the poor girl did not stir; only occasionally she moved her
hands and listened, listened all the time. Something cracked once
more in the forest; she started. This time the noise did not stop,
it was becoming more distinct, it was nearing. At last firm footsteps were heard. She straightened herself, and it seemed as if she
lost her courage, for her eyes began to quiver. The figure of a man
appeared through the undergrowth. She looked steadily, suddenly
flushed, and smiling joyously and happily, seemed about to rise,
but she immediately cast down her head again, turned pale, confused; and then she lifted her quivering, almost prayerful eyes to
the man as he paused beside her.

I looked at him from my hiding-place with curiosity. I confess
he did not produce a pleasant impression. He was, by all appearance, the spoiled valet of some rich young man. His clothes be-
tokened a claim to taste and smart carelessness. He wore a short
overcoat of bronze colour, which evidently belonged to his master,
and which was buttoned up to the very top; he had on a pink necktie with lilac-coloured edges; and his black velvet cap, trimmed with
gold stripes, was pulled over his eyebrows. The round collar of
his white shirt propped his ears up and cut his cheeks mercilessly,
and the starched cuffs covered his hands up to his red, crooked
fingers, which were ornamented with silver and gold rings, set with
forget-me-nots of turquoise. His red, fresh, impudent face belonged
to those which, as far as I have observed, are almost always repulsive to men, but, unfortunately, are often admired by women.
Apparently trying to give an expression of contempt and of weariness to his coarse features, he was ever closing his small, milky-grey
eyes, knitting his brows, lowering the corners of his lips, yawning,
and, with careless, although not too clever ease, now adjusting
his reddish, smartly twisted curls, now fingering the yellow hair
which bristled upon his thick upper lip. In a word, he was making
an insufferable display of himself. He began to do this as soon as
he noticed the young peasant girl who was awaiting him. He
advanced to her slowly, with long strides, then stood for a while,
shrugged his shoulders, thrust both hands into the pockets of his
coat, and, casting a quick and indifferent glance at the poor girl,
sank down on the ground.

" Well? " he began, continuing to look aside, shaking his foot
and yawning. " Have you waited long? "

The girl could not answer him at once. " Long, Victor Alexandrich," she said at last, in a scarcely audible voice.

" Ah! " He removed his cap, majestically passed his hand
over the thick, curly hair whose roots started almost at his eyebrows, and, looking round with dignity, covered his precious head

137*

again cautiously. " And I almost forgot all about it. Besides, you see, it's raining." He yawned again. " I have a lot of work to do; you can't look after everything, and he is in a bad temper. We are leaving to-morrow——"

" To-morrow? " said the girl, and fixed a frightened look upon him.

" To-morrow. Come, come, come, please," he replied quickly, vexed, noticing that she shook, and bowed her head in silence. " Please, Akulina, don't cry. You know I can't bear it " (and he twitched his flat nose). " If you don't stop, I'll leave you at once. What nonsense—to whimper! "

" Well, I won't, I won't," said Akulina hastily, swallowing the tears with an effort. " So you're going away to-morrow? " she added, after a brief silence. " When will it please God that I shall meet you again, Victor Alexandrich? "

" We'll meet, we'll meet again. If it isn't next year, it'll be later. My master, it seems, wants to enter the service in Petersburg," he went on, pronouncing the words carelessly and somewhat indistinctly. " And it may be that we'll go abroad."

" You will forget me, Victor Alexandrich," said Akulina sadly.

" No—why should I? I'll not forget you, only you had better be sensible; don't make a fool of yourself; obey your father. And I'll not forget you. Oh, no; oh, no." And he stretched himself calmly and yawned again.

" Do not forget me, Victor Alexandrich," she resumed in a beseeching voice. " I have loved you so much, it seems—all, it seems, for you. You tell me to obey Father, Victor Alexandrich. How am I to obey my father? "

" How's that? " He pronounced these words as if from the stomach, lying on his back and holding his hands under his head.

" Why, Victor Alexandrich—you know very well! "

She fell silent. Victor fingered his steel watch-chain.

" Akulina, you are not a foolish girl," he said at last, " so don't talk nonsense. It's for your own good, do you understand me? Of course, you are not foolish, you're not altogether a peasant, so to say, and your mother wasn't always a peasant either. Still, you are without education. Therefore you must obey when you are told to."

" But it's terrible, Victor Alexandrich."

" Oh, what nonsense, my dear! What is she afraid of! What is that you have there," he added, moving closer to her, " flowers? "

" Flowers," replied Akulina sadly. " I have picked some field tansies," she went on, with some animation. " They're good for the calves. And here I have some marigolds—for scrofula. Here, look, what a pretty flower! I haven't seen such a pretty flower in all my life. Here are forget-me-nots, and—these I have picked for you," she added, taking from under the tansies a small bunch of cornflowers, tied around with a thin blade of grass. " Do you want them? "

Victor stretched out his hand lazily, took the flowers, smelled them carelessly, and began to turn them around in his fingers, looking up with thoughtful importance. Akulina gazed at him. There was so much tender devotion, reverent obedience and love in her pensive eyes. She feared him, and yet she dared not cry, and inwardly she bade him farewell, and admired him for the last time; and he lay there, stretched out like a sultan, and endured her admiration with magnanimous patience and condescension. I confess I was filled with indignation as I looked at his red face, which betrayed satisfied selfishness through his feigned contempt and indifference. Akulina was so beautiful at this moment! All her soul opened before him trustingly and passionately; it reached out to him, caressed him, and he—— He dropped the cornflowers on the grass, took out from the side-pocket of his coat a round glass in a bronze frame and began to force it into his eye; but no matter how hard he tried to hold it with his knitted brow, his raised cheek, and even with his nose, the glass dropped out and fell into his hands.

" What's this? " asked Akulina at last, with surprise.

" An eyeglass," he replied importantly.

" What is it for? "

" To see better."

" Let me see it."

Victor frowned, but gave her the glass. " Look out; don't break it."

" Don't be afraid, I'll not break it." She lifted it timidly to her eye. " I can't see anything," she said naïvely.

" Shut your eye," he retorted in the tone of a dissatisfied teacher. She closed the eye before which she held the glass.

" Not that eye, not that one, stupid! The other one! " exclaimed Victor; and, not allowing her to correct her mistake, he took the glass away from her. Akulina blushed, laughed slightly, and turned away.

" It seems it's not for me." " Of course not! "

The poor girl maintained silence, and heaved a deep sigh.

" Oh, Victor Alexandrich, how shall I get along without you? " she said suddenly.

Victor wiped the eyeglass and put it back into his pocket.

" Yes, yes," he said at last. " At first it will really be hard for you." He tapped her on the shoulder condescendingly; she quietly took his hand from her shoulder and kissed it. " Well, yes, yes, you are indeed a good girl," he went on, with a self-satisfied smile; " but it can't be helped! Consider it yourself! My master and I can't stay here, can we? Winter is near, and to pass the winter in the country is simply impossible—you know it yourself. It's a different thing in Petersburg! There are such wonders over there that you could not imagine even in your dreams, you silly! What houses, what streets, and society, education—it's something wonderful!" Akulina listened to him with close attention, slightly opening her lips like a child. "However," he added, wriggling on the ground, "why do I say all this to you? You can't understand it anyway!"

"Why not, Victor Alexandrich? I understood, I understood everything."

"Just think of her!"

Akulina cast down her eyes. "You never spoke to me like this before, Victor Alexandrich," she said, without lifting her eyes.

"Before? Before! Just think of her! Before!" he remarked, indignantly. Both grew silent.

"However, it's time for me to go," said Victor, and leaned on his elbow, about to rise.

"Wait a little," said Akulina in an imploring voice.

"What for? I have already said to you, Good-bye!"

"Wait," repeated Akulina.

Victor again stretched himself on the ground and began to whistle. Akulina kept looking at him steadfastly. I could see that she was growing agitated; her lips twitched, her pale cheeks were reddening.

"Victor Alexandrich," she said at last in a broken voice, "it's a sin in you, it's a sin, Victor Alexandrich, by God!"

"What's a sin?" he asked, knitting his brows. He raised his head and turned to her.

"It's a sin, Victor Alexandrich. If you would only say a good word to me before leaving; if you would only say one word to me, miserable little orphan that I am——"

"But what should I say to you?"

"I don't know. You know that better than I do, Victor Alexandrich. Here you are going away—if you would only say one word—— What have I done to deserve this?"

"How strange you are! What can I say?"

"If only one word——"

"There she's always at the same thing," he muttered with vexation, and got up. "Don't be angry, Victor Alexandrich," she added hastily, unable to repress her tears.

"I'm not angry—only you are foolish. What do you want? I can't marry you! I can't, can I? Well, then, what do you want? What?" He stared at her, as if awaiting an answer, and opened his fingers wide.

"I want nothing—nothing," she replied, stammering, not daring to outstretch her trembling hands to him, "but only—at least one word, at parting!"

And the tears began to stream from her eyes.

" Well, there you are, she's started crying," said Victor indifferently, pulling the cap over his eyes.

" I don't want anything," she went on, sobbing and covering her face with her hands; " but how shall I feel now at home, how shall I feel? And what will become of me, what will become of me, wretched one that I am? They'll marry the poor little orphan to a man she does not like. My poor little head! "

" Oh, go on, go on! " muttered Victor in a low voice, stirring restlessly.

" If you only said one word, just one: ' Akulina—I——' "

Sudden heartrending sobs interrupted her. She fell with her face upon the grass and cried bitterly, bitterly. All her body shook convulsively. The long-suppressed sorrow at last burst forth in a stream of tears. Victor stood a while near her, then shrugged his shoulders, turned around and walked off with long strides.

A few moments went by. She became silent, lifted her head, looked around and clasped her hands; she was about to run after him, but her feet failed her; she fell down on her knees. I could not endure it any longer and rushed over to her; but before she had time to look at me, she suddenly seemed to have regained her strength, and with a faint cry she rose and disappeared behind the trees, leaving the scattered flowers on the ground.

I stood a while, picked up the bunch of cornflowers, and walked out of the wood to the open. The sun was low in the pale, clear sky; its rays seemed to have faded and turned cold; they did not shine now, they spread in an even, almost watery, light. There was only a half-hour left until nightfall, and twilight was setting in. A violent wind was blowing fast toward me across the yellow, dried-up stubble-field; the small withered leaves were carried quickly past me across the road; the side of the wood which stood like a wall by the field trembled and flashed clearly, but not brightly; everywhere on the reddish grass, and on the bracken, innumerable autumn cobwebs flashed and trembled. I stopped. I began to feel sad; it seemed as if a dismal fear of approaching winter was stealing through the gay, fresh smile of fading nature. High above me, a cautious raven flew by heavily, sharply cutting the air with his wings; then he turned his head, looked at me sidelong, and croaking abruptly, disappeared beyond the forest; a large flock of pigeons rushed past me from a barn, and suddenly whirling about in a column, they came down and set themselves busily to search the field—a sign of autumn! Some one drove past beyond the bare hillock, making much noise with an empty waggon.

I returned home, but the image of poor Akulina did not leave my mind for a long time, and the cornflowers, long withered, are in my possession at this day.

# FIODOR N. DOSTOYEVSKY
1822–1881

# THE HONEST THIEF

ONE morning as I was just starting for work, Agraphina, my cook, laundress, and maid-of-all-work, entered into conversation with me to my great astonishment. Up to that time she had been such a silent, simple woman, that, except for two words daily as to what she was to cook for dinner, she hadn't spoken in six years. At least I had heard nothing further from her.

" I came to you, sir," she began suddenly, " you should let the small room."

" What small room? "

" The one by the kitchen, of course."

" Why? "

" Why? Because people take lodgers, of course."

" And who will hire it? "

" Who will hire it? Why, of course, a lodger."

" But, my good woman, it's too narrow to place even a bed there. Who will live in it? "

" Why live there? Just sleep there and live by the window."

" What window? "

" You know as well as I do! The one in the hall. He can sit here and do whatever work he has. He can even sit on a chair there. He has a chair, and a table—everything."

" Who is he? "

" Oh, an excellent, experienced man. I will cook for him, and will only charge three roubles a month for board and lodging. . . ."

After long efforts I succeeded in finding out that some elderly man had induced or somehow got round Agraphina to take him in the kitchen as a lodger. Then she took it upon her to decide how it was to be done; otherwise, I know she would have given me no peace. Whenever she disapproved of something she at once became pensive, lapsed into deep melancholy, and continued so for two or three weeks. During this period she spoiled the food, neglected the washing, did not clean the floors, in a word, life was made unpleasant for me. I often remarked that these silent women are incapable of reasoning and remain obsessed with their own ideas. But whenever in some strange manner something like an idea or an enterprise had taken form in her feeble mind, to thwart or to refuse her was morally to kill her for a time, and as I liked my own peace of mind, I agreed at once.

" Has he, at any rate, a passport or something? "

" How d'you mean? Of course there is. An excellent man; promised to pay three roubles a month."

The next day the new lodger appeared in my modest bachelor quarters; but I did not grieve over it, rather I felt glad. I always lead the solitary life of a recluse. I have hardly any acquaintances and go out rarely. After ten years of solitary life, I am naturally used to loneliness, but ten, fifteen, or even more years of such solitude, with such a woman as Agraphina, in a bare flat, appeared an unalluring prospect! So under the circumstances another man was indeed a blessing from heaven.

Agraphina spoke the truth: my lodger was a retired soldier, which I saw at the first glance without looking at his passport. They are easy to recognise. Eustace Ivanitch, my lodger, came of a well-to-do family. We settled down well together, but what was better was that he had many interesting stories of his life which he told well. In the dull monotony of my existence such a raconteur was a treasure-trove. He made a considerable impression on me, but now follows the incident which brings about this story.

One day I was alone in the flat: and Eustace and Agraphina had gone out on business. Suddenly I heard something which seemed to me strange in the next room; I went in; there, indeed, in the hall stood a strange man, small in stature and wearing a smock without a coat in spite of the bitter autumn weather.

" What do you want? "

" Inspector Alexandrov: does he live here? "

" No, my friend; good-bye."

" The concierge said he lived here," said my visitor, retreating cautiously to the door.

" Get away, take yourself off."

Next day after dinner, when Eustace Ivanitch was trying a coat on me which he was altering, some one again came into the hall. I opened the door.

The gentleman of yesterday, under my very eyes, calmly took my short winter coat from the peg, folded it under his arm and rushed from the flat. Agraphina looked at him, her mouth wide open with astonishment, and did nothing to rescue the coat. Eustace Ivanitch dashed after the thief and returned ten minutes later completely out of breath and empty-handed. The man had absolutely escaped.

" Well, Eustace Ivanitch, no success? Lucky he left the greatcoat or we should have been in a nice mess, the rascal! "

But all this so upset Eustace Ivanitch that I quite forgot the theft in watching him. He couldn't get over it. He constantly threw down his work and related again and again how it all happened, how the man stood two paces off and took the coat under our very eyes in a most incomprehensible manner. Then he started work again, only to throw it down, and finally I saw him go off to tell the concierge about it and reproach him for such a thing happening in his house. Then he returned and started blaming Agraphina. Then again sat down to work and muttered to himself all the time about the theft. In a word, though he could work, Eustace Ivanitch was a most pertinacious busybody.

" He made a fool of us, Eustace Ivanitch," said I that evening, as I handed him a glass of tea, feeling so bored that I wished him to relate the story again, which, from constant repetition and the deep sincerity of the narrator, had begun to grow very comic.

" Fooled us, sir! Yes, it was a great pity, and in my opinion there is no worse crime in the world than theft. One works in vain, for another steals the result of your work, the labour of years. . . . Horrible! One hardly wants to talk of it. What d'you think of it, sir . . . isn't it pitiable? "

" Yes, it's true, Eustace Ivanitch; better to burn the thing than let the thief have it."

" Yes, as you say, but of course all thieves are not alike. It was once my strange lot to meet an honest thief."

" What, an honest one? What thief can be honest? "

" It's true, sir! The honest thief is not a thief. I only wished to say that the man seemed honest and stole. It was really rather sad."

" And how did it happen? "

" Yes, sir, it was about two years ago. I had been out of a place almost a year, and before I had secured one I fell in with an absolutely broken man. We met in an eating-house. He was a drunkard, a vagabond, a parasite, had held a position somewhere but had lost it long ago through drink. God knows what clothes he wore! Sometimes you wondered if he had a shirt beneath his great-coat; everything he laid hands on he drank. He wasn't a brawler; very gentle and kindly in character, but you soon saw how he craved for drink. Well, I foregathered with him, or rather he attached himself to me. And what a man he was! Like a dog, you go there—he follows; only once had I seen such a helpless creature! At first I allowed him to spend the night—why, I don't know; his passport was in order and the man himself all right. The next day I again let him stop the night, and the third day he came again, spent the whole day sitting in the window and stopped the night. Well, thought I, he's attached himself to me, and if I, a poor man, give him food and drink and a night's lodging, it's a millstone round my neck. Previously he had attached himself to some official in the same way. The two drank together, but

the official overdrank and died. He was called Emil, Emil Ileetch.
I thought and thought: what am I to do with him? Send him
away—I haven't the heart to, he's such a miserable, broken man.
And he's so silent; never asks for anything, just sits and looks at
you with dog-like eyes. This is what drunkenness makes a man,
I thought to myself: how shall I say to him, ' Be off with you,
Emil, you've no business here, you can't force yourself on anybody; soon there will be nothing to eat, how can I keep and feed
you? ' I sit and think, what will he do when I say this to him?
And I see how long he would look at me when he heard without
understanding my words, how, bent and ragged, he would get up
at length with his bundle in which he carried God knows what,
how he would arrange his overcoat to look all right and not show
the holes—for he was well brought up; how he would open the
door and go out, till I felt I could not cast him adrift. God knows
I might have been such a one myself. Wait, thought I, you
won't have much longer to stay with me. Soon I'm going, then
you won't find me again.

" Well, sir, we parted. When the late Alexander Philimovitch
(God rest his soul) was alive, he said to me, ' We are very pleased
with your work; when we return from the country we will engage
you again.' So I went to them again. He was a kind gentleman,
but died the same year. So, gathering my scanty belongings, I
left his house and hired a room from an old woman, her only spare
one; so, thought I, good-bye to Emil. But what do you think,
sir? Returning towards evening (I had been to see a friend), the
first person I saw in my room was Emil in his old great-coat, his
bundle by his side, sitting on my trunk, waiting for me . . . yes,
and reading a book of Church services, which he had borrowed from
the old woman to pass the time. He had found me! My hands
dropped: ' Well,' thought I, ' there's nothing to be done, why
didn't I send him away at first? ' I went straight up and asked:
' Have you brought your passport, Emil? '

" I sat down and began to think; what was I to do with this
man in my room? He must eat, though a drunkard does not eat
much. I felt certain he would go off on drinking bouts, yet I
knew I should feel sorry if he left me. So I decided to be his
benefactor. I will keep him, thought I, from evil and disaster,
so I said: ' Stop here, Emil, but you must do as I tell you.'

" I thought to myself I will teach you to do some work—not
all at once, but by degrees. I may find some ability in you,
because for any work only human ability is needed. I looked
quietly at him, and saw before me a man in the lowest depths. I
began to encourage him with kind words: ' Look to yourself,
Emil,' I said, ' and see if you can't do more for yourself. Enough
of this life! Look at your clothes, your overcoat is only fit for use
as netting; it's not right! It's time to learn honour.'

" Emil sat and listened to me for a long time with downcast
eyes and incapable of speech.  Then he sighed heavily.  ' Why do
you sigh? ' I asked.  ' Oh, nothing, Eustace Ivanitch, don't be
disturbed.  To-day two peasant women were quarrelling in the
street and one upset the other's basket of berries.'

" ' Well, what of it? '

" ' And the other knocked over the first one's basket of berries
on purpose, and kicked it with her foot.'

" ' Well, what of it, Emil Ileetch? '

" ' Oh, nothing, Eustace Ivanitch, it just happened.'

" ' Nothing, it just happened! '  Oh, thought I, my poor Emil,
you've been over-drinking.

" ' And then a gentleman dropped a bank note in the Sadovaya.
A peasant saw it and said: " Mine! " but another saw it and said,
" No, mine!  I saw it first "—so they started to fight, but a policeman came up, picked up the note, gave it to the gentleman, and
threatened to arrest both the peasants.'

" ' Well, what of it?  What is there important in it? '

" ' Oh, nothing.  The crowd laughed, Eustace Ivanitch.'

" ' Oh, Emil!  What do the crowd matter?  You have sold
your soul for a copper, I tell you.'

" ' How, Eustace Ivanitch? '

" ' Take some work, for the hundredth time, I say, take pity
on yourself and work.'

" ' What shall I do?  No one will take me.'

" ' For the reason that you were dismissed, Emil, because you
are a drunkard! '

" He was just cunning.  He would listen to me till it bored him,
then slink away.  Drink all day and return home drunk.  Who
gave him the drink, or from where he got the money, God only
knows.  I at least was not guilty.

" ' No, Emil,' I said to him, ' I can stand it no longer.  Enough
of this, d'you hear, enough!  Next time you come back drunk I
will turn you out to sleep on the stairs.'

" After hearing this Emil stopped two days at home, but slipped
away on the third.  I waited and waited, still he did not come
back.  I began to be alarmed.  What had I done to him?  Had
I frightened him?  Whither he had gone, God knew.  Night came,
no Emil.  In the morning I went out to the hall and saw him
lying there.  He lay there, his head on the step, absolutely stiff
with cold.

" ' What's the matter with you, Emil?  What are you doing
there? '

" ' You were angry with me the other day and threatened to
put me out on the stairs, so I was afraid to come in and lay here.'

" Then wrath and pity seized me.  ' Why don't you do some
work instead of lying on the stairs? '

" ' But what work can I do, Eustace Ivanitch? '

" ' You miserable wretch,' said I angrily, ' learn tailoring. Look at your coat! It's nothing to you that it's all in rags, so you wear it out on the stairs! Take a needle and try to mend it, you good-for-nothing drunkard! '

" Well, sir, he took a needle; I had spoken in derision, but he was frightened. He took off his coat, took some thread and tried to thread the needle, but in vain; his hands trembled, his eyes grew red, and at length he put it down and looked at me. . . .

" ' Let me help you, Emil,' said I. · ' I spoke scornfully to try and rouse your shame. Give up your weakness, and let's have no more nights on the stairs.'

" ' But what am I to do? I know I'm a drunkard and good for nothing! . . . To you my be—benefactor my heart is everlastingly! . . .'

" Suddenly his blue lips trembled as tears rolled down his white cheeks to his unshaved chin in a torrent. How they flowed! It was as if a knife had pierced my heart.

" ' Oh, you sensitive man! Who would have known it, who would have guessed it of you? '

" Well, sir, there is yet much more to tell. Events so miserable and sordid that you would despise them utterly, but I would give much if they had not happened. I had a pair of breeches of excellent material which I had made for a certain landowner, who, however, said they were too narrow and left them on my hands. I considered them valuable. In the market they would have fetched five roubles—much to a poor man. At that time Emil was passing through a severe, trying period. I watched him, a whole day he drank nothing, then a second, a third day, nothing passed his lips and he sat silent and disconsolate. Thought I, ' Either you have not wherewithal to buy it, or maybe you have turned over a new leaf.' This was the state of affairs when a big holiday came. I went out to vespers; came back—found Emil in the window, drunk and staggering. Alas! thought I, what a man, and went to my trunk for something or other. Looked in—no breeches! . . . I searched everywhere but could not find them. I rushed off to the old landlady and blamed her, for it was no use talking to a drunken man. ' No,' said the old woman, ' what do I want with your breeches? ' ' I don't know,' said I, ' but who has been here? ' ' No one has been here,' she answered, ' Emil Ileetch went out, but came in and is sitting up there. Ask him.' ' You didn't take those breeches for any reason, Emil, did you? ' said I, ' you remember the ones I made for the landowner.' ' No, Eustace Ivanitch,' answered he, ' I didn't take them.'

" What a state of affairs! Again I looked everywhere—no breeches! And Emil sat and swayed. I sat on the trunk straight opposite him, and at length caught his eye.

" ' No,' said he, ' you may think I took them but I didn't.'

" ' Where can they have got to, Emil? '

" ' No, Eustace Ivanitch, I haven't seen them at all.'

" I listened to him unheeding, crossed to the window, sat down and began to work at a waistcoat I was altering for some official in the house. I felt sick at heart and ready to let things slide, till Emil felt the anger that possessed me. Thus does a man who has participated in an evil act feel the approach of misfortune, as birds feel the oncoming storm.

" ' Eustace Ivanitch,' began Emil, and his voice trembled, ' to-day Anton Prokovitch, who married the other day . . .'

" I looked at him till he understood my thoughts. Getting up he walked to the bed and started shuffling round it. I waited while he kept on saying to himself : ' No, no, where can they have got to? ' I waited to see what would happen and saw him crawl under the bed. I could restrain myself no longer.

" ' What are you doing, crawling under there, Emil? '

" ' I was looking for the breeches. Perhaps they have fallen down somewhere.'

" ' You poor fool,' said I, ' what good d'you expect to do crawling about on your knees? '

" ' Well, why not, Eustace Ivanitch? I thought it would be well to look for them.'

" ' H'm, listen,' said I. ' What? ' answered Emil.

" ' Wasn't it you,' said I, ' who stole them from me like a thief and a rascal? '—for thus only could I account for his strange conduct.

" ' No, Eustace Ivanitch . . .' All this time he stopped under the bed. At length he crawled out. I looked at him—he was as white as a sheet. He went to the window and sat opposite to me for about ten minutes. ' No,' said he as he suddenly rose and approached me, and I see him now, white and guilty-faced, ' No, I never took them.'

" He was trembling all over and his fingers clutched his breast convulsively, his voice shook, so that I myself grew frightened and went to the window.

" ' Well, Emil,' I said, ' as you wish, and forgive me if in my stupidity I accuse you unjustly. And let the breeches be; we shall live in spite of the loss; we have hands, thank God, and will not sink to theft and steal from another poor man. We will earn our bread . . .!'

" Emil stood and listened to me, then sat down. There he sat the whole evening without stirring, and when I fell asleep he was still there. When I woke up in the morning he was lying on the bare floor, wrapped in his coat. Well, sir, I never liked him since then, and during those first few days hated him. It was as if my own son had robbed me and caused me grievous harm. And

Emil drank without a stop for two weeks till he was sodden with drink. He went out early and came back late, and for two weeks I never heard a word from him. Perhaps conscience pricked him, or he hoped to escape from himself. At length the orgy ended, all his money was finished, and again he sat at the window. For three days I remember he sat in silence. I looked at him; he was crying. The tears came copiously like a fountain, and it's a sad thing to see a grown man cry, especially an old man like Emil.

" ' What's the matter, Emil? ' I said.

" And he trembled all over. It was the first time I had spoken to him. ' Nothing . . . Eustace Ivanitch.'

" ' But good heavens, Emil, why are you sitting like that? ' He aroused my pity.

" ' I don't know, I wish to get some work, Eustace Ivanitch.'

" ' What kind of work, Emil? '

" Oh, any kind. Perhaps I shall find a position like I held before: I have already been to ask for one. I don't wish to abuse your kindness further; if only I can get a place I will repay you in full.'

" ' Enough of that, Emil! Let's live on as before.'

" ' No, Eustace Ivanitch, perhaps you still think . . . but I never took those breeches. . . .'

" ' Oh, well, my dear Emil, do as you please.'

" ' No, Eustace Ivanitch, I certainly can't live on here any longer.'

" ' But what's the matter with you? ' said I. ' Who's driving you away? '

" ' No,' answered Emil, ' it isn't right I should stay, I had much better go.' And, indeed, he rose and put on his coat.

" ' But what are you doing, Emil? Listen to reason. Where are you going? '

" Good-bye, Eustace Ivanitch, don't keep me back—I'm going. You have changed towards me.'

" ' How have I changed? You will be lost alone, Emil, like a small ignorant child.'

" ' No, Eustace Ivanitch. When you go out now you lock your trunk, and I notice it and it grieves me . . . better let me go and forgive me for bringing trouble on you.'

" What was I to do? The man went out. All day I expected him to return at evening—but no. Another day—no; a third—no. I got frightened and anxious; neither drank, ate, nor slept. The man had disarmed me entirely! Next day I started off and searched all the cabarets.—but in vain, he had vanished. ' Have you succumbed already? ' thought I. ' Perhaps the end came in a drunken fit and you are lying out somewhere like a rotted log.' Half dead, half living, I returned home. The next day I again searched in vain and blamed myself bitterly for allowing the poor helpless fellow to leave me. The fifth day (it was a holiday) the door creaked. I looked up and saw Emil enter, pinched and blue, his hair plastered with mud as if he had slept in the streets, while he had grown thin out of all knowledge. He took off his coat and sat down opposite me on the trunk. I rejoiced after my anguish at his loss. Naturally it was sad to see a man in his state. I began to soothe and comfort him.

" ' Well, Emil,' said I, ' glad to see you back. You were so late I almost went round the cabarets to look for you. Have you had anything to eat? '

" ' Yes, thanks, Eustace Ivanitch.'

" ' Enough to eat? Here is some of yesterday's supper left, some veal and a piece of bread. Eat it, it won't do you any harm.'

" I helped him, and saw he had not eaten for three days, so great was his appetite. It meant that hunger had driven him to me, and my thoughts hardened towards him. To finish his meal I brought some vodka.

" ' Well, Emil,' I said, ' let's drink to the holiday. D'you want some? It's excellent.'

" He stretched out his hand and seized it greedily, then stopped. I waited and watched. He lifted it to his mouth, spilling some over his sleeve; but it never reached his mouth, for he put it down on the table untasted.

" ' What's the matter, Emil? '

" ' No, thanks, Eustace Ivanitch, I don't want to drink any more.'

" ' Have you made up your mind to give it up, or is it just for to-day? '

" He was silent and his head dropped on to his hand as I watched. ' You're not ill, are you, Emil? '

" ' I'm not feeling very well.'

" I took him and placed him on the bed. How thin he had grown: his head burned and he shook with fever. I sat by his side all day: towards night he grew worse. I offered him some light food, saying, ' Try and eat or you will be worse.' He shook his head: ' No,' says he, ' I won't dine to-day.'

" The next morning I went for the doctor. Doctor Kostopravov, whom I knew, lived near by. I met him when working for the Bosomiagins, where he attended me. ' He's in a bad way,' said the doctor, and gave me some powders for him, but I didn't give the powders as I had no confidence in them. So the day passed.

" The end came as he lay opposite me; I was sitting in the window working, and the old landlady was lighting the stove. All were silent. I was grieving for him as for a son. I knew he was looking at me and had been trying to say something since morning, but did not dare. At length I looked at him and saw his eyes fixed on me with a look of unutterable anguish, but he looked quickly away when he met my gaze. 'Eustace Ivanitch.'

"'What is it, Emil?'

"'How much is my coat worth in the market?'

"'Well,' I said, 'I don't know, perhaps three roubles.' Though I knew full well they would only laugh at any one who tried to sell such useless rags, but I just said it to comfort him.

"'And I too thought they would give three roubles for it. It is a cloth coat. Are you sure they'd give three roubles?'

"'I don't know, Emil, if you take it you must start by asking for three.'

"He was silent for a little: then spoke again.

"'Eustace Ivanitch!'

"'What is it, Emil?'

"'Sell my great-coat when I die, don't bury me in it. It has some value and will do for you perhaps.'

"My heart was full of pity as I saw death approaching rapidly. Again we were silent and so an hour passed. He watched me the whole time till I looked at him and then his eyes always looked away.

"'Would you like some water, Emil?' I said.

"'Yes, please, Eustace Ivanitch.' He took it and drank eagerly.

"'Is there anything else you want?'

"'No, Eustace Ivanitch; I want nothing, but . . .'

"'What?'

"'Those . . .'

"'What, Emil?'

"'Those breeches . . . I took them from you . . . when . . .'

"'Well, God forgive you, Emil, rest in peace. . . .'

"The tears ran down my cheeks as I turned away.

"'Eustace Ivanitch. . . .'

"He was trying to speak, raising himself up as his lips moved. His face grew red suddenly as he looked at me, then in a flash he turned ghastly pale, his head fell back, he sighed once and gave his soul to his Maker."

# NICOLAI SCHEDRIN
1826–1889

# TWO LITTLE MOUJIKS

IT is midnight. A vast, gloomy hall, lighted only by a flickering tallow candle; two little boys, aged eight and eleven years, are sitting on the floor leaning against an oblong table. Death-like silence reigns; man and beast are both asleep. The little serfs alone dare not close their eyes before the return of their mistress, who is out visiting and detained late.

Midnight! The hour of ghosts, and that hall is so immense! Such dark corners! The children look at each other. The elder tries hard to assume an air of easy courage, while the little fellow of eight dries his wet blue eyes on his ragged sleeve. The solitary candle is wasting rapidly away. From time to time pale shadows flit across the frost-covered window-pane; the shutters creak and groan dismally. Outside great flakes of snow are whirled about by a furious wind.

The trembling children press closer to one another. In that white, spectral gleam they seem to trace the phantom of a soul in pain. In the " hou-hou-hou " of the winter wind they hear a cry from the unseen world.

The elder boy is named Vania; the little one Mischa. The latter is a slight, pale child, with blond hair and great blue eyes which glance timidly around the hall; when they rest upon the gloomy corners he turns paler still. Vania is a sturdy, black-eyed fellow, who would fain persuade little Mischa that he is not afraid—not in the least; " for I saw a ghost one day, a real ghost, and did not cry out, nor even feel frightened. Indeed, Mischa, I am not afraid," he repeated, starting nevertheless at the slightest sound. " I am only low-spirited, and I don't feel nearly so much so when you are with me."

" But then if we should be burned," murmured poor little Mischa.

" Burned! Oh, that is impossible! "—with such an assured air that Mischa is completely soothed.

" Tell me, Vania," said Mischa, after a pause, " does the touch of a sharp, cold knife hurt much? "

" It hurts a little, for the first moment, and then you don't feel it at all," replied Vania sententiously, stroking Mischa's blond curls with a reassuring touch.

" But, oh, don't you remember when the cook, Mihei, cut his throat? ' I am going to cut my throat,' he cried, and when he drew the knife across—oh, how the blood ran! "

" Oh, Mihei—never mind Mihei—he was an imbecile, for he did not die. He was cured by the doctors, and much good it did him, for he was beaten all the same. But we will manage better: when we cut our throats it shall be well done—they shall not cure us to be beaten again."

" And the knives—are they ready, Vania? "

" Ready? I have had them sharp and shining for three days. Are you going to draw back at the last minute, little coward that you are? "

Mischa did not answer, but drew a long, sobbing breath and fixed his scared blue eyes on the wasting candle.

" Shall I snuff it, Vania, for—for the last time? " he asked in a trembling voice.

" What is the use? Let it alone, and pay strict attention to what I am saying. If we do what we have sworn to do *now*, we shall go straight to heaven because we are little children and have not lived long enough to sin much; but Katerina Afanasievna will be punished for having driven us to it, and she will go to hell."

" And Ivan Vasilich—will he go there too? "

" Perhaps the good God may pardon him, for he would not be so wicked if left to himself."

" Then Katerina will be punished for her sins? "

" Oh, that she will, my little comrade," cried Vania exultingly. " They will hang her on a great iron hook and beat her with a knout until the blood flows; they will make her walk with naked feet over red-hot bricks; perhaps they will make her lick them, as she made poor Sienka a few days ago. Oh, yes, she will be beaten and tormented until it makes one's blood run cold to think of it."

" But how can she endure it? " murmured soft-hearted little Mischa, with awe-struck pity.

" They'll make her endure it. Down there, little brother, they pay no attention to cries and complaints; and whether you can bear it or not, you have to suffer all the same."

The dog in the outer court uttered a long, mournful howl.

" Oh! Tresor has scented a ghost! " exclaimed Mischa, turning pale.

" Nonsense! And suppose he has—are you not ashamed to be such a coward? "

" No, Vania, I am not a coward; but why does this dog always scent ghosts? "

"Ah, that is because a dog is friendly to man. Now, a horse has no idea about such things; but a dog understands—that is why he barks when a ghost is near."

"Vania," interrupted Mischa, "suppose we were to drown ourselves instead."

"How silly you are! Is this summer-time?"

"It is true, the water is cold—so cold—perhaps if we plunged in we could not bear it."

"Drown ourselves indeed! First, we would have to break the ice, and then no doubt you would try to get out, little coward. Then, too, what suffering! While the knife is quite another matter. Draw it firmly across your throat, and it is done. Only, your hand must not tremble."

"And shall we never be beaten any more?" queried little Mischa.

"No, no! Nobody will ever beat us again. The angels will take our souls, and carry them straight to the feet of our Father in heaven."

"And what will our Father say?"

"Our Father will say: ' My little serfs, why have you not waited patiently for the end? Why have you taken your lives? ' And we will answer: ' Dear Lord, it was so hard to live,' and we will tell Him all—how Katerina has beaten us again and again, till the blood flowed—beaten and tortured us."

Mischa listened eagerly; the agony that filled his little heart to bursting found vent in a flood of burning tears. Vania tried to comfort him.

"We will play her one last trick to-morrow. She expects a crowd of fine people to dinner, and I have hidden away every knife, so she cannot find one for her grand company to eat with."

But Mischa continued to weep. Vania snuffed the candle, and looked out of the window.

"What a wind, what a wind!" And then he began to hum the song, "O Night! O Sombre Night!" But Mischa sobbed louder when he heard the familiar strain.

"What a cry-baby you are!" exclaimed Vania impatiently. The striking of the clock broke the silence. Mischa dried his eyes and said timidly:

"Mistress will be here in a moment."

"Yes, you may be sure she will, but how pleasant it would be if we could go to sleep now!"

"No, no! For the love of Christ, Vania, I implore you, don't go to sleep."

"You are afraid?"

"Yes—y-e-s—I am afraid," stammered poor little Mischa.

"Idiot! how many times must I tell you there is nothing to be afraid of in this hall? If you wish I will go about and search "— but he took good care not to stir. There was a deep silence—one of those hushed pauses, when great waves of sadness seem to sweep over the soul. The boys gazed silently at the dying flame of the wasting candle. The dog howled again.

" Cursed dog," said Mischa.

" Where is Olia now? " demanded Vania suddenly.

Olia was Mischa's sister, a girl of eighteen who had disappeared six months ago, and no one knew what had become of her, though there had been much whispering and many conjectures in the household. Some said that she had fled to escape the daily martyrdom of her life, other that she had disappeared to hide her shame. All that was known was that one day she went to the river to wash some linen, and had never been seen again. The linen was found on the river-bank. Two days before she disappeared they had cut her hair off close to her head, as is customary when a young girl had gone astray. Olia had struggled desperately while it was being done. The mistress affirmed that the wicked Olia had drowned herself, not to escape ill treatment, but to hide her ill-conduct. Still a mystery hung over her fate. During the inquest the boldest among the household witnesses declared that Olia's daily life was a hard one, but the judge did not believe a word they said.

" You are summoned to speak the truth and not to lie," he admonished them, and thereupon he summoned Katerina herself. She declared that not only were her serfs well treated, but that they were even fed on meat. She brought forward witnesses who confirmed her statements. The judge hesitated, reflected, and made the following note: " The aristocrats of District R—— not only treat their serfs with great kindness, but actually feed them on meat."

" Why have you told such falsehoods? " he then said, turning to the first witnesses. But they stood pale and mute, biting their lips until the blood came. Katerina noticed this, and, overcome by such audacity, she thought proper to faint on the spot. The court rendered the following verdict:

" Disappeared on the morning of June twenty-fourth, from the Polianok estate, a girl, Olga Nilandrova, belonging to Ivan Vasilich, retired captain of cavalry; said girl was tall, fair, with flaxen hair, cut close, clear complexion, blue eyes, well-shaped nose and mouth, a tiny black mole on the left cheek. The military in the district to which the said girl belongs are ordered to deliver her to the court of District R——, to be held at the disposal of her owners."

And thus the affair was legally brought to an end. Katerina was more cautious for a while, but in a month or two resumed her former amusements. Was she looked upon as a wicked, hardhearted woman? No, indeed. Everybody visited her, and her salon was thronged every day. To be sure, everybody knew she was fond of amusing herself by punishing her serfs in many original, eccentric ways, but nobody judged her severely for that. Indeed, she was really extremely popular among her own circle for her gaiety, and her fascinating and gracious manners to her friends, whom she entertained charmingly.

One day she found a small beetle in the soup. She summoned her cook and with great coolness ordered him to swallow it, and none of the company was at all shocked.

Another time she said: "Sienka, go and lick the stove," and Sienka dared not disobey. She came back with a blistered tongue, her face crimson with pain, her hair scorched, and great tears rolling down her face.

"Idiot! What a fuss she makes," said one. "What a fool," said another, and all burst into peals of laughter. It was only the manner of the day, the fashionable way of entertaining one's guests.

The thought of his sister Olia weighed heavily on Mischa's childish heart. It had bowed his little form and blanched his cheek. Great tears now rose to his eyes as Vania continued:

"Olia has come back; she appéared to the mistress the other day."

"It is false," cried Mischa.

"It is true—she did come back. Matrena told us that the mistress rushed out of her room whiter than a sheet."

"It is false! Olia lives—she did not drown herself," sobbed Mischa.

"Oh, as to that, Mischa, she did drown herself as sure as two and two make four."

"It is false! It is false!" moaned Mischa.

"You baby! Why should you make such a noise about it? Are we not going to die in a few hours?"

Mischa was silenced. How many memories came back to him! He saw Olia as she used to come toward him, tapping his cheek and saying in her sweet, caressing voice: "Dear little simpleton." Or as she used to smile when bringing a new blouse she had just finished for him, and saying, "May you be happy while you wear it, little brother." And then he recalled the day when, her face disfigured with weeping, her beautiful hair cut short, she had rushed from the mistress's room—and that voice imploring mercy! He heard them still, those prayers interrupted by sobs: "Oh, spare me! Spare me! I'll never, never do it again. Oh, do not cut my hair, for Christ's sake!" And her one thrilling cry of agony and shame as the long, beautiful blond braids fell beneath the scissors! And in Mischa's anguish the scene came back with such piercing reality that he thought he saw Olia—that her spirit had indeed come back to torment the mistress, and even that she was there, close to him. He seemed to hear her voice murmuring: "Dear little brother."

around them. Before them yawned a deep ditch. There the blow was to be struck.

Vania sprang in first. Mischa followed, the dumb, imperious instinct of life growing stronger at every step he made. But would he dare to speak? Vania frightened him, but perhaps at this moment Vania, too, might feel one pang of regret for life; perhaps the same irresistible instinct was making itself felt in his soul, too. Although he was shivering with cold his brain seemed on fire.

Vania walked straight on, sharpening one knife against the other. The awful sound seemed to make Mischa's heart stand still, but he followed, submissive, blind, stupefied.

At daybreak the herdsman, buried in profound slumber, was rudely awakened by two passing moujiks, who told him they heard mournful cries for help proceeding from the ditch. " Batiouschki, help! Batiouschki, help! " resounded mournfully over the deserted field. They hurried to the ditch and found the two children —one half naked and both covered with blood. Vania lay still, cold and lifeless. His hand had not faltered, but had struck home firmly, surely. Mischa was still breathing; his little, trembling hand had indeed struck, but ineffectually. The instinct of life had spoken, and at the last moment had prevailed.

# THE SELF-SACRIFICING RABBIT

### Nicolai Schedrin

ONE day a rabbit incurred the displeasure of a wolf. You see, he was running along not far from the wolf's lair, and the wolf saw him, and called out: " Little bunny! Stop a minute, dear! " But the rabbit, instead of stopping, ran on faster than ever. So the wolf, with just three bounds, caught him, and said:

" Because you did not stop when I first spoke, this is the sentence I pronounce: I condemn you to death by dismemberment. But, as I have dined to-day, and my wife has dined, and we have stored up food enough to last us five days, you sit down under this bush and wait your turn. Then perhaps—ha! ha! ha!—I will pardon you! "

So the rabbit sat on his haunches under the bush, and never moved. He thought of only one thing—how many days, how many hours would pass before he must die. He looked towards the lair, and saw the glittering eyes of the wolf watching him. And sometimes it was still worse; the wolf and his wife would come out into the field, and stroll up and down close by him. They would look at him, and the wolf would say something to his wife in wolf language; then they would burst out laughing, "Ha! ha! ha! . . ." And all the little wolf-cubs would come with them, and run up to him in play, rub their heads against him, gnash their teeth. . . . And the poor rabbit's heart fluttered and bounded.

Never had he loved life so well as now. He was a highly respectable rabbit, and had chosen for a bride the daughter of a widowed lady-rabbit. At the moment when the wolf caught him by the neck, he was just running to his betrothed.

And now she, his betrothed, would wait, and think, "My squint-eyed one has forsaken me!" Or perhaps—perhaps she has waited —waited . . . and loved another, . . . and . . . or it may be . . . she, too, . . . playing, poor child, among the bushes, caught by a wolf! . . .

Tears almost choked the poor fellow at this thought. "And this is the end of all my warrens in the air! I, that was about to marry, had bought the samovár already, looked forward to the time when I should drink tea with sugar in it with my young wife,— and now, instead, what has befallen me! . . . How many hours now till death?" . . .

One night he fell asleep where he sat. He dreamed that the wolf had appointed him his special commissioner, and while he was absent, performing his duties, the wolf paid visits to his lady-rabbit. . . . Suddenly he felt some one touching his side; he awoke, and saw the brother of his betrothed.

"Your bride is dying," said he. "She heard of your misfortune, and sank at once under the blow. Her one thought now is, 'Must I die thus, and not say farewell to my beloved?'"

At these words the condemned one felt as though his heart would burst. Oh, why! How had he deserved his bitter fate? He had lived honestly, he had never stirred up revolutions, had never gone about with firearms, he had attended to his business— and must he die for that? Death! Oh, think what that word means! And not he alone must die, but she too, his little grey maiden-rabbit, whose only crime was that she had loved him, her squint-eyed one, with all her heart! Oh, if he could, how he would fly to her, his little grey love, how he would clasp his fore-paws behind her ears, and caress her, and stroke her little head!

"Let us escape," said the messenger.

At these words the condemned one was for a moment as if transformed. He shrank up altogether, and laid his ears along his back. He was just ready to spring, and leave not a trace behind. But at that moment he glanced at the wolf's lair. The rabbit's heart throbbed with anguish.

" I can't," he said; " the wolf has not given me permission."

All this time the wolf was looking on and listening, and whispering softly in wolf language with the she-wolf. No doubt they were praising the rabbit's noble-mindedness.

" Let us escape," said the messenger once more.

" I can't," repeated the condemned.

" What treason are you muttering there? " suddenly snarled the wolf.

The rabbits stood as petrified. Now the messenger was lost too. To incite a prisoner to flight—is that permitted? Ah! the little grey maiden-rabbit will lose both lover and brother; the wolf and the she-wolf will tear them both in pieces.

When the rabbits came to their senses, the wolf and the she-wolf were gnashing their teeth before them, and in the darkness their eyes shone like lamps.

" Your Excellency, it was nothing; we were just talking; . . . a neighbour came to visit me," stammered the condemned, half-dead with terror.

" Nothing! I dare say! I know you! Butter won't melt in your mouths! Speak the truth. What is it all about? "

" It's this way, your Excellency," interposed the bride's brother. " My sister, his betrothed, is dying, and asks, may he not come to say farewell to her? "

" H'm! It's right that a bride should love her betrothed," said the she-wolf. " That means that they will have a lot of little ones, and there will be more food for wolves. The wolf and I love each other, and we have a lot of cubs. Ever so many are grown up, and now we have four little ones. Wolf! wolf! shall we let him go to take leave of his betrothed? "

" But we were to have eaten him the day after to-morrow——"

" I will come back, your Excellency. I'll go like a flash; I—indeed. . . . Oh, as God is holy, I'll come back! " hurriedly exclaimed the condemned. And, in order to convince the wolf that he *could* move like a flash, he sprang up with such agility that even the wolf looked at him admiringly, and thought—

" Ah! if only my soldiers were like that."

And the she-wolf became quite sad, and said:

" See that, now! A rabbit, and how he loves his she-rabbit."

There was nothing for it; the wolf consented to let the rabbit go on *parole* with the stipulation that he should return exactly at the appointed time. And he kept the bride's brother as hostage.

" If you are not back the day after to-morrow by six in the morning," he said, " I'll eat him instead of you; then if you come I'll eat you too; perhaps, though, I'll—ha! ha!—pardon you! "

The squint-eyed one darted off like the arrow from the bow. The very earth quivered as he ran. If a mountain barred his way, he simply dashed at it; if a river, he never stopped to look

for a ford, but swam straight across; if a marsh, he sprang from
tuft to tuft of grass.  Not easy work!  To get right across country,
and go to the bath, and be married (" I will certainly be married! " he kept repeating to himself), and get back in time for
the wolf's breakfast. . . .

Even the birds wondered at his swiftness, and remarked:

" Yes, the *Moscow Gazette* says that rabbits have no souls, only
a kind of vapour, and there it goes."

At last he arrived.  Tongue cannot speak, neither can pen write
the rapture of that meeting.  The little grey maiden-rabbit forgot
her sickness at the sight of her beloved.  She stood up on her hind
paws, put a drum upon her head, and with her fore-paws beat out
the " Cavalier March "; she had been practising it as a surprise
for her betrothed.  And the widowed lady-rabbit completely lost
her head with joy; she thought no place good enough for her future
son-in-law to sit in, no food good enough to give him.  Then the
aunts and cousins and neighbours came running from all sides,
overjoyed to see the bridegroom, and perhaps, too, to taste the
good cheer.

The bridegroom alone was not like himself.  While still embracing his betrothed, he suddenly exclaimed:

" I must go to the bath, and then be married at once."

" Why should you be in such a hurry? " asked the mother
rabbit, smiling.

" I must go back.  The wolf only gave me leave of absence for
one day."

Then he told them all, and his bitter tears flowed as he spoke.
It was hard to go, and yet he must not stay.  He had given his
word, and to a rabbit his word is law.  And all the aunts and
cousins declared with one voice: " Thou speakest truth, O squint-
eyed one.  Once given, the spoken word is holy.  Never in all our
tribe was it known that a rabbit was false to his word! "

A tale is soon told, but a rabbit's life flies faster still.  In the
morning they greeted the squint-eyed one, and before evening came
he parted from his young wife.

" Assuredly the wolf will eat me," he said.  " Therefore be
thou faithful to me.  And if children shall be born to thee, educate
them strictly; best of all, apprentice them in a circus; there they
will be taught not only to beat the drum, but also to shoot peas
from a pop-gun."

Then suddenly, as though lost in thought, he added, remembering the wolf:

" It may be, though, that the wolf will—ha! ha!—pardon me! "
And that was the last of him they saw.

.　　.　　.　　.　　.　　.　　.　　.

Meantime, while the squint-eyed one was making merry and

getting married, great misfortunes were happening in the tract of country which divided him from the wolf's lair. In one place heavy rains had fallen, so that the river, which the rabbit swam across so easily the day before, overflowed and inundated ten versts of ground. In another place King Aaron declared war against King Nikita, and a battle was pitched right in the rabbit's path. In a third place the cholera appeared, so that quarantine was established for a hundred versts round. And, besides all that, wolves, foxes, owls—they seemed to lie in wait at every step.

The squint-eyed one was prudent; he had so calculated his time as to leave himself three hours extra; but when one hindrance after another beset him his heart sank. He ran without stopping all the evening, half the night; the stones cut his feet, the fur on his sides hung in ragged tufts, torn by the thorny branches, a mist covered his eyes, blood and foam fell from his mouth,—and still he had so far to go! And his friend, the hostage, haunted him constantly, as though alive before him. Now he stands like a sentinel in front of the wolf's lair, thinking: " In so many hours my dear brother-in-law will return to deliver me." . . . When the rabbit thought of that, he darted on yet faster. Mountains, valleys, forests, marshes—it was all the same to him. Often he felt as though his heart would break; then he would crush it down, by sheer force of will, that fruitless emotion might not distract him from his great aim. He had no time now for sorrow or tears: he must think of nothing but how to tear his friend from the wolf's jaws.

And now the day began to break. The owls and bats slipped into their hiding-places; the air became chilly. Suddenly all grew silent, like death. And still the squint-eyed one fled on and on, with the one thought ever in his heart: " Shall I come too late to save my friend? "

The east grew red; first on the far horizon the clouds were faintly tipped with fire; then it spread and spread, and suddenly—a flame. The dew flashed on the grass, the birds awoke, the ants and worms and beetles began to move, a light smoke rose from somewhere; through the rye and oats a whisper seemed to pass—clearer, clearer. . . . But the squint-eyed one saw nothing, heard nothing, only murmured to himself again and again: " I have destroyed my friend,—destroyed my friend! "

At last, a hill! Beyond that was a marsh, and in the marsh the wolf's lair. . . . Too late, O squint-eyed one, too late! . . .

With one last effort he put forth all his remaining strength, and bounded to the top of the hill. But he could go no farther; he was sinking from exhaustion. And must he fail now? . . .

The wolf's lair lay before him as on a map. Somewhere far off six o'clock struck from a church steeple, and every stroke of the bell beat like a hammer on the heart of the agonised creature. At the last stroke the wolf rose from his lair, stretched himself, and wagged his tail for pleasure. Then he went up to the hostage, seized him in his fore-paws, and stuck the claws into his body, in order to tear him in two halves, one for himself, the other for his wife. And the wolf-cubs surrounded their father and mother, gnashing their teeth and looking on. . . .

" I am here!—Here! " shrieked the squint-eyed one, like a hundred thousand rabbits at once; and he flung himself down from the hill into the marsh.

And the wolf praised him.

" I see," he said, " that a rabbit's word can be trusted. And now, my little dears, this is my command: Sit, both of you, under this bush, and wait till I am ready, and afterwards I will . . . ha! ha! . . . pardon you! "

# COUNT LEO N. TOLSTOY

1828-1910

# HOW MUCH LAND DOES A MAN NEED?

THE two sisters met in the country. The elder, a shopkeeper's wife, had come down to the peasant home of the younger. They talked endlessly over their tea. The elder sister had a very good idea of herself. Town life was better than country; she lived in some style; her children were well dressed; there was always enough to eat and drink, and in the evening you could go to the theatre.

The younger girl was not at all pleased at this. She thought that life in the country was better than in the town. She said, " I should not like to be in your place. Our life is stupid enough, but it is without trouble. You people have plenty of swank; but though you get on well, you may be ruined at any moment. Haven't you heard the proverb, ' Income and Loss are brothers '? You are well enough off to-day, but to-morrow you may be begging your bread at my door. Country life is in every way better; of course we are not rich, but we always have enough."

" You call that enough? " cried the town sister, contemptuously. " The beasts have enough to eat, and you live just as they do. There is no trace of refinement or comfort in your lives; and however hard your husband may work, he can never make things any different; you will die like the lower animals, even as you live."

" Well," answered the younger, " granted all that, we are content that it should be so. For, on the other hand, we have security in our lives. We need not toady to any man. But you town people are surrounded with insecurity and all sorts of dangers; you never know when the Evil One may entice away your husband to gambling or drink or even to worse vices; and then there is an end to all your money and all your comfort. You know I speak the truth."

Her husband, who was lying near the fire, had been listening to his wife's defence of peasant life. " It is all gospel truth," he thought approvingly. " I have been too hard at work all my life on my bit of earth for any such dangerous rubbish to find its way into my head. The only wickedness here is that it's so devilish hard

549

to get a bit of land. Just give me a tidy piece of ground, and I should have no fear of any one, not even of Old Nick himself."

When the two wives had finished their tea and their chatter, and had cleared away the tea-cups, they went to bed. Then the Devil, who had been listening all the time from the corner behind the stove, gave himself a quiet hug of satisfaction at the peasant's vain boast against him. "So, so! If he had a nice bit of land he would not fear Old Nick himself!" thought the malicious fiend. "We'll soon see about that! You shall have the land all right, and Old Nick will have both you and your land, my friend."

Near by Pakhom's cottage lived a lady who owned some hundred odd acres of land. Until recently she had been a good and easy mistress, and had kept a friendly understanding with the peasants on her land; but she had lately appointed an ex-soldier as her bailiff, and the peasants had a bad time of it under him. Pakhom began to find trouble and misery on every hand; in spite of all his acres, his horses would get into the standing oats; then his cow would break through the fence into a garden; and another time his calf would trespass in the lady's fields. Every time an offence of this sort occurred, Pakhom was heavily fined by the new bailiff; and it was of little avail that he scolded and punished his own servants, or tore out his hair in his anger. All summer his offences accumulated, so that he was glad when winter came, and he had to bring in his cattle to the yard. Stall feeding was hard enough, indeed, but at any rate there could be no more fines during the winter.

Before winter was over, however, a new terror came upon the peasants, which made all their hearts quail. It was whispered abroad that their lady was going to sell her land, and that the hated ex-soldier was to purchase it. "Alas," they told one another, "if he should get the land, our miseries will be greater than we can bear; he will inflict more grievous fines than ever upon us. What shall we do? For we cannot live but by the land!"

At last the peasants went in a body to their lady, and implored her not to let the bailiff have the land, but to sell it to them, promising to pay as much and more for it than he would have paid. She acceded to their request; and the peasants held a great meeting of their common council to decide on the best way to proceed in the matter of buying the land. Many meetings were held, and yet nothing could be agreed upon, and no progress at all was made. In the end it was arranged that each peasant should buy his own separate bit of land, as much or as little as he could afford. Their lady fell in with this arrangement, and Pakhom heard before long that twenty acres had been purchased by his next-door neighbour, who had only had to find half the amount in ready money and was to pay the remainder within a year. This kindled Pakhom's heart to envy, and he thought within himself, "Here are all our neighbours buying up the land, and presently I shall find myself cut off and left with nothing! ''

He talked the matter over with his wife. '' Every one is buying up land now,'' he said, '' and we ought to get a bit for ourselves. If we can't raise the price of ten acres, we are done, for the bailiff will have no mercy on us; we shall be beggared with his fines.''

They spent a lot of time planning how it was to be done. All their savings amounted to £10; and when they had sold the horse and most of the bees, and had hired out their son as a labourer, they managed to bring the total sum up to one-half of the purchase money. Pakhom managed to conclude an arrangement with the lady of the manor for a piece of fifteen acres, which he chose on account of a little wood included in it which he had long coveted. He walked into the neighbouring town and had the contract executed, paying down half the money and undertaking to complete the payment within two years; and so he got his land.

Pakhom then got his brother-in-law to lend him money for seed, and soon the land was tilled and sown. Fortune favoured him, and before the year was out he had paid off all he owed both to the lady of the manor and to his brother-in-law, and felt himself indeed a landowner. The earth that he worked so vigorously was his own bit of earth; the crops that he reaped, the hay, the stacks of firewood, the pasture for his beasts, were all his very own, and his heart swelled as he walked about over his possessions. He never tired of the joy of possession; never were such cornfields, such green grass, such wonderful flowery meadows. Nothing on the land was the same as before; the pride of ownership had transformed it into a veritable Eden.

Life had become very delightful to Pakhom, and for some time all was as merry as a song. Then a small cloud came up on the horizon, for the peasants began to let their animals trespass on his meadows and over his corn. Pakhom at first remonstrated, driving the cows out of the fields and the horses from amid the corn; and even when they took no notice, it was not for some time that he could bring himself to appeal to the law against them. But at last he lost patience, and in a burst of anger, prosecuted first one of them and then others, though his heart and his own experience told him that the peasants were driven to such courses by sheer poverty and misery and by no ill-will. '' Still, I cannot afford always to let it pass,'' he told himself. '' If this goes on I shall be brought to the workhouse myself. I must teach them that this has to stop.''

When Pakhom took to prosecuting the peasants, among whom he had lived so many years as an equal, they felt very sore about it, and soon began to work him ill out of real spite. His cherished wood was invaded one night, and all the young saplings were wantonly barked. And Pakhom, walking amid the desolation, and seeing the torn bark lying all around and the gaunt bare trunks gleaming white throughout the copse, grew pale with anger and with desire for vengeance on his enemies. Sheer malice had prompted such ruthless destruction, which could not content itself with cutting down a few trees, but must wantonly ruin the whole lot.

" If I could only get hold of the miscreant," he growled between his teeth, " he should pay dearly for this." Then he cast about in his mind, trying to fix the blame. " Simeon! " he thought at last, " it was certainly Simeon," and went off at once to Simeon's farm to have it out with him.

Simeon denied all his charges, and bitter recriminations ensued. The quarrel, however, strengthened Pakhom's suspicions into certainty, and he took out a summons against Simeon. There was a lengthy process in the Court, which finally decided that there was no real evidence against the peasants, and dismissed the case. Pakhom, whose anger at the decision became uncontrollable, vented it upon the magistrates, crying out, " You are upholders of criminals and thieves; if you were honest men yourselves you would not be afraid to punish the vagabonds." So the magistrates, as well as the peasants, became his enemies.

The village council soon became too hot to hold him; and at home he had more room than company, for all left him alone. Then a report began to get abroad that the villagers were going away in search of fresh land; and Pakhom thought to himself, " All the better for those who stay. I need not go away, for I shall be able to get hold of the land of those who go, and so make my estate complete; I am dreadfully cramped for room as it is."

One day a stranger, a peasant who was passing through the village, called at the house, and Pakhom, who happened to be at home, welcomed him, gave him a meal and a bed, and they had a long talk.

" Well, friend, and where are you going? " asked Pakhom.

The peasant told him that his home was in the district of the lower Volga, and that work was to be had there in plenty. So they fell to talking of these parts, and the peasant related how the land was being settled there. His own family, he said, had gone thither, had put down their names on the local land-roll, and had ten acres allotted to them. " The land is so fertile that barley grows higher than the horses' heads, and the ears are so thick that it only takes a few handfuls to make a small stack. I know one peasant who was as poor as Job when he went there, and he was given a plot of fifty acres. Well, last year one wheat-field alone brought him in £100."

Pakhom's excitement mounted to fever heat as he listened. Why should he stay here, where he only became poorer the harder he worked, when in this new place he might easily live so well? " I will sell my land and stock," he said, " and with the money I raise I will take up a large piece of land there, and go in for farming on a really big scale. It is a shame to stay in such a hole-and-corner place as this. I must go and see your place, first, however, to see for certain that all is as you say."

When summer came, Pakhom made his journey. He went by steamer down the Volga to Samara, and then walked the remaining forty miles to the specified place. Here he found everything just as it had been described to him, and all the peasants living on the fat of the land. Every fresh settler who came to the district was given ten acres of land free, and might buy as much as he wished of the very best land at six shillings an acre. Pakhom, after a full investigation, went back home in the autumn, sold his land, his house and buildings and all that he possessed, and had his name removed from the village roll. Then, when spring came, he and his family migrated to their new home.

Pakhom and his family settled in the largest village of the new district, and were inscribed upon its roll. He entertained all the most important people of the village, showed them his credentials, was accepted as a member of the community, and received fifty acres of land in various fields, being the portion allowed for five persons, together with the right of pasture on the common land. Pakhom then built a house and bought a lot of cattle; he had more than twice the amount of land he had had in the old place, and much better land; so that he lived now on a scale many times beyond his former style of life. There was any amount of meadow and arable land, and no limit to the number of cattle it was possible to rear.

Just at first, while his mind was filled with the new house he was building and with all the stock he was buying, Pakhom was altogether happy and satisfied; but it was not long before he began to feel that here too he was cramped and limited. He had conceived an ambition to grow Turkish wheat like some of his neighbours; but the land suited to this particular crop was very small in extent, and there was great competition for it. Most of the wheat had to be sown alternately with grass and fallow; a lot of the land was of too light soil for any crops but rye; and though every one wanted to get heavy soil and to grow wheat, there were only a very few who succeeded. Hence it was not long before jealousy and ill-feeling were produced, and quarrels broke out. The rich peasants held tenaciously to all that they had managed to get, and the poorer ones soon had to sell more and more of theirs to pay the taxes. Pakhom had sowed his land with wheat the first year, and had secured a fine crop; so that the next year nothing would satisfy him but to sow wheat again; but he was not able to secure more than a very little wheat land, and that of poor quality. He went, therefore, to a large farmer and rented more land; and this year he sowed wheat on a large scale; and once more he reaped a splendid crop. But there was still a fly in the ointment; the field was fifteen miles away, and as Pakhom went backwards and forwards between his house and his wheat, he was struck with envy of the peasant proprietors whose estates he passed on the way, and who all looked so prosperous. "That's the life for me," he told himself; "I should have all I could wish if only I could buy a holding and build my own farm on it." From that time his one idea was how to compass the complete purchase of a holding.

Five years passed away, years of great prosperity for Pakhom. He rented more and more land, and grew ever larger and larger crops of wheat; his wheat was excellent and the money began to roll in. Pakhom would now have felt that life was good indeed; had it not been for the bother of having to rent land every year, and the waste of time which the transaction involved. Wherever there was an extra good bit of land to be had, all the peasants would rush to get some of it; and if he wanted to get a piece it was necessary to be on the spot at the earliest moment, or there would be none left. One year Pakhom rented a great section of the common land, and had already ploughed it up, when the peasants, highly incensed, appealed to the law against him, and the land had to be restored. So Pakhom felt thwarted on every hand, because he had not land which was all his own property.

The problem of how to acquire land of his own occupied his mind night and day. He happened one day to meet a peasant who was faced with ruin, and had to sell his land for anything he could get for it. Pakhom at once determined to get it at a bargain, and after a lot of haggling, at last arranged to buy the whole of it, five hundred acres, for £100, one-half of which amount he agreed to pay down in cash. But as they were on the point of clinching the bargain, a trader who was passing stopped to ask a feed for his horses. Pakhom gave him tea, and was soon engaged in earnest conversation with him. He learned that the merchant had just purchased a huge estate of 5,000 acres from the Bashkirs, from whose country he was now making his way home, and that the whole estate had only cost him £100. Pakhom, fired with envy, induced him to tell the whole story of how the bargain was made.

"All you need do, is to get round the chiefs," said the trader. "I got my way by means of a present of ten pounds' worth of raiment and carpets and a chest of tea, and by treating all the notables with wine. They let me have the land, which lies alongside the river, and on the grassy steppes, for fivepence an acre."

Pakhom was greedy for information.

"The country of the Bashkirs," the merchant told him, "is of such vast extent that one could not possibly traverse the whole of it in a year, travelling all the time. The people are like children, quite simple and unsophisticated, and I should not wonder if you could get them to give you some of their land for nothing."

"If this is all true," thought Pakhom to himself, "I should be a fool to pay £100 for five hundred acres, and involve myself in debt too, when I could get all I want for the same sum."

Having learned carefully the way to the Bashkir country, Pakhom prepared to set out at once. He left his wife in charge of the farm, taking with him one of his farm servants. They went first to the nearest town, and there purchased all the presents that the merchant had suggested, such as clothes, tea, wine, and other things. Over five hundred miles they travelled, and came at last to the country of the nomad tribe of Bashkirs, who lived on the steppe beside a great river, and had their homes in tent-like caravans. He found that the merchant had described them and their country correctly. These simple people made no effort to grow corn, and never ate bread; but moved across the steppe with their vast herds of cattle and horses, the foals being fastened to the backs of the vans. Twice a day they rounded up the mares and milked them, and from the milk koumiss and cheese were made, but the cheese was different from any which Pakhom knew at home. These merry, hospitable people ate their mutton, drank tea and koumiss, and made every day a festival with music and gaiety. Strong, lithe and free-hearted, they welcomed every stranger, and the moment Pakhom appeared he was surrounded by a chattering throng, who could not speak a word of Russian, but whose kindly feelings were evident. As luck would have it, there was a man among them able to act as interpreter, and Pakhom soon made known his desire to purchase land from them. The Bashkirs were immensely pleased with Pakhom and his mission, led him away into the grandest of their vans, made him a comfortable seat with carpets and pillows, and gave him tea and koumiss to drink. A sheep was slain and cooked, and all did their best to feast him and make him welcome. Pakhom fetched out the presents he had brought with him, and gave them away among the men, who were more than ever pleased with him. They talked incessantly, and the interpreter told Pakhom the meaning of their eager chatter.

" The people are greatly taken with you," he said, " and as their custom is, they wish to give you whatever you may choose, in return for the presents you have made. Tell us, then, what is it that you most desire? "

" What I long for most of all," Pakhom answered, " is to possess a piece of your land. In our part, there is but little land to be had, and what there is is dreadfully poor, but you have any amount of land, and of such quality as I never saw before! "

The Bashkirs, on learning what Pakhom had said, held a long discussion among themselves; and though Pakhom could not of course understand a word, he could tell that something had amused them, by the way in which they all laughed. When they stopped speaking, and the interpreter explained their decision to Pakhom, they all sat looking at him while he listened.

"The people have decided," the interpreter said, "that since you have been so good to them, they are ready to let you have all the land you want; you have only to point out to them which is the land you would like, and you shall have it."

Pakhom saw, however, that an argument was taking place among the Bashkirs, and asked what was the matter. "There is a difference of opinion," the interpreter answered; "some of them think that the Chief must be consulted before anything can be settled about the land; the rest think that it can all be settled just as well without him."

While the discussion was still going on, a fine, tall man wearing a head-dress of fox-skin strode into their midst, at sight of whom talking ceased and all at once stood up respectfully.

"It is the Chief himself," explained the interpreter.

Pakhom opened his bundle and presented the Chief with a fine robe and five pounds of tea. These gifts were graciously received, and when the Chief had seated himself the Bashkirs reported all they knew about Pakhom. The great man listened with an occasional smile. Then, speaking in Russian, he said, "Very well, you are welcome to your choice of land. There is enough for all of us."

Pakhom was amazed and delighted, but a little suspicious. He was afraid that they might offer the land to-day, and to-morrow go back on their word.

"Thank you very much," he said. "Your land is indeed unlimited, and my wants are small. Yet it would be well that we should agree definitely with regard to my holding. Let us survey it accurately, so that I may have an unquestionable title to it. Only God knows how long any one of us may live; and though yourselves are to be trusted, you cannot answer for your sons."

Again that quizzical smile on the Chief's features. "Very good," he said; "let us make the matter absolutely certain."

"I was told," said Pakhom, "by a trader who came from here that you made a formal agreement about his land, and I ask no more for myself."

"Quite right," the Chief replied. "Here is one who can write, and we can go to the town and have the contract duly signed."

"What is your price?" Pakhom inquired.

"We ask always the same figure—£100 per day."

"But how can you sell it *by the day*? How can you measure land that way?"

"The matter is simple enough," was the reply. "We sell for £100 as much land as you can run round in one day."

The purchaser was astonished. "One can run round a great deal of land in one day!"

Again that queer smile. "All that you can compass will be yours.

But you must understand that if you fail to return before sunset to your starting-point, you get no land and you lose your money."

" How do you propose to measure my course? "

" We ourselves will remain at the place whence you set out. You will pursue your course, followed by mounted men who will set up posts at each place you indicate; and then a furrow will be ploughed from each post to the next. You choose your own course, but you must return before sunset to your starting-point. All that your circle includes will then be your own property."

This proposal was readily agreed to, and the adventure was fixed for dawn on the following day. Then followed a pleasant evening of conversation and the drinking of koumiss and of tea. A comfortable bed was prepared for Pakhom, and the Bashkirs left him to his slumbers, promising to meet at earliest dawn.

But sleep deserted the delighted purchaser. " What wonderful fortune! " he said to himself. " It will make a vast estate. The days are now the longest of the year, and to-morrow I can easily do fifty miles. A circuit of that length will include 10,000 acres. I shall be a wealthy man. With two teams of oxen and a couple of men I will plough up the choicest parts, and feed cattle on the rest." Not until it was nearly dawn did Pakhom fall into an uneasy sleep, haunted by a strange dream.

He seemed to be lying where he was in the van, and to hear a mocking laughter outside. He dreamed that he descended from the van, and found the Bashkir Chief sitting on the ground and shouting with uncontrollable laughter. " What amuses you so much? " he asked; and then, behold, it was not the Chief at all, but the trader who had stayed with him a few days before and had told him about the land. " Hullo," he inquired, " how long have you been down here? " But now it was no longer the trader, but the peasant from the Volga who had told him of his last venture. But now, again, it was not the peasant after all, but the Devil himself, with his horns and hoofs, laughing horribly at some object at which he was looking. And Pakhom crept nearer, and gazing, saw a dead man lying on the ground in shirt and trousers. The feet of the corpse were bare and its upturned face as white as a sheet. Looking more closely, Pakhom saw in his dream that the dead man was no other than himself. He awoke with a horrid cry; and after considering the absurdity of this nightmare, he looked out and saw the first light of dawn in the east. " I must look for my friends," he said. " It is time to start."

Calling his man, Pakhom ordered him to put in the horses, and set out to wake the Bashkirs. " Good morning," he said; " we must now go out to the steppe and measure off the land."

The tribe were soon gathered together, and in a few minutes were joined by the Chief. They breakfasted on koumiss, and offered

Pakhom tea; but he was in too great a hurry to wait. " Let us start, let us start! " he cried.

And so they all set out, some of them mounted and others in the light carts of the steppe; and they had no sooner reached the steppe than the dawn was ruddy in the sky. The tribe halted at the foot of a low hill, and ascending it, all stood there together. The Chief waved his hand over the horizon.

" There you are," he said. " The land is ours as far as you can see. Make your own choice."

Pakhom's eyes gleamed. The entire expanse was covered with waving grass. It was a vast level of the darkest and richest hue, and the watercourses were marked out by many-coloured bushes and stunted trees. The chief laid his fur cap on the ground at the summit of the hill. " There is your goal," he exclaimed; " put the money in my cap. Your man shall stand beside it. From here you start, and here you must return. The land that you surround to-day is yours."

Pakhom laid the money in the fur cap, took off his cloak, tightened his belt, placed a chunk of bread in his breast, tied a water-flask to his belt, fastened his boots more securely; and ready to set out, surveyed the land.

" It does not matter which way I start," he thought, " I will go westward." Then he stood looking toward the dawn, eager for the sun to rise above the horizon. The horsemen had now grouped themselves on the summit of the hill behind him. As soon as the disc of the sun came into view Pakhom turned his back on it and set out across the steppe, followed by the mounted men.

At first he kept an easy steady pace, and after the first mile he ordered them to plant a post. As he went on, his limbs became more supple and his pace increased, and before long another post had been set up. Looking backward now, he could still see the summit of the hill, and even the tribe grouped upon it, and guessed that he had come five miles at least. And now the pace began to tell. He was bathed in perspiration. He threw off his coat and tightened his belt again. He ran five miles more, and the sun grew very hot. It was quite breakfast-time. " Now I have done one stage," he thought; " four stages are as much as any one does in a day. I don't need to turn back yet, but I had better ease my boots." This made the running much easier, and the eager man, noticing how excellent was the land over which he passed, determined to do another five miles and then turn to the left. But as he went on, the quality of the land became better and better, and he could not turn aside from his straight course. When once he looked round, the hill was scarcely to be descried upon the horizon.

" I have done enough in this direction," he said at last. " I must turn in time." The heat was dreadful and he was very thirsty; so he raised his flask and drank eagerly, had another post fixed in the ground, and turned sharply to the left. Still he went onward through the stiff high grass. The heat was overwhelming, and the position of the sun showed that it was dinner-time. " I must rest," he said as he stood still and bit at his loaf, " but I must not sit down, for then I should lie down, and then I should go to sleep."

Having regained his breath, he forced the pace again. At first it was fairly easy, for the food had given him strength. But the sun beat down cruelly, and he was tired almost to death. " Stick to it," he said, " stick to it for an hour, and live like a king for the rest of your days! "

For ten miles he continued in this direction, and was just about to turn once more to the left, when he caught sight of a lovely cool well-watered dell. This at least must not be left out; it was perfectly adapted for growing flax. So again he went straight on, and passing the dell, made them set up another post, and turned his second corner. Pakhom looked away toward the hill, which was about fifteen miles away, and concluded that as the first two sides of his estate had been very long, this last one must be as short as possible. With long painful strides, he set out upon it. The sun had already begun to descend in the heavens. Thinking that he had got enough land at last, he ran swiftly towards the hill.

And now the work began to be very heavy. Again and again he stumbled and nearly fell. His limbs were in torment and seemed on the point of giving way altogether. He would have given anything for a rest; but that was now impossible, for the sun seemed actually to be falling down toward the horizon. And now for the first time a doubt began to form itself in his mind. " Have I made a fool of myself? " he wondered. " Have I tried for too much? What if I don't get there in time? Oh, how far it is! What if all this trouble should go for nothing! " He pulled himself up, and fell into a lame trot. His feet were bleeding. He threw away his boots, his flask, his hat. " I have been too covetous," he moaned; and his heart was filled with terror. His clothes, streaming with sweat, stuck to his limbs. His mouth and throat were dry and hot as a furnace. His lungs laboured like the bellows of a smithy, and his heart beat like the hammer on the anvil; and now he had a strange sense that his feet and legs no longer belonged to him. He had no more thought of the estate, but only feared dying of exhaustion. Yet, though he was afraid to die, he could not bring himself to stop.

What strange sound was this ringing in his ears? The tribe were shouting, encouraging him to run the race, and their friendly cries renewed his courage. One glance backward showed that the sun was touching the horizon, but a few minutes would be enough to bring him to the goal. The folk on the hill were waving their arms to him, and their shouts spurred his fainting strength. Very soon he saw the fur cap on the ground, which held the money, and beside it was the Chief, laughing. That dreadful dream came back to Pakhom. "My land is great and wonderful," he thought, "most wonderful and plenteous; but—will God let me enjoy it? Ah; I have lost myself, *myself!*"

Still giddily he stumbled on. One glance back at the sun showed that its great lurid disc was nearly gone; and when he had struggled to the foot of the hill, it had fallen quite below the horizon. The man groaned aloud, thinking that everything was lost; and then he suddenly realised that though he could not see the sun, it must still be visible from the summit of the hill. With a last effort he plunged upward, and staggered toward the fur cap. Yes, it was there still! Near it he gave way altogether, and falling on the ground stretched out his hands toward the prize.

"Well done, my lad; well done!" shouted the Chief of the tribe. "You have indeed won a great estate!"

Pakhom's man ran to his master to lift him up; but he found his master dead, with blood oozing from his lips. The servant moaned in despair; but the Chief still sat on the ground, swaying with inextinguishable laughter.

At last the Chief arose and took the money from the fur cap, saying to Pakhom's servant, "Dig, dig!" Then, with all his tribe, he went away.

The man was left alone with the body. He dug a grave and buried his master. The grave was just six feet long, for Pakhom had been six feet tall.

# THE LONG EXILE

## Count Leo N. Tolstoy

"God sees the truth, but bides His time."

ONCE upon a time there lived in the city of of Vladímir a young merchant named Aksénof. He had two shops and a house.

Aksénof had a ruddy complexion and curly hair; he was a very jolly fellow and a good singer. When he was young he used to drink too much, and when he was tipsy he was turbulent; but after his marriage he ceased drinking, and only occasionally had a spree.

Once, in summer, Aksénof was going to Nizhni [1] to the great Fair. As he was about to bid his family good-bye, his wife said to him:

[1] Nízhni Nóvgorod: it means Lower New Town.

" Iván Dmítrievitch, do not go to-day; I had a dream, and dreamed that some misfortune befell you."

Aksénof laughed at her, and said: " You are always afraid that I shall go on a spree at the Fair."

His wife said: " I myself know not what I am afraid of, but I had such a strange dream: you seemed to be coming home from town, and you took off your hat, and I looked, and your head was all grey."

Aksénof laughed. " That means good luck. See, I am going now. I will bring you some lovely presents."

And he bade his family farewell and set off.

When he had gone half his journey, he fell in with a merchant of his acquaintance, and the two stopped together at the same tavern for the night. They took tea together, and went to sleep in two adjoining rooms.

Aksénof did not care to sleep long; he awoke in the middle of the night, and in order that he might get a good start while it was cool he aroused his driver and bade him harness up, went down into the smoky hut, settled his account with the landlord, and started on his way.

After he had driven thirty miles, he again stopped to get something to eat; he rested in the vestibule of the inn, and when it was noon he went to the doorstep and ordered the samovár to be got ready; then he took out his guitar and began to play.

Suddenly a carriage with a bell dashed up to the inn, and from the equipage leaped an official with two soldiers; he came directly up to Aksénof and asked: " Who are you? Where did you come from? "

Aksénof answered without hesitation, and asked him if he would not have a glass of tea with him.

But the official kept on with his questions: " Where did you spend last night? Were you alone or with a merchant? Have you seen the merchant this morning? Why did you leave so early this morning? "

Aksénof wondered why he was questioned so closely; but he told everything just as it was, and asked: " Why do you ask me so many questions? I am not a thief or a murderer. I am on my own business; there is nothing to question me about."

Then the official called up the soldiers, and said: " I am the police inspector, and I have made these inquiries of you because the merchant with whom you spent last night has been stabbed. Show me your things; and, you men, search him."

They went into the tavern, brought in the trunk and bag, and began to open and search them. Suddenly the police inspector pulled out from the bag a knife, and demanded: " Whose knife is this? "

Aksénof looked and saw a knife covered with blood taken from his bag, and he was frightened.

" And whose blood is that on the knife? "

Aksénof tried to answer, but he could not articulate his words:

" I—I—don't—know—  I—  That knife—it is—not mine——"

Then the police inspector said: " This morning the merchant was found stabbed to death in his bed.  No one except you could have done it.  The tavern was locked on the inside, and there was no one in the tavern except yourself.  And here is the bloody knife in your bag, and your guilt is evident in your face.  Tell me how you killed him and how much money you took from him."

Aksénof swore that he had not done it, that he had not seen the merchant after he had drunk tea with him, that the only money that he had with him—eight thousand roubles—was his own, and that the knife was not his.

But his voice trembled, his face was pale, and he was all quivering with fright, like a guilty person.

The police inspector called the soldiers, commanded them to bind Aksénof and take him to the carriage.

When they took him to the carriage with his feet tied, Aksénof crossed himself and burst into tears.

They confiscated Aksénof's possessions and his money, and took him to the next city and threw him into prison.

They sent to Vladímir to make inquiries about Aksénof's character, and all the merchants and citizens of Vladímir declared that Aksénof, when he was young, used to drink and was wild, but that now he was a worthy man.  Then he was brought up for judgment.  He was sentenced for having killed the merchant and for having robbed him of twenty thousand roubles.

Aksénof's wife was dumbfounded by the event, and did not know what to think.  Her children were still small, and there was one at the breast.  She took them all with her and journeyed to the city where her husband was imprisoned.

At first they would not grant her admittance, but afterward she got permission from the chief, and was taken to her husband.

When she saw him in his prison garb, in chains together with murderers, she fell to the floor, and it was a long time before she recovered from her swoon.  Then she placed her children around her, sat down amid them, and began to tell him about their domestic affairs, and to ask him about everything that had happened to him.

He told her the whole story.

She asked: " What is to be the result of it? "

He said: " We must petition the Tsar.  It is impossible that an innocent man should be condemned."

The wife said that she had already sent in a petition to the Tsar, but that the petition had not been granted.  Aksénof said nothing, but was evidently very much downcast.

Then his wife said: " You see the dream that I had, when I dreamed that you had become grey-headed, meant something after all. Already your hair has begun to turn grey with trouble. You ought to have stayed at home that time."

And she began to tear her hair, and she said: " Ványa, my dearest husband, tell your wife the truth: Did you commit that crime or not? "

Aksénof said: " So you, too, have no faith in me! " And he wrung his hands and wept.

Then a soldier came and said that it was time for the wife and children to go. And Aksénof for the last time bade farewell to his family.

When his wife was gone, Aksénof began to think over all that they had said. When he remembered that his wife also had distrusted him, and had asked him if he had murdered the merchant, he said to himself: " It is evident that no one but God can know the truth of the matter, and He is the only one to ask for mercy, and He is the only one from whom to expect it."

And from that time Aksénof ceased to send in petitions, ceased to hope, and only prayed to God. Aksénof was sentenced to be knouted, and then to exile with hard labour.

And so it was done.

He was flogged with the knout, and then, when the wounds from the knout were healed, he was sent with other exiles to Siberia.

Aksénof lived twenty-six years in the mines. The hair on his head had become white as snow, and his beard had grown long, thin, and grey. All his gaiety had vanished.

He was bent, his gait was slow, he spoke little, he never laughed, and he spent much of his time in prayer.

Aksénof had learned while in prison to make boots, and with the money that he earned he bought the *Book of Martyrs*, and used to read it when it was light enough in prison, and on holidays he would go to the prison church, read the Gospels, and sing in the choir, for his voice was still strong and good.

The authorities liked Aksénof for his submissiveness, and his prison associates respected him and called him " grandfather " and the " man of God." Whenever they had petitions to be presented, Aksénof was always chosen to carry them to the authorities; and when quarrels arose among the prisoners, they always came to Aksénof as umpire.

Aksénof never received any letters from home, and he knew not whether his wife and children were alive.

Once some new convicts came to the prison. In the evening all the old convicts gathered around the newcomers, and began to ply them with questions as to the cities or villages from which this one or that had come, and what their crimes were.

At this time Aksénof was sitting on his bunk, near the strangers, and, with bowed head, was listening to what was said.

One of the new convicts was a tall, healthy-looking old man of sixty years, with a close-cropped grey beard. He was telling why he had been arrested. He said:

" And so, brothers, I was sent here for nothing. I unharnessed a horse from a postboy's sledge, and they caught me in it, and insisted that I was stealing it. ' But,' says I, ' I only wanted to go a little faster, so I whipped up the horse. And besides, the driver was a friend of mine. It's all right,' says I. ' No,' say they; ' you were stealing it.' But they did not know what and where I had stolen. I have done things which long ago would have sent me here, but I was not found out; and now they have sent me here without any justice in it. But what's the use of grumbling? I have been in Siberia before. They did not keep me here very long though——"

" Where did you come from? " asked one of the convicts.

" Well, we came from the city of Vladímir; we are citizens of that place. My name is Makár, and my father's name was Semyón.''

Aksénof raised his head and asked:

" Tell me, Semyónitch, have you ever heard of the Aksénofs, merchants in Vladímir city? Are they alive? ''

" Indeed, I have heard of them! They are rich merchants, though their father is in Siberia. It seems he was just like any of the rest of us sinners. And now tell me, grandfather, what you were sent here for? ''

Aksénof did not like to speak of his misfortune; he sighed, and said:

" Twenty-six years ago I was condemned to hard labour on account of my sins.''

Makár Semyónof said:

" But what was your crime? ''

Aksénof replied: " I must, therefore, have deserved this.''

But he would not tell or give any further particulars; the other convicts, however, related why Aksénof had been sent to Siberia. They told how on the road some one had killed a merchant, and put the knife in Aksénof's luggage, and how he had been unjustly punished for this.

When Makár heard this, he glanced at Aksénof, clasped his hands round his knees, and said:

" Well, now, that's wonderful! You have been growing old, grandfather! ''

They began to ask him what he thought was wonderful, and where he had seen Aksénof. But Makár did not answer; he only repeated:

" A miracle, boys! how wonderful that we should meet again! ''

And when he said these words, it came over Aksénof that perhaps this man might know who it was that had killed the merchant. And he said:

" Did you ever hear of that crime, Semyónitch, or did you ever see me before? ''

" Of course I heard of it! The country was full of it. But it happened a long time ago. And I have forgotten what I heard," said Makár.

" Perhaps you heard who killed the merchant? " asked Aksénof.

Makár laughed, and said:

" Why, of course the man who had the knife in his bag killed him. If any one put the knife in your things and was not caught doing it—why, it would have been impossible! For how could they have put the knife in your bag? Was it not standing close by your head? And you would have heard it, wouldn't you? "

As soon as Aksénof heard these words he felt convinced that this was the very man who had killed the merchant.

He stood up and walked away. All that night he was unable to sleep. Deep melancholy came upon him, and he began to call back the past in his imagination.

He imagined his wife as she had been when for the last time she had come to see him in prison. She seemed to stand before him exactly as though she were alive, and he saw her face and her eyes, and he seemed to hear her words and her laugh.

Then his imagination brought up his children before him; one a little boy in a little fur coat, and the other on his mother's breast.

And he imagined himself as he was at that time, young and happy. He remembered how he had sat on the steps of the tavern when they arrested him, and how his soul was full of joy as he played on his guitar.

And he remembered the place of execution where they had knouted him, and the knoutsman, and the people standing around, and the chains and the convicts, and all his twenty-six years of prison life, and he remembered his old age. And such melancholy came upon Aksénof that he was tempted to put an end to himself.

" And all on account of this criminal! " said Aksénof to himself.

And then he began to feel such anger against Makár Semyónof that he almost fell upon him, and was crazy with desire to pay off the load of vengeance. He repeated prayers all night, but could not recover his calm. When day came he walked by Makár and did not look at him.

Thus passed two weeks. Aksénof was not able to sleep, and such melancholy had come over him that he did not know what to do.

Once during the night, as he happened to be passing through the prison, he saw that the soil was disturbed under one of the bunks. He stopped to examine it. Suddenly Makár crept from under the bunk and looked at Aksénof with a startled face.

Aksénof was about to pass on so as not to see him, but Makár seized his arm, and told him how he had been digging a passage under the wall, and how every day he carried the earth out in his boot-legs and emptied it in the street when they went out to work. He said:

" If you only keep quiet, old man, I will get you out too. But if you give me away, they will flog me; but afterward I will make it hot for you. I will kill you."

When Aksénof saw his enemy, he trembled all over with rage, twitched away his arm, and said: " I have no reason to make my escape, and to kill me would do no harm; you killed me long ago. But as to informing about you or not, I shall do as God sees fit that I should do."

Next day, when they took the convicts out to work, the soldiers discovered where Makár had been digging in the ground; they began to make a search, and found the hole. The chief came into the prison and asked every one, " Who was digging that hole? "

All denied it. Those who knew did not name Makár, because they were aware that he would be flogged almost to death for such an attempt.

Then the chief came to Aksénof. He knew that Aksénof was a truthful man, and he said: " Old man, you are truthful; tell me before God who did this."

Makár was standing near, in great excitement, and did not dare to look at Aksénof.

Aksénof's hands and lips trembled, and it was some time before he could speak a word. He said to himself: " If I shield him— But why should I forgive him when he has been my ruin? Let him suffer for my sufferings! But shall I tell on him? They will surely flog him? But what difference does it make what I think of him? Will it be any the easier for me? "

Once more the chief demanded:

" Well, old man, tell the truth! Who dug the hole? "

Aksénof glanced at Makár, and then said:

" I cannot tell, your Honour. God does not bid me tell. I will not tell. Do with me as you please; I am in your power."

In spite of all the chief's efforts, Aksénof would say nothing more. And so they failed to find out who dug the hole.

On the next night, as Aksénof was lying on his bunk, and almost asleep, he heard some one come along and sit down at his feet.

He peered through the darkness and saw that it was Makár.

Aksénof asked:

" What do you wish of me? What are you doing here? "

Makár remained silent. Aksénof arose, and said:

" What do you want? Go away, or else I will call the guard."

Makár went up close to Aksénof, and said in a whisper:

" Iván Dmítritch, forgive me! "

Aksénof said: " What have I to forgive you? "

" It was I who killed the merchant and put the knife in your bag. And I was going to kill you too, but there was a noise in the yard; I thrust the knife in your bag, and slipped out of the window."

Aksénof said nothing, and he did not know what to say. Makár got down from the bunk, knelt on the ground, and said:

" Iván Dmítritch, forgive me, forgive me for Christ's sake. I will confess that I killed the merchant—they will pardon you. You will be able to go home." Aksénof said:

" It is easy for you to say that, but how could I endure it? Where should I go now? My wife is dead! my children have forgotten me. I have nowhere to go."

Makár did not rise; he beat his head on the ground, and said:

" Iván Dmítritch, forgive me! When they flogged me with the knout, it was easier to bear than it is now to look at you. And you had pity on me after all this—you did not tell on me. Forgive me for Christ's sake! Forgive me though I am a cursed villain! "

And the man began to sob.

When Aksénof heard Makár Semyónof sobbing, he himself burst into tears, and said:

" God will forgive you; maybe I am a hundred times worse than you are! "

And suddenly he felt a wonderful peace in his soul. And he ceased to mourn for his home, and had no desire to leave the prison, but only thought of his last hour.

Makár would not listen to Aksénof, and confessed his crime.

When they came to let Aksénof go home, he was dead.

# A CANDLE

## Count Leo N. Tolstoy

The incident took place at a time when the landowners were all-powerful. They were of various kinds; some of them feared God, and remembered death, and had pity on the poor; others, if I may use the word, were little better than dogs. But none of them was worse than the stewards who had risen from being serfs. They were like rulers who had risen out of the mud; and they made the life of the peasants intolerable.

A steward of that kind ruled over the estate of a great landlord. There were many peasants, much good land, plentiful water, and good meadows and woods. There was plenty for lord and peasants alike, but this landlord brought one of his serfs from another of his estates to be steward. This man was very overbearing and oppressed the peasants. He came with his wife and two daughters, who were married. He was already well off, and might well have lived a blameless life, had not covetousness led him into evil. He made the peasants do more than their proper day's work on the estate; and besides that he started a brickyard, forced both men and women to work upon it, and made a profit by the sale of the bricks. The peasants vainly complained to the landlord at Moscow; he sent them away disappointed, and did not bring the steward to book. The latter soon found out that the peasants had reported his actions, and quickly took his revenge, so that their state was worse than before. Moreover, some of the peasants were tale-bearers, so that the estate was soon in a very bad way, and the steward became more ferocious than ever. At last he became so hard and cruel that he was more feared than a wild beast. Men and women alike would hide from him as from a wolf, doing everything to escape his sight. Of course, the man soon saw this, and their fear only increased his rage. He pursued them with violence and oppression, so that their sufferings were unendurable.

It often happened that criminals of this kind were done to death, and the peasants began to mutter of assassination. They met furtively from time to time, and the bolder spirits would say: " Must our sufferings go on for ever? It is no sin to kill a man like him! " On one of these occasions, just before Easter, the peasants were gathered at the dinner in the forest, whither the steward had sent them to cut wood. " How are we to live? " said one. " The man will be the death of us. Neither our wives nor we can rest by day or night. Whenever he is angry he uses the whip. So Semyón died, and Anisim was tormented by the stocks. The same will be our fate. He will be here to-night and is sure to raise trouble. Let us pull him off his horse and hit him on the head with an axe and bury him like a dog. No one can ever know anything about it. But we must all stick together; no one must tell! "

These were the words of Vasili Minaef, who was angrier than any one else, for the steward beat him every few days and had taken away his wife to be his servant.

As expected, the steward came on horseback in the evening, and no sooner had he arrived than he began to scold. He found a few lime-branches among the cut wood. Now he had forbidden this wood to be cut. " Confess who did it," he said, " or I will beat you all." Then he ascertained whose pile contained the lime-wood. It had been cut by Sidor, and the steward beat him until the blood came. Then he beat Vasili because he had done too little work; and growling, went away.

That same evening the peasants met once more, and Vasili harangued them. " You are not men," he said, " but sparrows. You promised to stand all together, but when the opportunity comes all fear to act. When he beat Sidor you should all have joined and put him to death. But after promising to stand together, you are like sparrows who fly into the bushes when the hawk swoops down on one of them."

The anger of the peasants gathered force, and at last they determined to put an end to the steward. He told them on Good Friday that they must plough for the landlord on Easter Sunday, to prepare the land for oats. This was an unheard-of proposal. On Good Friday they met behind Vasili's cottage and consulted. " He has forgotten God," they said. " If he commands such sins we must kill him. We are lost in any case."

There was among them a very peaceable peasant named Piotr Mikhyeef, who did not at all agree to this. " Brothers," he said, " you are proposing a great sin. Nothing is worse than to kill a soul. What about your own souls? The misfortune is his, because it is he who does the evil. As for us, brothers, we must suffer in silence."

This counsel annoyed Vasili exceedingly. " You say that it is a sin to kill a man! You repeat the same thing again and again. Now it is a sin to kill an honest man, but God Himself has commanded that we should kill a dog like this one. A mad dog must be slain that men may be safe. It would be a greater wrong not to kill the steward who is our ruin. Even though it should bring us into trouble, we ought to do it for the sake of others. They will be grateful to us. You talk mere nonsense. It would be a greater sin for us all to work on Easter Sunday. Even *you* would not do that."

But the peaceful peasant was ready with his answer. " Certainly I will plough," he said, " when they send us, though I would not plough for myself. God will know where the sin lies. It only matters that we should not be forgetful of Him. God has not told us to render evil for evil, but to do exactly the opposite. If you do wrong, it is you who will suffer in the end. If you slay a man your soul will be stained with blood. You think that you will have killed a bad man, or that you will have destroyed a plague-spot, but in point of fact you will have done a far greater wrong to yourself. If you give way to fate, fate will give way to you." This speech had much effect, and the peasants were divided in opinion, some thinking that the steward should be slain, and others agreeing with Piotr that it would be better not to sin, but rather to bear their sufferings.

The peasants were celebrating the great festival of Holy Saturday when the village elder came round and informed them that the steward had given orders that all the men were to plough the oatfields on the following day. Together with police officials, he went all through the village, shouting to one man on the river and to another on the road, saying that every man must plough. The unhappy men mourned, but could only obey; and on the morrow they brought their ploughs and set to work. The first mass was being celebrated at church and all the air was full of the Easter festival, but the peasants were ploughing.

Late in the morning the steward arose and rode over to the farm. His family were dressed in all their best garments, horses were harnessed to the little carriage; they went and heard mass. On their return the servants made the tea, and when the steward came in they began to drink it. After the steward had finished his tea he lit his pipe and sent for the village elder.

" Have you set the men to work at ploughing? " he asked.

" I have," was the reply.

" And did all of them go? "

" Every one of them. I set them to work myself."

" That is very good, but I wonder whether they are really working. I want you to go and see, and tell them that I shall come out after dinner to see that each of them has covered sufficient ground, and has done it well too. If I have any fault to find, there will be no festival for them."

The village elder had not gone far when the steward called after him. He hesitated, wishing to give some order, but did not know how to choose his words. At last, with some hesitation, he brought it out.

" I want you to tell me what those scoundrels say about me. Find out which of them is grumbling and let me know what he says. I know the lazy villains; they hate working; and unless I kept them tightly in hand they would do nothing. They like feasting and holidays, but not ploughing. Just keep your ears open to what they say and report to me. I want to know all about it." At this the village elder mounted his horse and rode off to the fields where the peasants were working.

Now the steward's wife, a peaceable, tender-hearted woman, had overheard this conversation, and came to speak with her husband and plead for the peasants. In fact, she always stood up for them whenever she could.

" My dear husband," she said, " do take care you do not commit a sin on this great festival of Our Lord. Dismiss the men from their work, I ask you for Christ's sake."

But the brutal man only laughed at her. " It seems to me that you want a good thrashing," he growled. " How dare you meddle with my affairs? "

" My dear love," she said, " I dreamed about you last night; it was a dreadful dream. Do listen to me and dismiss the men."

" I shall have something to say about that," he replied; " if you give me any more cheek I will beat you. So take care! " He was very angry; and thrusting his pipe into her face, told her to fetch dinner. After an abundant repast, at which he drank freely, the steward called for the cook and made her sing, while he accompanied her voice with his guitar. He was still gaily chatting with the cook and playing his guitar, when the village elder returned to report upon the men at work.

" Are they ploughing? " asked the steward. " Will they get their task done? "

" They have done more than half of it already."

" And done it well? "

" Very well, sir. They dared not do otherwise."

" How does the ground look? "

" In excellent condition, and turns up easily."

After a long silence the steward resumed. " And what are they saying about me? No good, I suppose? "

The old man hesitated, but the steward called on him to speak freely. " Tell me everything; it is not your own words I ask you to repeat, but those of others. I will make it worth your while to tell the truth, but take care you don't hide anything. Here," he continued, addressing the cook, " give him a glass of spirits."

The old man, thus refreshed, took courage and spoke. " They don't speak any good, sir; they grumble a good deal."

" I dare say; but what do they actually say? "

" Always the same thing, sir,—' He does not believe in God.' "

" Who says that? " asked the steward scornfully.

" All of them. They say: ' He has sold himself to the Devil.' "

" Very good," said the steward, chuckling. " Now tell me, does Vasili say that? "

Unwilling as the elder was to tell tales of his companions, he had long been on bad terms with Vasili, and admitted that Vasili grumbled more than any of the others.

" Can't you speak out, man? " said the steward. " What does he say? "

" It is a dreadful thing to tell you. He says that you cannot escape a violent death."

" Aha, he's a fine fellow! I suppose he lies in wait for me? No, no, Vasili, you cannot touch me! I'll see about you, my man! Now, then, what does Tishka say? He, too, I suppose, the dog? "

" Yes, sir, they all say dreadful things, hateful."

" Come on, man. Don't be afraid to speak."

" Well then, if I must: they all say that you will burst asunder and your entrails will fall out."

The steward was hugely delighted and howled with laughter. " Aha, we shall see who will first meet that fate! Who is it says that? "

" No one has anything good to say; all are very threatening."

" What about Piotr? He grumbles too, I suppose? "

" No, sir; he alone among all the men has nothing to say. He is a deep fellow, is Piotr. I can't understand him."

" What do you mean? "

" All the men are working and talking about it. He is ploughing on the upper field. I came near him and heard him singing, and saw that he was carrying something very carefully; and there was a bright light between the handles of his plough, just as it might have been a tiny fire flickering. When I came near I saw a little candle, might be a twopenny one, standing burning on the cross-bar of the handles; and it would not go out for all the wind. Piotr, in his Sunday clothes, went up and down the furrows singing as they sing in church. With all the shaking the candle would not go out. I was close up to him when he lifted and turned the plough; and the candle burned steadily and would not go out."

" What did he say? " inquired the steward.

" Not a word, sir; he only looked at me, made the sign of the cross, and then began to sing."

" Did you not speak to him? "

" No, sir, but some of the men came up and began to chaff him, saying that his prayers would not save him from punishment for ploughing on a holy day."

" And did he speak? "

" Only these words—' On earth, peace to men of good-will.' And then he jerked the reins, and into his songs again, and the plough went away across the hill. And still that candle burned and would not go out, sir."

The steward laughed no longer, but throwing aside his guitar, let his head fall upon his breast, as he pondered this portent. Long he sat there before he sent away the cook and the old man; and then he lay down on his bed, and sighed and groaned as if he had been buried beneath a stack of wheat. His wife entered and spoke to him, yet could get no reply but this: " He has won the day; it is all up with me! "

The good woman seized on the opportunity. " Do dismiss the men, dear. Don't be afraid; no harm has been done."

" It is all up with me," the wretched man repeated; " he has won the day; he has conquered me."

His wife raised her voice imperatively. " Get up and dismiss the men, and all will be well. Get up while I saddle your horse."

The steward mounted at the gate, and rode forth to dismiss the men. As he came near the village a woman opened the gate for him; and as he rode down between the houses the street was cleared as if by magic, every soul running to cover, some within doors and others in their gardens. So he passed throughout the village and came to another gate. This was shut, and he failed to open it while mounted. He shouted again and again for some one to open it, but no one came forward. Dismounting, he set the gate wide open, and was about to mount his horse. His foot was in the stirrup, and he was just throwing himself into the saddle when the restive horse shied at a running pig and leapt sideways against the fence. The corpulent steward failed to reach the saddle, and was thrown forward upon a sharp post that supported the fence.

He fell with his belly right on its sharpened point; and it tore him open, and then he fell to the ground.

The men were returning in haste from their work, their mouths full of bitter sayings. When they came with their horses to the gate they saw the dead steward lying on his back with outstretched arms; his eyes were glazed, and his blood was about him like a pool, of which earth itself refused to drink. The terrified men urged their horses onward. But Piotr threw himself from his horse and, coming to the dead man, closed his eyes; then putting his horse into a cart, brought the body to the manor-house.

Having heard the whole matter, the lord of the manor remitted to his men their annual tax. And the peasants, for their part, knew that the power of God works by goodness and not by sin.

# THE THREE HERMITS

## Count Leo N. Tolstoy

A certain bishop set out to sea in a ship sailing from the city of Archangel to Solovki, a port on the River Dwina. With him were many going on pilgrimage to a holy shrine. There was a fair breeze, the sea was smooth and the skies blue. And as they fared forth over the waters the pilgrims held converse together, whether lying or sitting on the deck or taking their meals.

One morning the bishop came up on deck and paced to and fro upon the poop. Then, seeing the ship's company and passengers thronging the bow, he went forward to join them. A young lad was pointing away far over the sea, and those about him were listening to what he said. The bishop scanned the horizon to which he pointed, but could see nothing but the far glittering of the ocean. Approaching nearer to hear what the lad had to say, the bishop was saluted with great deference by all the company.

" Do not let me interrupt you, my brethren," he said. " I only wanted to hear what you are saying, my lad."

" The boy, a fisherman in these waters," said a trader, " has been telling us about certain hermits."

" What hermits? I should like to hear," said the bishop, taking his seat by the bulwarks. " What were you pointing at? "

" That little island just in sight on the port bow," replied the fisherman. " There are three hermits living there for the good of their souls."

" But where is this island? " the bishop inquired.

" Look, sir, right along my arm, just to the left of the little cloud. You will be able to see it."

The man of God peered forth across the glittering waters, but could make out nothing in the vast expanse. " I see nothing," he exclaimed. " What kind of hermits are they? "

" Some sort of monk," the lad replied. " I have heard of them often, and last summer I saw them." Then he told how he had been driven by contrary winds to the shore of the island, not knowing where he was. He had explored the island and had come upon a lowly mud cabin. Here he had found one of the hermits, and then the two others had come into the cabin. They had given him food and dried his clothes, and had helped him to mend his fishing-boat.

" What were they like? " the bishop inquired.

" Well, sir, the first I saw in the hut was a very, very old man, I should think a hundred years old; a tiny little man he was, with a round back, and he wore an old cassock. His beard was quite white, and he smiled, sir, smiled like the pictures of the saints. Then the next, he was old too, with a long yellow beard; taller, he was, and had a ragged coat; I can tell you he *was* strong; he could turn my boat over by himself. Lively and happy he was. Then the other was a great tall white man, white as the moon, and his beard came down to his knees. He was severe and sad to look at, and his eyes shone as out of caves. He wore nothing except a belt round his middle."

" What did they say? "

" They would hardly speak a word, sir, and said very little to each other; if one of them looked, *so,* the others would understand. I asked the tall one how long they had been there, and he frowned and looked angry and growled at me; but the little old, old man took his hand and smiled at him, and the big tall man was quiet then. And then the old man smiled again and said to me, ' You must excuse us.' "

While this story was going on the ship was gradually approaching the island. " There now, reverend Father," exclaimed the trader, " the island is quite plain now! " and pointed away over the sea. And this time the bishop was just able to make out a tiny dark speck, which was indeed the island. For long the man of God gazed upon it; then, taking some resolution, he walked aft and spoke to the steersman.

" What is that little island called? " he inquired.

" Well, sir, I don't suppose it has a name. There are many like it in these waters."

" I am told that certain hermits live on it. Do you know if that is the case? "

" You can't believe all you hear," the man replied. " They do say that there are hermits there, and that the fishermen have seen them. I am sure I don't know."

" I should like to put ashore," said the bishop, " and visit the hermits. Can it be done? "

" Well, your reverence, we cannot take the ship alongside," the man answered. " Of course you could land in the boat, but that is a matter for the skipper. There he is."

" Captain," said the bishop, addressing him, " I should very much like to see those hermits. Can you see your way to putting me ashore? "

The skipper was very unwilling to do anything of the kind. " It is easy enough, my lord," he said, " but it would only be a waste of time. I can assure you that they are not worth your trouble. I have been told that they are out of their wits; cannot understand what you say nor say anything themselves; little better than shell-fish."

" That may be," the bishop replied. " But I wish to land and am willing to pay for the time and trouble."

It was difficult to refuse a man of his dignity. The necessary orders were given; the ship was laid on the other tack and swiftly bore down on the island. They fetched a seat for the bishop, who then sat right in the bow and looked steadily at the island, while the ship's company gathered behind him. Soon the more far-sighted seamen made out the rocks, and presently the little cabin, and at last one of them thought he saw the three hermits. Then the skipper fetched his glass, and having studied the shore gave it to the bishop, saying, " Right you are. There are three men standing on a rock on the shore." The bishop took the glass and presently made out the three men, one very tall, the second shorter, and the third very short indeed, standing together on the shore and holding one another's hands.

Then said the captain: " We cannot go farther, sir. We must anchor here. If you still wish it you can go ashore in the ship's boat." So the helm was put down and the ship ran up into the wind; the anchor was thrown over and the sails lowered; and the vessel rolled in the swell of the sea. The boat was put over the side and manned by its crew; the bishop climbed down the ladder and sat in the stern; the oarsmen beat the water and the boat sped on its way like a stone from a sling. Plainer and plainer became these three old men standing together and holding one another's hands. Soon the boat came alongside the rocks; a seaman caught them with a hook, and the bishop climbed ashore. The hermits came forward and made obeisance. He gave them his blessing, and they bowed again. Then the bishop spoke:

" I have been told that you are living here as followers of Our Lord Christ, to worship God and to work out your salvation. By the grace of God I too am a servant of Our Lord, though an unworthy one, and have been called to be a shepherd of His flock. So I wish, if possible, to come and give you some instruction, for you are God's servants."

The hermits found nothing to say, but only looked at one another and smiled.

"Will you tell me," inquired the bishop, "how you seek your salvation and serve God?"

The two taller hermits sighed and looked toward that venerable ancient little one. And he in turn smiled and said, "O servant of God, we are not able to serve God. We serve ourselves by seeking our food."

"But how do you pray to God?" said the bishop.

Then the old man made reply, "This is what we say: *You are three; we are three; have mercy on us.*" And no sooner had he spoken than all three hermits lifted their eyes to the heavens and cried in chorus: "*You are three; we are three; have mercy on us.*"

The bishop was touched, and smiled. You have been rightly taught," he said, "about the Holy Trinity, but that is not the way to pray. Your devotion pleases me, my children. It is plain that you wish to serve God, but you do not know how to do so. Listen to me; let me teach you. I am not going to teach you my own words, but will teach you from Holy Scripture how God wishes all men to pray to Him." Then he explained to the hermits the mysteries of Revelation, telling them all about God the Father, God the Son, and God the Holy Ghost, and continued, "The Son of God came to earth to save us all and taught all men to pray thus,—Listen and say the words after me,—*Our Father.*"

One hermit repeated *Our Father,* and the second after him, and lastly the third also.

"*Who art in heaven.*"

The hermits tried to say, *Who art in heaven,* but none of them could make anything of it. The tall naked man's lips were ungovernable so that he could not speak. The most ancient of the three failed to make the words intelligible; and the other mixed them up hopelessly.

Undiscouraged, the bishop took his seat on a rock while the hermits stood before him, and they repeated that phrase after him until at last they had it by rote. All the long day until nightfall the bishop persevered, repeating every word a hundred times, until the hermits were able to speak each phrase. And when, as often happened, they got it all mixed up, he stopped them at once and began all over again. He did not leave them until they had learned the whole of the Lord's Prayer, and could repeat it together and separately.

Night had already fallen, and the moon had climbed up from the sea, before the bishop arose to say farewell. They made obeisance as before and he kissed them, enjoining them to pray as he had taught them. Then he entered the boat again, and as the seamen rowed him toward the ship the voices of the hermits followed him, shouting the *Our Father*. Having climbed aboard the ship, he could no longer hear the sound of prayer, but there in the moonlight were the three old men standing upon the shore.

The sails were set and the anchor raised and the swift ship sped on her course. Seated in the stern, the bishop still gazed at the rocky island. Soon he lost sight of the hermits; presently the island itself faded from vision; and there was only the sea with the wide pathway of the moon. The pilgrims were asleep, and there was not a sound on board. But there was no sleep for the bishop, seated alone in the stern, rejoicing in his good hermits and in the instruction they had received, and thanking God that he had been able to help them.

Thus he sat thinking, his eyes dazzled with the moonlight dancing on the waves, when he was suddenly aware of some gleaming white fleeting object coming down the pathway of the moon. Was it a sail, or some bird pursuing them? The bishop peered over the water. This strange object was swiftly gaining upon the vessel. It was not a boat, nor a bird, nor a fish, but rather like the figure of a man of great stature. Yet that could not be, for how could a man be fleeting over the surface of the waters?

The bishop hailed the steersman. "See, brother," he cried, pointing, "what is that?" But he knew already. The three hermits were fleeting over the sea with shining beards, and they overhauled the ship as though she had been at anchor. The frightened steersman left the tiller, and screamed, "God save us! The hermits, the hermits! They run as though upon the land!"

The alarm brought the whole ship's company on deck, and they clustered affrighted about the stern. And still the hermits, holding one another's hands, fleeting over the moonlit waters, waving to the vessel to lie to; and though they ran as on dry land their feet were not seen to move. Before ever the ship had run up into the wind the hermits had come up and scaled the side. Standing on deck before the astonished company, they said, "O servant of God, we have forgotten all, all that you taught us. We remembered it so long as we were repeating it; but when we stopped saying it for an hour, we had lost one of the words. We could not recall it, and presently the whole was gone. We remember not a word of it; please teach us again."

The bishop made the sign of the cross, and knelt before the hermits, saying, "God has accepted your prayer, O holy hermits. There is nothing I can teach you. Only, pray for us sinners." So he bowed himself before their feet.

For a moment the hermits stood, then turned and fleeted away over the sea. And next morning the deck was seen to shine where they had stood.

# ELIAS

## Count Leo N. Tolstoy

ONCE upon a time there lived in a remote Russian district a man of the name of Elias. His father had left him but little wealth, but had found a wife for his son, and had died a year later. Then Elias was the owner of seven mares, two cows, and twenty sheep. But as soon as Elias had become his own master he began to get on. He and his wife worked from dawn to sunset; he was more laborious than any other man, and grew richer year by year. After thirty-five years of arduous labour he had amassed great wealth. For now he had two hundred horses, a hundred and fifty cattle, and twelve hundred sheep; and employed many herdsmen and horsemen, and many dairymaids to make koumiss and butter and cheese.

Elias was the envy of all who knew him; and people used to say " What good fortune the man has! He has abundance of everything! " Even the best people began to make his acquaintance, and visitors came to him from far away. Elias gave a welcome to everyone, and plenty to eat and drink; there was always abundance of koumiss and tea and sherbet and mutton. As soon as a guest came a ram was killed, and if there was a large company they killed a mare.

Elias had two sons and a daughter; for the former he had procured wives, and his daughter had been given in marriage. So long as the father had been poor the sons had worked for him as herdsmen, but when wealth came the lads took to dissipation, and one of them to strong liquor. The elder fell in a drunken quarrel, and the younger came under the dominion of a proud wife and no longer respected his father, so that Elias had to portion him off and send him away. He gave him a house and herds of cattle, and thereby Elias lost much of his wealth.

And now troubles began to accumulate. Many of the old man's sheep perished by a fell disease. Then followed a year of drought such that no grass would grow, and for lack of hay many of his cattle died in the winter. Not long afterward a bandit tribe came and drove away most of his horses, so that Elias was impoverished yet further. He fell from one sorrow to another, and his natural strength was abated. At last, when he was seventy years old, he had to sell his furs and carpets and waggons; and then the day came when his last cow and last sheep had been sold, so that Elias had come down to nothingness. He realised that he had now

absolutely nothing, and that he and his wife must now live among
the very poorest. He had nothing to call his own but the clothes
he wore, a fur cloak, his hat and shoes; and his aged wife was
equally destitute. The son had gone away to a far country and the
daughter was dead; and there was no one to help the poor old
couple.

But a neighbour of theirs, Muhamedshah, was sorry for the
poor old folk. He was not rich, neither was he poor, but lived
comfortably and had a good heart. He did not forget that he had
eaten bread and salt with Elias; and touched with pity, he said
to him, " Come and live with me, Elias, together with your wife.
In summer you may do what you can in the melon-fields, and in
winter you may feed the cattle, while your wife does the dairy-
work and makes koumiss. I will give you both food and clothing,
and whatever else you may desire and ask for."

The grateful old man thanked Muhamedshah, and with his wife
dwelt in his house as a servant. It was hard enough at first, but
they soon became accustomed to it. So the aged couple lived and
did what work they were fit for. They were very profitable to
their master, because they themselves had been master and mistress,
and knew the right way of doing things; moreover, they were never
idle, but did all that they could. Only, their employer was sorry
to see his old friends fallen to so humble a state of life.

One day it happened that some of his relatives came to visit
Muhamedshah, and a priest came with them, and Elias was
ordered to choose a ram and prepare it for the table. The visitors
feasted on the meat and drank tea and then koumiss. They sat
with their host on cushions on the floor and had pleasant talk,
while Elias pursued his duties, and happened once to pass by the
open door. As he did so, Muhamedshah exclaimed, " Did you see
that old man who just now passed the door? "

" Yes," said one of the guests, " what about him? "

" There is this to tell about him. There was a day when Elias
was the wealthiest of us all. You have surely heard of him? "

" Of course I have heard of him," was the reply. " His reputation was all over the countryside."

" Well, he is nothing now. He lives here as my servant, and
his wife looks after the cows."

The visitor was amazed. He sighed, and shook his head and
exclaimed: " Surely fortune goes round like a wheel, raising one
upward and throwing another down! But tell me, is the old man
unhappy about it all? "

" Who can say? He is very quiet and gentle, and seems happy
enough."

" May I have a few words with him? " continued the guest. " I
should like to ask him one or two questions."

" Of course you may," the host replied, and sent for Elias.

The aged couple came to the door. Elias saluted his master and the visitors, muttered a prayer, and knelt down at the door, while the wife went to her mistress behind the curtain. Elias was given a cup of koumiss, and after drinking the health of the company, laid down the cup.

"Would you tell me, grandfather," said the visitor who had spoken; "does it not pain you, when you come among us, to remember your former happy and fortunate life, and to think of your present lowly position?"

Elias smiled. "You would not believe me, sir, if I were to speak of what is good fortune and what is misfortune. It would be better to ask my wife about this. Being a woman, she says all that is in her heart; she can tell you all that there is to know about your question."

The visitor turned toward the curtain, and said: "Tell me, old mother; what do you think about the good fortune of the old days and the troubles of the present?"

An aged voice came from behind the curtain. "This, sir, is what I think. My old man and I have lived together for fifty years. We sought for happiness, but could not find it. And this is only the second year in which we have wanted for nothing. We live as working people, and are really happy, and have need of nothing."

Not only the guests but even their host was amazed; he rose to his feet and drew aside the curtain to see the old wife. She was standing just behind it with her arms folded; she smiled as her eyes fell on her old man, and he returned the smile. "I mean what I say," she continued. "I am not jesting. For half a hundred years we sought for joy, and so long as we were rich we never found it. But now that we have nothing of our own and live among the peasants we have found greater happiness than I can say."

"What causes this happiness of yours?"

"This is what causes it, sir. So long as we were rich my old man and I had never a quiet hour together; we had no time to talk, nor to care for our souls, nor to pray to God; for we were burdened with endless cares. Often guests came to us, and we were concerned how to provide for each of them, and what presents to give lest we should go down in their esteem. We were always worrying lest the wolves should snatch our lambs and kids, or robbers drive away our mares; and even when we went to bed we stayed awake fearing that the sheep might smother the lambs. Then we would rise and walk about in the night, but no sooner had we set our minds at ease than a fresh question would come to us, such as how to procure hay or find pasturage for winter. So it went on and on. But this was not so bad as the quarrels between my husband and myself. He would say: 'We must do this,' and I would reply: 'No, we must do that,' and then we would fall into ill words, and so into sin.  So we lived, going on from care to care, and from one sin to another, and there was no happiness for us anywhere.

" And what about your present state? "

" My husband and I rise in the morning together and agree in everything; our talk is all loving; there is nothing to trouble us nor to dispute about; our only desire is to serve our master.  We are glad to work for his prosperity.  When we come up to the house we find dinner or supper or koumiss.  In cold weather there is a good fire and plenty of furs.  And we always have time to talk with one another, to care for our souls, and to pray to God.  We sought happiness for fifty years, and have only found it now."

The visitors laughed among themselves, but Elias continued: " My brothers, do not laugh; this is not a jest, but the very truth of human life.  In the first days my wife and I were foolish enough to weep that we had lost all; but now God has shown us the very truth; and we tell it to you, not to amuse ourselves, but that it may help you."

Then said the priest: " These are wise and true sayings.  Elias has spoken the very truth.  Moreover, every word of it is set forth in Holy Scripture."

The guests laughed no more, but thought deeply in their hearts.

# THE GRAIN OF WHEAT AS LARGE AS AN EGG

### Count Leo N. Tolstoy

Some children at play happened to find in a crack in the ground a curious object very like an egg, but with a groove running down it such as is found in a grain of wheat.  A wayfarer, attracted by its curiosity, gave the children a penny for it, and having brought it up to the city sold it to the King.  He then sent for the learned men of his Court and asked them what this object could be, and whether it was a grain of wheat or a hen's egg.  The men of learning thought deeply on the matter, but were still unable to give any reply.

But the question was soon solved.  This remarkable object was lying on the window-ledge when a bird alighted beside it and eagerly pecked at it, and so dug a cavity deep into its middle.  The by-standers were astonished to see that it was indeed a grain of corn.

So the men of learning went up to the King again and reported that it was a grain of wheat. The King was amazed, and commanded these learned men to find out in what place and at what time monster grain such as this had been grown.

The men of learning thought on the matter and consulted; they searched the volumes in their libraries, and all without result. They returned to the King's presence and said: " Your Majesty, we have not been able to find out, for our books contain nothing concerning this thing. It will be well to ask the peasants whether they have heard from their forefathers anything about the growing of wheat like this. So the King commanded that one of the oldest of the peasant elders should be fetched into his presence.

This aged man tottered painfully into the presence, supported by crutches. His face was white, he was without teeth and could hardly see. The King placed the grain of wheat in his hand. The old man turned it about, peered at it, and felt it over with his fingers, and at last formed some dim idea of its nature.

" Do you know, old man," said the King, " where corn like this is to be found? Have you ever grown wheat like this, or do you remember buying it? "

For long the old man made no reply. His hearing was almost gone, and his mind moved very slowly. But at last he raised his voice, saying, " No, sire, I have never sown nor reaped grain like this, nor bought of it in the market. All the corn we have had to do with has been of the small-grained kind. But perhaps my father may have heard tell of wheat like this. Let Your Majesty ask him."

So the King commanded them to fetch the old man's father, and they found him and brought him into the presence. This venerable man used but a single crutch, and had still the use of his eyes. The King put the grain of wheat before him, and one glance was enough for him. " Do you know, my venerable man," said the King, " where grain like this has been grown? Have you ever grown any like it, or bought it in the market? "

The venerable man was indeed hard of hearing, but was not nearly so deaf as his son. " No, sir," he replied, " I have never cultivated wheat like this; nor have I ever purchased any, inasmuch as we knew nothing about money in our time. Every man lived on the corn grown on his own land, and had wherewithal to furnish his neighbour's need. I do not know where wheat like this was grown. Ours was of larger grain and the yield was greater than that in the present day; but I have never seen anything like this. But I remember my father's saying that wheat was better and the grain larger in his time than it was in my day. It would be well to send for him."

So the King sent them to fetch the father of the venerable man, and soon they brought this ancient patriarch into the presence. This ancient man came before the King without any crutch; his footstep was alert, his eyes gleamed, and his speech was distinct. The King placed the grain of wheat in his hand.

The ancient grandfather glanced at it, and rubbed it between his fingers. " Holla ! '' he exclaimed; " this is a grain of the good old kind! '' He bit the grain and tasted it. " It is the very same," he said.

Then said the King, " Can you tell me, ancient grandfather, in what place and at what time they grew wheat like this? Have you ever cultivated this great wheat or bought of it in the market? ''

" In my time, sire," the ancient man replied, " all the wheat was just such as this is. My family and I always lived on grain like this. And all my youth I sowed and reaped and threshed this wheat."

Then replied the King: " Did you buy this corn, old man, or grow it in your old fields? ''

" In those days," returned the ancient man, " no one ever thought of so great a sin as the buying or selling of grain. None of us knew anything about money. There was as much wheat for every one as he could wish."

" Tell me once more, old man, on what land did you sow corn like this? Where were your fields? ''

Then answered the ancient grandfather: " My fields were as wide as God's own world. Wherever I drove my plough there was my land. The soil was free to every man. No one ever said: ' This is *my* land.' A man called nothing his own except the work of his own hands."

The King pondered and said: " I have yet two questions to ask. In the first place: Why can we not grow wheat like this in our day, though you were able to grow it in your day? And, secondly: Why does your grandson need two crutches, and your son one crutch, while you yourself, ancient as you are, have a light and firm step, and your eyes are bright, and your teeth are strong and sound, and your speech is distinct, and your voice is pleasant to the ear. Can you tell me, old grandfather, what is the meaning of all this, and why such things as these do not come to pass in our day? ''

Then answered the ancient patriarch: " Such grain as this no longer grows, and the aged are afflicted by every ill, because men no longer live only by the work of their own hands, but covet instead the property of their neighbours. In the days of old they lived far otherwise. In the days of old they walked with God, and peacefully ruled their own households, and had no desire for the possessions of others."

# CHILDREN WISER THAN THEIR FATHERS

### Count Leo N. Tolstoy

Easter was early that year, and people were still going about in sledges. The roofs were covered with snow, and streamlets were running all about the countryside. A large pool lay across the roadway between two cottages and had attracted two little girls, one a very tiny child and the other a little older, from these cottages. The two girls had both been dressed by their mothers in new frocks; the smaller child was in blue and the elder in yellow with a pretty pattern, and each had a smart handkerchief fastened about her head. They had finished dinner, and had run out to play by the pool and to show one another their little presents.

Then, of course, they wanted to paddle in the dirty water. The baby stole down to the edge of the pool in her dainty shoes, but her companion cried, " Stop, Malashka, don't go in, mother will be angry. Take off your shoes if you like, and I will take off mine too." So they took off their shoes and tucked up their frocks, and stole into the pool.

Malashka's ankles were soon covered, and she cried, " I am afraid; it is so deep! "

" Oh, no, it's quite safe," said Akulyushka. " It is no deeper in the middle. Come right across."

They approached one another, and the elder girl said, " Take care, Malashka, you are splashing too much. Do walk more gently."

But she had hardly spoken when Malashka's little foot made a great splash and wetted Akulyushka's pretty frock all over, and the water even wetted her face and got into her eyes. When Akulyushka saw that her frock was spoiled, she lost her temper and raged at Malashka, and flew at her with her little fists clenched. Thoroughly frightened, Malashka fled from the pool for the shelter of home.

At this moment, the mother of Akulyushka came past and saw her child's frock splashed from neck to knee. " What have you been doing, you dirty child? " she cried.

" It was Malashka," was the reply. " She did it on purpose."

The infuriated mother pursued Malashka and hit her on the head.

The child's cries rang down the street, and her own mother, running out from her cottage, fell to scolding the other woman, saying, " What right have you to hit my child? "

Soon the two were engaged in a hearty duet of abuse, and the cottagers all down the street came out and gathered in a crowd around them; the men all growling and the women all shrilling, and no one giving heed to any word of his neighbour. Curses and oaths were followed by blows, and there was a mob fight until the arrival of an aged woman, the grandmother of Akulyushka.

" Come, come, my children, this is too bad. This is no way to spend Easter. We ought all to be giving thanks, and not to be sinning with our words." Her appeal was in vain, and they even hustled the poor old woman. She would never have succeeded in calming them if it had not been for the two little girls. While the acrimonious conflict was still going on, the elder child had dried her frock and returned to the pool. Using a stone to excavate the earth, she began to throw it into the pool so as to send the water into the main street; and Malashka came out to help her dig a channel to direct its flow. Still the peasants argued and disputed, while the water ran down through the tiny ditch the girls had made and came at last to the feet of the angry peasants and the old woman who was trying to pacify them. The happy children were running one on each side of the little water-course which they had made.

" Stop it, Malashka, do stop it," Akulyushka cried, as well as she could for laughing. But the little one was unable to do anything or even to speak through happy laughter.

So they danced down beside their rivulet, delighted with a little bit of wood which was tumbling down its rapids; and so they danced right into the middle of the crowd.

Seeing this, the old woman raised her voice once more. " Have you no fear of God, that you quarrel so miserably? Here you are all angry and disputing about these two little girls, although they have forgotten all about it long ago, and—dear little hearts— are happily playing together again. Are they not wiser than you? "

The peasants, now silent, looked at the two children and were ashamed of their contentions. Then, laughing at their own folly, they separated and went home to their several cottages.

" Unless you become as little children, you cannot enter the Kingdom of Heaven."

# NICOLAI S. LESKOV

1831–1895

# THE GHOST OF THE ENGINEERS' CASTLE

I

HOUSES, like people, have their own reputations. There are houses that by general opinion are considered impure, that is, where there have been indications of some impure or, at any rate, incomprehensible power. Spiritualists have done much to explain such phenomena, but as their theories are not generally accepted the matter of haunted houses is still as obscure as ever.

In St. Petersburg, one of the many houses that possessed such an undesirable reputation was the characteristic castle of Paul, known at the present day as the Engineers' Castle. The mysterious manifestations, put down to ghosts and spirits, were observed almost from the very foundation of the castle. Even during the lifetime of the Emperor Paul, they say that the voice of Peter the Great would be heard there and that the Emperor Paul himself saw the ghost of his great-grandfather. The latter event was recorded in the foreign reviews that found space to write about the death of Paul, and in the latest Russian book by Mr. Kobeko, and no refutation appeared. It seems that Peter rose from his grave to warn his great-grandson that his end was near, and the prophecy was fulfilled.

However, Peter's ghost was seen on the walls of the castle, not only by the Emperor Paul but also by some of his suite: in a word, the house was sinister because it was haunted by ghosts and apparitions who spoke of terrible things that came true into the bargain. The sudden and unexpected end of the Emperor Paul—on which occasion people instantly recalled the ghosts met by the late Emperor in the castle—exaggerated still more the mysterious and forbidding reputation of the gloomy house. From that time the castle lost its former importance as a royal residence and, as they say, " went to the cadets."

At the present time this former palace is used by the cadets of the engineering department, but before that it was lived in by the former engineer cadets. This was a still younger crowd of boys not yet free from childish superstitions, who were, besides, sportive, mischievous, daring, and curious. Of course they all knew something of the terrible tales told of their gloomy castle. The children were very much interested in the details of these harrowing stories and fed on their terrors, while those who were sufficiently acclimatised loved to frighten the others. This was in great fashion among the engineer cadets, and the principals could in no way break them of this bad habit until an event occurred which cured them of it once and for all.

It is with this event that our story deals.

## II

It was especially the fashion to frighten the new boys, the " little ones " as they were called, who on their arrival would hear so many weird stories about the castle as to make them superstitious and timid to the extreme. They were most afraid of a certain room at the end of a corridor that had served as bedroom to the Emperor Paul, where he had gone to bed one night quite well, and had been carried out dead next morning. The " old boys " maintained that the spirit of the Emperor haunted that room and came out of it every night to inspect his beloved castle, and the " little ones " believed it. The room was always securely fastened with several locks, but to a spirit no lock or bar is of significance. Besides, it was said that it was possible to get into the room, and this turned out to be true. At any rate, a few of the older cadets managed to get in, and continued to do so until one of them committed an outrageous piece of mischief for which he had to pay cruelly. He opened some sort of secret aperture into the terrible bedroom and managed to hide a sheet there. At night he went there, covered himself from head to foot in the sheet, and stood by the dark window that looked out into Sadov Street, where he could be seen by any one who happened to be walking or driving past.

In playing the part of a ghost, the cadet certainly managed to bring terror upon many superstitious people who lived in the castle or who happened to pass by it and see the white figure, all taking it for the shade of the late Emperor.

This piece of mischief continued for several months, and caused a persistent rumour that the Emperor Paul walked about his bedroom at night and looked out on St. Petersburg from this window. Many were certain that the white ghost at the window shook his head and bowed to them more than once; the cadet, of course, was capable of doing these things. All this caused general discussion and prophetic explanations, and ended with the culprit who had caused this anxiety being caught red-handed. He received " exemplary corporal punishment " and disappeared for ever from the institution. There was a rumour that, at one of his appearances at the window, the hapless cadet had the misfortune to frighten some important person who happened to be passing by, and that was why he was so severely punished. To put it more bluntly, the cadets said that the unfortunate boy had " died under the rod," and as at that time such a thing was not looked on as impossible, this, too, was believed and the cadet himself became a new apparition. His comrades began to see him " slashed all over," with a wreath on his forehead, and on the wreath was written the inscription :

> I did but taste a little honey, and lo, I must die!

The allusion is very touching if one recalls the Biblical story from which it is taken.

After this cadet's downfall, the bedroom that was the cause of all the terror in the Engineers' Castle was thrown open and put to such a use as to destroy its uncanny reputation, but nevertheless the tradition of the ghost lived on for a long time. The cadets continued to believe that their castle was haunted by a ghost that appeared at night. This was the general conviction held equally by young and old cadets, with the difference, however, that the younger ones believed blindly in the apparition while the elder ones sometimes personally arranged its appearance. This did not prevent those responsible for the apparition from being afraid of it. In the same way " false makers of miracles," who produce the miracles themselves, bow down before them and believe in their reality.

The young cadets did not know " the whole story," about which it was strongly forbidden to speak after the event of the cruel corporal punishment, but among the older cadets there were some who had been either whipped or flogged and knew the whole secret of the apparition. This gave the elders great prestige, which they enjoyed until the years 1859 or 1860, when four of them went through a very trying ordeal which I shall relate from the story of one of the participants in the misplaced joke at the coffin.

III

In 1859 or 1860, General Lamnovsky, the head of the Engineers' Castle, died. He can hardly be said to have been beloved by the cadets, and it was said that he did not enjoy a good reputation with the governors. They had many reasons for this; they found that he treated the boys in a severe, unsympathetic manner, did not investigate their needs, did not trouble himself about their food, and, above all, was troublesome, quarrelsome, and severe in petty things. In the corps it was said that, left to himself, the general would have been still harsher had not his unreasonable severity been mitigated by his angelic wife, whom no one had ever seen because she was always ill, but who was considered the good genius, protecting every one from the general's extreme ferocity.

Together with his severe disposition, General Lamnovsky had exceedingly unpleasant manners. Some of them were comic, and these the children seized on, and when they wanted to imitate the unpopular head they would take off one of his absurd habits, exaggerated to caricature.

One of the general's most comic habits was that, when making a speech or doing something imposing, he always stroked his nose with all the fingers of his right hand. This, according to the cadets, made it appear as though he were " milking the words out of his nose." The deceased was not distinguished by his eloquence, and it would sometimes happen that he would be at a loss for a word to point a homily, and at every such pause the " milking " would increase, at which the cadets would be unable to maintain their seriousness, and would begin to exchange smiles. Noticing this insubordination, the general would grow still angrier and punish them. Thus the relations between the general and the cadets grew worse and worse, and through it all, according to the cadets, " the nose was most to blame."

Having no love for Lamnovsky, the cadets lost no opportunity of annoying him or of revenging themselves on him and of impairing his reputation with his new colleagues. For this purpose they spread a rumour in the corps that the general had dealings with the black art, and made demons carry the marble for a memorial he had erected in some building, the Isaac Cathedral, I believe. But as the demons were tired of the work, the story goes on, they were anxiously waiting for the general's death, which would bring them their freedom. And to make this more credible, on the evening of the general's nameday the cadets caused him a great deal of unpleasantness by arranging a mock funeral. It was arranged so that when the guests began to arrive in Lamnovsky's private quarters a mournful procession marched down the corridor of the cadets' quarters. The cadets, covered in sheets, with candles in their hands, singing dirges, were carrying a bier on which lay the dummy of a man with a long-nosed mask. The ringleaders who had arranged this ceremony were discovered and punished, but on Lamnovsky's next nameday the unpardonable jest of the mock funeral was repeated. Thus things went on until the year 1859 or 1860, when General Lamnovsky really died and it was necessary to arrange a real funeral. According to the custom of the time, the cadets had, in turn, to be on guard at the coffin, and it was then that there happened the terrible event that frightened the very heroes who, for so long, had been frightening others.

## IV

General Lamnovsky died late in autumn—in November—when St. Petersburg has a most man-hating appearance; cold, penetrating damp, and mud; the peculiar misty, foggy light has a depressing effect on the nerves and through them on the brain and imagination. All this produces an abnormal inner disturbance and excitement. Molechott, in his learned deductions on the influence of light on life, could have got some very curious data from us at this time.

About the time that Lamnovsky died the days were particularly depressing. The deceased was not carried into the castle church, as he was a Lutheran; the body was placed in the large, mournful drawing-room in the general's quarters, and it was here that the cadets had, in turn, to be on guard. In the church, according to the Orthodox custom, there was one mass for the dead during the day and another in the evening. All the inmates of the castle, cadets and servants alike, had to appear at both services, and this rule was observed strictly. In consequence, when a service was going on in the church, all the inmates of the castle were gathered there, and the rest of the enormous house, with its long corridors, was quite deserted. In the drawing-room there was no one except the relief guard, who, in parade dress and with rifles, were watching the coffin.

An uncanny weirdness was over the place; all felt uncomfortable and began to be afraid of something; and then they began talking of people " rising " and " walking " again. It became so unpleasant that they began to stop each other, saying: " Shut up, do! Damn your stories! You only ruin your own and other people's nerves." Then they would start again in the same strain, and be again repressed. Towards evening they were all afraid. Their fear became particularly acute when one of them called out plaintively for " Batya," one of the priests.

The priest made them feel ashamed of their joy in the general's death. He had a gentle way, but he understood how to touch their feelings.

" He walks," he said, repeating their words. " You do not and cannot see him, but he has a power which you cannot escape. He is the grey man. He does not arise at midnight, but in the twilight when everything turns grey and every one wants to express the evil in their thoughts. This grey man is conscience. I advise you not to disturb him with your petty joy over another's death. Every man loves some one, pities some one,—take care that the grey man does not take some of those you love and give you a severe lesson."

The cadets took this to heart, and as it began to get dark that day they began peering round for the grey man. We know that in the twilight all sorts of sensitive feelings arise in the heart—a new world arises to take the place of the one we knew by day; well-known objects of familiar form become fanciful, incomprehensible, and even terrible. At such a time every sensation seems somehow to try to find for itself a vague enhanced expression; the moods of thought and feeling are constantly wavering, and in this strange, crowded discord, all the inner world of man begins its work of fantasy; the world turns into dreams, and dreams into the world. This is alluring and terrifying; the more terrifying it is, the more alluring and enticing it becomes.

The majority of the cadets were in such a condition, particularly when on night duty at the coffin. On the last evening before the funeral, many high personages were expected to mass in the church, so that besides the ordinary inmates of the castle there was a large number of people from the town. Even every one from Lamnovsky's household went to the Russian church to see the gathering of the famous people. The dead man remained alone with four young guards. The guard consisted of the cadets G——, B——, Z——, and K——, all still living happily and now occupying important military as well as social positions.

## V

Of the four youngsters composing the guard, one particularly, K——, was a most mischievous scamp who had annoyed the late Lamnovsky more than all the rest, and the general, in his turn, had punished K—— more than any one else. The deceased particularly disliked K—— because he could mimic him beautifully about the " milking of the nose," and because he had taken an active part in the arrangement of the funeral processions that took place on the general's namedays.

On the occasion of the last of these processions K—— had himself played the part of the general, and had even made a speech from the coffin with so many grimaces and in such tones as to amuse every one, even the officers sent to scatter the mock procession.

It was known that this event had brought the late Lamnovsky into an extreme fit of wrath, and among the cadets there was a rumour that the enraged general had sworn " to punish K—— so that he would remember it for the rest of his life." The cadets believed this, and taking into consideration the well-known character of their head, did not in the least doubt that he would carry out his oath. For a whole year K—— had been looked upon as " hanging by a hair," and as by the liveliness of his nature it was difficult for this cadet to keep away from dangerous and risky escapades, his position was considered very precarious, and it was expected by everybody that some day K—— would be found out in something, and then Lamnovsky would make short work of him and bring all his might to bear on the famous " I will make him remember for the rest of his life."

K—— was so greatly afraid of the head's threats that he made desperate efforts over himself, like a drunkard does over wine; he avoided all pranks, a thing that made the others quote the old proverb to him, " A peasant may not drink for a year, but when the devil seizes him he drinks without stopping."

The devil seized K—— at the general's very coffin. The latter was reposing without having fulfilled a single one of his threats. The general was no longer terrifying to the cadet, and the boy's long pent-up playfulness at last came out, breaking out like an overstrained spring. He simply went mad.

### VI

The last mass for the dead man, at which all the inmates of the castle were to be present, was fixed for seven o'clock in the evening, but as certain famous people were expected, after whom it would not have been decorous to enter the church, they all went much earlier. In the dead man's drawing-room there only remained the youthful guard, G——, B——, Z——, and K——. There was not a soul in any of the large neighbouring rooms.

At half-past seven the door opened, and the adjutant appeared for a moment, to whom there happened an absurd incident that increased the general weirdness. The officer, going up to the door, was either alarmed at his own footsteps, or imagined that some one was running after him; at first he stopped to let the person pass, and then cried out suddenly:

" Who is that? Who is that? " and quickly thrust his head through the door.

The second half of the door shut of itself and made him cry out again as though some one had seized him from behind. Needless to say that he went away after that, casting a quick anxious glance over the mournful room, and guessing by its deserted state that every one was in church, he again shut the door, and loudly clanking his sword, he ran down the corridor to the church as fast as he could.

The cadets standing by the coffin noticed that even the grown-ups felt there was something to be afraid of, and fear is infectious to all.

### VII

The cadet guard listened to the sound of the retreating footsteps and with every step they felt themselves more deserted—as though they had been immuned with the dead man for some unforgotten, unforgiven insult, and for which he would arise and revenge himself. And this indeed he did, in the manner of the dead. . . . It was only necessary to have the proper hour—the mystic hour of midnight,

> When the cocks crow
> And the dead roam about in the darkness. 

But they were not going to remain there until midnight, they would be relieved, and besides, they were not only afraid of the dead but also of the grey man who walks in the twilight.

Now it was dense twilight; the dead man was in his coffin and all around was the weirdest stillness. Outside the wind blew with a raging fury, beating the heavy autumn rain against the huge windows, in terrific gusts, smiting the leaves against the tiles in the angles of the roof; the chimneys moaned and howled. All this did not conduce to sobriety of feelings or calmness of reason. The oppression of these sensations was made still worse for the youngsters by the fact that they had to stand and maintain a strict silence: everything was in a state of alarm; the blood rushing to the head beat against the temples so that the sound it produced was like the monotonous grinding of a mill. Those who have experienced this sensation will know it well; it is as though a mill were grinding, not grain, but its very self. This soon brings a man into an oppressive nervous state, and it is rather like the feeling inexperienced people have when going down the shaft of a mine as the customary daylight suddenly changes to the murky light of lamps. . . . To maintain silence becomes impossible—you are seized with a desire to hear your own voice, or to crawl under something and hide, or do most unreasonable things.

## VIII

One of the four standing at the general's coffin, K—— himself, feeling this sensation, forgot discipline, and whispered as he stood with his rifle:

" Ghosts are coming to us for Papka's nose."

Lamnovsky was sometimes called " Papka " in fun, but the joke failed to amuse the others, in fact it increased the general weirdness. Noticing this, one of them said to K——:

" Shut up! We are frightened enough as it is," and all looked anxiously towards the shroud that covered the dead man's face.

" That was why I said it," K—— replied. " As for me, I am not a bit afraid; he can't do anything to me now. You must be above such prejudices and not be afraid of such nonsense—a corpse cannot harm you; I'll show you."

" Don't, please! "

" Yes, I will!  I'll show you that Papka can't do anything to me now not even if I take hold of him this minute by the nose."

And with this unexpected remark, K—— put his rifle under his arm, walked quickly up the steps of the catafalque, and taking the dead man by the nose, called out loudly and merrily:

" Oh, Papka, you are dead and I am alive!  I am pulling your nose and you can't do anything to me! "

His comrades were stunned by this prank; they had scarcely time to utter a word when suddenly they all heard, plainly and distinctly, a deep, painful sigh.  It was like the sound of air escaping from an inflated rubber air-cushion when the valve is loose, and this sigh, it seemed to all, came from the very coffin.

K—— seized his gun quickly and flew down the steps of the catafalque with a loud clatter; the other three, scarcely knowing what they were doing, put down their guns to defend themselves against the rising dead.

But this was not all; the dead man not only sighed, but actually either ran after the mischievous boy who had insulted him or caught him by the hand, for a whole wave of the muslin on the coffin came down after K—— and he could not extricate himself from it. With a loud cry he fell to the ground. . . . The wave of muslin was really an inexplicable and terrifying phenomenon, the more so as now the dead man lay completely uncovered, his hands folded over his breast.

The boy lay on the floor; he dropped his gun and, covering his face with his hands, made the most awful groans.  He was evidently in full possession of his senses and just waiting for the dead man to dispose of him in his own fashion.

Meanwhile the sigh was repeated, and a faint rustling was heard. It was a sound that might have been produced by the rubbing of one linen sleeve on another.  Evidently the dead man was moving his hands—and suddenly there was a gentle noise followed by a draught of air that blew over the candles, and at the same moment, in the moving curtains that covered the door, an apparition appeared.  It was the grey man!  Yes, to the eyes of the terrified boys there was presented an apparition in the form of a man.  Was it the soul of the dead man in a new shape that he had acquired in the other world—from which he had returned for a moment to avenge the insult? or was it the still more terrible guest, the spirit of the castle, who had come out of the floor of the next room from out the earth?

IX

The apparition was no trick of the imagination; it did not disappear nor remind one by its form of Heine's description of the " Mysterious Woman " he had seen.  At the same time, this apparition, like Heine's woman, seemed like a corpse with a human soul imprisoned in it. Before the frightened boys there was an extraordinary emaciated figure, all in white, but in the shadow it appeared grey. It had a terribly thin pale face, and a long, thick, tangled mass of hair which also was grey and which, flowing down in disorder, covered the bosom and shoulders of the apparition. . . . The swollen eyes were bright and sparkled with a feverish fire. They looked out from deep hollows like two living coals of fire. The apparition had thin emaciated hands, like those of a skeleton, and with these hands it was holding on to the heavy drapery over the door. Convulsively clutching the material in feeble fingers, these hands produced the dry rustling heard by the cadets.

The apparition's lips were black and parted, and through them at intervals there issued with a whistling and wheezing that half groan, half sigh that the cadets had first heard when K—— had held the dead man's nose.

## X

Seeing this terrible apparition, the three guards who remained standing were petrified in their defensive attitudes. They were more afraid than K——, who lay on the floor entangled in the shroud.

The apparition paid no heed to this group. Its eyes were fixed on the coffin where the dead man lay completely uncovered. It swayed gently from side to side, evidently trying to move. At last it succeeded. Supporting itself against the wall, the apparition moved slowly, with halting steps, towards the coffin. Its movements were terrible. Shuddering convulsively at each step, and trying, with pain, to draw air through those parted lips, it emitted from its chest those awful sighs that the cadets had thought issued from the coffin. Another step, and another; it was nearer; at last it had approached the coffin, but before walking up the steps of the catafalque, it stopped, and taking the trembling K—— by the hand with its gentle dry fingers it disentangled the shroud that had got caught in one of the unfortunate boy's buttons, then, looking at him with an expression of unutterable sadness, waved an admonishing finger and made the sign of the cross over him. . . . Then, scarcely able to stand on its trembling legs, it walked up the steps of the catafalque, and catching hold of the edge of the coffin it put its skeleton arms around the dead man and burst into sobs. . . . It seemed as though the two dead were embracing in the coffin, but soon this ceased. Sounds of life were borne from the other end of the castle; the mass was over and the vanguard was hurrying from the church to the general's quarters, to be there before the arrival of the dignitaries.

## XI

The cadets heard firm footsteps approaching down the corridor, and from the open door of the church sounded the last notes of the funeral hymn. The sudden change of impressions caused the cadets to gain courage, and the force of habitual discipline put them in their proper places and positions.

The adjutant, the last person who had looked in before mass, was the first to run in hastily.

" My God! How did she get there? " he cried.

The inert body in white, with the tangled grey hair, was lying with its arms round the dead man and seemed herself to be no longer breathing. The matter was explained. The apparition that had frightened the cadets was the late general's widow, herself at death's door. From extreme weakness, she had for long not been able to rise from her bed, but when all had gone to the State mass, she crawled from her own death-bed and, supporting herself with both hands against the wall, had appeared at the dead man's coffin. The dry rustling that the cadets had taken for the movement of the dead man's sleeves was her touch against the wall. Now she was in a deep faint, in which condition the cadets, by the order of the adjutant, carried her out in an armchair into the next room.

This was the last night in the castle, and according to the man who told the story it left a lasting impression. " Since that event," he said, " we could never bear to see any one pleased at another's death. We always remembered our unpardonable prank and the blessing hand of the last ghost of the Engineers' Castle, that alone had the power to forgive by the holy right of love. From that time fear of apparitions disappeared from the corps. The one we had seen was the last."

# NICOLAI V. USPENSKY
### 1837–1889

# THE VILLAGE SCHOOL- MASTER

'AN elderly gentleman, sitting on the verandah of his house, called to a workman who was passing with a water-cart:

" Hi! Prokòfyi! Prokòfyi! "

The cart stopped.

" Are you deaf? "

" The wheels makes such a noise, Grigòryi Naòmich; one can't hear anything. They wants greasing."

" Oh, they're all right. What have you got there? water? "

" Yes, sir."

" From the pond? "

" Yes, sir."

" All right," said the master after a moment's pause, " you can go."

A soldier came up to the verandah.

" Wish your honour good-day! "

" Who are you? "

" From Verkhogliàdov in the Merkoùlovsky district; perhaps you know it?—by the river Kostra . . ."

" What d'you want? "

" I'm looking for a place, sir, as doorkeeper, or bailiff."

" What have you been up till now? "

" Well, when I served in the army I used to be postillion for the commander; then, in Mouràvki, I was cook for the examining magistrate. I'm a Jack-of-all-trades, your honour—gardener, whipper-in, cook—anything you like! "

" Can you break stones? "

" Why, no, your honour, I can't do that kind of work! "

" Why? "

" Well, you see, the army life breaks a chap down so; I was in a line regiment, not in the guards, and a man never gets over that."

" Oh, you're healthy enough, I can see that, and yet you want

597

to do such little fiddling work! What sort of career is it to be a bailiff or a whipper-in? " . . .

" Surely, your honour, it's better than stone-breaking! "

" I think stone-breaking a very fine occupation. . . . H'm. . . . Have you recommendations from your former employers? "

" No, your honour."

" I can't take you without a character, my good man."

" Yes, sir, you're quite right, sir."

" Perhaps you're some good-for-nothing fellow—a thief or drunkard for all I know. . . ."

" Just so, your honour."

" You must bring me a character."

" Yes, sir; good-morning, sir."

The soldier went away. Presently the steward came up to his master and announced—

" If you please, sir, a strange gentleman came while your honour was asleep; he calls himself a village schoolmaster."

" Where is he now? "

" Sitting in the office."

" Let him in."

There came on to the verandah a sunburnt man of about forty, in a nankeen coat and high boots. The master of the house offered him a chair.

" Who are you? "

" Schoolmaster from the Pobiràkhinsky district, from the village of Bezzùbov. I humbly venture to trouble you with a request; can I not obtain some kind of situation? "

" I don't want a schoolmaster," said the owner of the house.

" I can take other situations. I have heard that you are looking for a clerk? "

" Why did you leave your situation in Bezzùbov? "

" The school was destroyed by fire."

" Long ago? "

" On All Souls' Day. The cause is not known—the whole village was burnt down."

" Yes, one is constantly hearing of fires nowadays. A village close to us has been burnt down too. . . . Allow me to ask, though, how did you become a teacher? "

" After completing my education I lived in my brother's house in the village of Khmyèlnoye. I diα not work, but he supported me. Then I took a situation as tutor in a country gentleman's house at Ogoùrtzov, at a salary of two roubles a month. But I did not stop with him long, and while there I served chiefly as coachman. . . ."

" But why? "

" Because my pupil did not like studying, and his parents let him have his own way, and employed me temporarily as coach-man. . . ."

" That's strange! "

" I did the work properly! I had no choice. . . ."

" How much did you get for it? "

" Nothing! only board and lodging, and a cast-off dressing-gown that the gentleman gave me. In that dressing-gown I went back to my brother, and he said: ' What are you hanging about here for, doing nothing? Can't you set to and learn something, if it's only singing?—you might get to be choir-master in time.' So I began to study singing, and then my brother got tired of hearing me. ' Confound it all! ' he said, ' I'm sick of this; go home to father.' Well, then, I went home. Of course my people abused me:—' Always hanging about in the way! We've had enough of this! ' What would you have me do, sir, when I couldn't get a situation anywhere? I thought one time of going into a monastery; but just then I got a letter from my brother telling me to come to him. I went, and he said, ' The prince's steward wants to start a choir. You must engage yourself as choir-master.' I asked him how did he suppose I was to do that when I didn't know how to sing myself? But all he would say was: ' Don't be afraid! you'll learn in teaching your class.' So I took the post. They gave me a tuning-fork——"

" May I ask," interrupted the gentleman, " whether you were attired in the dressing-gown? " . . .

" No, in my mother's cloak; the dressing-gown was worn out. . . . It was a short cloak, . . . home-made. . . ."

" Well, and how did you get on? "

" Very well. There was quite a fair choir. My brother sang tenor; Iván Alexèyich (at the present moment a teacher of patrology and hermeneutics) bass; then there were a few more volunteers. We got perfect in ' Kol Slàven,' [1] and two sort of . . . a . . . choral part-songs, ' Vzyde ' and ' Polozhil yesi.' The steward was quite surprised at us; he was a critic in musical matters; and he wrote a letter to Moscow, to the prince, about a salary for the choir-master. Meanwhile we began to practise ' Kto Bog? ' and ' Kheruvìmskaya Razòrennaya ' [2] . . . All of a sudden the prince wrote back, ' I don't want a choir; I am going away for my health.' . . .

" So after that I got appointed at the village school at Bezzùbov. The people there are very poor; many of the peasants used to sleep in their ovens in winter-time. One day the priest came into a cottage to bless the household; he looked round, and there was no one there, so he began to sing the *tropar*.[3] Suddenly the people crawled out from the oven and came up to kiss the crucifix.

---

[1] Russian hymn.    [2] Russian sacred songs.
[3] Special canticle on a Saint's day.

. . . A good many of my pupils went about begging. For all that, though, a great gentleman from St. Petersburg passed through our village, and he said the people were not averse to education —really."

" Do you mean that ironically? " asked the master of the house.

" Oh dear no! "

" Of course, even a poor man may desire education; just take the case of Lomonòsov: he was a peasant and became an academician."

" Exactly so."

" Well, what else did the great gentleman from St. Petersburg remark? "

" He said that it would be a good thing for our administration to introduce a uniform for the scholars."

" A capital idea! " exclaimed the master of the house; " there ought to be discipline in a school. Without discipline no institution can exist. H'm. . . . What subjects were taught in your school? "

" We used the New Testament in the Russian and Slavonic tongues, a hundred and four selections from the Old and New Testaments, the ' Elements of Christian Doctrine,' ' Examples of Piety,' and the Breviary for the children to learn by heart; the first hour's division [1] of the Thirty-third Psalm, and the Book of Six Psalms, with ' All that has breath.' "

" Is that all? "

" No, we had a library, containing the following books:

" ' Selected Passages from Schreck's " Universal History." '

" ' The Programme for Acceptance into the Military Service.'

" ' Food for the Mind and Heart.'

" The Psalter, without red lettering.

" The Breviary, with red lettering.

" A work of Glinka, entitled, ' Hurrah.'

" ' The Life of St. Prokopius the Natural.'

" ' Reader for the People.'

" ' Domestic Conversations.'

" ' The Clever Reader.'

" And a few others."

" The books are good," remarked the gentleman; " I'll order ' Domestic Conversation ' and the ' Clever Reader ' myself. How long did you retain your post? "

" Eight years. I received no rise in my salary for the whole time. One day the inspector came, and he asked, ' How long have you been teaching here? ' ' Eight years,' said I. ' Has your salary been raised? ' ' No,' said I; ' I receive the minimum salary.' ' Why is that? ' ' I don't know.' Then he turned to the chief of the district and said, ' The teacher is to receive a rise

[1] In the Greek Church the psalms are divided up into a kind of rosary.

in his salary.' The inspector observed, too, that the schoolhouse garden was neglected, and ordered it be put to right, saying ' that it would then have a favourable moral influence on the minds of the scholars, who would, in time, become agriculturists.' "

" I agree with him. The bad tendencies must be restrained in these people from the very tenderest years."

" The inspector ordered flowers to be planted in the garden——"

" H'm, in my opinion that is superfluous. He should have had birch trees planted; that would have influenced the pupils more favourably."

" There were birch trees already——"

" Ah! Birch trees are as valuable as the ' Clever Reader ' and ' Domestic Conversations.' Are you married? "

" I should have liked to marry, but I was afraid to. The parish clerk of Ogoùrtzov offered me his sister-in-law in marriage. I knew her—she was a first-rate girl. I went to see her."

" Was she clever? "

" A-a! Really, sir, I don't know whether she was clever or not."

" But you talked with her? "

" Oh, yes, of course! I said, ' We are acquaintances, Olga Mitrevna.'

" ' Oh, yes,' she said, ' I am quite aware of that.'

" ' I have been brought here,' said I, ' to ask you in marriage.'

" ' Indeed! ' said she.

" ' Do you know where I have seen you? At a christening at Ogoùrtzov,' said I, and she answered:

" ' Yes, I remember. And you are from Khmièlnoye? '

" ' Yes,' said I.

" ' Ah! the scenery is pretty round there.'

" And that was about all her cleverness! . . . Her father kept on begging me to marry quickly, because a man can't live properly without some one to keep his house. ' We shall get on much better together,' she used to say. . . . So we stayed up till dawn, singing and dancing."

" Sacred songs? "

" No, sir, various—sacred and secular."

" ' Well, and did your betrothed sing? "

" No; afterwards, when I left her—she sang that romance—you know—

> 'Twas my fault for thus betraying
> All too soon my love to thee;
> Now thou hast beheld my weakness,
> Ah! thou hast forsaken me."

" That's to say you jilted her? "

" I don't know—anyway, I hadn't anything to keep her on."

" H'm—so you say the school was burnt down? "

" To the ground."

" And are all the books and things burnt too? "

" No; they were saved. The fire was in the day-time, and our people had time to get the books out."

" That's good. So I suppose it will soon be built again, and you can go on being teacher? "

" I don't wish to take that work."

" Why not? "

" I'm sick of it! You wouldn't believe me, I've often thought of putting an end to myself."

" So you prefer to be a clerk? "

" Yes, sir."

" H'm'm—I am sorry that I can't help you; it's true that I've just dismissed my clerk, but I don't want another. You see, in these times one must look after everything oneself. I do all my accounts myself. Now, I have a vacancy for a bailiff, but you wouldn't care for that . . . the salary is so small . . . three roubles a month."

" That is very little," said the teacher.

" There you see! and I don't want a clerk. Besides, I can't understand why you don't wish to be a teacher."

" I can't stand it, indeed I can't! "

" It's true that the root of learning is bitter, but, you see, the fruits are sweet. . . . No, I would advise you to disseminate instruction among the people. . . . At the present time, when education has become a positive necessity, we ought all of us to assist in the work, to the limit of our powers. For my part, I am quite willing to do what I can. I will make a donation of books to your school. Here! Aliòshka! Fetch the hamper that stands under the ante-room sofa."

The footman brought in a hamper of books, gnawed all over by rats.

" Now," said the gentleman, "here's a book for you, ' Nature's Vengeance,' a capital book; I've forgotten what it's about. Ah! and here . . . ' The Oath, taken at the Holy Sepulchre.' . . . In fact, you can have the whole lot. When your new school is built, kindly range all these works in your library with an inscription: ' Presented by Mr. Yàkov Antònovich Svinooùkhou,[1] the squire of Prokhòrovka.' Posterity will remember me. . . . I am very glad that fortune brought you here, otherwise my books would have lain by uselessly, but now they will do good; and not to one generation only, but to future ages. . . . Hi! Aliòshka. Tell the man to harness a horse and conduct these books and the schoolmaster with them to the village of Bezzùbov."

.        .        .        .        .        .

Two months later the new school was built. The educational library had been enriched by the following works, the gift of Mr. Svinooùkhov:—

[1] Literally "Pig's ear."

" The Correspondence of the Nobility of Hell."
" Hunting with the Hounds."
" The Russian Theatre."
" Nature's Vengeance."
" The Works of Bulgarin."
" Political and Moral Fables."
" *The Moscow Gazette.*"
" A New Latin Alphabet."
" Words to Scholars, Concerning the Attributes of True Wisdom."
" A Guide to Didactics."
" A Short Dissertation upon the Rules of True Wisdom."
Etc., etc.

Nothing was wanting, except a teacher.  The former teacher, it is said, had hanged himself.

# DMITRI MAMIN-SIBIRIAK
b. 1852

# IN THE HEART OF THE URALS

## I

THE village of Shalaika was situated in the very heart of the forest on the high bank of the river Chusovoi. The road for vehicles ended at Shalaika, and beyond it there was no road. No one ever came to Shalaika except the priest who lived on the Borovsky Works some twenty miles away, and whenever he came he invariably expressed his surprise that all the inhabitants of the village were surnamed Shalaev. Rightly speaking, there were no surnames, merely a nickname after the village.

" How shall I enter you in the book? " the priest would ask. " For instance, in the present year, three Ivan Shalaevs have died and three Ivan Shalaevs were born, and last year we had the same thing happen with Matrenas—two Matrenas died and two were born! You seem to mix them all up."

" It has been so from time immemorial," the elder explained, " all are Shalaevs and there is an end to the matter. Our great grandfather was called Shalaev and we are all called Shalaev after him. The authorities also are vexed about it. Some five years back, I took our young fellows who were called up for soldiers, and, as though on purpose, they turned out to be three Sidors, and all were Ivanitch. The military commander got quite angry."

" We must invent some surname though," the priest said. " It will be more convenient for you."

" What do we want surnames for, father? We have lived in the forest from time immemorial and know each other well. . . . And as for the dead, the Lord our Father will be able to distinguish them for what they are worth without our help."

From the distance, Shalaika was very beautiful, especially when seen from the river—the huts shone in the sun like firm white teeth, each more beautiful than the other, thanks to the forest that was near at hand and surrounded the village like a massive green wall. There was little ploughing, for the Shalaevs mostly worked in the forest, and in the mountains the summers are cold and the soil not very fertile. If hay were needed, it could be cut in the glades of the forest or on the banks of the river Chusovoi. There were twenty-seven dwellings in Shalaika, and the Shalaevs were like a huge family, all related to one another.

Pimka's hut stood right by the river-bank, that is to say, almost on a cliff. In the summer the river could be seen from the little window for about five miles, for there was a reach here. By the river stretched the limitless forest, and no one in Shalaika knew where it ended, as though the village were at the very end of the earth. Pimka was in his tenth year and he had not been anywhere or seen anything except his own village. It must be said that the Shalaevs were very fond of their village and even proud of it too. When the young fellows were called up as soldiers they took leave of their native village with such tears as were not shed by St. Petersburg or Moscow recruits. One would have thought that the only possible place to live in was Shalaika. Pimka remembered how his elder brother Yefim had gone off as a soldier with the other young fellows and had also cried like the others.

" Leave off, you fools! " Uncle Akintich said to them, " why are you crying? You are not going to live with wolves, but with kind people; you will, at any rate, see how other people live and learn from them. Passing the whole of your lives in the forest at Shalaika is not such a great joy! " No one believed the soldier Akintich. It was all very well to talk after you had finished your service. If it was so very pleasant in those strange lands, then why did he come back again to Shalaika? Akintich lived with Pimka's father, because his own family had somehow got separated; the old people had died, his sisters had got married, and he could not get on with his married brothers. Pimka was passionately fond of the soldier Akintich, who knew everything and could tell such good stories, even better than grandmother, who only knew fairy stories about " long ago." When brother Yefim went away as a soldier, Akintich took his place. Though the family was large, there were only two real workers, father Yegor and the second brother Andrei. There was also grandfather Tit, but he could no longer go out to work, and lived for the most part in the forest, which he very rarely left. The women were not counted. The mother Avdotia looked after the house, and the elder sister Domna was " not quite right " in her mind. This is what had happened to Domna. One summer the women had gone out to gather raspberries in old Matugin's charcoal works, and Domna was with them. She was still quite a child, and somehow strayed from the company. The women hunted high and low but could not find her. For three whole days they searched the forest round the village and then came to the conclusion that she had been torn to pieces by a bear. On the fifth day, grandfather Tit found her, hidden on a silver birch to which she was clinging and making no sound. The old man could scarcely get her down, and brought her home half dead. From that time Domna had not been quite right in her mind. She never spoke, no matter what was said to her. She worked when her mother made her, and generally was like a small child. The village children loved to tease her. They would come in a crowd shouting:

" Domna, show us how the werewolf laughed."

They had only to say this, and Domna would begin to laugh wildly, rolling her eyes and looking terrible. It was thought that she had seen a werewolf and he had frightened her with his laughter. Besides Domna there were some other children, but these were quite tiny and did not count at all.

The whole of Shalaika worked in the forest, including Pimka's family. Even grandfather Tit worked at the charcoal works under father Yegor. Some cut the wood and carted it to the river, where it was placed on rafts, some rowed it to the lower wharves. The work was not light, but all were used to it and desired nothing better. And what more can a man want after he is fed, clothed, and warm? Pimka knew that he too would work in the charcoal works, and often said to his father:

" Father, when will you take me to the forest? "

" Wait, your time is before you, Pimka. . . . You will work in the charcoal works when the time comes."

And Pimka waited. It seemed to him that when he departed for the charcoal works he would be grown up. The works were about twenty miles away, and you could only go there over the winter roads. Grandfather Tit sometimes stayed there all summer. Pimka was disturbed by one thought only. In the forest they " bewitch " you as Domna was bewitched. You have to look out and see that the werewolf does not make you lose your way in the forest. However, the werewolf played his pranks even in Shalaika, particularly near the Chusovoi. Many times had grandmother Akulina heard him sighing in the night, and once he had killed a woman at the hay-making. Still more terrible was the werewolf's wife who had lived in the waters of the Chusovoi. Even the grown-ups were afraid of her; when she splashed about in the water, the sound could be heard from afar. She loved to look for children who happened to be bathing in the river on hot summer days; she would seize them and carry them away to her pool. Every one knew that she lived in a pool about a mile from Shalaika, where the bottomless river flowed under a high cliff. Grandfather Tit had seen her with his own eyes, only he did not like to talk about it; she was quite black, covered with hair, and had eyes like those of a wolf. Only the soldier Akintich was not afraid of either the werewolf or his wife and even went at night to fish in the pool.

" The old woman tells you foolish things, Pimka," he said gently.

" Don't you be afraid of anything—of nothing at all; and you will never be frightened. Do you understand? "

" And suppose the werewolf's wife catches hold of my leg? " Pimka asked.

" She won't; but if she does, hit her in the jaw. The werewolf, too, is all nonsense. Should he sigh, you sigh too; if he cries like a baby, you cry. Let him frighten women, but don't you fear anything, Pimka, and you will never be frightened."

We have already said that no one ever came to Shalaika and there was nowhere further to go. Of " strange folk " occasionally some charcoal contractor would come or sometimes a hunter who lived by catching wood-hens and squirrels in late autumn. The soldier Akintich also did a little hunting in his spare time, and made friends with all the hunters. They always stayed at Yegor's hut. Pimka, lying in the loft, loved to listen to the hunters' tales, especially when they talked of the pranks of bandy-legged bruin. Grandfather Tit had killed more than a dozen bears, but he did not like to speak of it. He had given up hunting when the last bear had so mauled his leg that he remained lame for the rest of his life. Akintich, after a couple of drinks, would boast of his feats and would tell the hunters imaginary tales of his prowess, until brother Yegor would stop him:

" That will do, brother Akintich. . . . You have exaggerated enough."

The gayest time in Shalaika was spring, when a caravan would come down the Chusovoi. The river rose about two feet, and over it hundreds of boats sped along quickly. All the village came out on the banks to watch. Pimka, too, looked on, thinking of the places to which the boats were going, and of the people there. Akintich was the only man in the village who had even been in a boat, and he told wonderful tales of how the river beat against the banks, how boats struck on rocks and people were drowned. Akintich knew everything there was to know in the world, and would mention some wonderful places where the boats were going.

" The people who live there are rich, brother," he would explain. " They will buy everything that you care to bring: timber and iron and copper, squirrels and wood-hens—you have only to take them there. The houses there are built of stones and there are steamers on the river."

## II

Pimka was in his thirteenth year when his father said to him: " Well, Pimka, you must get ready to come to the charcoal works. It is time, my son, that you turned into a peasant."

It was at the beginning of the winter, when the winter roads were forming. Pimka was glad, yet afraid. In the charcoal works there were of course no werewolves, but there were bears. He told no one of his fears, because a real peasant was not afraid of anything. In the summer the mother had prepared the future peasant's garments; a short sheepskin coat, gauntlets, and long felt boots, and the kind of cap that a real peasant should wear. Sometimes the frosts were so terrible in the winter that the birds froze in the air, and the only protection for one was dogskin. The charcoal workers who took the charcoal to the Borovsky suffered terribly, and sometimes a man would have his nose or ears frozen. His mother was sorry for Pimka and cried when she took leave of him.

"Mind you don't catch cold, Pimka. . . . You are going to live in camp and the draughts there are terrible."

"Don't be afraid, mamma," Pimka replied gaily. "I shall live with Akintich, and he knows everything. . . . He and I are going to kill bears."

"That's right, mind you don't get your ears frozen."

"I will let him do the cooking," explained his father. "Why should he waste his time at home when there is work to do there? You can't make a cook out of a cat, can you, Pimka? Grandfather Tit will be pleased to see you. Old and young—and you will live in camp."

"I am not afraid of anything, father."

"Why should you be afraid? You are going to live with other people."

The road to the charcoal works ran through the forest and pleased Pimka very much. The snow had only just fallen and the bogs were not yet properly frozen. They travelled in the cart plaited out of bushwood by grandfather Tit. The old man had remained in the forest the whole summer, making sleighs out of birch and plaiting carts. He could make everything for the charcoal works or for the house: hatchets for the men, troughs and rolling pins for the women—all were useful. The forest was only just covered by its first snow. The slumbering birches stood in rows, one behind the other, like soldiers. On old clearings there stood young aspens and birches, which, in the winter, had a very bare appearance. The father drove the horse, saying every now and then to Pimka:

"Look, there is a hare's trail! See the little dents he has made in the snow. They make such patterns that you can't mistake them. And there a fox went by; the fox, like the sheep, covers its traces with its tail."

At one place Yegor stopped the horse, stared for a long time at the trail, and then said:

"A pack of wolves went by here. . . . They are like soldiers, my son, each walks in the same footsteps. A whole pack went by, yet there is only a single trail. Our wolves are not dangerous because they get plenty of food in the forest. They catch hares, wood-hens, and moor-hens. They are cunning beasts!"

At another place Yegor pointed out a big trail to Pimka, and explained what it was:

" That was a moose-deer. See how he hurried away. Our soldiers must try to get him—he would feed the lot of us, and we could sell his skin at the works. I must tell him and he will go after its trail."

It was night when they got to the charcoal works. Pimka was huddled up at the bottom of the cart and was dozing. The clearing could be seen from a distance by the light cast by the burning piles of wood. To one side stood four huts. Yegor went to the one occupied by grandfather Tit. When still some distance away, the guests were greeted by the barking of the dog Liska, who looked very sheepish when she recognised the horse. With the sound of the barking, persons appeared from all the huts.

" Is that you, Yegor? "

" Yes, it is I. . . . Look at the animal I have brought you. Pimka, come out."

Akintich came forward and pulled Pimka from the cart, but the boy could not wake up. When Akintich shook him, the boy felt very cold. In the hut, grandfather Tit was watching the pot of porridge on the fire, cooking for that night's supper. When he caught sight of his grandson the old man was very pleased.

" Come, come, sit down like a visitor," he said. " Are you cold? Wait, when you have eaten some porridge you will be quite warm."

It was a large, low hut without windows or chimney. The rear half was taken up with large bunks of yew. To the right of the low door a fireplace had been built out of big stones. In the place for a chimney there was a hole in the roof, and the hut was filled with smoke so that it was impossible to stand, and Pimka began coughing violently as he swallowed the smoke. The walls and ceiling were covered with soot.

" Don't you like our place? " Akintich said teasingly. " Sit down on the floor, Pimka, near grandfather."

Old Tit was immensely pleased with his grandson, and made him sit down near him on a log of wood. The old man was about eighty, and his grey beard had turned yellow, but he was still strong and did not take second place in work with the youngest peasant. Unfortunately, however, his back had begun to ache and he had constant pains in his legs.

" Another hand for you, grandfather," the peasants who had gathered in the hut said in fun. " When it comes to eating, he will make an excellent assistant."

All the wood-cutters and wood-burners looked like chimney-sweeps owing to the life in the charcoal camp. It was all the same whether you washed or not, you could not get away from the soot. They were all pleased to see a new face, and teased the youngster in every way they could think of. But Pimka was perfectly happy. The peasants were all his own people and he knew them all by sight. Pimka's father had brought all sorts of things with him, and these he handed out—bread for one, a coat for another, a shirt for a third.

Pimka ate his porridge with more relish than he had ever experienced before in eating, and instantly fell asleep sitting on the log beside his grandfather.

" Well, we must put the youngster on the feather-bed," said Akintich jestingly, making a bed for him out of hay on a bunk. " We will put some green down here so that he can sleep well."

He carried the sleeping Pimka over in his arms, laid him on the hay, and covered him over with his coat.

" How sleepy the young beggar is! " said the peasants. " He must have got cold on the way, and coming straight into the warm room sent him off; besides, he is tired."

One after another the peasants left grandfather Tit's hut. All had to rise early in the morning.

On the following morning Pimka was awakened early by the terrible cold. It was warm in the hut so long as there was a fire, but as soon as the fire went out, the heat escaped through the hole in the roof and through the badly fitting door. It was terrible waiting until the fire gave out some heat and the smoke began to come. Then grandfather Tit climbed on to the roof and covered the hole with a piece of yew bark and some maple leaves over the top. It was either very cold or very hot in the hut.

The work in the camp was already in full swing when Pimka emerged from the hut. Grandfather Tit was harnessing the new sledge just outside the door. Somewhere in the forest the axes cutting the frozen wood could be heard, and in the clearing there were about ten smoking piles. These piles were about seven feet high and four feet broad. The wood was placed upright in the centre and allowed to burn or rather smoulder slowly. The whole secret consisted in not letting the wood rot, so as to get firm charcoal. The piles burned for about two weeks until all the wood was turned into charcoal. Every group of piles had its stoker, who had to look after the whole set. All the work would be wasted if the fire were allowed to burn through the sods, as then the wood burned right away. The stokers never left their piles, day or night. This was the most difficult and responsible work. The wood-cutter ran no risks, nor did the carrier, but the stoker was responsible for all. Only the most experienced workmen became stokers. From a distance the piles looked like huge ant-hills, with the difference that no smoke issued from the latter, while from the former a thick smoke rose night and day. A burnt-out pile had to be left for quite a long time until the charcoal was quite cold. Grandfather Tit had been a stoker for forty years and now his son Yegor had taken his place.

From the very first day Pimka adapted himself to the conditions of the camp life. They rose at daybreak, ate whatever there was, and then worked till dinner. After dinner there was a little rest, and then work again as long as there was light. Everybody's task was hard, and only those accustomed to it could stand it. The wood-cutters reeled home like drunken men, so tired were their backs and hands. The wood-carriers dropped on the road, especially in the hard frosts when the cold beat against their faces. And it was worse still to live in the dark huts, with poor food, black bread, and something hot—generally porridge. How could a peasant arrange for cooking?

" What a life! " the soldier Akintich would grumble, his years of service having disused him from the heavy work. " I'll throw it all up and go away somewhere. The worst of it is that there are no baths. . . . You look as if you've just got out of a chimney."

The whole camp dreamt of baths and envied every one who went to the village. Going to the village meant having a bath. They went in turns, and the whole winter through each man would have been twice only. Pimka had only been in camp a few days when he grew terribly home-sick. It was hard living in the forest, and the boy agreed with uncle Akintich that it was better to go away anywhere. Pimka even cried when there was no one to see him.

## III

The most trying time was holidays. Of course they could have gone to Shalaika for the day, but they did not like to tire the horses unnecessarily. It was about forty miles there and back, over a bad forest-road. It was wicked to work on a holiday, so they killed time somehow or other. It was wearisome sitting in the dark huts all day, so they gathered in the " street." They lit a big fire, sat round it and talked. The principal talker was of course Akintich, who had been to Moscow in his soldiering days. The others had never been farther than the Borovsky works. Akintich, too, loved to tell impossible tales.

" Mind you don't tell us lies, soldier! " the peasants would say.

" Why should I tell lies? You have never seen anything, that is why everything seems so wonderful to you. Take a steamer, for instance. It is enormous! A thousand people could go in it, and it does not even trawl a single boat after it. The whole of Shalaika could go in it at the same time. And then there is the railway train, that is even more wonderful—one whistle, and away you fly. That, too, can take ever so many people and all sorts of things. You have hardly time to look round when there goes another whistle and this means that you have arrived. If only there were a railway to Borovsky you could get there in an hour, whereas now you crawl along for eight and get tired on the way."

" You are telling lies, soldier! "

" How can I talk to you if you won't understand anything? "

To Pimka, too, it seemed that the soldier lied, especially when he described the mode of life in various towns. To Pimka it seemed that all people must chop wood and make charcoal, and here were suddenly stone houses, stone churches, steamers, trains, and such-like wonders. The peasants sometimes made fun of the soldier.

" Have you flown in the air, soldier? It won't cost you any more to say so."

Then Akintich would grow angry and begin to quarrel. He was quite absurd when he got angry, and all laughed.

" I shall go away from you, and that will be the end of things! I am tired of living with you in darkness. I'll go to the town, and become a handyman to a merchant. The work is very easy; you have to sweep the yard, carry the wood, groom the horse, and that is all. You can go to the baths every day if you like. Your clothes are clean, and you get as much food as you want. You get soup with plenty of fat, and porridge in which the spoon will stand up. But the nicest thing of all is tea. . . . I can't tell you how much I love tea, brothers! "

" How do they prepare it, this tea? "

" It is a kind of herb—Chinese."

" Do they put groats or beef with it? "

" Heavens! What can one do with you? You don't seem to understand anything. They drink tea with sugar! Do you understand now? But how can you? Take a lamp now. You have never seen one, but it is a most necessary thing. In Shalaika we use splints, but enlightened people have lamps. It is like a small glass bowl filled with an oil called kerosene, a wick is put in, you take a match and you get a light! The best thing about it is that you can make the light weaker or stronger as you will, not like a tallow candle. . . . Do you understand now? "

" It is sinful, all this," grandfather Tit said. " Suppose I drink this tea of yours, eat soup and porridge, go away in trains and steamers, who will do the work, eh? Suppose I run away from hard work, then you, then Pimka, and after us the whole of Shalaika, who will make the charcoal? "

" Your charcoal is of no use to any one, grandfather," the soldier said. " There is the mineral coal which they get straight out of the earth."

" Who put it there for you, eh? Oh, soldier, soldier . . . another story of yours."

Grandfather Tit did not like Akintich, because of his frivolity and because he had become spoiled in service and loved to talk about the easy life there. The man had got quite unaccustomed to real peasant labour. The old man often quarrelled with Akintich on account of his soldier's pipe and frequently chased him out of the hut. No one smoked in Shalaika, and the peasants took advantage of this to complain to the old man.

" Grandfather, the soldier says that in the town every one smokes and they even put tobacco in their noses."

" Nonsense, it is not true," grandfather said. " It is a sin to listen to such things. He doesn't like work, that is the chief reason. That is why he does not know that God loves him who labours. What sort of a man would I be if I did not work? Every creature must do its work, according to its needs, because nests must be built and the young must be fed."

" In towns they work according to their need, grandfather," exclaimed the soldier, " only there the work is cleaner than ours. . . . They do not work less than we do . . . perhaps more. Not every one need make charcoal—there are many other trades. Some make cotton and cloth, others boots, and others are locksmiths."

" That is all nonsense! " grandfather said. " In the olden days they lived without cotton, and cloth was woven by the women at home. It is all nonsense! The principal workman is after all the peasant who sows the corn. You can't live without bread, and the rest is all nonsense. Indulgence . . ." Pimka began to think of how other people in this wide world lived. If he could only look at them—with one eye only! Perhaps the soldier did not lie. He had told them of places where there was no winter, and that he had seen, with his own eyes, the biggest animal in the world, an elephant, that was as big as a huge bath. Pimka's childish curiosity was satisfied by an unexpected event.

One day the whole camp was in a deep sleep. There was a hard frost and even the dogs went into the huts. Suddenly, in the middle of the night, Liska growled angrily. He had particular growls for beast and for man, and now his growl was for man. Soon loud voices were heard. It was a party of railway engineers who were surveying a road for a new railway. There were about ten of them; two engineers, their assistants, simple peasants—and a guide. The latter had lost his way, and had brought the party to the camp instead of to Shalaika. The soldier Akintich shot out and invited the chief into his hut.

" Welcome, Your Honour. We will do the best we can for you. We will light a fire in a moment and boil some water. You must excuse us, Your Honour."

This was the first time that Pimka had ever seen strangers, and he stared at them as though they were from another world, with all the wonder of a young barbarian. Then he was struck by the alacrity with which Akintich looked after the guests, excusing himself at every step. The chief was angry, however—angry with everything: with the sooty hut, the smoky fire, with the guide who was responsible for their having lost their way, and even with the hard frost of the forest.

" It certainly does smoke, Your Honour," Akintich said, " and the frost is very bad indeed. . . . You must excuse us because we live in the forest and know no better, Your Honour."

" Have you been a soldier? " the chief asked.

" Yes, Your Honour . . . I have been to Moscow. Yes. . . . And here—you must excuse us—there is only the forest and ignorance."

Pimka saw the gentlemen drink tea, eat their own food, and smoke cigarettes. He even tasted the tea himself, that is, he ate several leaves and decided that the soldier had lied. There was no sweet taste, it was only a weed, and black.

Early in the morning the party went on farther. Akintich himself accompanied them, not knowing what to do to please the gentlemen.

" It is as though a snake were uncurling itself," grumbled grandfather Tit, shaking his head. " Ah, soldier, soldier, you will betray the lot of us! "

The chief grumbled the whole morning: it was cold in the hut, and the water in the pot smelt badly; the dogs had barked all night, —he was discontented with everything. Pimka stood with his mouth open, fearing that the chief might strike him. However, things went off smoothly.

When the guests departed, the camp seemed empty, it was so quiet. The whole camp gathered in a crowd to discuss the departed guests.

" And the soldier foretold all this," Pimka's father said. " The railway—and here it has come to us."

The peasants wondered whether it would be good or bad for them when the railway ran through their forest.

" Of what use will a railway be to us? " grandfather Tit grumbled. " It is only indulgence, and probably sinful. . . . Ah, it is time I were dead. . . ."

Exactly three years later, an iron railway bridge stretched across the Chusovoi a little below Shalaika, and the soldier Akintich was appointed watchman. He had his own sentry-box, a samovár, and a new pipe. He was perfectly happy.

The whole of Shalaika turned out to see the first train go by— even grandfather Tit. The old man no longer went to the charcoal camp, because he was too ailing. He gazed for a long time at Akintich, who was pacing up and down outside his sentry-box, with a green flag in his hand, and at last the old man said:

" That is the very place for you, Akintich. No work at all and you get wages for nothing."

Pimka trembled all over when the sound of the first train was heard in the distance. Soon it crawled out from behind the mountain like an iron serpent, and emitted its first shriek, destroying for ever the stillness of the forest. Akintich drew himself up erect in military fashion and, raising his flag, cried to the first train: "Zdravia jelaem!" [1]

# "THERE IS NO REPLY"

## Dmitri Mamin-Sibiriak

### I

"AND you say we shall have an apple orchard also?" she asked, dexterously applying the pencil beneath the left eyelid.

"Yes—and the apple trees are lovely in full bloom," he replied, watching her as she quickly went on with her make-up.

"And the Volga flows below?"

"My estate lies on the very slope of the hill. There is a fine view from the verandah, and in spring the Volga spreads out for more than seven versts."

"Very nice, indeed—that is, the slope of the hill, the spreading of the Volga, and the blossoms of your apple trees—it is all very beautiful. But, do you know, there is something your orchard lacks?"

She turned her painted face and looked at him with smiling eyes. It was a remarkable face, which drew him to her like an electromagnet. What beautiful eyes she had, grey and lustrous, a rosebud mouth showing with every smile two lines of pearly teeth; pink, shell-like little ears; a charming dimple in the chin; a small but beautifully sculptured brow; everything, even to the tiny birthmark on the left cheek, was lovely and like a picture in its living frame of soft, slightly curling fair hair with a golden glint in it.

"Yes, the only thing your garden lacks is orange-blossoms," she said slowly, drawling the words.

He did not catch her meaning, and replied quite seriously:

"Orange-blossoms? Oranges do not grow in our climate."

"Really? Ah, why did you tell me that? I think orange-blossoms are so beautiful, something like a lily, emblematic of youth and purity."

He still did not catch her meaning, and his face wore the same confused smile. She playfully struck him on the shoulder with her fan and said in a more serious tone:

[1] The Russian military greeting from soldiers to their officers.

" Well, and what should we do in your garden? "

" We should roam in it every day."

" And upon the estate? "

" Oh, we should settle down and live upon it pleasantly and peacefully."

She threw back her head and laughed. He could see her beautifully sculptured neck, her rounded breast, her sloping shoulders which were shaking with laughter.

" Roam in a garden—live on an estate! " she repeated, wiping the tears of laughter from her face. " See, you have spoiled my whole make-up. Oh, you dear child! How old are you? "

" I shall soon be twenty-three."

" A beautiful age. I can only be envious of you. And how old do you think I am? But, after all, better not try to guess. In fact, I myself am beginning to forget my chronology."

They were in the dressing-room of one of the merry summer theatres of St. Petersburg. Upon the small strip of paper pasted on the outside of the door was written: " Maria Ivanovna Guliaeva." The interior of the room struck a newcomer with its look of poverty. The walls were built of the badly joined boards of an old boat, full of holes from the pulled out wooden spikes, through which a continual draught entered in spite of the plugs of rags, wadding, and paper. The furniture consisted of a dilapidated sofa, a couple of chairs, a toilet-table, and a washstand. In a corner several theatrical costumes hung in artistic disorder. The stale air was impregnated with the smell of eau de cologne, face powder, and cheap, strong perfumes. The only window, facing the garden, was curtained with a piece of muslin yellow with age. During the performance, when Maria Ivanovna was dressing, the window had, as a matter of course, to remain closed; during the rest of the day and night there was no necessity for keeping it open. But even such a dressing-room was a certain luxury which only the " stars " of summer-garden companies could obtain. Maria Ivanovna had already reached that period when an actress struggles desperately against the mercilessly approaching " artistic " age. She well knew that her reign would not last long, but she was as yet queening it on the stage of the summer-garden theatres, thanks to her great name. In every walk of life and in every profession there are great names.

The young man who stood before her was neither handsome nor plain. He was only young, young with an uncorrupted youth. A thick, blond little beard gave him a more steadfast and mature appearance than his years warranted, and his earnest brown eyes looked unusually simple and trustful. Judged by his elegant summer clothes and general well-groomed appearance he could be easily classified as belonging to people of " society." Maria Ivanovna, who had studied well her summer-theatre zoology, noticed that from the first. She liked his air of breeding, and allowed him to visit her in her dressing-room. But to-day he surprised her so much that even she lost control over herself while trying to impart a jesting tone to his proposition.

"Please do not forget that I have spoken in all seriousness," he remarked in a slightly dulled voice; his throat had become parched from excitement.

"Yes? Oh, yes—please do not bother me with your jests. It soon will be my turn. What shall I sing for you?"

"Whatever you please."

"Very well, I know just what you care most to hear."

She wanted to say something more, when some one tapped at the door; it was the call of the stage manager. She rose quickly from her seat, gathered her long train, and, rustling her silk skirts like a snake in its dry skin, hurriedly left the room. Going through the dirty, sparsely lighted corridor, she smilingly repeated to herself:

"Oh, what a funny creature! How foolish he is—the dear!"

The door of the dressing-room remained open, and he could hear the deafening applause and that remarkable noise of a human crowd which recalls the roar of sea-breakers. She had appeared before the footlights, and the public were greeting her with a voice like that of a bloodthirsty, hungry beast to whom a piece of fresh meat is flung. They quieted down soon, and the first words of the romance which he loved so well reached his ears.

He listened numb with excitement, absorbing with intoxicated delight every note. Yes, she was singing for him, confessing her love in another's words.

The sounds ceased. A brief pause and again a storm of applause like the thousand-voiced echo of a summons and a caress. He rose and began to walk quickly up and down the dressing-room. In his heart also raged a tempest, but a silent one, like a gathering storm. Oh, how he hated it all now—this madly roaring mob and the whole setting of this low cabaret, even the air impregnated with the peculiar miasmas of unrestrained debauch. The place was a putrid swamp emanating vile, poisonous stenches and corrupting everything that dared to come close enough—and she, this pure water lily, whose chaste whiteness could not be ruined by all the miry poisons together! A low cabaret and the first lisp of love!

The public continued their violent clamour, forcing her to sing song after song. Maria Ivanovna sang pieces from *The Geisha* and the new gipsy songs which were then the rage.

She returned to the dressing-room tired out, with red spots on her face and eyes troubled. In her hand she held several visiting cards, which she carelessly threw upon the toilet-table. To the dumb question in his eyes she wearily replied:

"Oh, these are all invitations to suppers in private rooms. My

140*

dear admirers seem to think that I have seven stomachs, like a dromedary. And all of them are our esteemed provincials, fathers of families and elderly men. At home they would be ashamed to take supper with a singer in a private room, but here, where no one knows them, they are glad to take advantage of the opportunity to enjoy themselves." Catching an expression of jealousy in his eyes, she quickly added, with a smile: " Don't be afraid; you have no rivals. I want to be only my own self to-day; it is an almost unobtainable luxury for me. Only one evening to be my own self——"

Then she put her round, white arms upon his shoulders and, gazing searchingly into his eyes, whispered, " And I do not receive a declaration of love and an offer of the hand and heart every evening."

He dropped his eyes, and she felt she had been wanting in tact.

## II

After the performance they walked over to the farthest end of the summer garden, where, in a low, stone building, were the private rooms of the garden restaurant. She took his arm and looked around continually, as if fearing to meet an acquaintance. He also felt her fear, and attentively scanned the faces of the people. They met two actors—one stout and red-faced, the other a handsome, dark man with bold, black eyes. The two exchanged glances, and the stout man whispered something which evidently concerned Maria Ivanovna. The handsome actor only smiled with his eyes and shrugged his shoulders.

" The scoundrels! " thought Maria Ivanovna, hurrying her steps.

The private room looked like all such places—a pothouse den. A motley collection of dirty, dilapidated furniture, a dim, scratched mirror, a carpet worn and soiled, and so on. At the door of the room they were overtaken by the box-opener, who stealthily tried to hand two more visiting cards to Maria Ivanovna, but she pettishly pushed him away.

" Enough, enough! Tell them I am dead—yes, dead."

When the door closed after them she sank into a chair.

" How tired I am! " she said in a weary voice. " If you could only know! By the bye, I have forgotten your name—forgive me."

" Pavel Konstantinich Ruzhishchev."

" Yes, yes; please forgive me. I have such a bad memory, and besides——" She was going to add, " And I have so many acquaintances and new ones every day," but she caught herself in time. He looked over the menu, not knowing what to offer her.

" Pavel Konstantinich, to-night I would like to choose for myself something cheap and plain: a plate of beet soup, sausages and cabbage, or creamed liver——''

'' And I wanted to order a steamed sterlet.''

'' Ah, no, I am sick to death of all these delicacies. I want something simple.''

'' And the wine? ''

'' No wine at all—order a bottle of cheap beer. Let us eat like a pair of student comrades. I shall order some nice hot sausages —you know the kind, those you can slice in fine round slices with the skin on—and a piece of cheap domestic cheese that crumbles under the knife. That will be splendid! ''

He laughed contentedly at her whims and fantasies. And the waiter who received the order looked at him contemptuously—was this the way to treat Maria Ivanovna? Their first star, and—a bottle of beer!

'' Splendid, first-rate! '' she continually kept repeating, gazing at Pavel with narrowed eyes.

She took off her lace cape and approached the window, through which the noise of the public, now scattered over the whole garden, reached them like a far-away rumble.

'' We should have gone away from here and supped somewhere at a cheap little restaurant,'' she murmured meditatively, '' where the air is always saturated with the smell of burned butter, fried onions, and herring. But I think all the restaurants except the most expensive ones are closed at this time of night.''

The supper turned out a very homely affair. Maria Ivanovna, who usually took a tiny glass of vodka at night '' for the nerves,'' as she explained, looked very charming with her slightly heightened colour. The impression was marred only by the traces of make-up near the eyes. Pavel looked at her admiringly, and listened attentively to the endless flow of her feminine prattle.

'' Am I wearying you? '' she asked him several times, with a kind of guilty smile. '' And I would like to tell you everything— that is, not quite everything, but what would interest you. I was born and brought up far from here, in the South. My family was neither poor nor well-to-do, but middling—managing to pull through somehow or other. My childhood was spent tediously and uninterestingly till I passed the fourth form at school—I was then just fourteen years of age, but I looked much older, and my short, brown dress-uniform gave a sort of piquancy to my whole appearance. Oh, I very early found out my personal value—probably this was the real reason for all the misfortunes of my subsequent life. You men cannot imagine how joyfully the woman awakes in the girl-stripling. Why are you sitting in that chair, Konstantin Pavlowich? ''

'' Pavel Konstantinich.''

'' Pardon me—come, sit here, close by me on the sofa; let us

touch glasses! Yes, it was very nice. I can see myself now, just
a bit of a girl. I was splendidly built and had a long, thick,
luxurious braid of hair, a wonderful complexion, and beautiful,
gentle eyes. I can speak of myself like that now because it was
so long ago that I can talk of myself as if I were an entire stranger,
as I would speak of those young girls whom I often meet in the
street and in whose beauty I take such delight. Come, sit close
by me, closer! What a strange man you are! But wait, I will
move nearer myself—so! "

Her shoulder almost touched his, and he could feel the warmth
of her body and the odour of powder. He was slightly dazed, and
his eyes became overcast with a mist. It was at the same time
painful and pleasant, and he felt like telling her so, and in such
wonderful language—in words which are as difficult to grasp as
one's shadow. And she prattled on, sipping the beer from her
glass and bestrewing her dress with cheese crumbs.

"You have noticed, Konst—that is, Pavel Konstantinich, the
expression of human eyes? How beautiful they are in children—I
mean, very little children! In boys this purity of expression is lost
at a very early age, but girls preserve it till nearly sixteen. Yes,
exactly, purity. It is as pleasant to gaze into such eyes as it is to
gaze into calm waters unruffled by the wind. In such eyes one sees
the whole soul, while it is as yet pure and untroubled. Yes, and
thus I was passed into the fifth form; and afterward, when I passed
into the sixth, I began to feel uncomfortable in my short frocks."

She sighed and leaned her head on the back of the sofa with half-
closed eyes. He took her hand and softly patted it. She did not
draw it away nor open her eyes. In a sweet drowsiness Maria
Ivanovna continued to see herself a half-grown girl.

"Yes, it was a beautiful time," she whispered, as if awaking
from sleep. "And afterward——"

"I know what happened afterward," he interrupted. "That
is, I can guess——"

She was suddenly possessed by a passionate longing to tell him
everything, to tell the story of her whole life, to him, who was so
gentle and good and pure, and who ought to know what kind of
a woman he wanted to bring to his ancestral home, into his beloved
apple orchard. It was true he would turn away from her in
disgust, but that was preferable to base deceit. Oh, she had lied
so much, lied her whole life long, every word she had uttered was
a lie. When he first proposed marriage to her she had taken it
for one of those jests that are often essayed for closer intimacy with
such women as she. In her life history she had had several such
experiences. But this time she felt with her whole being that he
meant it earnestly, as she felt his wonderful gaze—he looked at her
also with his whole body, with every drop of his pure, uncorrupted
blood.

For a few moments they were silent, but the silence was more eloquent than words; he understood what she was thinking of and forestalled her.

" Yes, I know," he said, choosing his words with difficulty. " I know that you have a past. But it does not concern me. I do not want to know it. There are feelings which cleanse everything, just as fire clears metal from rust. I am fully conscious of the step I am taking and what I intend to do. But one condition I beg of you, for the love of God—never, not with a single word, mention that past! " It would pain me very much, horrify me to hear it—especially from you."

She was silent, feeling suddenly a queer dizziness, and it seemed as if she saw many-coloured disks whirling before her eyes.

" No, never, never! " he repeated, firmly pressing her hand. " A human being should not be judged by his mistakes, but by his heart."

He spoke further in the same strain, seriously and simply, like a brother to a sister, while from the garden the clamour and noise of the revellers and the sound of music came up to them. To Maria Ivanovna it seemed as if the great crowd were calling to her, and she wanted to hide herself far, far away, leaving behind for ever the Maria Ivanovna whom this public knew and whom it considered its property. Thus think the sick, who dream of going away in the vain hope of leaving their sickness behind them.

" You are good and noble," she said in a motherly tone. " There are so very few really good people in the world. No one can become good—it is in one's blood. Your father and mother must also be good people."

" Yes, they are."

They sat very late into the night, speaking quietly of trifles which had suddenly gained an unwonted importance in their eyes. On parting she kissed him. It was their first kiss, and she was surprised to find her heart beating faster than usual.

It was a white, moonless night. Only a few late guests were left in the garden. From one of the private rooms came the sounds of a drunken quarrel. Tired waiters hurried past with trays upon which were piled empty dishes and bottles. The air was filled with the fumes of drunken revelry.

Pavel escorted Maria Ivanovna to a carriage and helped her in.

" I do not like to be accompanied home," she informed him gently, with an enigmatic smile.

### III

The following nights were also white and moonless, those white nights of St. Petersburg.

Maria Ivanovna was very miserable. She felt as if something were pressing on her. She wept and was angry with herself.

" You old fool, you old fool! "

She went to the mirror and, looking intently at her slightly faded face, smiled bitterly.

" Old, quite old."

There had been a time when Maria Ivanovna laughed at the women age had caught in its merciless grasp, who yet tried desperately to appear young. And now her turn had come! Time knows no pity. She caught her head in both her hands, cursed herself and again wept. She was of a different mind about the matter ten times a day. She would certainly never marry Ruzhishchev; that would be simply ridiculous—a husband of twenty-four and a wife of thirty-seven—a whole abyss of thirteen years. No, she would just go on loving him, simply and without any obligations on his side, for so long as his love might last—a year, maybe two. To be superfluous, to be unloved—that would not matter; but to be ludicrous was more than she could bear. On the other hand, do not old men marry very young girls? There are marriages based upon mutual respect, and there are some men who love only once in their lives and find in their wives the better part of themselves. Was it possible that she might die in the height of their happiness and he also? And, after all, she could always leave him as soon as she noticed a change in his feelings and give him back his full liberty.

Her infatuation was no longer a secret among her comrades of the profession. She was met with meaning smiles, and the stout comedian Butusov paraphrased a well-known French jest: " Our Maria Ivanovna wants to exchange her forty-franc piece for two twenty-franc pieces; one cash down and the other on credit. That is called the conversion of a domestic loan."

Her good friends certainly did their best to acquaint Maria Ivanovna with all this tittle-tattle and the cheap witticisms circulated about her. She was exasperated, but had always the same reply : " They do not understand, therefore they are angry."

Among the members of the International chorus there was a fair young girl by the name of Tania. She was a newcomer on the stage and had not as yet lost her maidenly modesty. Maria Ivanovna took an interest in her, and often invited her into her dressing-room to pin a bunch of fresh flowers on her corsage or to give her a box of bon-bons.

Tania looked up to Maria Ivanovna as to an unattainable ideal. She waited for her in the corridor before going on the stage, caught her every glance, and followed her with loving eyes. This mute adoration highly amused Maria Ivanovna, and she instinctively pitied the lovable girl. After listening for some time to the gossip in the wings, Tania watched for Maria Ivanovna in the corridor and, assuring herself that she was alone, went uninvited into the dressing-room.

" Do you need anything, Tania? " asked Maria Ivanovna.

" No—that is, yes," the girl said, confused; then she faltered: " They all say that you are in love."

" Oh, what foolishness, Tania! And why must you repeat what others are saying? "

" But I know, Maria Ivanovna, that you are in love."

" Well, let us suppose that it is so—what of it? "

" I wanted to ask you how it feels."

Maria Ivanovna broke into a merry peal of laughter.

" Oh, you little silly! I suspect you are in love, too? "

" I do not know. I am being courted by two men: the head boxkeeper and the hairdresser."

" And whom do you love? "

" I like them both the same."

" Ah, you foolish, foolish little girl! If you like them both, then you do not love either one. You can love but one. Your time has not yet come, Tania. When one loves one asks no one about it."

Maria Ivanovna took the ingenuous girl in her arms and kissed her many times.

" Everybody loves you, Maria Ivanovna. Everybody courts you," whispered Tania, pressing her fair little head on Maria Ivanovna's shoulder; " you do not want to tell me, but you know everything. The boxkeeper went on a spree from sheer despair, and Alfred, the hairdresser, is threatening to blow his brains out, and I do not know what to do."

Maria Ivanovna laughed heartily as she told Ruzhishchev about this, but Ruzhishchev found little in it to laugh at.

They met every day. Ruzhishchev, as if in duty bound, spent every evening in the garden. He knew by sight not only all the artists, boxkeepers, and waiters, but even the hangers-on and habitués of the garden, and the closer his contact and acquaintance with the place the more he hated it. It was all horrible, ugly, and hopeless. He suffered terribly at the sight of the actors and actresses who were employing all the tricks of their trade for the edification of the drunken crowds. The boldness of the actresses as they vied with each other especially distressed him.

Maria Ivanovna was no better than the rest when she sang her spicy chansonettes, accompanied with gestures and intonations. Her painted face, her neck and arms covered with false diamonds, her bold smiles and gestures horrified Ruzhishchev. At supper every evening he would repeat the same words to her:

" Maria, let us go away from here. It is terrible! You cannot imagine how it hurts me to see you grimacing upon this accursed stage. I no longer recognise you. Your face becomes strange, and your smile, your motions, your voice——"

" My dear, it is simply because you are not used to it. Our cynicism does not exist for ourselves personally; we do not feel it

any more than the hucksters and fishmongers in the market do the
continual abuse and cursing in which they indulge with so much
gusto on the least provocation: they are used to it, and therefore do
not care. As to my leaving at present, I cannot do it; my contract
will not permit it; I should have to pay a large forfeit."

" I will pay the forfeit."

" But my reputation? What manager would engage me again
if I once broke my contract? Our artistic reputation is our whole
capital. To-day you love me, and everything is well; but who
knows what may happen to-morrow? "

" For the love of God, Maria, do not speak like that! "

Ruzhishchev was too modest to talk much about himself and his
private affairs; but in the theatrical world in which Maria Ivanovna
lived there are no secrets, and Maria Ivanovna knew through others
that he was the only son of a very wealthy landowner on the banks
of the Volga, had graduated from a university, and served in one of
the minister's offices without remuneration.

There was one man, a very questionable character, whose business
lay with the actors at summer gardens and cafés chantants. He wore
a high hat and gold spectacles, and spoke several languages. He
seemed to know everything and everybody, and served the actors—
especially the women—in the capacity of theatrical agent. His
name was Astmus. Rumour gave him a very shady reputation and
held him as ready for any kind of rascality. His speciality lay in
procuring profitable acquaintances for his clients, writing laudatory
criticisms, and circulating scandals or slanders. Maria Ivanovna
had known him for several years and had often made use of his
services. She now feared him with a deadly fear. She knew that
Astmus was intimately acquainted with the whole of her turbulent
life, and could spoil her growing happiness in a moment by a few
anonymously written lines.

Astmus himself thoroughly understood the situation, and behaved
toward her with provoking familiarity.

" So, so; we have a nice little love affair, Maria Ivanovna? " he
jested, looking straight at her with his cruel eyes. " Well, you
must not lose valuable time, my dear. You can depend on my discretion, because I am the living grave of all women's secrets. That
is my principle, Maria Ivanovna. But why do I tell you this? You
have had enough opportunities to find out how honest I am in my
dealings. By the bye, Maria Ivanovna, you could easily win my
friendship by doing me a small favour. You know the little chorus
girl Tania. I like her extremely, but she chooses to play the prude,
taking offence at the least hint. If I could meet her at your rooms—
accidentally, of course—well, what do you say? Besides, I am well
aware that she adores you, and you, like a clever and practical
woman, could easily influence her."

" Pardon me, Monsieur Astmus," Maria Ivanovna sharply interrupted him, red with anger. "I have nothing to do with affairs of that sort."

"You are afraid of a new rival, my dear, eh? Oh-h-h! I really didn't expect it."

After this conversation there was nothing for her to do but run away from the place as quickly as possible. Yes, run—not leave it but run.

IV

Ruzhishchev was beside himself with joy when she told him that she had decided to leave the stage.

"I sing to-day for the last time," she declared, watching him with eyes beaming with joy. "To-morrow I shall announce it to the manager. I am a little conscience-stricken, because I am leaving at the height of the season. After all, I have been a good attraction, and the public liked me. My leaving may have a detrimental effect upon the business of the whole company."

"My beloved, somebody will surely be found to replace you."

"You forget that I shall have to pay a large forfeit—something like six thousand roubles. I have only two thousand, which I had saved up for a rainy day."

"Do not worry about money."

"It looks very much as if you were ransoming your future wife out of captivity!"

"Precisely. You are perfectly right! And so this is your last appearance?"

"Yes, my beloved. And to-night we shall sup for the last time in the cabaret."

They embraced lovingly. She turned to her make-up while he went out into the theatre to look on for the last time at his shame. The low cabaret, with its hangers-on, confidence tricksters, and revelling elderly provincials, who came to the capital on business—everything vanished from before his eyes like a bad dream. Ruzhishchev could not even distinguish the various faces—everything was mixed into one absurd living and moving spot, like a drop of infected blood under a microscope. "Oh to escape from here into the fresh air!" he thought. "Oh to be able to carry away my happiness to the banks of my native Volga!"

It seemed to him as if time had stopped—like flowing waters meeting an irresistible barrier in their way. Maria Ivanovna was the last on the programme, and the public, as if anticipating the speedy retirement of its idol, was tireless in calling her before the curtain.

Ruzhishchev kept continually repeating to himself: "Enough! Enough! Leave her alone!"

He was surprised at Maria Ivanovna's whim to sup for the last time in a private room of the garden restaurant. In his opinion they should have run away from there without one backward glance.

But who can account for a woman's caprices? Besides, she probably intended it as a last good-bye to the past, a last tribute to a bad habit.

He awaited her in his private room, which somehow did not appear to him to-night so dirty and disgusting as usual.

She came rather late, looking happy, agitated, and joyful.

" Is everything done with? " he asked.

" Yes."

" Did you see your manager? "

" For a moment. I told him what I intended to do. Let us not speak of it," and she laughingly tossed half-a-dozen visiting cards on the table.

" Those dear old men from the provinces won't leave me in peace," she explained, making a wry face. " Oh, how I despise them—I hate them from my very soul. It is not the young who are depraved and debauched, but these esteemed fathers of grown-up families, these virtuous husbands, these living examples of family happiness."

She could have told him also that some of these cards were delivered through the friendly offices of Monsieur Astmus, who was the go-between.

Again they ordered a plain student's supper, and sat on the sofa, holding each other in a close embrace and recalling the details of their first meeting. Maria Ivanovna gazed at Ruzhishchev with loving eyes.

" Heavens, how quickly it has all happened! " she exclaimed. " Just like a dream! Let us see, how was it we became acquainted? I really cannot recollect."

" Oh, well, how we became acquainted is not very interesting. It was in just such a private room as this. Have you forgotten? "

" Let me see; you had two old men with you. Yes, one of them was such a funny creature, a little bit of a man, and he said his name was Dr. Kinderbalsam. He told me that he had formed your acquaintance only that very evening here in the garden."

" No, he was only humbugging you, Maria." Ruzhishchev laughed and added: " This must be our little secret, Maria—you see, my father is a very good and kind man, but sometimes he likes to go on a spree! "

She tore herself away from his arms, sprang up from the sofa, and trembling all over, her face white, said in a choked voice:

" That—that was your—father? "

He rose, took her hands in his and tried to draw her back upon the sofa.

" Yes, my father. He is a very good man, though he has his little shortcomings."

" Father! " she repeated, listening to the sound of her own voice. " Father! "

Again she tore herself away from him and sank, weak and helpless, into a chair.

"Maria, Maria, what ails you? Such nonsense——"

But she made no reply and only covered her face with her hands.

"Maria, you will forgive him! It is such a trifle! "

But she could only groan and press her head in her two hands.

"It is nothing. I often have them," she explained, without removing her hands—" violent pains in the head. Do not be angry.
I must go home immediately. You will receive here my final decision to-morrow evening. I must first speak with the manager."

"I will accompany you, Maria."

"Oh, for the love of God, don't; it is unnecessary! " Maria
Ivanovna exclaimed in a frightened voice. "Tania will see me
home."

He escorted her back to her dressing-room. Tania, who was
ready to start for home, was delighted at the thought of accompanying Maria Ivanovna and sitting with her alone in a carriage. Ruzhishchev helped them into the carriage and remained standing on
the pavement long after. He could not make it out. Maria
Ivanovna had gazed so long into his eyes at parting and had embraced him so lovingly.

As soon as the carriage rolled off, leaving Pavel behind, Maria
Ivanovna broke out into bitter weeping, unheeding the crowds of
people thronging the pavements on their way from the gardens.

"Maria Ivanovna! Darling, what ails you? " murmured the
frightened Tania, embracing her adored one. "Maria Ivanovna,
tell me! "

Maria Ivanovna looked at her with wild eyes, and wiping away
the tears that were rolling down her face, she said in a choked voice:

"There is no longer any Maria Ivanovna. She is dead. Oh, my
God! So this is how retribution has overtaken me! "

"Darling Maria Ivanovna, men are all like that—they are all
deceivers."

"Ah, it is not that, Tania. He is noble and pure. You will stay
with me to-night, will you not? I am afraid. I cannot explain to
you what has happened."

The distance from the garden to Maria Ivanovna's rooms was
very short—a few streets only, but it gave her time to think it all
over and arrive at a decision. Thoughts chased each other quickly
through her head as if storm-driven. And the fatal word "father"
was beating in her brain like a hammer. Yes, father! she could
see him before her at that very moment, and it sent a shiver
through her whole body. After she had formed his acquaintance,
brought about by Astmus, in a private room of the garden restaurant, he had visited her several times at her rooms, bringing her
flowers, bonbons and costly trinkets. He was a well-preserved, provincial old man, brimming over with the joy of life. And each time

after the visit of Dr. Kinderbalsam Maria Ivanovna found on her little night-table under her powder-box a hundred-rouble note. These facts burned in her now like a red-hot iron. She could hear the voice of Dr. Kinderbalsam:

" The young men of to-day are no good. What do they understand, the striplings! But Dr. Kinderbalsam is a specialist in women, for whom the best prescription is a nice cheque or banknote, easily filled by a first-class jeweller."

Maria Ivanovna felt that she was drowning in this mire in which she had wallowed all her life. Could she marry the son after this? Enough! And she, such a low, vile, disgusting being, dared to love! No, there was no punishment too heavy for her!

On the evening of the next day Ruzhishchev sat impatiently awaiting the promised reply from Maria Ivanovna. Tania found him in the garden and silently handed him an envelope. He opened it, and found written on a single sheet the laconic phrase of Marguerite Gautier: " There is no reply."

# VLADIMIR KOROLÉNKO

B. 1853

# EASTER EVE

It was Holy Saturday, one year in the 'eighties.

Evening had long since enfolded the silent earth. The ground, warmed during the day by the rays of the sun, was now cooling beneath the invigorating influence of the night-frost. It seemed as if sighing, while its breath, forming a silvery mist, rose glistening in the rays of the starlit sky, like clouds of incense, to greet the approaching feast.

All was still. In the cool night-breeze the small provincial town stood silent, waiting to hear the first stroke of the bell from the high cathedral tower. But the town was not sleeping; a spirit of expectancy brooded beneath the veil of darkness, breathing through the shadows of the silent and deserted streets. Now and then a belated workman, who had just escaped from his servile task ere the festival began, passed, hurrying on his way; once in a while a cab rattled by, leaving silence behind it. Life had fled indoors and hidden itself, in mansion and hovel, from whose windows the lights shone far out upon the street, while over the city and the fields hovered the spirit of Resurrection.

Although the moon stood high above the horizon, the town still rested in the broad, deep shadow of a hill, crowned by a gloomy and massive edifice, whose peculiarly straight and severe outlines were sharply defined in the golden atmosphere. The sombre gates were hardly to be distinguished amid the gloom of its deeply shadowed walls, while the towers on the four corners stood out boldly against the azure sky, and gradually over all the moon poured its flood of liquid gold.

Suddenly on the sensitive air of the expectant night came the first stroke from the high cathedral belfry; then another, and still another. A minute later and the whole air throbbed and swelled, as the countless bells rang out, uniting in one harmonious peal. From the gloomy building overshading the town came a faint, broken harmony, that seemed to flutter helplessly in the air, and thence to rise into the ethereal light, and join the mighty chorus. The singing ceased, the sounds dissolved in air, and the silence of the night gradually resumed its sway; a faint echo seemed to hover for a while, like the vibration of an invisible harp-string. Now the lights were gradually extinguished, the church windows shone forth brightly, and Earth seemed ready to proclaim once more the old tidings of peace, love, and good-will.

The bolts of the dark gates in the gloomy building creaked, and a band of soldiers, with clanking arms, sallied forth to relieve the night sentinels; on approaching the corners, they would halt, and a dark form, with measured steps, would detach itself from the rest, while the former sentinel took his place in the ranks, and the soldiers went on their way, skirting the high prison wall, that glistened in the moonbeams.

As they reached its western side, a young recruit stepped forward from the ranks to relieve the sentry who was posted there; a rustic awkwardness still showed itself in his movements, and his young face betrayed the absorbed attention of a novice who was to occupy for the first time a responsible post. He faced the wall, presented arms, made two steps forward, and shouldering his rifle, stood beside the sentry he was to replace. The latter, turning slightly toward him, repeated the usual formula, in the sing-song tone of discipline:

" From corner to corner. Keep watch! Do not sleep or doze! " He spoke rapidly, while the recruit listened with close attention, and a peculiar expression of anxiety and sadness in his grey eyes.

" You understand? " asked the sergeant.

" Yes, sir! "

" Then, look out! " he added sharply; but, suddenly changing his tone, he said, good-naturedly:

" Don't be afraid, Faddeyef; you are not a woman! I hope you are not afraid of the Lyeshy! "

" Why should I be afraid of him? " replied Faddeyef. Then he added: " But I tell you, boys, I have some misgiving."

This simple and almost childish confession made the soldiers laugh.

" There's simplicity for you! " exclaimed the sergeant, in tones of contempt. Then giving the order, " Shoulder arms! March! " the sentries, with measured tread, disappeared around the corner, and the sound of their footsteps was soon lost in the distance. The sentinel shouldered his rifle, and began to pace along the wall.

Inside the prison, at the first stroke of the bell, all was in motion. It was long since the sad and gloomy prison night had witnessed so much life. It seemed as if the church bells had really brought tidings of liberty; for the grimy doors of the cells opened in turn, and their occupants, clad in long grey garments, the fatal patches on their backs, filed in rows along the corridors, on their way to the brilliantly lighted prison church. They came from all directions —from right and left, descending and ascending the stairway; and amid the echoing footsteps rang the sound of arms and the clanking of chains. On entering the church, this grey mass of humanity poured into the space allotted to it, behind the railing, and stood there in silence. The windows of the church were protected by strong iron bars.

The prison was empty, except in the four towers, where, in small, strongly bolted cells, four men, in solitary confinement, were restlessly pacing to and fro, stopping once in a while to listen at the keyhole to the snatches of church-singing that reached their ears.

And, beside these, in one of the ordinary cells, in a bunk, lay a sick man. The governor, to whom this sudden illness had been reported, went into his cell as they were escorting the prisoners to church, and, leaning over him, looked into his eyes, that were gazing fixedly before him, and in which shone a peculiar light.

" Ivanof! Ivanof! " he called out to the invalid.

The convict never turned his head, but continued muttering something unintelligible, moving his parched lips with difficulty.

" Carry him to the hospital to-morrow! " said the governor, as he left the cell, appointing a sentry to guard the door. The latter, after a close examination of the delirious patient, shook his head, saying as he did so: " A vagrant! Poor fellow! you are not likely to tramp any more! " The governor continued his way along the corridor, and entered the church, taking up his post by the door, where, with frequent genuflexions, he listened devoutly to the service. Meanwhile the mutterings of the unconscious man filled the empty cell.

He did not seem old; on the contrary, he looked strong and muscular. He was delirious, apparently living the past over again, while a look of distress disfigured his face. Fate had played him a sorry trick. He had tramped thousands of miles through the Siberian forests and mountains, had suffered countless dangers and privations, always urged onward by a consuming home-sickness, and sustained by one hope—that he might live to see his native place, and be once more with his own people, if it were but for a month, or even a week. Then he would be resigned, even if he had to go back again. But it chanced that, when only a few hundred miles from his native village, he had been recaptured and confined in this prison. Suddenly his mutterings ceased. His eyes dilated, and his breathing became more even. Brighter dreams flitted across his fevered brain. The forest moans. He knows it well, that moaning; monotonous, musical, and powerful. He can distinguish its various tones; the language of each tree: the majestic pine, dusky green, rustling high overhead; the whispering cedars, the bright, merry birch, tossing its flexible branches; the trembling aspen, fluttering its timid, sensitive leaves. The free birds sing; the steam rushes across the stony chasm; and a swarm of gibbering magpies, the detectives of the forest, are soaring in the air over the path followed by the vagrant through this almost impenetrable thicket.

It seemed as if a breeze from the free forest were wafted through the prison cell. The invalid sat up and drew a long breath, gazing intently before him, while a sudden gleam of consciousness flashed into his eyes. The vagrant, the habitual fugitive, beheld before him an unaccustomed sight—an open door!

In his frame, enfeebled by disease, a powerful instinct sprang to life. His delirium either disappeared or centred itself on one idea, which, like a ray of sunlight, illumined the chaos of his thoughts. Alone, and with an open door! In a moment he was on his feet. It seemed as if the fever had left his brain, and was only perceptible in his eyes, which had a fixed and menacing expression.

Some one had just come out from the church, leaving the door ajar.

The strains of the harmonious singing, subdued by the distance, reached the ear of the vagrant, and then died away. His face softened, his eyes grew dim, and his imagination reproduced a long-cherished scene: A mild night, the whisper of the pines, their branches swaying above the old church of his native village, a throng of countrymen; the lights reflected in the river, and this same chant! He must make haste with his journey, that he may hear this at home, with his family!

All this time, in the corridor, near the church door, the governor prayed devoutly, kneeling, and touching his forehead to the ground.

Meanwhile, the young recruit paced to and fro on his beat along the prison wall, which glowed with a phosphorescent light. A broad, level field, recently freed from snow, lay before him.

A light wind rustled through the tall grass, inclining him to a sad and pensive mood.

The moon hung high above the horizon; the expression of anxiety had vanished from Faddeyef's face. He stopped by the wall, and, setting his rifle on the ground, rested his hand on the muzzle, on which he leaned his head, falling into a deep reverie. He could not yet wholly grasp the idea of his presence in this place, on this solemn Easter Eve, beside the wall, with a rifle in his hand, and opposite the vacant field. He had by no means ceased to be a peasant; many things clear to a soldier were to him incomprehensible; and he was often teased by being called " a rustic." But a short time ago he was a free man, had the care of a household, owned a field, and was at liberty to work when and where he pleased. Now, an indefinite, inexplicable fear beset his every step and movement, forcing the awkward young peasant into the groove of strict discipline. At this moment he was alone. The bleak landscape before him, and the wind, whistling through the dry grass, made him dreamy; and memories of familiar scenes passed through his mind. He seemed to see his native village! The same moon shone above it, the same breeze blew over it; he saw the lighted church, and the dark pines tossing their green heads—

Suddenly he became conscious of his present surroundings, and surprise kindled his blue eyes, as though he were questioning, " What are these—this field, this wall, and rifle? " For an instant he realised where he was, but in another moment the whistling breeze wafted him back to familiar scenes; and again the soldier dreamt, leaning on his rifle.

All at once, close beside him, appeared a head over the top of the wall, the eyes glimmering like two coals. The vagrant peered into the open field, and beyond it to the shadowy line of the distant forest; his chest expanded as he greedily inhaled the refreshing breath of " mother night." He let himself down by his hands, gently gliding along the wall.

The joyful ringing had awakened the slumbering night. The door of the prison church was opened, and the procession moved into the yard. In waves of melody the singing poured forth from the church. The soldier started, lifted his cap, and was about to make the sign of the cross, when he suddenly stopped, with his hand raised in the act of prayer, while the vagrant, having reached the ground, swiftly began to run toward the tall grass.

" Stop, pray, stop, my dear fellow! " exclaimed the soldier, in a terrified voice, as he raised his rifle. At the sight of this grey figure fleeing from pursuit, all his shapeless and terrible fears took a definite form. " Duty—responsibility! " flashed across his mind, and, raising his weapon, he aimed at the fugitive. But before pulling the trigger he pitifully shut his eyes.

Meanwhile, above the town there rose, hovering in the upper air, a harmonious and prolonged chime, marred only by the prison bell, that trembled and fluttered like a wounded bird; and from beyond the wall the sounds of the joyous chant, " Christ is risen," reached far into the field. Suddenly, above all other sounds, came the report of a rifle, followed by a faint, helpless groan, like a plaintive and dying protest. Then for a moment all was still; and only the distant echoes of the vacant field repeated with a sad murmur the last reverberation of the shot amid the silence of the terror-stricken night.

# THE OLD VERGER

### Vladimir Korolénko

It is growing dark.

The little village, sheltering under the pine forest above the distant river, is bathed in that peculiar twilight of starry spring nights when thin mists, rising from the ground, deepen the shadows in the woods and cover the open space with silvered azure smoke. . . . All is still and sad. The village is quietly dozing.

The dark outlines of the wretched huts are scarcely distinguishable; here and there a light twinkles; occasionally a gate creaks; an alert dog barks; now and again, from out the dark mass of gently rustling woods, the figures of pedestrians stand out; a horseman rides by; a cart scrapes along. The inhabitants of the forest villages are about to go to church to celebrate the Easter Festival.

The church stands on a little hill in the middle of the village; its windows are illuminated by candles; the belfry, old, high, and dark, stretches into the azure.

The staircase creaks . . . the old verger Mihaitch is mounting to the belfry tower, and soon his lantern is hanging in space, like a fallen star.

The old man finds it hard to climb the winding stairs. His old legs refuse to carry him; he, too, is worn out—dimly see the eyes. . . . . It is quite time for him to rest, but God does not send death. The old man has buried sons and grandsons, accompanied the young and the old to the grave, but himself lives on. How hard it is! Many times he has heralded the Easter Festival, so many that he has lost count of the number of times he has waited at the appointed hour in this same belfry. And God has brought him again. . . . The old man leans his elbows on the rail and looks down from the belfry. Below, the graves in the churchyard are just discernible in the darkness; the old crosses seem to guard them with their outstretched arms. Here and there, birches not yet covered with leaves, bend over them. To Mihaitch is borne aloft the fragrance of young buds; all seems enveloped in the calm stillness of eternal sleep. . . .

What will happen to him next year? Will he again mount up here under the copper bell and wake the night with resounding blows or will he lie down . . . there, in a dark corner of the church-

yard under a cross?   God knows. . . .   He is ready; in the meantime God has granted him to meet another festival.   " The Lord
be praised! "   The old lips whisper the habitual formula, and
Mihaitch looks up at the millions of bright fires in the starry
heavens, and crosses himself. . . .

" Mihaitch!   Mihaitch! " another old, quavering voice calls
from below.   The aged deacon looks up at the belfry, shading his
blinking tearful eyes with his hand, but does not see Mihaitch.
" What do you want?   Here I am," the verger replies, leaning
out of his belfry.   " Can't you see me? "
" No, I can't.   Don't you think it's time to strike up?   What
do you think? "
Both looked up at the stars.   Thousands of God's candles twinkle
down on them.   Fiery Venus is already high in the sky.   Mihaitch
ponders a moment.
" Not yet; I'll wait a little. . . .   I know when to begin."
He knows.   He needs no clock; God's stars tell him the hour. . . .
The earth and the sky, the white cloud softly floating in the azure,
the dark forest inarticulately murmuring, the lapping of the unseen
river down below—all this is familiar to him—all this is akin to
him . . . it is not in vain that he has passed his whole life here. . . .
Before him the distant past comes to life. . . .   He recollects how
he mounted to the belfry for the first time. . . .   Good God!   How
long ago that was . . . how long ago. . . .   He sees himself, a fair
little boy with sparkling eyes; the wind—not the kind that raises
the street dust, but a peculiar wind blowing high over the earth,
flapping its unseen wings—ruffling his hair. . . .   Below, far far
away, little people were walking to and fro . . . the village houses
looked so small, too, and the woods had receded into the distance.
The round glade on which stood the village had seemed so big
as to be almost limitless.   " Ah, there it is!   All there! " smiles
the grey old man looking out at the small glade.
" Such is life! . . .   In youth you see no end to it. . . .   Ah,
there it is! "   He sees it vividly, from the beginning to the very
grave he has chosen for himself in the churchyard. . . .   Well . . .
God be praised. . . .   It is not time for rest yet. . . .   The weary
road has been trodden honestly and the moist earth is his mother.
. . . Soon, oh soon!

However, it is now time.   Looking up at the stars, Mihaitch
straightens himself, takes up his hat, crosses himself, and collects
the bell ropes. . . .   In a moment the night air vibrates with the
resounding stroke . . . another . . . a third . . . a fourth . . . one
after another flow the slow, powerful melodious notes, filling the
expectant night
The ringing ceases, and in the church the service begins.   In

former years Mihaitch always went down and stood in a corner by the door to pray and listen to the singing, but now he stays up above. It is hard for him—and besides, he feels a kind of weariness. He sits down on the bench and, listening to the dying vibrations of the copper bell, becomes lost in thought. Of what is he thinking? He himself could not say. The belfry tower is lit up faintly by his lantern; the deep resounding bell is merged into the darkness. Below, from the church, a faint sound of singing can occasionally be heard; the night wind stirs the bell-ropes. . . .

The old man lowers his grey head on to his breast. Disconnected pictures float before him. They are singing the " Tropar," he thinks, and sees himself also in the church. There are many young voices in the choir; the old priest, gentle Father Naum, intones the prayers in a trembling voice. Hundreds of peasants' heads bow repeatedly like ears of corn before the wind . . . the peasants cross themselves . . . all familiar faces and yet there are dead. . . . Where is it, this happiness? . . . The aged brain quickens, like the final flicker of a dying fire; his thought glides in bright, swift rays lighting up all the by-paths of his past life . . . unbearable labour, sorrow, care . . . Where is it, this happiness? The heavy burden bends the powerful back, wrinkles the young face, and teaches how to sigh. . . .

He seems to see his sweetheart, standing, with humbly bent head, to the left among the village women. She was a good woman. . . . Peace be to her soul! and she had suffered much sorrow and pain. . . . Want and work, continual womanly sorrow, withers a woman's beauty and dims her eyes; a constant expression of dull fear of the unexpected blows of life is visible midst her immense beauty. . . . Where is her happiness? . . . Only one son remained to them—their hope and joy, and he had suffered human injustice. . . .

Here he was, his cup overflowing with sorrow, pressing down the earth on her grave, watering it with his bitter orphan's tears; quickly he crosses himself and bows his head in the dust. . . . Mihaitch's heart overflows in the clearness of his memories, and the dark images of the ikons look down austerely from the walls on human sorrow and human injustice. . . It has all gone. . . . It is all in the past. . . . And now the whole world for him is centred in this dark tower where the wind blows in the darkness stirring the bell-ropes. . . . " God will judge you. . . . God will judge," whispers the old man, lowering his grey head; and the tears course softly down his cheeks. . . .

" Mihaitch! Mihaitch! Have you gone to sleep? " they call from below.

" What? " he asks, quickly jumping to his feet. " Lord, I have been asleep. What a disgrace! " . . . With unusually quick movements he gathers together the ropes. Below, the peasants are moving about, like a colony of ants. The choir, sparkling in their golden gowns, are filling the air with song. They have passed the cross near the church, and to Mihaitch is borne the joyful cry " Christ is risen from the dead! " The call penetrates the old man's heart like a wave . . . and it seems to him that the tall candles burn brighter in the darkness; the crowd is more excited; the choir sings louder. The wind seizes the waves of sound and lifts it on high, mingling it with the loud, triumphant bells. . . .

Never before has old Mihaitch rung as he does now. The old overflowing heart seems to have entered the inanimate copper, and the bells seem to sing, laugh, and cry; they form a wonderful crown of sound carried on high to the starry heavens. The stars shine brighter, and the trembling sounds mingle together and fall to earth again in loving embrace. . . . The big bass calls loudly, drowning the earth with its powerful tones: " Christ is risen! "

The two tenors, trembling with the alternate strokes of the iron clappers, ring out joyfully: " Christ is risen! " The small bells, as though in a hurry not to be left behind, chime in between the larger ones and sing after them like little children: " Christ is risen! " The old belfry seems itself to vibrate, and the wind, fanning the old verger's face, flutters its wings and repeats: " Christ is risen! "

The weary heart forgets about life so full of sorrow and care . . . the old verger forgets that life for him means only the cramped belfry tower, that he is alone in the world like an old tree beaten down by rough weather. . . . He listens to the sounds as they cry and sing, rising to the sky and falling to the pale earth, and it seems to him that he is surrounded by sons and grandsons, that their voices, young and old, mingle in one chorus, and sing to him of the joy and happiness that he has never seen. . . . He pulls at the ropes and the tears flow down his cheeks and his heart beats with the illusion of happiness. . . .

And below people listen and say to one another that never before has Mihaitch rung so beautifully. . . . Suddenly the big bell vibrates uncertainly, then ceases. The accompanying bells, confused, trill out in an unusual peal and break off as though listening to the long sad note that, trembling and crying, gradually dies away in the air. . . .

The old verger drops helplessly on to the bench, and two last tears roll gently down his cheeks.

" Hi, send for a relief, the old verger has finished his task! "

# VSEVOLOD M. GARSHIN
1855–1888

# THE RED FLOWER

*(In memory of Ivan Sergaevitch Turgeniev)*

## I

" In the name of His Imperial Majesty, His Highness the Emperor
Peter the First, I proclaim a revision of the whole madhouse! "

These words were uttered in a loud, harsh voice. The hospital
clerk entering the invalid's name in a large shabby book at a table
covered with ink, could not repress a smile. But the two young men
who accompanied the invalid did not smile; they could scarcely
stand after two sleepless days and nights alone with the madman
whom they had just brought by rail. At the station before the last,
the fit of madness had increased; a strait-waistcoat had been procured and put on the patient with the aid of the conductor and
some gendarmes. Thus he reached the town and thus he had been
brought to the hospital.

He had a terrible appearance! Over the grey garments that he
had torn to shreds during his fit, a broad cut jacket of coarse sail-
cloth was stretched across his waist; the long sleeves kept his arms
crossed over his chest and were tied behind. The swollen, wide-
open eyes (he had not slept for ten days) burnt with a bright unwavering blaze; a nervous shuddering caused the corner of his lower
lips to tremble; the tangled curly hair fell crookedly over his forehead; with quick heavy tread he paced the office from corner to
corner, glancing inquisitively at the old shelves filled with books
and papers and the chairs covered with American cloth, and from
time to time looked at his companions.

" Take him to the section on the right."

" I know, I know. I was here with you last year. We looked
over the hospital. I know everything; it will be difficult to deceive
me," the invalid said.

He turned to the door. The warder opened it for him; with the
same quick resolute tread he walked out of the office, his insane
head raised, and almost at a run, went to the right to the division
for the mentally deranged. His companions could scarcely keep
up with him.

" Ring the bell, I cannot; you have bound my hands."

The porter opened the door and the travellers entered the hospital. It was a large stone building of an old Government type. Two large rooms, one a dining-room, the other a general sitting-room for the quieter invalids, a broad corridor with glass doors leading out into the garden, with a flower-bed and about twenty separate rooms where the invalids lived—this composed the first floor; here also there were two dark rooms, one padded, the other lined with boards, where they put the restive inmates, and a large gloomy vaulted room that was the bathroom. The upper floor was occupied by the women, whence came discordant sounds, broken by yawns and groans. The hospital was built for eighty inmates, but as it served several surrounding counties, it actually contained about three hundred. In the small rooms there were as many as four or five beds. In winter, when the patients were not allowed out and all the iron-barred windows were tightly shut, it was unbearably stuffy in the hospital.

The new patient was taken to the bathroom. Even on a healthy man this room would have produced a great impression, but on an unhinged, excited imagination the impression was greater still. It was a large vaulted room with a stone floor, lighted by one corner window. The walls and vaults were painted dark green, and in the dirty black floor were sunk two stone baths filled with water. A huge copper stove, with a cylindrical boiler for heating the water, and a whole system of copper pipes and taps occupied the corner facing the window. To an unhinged mind all this must have created an unusually gloomy, fantastic atmosphere, and the warder in charge of the bathroom, a stout, silent southern, with a gloomy countenance, increased the impression.

And when the invalid was led into this terrible room to be bathed, and, in accordance with the principal doctor's system of cure, to have a fly-blister put on the back of his neck, terror and anger took possession of him. Absurd thoughts, each more wonderful than the preceding, flew through his brain. " What is this? The Inquisition? The place of secret punishment where his enemies had decided to make an end of him? Perhaps it was hell itself? " At last it entered his head that he was being tried in some way. He was undressed despite his desperate resistance. With the increased strength of his madness, he easily tore himself from the hands of the few warders, so that they fell on the floor; at last, four of them knocked him down and, seizing him by hands and legs, put him into the warm water. It seemed boiling hot to him, and there flashed through his disordered brain a disconnected, fragmentary thought of trial by boiling water and molten iron. Held firmly by the warders, he kicked feverishly with legs and hands, panted, gulped down the water, and shouted out disconnected words impossible to imagine unless one had heard them. There were prayers and curses. He screamed as long as his strength lasted, and at last, with hot tears flowing down his cheeks, he softly uttered a sentence that had no connection with his former words:

" Holy martyr Giorgi! Into thy hands I deliver my body, but my soul—never, oh, never! "

The warders still held him, though he had calmed down. The warm bath and bladder of ice on his head had performed their task. But when they took him out of the bath, almost unconscious, and placed him on the tabouret to put the blister on him, mad thoughts came back, and his remaining strength broke out.

" Why? What for? " he shouted. " I have never wished harm to any one. Why do you want to kill me? O-o-oh! oh, God! Oh, ye martyrs who died before me, save me, I pray! " . . .

The hot contact at the back of his neck caused him to struggle desperately. The warders could not manage him, and did not know what to do. " We can't do anything," said the soldier performing the operation. " We must rub."

These simple words made the patient shudder. " Rub . . . Rub what? Rub whom? Me? " he thought, and in deadly terror shut his eyes. The soldier took up a rough towel by both ends, and rubbing firmly, passed it quickly over the back of his neck, tearing off the blister and the upper skin, and leaving a bare, raw place. The pain of this operation, unbearable even to a calm, healthy man, seemed the end of everything to the patient. With a desperate movement of his whole body he tore himself out of his warder's hands, and his naked body rolled down the stone slab. He thought they had cut off his head. He wanted to cry out, but could not. He was carried out on a stretcher in an unconscious state that gave place to a deep, dead long sleep.

II

He awoke in the night. All was quiet; from the adjoining large room could be heard the breathing of the sleeping patients. Somewhere in the distance, a patient who had been in the dark room for the night was talking to himself in a monotone; upstairs, in the women's quarters, a hoarse contralto was singing some wild song. The patient listened to all these sounds. He felt a terrible exhaustion and weakness in all his limbs; his neck hurt frightfully.

" Where am I? What is the matter with me? " flashed through his brain. And suddenly, with unusual clearness, he saw the last month of his life, and he understood that he was ill and what his illness was. He recollected the crowds of absurd thoughts and acts, and it made him shudder. " But it is all over now, thank God, all over! " he whispered, and dropped off to sleep again.

The open window behind the iron bars looked out into a narrow lane between the tall buildings and a stone wall; no one ever used

this lane, and it was thickly overgrown with wild bushes and lilac
which, just then, were in full bloom. . . . Behind the bushes, right
in front of the window, was a dark, high wall; the tops of the trees
in the large garden, bathed in moonlight, peeped over it. On the
right there towered the white hospital edifice with its iron-barred
windows lit up from within; to the left, the white moonlit dead
wall of the mortuary. The rays of the moon streamed through
the iron bars of the window on to the floor in the middle of the
room, and lit up part of the bed and the pale, worn face of the
patient, who lay with eyes closed; now there was nothing mad
about him. He slept the deep, dreamless sleep of an exhausted
man, without movement, almost without breathing. At intervals
he would wake in full possession of his senses, as though perfectly
well, but in the morning he was the same madman.

### III

" How do you feel? " the doctor asked him on the following
day.

The patient, who had only just awakened, was lying under the
bed-clothes.

" Splendid! " he replied, jumping up and putting on his slippers
and dressing-gown. " Splendid! except for this! "

He pointed to the back of his neck.

" I cannot turn my head without pain, but that is nothing.
Everything is well if you only understand it, and I do understand."

" Do you know where you are? "

" Of course, doctor! I'm in the madhouse. But if you understand, it makes no difference, none whatever."

The doctor looked fixedly into his eyes. His handsome nurtured
face, with the well-kempt golden beard and calm blue eyes gazing
out of gold spectacles, was motionless and impenetrable. The
patient went on:

" Why do you look at me so intently? You cannot read what
is in my soul, but I can read clearly what is in yours! Why will
you do harm? Why have you gathered together this crowd of
unfortunate beings and keep them here? To me it doesn't matter,
I understand and am calm, but they? Why these tortures? To
a man who has reached the state when he has a great idea in his
brain, a universal idea, it makes no difference where he lives or
what he feels. Even life and death are of no consequence . . .
isn't that so? "

" Perhaps," the doctor replied, sitting down in a chair in the
corner of the room so as to get a good view of the patient, who
was pacing the room quickly from corner to corner, shuffling his
large horse-skin slippers and waving the skirts of his dressing-gown
made of some cotton material with broad red stripes and large

flowers. The assistant surgeon and the inspector who accompanied the doctor continued standing by the door.

" And I have it! " the patient exclaimed. " When I discovered it, I felt myself reborn. Feelings grew more intense, the brain worked as never before. What I had reached before after much theory and speculation I now know intuitively. I have, in fact, reached what has been arrived at philosophically. I experience in myself the great idea that space and time are illusions. I live in every age. I live without space, everywhere or nowhere as you please. For that reason it is all the same to me whether you keep me here or let me go, whether I am free or bound. I noticed a few others like me here, but for the rest their position is terrible. Why don't you let them go free? To whom is it necessary? . . ."

" You say," the doctor interrupted, " that you live outside space and time. However, you cannot but admit that you and I are in this room, and that at present "—the doctor pulled out his watch— " it is half-past ten, May the 6th, 18—. What do you say to that? "

" Nothing. It is all one to me where I am and when I live. And if it is all the same to me, doesn't that mean that I am everywhere and at all times? "

The doctor smiled.

" An unusual logic," he said, rising. " However, you are right. Good-bye. Wouldn't you like a cigar? "

" Thank you." The patient stopped, took a cigar, and nervously bit the end off. " This helps thought," he said. " This is the world in miniature. At one end is alkali; at the other, acid. So, in the universe, opposing causes are balanced and neutralised. Good-bye, doctor."

The doctor went on farther. The majority of the patients were waiting for him, stretched out in their hammocks. No chiefs are ever accorded such respect from their subordinates as a mental specialist gets from his patients.

The lunatic, left alone, continued jerkily pacing his room from corner to corner. They brought him tea, and, without sitting down, he drank off, at one gulp, a large mugful and almost in an instant ate a large piece of white bread. Then he went out of the room, and for several hours on end paced, with his quick, heavy tread, from one end of the building to the other. It was a rainy day, and the patients were not allowed out into the garden. When the assistant surgeon came to look for the new patient, they pointed him out at the end of the corridor. He was standing and gazing fixedly at a flower-bed through the glass door that led out into the garden. His attention was taken by a flower of an unusually bright, ruby shade, a kind of poppy.

" Will you please come and be weighed? " the assistant surgeon said, touching him on the arm, and when the patient turned towards him the surgeon nearly dropped with fright, so much wild anger and hatred burned in those mad eyes. But, catching sight of the surgeon, the patient immediately changed the expression on his face and followed obediently, without a word, as though deep in thought. They went into the doctor's study, and the patient got on to the small weighing machine of his own accord; the assistant surgeon, after weighing him, entered his weight—109 pounds—against his name in a book. On the following day it was 107, and on the third day 106.

" If he goes on like that, he will not last long," the doctor said, and ordered him to be fed as well as possible. Yet, notwith-standing the patient's tremendous appetite, he grew thinner every day, and every day the number of pounds entered by the assistant surgeon diminished. The patient scarcely slept, and passed whole days in constant movement.

### IV

He knew that he was in a madhouse; he knew even that he was ill. Sometimes, as on the first night, he would awake amid the stillness, after a day of impetuous movement, aching in every limb, and with a terrible heaviness in his head, but fully conscious. It may be that the absence of impressions in the stillness of the night, the slow working of the brain on first waking up, caused him in such moments to understand his position and regain his normal state. But the day arrived; together with the light and the awakening life of the hospital, waves of impressions that his dis-ordered mind could not cope with swept over him, and he was again mad. His condition was a strange mixture of perfect judgment and absurdities. He knew that he was surrounded by invalids, yet at the same time, in every one of them he saw some mysterious person who was hiding or being hidden, whom he had known or of whom he had read. The hospital was inhabited by people of all ages and all countries. There were the living and the dead, the famous and mighty ones of the world, the soldiers killed in the last war but resurrected. He imagined himself in some enchanted magic circle, where all the powers of the world were gathered together, and with a divine ecstasy imagined himself the centre of the circle. All his comrades were gathered together in order to accomplish the task that appeared to him vaguely as a gigantic undertaking to destroy evil on earth. He did not know in what it consisted, but felt himself strong enough to accomplish it. He could read the thoughts of others, and see in things their whole history; the large elms in the hospital garden told him whole legends of the past, the building, that really was fairly old, he imagined had been built by Peter the Great, and was convinced that the Tsar had lived in it at the time of the battle of Poltava. He read this in the walls, in the crumbling plaster, in the bits of brick and tile he found in the garden. He peopled the little mortuary with multitudes of people long dead, and peered intently through the window of its cellar that looked out on the garden, seeing in the light, unevenly reflected through the dirty coloured glass, familiar features that he had seen somewhere, in real life or in portraits.

Meanwhile, fine clear weather set in and the patients spent whole days out in the fresh air in the garden. Their portion of the garden, though not large, was thickly overgrown with trees, and planted with flowers wherever possible. The inspector made all those who were capable of it do some work in the garden. For whole days they shoaled and scattered the paths with gravel, trimmed and watered the beds and flowers, tended the cucumbers, pumpkins, and melons, planted with their own hands. The corner of the garden had several thick cherry trees, farther on there stretched an avenue of elms, and in the middle, on an artificial mound, was the most beautiful flower-bed in the whole garden. Bright flowers grew round the border of this bed, and in the centre was a patch of large rare dahlias, yellow ones with red spots. The whole garden spread out round this bed, and one could see that many patients attached some mysterious significance to it. In the garden were all the flowers met with in Little Russia—tall roses, bright petunias, tall tobacco plants with their small pink blossoms, mint, amaranth, geraniums, and poppies. Here, too, not far from the porch, grew some poppies of a particular kind. They were smaller than the usual and were distinguished by their extraordinarily bright ruby colour. This was the flower that had attracted the patient's attention when he had looked out on the garden through the glass doors on the day after his entrance into the hospital.

On going out into the garden for the first time, the first thing he did, before ever leaving the porch, was to stare fixedly at the bright flowers. There were only two of them, and as it happened they grew away from the others in an uncultivated patch, and were surrounded by thick tall grass and goose-foot.

The patients came out of the door one after another, while a warder handed each a thick white knitted cotton cap with a red cross on the front. These had come from the wars and had been bought at an auction, but the invalids, of course, attached a mysterious significance to the red cross. The patient took off his cap, looked at the cross and then at the flowers. The latter were brighter. " It is triumphant," he said, " but we will see."

And he came out of the porch. Looking round and not seeing the warder who stood behind him, he stepped over the border and stretched out his hand to the flower but could not decide to pluck it. In his extended hand he felt a stinging fire that spread over his whole body, as though waves of some unknown power emanated from the red petals and penetrated through him. He moved nearer, and putting out his hand, almost touched the flower, but the flower, so it seemed to him, defended itself by exhaling a most deadly poisonous vapour. His head was in a whirl and he made a last desperate effort to seize the stalk when suddenly a heavy hand was laid on his shoulder. It was the warder who had seized him.

" You mustn't pluck the flowers," the old southerner said, " and you mustn't walk on the border. There are many of you madmen here, and if each of you took a flower there would be nothing left of the garden." And he held him firmly by the shoulder.

The patient looked into his face, silently freed himself from the hand, and walked down the path in a state of excitement.

" Oh, unfortunate ones! " he thought. " You do not see, you are so blind that you even defend it. We will measure our strength, if not to-day, then to-morrow. And if I perish, what difference does it make? "

He walked about the garden until the evening, making acquaintances and carrying on strange conversations, in which each person he happened to be talking to heard only the answer to his own mad thoughts, expressed absurdly in mysterious words. The patient walked about, first with one comrade, then with another, and at the end of the day was more than ever convinced that " everything was ready," as he said to himself. Soon, soon, the iron bars would fall and all these exiles would go from this place and hurry away to the ends of the earth, and then the whole world would tremble, throw off its worn crust, and appear in a new wonderful beauty. He had almost forgotten about the flower, but just as he was leaving the garden and going up the steps to the door, he again caught sight of those two red sparks among the darkening grass that was already covered with dew. Then he receded from the crowd, stood behind the warder, and waited for a propitious moment. No one saw him jump over the border, pluck the flower and hide it in his bosom under his shirt. When the fresh dewy leaves came into contact with his body, he turned as pale as death, and opened his eyes wide in horror; a cold perspiration bathed his forehead.

In the hospital the lamps were lit and most of the patients lay on their beds waiting for supper, while a few restless ones hastily paced the rooms and corridors. Among these was the patient with the flower. He walked about feverishly, pressing his hands over his breast. It seemed as though he wished to crush the hidden flower. When meeting any of the others, he walked far away from them, fearing even to touch them with the hem of his garments. " Don't come near me! Don't come near me! " he cried, but in the hospital no one took any notice of such exclamations! He walked quicker and quicker, his strides grew longer and longer; for a whole hour he walked in a kind of fury.

" I will harass you! I will strangle you! " he said deeply and viciously, and occasionally he ground his teeth.

Supper was served in the dining-room. On the large bare tables they placed big painted and gilt wooden bowls containing wheaten porridge. The patients sat down on the benches, and were given a hunk of black bread. Eight of them ate out of each bowl with wooden spoons. The few who were privileged to a better diet were fed separately. Our invalid, quickly swallowing his portion given him by the warder who had called him to his room for that purpose, was not contented with it, and went into the general dining-room.

" Can I sit down here? " he asked the inspector.

" Haven't you had any supper? " the inspector asked, pouring some more porridge into a bowl.

" I am very hungry, and I must gain strength. I depend entirely on food. I do not sleep at all, as you know."

" Have some more then, my friend. Taras, give him a spoon and some bread."

He sat down by one of the bowls and ate a large portion of porridge.

" Enough, enough," the inspector remonstrated at last, when every one had finished supper and our patient was still ladling porridge out of the bowl with one hand, holding the other firmly over his breast. " You will over-eat yourself."

" Ah, if you only knew how much strength I need, how much strength! Good-bye, Nikolai Nikolaevitch," the invalid said, rising from the table and pressing the inspector's hand. " Good-bye."

" Where are you going? " the inspector asked with a smile.

" I? Nowhere. I am staying here, but to-morrow, perhaps, we shall not see each other. Thank you for your kindness," and once again he pressed the inspector's hand. His voice trembled, and tears started to his eyes.

" Calm yourself, my friend, calm yourself," the inspector said. " Why these gloomy thoughts? Go to bed and have a good sleep. You should sleep more. If you slept well, you would soon get better."

The patient sobbed. The inspector turned to order the warders to clear the tables. Half an hour later, every one in the hospital was asleep except one man, who lay fully dressed on his bed in the corner room. He was trembling as in a fever, and beating his breast convulsively, smothered, as he thought, in an odourless, deadly poison.

## V

He did not sleep the whole night. He had plucked the flower because it seemed to him he was bound to do it. At his first glance through the doors the red petals had attracted his attention, and he imagined that he had, at that moment, realised his mission on this earth. In this bright red flower was gathered together all the evil in the world. He knew that opium was made from poppies, and it may be that this thought, spreading and taking on a monstrous form, made him create this terribly fantastic illusion. The flower embodied all evil to him; it had drunk all the innocent blood that had ever been spilt in the earth—that was why it was so red—all the tears and all the sorrows of mankind. It was a mysterious, terrible being, Antichrist, that had assumed this humble, innocent form. It had to be torn up and crushed. But that was not sufficient. The evil must not be allowed to escape again into the earth. That was why he had hidden it in his bosom. He hoped that the flower would have lost its strength by the morning. The evil in it would penetrate into his breast, into his soul, and there be either conquered or conqueror, in which latter case he would die; but he would die like a gallant soldier, the supreme warrior of mankind, because, until now, no one had dared to engage all the evil of mankind in single combat.

"They did not see it, but I did. Can I let it live? Better that I should die." And he lay there, growing feebler in his illusory battle, ever growing feebler. In the morning the assistant surgeon found him scarcely alive. But in spite of this, in a little while his animation came back, he jumped out of bed and, as before, ran about the hospital talking to the other patients and to himself louder and more disconnectedly than ever. He was not allowed out into the garden, and the doctor, seeing that he kept on losing weight, did not sleep, and walked about incessantly, ordered a hypodermic injection of morphia. The patient did not resist—fortunately his mad thoughts of the moment favoured the injection. He soon went to sleep and the furious movement ceased, the sound of his own loud jerky footsteps vanished from his ears. He forgot himself and ceased to think of anything, even of the second flower that had to be plucked.

However, about three days later he plucked it before the very eyes of the warder, who was too late to stop him. The warder tried to catch him, but with a loud, triumphant yell the patient tore into the hospital, up to his room, and hid the flower in his bosom.

"Why do you pluck the flowers?" the warder asked, running into the room. But the patient, who was already lying on his bed in his usual pose—hands crossed over his breast—began to talk such nonsense that the warder merely took off the white cap with the red cross that the other had forgotten in his haste, and silently left the room. The illusory battle began again. The patient felt the evil oozing out of the flower in snaky crawling streams. They enveloped and oppressed him, crushed his limbs and filled his body with their terrible contents. He wept and prayed to God

in the intervals between cursing his enemy.  Towards evening the
flower was quite withered.  He crushed the withered flower under
foot and, picking up the pieces, took them into the bathroom.
Throwing them into the red-hot stove, he stood watching his enemy
frizzle and shrivel up until nothing was left but tender white ash.
He blew at this and it vanished.

On the following day the patient was worse.  Terribly pale, with
sunken cheeks and sunken blazing eyes, he continued his mad walk
from end to end of the hospital.  His gait was uncertain, he often
stumbled, but he kept on talking, talking without end.

" I would rather not use force," the older doctor said to his
assistant.

" But it is absolutely necessary to stop this activity.  He only
weighed ninety-three pounds to-day.  If it goes on like that any
longer, he will be dead in a couple of days."  The older doctor grew
thoughtful.  " Morphia?  Chloral? " he said half-interrogatively.

" Yesterday the morphia had no effect on him."

" Very well, tell them to bind him.  However, I doubt whether
he will recover."

## VI

And the patient was bound.  He lay on his bed in a strait-
waistcoat, firmly bound with broad linen bands to the folding iron
bedstead.  But the mad desire for movement had not ceased; it
had, if anything increased.  For several hours he tried obstinately
to free himself from his fetters.  At last, with a tremendous effort,
he managed to tear one of the bands, freed his legs, and, wriggling
off the bed, began pacing the room with bound hands, shouting out
wild, incomprehensible words.

" Damn you! " the warder exclaimed as he entered the room.
" Gretsko!  Ivan!  Help!  Quickly!  He's unbound himself! "

The three attacked the patient, and a long struggle ensued, a
struggle tiring for the attackers and painful for the man defending
himself and losing the remainder of his strength.  At last he was
thrown on the bed and bound tighter than before.

" You do not understand what you are doing! " he cried,
gasping.  " You will perish!  I have seen a third just coming up.
Now it is out.  Let me finish my task!  I must kill it, kill it, kill
it!  Then all will be finished, all saved.  I would send one of you,
but only I can do it.  You would die from the very contact! "

" Be quiet, sir, be quiet! " said the old warder who had remained to keep guard by the bed.

The patient suddenly quietened.  He had decided to deceive
the warders.  They kept him bound all day, and left him in that
position for the night.  After giving him his supper, the warder
made a bed for himself near the patient, and lay down.  In a

minute or two he was sound asleep and the patient began his work. He doubled up his whole body in order to reach the iron bar at the foot of his bed, and touching it with his wrists, beneath the strait-waistcoat, began to rub the sleeves against the irons, quickly and firmly. In a little while the sailcloth gave way and he put out his forefinger. Then the work went much faster. With an adroitness and litheness impossible in a normal man he untied the knot behind him that held the sleeves, unlaced the strait-waistcoat, and after this for a long time listened to the warder's snoring. But the old man slept soundly. The patient took off the waistcoat and unbound himself from the bed. Now he was free. He tried the door; it was locked from within, and the key was probably in the warder's pocket. Fearing to wake the warder, he decided not to hunt in his pockets, but to get out of the room through the window.

The window was open; it was a still, warm, dark night, and the stars shone in the black sky. He gazed up at them, distinguishing the familiar constellations, and rejoicing that they sympathised with him, as it seemed to him. Blinking, he saw the multitude of rays they sent him, and his mad resolution grew firmer. He had to bend the thick iron bars, climb out through the window into the lane overgrown with bushes, and climb over a high wall. Then there would be the last struggle, and afterwards—perhaps death.

He tried to bend a bar with his bare hands, but the iron did not yield. Then, twisting the strong sleeves of his strait-waistcoat into a cord, he put it round the bar and hung on with all his weight. After desperate efforts that used up nearly all his remaining strength, the bar gave way and a narrow opening was made. He squeezed through it, grazing his elbows, shoulders, and bare knees, wound his way among the bushes, and stopped before the stone wall. All was still; the night lights shone faintly out of the windows of the large building, but no one could be seen within. No one had noticed him; the old man guarding his bed was probably in a deep sleep. The stars twinkled, sending their rays into his very heart.

"I am coming to you," he whispered, looking up at the sky.

Tearing himself at the first attempt, with broken nails, bleeding hands and knees, he began to look for a more suitable spot. There, where the wall joined the wall of the mortuary, a few bricks had fallen out. The patient felt these hollows and made use of them. He climbed on to the wall, caught hold of the branch of an elm that grew on the other side, and quietly got down to the ground from the tree.

He set off quickly for the familiar spot near the porch. The dark head of the flower, its petals folded, could be seen clearly on the dewy grass. "The last!" he whispered. "The last! To-day it is victory or death. But it is all the same to me. Wait," he said, glancing up at the sky. "I shall soon be with you."

He plucked the flower, squeezed and crushed it, and holding it

141*

in his hand, returned to his room by the way he had come. The old man was still asleep. The patient hardly reached his bed before he dropped down on it, unconscious.

In the morning he was found dead. His face was calm and serene; the worn features, the thin lips and sunken closed eyes, expressed a kind of proud happiness. When he was laid on a stretcher, they tried to open his hand and take out the red flower, but the hand was rigid, and he carried his trophy to the grave.

# FOUR DAYS

### VSEVOLOD M. GARSHIN

I REMEMBER how we ran about the wood amid the whistling of the bullets, how the branches crashed and fell as they were struck, how we fought through the hawthorn bushes.

The bullets came faster. Through the edge of the wood in many places there was a glimpse of something red. Siderov, a little soldier of the first company ('' How did you get in with our gang? '' flashed through my mind), suddenly sat down on the ground and looked at me with large frightened eyes. A stream of blood flowed from his mouth.

Yes, I remember that well. I remember too how, almost at the edge of the wood among some thick bushes, I came across *him*. He was a big fat Turk, but I went straight at him though I was small and weak. There was a bang; some large thing, as it seemed to me, flashed past; there was a ringing in my ears.

'' He has fired at me,'' I thought. At the same moment, with a cry of horror he backed against a thick clump of hawthorns. He could have got round the clump, but in his terror he forgot everything and scrambled among the prickly branches. With one blow I knocked the gun out of his hand, with another I drove home my bayonet.

There was a cry, a groan, and I ran on farther.

Our men were shouting '' Hurrah! '' Some were falling, others were firing. I remember how I too fired several shots when we got out of the wood into the open fields. Suddenly the hurrahs grew louder and we all moved forward. That is to say, our men moved forward, for I remained behind. It seemed so strange to me. And stranger still when suddenly everything vanished, the shouting and the firing ceased. I did not hear anything; I could only see something blue. It must have been the sky. A moment later even that vanished.

I had never found myself in such a strange position before. I must have been lying face downwards, for as I gazed about I could see little pieces of earth. A few blades of grass with ants crawling from one to another just below my head, a few wisps of hay left over from last year, that was the extent of my world. And I could only see out of one eye, for the other was shut down tightly by something hard, the dead twig, no doubt, on which my head was resting.

I was very uncomfortable and could not understand why it was that I was unable to move. And so the hours went by. The only sounds I could hear were the chirp of the grasshopper and the humming of the bee.

At last I made a terrific effort, pulled out my right arm, on which I had been lying, and, resting on both hands, I tried to raise myself on to my knees.

A pain as sharp and quick as lightning flashed through my body from my knees upwards, and I fell down again.

Once more there was darkness—nothingness.

I awoke. Why do I see the stars which shine so brightly in the dark blue Bulgarian sky? Am I not in camp? Why did I come out of the tent? I try to move and feel a horrible pain in my legs.

I must have been wounded on the battlefield. Badly, I wonder? I felt my legs at the place where they hurt; both were covered with congealed blood. When I touched them the pain grew worse. It was a pain like incessant toothache, gnawing at one's very soul.

There was a ringing in my ears; my head felt heavy. In a vague kind of way I seemed to know that I was wounded in both legs. How is it? Why did they not pick me up? I wonder if the Turks beat us? Gradually at first, and then more clearly, until I came to the conclusion that it must have been the Turks who were beaten. We could not have been beaten, for I fell (of course I had no distinct recollection of falling; I only remembered how the others ran ahead and I could not run, but stayed behind with something blue before my eyes) in the open field on the top of the little hill, the very place our little commander had pointed out to us.

" We must get there, boys," he had shouted in his ringing voice, and we had got there, which proves that we were not beaten.

Why didn't they pick me up? In an open field like this they could easily have seen me. I wonder if there are any others here? The bullets were so thick. I must turn my head and look around. I could move my head more easily now; I must have fallen over on my back after my first attempt to raise myself on to my knees. That was why I could see the stars.

I tried to sit up, a difficult thing to do with two wounded legs. I had almost given up the attempt in despair when at last, after an excruciating twinge that brought the tears to my eyes, I succeeded and sat up.

Overhead was the dark blue sky. A large star and several smaller ones were twinkling round some tall dark object. It was a clump of bushes. I was among bushes and had been overlooked! My hair stood on end. But how did I manage to get among the bushes when I had fallen in the open field? I must have crawled in here myself. How strange I should have been able to get so far when now I can scarcely move. Perhaps I was only wounded in one leg then, and a stray bullet found me here.

A pale rosy light came over the sky. The large star grew fainter, several smaller ones disappeared. The moon rose. How nice it would be to be at home!

A strange weird sound reached me as of some one moaning. Yes, it was moaning. I wonder if there is some one else lying near by with wounded legs, or perhaps with a bullet in his stomach? The sound seemed quite close and yet there was no one near me.

My God! it was I that was moaning! Softly, plaintively! Is the pain really so bad? It must be, but I do not feel it because my head is dazed and as heavy as lead. I had better lie down and sleep—sleep . . . only shall I ever wake up again? What does it matter, though?

Just as I was about to lie down again, a broad streak of moonlight lit up the place where I was lying, and I caught sight of some large dark object lying a few paces away. Another wounded man. Various objects on him flashed in the moonlight; it might have been the buttons on his uniform or his arms. Was it a corpse, I wonder!

All the same, I will lie down. . . .

It is impossible! our men could not have gone. They are here. They have beaten the Turks and are occupying this position. But why is there no sound of talking, no crackling of twigs? I suppose I am too weak to hear them, but they must be here? "Help! Help!"

Wild senseless cries escape me, but there is no answer. They resound strangely in the night air. All else is still. Only the crickets keep up their incessant chirping. The moon looks down on me sadly with her big round face.

If the man over there had been alive, my cries would have awakened him. He must be dead. I wonder if he is one of our men or a Turk? My God, what difference does it make? And sleep once more descended upon my swollen eyelids.

I lay still with my eyes closed though I had been awake for a long time. I did not want to open them because I felt the strong sunlight through my closed eyelids and was afraid my eyes would not stand the glare. Besides, it was better not to make a movement of any kind.

Yesterday (was it yesterday?) I was wounded. A day has gone by; others will go by and I shall die. It does not matter! It is better not to move! I will lie here quietly. If only I could stop my brain from working, but thoughts and recollections will come crowding in one after another. However, this will not continue for long; the end will soon come. There will be a few lines in the papers to say that our losses were insignificant; so many wounded, and killed a private volunteer of the name of Ivanov. No, they will not remember my name, but simply say "One killed, one private," like that little dog! . . . The incident suddenly flashed through my mind. It happened a long time ago. However, the whole of my life, everything that had taken place before I found myself lying here, seemed long ago. I was walking along the street when I came across a crowd of people who stood surrounding a little white object covered with blood that was whining piteously. It was a pretty little dog that had been run over by a tramcar. The dog had died, just as I shall die. A porter who was holding forth to the crowd took the little dog by the scruff of the neck and carried it away. The crowd dispersed.

Will some one come and carry me away? No, I shall lie here and die. How nice it is to be alive. . . . How happy I was that day when the little dog was run over. I remember how I walked along in a state of rapture. What torture it is to think of these things now! Former joy is present pain. . . .

The pain and torture are bad enough without these recollections that cause despair. Despair is worse than any wound.

It was getting hot. The sun was scorching. I opened my eyes and saw the same bushes, the same sky, only this time I saw them by the daylight.

And there is my neighbour. Yes, it is a Turk—a dead Turk. How huge he is! I seem to recognise him. It is the same . . . Near me lay a man whom I had killed. Why had I killed him? He is lying there dead, covered with blood. Why did fate bring him here? Who was he? Perhaps, like me, he too had an old mother. For how long will she sit by the door of her wretched hut and look towards the north, watching for the return of her beloved son, her supporter and bread-winner?

And I? I too . . . I would have changed places with him. How happy he must be! He does not feel the pain of his wound, nor despair nor thirst. The bayonet had pierced straight through his heart.

In his uniform was a large blank hole surrounded with blood. I had done that!

I did not want to do it. I had no ill-feeling against any one when I came out to fight. The thought that I should have to kill did not occur to me. I imagined that I should expose my own breast to the bullet and nothing more.

And what had happened?   Fool! fool!

That poor unfortunate Arab (he had on an Egyptian uniform) was even less guilty than I.  He had probably never heard of Russia or Bulgaria before he was put into a ship and sent off to Constantinople.  He was ordered to go and he went.  Had he refused, he would have been flogged, or some Pasha or other might have put a bullet through him.  He had made a long weary march from Constantinople into Rumania.  We attacked him and he tried to defend himself, but seeing that we were not afraid and kept on advancing in spite of his English Martini rifle, his courage had failed him.  When he had wanted to run away, a little man —so little that he could have killed him with one blow of his swarthy fist—jumped at him and plunged a bayonet through his heart.  How was he to blame?

And how was I to blame though I had killed him?   How was I?

And why am I tortured by thirst?  Thirst! who knows what thirst really means?  Even when we had marched through Rumania, doing forty miles a day, with the thermometer over 100°, I did not experience what I feel now.  Ah, if only some one would come!  Stay!  There must be water in that gourd the Turk has!  But how can I get to him?  What efforts I shall have to make!  All the same I will try!

I attempt to crawl, dragging my legs behind me.  My weak hands will hardly pull my heavy body.  The Turk lies about four yards away, but the distance seems greater to me than if it had been four miles.

Still, I must get there.  My throat is parched and burning as though on fire.  I would assuredly die sooner without water.  Yet —something might turn up. . . .

So I attempt to crawl.  My legs seem fixed to the ground and every movement causes excruciating pains.  I moan and cry aloud but still persist.  I get there at last.  Here is the gourd. What a lot of water!  More than half full.  It will last me a long time . . . until death!  My victim has saved me.  I try to un-strap the gourd, leaning on one elbow, when suddenly I lose my balance and fall face downwards on my saviour's breast.  He gives off a strong, unpleasant odour.

I drank my fill.  The water was warm, but still wholesome, and besides there was so much of it!  It will enable me to last out several days longer!  I recollected how some one had said that a man could live for more than a week without food if he had water; also how a man who had tried to commit suicide by starvation had lived a long time because he had drunk water.

Well, and if I continue to live for another five days, what dif-ference will it make?  Our men are gone, the Bulgarians have retreated and there is no road near by.  Clearly I am bound to die; only instead of suffering for three days I shall prolong it for a week. Would it not be better to make an end? I glanced at my neighbour's rifle, a splendid specimen of English make. I had only to put out my hand and in the twinkling of an eye all would be over. A little heap of cartridges lay near him—he had had no time to use them all.

Shall I make an end or wait? For what? deliverance? death? To wait until the Turks come and pull the skin from my wounded legs? It would be better to kill myself. I must keep up my spirits and fight to the end—as long as my strength holds out. If some one finds me I shall be saved. Perhaps my bones are not broken and I can be cured. I may once more see my native land, my mother, Masha . . . Ah God! I hope they never know the truth. Let them think I was killed outright. What would they feel if they knew that I suffered like this for two, three, four days!

My head feels dizzy. The journey across to my neighbour has sapped all my strength. And then this horrible smell. How black he has turned! What will he be like to-morrow or the day after? I haven't strength enough to move away from him. I will rest a little and then crawl back to my old place away from the bad smell.

I lay there, unable to move. The sun scorched my face and hands. If only I could cover myself with something, or night would come. It will be the second night, I think. My thoughts are confused. I lose consciousness. . . .

I must have slept a long time, for when I awoke it was night. Nothing had changed. The pain was just as bad, and my neighbour was still lying there large and immovable.

I could not keep from thinking of him. Did I really give up all that was dear to me, tramp a thousand miles, suffer cold, hunger, heat, merely to deprive this unfortunate man of his life? And have I done anything to help the course of the war by committing this murder? Murder! Yes, I am a murderer.

When I made up my mind to go to the war, my mother and Masha did not attempt to dissuade me from it, though they wept. Wrapped up in my idea, I gave no heed to their tears. I did not understand them (though I do now). What harm I had done to these nearest me! (And what is the use of knowing when I cannot bring the past back again?)

(I remember now what some of my friends had thought of me! " Fanatic! " they had said. " He does not know himself why he is going! " How could they have said that? How could they reconcile their words with their conceptions of heroism, patriotism, and such ideals? According to their standards I possessed these qualities, yet they called me " Fanatic.")

I remember how I went to Kinenev, and they gave me my kit, and I set out with thousands of others, a few of whom were, like myself, volunteers. The rest would have stayed at home had they been free to do so. Yet, like us, they went on unthinkingly, did their thousand miles, and fought even better than we did. They fulfilled all their duties although they would have abandoned everything and gone off had they been allowed. Towards morning, a keen wind sprang up. The bushes began to rustle. The sleepy birds awoke. The stars grew dim. The dark-blue sky turned paler and fleecy clouds began to cover it. The grey semi-darkness lifted from the earth. It was the third day of my . . . what shall I call it? . . . life or purgatory here.

Three days . . . how many more remained? Not many, I should think. I was very weak and could not even move away from the corpse. Soon he and I will be alike, and then he will no longer be unpleasant. I must drink some water. I shall drink three times a day: in the morning, at noon, and in the evening.

The sun rose. Its huge disk, partly hidden by the dark branches of the bushes, was blood-red. It promised a hot day.

" My neighbour . . . what will happen to you to-day? You are horrible enough already."

Yes, he was horrible to look at. His hair had begun to fall out. His skin, dark by nature, had turned a pale yellow and, drawn tightly over his swollen face, had burst by his ears. In the raw places worms were crawling. His feet were so swollen as to be too large for his boots, and flesh protruded between the laces. He was bloated all over. What effect would the sun have on him to-day? To lie near him was unbearable. I must crawl away at any cost. But I—how could I?

I could still lift my hand, open the gourd, and drink some water, but to move my heavy cumbersome body was another matter. But I must move if ever so little, even if it takes me an hour.

I spent the whole morning in the attempt to crawl away. The pain was terrible, but I paid no attention—I was used to it. I had forgotten what it was like to feel normal and healthy. At last I reached my former place. I had hoped to get some fresh air (if one can talk of there being air within a few yards of a decaying corpse), but the wind had changed and carried the disgusting smell towards me. My empty stomach began to contract, causing a sickening pain; all my organs seemed to turn over. And still that fetid, infected air came towards me.

I was in despair and cried aloud.

Utterly crushed and broken, I lay there half unconscious, when suddenly . . . was I mistaken? was it my disordered imagination? I don't think so. Yes, there was a sound of voices, the clatter of horses' hoofs, and the voices of men. I was about to cry out but checked myself. Supposing they were the Turks? To my present sufferings would be added still worse ones, so horrible that it makes one's hair stand on end even to read of them in the papers. They will skin me alive, roast my wounded leg . . . that would be bad enough, but they might even invent something worse. Was it better dying at their hands than here alone? But what if it be our men? Oh, those cursed bushes! why do they surround me like a thick hedge, so that I can see nothing through them? There was only a little opening like a small window through which I got a glimpse of the glade in the distance. A stream flowed through it, the same stream at which we had quenched our thirst before the battle. A sandstone slab placed across it served as a little bridge. They will probably cross it. The voices ceased. I did not recognise the language they used: my hearing had become weak. Heavens! if only they are our men! I will call out to them; they will hear me even from the stream. I will do it even though I risk falling into the hands of the barbarians. Why are they so long in coming? My impatience was exhausting me. I did not even notice the smell of the corpse although it was no better than before.

Suddenly, by the little bridge, I caught sight of some Cossacks! Blue uniforms, red stripes, and bayonets. There was about fifty of them. At the head, on a fine horse, rode the dark-bearded captain. As soon as the last man had crossed the stream the captain turned in his saddle and shouted " Quick march! "

" Stop! Stop! For God's sake! Help! Help, comrades! " I cried, but the stamping of dozens of horses, the clanking of the sabres, the noisy chatter of the men, drowned my voice and they did not hear me!

Oh God! In my weakness I fell on my face and sobbed aloud. The gourd toppled over and the water began to trickle out—the water that meant life and salvation; but I did not notice it until there was only about half a glassful left, and the rest had been absorbed by the dry parched soil.

This last stroke quite numbed me. I lay quite still with half-open eyes. The wind was constantly changing, sometimes giving me a breath of fresh air and then carrying the horrible smell towards me. By this time my neighbour had become too horrible for description. Once when I opened my eyes to look at him I was terrified. The flesh on his face was already eaten away, only the bones remained. That constant bony grin was too horrible to contemplate, yet I had many times handled a skull. This skeleton in uniform, with its shining buttons, made me shudder. " Such is war," I thought; " war as it actually is."

The sun was hot and scorching as before. My face and hands were long burnt. The water was all gone. I had intended to drink the remainder in little sips, but my thirst was so overpowering that I emptied the gourd at one gulp. Ah! Why did I not call out to the Cossacks when they were nearer? Even had they been Turks, it would have been better than this. At most they would have tortured me for an hour or two, whereas now I do not know how long I shall have to lie and suffer here.

Mother! Dear mother! If you knew you would tear your grey hair, you would beat your head against the wall and curse the day on which I was born. You could curse the whole world for inventing such a torture as war!

But you are no doubt with Masha and do not know my plight. Good-bye, mother; good-bye, Masha, my sweetheart, my love! Ah how hard, how bitter it is! Something is gripping my heart! Again I see that little white dog! The porter had no pity on it, knocked its head against a wall and threw it on a rubbish heap. It was not quite dead, and must have lain there in agony for a whole day. And I am still more unfortunate, for my agony has lasted three days. To-morrow will be the fourth, and after that will follow the fifth, the sixth. . . . Where art thou, Death? Come, come and take me! But Death does not hear.

And I lie there under the blazing sun without so much as a drop of water to cool my burning throat, while the corpse is infecting me. Millions of worms are crawling over him. When they are finished with him nothing but his bones and his uniform will remain. Then my turn will come and I shall fare no better than he.

The day went by, and the night, but no change. Morning came and still no change. Another day will come. . . .

The bushes swayed and rustled gently. " You will die, die, die," they seemed to be murmuring. " You will never see your home, never, never, never," the bushes on the other side replied.

" You will never find any there—" I heard a loud voice suddenly near me.

I started and came to myself in an instant. The gentle blue eyes of Hakoolev, our corporal, were looking down at me from among the bushes.

" Bring the spades! " he shouted. " Here are two more. One of our men and one of theirs."

" You will not need spades—don't bury me. I am alive! " I wanted to cry out, but only a faint moaning escaped my parched lips. " My God! Can he be alive? Mr. Ivanov! Here, boys! Quickly! Our gentleman is alive—call the doctor! "

In an instant they were pouring water down my throat—vodka and something else. Then all vanished.

The stretcher moved along with a gentle swing, with a motion soothing as a lullaby. One moment I am awake, the next, again unconscious. My bandaged wounds no longer hurt me.

An inexpressible feeling of joy pervaded my whole body.

" Stop! Lower! Men of the four relief, March! To the stretcher! Take hold! Lift! "

Thus commanded Peter Ivanitch, our field hospital captain, a tall, gaunt, good-natured man. He was so tall that as I raised my eyes to look at him I could only see his enormously long beard and his shoulders, though the stretcher was being carried by four tall soldiers.

" Peter Ivanitch! " I whispered.

" What is it, old man? " He leaned over me.

" Peter Ivanitch, what did the doctor say? Shall I die soon? "

" Nonsense, Ivanov! You are not going to die. Not a bone in your body is broken. Lucky beggar! All your bones and arteries are whole. How did you manage to exist these three and a half days? What did you eat? "

" Nothing."

" And drink? "

" I took the Turk's gourd. I can't talk much now; I will tell you later."

" Well, God be with you, comrade. Try to sleep."

Again sleep, oblivion. . . .

I awoke in the field hospital. The doctor and a nurse were standing over me, and beside them was a famous professor from St. Petersburg who was bending over my legs. His hands were stained with blood. For a while longer he occupied himself with my legs and then he turned to me.

" God has been good to you, young man! You will live. We have only cut off one of your legs, but that is nothing serious. You may speak if you want to."

I spoke, and told them all that I have written here.

# THE SIGNAL

## Vsevolod M. Garshin

Semen Ivanov served as a surfaceman on the railway. His cabin was twelve versts distant from one station and ten from the other. The year before, a large weaving mill had been established about four versts away, and its tall chimneys looked black from behind the trees of the wood; and nearer than this, apart from the other cabins, there was no human habitation.

Semen Ivanov was a sickly, broken-down man. Nine years before he had gone to the war: he served as orderly to an officer and had remained with him during the whole campaign. He starved and froze, and baked in the hot sun, and marched from forty to fifty versts in the frost or in the burning heat. It also happened that he was often under fire, but, thank God, no bullet ever touched him.

Once his regiment was in the first line; for a whole week the firing was kept up constantly on both sides: the Russian line on this side of the hollow and the Turkish lines just across, and from morning till night the firing was going on. Semen's officer was also in the front lines, and three times a day, from the regimental kitchens in the hollow, Semen carried the hot samovar and the food. Semen walked through the open space while the bullets whistled over his head and cracked the stones. Semen was afraid, but he went on; wept, and went on. The officers were very much satisfied with Semen's services: the officers always had their hot tea.

Semen returned from the war without a wound, but with a rheumatic pain in his legs and arms. And he had suffered a good deal of sorrow since that time. His old father died soon after his return, then his little son, a boy of four, also died from some throat trouble; and Semen was left alone in the world with his wife.

Their work on the little piece of land allotted to them also proved unsuccessful, it being too hard for a man to till the soil with swollen arms and legs. And so they could not get along in their native village, and decided to go into new places in search of better luck. Semen lived with his wife on the Done for some time, and in the Government of Cherson; but somehow they could not get along very well anywhere. At last his wife went into service, and Semen continued his roving life as heretofore.

Once he happened to go by rail, and at one station he noticed the station-master, who seemed rather familiar to him. Semen looked at him intently, and the station-master also peered into Semen's face. They recognised each other: it was an officer of his regiment. "Is it you, Ivanov?" said the man.

"Yes, Your Honour, my very self."

"How did you get here?" And so Semen told him the story of his misadventures.

"Well, where are you going now?"

"I cannot say, Your Honour."

"How is that, you absurd fellow; you cannot say?"

"Just so, Your Honour, because I have nowhere to go to. I must look for some kind of employment, Your Honour."

And the station-master looked at him for a moment and fell to thinking, then said to him: "Well, brother, stay here at the station in the meantime. But it seems to me that you are a married man? Where is your wife?"

"Yes, sir, I am married; my wife is serving at the house of a merchant at Kursk."

"Well, then, write to your wife to come here. I shall get a free ticket for her. We shall soon have a vacant cabin on the line, and I will ask the division-superintendent to give you the place."

"Many thanks, Your Honour," replied Semen.

And so he remained at the station, helping in the station-master's kitchen, cutting wood, sweeping the courtyard and the platform. In two weeks his wife arrived, and Semen went on a hand-car to his new home.

The cabin was new and warm, wood he had in plenty, the former watchman left a small garden, and there was a little less than one and a half acres of arable land on the two sides of the line. Semen was overjoyed: he began to dream of a little homestead of his own, and of buying a horse and a cow.

He was given all the necessary supplies: a green flag, a red flag, lanterns, a signal-pipe, a hammer, a spanner for tightening the screw-nuts, a crowbar, shovel, brooms, nails, bolts, and two books with the rules and regulations of the railroad. At first Semen did not sleep at night, for he was continually rehearsing the regulations. If the train was due in two hours, he had already gone his rounds, and would sit on the little bench at the watch-house and look and listen: were not the rails trembling, was there no noise of an approaching train?

At last he learned by heart all the rules; though he read with difficulty and had to spell out each word, nevertheless he did learn them by heart.

This happened in summer: the work was not hard, there was no snow to shovel, and, besides, the trains passed but rarely on that road. Semen would walk over his beat twice in twenty-four hours, would tighten a screw here and there, pick up a splinter, examine the water-pipes, and go home to take care of his little homestead. The only thing that bothered him and his wife was: no matter what they made up their minds to do, they had to ask the permission of one official, who again had to lay the matter before another, and when permission was at last given the time had already passed, and it was then too late to be of any use to them. On account of this, Semen and his wife began, at times, to feel very lonely.

About two months passed in this way; Semen began to form acquaintance with his nearest neighbours, surfacemen like himself. One was already a very old man, whom the railway authorities had long intended to replace; he could hardly move from his cabin, and his wife attended to his duties. The other surfaceman, who lived nearer to the station, was still a young man, thin and sinewy. Semen met him for the first time on the permanent way half-way between their cabins, while they were making their rounds; Semen took off his cap and bowed. "Good health to you, neighbour," he said.

The neighbour looked at him askance. "How are you?" he replied, turned, and went his way.

The women also met afterwards. Arina, Semen's wife, greeted her neighbour affably, but this neighbour, also not of the talkative kind, spoke a few words and walked away. On meeting her once, Semen asked:

"Why is your husband so uncommunicative, young woman?" After standing for some time in silence, she said: "But what should he talk to you about? Everybody has his troubles—God speed you."

But after another month had passed, their intimacy grew. Now, when Semen and Vasili met along the line, they sat down on the edge, smoked their pipes, and told each other of their past life and experiences. Vasili spoke but little, but Semen told of his campaign life and of his native village.

"I have seen plenty of sorrow in my time, and God knows I am not so very old either. God has not given us much luck. It just depends: the kind of a lot the dear Lord portions out to one—such he must have. That is the way I make it out, Vasili Stepanich, little brother."

And Vasili struck the bowl of his pipe on the rail to empty it, and said: "It isn't luck nor fate which is eating your life and mine away, but people. There is not a beast more cruel and rapacious than man. A wolf does not devour a wolf—but man eats man alive."

"Well, brother, wolf does eat wolf—that is where you are wrong."

"It came to my tongue, so I said it; anyhow there is not a more cruel beast. If it were not for man's viciousness and greed, 'twould be possible to live. Every one is on the look-out to grasp at your vitals, tear off a piece, and gobble it up."

"I don't know, brother," said Semen after thinking a bit. "Maybe it is so; but if it is so, then the great God ordained it in this way."

"And if it is so," spoke Vasili, "then there is no use of my speaking to you. A man who attributes to God every kind of iniquity, and himself sits and patiently bears it, cannot be a man, brother mine, but an animal. There you have my whole say!" And he turned and went off without even saying good-bye. Semen rose also and called after him: "Neighbour, what are you abusing me for?"

But the neighbour did not even turn round, and went his way.

Semen looked after him till he was lost from sight at the turn of the road, then he returned home and said to his wife: "Well, Arina, what a venomous man that neighbour of ours is!" Nevertheless they were not angry with each other; and when they met again they spoke as if nothing had happened and on the very same topic.

"Ah, brother, if it were not for the people, we should not sit here in these cabins," said Vasili.

"Well, what if we do live in a cabin? It is not so bad to live in one, after all."

"Not so bad to live, not so bad—— You have lived long, but

gained little; looked at much, but seen little. A poor man, no matter where he lives, in a railway cabin or in any other place, what sort of a life is his? Those leeches eat your life away, squeeze all your juice out, and when you have grown old they throw you out like some swill, for the pigs to feed on. How much wages do you get?"

"Well, not much, Vasili Stepanich, twelve roubles."

"And I thirteen and a half. Allow me to ask you why? According to the by-laws of the administration, every one of us is supposed to get the same amount—fifteen roubles a month, and light and heat. Who was it that allotted you and me twelve, or say, thirteen and a half roubles? Allow me to ask you? And you say it is not so bad a life? Understand me well, it is not about the three, or one and a half roubles I am wrangling about, but even if they paid me the whole amount—— Last month I was at the station when the director happened to pass. I saw him there. Had the honour. He occupied a whole private car by himself; at the station he alighted and stood on the platform, looking—— No, I will not stay *here* long; I shall go where my eyes lead me!"

"But where will you go, Stepanich? Let well alone. You will not find it much better anywhere. You have a home here, warmth, and a bit of land. Your wife is an able workwoman——"

"Land! You ought to see the land I have—why, there isn't a stick on it. This spring I planted some cabbages. Well, one day the section-inspector passed: 'What is this?' he says. 'Why did you not report it? Why not have waited for permission? Dig it up at once; not a trace must be left of it.' He was half boozed. At another time he would not have said a word. Three roubles fine!"

For some moments Vasili pulled at his pipe in silence, then said in a low voice: "It needed but little more and I should have made short work of him."

"Well, neighbour, you *are* a hot-head, I can tell you."

"I am *not* hot, I am only speaking and considering everything from the point of justice. But he will get it from me yet, the red-mug; I shall complain to the superintendent of division. We shall see!"

And he did in fact complain.

One day the superintendent of the division came to make a preliminary inspection of the line. In three days' time very important gentlemen were expected from St. Petersburg to make an inspection of the road; everything had to be made ship-shape; some new gravel was ordered before their arrival, added, levelled, and smoothed out, the sleepers were examined, the nuts tightened, the verst-posts newly painted, and the order was given that some fine yellow sand be strewn over the crossings. A wife even drove her old man out of the nearest cabin, which he almost never left, in order to trim a little tiny grass-plot. Semen worked a whole week to bring everything into first-rate order, even mended his coat and burnished his brass badge till it shone. Vasili also worked hard. At last the superintendent arrived in a buzzing hand-car, worked by four men and making twenty versts an hour. It came flying toward Semen's cabin, and Semen sprang forward and reported in military fashion. Everything appeared to be correct.

" Have you been long here? " asked the official.

" Since the second of May, Your Honour."

" Very well, thank you. And who is at Number 164? "

The inspector, who rode with him on the car, replied : " Vasili Spiridov."

" Spiridov, Spiridov—— Oh, the one you reported? "

" The very same."

" Very well, let us have a look at Vasili Spiridov. Go ahead."

The workmen leaned upon the handles and the car sped away down the line. " There will be a fight between them and the neighbour," thought Semen, looking after the disappearing car.

About two hours later Semen went on his rounds. He saw that some one was coming toward him, walking along the line, and there was something white visible on his head. Semen strained his eyes to see. It was Vasili; in his hand he carried a stick; a small bundle was slung across his shoulders, and one cheek was tied up with a white handkerchief.

" Where are you going, neighbour? " Semen shouted to him.

When Vasili approached him closer, Semen saw that he was as pale as chalk and wild-eyed; and when he began to speak his voice broke.

" I am off to the city," he said, " to Moscow—to the head office of the administration."

" To the administration—— Is that it? You are going to make a complaint, are you? Better not, Vasili Stepanich. Forget it——"

" No, brother, I will not forget it. It is too late to forget. You see, he struck me in the face, struck me till the blood flowed. As long as I live, I will not forget it, nor let it go at this."

" Give it up, Stepanich," Semen spoke to him, taking hold of his hand. " I speak truth : you will not make things better."

" Who speaks better! I know myself that I will not make them better; you spoke truly about fate—you did. I shall not do much good to myself, but one has to stand up for justice."

" But won't you tell me how it all came about? "

" How it all came about——? Well, he inspected everything, left the car on purpose to do so—even looked inside the cabin. I knew beforehand that he would be strict—so I had everything in first-class order. He was just going to leave when I came out with my complaint. He immediately burst forth : ' Here,' he said,

' is to be a Government inspection, and you dare come forward with your complaints about your vegetable garden! We are expecting privy councillors, and you come with your cabbages! ' I could not control myself and said a word—not so very bad either, but it seemed to offend him, and he struck me—— And I stood there as if it was the most usual thing in the world to happen. Only, when they went off, I came to my senses, washed off the blood from my face and came away."

" And what about the cabin? "

" My wife is there, she will take care of the work; and, besides, the devil take their road, anyway! Good-bye, Ivanich," he said to Semen on taking leave of him; " I don't know if I shall find justice for myself."

" You don't mean to tell me that you will go on foot? "

" I shall ask them at the station to let me ride in a goods train; to-morrow I shall be in Moscow."

The neighbours took leave of each other and each went his way. Vasili stayed away for a long time. His wife did all the work for him, sleeping neither night nor day, and looked very worn and exhausted. On the third day the inspectors passed: an engine, guard's van, and two private cars, and Vasili was still absent. On the fourth day Semen saw Vasili's wife; her face was swollen with incessant weeping and her eyes were very red. " Has your husband returned? " he asked her. She only waved her arm, but did not utter a word.

．　　．　　．　　．　　．　　．　　．　　．

When still a little boy Semen had learned how to make willow pipes. He burnt out the pith, drilled out where necessary the tiny finger-holes, and finished the whistle of the pipe so artistically that almost anything could be played on it. At odd moments he now made lots of such flageolets and sent them by an acquaintance of his, a guard, to the city, where they were sold at a penny each. On the third day after the inspection he left his wife at home to meet the six o'clock train, took his knife and went into the woods to cut his willow sticks. He came to the end of his section, where the road made a sharp turn, descended the embankment and went up the hill. About a half verst farther was a large bog, around which grew splendid shrubs for his pipes. He cut a bundle of sticks and went home, again walking through the wood. The sun was already low; and a death-like quiet reigned all about; only the chirping of the birds could be heard and the crackling underfoot of the wind-fallen wood. A little more and he would reach the railway line; suddenly it seemed to him as if he heard coming from somewhere the clang of iron striking on iron. Semen hurried his steps. " What can it be? " he asked himself, knowing that no repairs were going on in that section at that time. He reached the edge of the wood.  Before him rose high the embankment of the railway; and he saw on the top, on the line, a man squatting down at work on something.  Semen began to ascend the embankment very quietly, thinking that some one was trying to steal the bolt-nuts, He saw the man rise; in his hand he held a crowbar; he quickly shoved the crowbar under the rail and gave it a push to one side.  Semen felt everything grow dim; he tried to shout, but could not.  He saw that it was Vasili, and made a dash for the embankment, but Vasili was already rolling down the other side of the embankment with spanner and crowbar.

"Vasili Stepanich!  Little father, friend, come back!  Give me the crowbar!  Let us put the rail in place; no one will ever know.  Come back, save your soul from a great sin! "

But Vasili did not even turn round, and went on into the woods.

Semen remained standing over the dislocated rail, his sticks lying in a heap at his feet.  The train which was due was not a goods, but a passenger train, and he had nothing to stop it with: flag he had none.  He could not put the rail into its right place; with bare hands one cannot fasten in the rail spikes.  He had to run, run for dear life to his cabin for the necessary tools!  God give him strength!

And Semen started to run breathlessly toward his cabin.  He ran —now, now he would fall—at last he left the wood behind, he had only about seven hundred feet left to his cabin—suddenly he heard the factory whistle.  Six o'clock, and at two minutes past six the train would pass.  Great God!  Save the innocent souls!  And before his eyes he seemed to see how the left wheel of the engine would strike the cut rail, quiver, slant to one side, and tear the sleepers, knock them all to splinters; and just here is the rounded curve, and the embankment; and the engine, the cars, all would go pell-mell down, down from the height of seventy-seven feet, and the third-class cars were crammed full of people, little children among them.  Now they were sitting tranquilly, not thinking of anything.  O Lord, teach him what to do!  No, he would not be able to get to the cabin and return in time.

Semen gave up his intention of running to the cabin, turned and ran back quicker than he had come, his head in a whirl.  Not knowing himself what would happen, he ran up to the cut rail: his sticks lay scattered all around.  He bent down and took one of the sticks, not understanding himself why he did it; and ran farther.  And it seemed to him that the train was already approaching.  He heard a far-away whistle, heard the rails begin to quiver measuredly and quietly: he had no more strength left to run.  He stopped about seven hundred feet from the fatal spot: suddenly he became illumined, as it were, by a thought.  He took off his hat, took from it a handkerchief; took out his knife from his boot-leg and crossed himself.  God's blessing!

He slashed his left arm a little above the elbow with his sharp knife; the blood spurted down in a hot stream; he dipped his handkerchief in it, smoothed it out, tied it to his stick, and displayed his red flag. He stood waving the flag; the train was already in sight. The driver did not see him, he would come nearer, but at a distance of seven hundred feet he would not be able to stop the heavy train!

And the blood was pouring and pouring—— Semen pressed his hand to his side, but the blood would not stop; evidently he had made too deep a cut into the arm; his head was beginning to turn; he was getting dizzy, as if black flies were swimming in his eyes; then everything became altogether dark, and loud bells were ringing in his ears—— He no longer saw the train, no longer heard the noise: only one thought predominated: "I shall not be able to keep on my feet, shall fall down, drop the flag; the train will pass over me!—— Dear God, help, send some one to relieve me——" His soul became a void, and he dropped the flag. But the bloody flag did not fall to the ground: some one's hand caught it and raised it aloft in front of the oncoming train. The driver saw him and brought the engine to a stop.

. . . . . . . .

The people came rushing from the train; soon they gathered into a crowd; before them lay a man, unconscious, covered with blood; another man stood beside him with a bloody rag tied to a stick.

Vasili surveyed the crowd and lowered his head.

"Arrest me," he said; "it was I who cut the line."

# ATTALEA PRINCEPS

## Vsevolod M. Garshin

IN a certain large town there was a botanical garden, and in this garden was a large glass-house. The house was very beautiful, with its tall graceful columns and delicately wrought arches, particularly in the evening when the setting sun bathed it in rosy light and the fiery reflections danced and mingled together like the colours in some large precious stone. The plants within could be seen through the thick transparent glass, and though the house was large they were very crowded in it. Their roots were massed and tangled together, and they all fought one another for every available drop of water and every scrap of nourishment. The trees pushed their branches in among the palm leaves, bending and breaking them, and in their turn being bent and broken against the iron frames

Though the gardeners were always busy, cutting, pruning, and training, they accomplished but little; for the growth, space and freedom were necessary. The plants were beautiful delicate things, natives of the hot countries; they dreamed of their homes and longed to be there. No matter how transparent the roof, it was not the blue sky. In winter, when the glass was covered with frost and snow, it was quite dark in the house. The wind would hoot and beat against the frames, making the plants tremble with fear. They would listen to the roar, and think of another wind, warm and moist, the wind of their beloved home countries. They longed to feel it fanning them once more, shaking their branches and playing with their leaves. But the air in the house was still; unless perhaps some heavy storm would break the glass and let in a cold, sleety draught that made the leaves turn pale, shrivel up, and die.

The glass, however, was soon mended. The director of the gardens was a learned botanist of great repute, who would not permit of disorder, though actually he spent most of his time in a little glass laboratory, over his microscope.

Among the plants there was a lovely palm, more beautiful than all the rest. The director in his little laboratory gave it the Latin name of " Attalea." This was not its real name, but then, the botanists did not know its real name, so a little wooden label bearing the name " Attalea " was attached to its trunk.

One day there came to the garden a native of the country where this palm grew. When he caught sight of it he smiled, for it made him think of his home.

" Ah! " he exclaimed, " I know this tree," and mentioned its proper name.

" I beg your pardon," the director called out from his laboratory, though he was at the moment engaged in dissecting some little stalk, " there is no such palm as you have just mentioned; the one you are referring to is ' Attalea Princeps,' a native of Brazil."

" Oh, yes," the Brazilian said, " I daresay the botanists call it Attalea, but it has a real name of its own."

" A real and proper name is one that has been given by science," the director said drily, shutting the door of his laboratory, so as not to be disturbed by people who were too stupid to understand what was said to them.

The Brazilian stood for a long time gazing at the palm. A feeling of sadness came over him. He thought of his own country, of her lovely woods and sun and sky, of her wonderful beasts and birds, her vast pampas and glorious southern nights. It seemed to him that he had never been happy anywhere but at home, and he had been all over the world. He touched the palm with his hand, as though bidding it good-bye, then left the garden, and on the following day took ship for home. But the palm remained behind. She felt lonelier and sadder than ever.

For thirty feet she soared above the tops of the other trees, who did not like her, but envied her and considered her proud.

Attalea's height was only a source of grief to her: and besides, they were all together while she was quite alone. She remembered her home more than did the others, perhaps, because she was nearer to the hateful glass roof that had taken the place of her home.

Occasionally she would get a glimpse of something else. It was the sky, though strange and pale, yet it was the real blue sky.

When other trees gossiped among themselves Attalea would remain silent. She was always thinking how nice it would be to be out, even under that pale blue sky.

" I wonder whether they are going to water us soon," said a sago palm, who was very fond of moisture; " I am simply parched to-day."

" I am surprised at what you say, neighbour," said a large cactus; " I should have thought the quantities of water you get every day would have been enough for you. Just look at me; I get very little, and yet I am always fresh and succulent."

" We are not so frugal; we cannot grow on poor, dry soil like you cacti; we are not accustomed to living anyhow. Besides, no one asked your opinion."

The sago palm felt hurt and lapsed into silence. " As for me," the cinnamon remarked, " I am fairly contented with my position. It is dull here, of course; but at any rate one is not afraid of being skinned."

" We are not all of us skinned, you know," a stately fern observed. " To some people I daresay even this prison must seem like a paradise after the miserable existence they have been accustomed to outside."

The cinnamon was offended and began a dispute. Some took her side, others that of the fern, and a quarrel ensued; had they been able to move from their places a battle would have followed.

" I wonder why you all quarrel like this! " Attalea interposed. " It is so senseless! All this bitter feeling and irritation merely adds to your misfortunes. You had much better leave off and listen to me. I have a suggestion. Let us begin growing taller and broader; let us spread our branches and lean against the frames with all our weight, so that the glass will be shattered into a thousand pieces and we can get out into the open. Of course, if we send out one little shoot, it is soon cut off, but what could they do against a hundred strong, determined branches? We have only to work together in a friendly manner and we are sure to succeed."

No one interrupted the palm. All were silent, not knowing what to say. At last the sago palm gained courage.

" What nonsense! " she said.

" What nonsense! What nonsense! " they all echoed in one voice, each endeavouring to show Attalea how absurd the plan was.

" An unheard-of idea! Absurd! Ridiculous! "

" The frames are very strong; we could not possibly break them. And even if we did, what then? Men would come with choppers and knives and cut off our branches. They would come and mend the frames and everything would go on as before. The only difference would be that we should lose some of our limbs."

" As you please," Attalea replied. " Now I know what to do. I shall not trouble you any more. You can live as you choose; go on grumbling at each other and quarrelling about the amount of water you get, and remain for ever under this glass roof. I will find a way for myself. I am determined to see the sun and the sky, not merely through this iron grating and glass, and I shall certainly see them." And the palm looked down haughtily from her green summit on to the mass of foliage spread out beneath her. No one ventured to speak, only the sago palm whispered to a neighbour.

" We shall see how they will cut off her big stupid head, and then she will not be quite so conceited." Though they remained silent, one and all were angry with Attalea for her proud words. Only a little creeper approved of what she had said. It was the poorest, humblest little plant in the whole house, and had pale, flabby, little drooping leaves. It had no distinguishing feature of any kind; its only use in the house was to cover up the bare soil. It wound itself about Attalea's feet as it listened; her words seemed to be right. It had never known the south, but it also loved air and freedom, and looked upon the glass-house as a prison. " If an insignificant little creeper like myself can suffer through the loss of my grey sky, pale sun and cold rain, what must be the feelings of such a beautiful, powerful tree like Attalea? " it thought, as it wound itself caressingly about the palm.

" If I were a big tree, I would take her advice. We would grow up together and attain our freedom. The others would see that Attalea was right."

Unfortunately it was not a big tree, but only a humble, drooping little creeper. It could only wind itself still closer about Attalea's trunk, whisper words of love, and express a desire for the success of her undertaking. " Of course, it is not so warm with us, the sky is not so clear nor the rains so invigorating as in your country, but even we have a sky and sun and wind, such as they are. We have no such stately trees like you and your neighbours, with such large leaves and beautiful flowers, but we have some very nice trees like the fir, the yew, and the silver birch. A poor little creeper like myself can never hope to attain freedom, but you are so big and strong. Your trunk is firm and you have not much further to grow before you reach the glass roof. You will easily shatter it to pieces and once more see God's world. Then you must tell me if it is as beautiful there as it used to be. I shall be quite satisfied even with that."

" But why won't you come out with me, little creeper? My trunk is firm and strong, lean on it and climb up to me. I can carry you easily."

" Oh no! How could I? See what a sickly, weak, little thing I am! I cannot even lift one little shoot. No! I am not fit to be your comrade. Go on growing! I wish you happiness! The only thing I ask of you is that when you are free you will sometimes remember your little friend." Then the palm began to grow. Former visitors to the house were amazed at her enormous size, and with each month Attalea grew higher and higher. The director of the garden put this down to his excellent treatment, and was proud of his knowledge and the success of his work.

" Why, look at Attalea Princeps," he would say. " A specimen of her size is rarely met with even in Brazil. We apply all our knowledge so that the plants may develop here just as freely as in their native lands, and I think we have attained some measure of success." And with a self-satisfied expression he tapped the trunk of the tree with his cane, the blows resounding through the whole house. The leaves of the palm trembled. " He imagines that I grow for his pleasure," she thought. " Let him go on thinking so "; and had she been able to express her thoughts aloud the director would have been surprised at her pain and wrath.

She continued growing, using up all her sap to increase her height, and denying the nourishment to her roots and leaves.

Sometimes it would seem to her that the distance between her and the room remained the same, then she would strain with all her might. The frames were getting closer and closer, and at last a young leaf came into contact with the cold glass and iron.

" Look! Look! " the other plants exclaimed; " see where she has got to! Will she really do it? "

" How she has grown! " a stately fern remarked.

" I do not see anything to wonder at. If she had only grown as stout as I am that would have been another matter," observed a plant which had a trunk like a barrel.

" What is the use of stretching? She will not accomplish anything by that. The iron gratings are strong and the glass is thick."

Another month went by and Attalea was still growing higher and higher, until at last she was leaning against the iron frames. There was no more room for her to grow. Her trunk began to bend, her foliage at the top doubled up, the cold iron joints cut into the tender flesh of her young leaves, destroying their beauty. But the palm had no pity for her leaves, and notwithstanding the discomfort she pressed heavily against the iron frames until at last they began to give way, though they were made of solid iron. Trembling with excitement, the little creeper watched the proceedings.

" Does it not hurt you? " she asked the palm. " As the frames are so strong would it not be better to abandon your project? "

"Hurt me! what does that matter when I *want* my freedom! Did you not encourage me? " the palm replied.

"Yes, I did encourage you, but I had no idea how difficult it would be. It pains me to see you suffer like that."

"You need not pity me, little weakling. I am determined to be free or die."

At this moment there was a loud crash. The thick iron frames had given way at last. There was a shower of glass splinters, and one struck the director's hat as he was coming out of his laboratory.

"I wonder what has happened? " he exclaimed nervously, when he saw the pieces of glass flying through the air. He stepped back a little and looked up at the roof. Attalea's beautiful crown, now straight once more, stood out proudly at the top.

"Is this all? " she thought. "Was it for this that I worked and suffered for so long; this that I considered my highest goal? "

It was about the middle of autumn when Attalea put her head out of the hole she had made in the roof. There was a fine drizzle, half rain, half snow; the wind was chasing the low-hanging clouds, and it seemed to Attalea that they would carry her away with them. The trees were already bare and looked like terrible ghosts. Only the firs and the yews were still green. They looked solemnly at the palm, as much as to say, "You will freeze to death. You do not know what frost is; you are not hardy like us. Why did you come out of your warm house? "

And Attalea realised that this was the end.

She began to freeze. "Should she go back under the roof again? " But it was too late. She would have to stay there in the cold wind and snow, look out at the grey sky, the poor country, the dirty yard belonging to the garden, the huge dull town that could be seen through the mist, until, down there in the warm, men would decide what to do with her.

The director ordered the palm to be cut down.

"Of course, one could build a dome over her," he said, "but what would be the use? She would only break it again. Besides, it would cost too much. She had better be cut down." Attalea was tied up with ropes, so that she should not fall and break the walls of the house, then she was cut down very low, right by the roots. The little creeper wound about her trunk did not want to part with its friend and also fell under the axe. When the palm was removed, lying near her roots were the bruised little shoots and leaves of the creeper. "Take away that rubbish! " the director said. "It is getting yellow, and the axe has cut it up too much. Put something else in its place."

One of the gardeners pulled the little creeper out by the roots with one skilful stroke of his spade. He put it in a basket, took it out to the yard, and threw it on the dead palm that was lying in the dirt, already half-covered with snow.

# IGNATI N. POTAPENKO

# BIGGER THAN YOURSELF

From the wide-open gate of a tall many-storeyed house a man walked out into the street. It would be more correct to say that he shot out. Turning to the right, he did not walk along the pavement as people do ordinarily, but strode along.

As a matter of fact there was nothing particularly striking about the man. He was of middle height, broad-shouldered though not stout, and very healthy looking—his broad chest in particular bearing witness to that. His face was insignificant, one that would not attract attention or be easily remembered. The features were neither large nor small, neither handsome nor ugly, just medium—so to speak. He wore a beard—dark, with a red tinge in it, as though burnished by the sun; had side-whiskers on his cheeks, and a thin moustache. Notwithstanding the commonplace features of this man who had shot out of the gate of the tall house, all the passers-by stopped and stared at him curiously as he strode along.

He seemed, for the amusement of the public, to have gathered together purposely the strangest collection of apparel. He wore high boots with thick soles, that resounded loudly on the stone pavement. The boots came right over his knees, and his trousers were tucked into them. His broad pea-jacket, made of some strange home-spun the colour of camel skin, was open, and even when the air was still, its skirts standing out on either side of him looked as though they were blown out by the wind. Large glass buttons sparkled on his velvet waistcoat, and his neck was enveloped in a bright red shirt with a slanting opening. His thick, unkempt hair hung over his shoulders, and to crown the whole effect, he wore a black felt hat with an unusually wide brim. If we add that in his right hand he carried a thick stick which he had himself cut recently in the nearest wood and that he flourished his clenched left hand—that he wore a frown and two severe wrinkles on his forehead, it will be understood why the passers-by stepped to one side and stared at him so curiously.

His name was Fiesov, and there was hardly an inhabitant of the town that did not know him. It is true that he had been bred and born in that town and had lived there for twenty-four years, yet in all this time he had not accomplished anything outstanding. Yet he had a name and fame that no one would have dared to impugn.

Before he had shot out of the gate of the tall house and stalked along the street, Fiesov had had a certain interview. It took place on the fourth floor of the tall house, and inadvertently had a fateful significance.

In addition to the usually fierce expression of his face—which seemed as though he wished, with one blow of his hand, to strike all mankind on the cheek—two things were plainly visible: unwavering resolution and sarcasm. Fiesov showed his teeth and raised his clenched fist. Every one could see that.

For the sake of clearness and the full explanation of subsequent events, we will describe the scene that took place on the fourth floor of the tall house. It had happened only a quarter of an hour before. Fiesov had gone through the gate, also with resolution in his face, but without sarcasm. One might have noticed even that there was less resolution in his legs than there was in his face. But when he had walked through the yard, entered the hall, and was walking up the stairs, firmness entered his legs and chest, a thing, as is known, that always happens in the last moment before a decisive battle.

Getting up to the fourth floor he rang the bell without the slightest hesitation, and when the door was opened, he asked the maid with assurance:

" Is Varenka at home? "

He was told that she was, and entered. He put his stick in a corner of the miniature hall, took his hat with him, and followed the maid into the drawing-room. No one was there, and the two doors, one to the left and one to the right, were firmly shut. It was a tiny room, long and narrow, and had one window. There was a small couch in a loose cover of sail-cloth to protect the upholstery beneath, one arm-chair, several other chairs, and a table. Poverty glanced out of every corner and from every crack of the floor, from which the stain was wearing. On the shelf stood some cheap objects of art, such as clay jugs, glass baskets, sea-shells, and empty scent-bottles. In the midst of them was a round mirror that distorted the face of any one that happened to look in it.

Fiesov paced the room, and the old floor groaned and trembled beneath his tread. Passing the mirror he glanced at it and became convinced that his face was pale. He grew angry with his face for being pale.

The bright rays of the summer sun streamed into the window from the street. It was hot and stuffy. His forehead shone with perspiration.

When the door to the right opened, he stopped suddenly and stared at the girl who entered. His eyes were small, sharp, and penetrating. The girl looked very young. There was something

childish about her rather pale face. Small and thin, she wore a
grey knitted shawl that hid her neck, shoulders, bosom and both
hands.

" Oh, it is you, Misha! " she said in amazement, opening wide
her large blue eyes, and she seemed not at all pleased to see him.

" Yes . . . yes . . . I! " Fiesov replied, remaining in his original
attitude with his original expression.

" But why? " she asked, looking away. " You told me that
you would not come for a long time and would avoid me until . . .
this would pass."

She had a soft caressing voice, but she was apparently trying to
make it softer still in her anxiety not to offend her visitor.

" Yes, I thought I could, but later I became convinced that I
couldn't . . ." Fiesov said, in the tones of a man sentenced to
death. " And so I have come for the last time. I tell you,
Varenka, that you alone are capable of bringing me to that broad
path of useful social activity to which I am so strongly drawn. . . .
And without you, without your support, I shall fall into an abyss
from which I shall never rise. . . ."

A faint smile, that instantly vanished, appeared on the girl's thin
lips.

" You exaggerate, Misha. Isn't that so? . . ." she said simply.

" You will soon be convinced that I don't! "

She shook her head.

" But, really, Misha . . . let us put this aside. . . . I can't. . . .
What can I do? I like you very much, but not in the way you
want me to do. I know you too well, Misha."

" You do not know me if you prefer some foppish nonentity in
a fashionable coat and grey gloves to me! "

Varenka blushed faintly.

" I assure you, you are mistaken. I don't prefer any one else
at all. . . . You are quite mistaken."

" But I shall perish without you. . . . Do you hear? . . . I
have decided . . . yes, I have decided to die! " Fiesov said, trying
to make his rather thin voice sound deeper.

" Oh, don't! " Varenka said, with a sweet smile. " That will
never be; you are not capable of it, Misha! And really . . . it
only seems to you . . ."

" Is this your last word? "

" I have told you so already, Misha! . . . When a few weeks
have gone by, you too will see that you did not love me. You too
cannot love me, just as I cannot love you. We know each other
too well. You will only thank me . . ."

" No . . . perhaps some one else will say that for me. . . ."

" Really, Misha, you are quite incorrigible! "

" Yes, I am incorrigible . . . incorrigible because I cannot enjoy
an empty, commonplace life, because my soul is guided by ideals,

and because even those nearest to me, those whom I value most on earth, either cannot or will not understand me. . . . But you will understand, Varenka, you will understand when it is too late. . . . Good-bye!"

This small speech was made with warmth, with sparkling eyes and trembling voice. Fiesov was about to turn and go out, when he suddenly noticed a smile on Varenka's lips, a smile that she took no pains to hide.

"You are amused! In vain, I assure you!" he said.

"Not at all. I simply recalled what mother said about you. She said that you were very nice but had one failing—that you wanted to be bigger than yourself."

"Well, soon your mother and all of you will see that you were mistaken! . . . Good-bye!"

He turned right round and, seizing his stick in the hall, went out. He ran madly down the stairs and into the street in the manner in which we met him.

He flew home as fast as possible. He had a mother and sister in the town. They possessed a small income on which they lived free from want. But Fiesov did not live with them. It was already seven years since—being about to pass from the seventh to the eighth form—he left school and took rooms for himself. He considered the life led by his mother and sister too bourgeois.

"In the morning there is tea, at mid-day coffee and cream, dinner at three, tea again at seven, supper at ten, and bed at eleven, and so on every day of one's life! The devil knows what it all means!" he said, and decided to live by himself. He had, by the way, a little money of his own, the interest on which was sufficient to keep him. This act of his grieved his mother and sister, but that was of little consequence, since all his acts grieved them. The first grief he caused them was when he threw up his school. It was an inexplicable decision on his part, as he had passed the seventh form, and well, too.

"Why?" he was asked.

"Because, had I remained in the eighth form, it would have looked as though I were trying for a diploma, and that is commonplace. Every one does that."

And all these griefs came largely because "that is commonplace, every one does that." Settling in a furnished room, he at once introduced an order that was not at all like the order maintained by the rest of the world. There was a bed, but he ordered it to be removed, and slept on some kind of animal skin. He kept his books in the chest of drawers, while his linen was strewn about on the window-sill, on the writing-table, and sometimes even on the floor. The first thing in the morning, he ate a large piece of meat, and thus fortified himself until the evening, considering it a low occupation to spend much time over food—"a commonplace that

everybody does." Then he eliminated from his toilet all the appur-
tenances considered necessary by ordinary folk, and made himself
into such a scarecrow that his poor female relatives fainted at the
sight of him. In the course of time he toned down some of the
extremes and made his toilet more seemly, but his compromise did
not carry him far enough to wear a starched collar, ordinary boots,
or a hat with a less startling brim. Later, he began to reject
practically everything that people considered comfortable, and as
a result suffered real privations.

With it all he was quite sincere, and did everything from pure
motives. From the time he was fourteen, there had grown in his
heart a vague feeling that always kept him in a nervous state.
Nothing satisfied him, and he was always hankering after something. As the years went by, this feeling grew to a painful degree,
but became no clearer. It seemed as though an ulcer had grown
in his breast and threatened all his body. Sometimes he was possessed by a feeling of universal love, and wanted to perform some
act that would instantly save all mankind. However, he had no
clear idea from what evil mankind was to be saved. Sometimes a
fury seized him and he would be possessed with the desire to
commit some great evil, also of a kind that would shake the earth
and startle all its inhabitants. As a result, he would pursue his
studies by fits and starts; sometimes he would abandon books
for weeks at a time, at others seize them and learn his lessons so
well as to astonish his masters. His capabilities were not very
great, but determination helped them considerably.

There were not a few incidents in his life when glory seemed to
approach him as it were, and he was separated from it only by the
smallest interval. Once when he was walking by the river-bank he
heard the cry of a drowning boy who was battling with death. The
quick current was bearing him away to the depths. Our hero overflowed with benevolence. His eyes lit up, he rushed towards the
river and began to take off his clothes. He removed his coat, his
hat, his waistcoat, and by the time he got to his shirt, decided that
it was not worth while risking his life for such an insignificant act,
for the sake of saving the life of some perhaps worthless boy.
Meanwhile a crowd had gathered, and a long-bearded workman
stepped out, and without stopping to consider for a moment,
plunged into the water as he was and began to swim. The workman saved the boy, while Fiesov remained on the bank waiting
for the great deed with which he would save all mankind in one
effort.

And as the occasion for such a deed did not arrive, and the
ulcer in his bosom grew larger, he was constantly tossed from
side to side: committed eccentricities; quarrelled with the police in
the street when he was informed that " strangers were not
admitted," when they " insulted his human dignity "; entered into

disputes with neighbours at the theatre when they did not approve
of an actor over whom he was in ecstasies; spoke excitedly, nervously, and loudly everywhere, of everything, and to every one,
stamping his feet, banging his stick, and waving his arms.  The
only thing he accomplished was that he was considered an incorrigible crank by some, and a madman by others.

But all were mistaken in him.  The real trouble was that he was
very vain; he wanted to accomplish something great, whereas his
powers were small.  Nature frequently produces such contradictions, endowing with brilliant abilities a man who desires nothing
of life but dinner, supper, and a warm bed, and putting into the
heart of a weak " average man " the desire for great deeds.

Fiesov had many friends who were sincerely fond of him, but
all thought of him with a smile.  In reality he was a good fellow,
sensitive to every kindly impulse, ready to give up anything to a
man in want; all knew and valued this quality in him.

With Varenka he had been friendly from childhood, when suddenly a misfortune happened to them; he fell in love with her, and
so violently that life without her seemed unbearable.  There were
long conversations, heated explanations, when with the heat of a
lover he proved to Varenka how she must love him, how she
was destined to make his life fruitful, that from that very moment
he would give up his indefinite wanderings and begin his great
work—though what it was to be he could not say.  But that did not
matter, it would become clear of itself.  Love illuminates everything.  Love is the most powerful lever in life!

But Varenka could not convince herself of this.  She looked on
Fiesov as a spoilt child that kindled itself with words but was
incapable of any definite work.  She fully shared her mother's
opinion, that he was a good man, but that it was a pity he wanted
to be larger than himself.  The most important thing, though, was
that Varenka, while appreciating his good qualities, did not love
him.  She told him so, and we witnessed their last resolute explanation.

Fiesov reached home.  The maid who opened the door noticed
something peculiar about him, but paid no special attention.  She
announced in the kitchen that " Fiesov has just come in furious.
. . . As soon as he got in his room he began pacing up and down,
from corner to corner, stamp, stamp, stamp, like the blows of a
hammer."  But in the kitchen they paid no attention to that.  The
housemaid and the other members of the kitchen could scarcely
guess that the peculiar thing in Fiesov's face was nothing less than
resolution, final and irrevocable.

Yes, he had decided.  And what if he were pacing his room
instead of sitting down to his writing-table, that looked more like
a shop counter?  Of course, he had many things to think over,
very many.  To disappear from the face of the earth without ex-

pressing himself from the depths of his soul, was far from his intention. If they could not value his life (he had Varenka in his mind), then they should value his death. But all this must be thought over so as to express his soul in a few words. He had no worries of any kind. His belongings and small capital would naturally go to his mother. There was no need to bother about that. He would have liked to bequeath it to mankind, but nothing would have come of it. Besides, humanity might go to the devil, since it did not appreciate his strivings (here too he meant Varenka).

At last he sat down by the table and began to write. The first letter was addressed to Varenka, and we give it, word for word:

" Varenka—I should have desired my death not to cause you pain. I should have liked you to greet the news with a smile; I should have liked your whole life to be one constant smile. I loved you. I speak as one dead, because, though the hand that pens this letter is still moving, I am already dead—yes, dead. You alone could have awakened me to life, but you did not wish to. God be with you! Reviewing my whole life, I see that no one understands my aspirations. I had friends, but they liked me superficially. No one knew my soul, no one could look into it and see the impetuous strivings after the Ideal that never gave me peace. Oh, Varenka! I dreamt that you were an exception. I dreamt that you were more clear-sighted than the rest, but I was mistaken; you are just as short-sighted as the others. What is the use of living when your beloved refuses you support? Life consists of days and days, of breakfasts, dinners, suppers and sleep, of commonplace interests, commonplace occupations and commonplace conversations. Is it worth while living only for this? Humanity? Oh, my God! Humanity! It prizes its commonplaces and is ready to stone its prophets. No, there is nothing great in life, and it is not worth while living for pettiness, that is, to spend life's energies in rising from bed, dressing, eating and cooking food, moving about, wagging one's tongue, and so on. And so it is settled. The thing you would not believe has happened. Varenka, I loved you with a holy love of which only the chosen are capable. But when you read this letter, I shall no longer be on this earth. Forgive me, and may God forgive you. Be happy.—Yours,

M. Fiesov."

His hand flew swiftly over the paper. His bruised soul overflowed in phrases, naturally and easily. Having finished it, he reread the letter once, twice, and a third time. It was expressive and strongly put. Varenka would be sorry and realise what she had lost.

Then he began a letter to his mother and sister. This was shorter:

" Because interests that were incomprehensible to you prevented me from expressing my feelings, do not imagine that I did not love you. I love you tenderly and fear more than anything that this news will drive you to despair, since I know that you, too, loved me. But alas, that love could not bind me to life! There is a higher love that lives only in the hearts of a few, but it does not meet with sympathy and dies with those hearts. All my belongings in things and money I bequeath to you. When you read this letter, I shall no longer be on the earth. Gather together all your strength to bear your loss bravely —Your  MICHAEL."

This letter, too, he read more than once, and found it touching and noble. Then he took several sheets of paper, and writing a few lines on each, addressed them to his various friends. All these letters had the same contents, and merely stated the bare facts of the case. They said:

" MY FRIEND H.—When you read this letter I shall no longer be on this earth. Life without love and glory, life without great deeds is not worth a movement of the finger, and so I die as simply and easily as I sit down to dinner.—Yours,  FIESOV."

When he had finished all the letters to his friends (and there turned out to be two dozen of them) and got up from the table, his forehead and neck were bathed in perspiration, but he never even thought of taking his handkerchief from his pocket and wiping it off. When one has decided to die, one does not think of such nonsense.

He put the letters into envelopes, addressed them, and went out into the street. There was a post-office near by where he bought a number of stamps, which he fixed on to the envelopes. Then going up to the letter-box he dropped them in, one by one, unhesitatingly and with a firm hand. When one has made an irrevocable resolution, one does not stop at trifles. Then he returned home. . . .

People meeting him on the way walked past him without taking the slightest interest in him. He felt that the world, with its commonplace, empty life, seemed to walk away from him; he no longer felt himself to be a member of that big family called humanity.

He went home, entered his room, and locked the door. Pulling out the table-drawer, he took out a revolver, wiped it, examined it carefully, and being convinced that it was in perfect order, loaded it with six cartridges and put it on the table.

" And so all is ready! All is ready! " he thought. " One movement of my hand, a light pressure on the trigger, and life, with all its enigmas and enthusiasms, is over! How simple it is! "

He was very pleased with the idea that the question should be decided so simply. He took the revolver, put it against his temple, then removed it some distance and . . . for the time being, did not shoot; he was only trying it, so as not to make a mistake, and through some negligence, remain alive. " So," he said, and again put the revolver on the table.

For some reason he wished to review all the events of his life. However, this was always done on such occasions. When you finally take leave of something, you try to see clearly what it is you are losing. He paced up and down the room. Picture after picture rose before his eyes. There were many absurdities and stupidities, but so much noble fire, so much persistency and determination, so much strength. And it would all be wasted, go down to eternity with him at his last breath.

He walked up and down for two hours. The sun rose and the street lamps were extinguished. He felt hungry. It was somewhat strange. . . . But, after all, there was really nothing strange about it. His organism had gone through a terrible ordeal; in a few hours it had lived through a lifetime! Besides, he never ate anything after his morning beef-steak.

At first he wanted to deny his organism the satisfaction of this purely animal desire, in which there was nothing lofty. It was even incongruous, somehow, to be thinking of food a few hours, perhaps minutes, before death. But he was so irresistibly drawn towards the little low cupboard where his provisions were kept, that he could not control himself. He opened the door, and suddenly, in a terrible fright, jumped back against the opposite wall. A mouse had jumped from the cupboard and scampered into its hole in a corner of the room. He was unutterably afraid of mice.

It flashed through his mind that to be afraid of such a silly thing in his position was somewhat unseemly. All the same, he was afraid of mice and remained by the wall until his last enemy, his enemy at death's door, had disappeared into its hole.

Then he again approached the cupboard, took out some sausage, an open tin of sardines, a half-empty bottle of beer and a small bottle of vodka. He put all these things on the table, drank a little vodka, and began to eat with excellent appetite.

" Of course this does not change the facts of the case at all," he thought, and lit a candle. Feeling a little tired, he sat down in an arm-chair and became lost in thought. He was thinking of the same thing, that is, his past life as well as the future did not exist for him. . . .

At nine o'clock in the morning of the following day there was a large concourse of people in the corridor of the house where Fiesov lived. All those friends of Fiesov's who had received his letter appeared there with peculiarly anxious faces; Varenka ran up, pale

142*

and excited; Fiesov's mother and sister drove up in a cab, both in a half-fainting condition. The landlord was also there, as well as a policeman and the district inspector.

As the fatal event was known to every one, they dispensed with preliminary attempts to get the door open and immediately employed a locksmith. While the locksmith was engaged on the lock, a restrained whispered conversation went on in the corridor. The landlord of the house expressed the opinion that the event was to be expected, and that in general Fiesov was capable of anything. The district inspector agreed with him. " Oh yes," he said, " he was bound to come to some such end; you know he has long been under observation at the police station." He was evidently of the opinion that every one who was under police supervision was bound to commit suicide. Varenka was crying and blaming herself as the chief cause of the catastrophe. The rest were perplexed, growing gradually accustomed to the idea that Fiesov was bound to have acted in that manner.

The locksmith turned to the district inspector. " It is ready, sir."

The inspector put his hand on the handle of the door, opened it cautiously, and walked in, followed by all the people gathered in the corridor.

For a moment all were dumbfounded at the picture before them. No one understood anything. Fiesov was sitting in an armchair, his long legs in their big boots being stretched out beneath the table. His head, resting against the back of the chair, hung to one side. On the table near him lay a revolver. The only strange thing was that there was no sign of blood anywhere, and his face was red and not pale, while it even seemed that there was perspiration on his forehead. His long hair fell untidily to one side.

" He still breathes! " some one remarked, noticing that Fiesov's powerful shoulders rose and fell like a wave on the sea.

" He breathes! He breathes! " they all cried out in chorus under the presidency of the district inspector, who, being by his calling unafraid of dead men, moved towards the table, and suddenly jumped back.

Fiesov rose up to his full height, and rubbing his eyes, looked at his guests.

He evidently could not make out what it was all about.

" What the devil is the matter? " he said at last, in a sleepy voice. " Or am I dreaming? "

" Mr. Fiesov, you informed your friends that you were going to lay hands on yourself," the district inspector said. " It is not fitting to make a jest of such a thing. You may even have to answer for it. . . ."

Fiesov suddenly remembered everything.

" The devil! Of course! How is it I went to sleep? Eh? " he said, seizing his head. " Well . . . well . . . I suppose it is fate."

To-day he hadn't the slightest desire to die. A good sleep had, like a hand, taken from him his mood of yesterday.

The inspector walked out, severely followed by the policeman, while Fiesov's friends stayed behind to congratulate him on his fortunate and miraculous escape from death.

.          .          .          .          .          .

Five years later, Fiesov might have been met every morning at nine o'clock making his way to a certain office, and at three o'clock on his way back. He was smartly dressed, wore short hair and a bowler hat. Being at last convinced that you cannot make yourself bigger than you are, he resigned himself, took a place in a business office, and began to live as all do.

There were rumours that Varenka was no longer averse to accepting a proposal from him if he made it now, and as he still preserved his former attachment towards her, there is no doubt that the proposal was made and that the marriage took place.

# ANTON P. CHEKHOV

1860–1904

# DARLING

OLIENKA, the daughter of the retired civil servant Plenianikov, sat musing outside in her little porch. It was hot; the tiresome flies were very persistent; it was pleasant to think that it would soon be evening. Dark, rain-laden clouds were coming up from the East, whence every now and again the distant rain could be seen.

In the middle of the yard stood Kukin, theatrical producer and proprietor of " The Tivoli " pleasure gardens, who lodged in a wing of the house. He stood looking out on the sky.

" Again! " he said in a tone of despair. " It is going to rain again! Every day, rain! rain! It seems to rain out of sheer perversity. It spells ruin to me! Every day of it means a terrible loss! "

He clasped his hands and turned to Olga Semionovna:

" It is enough to make a man cry! You work and strive and worry; you lie awake at night, thinking out ways and means of improving things, and what is the result? First you have the stupid ignorant public; you give it the best little operettas, cantatas, beautiful duets, but do you think it appreciates them? Do you think it understands them? Not a bit. What it wants is low comedy. Give it something vulgar. And then, look at the weather! Every evening it rains. It has been raining steadily from the 10th of May and all through June. It is simply dreadful! The public does not come, but the artists will not forgo their pay nor the landlord his rent."

On the following day, when, towards evening, the clouds began to gather again, Kukin held forth with a hysterical laugh:

" Well, let it rain! Let the garden get flooded with water, and may I drown in it, so that I shall have no more happiness in the next world than in this. Let the actors sue me! I don't care! Let them sentence me to hard labour in Siberia! To the scaffold! Ha! Ha! Ha! "

The same thing was repeated on the third day.

Olienka would listen seriously to Kukin, not saying a word, and sometimes her eyes would fill with tears. In the end she was touched

by Kukin's misfortunes and fell in love with him. He was small
and thin, had a reedy Jewish voice, a waxed moustache, and a
yellow face that bore a perpetual expression of despair, but still he
inspired in her real, deep love. She could not exist without love,
and was always in love with some one or other. Once it was her
father, who was now an invalid in an arm-chair, who sat in a
dark room battling for breath. Then it was her aunt, who lived
at Bransk, and came to visit them twice a year, and earlier, when
she was still at school, she had been in love with her French master.

Olienka was a healthy, quiet, good-natured, kind-hearted girl.
Looking at her plump rosy cheeks, her soft white neck with the
mole on it, her good-natured smile that never failed to appear when
something pleased her, men would say to themselves, " Yes, she
is quite pretty," and respond to her smile, while lady guests would
sometimes, in the middle of a conversation, seize her by the hand
and exclaim, in an outburst of affection, " You darling! "

The house (in which she had lived since her birth) was situated
on the outskirts of the town, in Gipsy Lane, not far from the
" Tivoli " gardens. In the evenings she could hear the music in
the gardens and the noise of the fireworks in the air, and it seemed
to her that there Kukin was battling with his fate and assailing his
principal foe—the indifferent public. A sweet trembling would
come over her heart, the desire for sleep would leave her, and when,
towards morning Kukin returned home, she would tap gently at
her window, put out her head and give him a gentle smile.

Soon he proposed to her and they were married. When he was
privileged to see her white neck and full round shoulders, he clapped
his hands and exclaimed, " You darling! "

He was happy in his own way, but as it rained on his wedding
day, the look of despair did not leave his face.

After the wedding they lived together very happily. She would
sit in the box-office, see that the gardens were tidy, keep the
accounts, and pay the wages; her rosy cheeks and sweet naïve smile
now shining from the little box-office window, now from the wings
of the stage, now from the buffet. And she went about telling her
acquaintances that there was nothing more necessary or important
in the world than the theatre, and that it was the only thing that
afforded true pleasure and made one cultured and humane.

" But do you think the public sees this? " she would ask.
" What it wants is low comedy! Yesterday we gave a performance
of *Faust*, and would you believe it, all the boxes were empty. If
Vanotchka and I had put on some vulgar piece the theatre would
have been packed. To-morrow Vanotchka and I are producing
*Orpheus in Hell*. You must come and see it."

Everything that Kukin said she repeated. Like her husband, she
too despised the public for its boorishness and indifference to art.
She would interfere at rehearsals, correct the actors, supervise the

behaviour of the musicians, and when an adverse criticism appeared in the local paper, she would cry bitterly and rush off to the editor to protest and explain.

All the actors liked her; they used to call her " Vanotchka and I," or " Darling." She was very good to them, would lend them small sums of money, and if it so happened that she was sometimes deceived in one of them, she would indulge in a good cry all by herself, but would never complain to her husband.

In the winter, too, they lived together happily. They took the town theatre for the season and let it out for short periods to little Russian touring companies, to conjurors, or to local amateurs. Olienka filled out and literally shone with contentment, while Kukin grew thinner and more yellow, and would go about complaining of his losses, though in reality his affairs went remarkably well the whole winter. He used to cough at night, and his wife would give him raspberry syrup, lime-flower tea, or she would bathe his forehead with eau-de-Cologne and wrap him up in her soft shawls.

" What a dear you are! " she would say quite sincerely, stroking his hair. " How handsome you are! "

In Lent he went to Moscow to get together a company, and she, left alone, could not sleep at nights, but would sit at the window gazing at the stars. At such times she would compare herself to the hens that were restless and could not settle down at night without a rooster.

Kukin was detained in Moscow. He wrote saying that he would return by Holy Week, and made arrangements regarding the " Tivoli." But on Monday of Passion Week, late at night, there was a loud ominous knock at the gate—Boom! Boom! Boom!' The sleepy cook, shuffling along in her bare feet, went to open it.

" Open, please! " a deep voice said from the other side of the gate, " there is a telegram for you."

This was not the first time Olienka had received a telegram from her husband, but, somehow, she grew cold all over. With trembling hands she tore open the telegram and read the following words, " Ivan Petrovitch died suddenly to-day. We await instructions for funeral on Tuesday."

The signature was that of the manager of the company.

" My darling! " Olienka sobbed aloud. " My own dear Vanotchka! Why did we ever meet? Why did I get to know and love you? Why have you left your poor unfortunate Olienka? . . ."

Kukin was buried on Tuesday in Moscow at Vagankov cemetery. Olienka returned home on Wednesday, and reaching home, she threw herself on her bed, crying so loudly that her plaints could be heard in the street.

" Darling! " said the neighbours, crossing themselves; " Darling Olga Semionovna is bewailing her husband."

One day, three months later, when Olienka was returning from church dressed in deep mourning, one of her neighbours, Vassily Andreyitch Pustovalov, who was also returning from church, happened to be walking at her side. He wore a straw hat and white waistcoat, across which hung a gold chain, and looked more like a country squire than a merchant.

" Everything has its meaning," he said gravely, with a sympathetic tone in his voice. " If some one near to us happens to die, it is by the will of God. We must think of ourselves and bear our sorrows humbly."

He accompanied Olienka right to her door and there left her. For the rest of the day she could hear his steady voice, and she had only to close her eyes in order to see his dark beard. She had taken a great liking to him. Apparently she, too, had made an impression on him.

Not many days later, a certain old lady whom she knew but little, came to take coffee with her, and no sooner was she seated than she began talking of Pustovalov, saying what a good, respectable man he was, and that many women would be only too glad to get the chance of marrying him. Three days later Pustovalov himself came to visit her. He did not stay for more than ten minutes or so, and said very little, but Olienka fell in love with him, so deeply, that she lay in a fever the whole night and could not close her eyes. The following morning she sent for the old lady. Soon she was engaged and not long after she married.

After the wedding Pustovalov and Olienka lived together happily. He would work in his office until dinner-time, after which he would go out on business and Olienka would take his place until the evening, making up accounts and attending to the despatch of goods.

" Timber is getting twenty per cent dearer every year," she would say to her customers and acquaintances. " Why, not long ago we used to sell local timber entirely, now Vasitchka has to go and buy it in the government of Mogilev. And what an awful tariff we have to pay! " she would exclaim, holding her hands up in horror. " What a tariff! "

It seemed to her that she had dealt in timber for years and years, and that the most important and necessary thing in the world was timber. She would pronounce the technical terms, like beam, plank, joist, deal, batten, etc., with a touching sense of kinship.

In her dreams at night she would see mountains of boards and planks, and long chains of carts carrying timber out of the town. Once she dreamt that a whole regiment of beams invaded the yard, and a fierce battle ensued. The planks and beams struggled with one another, falling in heaps with a tremendous crash and getting up again. She cried aloud in her sleep, and Pustovalov said gently, " Olienka, dear, what is the matter with you? Cross yourself! "

What her husband thought, she thought also. If, for instance, he thought that it was too hot in the room, or that business was slack, she thought so too. Her husband did not care for outside amusements, and would stay at home even during holidays, and she would always stay with him.

" You are always at home or at the office," her friends would say to her. " Why don't you go to the theatre or the circus occasionally? "

" Vasitchka and I have no time for the theatre," she would reply solemnly. " We are hard-working folk, and have no time to waste on nonsense. Besides, what good is there in a theatre? "

On Saturday evenings Pustovalov and Olienka would go to church, and on all feast days to early service. They would return home from church side by side, their faces the embodiment of kindliness. They were both slightly perfumed, and Olienka's silk dress rustled pleasantly. When they got home they would have tea and milk-bread, with various jams, and afterwards pies. Always about mid-day an appetising smell would issue from their door, past the gate, into the street,—a smell of soup, roast lamb or duck, varied on fast days by that of fish. One's appetite was always whetted on passing their gate. In the office a samovar was always ready, and the customers were given tea and rolls. Once a week husband and wife would go to the baths and return side by side, both very red.

" We have nothing to complain of : we live very well, thank God! " Olienka would say to her acquaintances. " God grant every one such happiness as Vasitchka and I have."

When Pustovalov went away to Mogilev to buy timber, she felt very lonely, and would lie awake, crying, the whole night. Sometimes, in the evening, Sinerdin, a young army veterinary surgeon who lodged in the wing of her house, would come and sit with her. He would talk or play cards, and amuse her for a while. She was especially interested to hear about his own private life. He was married and had a little boy. He did not live with his wife, for she had deceived him, but sent her a monthly allowance of forty roubles for the boy. When he talked of his family Olienka would sigh, shake her head, and feel very sorry for him.

" God be with you," she would say as she bade him good-night and accompanied him to the top of the stairs with a candle. " Thank you for trying to amuse me. God grant you health. Our holy Mother . . ."

She expressed herself in the same grave, solemn manner as her husband. When the veterinary surgeon had gone down the stairs and was already out of the door she still called after him:

" Do you know, Vladimir Platonitch, you should try to get reconciled to your wife. You should forgive her, if only for your boy's sake. Boys understand so much."

And when Pustovalov returned, she told him in a whisper about the veterinary surgeon's unhappy married life, and they both sighed and shook their heads, and talked about the boy, whom they feared must miss his father. Then, by some strange bond of sympathy, they both fell on their knees before the holy image, bowed down to the ground, and prayed that God would bless them with children.

Thus the Pustovalovs lived quietly and peacefully in love and concord for six years, when one winter day, Vassily Andreyitch having gone out without a hat on after drinking some hot tea, caught a chill and took to his bed. The best doctors attended him, but the illness ran its course, and he died after four months. Olienka was again a widow.

" Why did you leave me, darling! " she sobbed at the funeral. " How can I live without you, poor unfortunate wretch that I am? Good people pity me, a poor orphan. . . ."

She dressed herself in deep mourning and gave up wearing a hat and gloves. Rarely did she go out of the house, and then only to church or to visit her husband's grave, and she lived at home like a nun. It was not until six months after her husband's death that she put off her widow's weeds and opened the shutters of her windows. Sometimes, in the morning, she would be seen marketing with her cook, but as to how she lived at home and what was happening there, people could only guess. They guessed by such signs as, for instance, that she was seen taking tea in the garden with the veterinary surgeon, and that he read the paper aloud to her; that once, when she met an acquaintance in the street, she was reported to have said:

" We have no adequate veterinary supervision in our town, and as a consequence disease is frequent. For instance, one hears of people falling ill through drinking bad milk, or by being infected by horses and cows. We ought to be just as careful about the health of our animals as we are of our own health."

She repeated the veterinary surgeon's words and held all his opinions about everything. It was clear that she could not live without an attachment, and had found her happiness in the little wing of the house. Neither she nor the veterinary surgeon spoke to people about their new relations, and tried to keep it secret, but they were not successful, for Olienka could have no secrets. When his colleagues from the regiment came to visit him, she would give them supper and pour out their tea; at the same time she would talk about the plague that had attacked the cattle, and complain about the town slaughter-house, while the veterinary surgeon would feel very uncomfortable, and as soon as the others had gone would seize her by the hand and whisper angrily:

" I've told you not to talk about things you don't understand! When my colleagues and I are talking, I must ask you not to interfere. This is too much! "

She would look at him in amazement and ask anxiously:
" But, Volodotchka, what can I talk about? " and with tears
in her eyes she would put her arms round him, beg him not to be
angry, and they would make it up.

However, this happiness did not last long. The veterinary
surgeon departed with his regiment, departed for ever, as he was
stationed far away, near Siberia. And Olienka was left alone.

Now she was quite alone. Her father had died some time before,
and his chair, covered with dust and with one leg broken, reposed
somewhere in the garret. She grew thin and plain, and when
people met her in the street they no longer looked at her nor greeted
her with a smile as of old. Clearly her best years had gone by, and
she had begun some new kind of life, strange and unknown, about
which it was better not to think.

In the evenings Olienka would sit at her little porch and listen to
the music and the fireworks at the " Tivoli," but it meant nothing
to her. No longer did it inspire thoughts. She would look out on
her empty yard, thinking of nothing, desiring nothing, and when
night came she would go to bed and dream of the empty yard. She
ate and drank almost mechanically.

And what was worse than all, she no longer had any opinions.
She saw the objects around her and understood all that went on,
but she could not form any opinion about these things, and did not
know what to talk about. How awful it is not to have opinions!
For instance, you see a bottle, or it rains, or a peasant drives by
in a cart, but why the bottle stands there, or the rain falls, or the
peasant passes, what meaning there is in these things, you could
not say for a thousand roubles. In the days of Kukin and Pustovalov, and later, in the time of the veterinary surgeon, Olienka
would have explained everything. and given her opinions on any
subject, but now her mind and heart were as empty as her yard.
It was as bitter and painful as gall.

Little by little the town expanded on all sides. Gipsy Lane was
now called a street, and in place of the " Tivoli " gardens and the
timber yards there were little streets of houses. How quickly time
flies! Olienka's house was no longer white, the roof was rusty and
the garden filled with weeds. Olienka herself grew old and plain.
In the summer she would sit at her little porch, her soul as sad and
empty as ever, and in winter she would sit by the window and look
out upon the snow. With the coming of spring, when the wind
carried the sound of the church bells towards her, a gleam of
memory would remind her of the past. A sweet pain would come
over her, and her tears would flow abundantly, but this would be
only for a moment. Again there was emptiness, and she did not
know why she lived.

Briska the black cat would purr and rub herself against her mistress, but Olienka was not moved by these caresses. That was not

what she desired. She wanted the kind of love that would absorb all her being, her soul, her reason; give her thought and an understanding of life; the kind of love that would warm her aged blood. She pushed Briska from her with annoyance, saying:

" Go away! Go away! I don't want you here! "

And so the days and the years went by without so much as a single joy, idea, or even opinion. What Mavra the cook said was quite good enough for Olienka.

One fine hot day, towards evening, when the cattle were being driven home and the yard was filled with clouds of dust, some one knocked at the gate. Olienka herself went to open it, and when she looked out she stopped short, bewildered. Outside stood the veterinary surgeon Sinerdin, already grey, and in civilian dress. Suddenly she remembered everything, and bursting into tears embraced him. She did not say a word, and was so excited that she did not know how they got into the house and sat down to tea.

" My dear Vladimir Platonitch! " she murmured, trembling with joy, " whence did the Lord send you? "

" I want to settle down here for good," he began. " I have retired and want happiness in freedom in my old age. Besides, it is time my boy went to school; he is growing up. You know, of course, that I am reconciled with my wife."

" Where is she? " Olienka asked.

" She is at the hotel with the boy, and I am hunting for lodgings."

" But, my dear, you can have the whole of my house! What do you want with lodgings? And I will not take anything from you," Olienka went on excitedly, and burst into tears again. " You can live here; the little wing will be enough for me! What joy, my Lord! "

The next day the roof was being painted and the walls whitewashed. Olienka went about with her arms akimbo, giving orders. On her face shone the former smile—she seemed to have become alive again, grown younger, as if awakened from a long sleep.

The veterinary surgeon's wife arrived, a thin, ugly, disagreeable woman with short hair, and with her the boy Sasha, a chubby little fellow of nine, with clear blue eyes and dimpled cheeks. He had scarcely entered the yard when he ran up to the cat, and soon there was heard his merry laugh:

" Auntie, is this your cat? " he asked Olienka. " When she has kittens will you give us one of them? Mamma is afraid of mice."

Olienka talked to him and gave him tea; a sweet emotion pervaded her, just as if he had been her own son. And when, in the evenings, he used to sit at the table repeating his lessons, she would look at him with affection and pity and whisper:

" My darling beautiful boy . . . little one . . . how clever and pretty you are! "

" An island," he read out, " is a piece of land surrounded entirely by water."

" An island is a piece of land . . ." she would repeat, and this was the first opinion she had expressed with conviction after all those years of silence and absence of thought.

She had her opinions now, and at supper would talk to Sasha's parents about how difficult it was for children at school nowadays; that still scholastic training was better than home teaching; that after passing out of school one could do what one liked, go in for medicine or engineering.

Sasha was sent to school. His mother went off to Kharkov to her sister's and never returned, and his father was out every day seeing cattle and would sometimes not come back for two or three days at a stretch. It seemed to Olienka that the boy was quite neglected, that he was superfluous in the house, and that he would die of hunger, so she took him to her side of the house and installed him there in a little room.

Six months had gone by since Sasha came over to her wing of the house. Every morning Olienka goes into his room while he is still asleep with his cheek on his arm. She scarcely breathes, and it pains her to wake him.

" Sasha! " she says at last, softly, " get up, dear; it is time to go to school! "

He dresses himself, says his prayers, and then sits down to breakfast. He drinks three cups of tea, eats two rolls and some French bread and butter. He is not quite awake yet, and feels a little cross.

" Sasha, dear, learn your fable properly," Olienka says, with a look as though she were sending him off on a long journey. " What a trial you are to me! Try, dear, and do well. Obey your masters . . ."

" Oh, do leave off! " answers Sasha.

Presently he is on his way to school, a little boy in a big cap, with a satchel on his back. Olienka follows him softly. " Sashinka! " she calls after him. He turns round and she thrusts a date or a caramel into his hand. When he turns the corner of the street leading to his school, he feels ashamed that a big, tall woman should be following him; he turns round and says:

" Auntie, you had better turn back now; I can go on alone from here."

She stops and watches him until he disappears within the school gates. Ah! How she loves him! Not one of her former loves has been as deep, nor was her soul ever so utterly subjected with such disinterestedness and consolation as now, when more and more there awakened in her the feeling of motherhood. For this strange boy she would have given up her life with the greatest of pleasure, thankfully. Why? Who can tell?

She goes home after having seen Sasha safely to school, so quiet and peaceful and contented; so full of love. Her face, that has grown younger in the last six months, shines radiantly. Acquaintances meeting her feel a pleasure at the sight of her and say:

" Good morning, darling Olga Semionovna! How are you getting on, my dear? "

" Lessons are so hard for children at school nowadays," she says on meeting an acquaintance marketing. " It is no joke. Yesterday in the first form they had to learn a fable off by heart, as well as do some Latin translations and a problem. . . . What do they expect of a child? "

And she begins to talk of the masters, the lessons, the text-books, repeating Sasha's opinions.

At three o'clock they have dinner together; in the evening they do the home work, and cry together. Putting him to bed, she makes the sign of the cross over him many times, murmuring a prayer, and when she herself goes to bed, ponders over the future, distant and vague, when Sasha will have finished his education and become a doctor or an engineer; when he will have his own house and carriage, marry and have children. . . . She begins to doze, still worrying over these things, the tears running down her cheeks from out her closed eyelids. The black cat is lying at her side, purring.

Boom! Boom! Boom!

Suddenly, there is a knock at the gate. Olienka starts up and can scarcely breathe for fear; her heart is hammering. A few seconds go by and the knocking is repeated.

" It must be a telegram from Kharkov," she thinks, shaking like a leaf. " The mother wants Sasha back. . . . Ah, God! " She is in despair; her head and hands and feet have gone quite cold. It seems to her that she is the most unfortunate being in the whole world. Another minute goes by and voices are heard. It is the veterinary surgeon returning from his club.

" Thank God! " she says to herself.

Gradually that oppressive feeling leaves her; again she feels light-hearted. She lies down, thinking of Sasha, who is sleeping soundly in the next room, and every now and again she hears him talking in his sleep:

" I'll give it to you! "    " Get away! "    " Don't fight! "

# THE ENCASED MAN

ANTON P. CHEKHOV

In a shed belonging to Prokoffy the elder, on the outskirts of the village, the belated hunters were preparing for bed. There were two of them, a veterinary surgeon, Ivan Ivanitch, and Burkin, a schoolmaster. Ivan Ivanitch had a curious double surname, " Chimsha Gimalaisky," and as it did not fit him, he was known over the whole country merely by his Christian name and patronymic. He lived near the town, at the stud, and had come down to enjoy the fresh air. Burkin, the schoolmaster, stayed with Count P—— every summer, and therefore was quite at home in the place.

They could not sleep. Ivan Ivanitch, a tall gaunt old man of sixty, with a long moustache, was sitting by the door of the shed, smoking his pipe. The moon shone full on his face. Burkin lay inside on the straw, and in the darkness could not be seen.

They touched on various topics. Among other things, they talked about the elder's wife, Mavra. She was healthy and not at all stupid, yet she had never in her life been out of the village, nor had she seen a town or a railway train. For the last ten years she had sat at home by the stove all day and come out only at night.

" There is nothing astonishing in that! " Burkin remarked. " There are many people in the world who are solitary by nature and who try to withdraw into their shells like a crab or a snail. It may be a type of atavism, a reversion to the time when our forefathers were not yet social animals, but lived alone in caves; or perhaps it is merely one of the many aspects of human character—who knows? Of course, I am not a scientist, it is not my business to bother about such questions, but it seems to me that people like Mavra are not rare in this world. Here is an example. About two months ago, there died in our town a certain man by the name of Belikov, a Greek master and colleague of mine. Perhaps you have heard of him. He was distinguished by the fact that even in fine weather he invariably went about wearing goloshes and a padded overcoat, and carrying an umbrella. His umbrella was always in a sheath, and his watch in a grey leather pocket. When he brought out his pocket-knife to sharpen his pencil, that too was in a case; even his face seemed to be in a case, as it was always hidden inside his high collar. He wore dark spectacles, a comforter, and cotton-wool in his ears. When he took a cab he always asked the driver to put up the hood. In a word, this man was constantly striving to envelop himself, to make a case for himself, so to speak, that would protect him from all outside influences. Reality irritated and frightened him, and held him in a perpetual state of anxiety. It may be, that in order to justify his timidity, his dislike for reality, he always praised the past and things that had never existed. The dead languages that he spoke were at bottom no more than the goloshes in which he hid himself from the realities of life.

" ' How beautiful and musical the Greek tongue is! ' he would say, with a sentimental expression; and as though to give proof to his words, he half closed his eyes and raised one finger when he pronounced the word ' Anthropos! '

" His thoughts too, Belikov tried to enclose in a case. The only things he could clearly understand were circulars prohibiting something or other and articles of the same nature. If a circular forbade a boy to be out in the street after nine o'clock in the evening —or an article spoke against the love of the flesh, then for him it was quite clear and definite—something was forbidden and there was an end to it. To him there was always a doubtful element about positive decision and permission—something unutterably lazy. If a theatrical society was formed in the town; if a reading were arranged or a tea-party made up, he would always shake his head and say quietly:

" ' This is all very fine, but I am afraid something or other may happen.'

" Any transgression or departure from the ordinary rules of convention made him feel wretched, though one might have wondered what it could possibly matter to him. If one of his colleagues happened to be late for morning prayers; if he heard of the pranks of some boy or other; if one of the mistresses was seen walking in the evening with an officer, he became hugely excited and would go about saying something or other was sure to happen.

" At our staff conferences he oppressed us all with his cautiousness and suspiciousness, his stereotyped precautions regarding the boys' and the girls' school.

" He would complain that the boys behaved badly and were noisy in class; that it might get to the ears of the principal and that something or other would happen; that if Petrov of the second form and Yegorev of the fourth were expelled, then things might be better. What did we think? With his sighs and lamentations, his smoked glasses on his tiny pale face—a face as small as that of a polecat, he oppressed us all. Petrov and Yegorev were taken in hand, put under arrest, and in the end both were expelled from school. He had a curious habit of visiting us regularly in our own quarters. He would come to a man's rooms, sit down silently as though on the look-out for something, stay like that for an hour or two, and then go away without a word. This is what he called

' maintaining good relations with his colleagues.' One could see that these visits were irksome to him, and that he only kept them up out of a sheer sense of duty.

" All the masters stood in awe of him, and so did the principal too. Imagine our men, fairly clever, respectable fellows, all brought up on Turgeniev and Schedrin, and then this man who always went about with his umbrella and goloshes, ruling the school with an iron hand for the space of twenty-five years! And not only the school; he ruled the whole town! The ladies would be afraid to arrange private theatricals or Saturday evening parties for fear that it should get to his ears; they were actually afraid to indulge their palate or to join a game of cards in his presence. Owing to the influence of such people as Belikov, for the last ten or fifteen years every one was afraid of doing anything at all in our town. One was afraid of talking too loudly, of writing letters, of making acquaintances, even of learning to read and write. . . ."

Ivan Ivanitch, wishing to make a remark, cleared his throat, puffed at his pipe, and said hesitatingly:

" Yes; clever, respectable men who read Schedrin, Turgeniev, Buckle, and so on, yet they gave in, submitted. . . . That is the point."

" Belikov lived in the same house where I did," Burkin continued. " His door was opposite mine; we saw a good deal of each other and I knew all about his domestic life. It was the same thing at home, dressing-gown, night-cap, shutters, bolts, a whole heap of restrictions and limitations, and oh! if something or other should happen? Fast fare was supposed to be bad for him, rich fare impossible, so they said he used to eat fish cooked in butter—a diet that could hardly be called plain on the one hand or rich on the other. He was afraid of having a woman servant in the house for fear of getting a bad name, so he kept a man-cook, Afonasy by name, an old fellow of sixty who was a drunkard and half-witted, and had been an officer's servant and could cook after a fashion. He would stand by the door with arms crossed constantly mumbling the same sentence:

" ' How they do increase nowadays! '

" Belikov's bedroom was very small, just like a box, and his bed was enclosed by curtains. When he got into bed at night, he would pull the bed-clothes right over his head. It was hot and stuffy, the stove roared, the wind shook the tightly-closed doors; sighs came from the kitchen, ominous sighs. . . .

" He lay in bed under the bed-clothes trembling with fear. He was afraid that something or other would happen; that Afonasy would cut his throat or that thieves would get in; even when he went to sleep he was troubled by unpleasant dreams. When in the morning we walked to school together, he was pale and depressed, and one could see that the idea of going into the school with its many people was a source of terror to him, was repugnant to his whole being. Even my presence was irksome to his solitary nature. ' The class-rooms are very noisy,' he would say as if trying to find an excuse for his depression. ' I don't know what things are coming to.' And would you believe it, this Greek master, this encased man, very nearly got married! ''

" Not really! You're joking! ''

" Yes, he nearly did, though it may seem remarkable to you. A new Master was appointed for history and geography, a fellow from Little Russia by the name of Michael Savitch Kovalenko. He did not come alone, but brought his sister Varenka with him. He was a tall young man, with a swarthy complexion and large hands; you could tell from the look of him that he had a bass voice, and it really was as deep as though it issued from a barrel—Ber! Ber! Ber! His sister was no longer young—about thirty—tall and graceful, with red cheeks and dark brows, as pretty a girl as one could wish to see. She was jolly and boisterous, very fond of laughing. At the smallest trifle she would burst into a ringing laugh—' Ha! ha! ha! '

" I remember that the first occasion on which we really had an opportunity of becoming acquainted with the Kovalenkos was at a birthday party given to the principal. Amidst the dry, uncomfortable pedagogues who even go to parties out of a sense of duty, we suddenly saw a new Aphrodite born out of the foam. She came in with her arms folded, laughed, sung, danced. She sang ' The Winds Blow ' with great feeling; then another song and another until we were all charmed, even Belikov. He sat down near her and remarked with a sentimental smile:

" ' The tongue of Little Russia by its softness and its music reminds one of ancient Greek.'

" She felt flattered by this and began talking enthusiastically about her Province of Gadvansk; of the farm-house where her mother lived; of the lovely cherries they grew, and melons and pumpkins (melons and pumpkins she called by their quaint Little Russian names), and of the delicious soups they made—so delicious that they made your mouth water.

" As we sat listening to her, suddenly, for some unknown reason, the same thought came into our minds.

" ' It would be nice to get them married! ' the principal's wife whispered to me.

" It was brought home to us immediately that Belikov was not married, and it seemed strange to me that we had not been conscious of this till now; and had completely overlooked this important possibility in his life. ' How does he bear himself towards women, and what does he think of marriage? ' Formerly, this had not interested us in the least; it may be because it never occurred to us that a man who always wore goloshes and always slept in a curtained bed could possibly fall in love.

" ' He is well over forty and she is thirty . . .' the inspiration of the principal's wife began taking shape. ' I think she would accept him.'

" You don't know the things we do in the provinces out of sheer boredom, what unnecessary, stupid things! I daresay it is because we never do what is necessary. For some reason we were all seized with an irresistible desire to see Belikov married, though he was the sort of man you could not imagine with a wife. The principal's wife, the inspector's wife, all the women connected with the establishment became immensely interested, got to look brighter even, as though they had suddenly discovered an aim in life.

" The principal's wife took a box at the theatre, and there was Varenka with a lovely fan, smiling and happy, and by her side Belikov, small and bent, looking as though he had been dragged from his house. I gave a party; the ladies insisted that Belikov and Varenka should be invited. In a word, the machine was set in motion. Varenka was very nearly married. Life at her brother's was not very gay—it was generally known that they were always bickering and quarrelling. This is a typical scene. Kovalenko would be striding down the street, a tall lanky fellow in an embroidered shirt, his hair crowding out from under his cap on to his forehead; in one hand would be a parcel of books, in the other a thick knotted walking-stick.

" Behind would follow his sister, also carrying an armful of books. ' But, Michael, you've not read this one! ' she shouts after him, ' I'm sure you haven't! '

" ' I tell you I have! ' Kovalenko shouts back angrily, banging his stick on the pavement.

" ' Oh dear, Minchick, why will you get angry! Our discussion is merely a matter of principle.'

" ' I tell you I've read it! ' Kovalenko bawls still louder, again banging his stick on the pavement.

" As you may imagine, it was much worse at home. The girl of course got tired of such a life, and longed for a home of her own; and besides, she was getting on in years. There was no chance for her; she had to marry whom she could, and even the Greek master was not to be despised. I daresay most of our girls marry merely for the sake of marrying. However, be that as it may, Varenka began to show a distinct preference for Belikov.

" As for Belikov, he used to visit Kovalenko in the same way that he did us. He would arrive and sit down without speaking. He would keep silent while Varenka sung to him ' The Winds Blow ' or gazed pensively at him with her dark eyes, or suddenly burst out with her ' Ha! ha! ha! '

" In love affairs, particularly when there is a question of

marriage, suggestion plays an important part. All of us—my colleagues and the ladies—took to proving to Belikov that he ought to marry—that there was nothing to do in life but marry. We congratulated him, and with serious mien would utter such commonplaces as that marriage was a serious step. Besides, Varenka was not a bad-looking girl, was the daughter of a councillor of state, and, most important of all, was the first girl who had been nice and kind to him. In the end his head was turned and he decided to marry."

" At that stage you ought to have taken his goloshes and umbrella from him," Ivan Ivanitch remarked.

" We found that impossible. He put Varenka's photograph on his table, and used to call on me often to talk about her, about family life, about what a serious step marriage was. He visited Varenka frequently too, but did not change his mode of life one atom. On the contrary the thought of marriage seemed to have a depressing effect on him; he got thin and pale and retreated still further into his shell.

" ' I like Varvara Savishna,' he would say to me with a faint smile, ' And I think every man should marry, but . . . it all happened so suddenly . . . I must consider.'

" ' What is there to consider? ' I said to him. ' Marry and get it over! '

" ' No, marriage is a serious step; one must weigh carefully all the duties and responsibilities it implies—so that nothing untoward should happen afterwards. I am so disturbed I cannot sleep at nights. To tell the truth, I am afraid she and her brother have such queer ideas, they look at things in such an unusual way. . . . And then, she is so rash. You may marry, and, without foreseeing it, let yourself in for something or other.'

" He kept on deferring the proposal, much to the disgust of the principal's wife and all the other ladies, while he duly weighed his future duties and responsibilities. At the same time he used to walk with Varenka every day, perhaps because he thought it was expected of him, and would call on me every evening to talk about family life.

" As far as one can conjecture he would have proposed to her in the end, and there would have followed one of those absurd marriages that take place by the thousand in our midst, either because people are bored or that they have nothing better to do. But suddenly there happened a tremendous scandal. I must first tell you that Varenka's brother Kovalenko took a deep dislike to Belikov the first time he met him, and could not endure the sight of him.

" ' I can't understand why you want to talk to that spy, that little worm. How can you fellows live here? The very atmosphere is suffocating. Do you call yourselves teachers? You are too hide-bound. You do not worship at the temple of science, but at the court of decorum—you reek with stagnation like one of our policemen's sentry-boxes. No, brothers! I'll stay another six months with you and then return to my farm to fish for crabs and relearn to talk Little Russian! '

" Another time he would laugh till the tears came to his eyes; first in a deep and then in a thin voice.

" ' Why does he come to my house? ' he would ask me. ' What does he want of me? He just sits and stares.'

" He even nicknamed Belikov ' The Spider,' and when one day the principal's wife hinted that it would be a good thing for his sister to marry such a ' reliable ' man whom every one respected, he frowned and muttered, ' It's not my business. She can marry a viper if she chooses. I don't like meddling in other people's affairs.'

" Now listen to what happened later. Some mischievous person made a caricature of Belikov walking along with an open umbrella, turned-up trousers, and goloshes; on his arm was Varenka, and underneath was written ' Anthropos in love.'

" The artist had seized his expression wonderfully well. He must have spent many nights at the work. Every one received a copy—all the masters and mistresses, the civil servants—even Belikov himself got one. The caricature had a very depressing effect on him.

" We had come out of the house together. It happened to be the first of May, and we had all—masters and boys—agreed to meet at the school and then go out of the town into the woods. He was gloomier than ever.

" ' What horrid, spiteful people there are in the world,' he said, his lips trembling.

" I felt quite sorry for him. As we walked along, who should overtake us but Kovalenko on a bicycle, followed by Varenka, also on a bicycle, flushed and red, but jolly and happy. ' We'll go on ahead,' she called out to us. ' What awfully jolly weather! ' Both passed out of sight. Belikov turned from green to white and appeared quite stunned. He stood still and looked at me. ' What is the meaning of that? ' he asked; ' or do my eyes deceive me? Is it proper for schoolmasters and women to ride bicycles? '

" ' What is there improper about it? ' I asked. ' Why shouldn't they cycle if they want to? '

" ' But how is it possible? ' he exclaimed, amazed at my coolness. ' What are you saying? '

" He was so overcome that he refused to go any farther and returned home.

" On the following day he was continually rubbing his hands together nervously, and from his face one could see that he was not well. He even absented himself from his work, a thing that had never happened to him before. He had no dinner either.

Towards evening he clad himself warmly, though it was quite hot summer weather, and set out for the Kovalenkos.' Varenka was not at home, but her brother was in.

" ' Won't you sit down, please? ' said the brother coldly, with a frown. He had been roused from an after-dinner nap and was sleepy and in a bad humour.

" Belikov sat silent for about ten minutes and then began: ' I came to unburden my heart to you. I am very unhappy. Some libellous person has had the audacity to make a caricature of me and of some one else who is very dear to us both. I consider it my duty to inform you that I am not to blame in the matter. . . . I have never given the least occasion for such an insult. On the other hand, I have all along behaved as an honourable man should do.'

" Kovalenko almost boiled over with rage, but said nothing. Belikov, too, sat silent for a moment, and then continued in a soft sad voice:

" ' I have another thing I want to say to you. I have been at my work now for a long time, while you are only just beginning. I consider it my duty as an older colleague to advise you. You ride a bicycle, and such an amusement is not proper to one who has the education of children.'

" ' Why, may I ask? ' Kovalenko said in his bass voice.

" ' I should have thought it was unnecessary to explain, Michael Savitch, the reasons are so obvious. If the masters ride bicycles, what must one expect from the boys? Nothing remains for them but to walk on their heads. Besides, when a thing is forbidden by a circular it stands to reason it is impossible. I was horrified yesterday when I saw your sister. I could scarcely believe my eyes. For a lady to ride a bicycle is positively dreadful.'

" ' May I ask what it is you want? '

" ' I only want to advise you, Michael Savitch. You are a young man; your future is still before you. You should conduct yourself with caution. You make many, many mistakes. You wear embroidered shirts, always go about the streets carrying bundles of books, and then there is the bicycle! The principal is sure to get to know that you and your sister cycle, and from him to the governors . . . what good is there in it? '

" ' That my sister and I cycle is nobody's business but our own! ' Kovalenko said, turning purple with passion. ' And whoever dares to meddle in my domestic and private affairs does so at his own risk! '

" Belikov turned pale and rose from his chair.

" ' If you adopt that attitude I cannot continue,' he said. ' And I must ask you never to express yourself in such terms about the principal and governors in my presence. You should be respectful to your superiors.'

" ' Did I speak ill of my superiors? ' Kovalenko asked, looking at him with rage. ' Please leave me in peace. I am a plain honest man and have no desire for further intercourse with men of your stamp. I do not like sneaks.'

" Belikov fidgeted nervously and began to put on his coat quickly, an expression of horror on his face. It was the first time in his life he had been spoken to so rudely.

" ' You can say what you like,' he observed, as he walked out on to the staircase landing. ' But I must warn you that in case by chance any one may have overheard our conversation, I must repeat its contents to the principal . . . the chief points, that is. It is my duty to do so.'

" ' Get along then! Make haste and tell him! '

" Kovalenko seized him by the collar and pushed him out; Belikov rolled down the stairs, his goloshes clattering as he fell. The staircase was steep and winding, but he reached the bottom unhurt. When he reached the bottom he immediately felt to see whether his spectacles were safe.

" As luck would have it, just as he rolled down, Varenka and two ladies happened to come in, and they stood at the bottom and watched him fall. To Belikov this was worse than anything. He would far rather have broken his neck, or his legs, than have appeared ridiculous. The whole town would know now! Something or other was sure to happen! Some one would draw another caricature, and the upshot would be that he would be requested to resign! . . . When he got up, Varenka recognised him, and seeing the absurd expression on his face, his crushed coat and goloshes; not understanding what had happened and thinking that he had slipped accidentally, she could not contain herself but burst out laughing, ' Ha ha! ha! '

" With this jolly ' Ha! ha! ha! ' everything was ended; the engagement, even Belikov's earthly existence. He did not hear what Varenka said; did not see anything. When he got home, the first thing he did was to remove her portrait from the table, then he went to bed and never got up again.

" Two or three days later Afonasy came and asked me whether the doctor had not better be sent for as something or other was wrong with his master. I went into Belikov's room. He was lying inside the curtained bed, muffled in the bed-clothes and perfectly silent. When I asked him a question, he would reply ' Yes ' or ' No ' and not another word. He lay in bed and Afonasy circled round him, solemn, gloomy, and smelling of vodka like a public-house.

" In a month Belikov died. We all went to his funeral; that is, the two schools and the seminary. When he lay in his coffin he had a gentle, pleasant, almost happy expression as though he were glad that at last he had been put into a case which he need never leave,

Yes, he had attained his ideal! And, as if in his honour, it rained on the day of the funeral, and we all had goloshes and umbrellas. Varenka, too, was present, and when the coffin was lowered she sobbed aloud. I have noticed that at a funeral people either laugh or cry, a halfway mood is unknown. I must confess that to bury people like Belikov is a great pleasure. When we returned from the cemetery we tried to look humble—no one dared to give expression to this feeling of joy—a feeling akin to that we experienced as children when our elders went away and we were left to roam about the garden in perfect liberty for hours on end. Ah, liberty! liberty! A mere suggestion, a faint hope of her, gives wings to the soul! Don't you think so?

"We returned from the cemetery in a good frame of mind, but scarcely a week went by before life went on exactly as before, uninteresting, wearying, senseless; a life with no restrictions printed in circulars, yet with no proper freedom. We were no better off than before. Belikov was buried, but how many other men in cases remained in the world, and how many more were yet to come!"

"That is just the point," Ivan Ivanitch said, lighting his pipe.

"How many more are to come!" Burkin repeated.

The schoolmaster came out of the shed. He was a stout little man, quite bald, with a long beard that reached nearly down to his waist. Two dogs followed him out.

"What a moon!" he said, looking up. It was midnight. On the right the whole village could be seen; a long street that stretched out for about four miles. Everything was immersed in a quiet, deep sleep; not a movement or sound; it was hard to believe that nature could be so still. When, on a moonlit night, you see a broad village street with its huts, hayricks, and willows, a tranquil feeling pervades you. In this quietude, hidden by the shadows of night from labour and worry and grief, the village looked peaceful and sad and beautiful, and it seemed that the stars looked down at it affectionately, that there was no evil in the world, and that all was well.

To the left, on the edge of the village, a large field stretched out; it continued in the distance, as far as the horizon, and in its breadth, filled with moonlight, there was also no movement or sound.

"That is the point," Ivan Ivanitch repeated. "And we who live in stuffy crowded towns write unnecessary articles, play bridge —aren't we in a kind of case? If you like, I will tell you a story illustrating this."

"No, thank you; it is time for bed; to-morrow will do," Burkin objected.

They went into the shed and lay down on the straw. As they were dozing off came the sound of light footsteps: tap, tap . . . some one was walking near the shed—walking a few steps, then stopping, and then again tap—tap.

The dogs growled.

" That is Mavra," Burkin said.

The footsteps ceased.

" See how people lie," Ivan Ivanitch went on, turning on his other side; " and then to be called a fool for enduring the lie; bearing the insult and humiliation, not daring to assert that you are on the side of honesty and freedom, but to lie and smile yourself; all for the sake of a piece of bread and a warm corner, or for some office that isn't worth a penny—no, it is impossible to go on being like that! "

" How you do wander off, Ivan Ivanitch! " the schoolmaster said. " Let us go to sleep."

In ten minutes Burkin was asleep, but Ivan Ivanitch kept sighing and tossing from side to side. After a little while he rose and, sitting down again outside the hut, lit his pipe.

# IN EXILE

## Anton P. Chekhov

OLD Semion, nicknamed the Wiseacre, and a young Tartar whose name nobody knew, sat by the fire on the river-bank. The other three ferrymen lay in the hut. Semion, an old man of sixty, gaunt and toothless, though broad-shouldered and healthy, was drunk. He would have gone to bed long ago had it not been for the flagon in his pocket and the fear that his companions in the hut would ask him for vodka. The Tartar was ill and tired. Wrapped in his rags, he was expatiating on the glorious life at Simbirsk, and the beauty and wit of the wife he had left behind him.

" Of course, you can hardly call it paradise here," the Wiseacre remarked. " You can take it in at a glance—water, bare banks, and clay everywhere, nothing more. Holy Week has long gone by, and there is still ice on the river, and this morning it snowed."

" Misery! Misery! " the Tartar moaned as he glanced around apprehensively.

Ten paces below lay the river, cold and dark, beating against the high clay bank as it wended its way swiftly to the distant sea.

Close to the bank lay a barge. On the other side little fiery serpents crept along, now dying out, now blazing up. It was last year's grass burning. And behind the serpents of fire darkness again.

The Tartar looked up at the sky. There were as many stars as
in his own country, just the same darkness about him. But there
was something lacking. At home in Simbirsk the stars were
brighter and the sky was different.

"Misery! Misery!" he moaned again.

"You will get used to it," the Wiseacre said with a laugh;
"you are young and foolish still. Your mother's milk has scarcely
dried on your lips. It is only your folly makes you think there
is no one more unfortunate than you. A time will come when you
will say, 'God grant every one such a life as this!' Look at me
now. In a week's time the river will be open; we will launch the
small ferry-boat, and you will all go wandering off over Siberia,
while I shall stay here rowing from bank to bank as I have done
for twenty-two years day in, day out. And nobody here except
the fish under the water and I above it. Yet, thank God, I do not
want for anything. God grant every one such a life!"

The Tartar heaped wood on the fire, huddled closer to it, and
said: "My father is ill. When he dies my mother and wife are
coming to join me here. They promised me they would."

"What do you want with a wife and a mother?" the Wiseacre
asked. "It is folly, brother. The devil put these notions into
your head. Do not listen to him. If he talks to you of women,
say you do not want them; if he begins about freedom, answer in
the same way. You need nothing; neither father, nor mother,
nor wife, nor freedom, nor hearth, nor home; you want none of
these things, curse them!" Wiseacre took a sip from his bottle
and continued: "I am not a common peasant, brother. My
father was a deacon, and when I lived in freedom at Kursk I
went about in a frock-coat, but now I have brought myself to such
a point that I can sleep naked on the bare earth, and eat grass if
necessary. God grant every one such a life! There is nothing I
want, no one that I fear, and I know that there is no richer or
freer man in the whole world. As soon as they sent me here from
Russia, I made up my mind from the very first day not to want
anything. The devil talked to me also about wife, home, freedom,
but I answered back persistently: 'I don't want anything!' I
stuck to that view and, as you see, I live well and am contented.
Give way to the devil one inch, and you are lost beyond salvation;
you will sink in the slough and never emerge. It is not only our
brother the peasant who goes under, but even men of birth and
education. About fifteen years ago a certain gentleman was sent
here from Russia. He would not share up with his brothers, and
there was some trouble about a forged will. Some said he was a
prince's or a baron's son, but perhaps he was only an ordinary
civil servant—who knows? Anyhow, he came here, and the first
thing he did was to buy himself a house and some land in Mihort-
irsk. 'I want to live by the sweat of my brow,' he said, 'I am

no longer a gentleman, but only a settler.' 'Well, God help you,' I said. 'It is a good wish!'

"He was a young man then, and loved to fuss and worry. He did his own farming and fishing, and would think nothing of riding sixty miles on horseback. But then came the misfortune. From the very first year he began to make a practice of riding into Girino to the post-office. He would stand on my boat, sigh, and say, 'Oh, Semion! why are they so long sending me money from home?' 'You have no need of money, Vassily Sergeyevitch,' I would say. 'What is the use of it to you? Give up your past, forget that it ever existed, and begin life anew. Do not listen to the devil;' I warned him; 'he means no good and will only put a halter round your neck. Now it is only money you want, later you will look round and desire something more; then another thing will occur to you and another. . . . If you want to ensure happiness to yourself, take my advice and desire nothing. If fortune has treated us badly, we must not bow down before her and beg for charity, we must despise her and laugh at her, and presently she will laugh with us.' So I would speak to him. . . . A year or two later I was again ferrying him across. He was laughing and rubbing his hands! 'I am going to Girino to meet my wife,' he said. 'She has taken pity on me and has come over. How good and kind she is!' He could scarcely contain his joy.

"A day or so later he returned with his wife. She was a young, beautiful woman, wore a hat, and had a little baby girl in her arms. There were stacks of luggage of all kinds. Vassily Sergeye-vitch was fussing round her. He could not take his eyes off her; could not praise her enough.

"'Well, brother Semion,' he said to me, 'life is not so bad even in Siberia!' 'You won't always think so,' I said to myself. And from that time onward he used to go every week to Girino to see whether money had been sent him from Russia. Of money he wanted no end. 'For my sake,' he said to me, 'she is burying her youth and beauty in Siberia, and is sharing my miserable life. In return I must procure her every enjoyment possible.' To make things gayer for her, he sought the acquaintance of the officials, and of all kinds of people. And, of course, all this company had to be provided with food and drink. A piano was installed, and a little lap-dog for the sofa—curse it. In a word, luxury, extrava-gance. The lady did not stay long with him. How could she? Everywhere was mud and water; it was cold; there was no fruit or vegetables, and the people were ignorant, drunken persons with no culture. Of course she got tired of it; she was a lady spoiled by the city life. And her husband, too, was no longer a gentleman, just a settler—no honour in that.

"Three years went by. I remember on Assumption Eve I heard some one calling from the opposite bank. I rowed across, and there was the lady wrapped up to the ears and accompanied by a young man, one of the officials. They had a troika! I rowed them across; they got into the troika and rode off. There was no one else in sight. Next morning Vassily Sergeyevitch rode up in haste. ' Semion, did my wife cross over with a man in glasses? ' he asked. ' Yes,' I answered; ' you may as well seek to capture the wind in the field.' He followed them for five days. When he returned he dropped into the boat and beat his head against the side. ' This is what you get,' he sobbed. ' Life is not so bad, even in Siberia! ' I reminded him with a smile. And he continued to wail. After this he wanted his liberty. His wife had returned to Russia, and he wanted to see her, to persuade her to return to him. Well, brother, from that day he spent his time riding from the post-office to the town authorities. He sent off petition after petition, begging to be allowed to return to Russia. One telegram alone cost him a hundred roubles. He sold his land, mortgaged his house to the Jews. His hair grew grey, his shoulders bent, and his face grew as yellow as though he had consumption. When he was speaking to you, a lump would rise in his throat, and the tears would come into his eyes.

" Thus he lived for eight years until at last he forgot it all and came to life again. He had found a new consolation. His daughter, you see, was growing up. He simply doted on her. And truth to tell, she was not at all bad looking—pretty, dark-browed, high-spirited. Every Sunday he would take her to the church at Girino. They would stand in the boat side by side, she smiling and he not able to take his eyes off her. ' Yes, Semion,' he would say, ' life is not so bad in Siberia. Even in Siberia one can be happy. See what a pretty daughter I have! You won't find a prettier lass within a thousand miles.' ' Yes, she is certainly pretty,' I replied, while to myself I thought, ' You wait a bit . . . she is young and hot-blooded, she wants to live: and what kind of a life is there here? '

" Anyway, brother, the girl began to pine. She grew listless and ill, and now she can scarcely stand on her legs. Consumption, they say it is. There, brother, is your Siberian happiness. That is how people live in Siberia. The father took to hunting after doctors and bringing them to see his daughter. If he only hears of a doctor or quack, no matter if he has to go two or three hundred miles, he instantly sets off to fetch him.

" I cannot tell you how much money he has spent on doctors. It would have been more worth while to have drunk it all away. She will die just the same. Nothing can save her. And then he will be utterly lost. He will either hang himself in despair or try to escape to Russia. If he runs away, they are certain to catch him; then there will be a trial, penal servitude, perhaps a halter. . . ."

" It was fine: it was good," the Tartar murmured, shuddering with cold.

" What was fine? " the Wiseacre asked.

" Wife, daughter. . . . What does despair or penal servitude matter when he has had his wife and daughter? . . . You say a man should want nothing; that is misery. His wife lived with him for three years—that was a gift from God. To have nothing is misery—but those three years were good. You don't understand."

Shivering with cold, and trying to find the correct Russian words to explain himself, the Tartar went on to say how he hoped God would never let him fall ill and die in a strange land to be buried in that cold red earth; that if his wife came to him, even only a single day, a single hour, for such happiness he would be prepared to undergo untold tortures and would thank God for them. One day of happiness was better than nothing at all.

And again he talked of his beautiful, clever wife whom he had left at home until he bowed his head in his hands and burst into tears. He assured Semion that he was not guilty and was unjustly sentenced. It was his brothers and his uncle who had stolen the person's horses and half killed the old man. But he had been accused unjustly. The three brothers had been sent to Siberia while the rich uncle remained at home.

" You will get used to it," Semion drawled.

The Tartar said nothing but, through eyes full of tears, gazed at the fire. His face bore a perplexed, hunted expression as though he did not understand why he found himself there in the darkness and cold among strangers, far from his own people in Simbirsk. Wiseacre lay down by the fire, smiling to himself and humming an air.

" What happiness can she have with her father? " he continued after a while. " She is a consolation to him and he loves her, it is true, but he must be none too easy to get on with, a crotchety, severe old man. And a young girl does not want severity. She wants kisses, ha! ha! ha! and perfumes and pomades. Yes, it's not an easy business! " Semion sighed, as he got up with difficulty. " The vodka is all gone, that means time for bed. Eh, brother? I'm going. . . ."

Left alone, the Tartar heaped more wood on the fire and, gazing into the flames, dreamt of his native village and his wife. If she would only come to him for a month, for a single day, he would not mind if she went back again. A month, or even a day of happiness was better than nothing. Suppose she kept her promise and came out to him, how would he support her? Where could she live? " If you have nothing to eat, how can you live? " he asked aloud. Working a whole day and night at the oar he only made ten kopeks. It is true he sometimes got extras in the way of tips, but the ferrymen pooled all such money and shared it out

among themselves. They gave the Tartar nothing, however, and
only scoffed at him. And it was terrible to suffer from hunger
and cold. . . .

Now, when he was trembling with cold, and very bone in his
body was aching, he should have gone into the hut to sleep; but it
was even colder there in the hut, for he had nothing wherewith to
cover himself. Here he had no protection, but there was at any
rate the fire. In a week, when the waters would have quite fallen,
they would begin to use the small ferry-boat, and none of the ferrymen, except Semion, would be wanted. Then the Tartar would
tramp from village to village begging for food and work. His wife
was only seventeen. She was pretty, and spoilt and shy. Would
she, too, have to tramp from village to village, brazenly, and ask
for bread? No, no, it was too terrible to think of. It was getting
light; the barge, the trees and the water stood out plainly. Turning
round, you could see the clayey slope with the thatched hovel at
the bottom, and beyond that the village huts. The cocks in the
village were already crowing.

The red clayey slope, the barge, the river, the strange unfriendly
people, hunger, cold, sickness—perhaps these things were not—
perhaps it was all a dream, the Tartar thought. It seemed to him
that he was asleep and heard the sound of his own snoring. Of
course he was back at home at Simbirsk; he had only to call out to
his wife and she would answer . . . and his mother was in the next
room. . . . What terrible dreams people have! How do they
come? The Tartar opened his eyes. What river was that? The
Volga? It was snowing.

" Hi, there! " some one shouted from the opposite bank.
" Ferry, please! "

The Tartar woke with a start and went for his mates. Pulling
on their torn coats and swearing in their hoarse, sleepy voices, the
ferrymen hurried down to the bank. Called from their sleep, the
river, over which a cold wind was blowing, seemed very uninviting
to them, and reluctantly they got into the boat. The Tartar and
three of the others took the oars that in the darkness looked like
the claws of a crab. Semion threw himself on his stomach across
the helm. From the other bank the shouting continued, and twice
a revolver shot was heard. Whoever it was must have thought
that the ferrymen were either asleep or had gone to the village
public-house. " All right, you've plenty of time! " Wiseacre said
in the tone of a man who was convinced that there was no need to
hurry in this world—that there was no sense in it anyhow.

The huge clumsy barge left the bank and moved along slowly
between the overhanging branches of the willow. Except for the
passing of the trees the barge seemed to be at rest. The ferrymen
pulled at the oars with a measured stroke. Wiseacre, lying across
the helm and making a bow in the air, swayed from one side to the

other. In the half light it seemed as if they were sitting on some enormous prehistoric beast with huge claws and floating away with it into the cold, desolate country that one sees in nightmares. The trees were left behind; they gained the open water. The measuring of the oars could already be heard from the further bank.

"Quicker! Quicker!" the stranger shouted across the water. Ten minutes later the barge bumped heavily against the landing stage. "It snows, snows all the time," Semion grumbled, as he wiped the snow from his face. "God knows where it all comes from."

On the bank stood a frail little man wearing a short fox-skin coat and a white lambskin cap. He stood immovable, a little way from his horse. He had an absorbed, gloomy expression as though he were trying to recollect something and was angry with his disobedient memory. "I am hurrying to Anastasevka," he said, when Semion approached him and took off his cap with a smile. "My daughter is worse. They say a new doctor has been appointed there."

The cart was dragged into the barge and the ferrymen started back. The man whom Semion called Vassily Sergeyevitch stood stock still all the time, biting his full lips and staring straight before him. When the driver asked him for permission to smoke, he made no reply, just as if he had not heard.

"Life is not so bad, even in Siberia!" Semion said maliciously, as he lay over the helm. Wiseacre's face wore a triumphant expression, as though he were rejoicing that things had turned out as he had predicted. The miserable, helpless expression of the man in the fox-skin coat seemed to afford him great delight. "You will find it muddy, travelling in this weather," he remarked when the horses were being harnessed. "You should have waited another week or so till it got drier. Or better still, not go at all. What is the use of going? People rush about, year in year out, and nothing ever comes of it. Don't you think so?" Vassily Sergeyevitch tipped the ferrymen without a word, got into the cart, and drove off.

"Gone for the doctor again!" Semion said, slapping his hands to get them warm. "You can as easily get a doctor worth anything as capture the wind in the field or catch the devil by his tail—curse him! Lord! How stupid people are. Forgive an old sinner!"

The Tartar walked up to Wiseacre and, for a moment, stood looking at him with hatred and disgust. Shivering with cold, and in his excitement bringing in Tartar words, he burst out: "He is a good man—good—and you are vile—wicked. He has a good soul and you are a beast! A vile beast! He is alive while you are dead! God made man that he might know joy and sorrow and despair, but you desire nothing. . . . You are a stone, a piece of clay. A stone needs nothing and neither do you. . . . You are a stone! God loves that poor man, but not you! " They all laughed, and the Tartar, with a forlorn movement, drew his rags closer round him and went back to the fire. Semion and the others went towards the hut.

" It's cold! " one of the ferrymen said in a hoarse voice, as he stretched himself on the straw that covered the damp clayey floor. " To be sure it is! " another agreed. " A convict's life! "

All lay down. The wind burst the door open, driving in the snow. No one was inclined to get up and shut it—they felt too cold and lazy. " I'm all right! " murmured Semion, as he dozed off. " God grant every one such a life! "

" You must be a convict seven times over, even the devil would not have you! " From without came a sound as of a dog whining.

" What's that? Who is there? "

" It is the Tartar, crying." " What a fool! "

" He will get used to it! " said Semion, and dropped off to sleep. The others quickly followed his example. The door remained open.

# AT HOME

## ANTON P. CHEKHOV

" SOME one called from Gregorev's for a book, but I told them you were not at home. And by the way, Yevgeny Petrovitch, I really must ask you to talk seriously to Serioja. Both to-day and the day before yesterday I discovered him smoking, and when I attempted to scold him, he put his hands over his ears and shouted so loudly as to drown my voice."

Yevgeny Petrovitch Bikovsky, the district public prosecutor, who had only just returned from a sitting and was taking off his gloves in his study, looked up at his boy's governess and laughed. " Serioja smoking! " . . . He shrugged his shoulders. " I can imagine the little imp with a cigarette! How old is he? "

" Seven. Of course you may not think it serious, but smoking at his age is a bad, injurious habit, and such habits should be eradicated from the very beginning."

" I quite agree. Where does he get tobacco from? "

" From your table."

" Really? In that case you had better send him to me."

When the governess had gone, Bikovsky sat down in his arm-chair by the table, closed his eyes and fell to musing. His imagination pictured Serioja with a huge cigarette about a yard long, enveloped in clouds of tobacco smoke. The picture brought a smile to his lips. At the same time the anxious, serious face of the governess reminded him of a time long gone by in the half-forgotten past when smoking in the nursery or at school inspired in parents and masters a strange and somewhat puzzling feeling of horror. The word horror exactly describes it. Such boys were flogged or expelled from school; their lives were made a burden to them; yet not one of the masters nor the parents could have told you exactly what harm there was in smoking, nor why it was considered such a crime.

A great many clever grown-up people, too, fought against the tobacco habit without precisely knowing why.

Yevgeny Petrovitch recalled how the headmaster of his school, a learned and kind-hearted old man, would turn quite pale with fright if he discovered a boy smoking. He would instantly summon a council of masters, and the culprit would forthwith be expelled.

Such seems the law of everyday life! The more intangible the evil, the more fiercely it is combated.

Yevgeny Petrovitch brought to mind the cases of two or three victims, and could not help thinking that the punishment wrought consequences far more evil than did the crime. A living organism is capable of adapting itself to any environment, else otherwise human beings would realise at every turn how normal activities were based on hypotheses that could not be proved; and how little was really known of the fundamental truths in such branches as education, law, literature. . . .

These and similar thoughts, the workings of a tired brain that craved for rest, began to float through his mind. They came crowding one after another, disconnected, remaining only on the surface without penetrating the depths.

To a man whose whole time is taken up by legal affairs and whose mind is constantly set in one direction, such homely, wandering thoughts as these produce a comfortable, soothing effect.

It was nine o'clock in the evening. In the flat above, on the second floor, some one was pacing the room, to and fro, from corner to corner, and in the flat above that, two people were playing a duet on the piano. The man who was pacing the floor —judging by his nervous tread—must have been tortured by some tormenting thought, or perhaps by a toothache, while the monotonous duet embued the evening stillness with a certain drowsiness that was conducive to lazy thinking. In the nursery Serioja and the governess were talking together. " Papa has come! " the boy sang. " Papa has come! Papa! Papa! "

" *Votre père vous appelle,* go at once! " the governess piped in a thin little voice like that of a frightened bird. " Do you hear? "

" What can I say to him after all? " Yevgeny Petrovitch asked himself. But before he had time to invent anything to say to his son, Serioja, a boy of seven, entered. It was only by his clothes that one could distinguish that he was a boy and not a girl. He was frail, fair-skinned, and fragile. He seemed like some exotic flower, and everything about him was soft and gentle; his looks, his gestures, his curly hair, even his little velvet coat. " Good evening, papa! " he said in a soft voice, climbing on to his father's knee and kissing him. " Did you want me? "

" One minute, Sergey Yevgenitch," the father began, gently disengaging the boy's arms. " Before we can think of kissing, you and I must have a serious talk. I am very angry with you and don't love you any more. Understand that I don't love you—you are no longer my son—yes . . ."

Serioja looked intently at his father, then transferred his gaze to the table and shrugged his shoulders.

" What have I done to you? " he asked in perplexity, blinking his eyes. " I did not go into your study once to-day and have not touched anything."

" Natalia Semionovna has just informed me that you smoke. Is it true? Do you smoke? "

" Yes, I smoked once. It is true! "

" There now, you are telling a lie into the bargain," the public prosecutor said, frowning in order to hide a smile. " Natalia Semionovna caught you twice. You have been discovered in three bad actions—smoking, taking another person's tobacco, and lying. Three bad faults."

" Oh, yes! " Serioja recollected, his eyes dancing. " It is quite true; I did smoke twice, once to-day and once before that."

" You see, you yourself admit it was not once but twice. . . . I am very angry with you. You used to be a good boy; and now you appear to have become bad."

Yevgeny Petrovitch rearranged Serioja's collar, thinking, " What else shall I say to him? "

" It is not right," he continued. " I did not expect it of you. In the first place you have no right to take tobacco that does not belong to you. Every man has the right of enjoying his own property, but if he takes something that is not his own, then he is a bad man! For instance, Natalia Semionovna has a trunk full of dresses. It is her own trunk, and that means that we—that is, you and I—have no right to touch it as it does not belong to us. Do you follow? Again, you have little horses and pictures . . . I do not take them, do I? Perhaps I should like to have them . . . but I know they are yours and not mine."

" You can take them if you like! " Serioja said, raising his eyebrows. " Don't mind me, papa, take them! That little dog you
143*

have on the table is mine, but I don't care . . . let it stay
there! ''

"You don't understand," Bikovsky said. "You gave me the
dog, so now it is mine and I can do what I like with it, but I did
not give you the tobacco. The tobacco is mine." (I shall never
be able to make him understand this way, the public prosecutor
thought. Impossible! It's quite useless!) "If I want to smoke
tobacco that does not belong to me, then first of all I must
ask permission." Lazily connecting his sentences, choosing childish words, Bikovsky set out to explain to his son the meaning of
private property.

Serioja fixed his gaze on his father's chest, listening attentively.
He loved to sit talking with his father in the evenings. Then he
rested his elbows on the table, half-closed his eyes, and transferred
his gaze to the paper and ink-pot. Then it wandered round the
room and settled on the paste-bottle.

"Papa, what is paste made of? " he asked suddenly, lifting the
bottle up to inspect it.

Bikovsky took the bottle from him, put it back on the table,
and continued: "And secondly, you smoke. . . . That is not
good. Just because I happen to smoke, it does not mean that
you may do so. I smoke, knowing that it is bad for me. I scold
myself for it. . . . (What a subtle teacher I am! thought the
public prosecutor.) Tobacco is bad for the health, and a man
who smokes dies sooner than he would otherwise have done.
Smoking is particularly bad for a little boy like you. You
have a weak chest, you are not strong yet, and in delicate people
tobacco causes consumption and all sorts of diseases. You remember Uncle Ignaty? Well, he died of consumption. Had he not
smoked he might have been alive to-day."

Serioja gazed at the lamp pensively, touched the shade with
his finger and sighed.

"Uncle Ignaty played the violin well! " he remarked. "The
Gregorevs have his violin now."

Serioja put his elbows on the table, rested his head on his hands
and grew thoughtful. By the expression on his face one could see
that he was following the trend of his own thoughts. A look of
sadness mingled with terror appeared in his large blinking eyes. No
doubt he was thinking of death that had so recently taken his
mother and his uncle Ignaty. Death bears mothers and uncles
away to the other world, but their children and their violins remain.
The dead live in heaven, somewhere near the stars, and look down
on the earth. Do they feel the separation?

"What else can I say to him? " Yevgeny Petrovitch was thinking. He is not listening to me. Obviously he does not consider
his action or my arguments as serious. How can I make him
understand? "

The public prosecutor got up and began to pace the room.

" In my young days these questions were settled very simply," he reflected. " Every boy found smoking was whipped. This cured the poor spirited and cowardly; but the braver and more intelligent of them took to hiding their tobacco in their boots, and smoking in the sheds. When discovered there and punished a second time, they went off to the river to smoke, and so on until the small boy grew into a man. To keep me from smoking my mother used to bribe me with money and sweets. Now such methods are considered immoral and are despised."

Taking his stand at the very base of reason, the modern pedagogue strives to make the child realise the idea of " good," not as connected with fear or vanity, but as an end in itself.

While he was thus pacing up and down, Serioja knelt on his chair, and leaning over the table began to draw. Some drawing-paper and a blue pencil always lay ready for him on the table, so that he should have no temptation to touch his father's papers, or the ink.

" When cook was chopping the cabbage to-day she cut her finger," he remarked, while drawing a house. " She screamed so loudly that we were all terrified and rushed into the kitchen. She was stupid! Natalia Semionovna told her to put her finger in cold water, but she would suck it. . . . How could she put her dirty finger into her mouth! It's not nice, is it, papa? "

Then he went on telling his father how at dinner-time a barrel-organ man had come with a little girl who had danced to the music.

" He has his own thoughts," the public prosecutor mused. " He lives in his own world and sets his own standard of what is important and what is not. To fix his attention and awaken his consciousness, it is not sufficient to imitate his words, one must know and understand his way of thinking. He would have understood me easily enough had I really been sorry about the tobacco, or had I been hurt, or cried. . . . Mothers bringing up their children know unconsciously how to feel with them, to cry with them, to laugh with them. . . . You can achieve nothing with logic and moralising. Well, what shall I say to him now? What? "

And it seemed strange and absurd to Yevgeny Petrovitch that he, an experienced lawyer, who had spent half his life cross-examining and sentencing, should be at a loss what to say to the boy.

" Listen; give me your word of honour that you will never smoke again," he said.

" Word of honour! " Serioja sang out, pressing hard on his pencil and bending over his drawing. " Word—of—hon—our— word . . ."

" I wonder whether he knows what ' word of honour ' means? " Bikovsky asked himself. " No, I am a bad mentor! If a teacher, or one of my colleagues, could only look into my mind just now,

they would consider me soft and suspect me of too much theorising.
. . . At school or in court these troublesome questions are settled
much easier than at home. Here you deal with people whom you
love with all your soul, and love is exacting; it complicates the
question at issue. If the boy were not my own son—say a pupil,
or a prisoner, I should not be afraid; my thoughts would not
wander like this."

Yevgeny Petrovitch sat down by the table and pulled one of
Serioja's drawings towards him. The drawing represented a house
with a crooked roof and showed a column of smoke that zigzagged
like forked lightning to the very top of the paper. Beside the
house stood a soldier, with two dots for eyes placed in the middle of
his face, and holding a gun that looked like the figure 4.

" A man cannot be taller than a house," the public prosecutor
said. " Look, the roof of the house only reaches to his shoulder."
Serioja climbed on to his father's knee and snuggled into a comfortable position.

" But, papa," he said, looking at his drawing. " If you draw
the soldier smaller, you cannot see his eyes."

Should he correct him? From daily observation of his own son
the public prosecutor was convinced that children, like savages,
have their own conceptions in art, which in their various forms are
quite incomprehensible to adults. Judged by adult standards,
Serioja would have appeared abnormal. He thought it proper
and reasonable to draw men taller than houses, and to portray by
means of his pencil not only objects but also sensations. Thus he
represented the sound of an orchestra as sphere and smoke; and
the sound of a whistle as a spiral thread. In his mind sound was
intimately connected with form and colour; thus, when colouring
the letters of the alphabet, he invariably made L yellow, M red,
A black, and so on.

Throwing down his drawing, Serioja settled himself comfortably
once more and began toying with his father's beard. At first he
smoothed it down carefully, then, parting it, he arranged it in the
form of side whiskers.

" Now you look like Ivan Stepanovitch," he said. " And now
you will look like our Swiss. Papa, why does a Swiss always stand
by the door? Is it to frighten thieves away? "

The public prosecutor felt Serioja's breath on his face, and his
beard touched the boy's cheek. A warm, gentle feeling arose in his
heart, as though not only his hands but his whole soul was lying on
Serioja's velvet coat. He gazed into the boy's large dark eyes,
and it seemed to him that out of those deep wells there looked out
at him his mother, his wife—and all that he had ever loved.

" How could I whip him? " he thought. " Of what use to
think out a punishment for him? I am no good as an educationa-
list. At one time people were simpler, theorised less and decided

things boldly. Now we think too much—logic has conquered us.
. . . The more developed a man is, the more he speculates and
falls into subtleties, the more undecided and doubtful he becomes,
the less confidence he has; he approaches questions more timidly.
And really, what courage a man must have in order to teach,
judge, write ponderous tomes. . . .'' The clock struck ten.

'' Well, boy, time for bed! '' he said. '' Say good-night and go
along.''

'' But, papa,'' Serioja said, making a move. '' I want to stay
a little longer. Tell me something. Tell me a story.''

'' Very well, only you must go to bed directly I have finished.''

On fine evenings Yevgeny Petrovitch would often tell Serioja
stories. Like most busy men he did not know a single poem or
story by heart, so that he had to improvise each time. He would
always begin with the formula, '' Once upon a time in a certain
kingdom,'' and then would follow some innocent nonsense or other.
The scenes and characters came at random impromptu, while the
plot and moral came of their own accord, so to say. Serioja loved
these improvisations, and his father had noticed that the simpler
the plot the more strongly it impressed itself on the boy.

'' Listen,'' he began, raising his eyes to the ceiling. '' Once
upon a time, in a certain kingdom, there lived an old king with
a long grey beard and . . . and such a long moustache. Well, he
lived in a palace of crystal that shone and sparkled in the sun like
a huge mass of clear ice. The palace, my boy, stood in a large
garden where you must know grew oranges . . . figs and cherries
. . . tulips, roses, lilies of the valley—and brilliantly-coloured
birds sang all day. On the trees there hung little glass balls that
tinkled in the wind so sweetly that it was a pleasure to listen to
them. Glass gives a softer sound than metal. Well, what else was
there? There were also fountains . . . you remember there was a
fountain in Auntie Sonia's garden in the country? Well, the
fountains in the king's garden were exactly like that, only ever so
much larger, and the spray from them reached to the very top of
the highest poplar.''

Yevgeny Petrovitch thought a moment, and then continued:

'' The old king had an only son and heir to his throne—a little
boy, just like you. He was a good boy. He was never cross, went
to bed early, never touched anything on the table—and . . . was
altogether a clever boy. He had only one fault . . . he smoked.''

Serioja listened attentively, his eyes blinking as they gazed
straight into his father's. '' What next? '' the father asked himself. Then, after a little uncertainty, ended the story thus:
'' Through smoking the king's son fell ill with consumption, and
died when he was only twenty. The infirm and aged monarch was
left alone, utterly helpless. There was none to govern the kingdom nor to protect the palace. Enemies came and killed the old

king, and destroyed the palace, and now in the garden there are
no longer any cherries or birds or little glass balls . . . you see,
boy. . . ."

Such an end appeared to Yevgeny Petrovitch as too naïve and
absurd, but on Serioja it created a great impression. Again an
expression of sadness and fear came into his eyes. For a moment
or two he sat gazing pensively at the dark windows, then shuddered
and said in a lowered voice:

" I will not smoke any more . . ."

When the boy had bidden him good-night and had gone to bed,
the father began pacing quietly up and down the room, a contented
smile on his face.

" People would say it was beauty and the artistic form that
affected him," he thought. " Even if that were so, it is not consolation. After all, it was not a fair means . . . why must truth
and morals be presented, not in the naked form, but gilded and
sugared like a pill? It is not rational. It is falsehood, deceit,
trickery . . ."

He recalled how, when he had to make a speech to a jury, instead
of giving them an analysis of the facts, he gave them a vivid
account of the case; and how people get their ideas on life, not
by reasoning and self-analysis, but by reading novels and historic
romances.

Medicine must be sweet, truth beautiful. . . . Man has accustomed himself to that since the days of Adam. . . . However
. . . perhaps that was natural and was as it should be. . . . There
are many delusions and illusions in nature. . . . He sat down to
work, but these idle homely thoughts long strayed through his
mind. Above, the piano had stopped, but the inmate of the
second floor was still pacing from corner to corner. . . .

# IN THE COACH-HOUSE

## Anton P. Chekhov

### I

It was ten o'clock at night. Stepan, the coachman, Michael, the
dvornik,[1] the coachman's little grandson, Aleshka (who had come
from the village on a visit to his grandfather), and Nikander, an
old man of seventy whose nightly custom it was to call at the house
on the chance of selling his herrings, were seated around a lantern
in the great coach-house, and playing at korol.[2] Through the open

[1] Gatekeeper or porter.          [2] " King "—a card game.

doors of the coach-house there could be seen the spacious courtyard of the mansion in which the gentry lived, the gates of the court-yard, some outbuildings, and the dvornik's lodge. All was shrouded in darkness, except that four windows in a wing tenanted by lodgers were brightly lit up, and causing the shadows thrown by the up-turned shafts of a number of carriages and sledges to mingle with the shadows thrown by the card-players where they hovered and darted over the walls and doors of the coach-house. Behind a thin partition-wall which divided the coach-house from the stable there were standing several horses, and everything was redolent with the smell of hay, added to a not over-pleasant odour of herrings which proceeded from old Nikander.

" He is lying unconscious," said the dvornik. " Without doubt he will die. Aleshka, you little pig, do not look at my cards, or I will box your ears for you! Yes, the doctors have gone, and his father and mother have arrived. They did so but a short while ago. 'Tis a most pitiful affair, and I pray to God He may avert it! 'Tis said the gentleman is an only son. What a misfortune, to be sure! "

All except Aleshka, who was absorbed in the game, glanced at the brilliantly lighted windows in the wing.

" To every man his fate," pursued the dvornik. " Of course, there will be an inquest held. Yet what do *I* know about the affair? What did *I* see? This morning the gentleman sent for me, and, handing me a letter, said: ' Put this in the post.' Even as he spoke his eyes were full of tears. Neither his wife nor his children were at home—they had gone for a walk. Well, while I was gone with the letter he shot himself in the temple with a revolver, and I returned to find the coachman's wife shouting the news about the courtyard! "

" Then the gentleman has committed a great sin," said the herring merchant hoarsely, with a jerk of his head. " Yes, a very great sin."

" It must be that he had lost his reason through over-study," added the dvornik, taking a trick. " He used to sit up whole nights over his books. Play away, peasant. He was a good-look-ing gentleman, too—tall, fair-haired, and dark-eyed. Also, he was a most respectable lodger."

" 'Tis the female sex which brings such things about," remarked the coachman as he capped the king of diamonds with the nine of trumps. " Maybe he loved some woman other than his wife? Or maybe his wife had grown cold to him? Such is often the way."

## II

Suddenly a wailing voice resounded through the stillness.

" He is gone," said the dvornik laconically. " They have sent to the hospital for the layers-out."

" The Kingdom of Heaven and eternal rest be with him! " whispered the coachman, crossing himself.

Glancing at his grandfather, Aleshka did the same.

" Nay, 'tis not right to remember such folk," put in the herring merchant.

" Why not? "

" Because 'tis a sin to kill oneself."

" True," assented the dvornik. " Therefore his soul will go straight to Hell, to the Unclean One."

Rising, the old man picked up his pack. " The same thing happened to our mistress, the general's lady," he continued, as he settled the pack more comfortably over his shoulders. " In those days we were her serfs. Well, her eldest son went out of his mind, and shot himself in the mouth with a pistol. According to the law such persons are to be buried outside a graveyard, and without priest or requiem; but, to avoid such a scandal, our mistress bribed the police and the doctors to give her a paper which said that her son had committed the deed in a fit of delirium, and without knowing what he was doing. Yet, such things *can* be done for a consideration. So they buried him with priests and full rites and music, and he was laid beneath the church. A month went by—two months—yet nothing happened. Then, during the third month, it was reported to the general's lady that the watchmen of the church had come to see her. What could they be wanting? As soon as they were brought into her presence they fell down upon their knees before her. ' Your Excellency,' they cried, ' we cannot go on with our task. All night your son lies wailing beneath the church! ' "

Aleshka shuddered, and pressed his face close to his grandfather's back, that he might not see the windows.

" At first our mistress would not listen to the watchmen," continued the herring merchant. " Yet after a while the watchmen came to her again, and with them came the deacon of the church, for he too had heard the wailing. Then the general's lady perceived that it was going to be a bad business; so, having called the watchmen into her private room, she said to them: ' Here are twenty-five roubles for you, my friends. Do you, in return, go quietly by night, and dig up my unhappy son again, and bury him outside the graveyard.' Yes, and probably she handed them also a glass apiece. Well, the watchmen did as she had bidden them; and though the gravestone, with its inscription, remains in the church to this day, the general's son himself lies buried without the precincts. May the Lord pardon us for our sins! Only one day in the year may one pray for such folk, and that day is Trinity Sunday. Also, though one may not give alms for them, one may feed the birds to gain rest for their souls. So every third day the general's lady used to go to the cross-roads for that purpose; and one day she beheld there—though whence come no one knows—a black dog! It leapt upon the bread and devoured it, and what that dog was there can be no doubt. For the next five days our mistress remained as one distracted—she ate and drank nothing whatever. Then suddenly, when in the garden, she fell upon her knees, and prayed, and prayed. . . . Well, good-night, my friends, and may God and the Queen of Heaven be with you all! Come along, good Michael, and open me the gates."

So saying, he departed with the dvornik, and the coachman and Aleshka also stepped outside, rather than be left alone in the coach-house.

III

" A man has lived, and a man has died," said the coachman as he glanced at the lighted windows with their hovering shadows. " This morning the gentleman was walking about this very yard, and now he lies there a corpse! "

" Yes; and for us, too, the time will come to die," added the dvornik, moving away with the herring merchant. Presently the pair became lost to view in the darkness.

Not without some diffidence, the coachman, followed by Aleshka, approached the lighted windows. A very pale lady, with large, tear-filled eyes, was helping a grey-headed, handsome gentleman to move a couple of card-tables into the centre of the room—probably to serve as a resting-place for the body. On the green baize of the card-tables figures, written in chalk, were still visible, while the coachman's wife—the same woman who, in the morning, had run screaming about the yard—was standing a-tiptoe on a chair, and endeavouring to cover over a mirror with a sheet.

" Grandfather, what are they doing? " asked Aleshka in a whisper.

" They are about to lay him on those tables," answered the coachman. " But let us go, little one; it is bedtime."

Grandfather and grandson returned to the coach-house, said their prayers, and pulled off their boots; after which Stepan lay down in a corner of the floor, and Aleshka betook himself to one of the sledges. The doors of the coach-house had been closed, and a strong smell of oil was proceeding from the extinguished lamp. After a while Aleshka raised his head, and looked around him. Through the crack between the doors the four lighted windows were still visible.

" Grandfather, I am afraid! " the little boy called out.

" Nay, nay. Go to sleep; go to sleep."

" I tell you I am afraid! "

" What are you afraid of? Oh! the little fool! "

For a moment there was silence. Then Aleshka leapt from the sledge, and, weeping loudly, ran across to his grandfather.

" What is it? What is the matter with you? " asked the startled coachman as he too rose to his feet.

"He is wailing, grandfather! He is wailing!"

"Who is wailing?"

"The gentleman, grandfather! I am afraid! Do you not hear him?"

The coachman listened.

"'Tis only the women mourning," he said. "Run away, little fool. Yes, 'tis only the mourners lamenting the dead man."

"Nay, but I want to go back to the village," continued the boy in a paroxysm of sobbing and trembling. "Grandfather, *do* let us go back to the village, to mamma's! *Do* let us go, grandfather dear, and God will send you the Kingdom of Heaven in return!"

"Oh, the little donkey! But nay, nay. Say no more, say no more. Hold your tongue for a moment while I light the lantern. The little idiot!"

The coachman felt for his matches, and lit the lantern. Yet even then the light failed to reassure Aleshka.

"Grandfather, *do* let us go back to the village!" he begged again through his tears. "I am so frightened here! Why did you take me away from the village, you bad man?"

"What? *Whom* are you calling a bad man? How dare you address your grandfather in such a manner? I shall have to flog you for it!"

"Flog me, grandfather—flog me as hard as Sidor's goat if only you will be kind to me and take me back to mamma's!"

"Now, now, little grandson," whispered the coachman soothingly. "There is nothing to be afraid of, or I, too, should be afraid. Say a prayer to God."

IV

The doors creaked, and the dvornik's head showed itself.

"What? Not asleep yet, Stepan?" he asked as he entered. "I myself am not likely to get much sleep to-night. All night long it will be a question of opening and shutting the gates. But what are you weeping for, Aleshka?"

"He is afraid," the coachman answered for his grandson.

Once more a short, wailing cry sounded through the air.

"They are mourning the dead man," commented the dvornik. "His mother cannot believe her eyes. Truly 'tis a terrible thing for a man to kill himself!"

"Is the father there too?"

"Yes; but he sits quietly in a corner. As for the children, they have been sent away to some relatives. . . . Well, Stepan, shall we cut for trumps again? Eh?"

"I'm your man," replied the coachman, scratching himself. "And do you, Aleshka, run away and sleep. You are nearly old enough to get married, yet there you stand blubbering, you little rascal! Now, run away, little grandson—run away and sleep."

The dvornik's presence had partially reassured Aleshka, so he returned—though not over-boldly—to the sledge, and lay down. Until sleep overcame him he could hear occasional whisperings of:

" It is I to play. I go so much."

" It is I to play. I go so much."

Then in the courtyard a bell rang, and a door creaked as though it were saying, in its turn, " It is I to play. I go so much." When at length Aleshka saw the dead man in his dreams, and, terrified at his eyes, leapt up in a renewed fit of weeping, morning had dawned, his grandfather was asleep and snoring, and the coach-house no longer seemed a place to be afraid in.

# THE CHORUS GIRL

## Anton P. Chekhov

Once, when she was younger, prettier, and had a better voice, her admirer, Nikolai Petrovitch Kolpakov, was sitting in the entresol of her summer cottage. It was unbearably hot and stifling. Kolpakov had just dined and had drunk a full bottle of cheap port; he was out of sorts and not very well; they were both suffering from ennui and were waiting until it should become a little cooler, so that they could go for a walk.

Suddenly and unexpectedly the bell rang. Kolpakov, who was in his shirt-sleeves and slippers, sprang from his seat and looked questioningly at Pasha.

" Probably the postman—or maybe one of the girls," she said.

Kolpakov would not feel embarrassed in the presence either of the postman or of Pasha's friend; but, to guard against a possible emergency, he caught up his clothes and boots in one hand and went into the next room, while Pasha ran to open the door.

To Pasha's great surprise she found there an unknown, young and beautiful woman, dressed with exquisite taste and evidently a lady.

The stranger was very pale and breathed hard, as if she had just climbed a very long flight of stairs.

" What can I do for you? " Pasha asked.

The lady did not reply at once. She made a step forward, slowly looked around the room and sat down in a way that clearly showed she was tired out. Then she moved her pale lips in an effort to say something.

" Is my husband here, at your house? " she asked at last, lifting to Pasha a pair of large eyes with lids red from weeping.

" Whose husband? " Pasha whispered.

" My husband—Nikolai Petrovitch Kolpakov."

" No, no, madame—I—I do not know any husband."

A moment passed in silence.  Several times the stranger touched her pale lips with her handkerchief and held her breath, as if to repress an inner shivering.  Pasha stood riveted before her and looked at her in perplexity.

" So you say he is not here? " asked the lady, with a stronger voice and smiling with a strange kind of smile.

" I—I do not know whom you are asking about."

" You are a nasty, odious, vile creature," the stranger began, looking at Pasha with hatred and disgust.  " Yes, you are abominable, and I am glad, very glad, that at last I have the opportunity to tell you so! "

Pasha felt that she was making an impression of something nauseatingly ugly on this lady, all in black, with her thin, white fingers.

" Where is my husband? " continued the lady.  " But, after all, what does it matter if he is here or not?  But I must tell you that his embezzlements have been discovered and they have begun a search for Nikolai Petrovitch, and he will be arrested.  See what you have done! "

The lady rose to her feet and walked about the room in great excitement.

" To-day he will be found and arrested," she went on, with a sob, and the sound showed how grieved and outraged she was.  " I know who brought him to this horrible pass!  You odious, low, miserable, lewd, mercenary creature! "  The lady's lips curled and her nose wrinkled in disgust.  " I am helpless—listen to me, you low woman!—I am helpless, you are stronger than I; but there is One who will defend me and my children!  God sees everything; He is just!  He will call you to account for every one of my tears, for all my sleepless nights!  There will come a time when you will remember my words! "

Again there was silence.  The lady walked to and fro wringing her hands, and Pasha stood and stared at her as stupidly as before, not understanding what it all meant and awaiting something terrible at her hands.

" I do not know anything, lady," she said at last, and suddenly burst into tears.

" You lie! " cried the visitor, her eyes flashing angrily.  " I know all.  I know he has spent every day of the last month at your house! "

" Well, what of that?  I receive many guests at my house, but I do not compel anybody to come.  They come of their own accord."

" I tell you that his swindle has been discovered!  He has spent other people's money—for such as you!  For *you* he has committed a crime! Listen to me!" the lady cried, stopping determinedly before Pasha. "You cannot have any principles; you live only to bring misfortune—that is your aim; but I cannot think that you have fallen so low that you have lost every vestige of human feeling! He has a wife and children; if he should be found guilty and sent to Siberia, I and his children will die of hunger. Do you understand what it means? But there is a way to save him and all of us from poverty and disgrace. If he should bring them to-day the nine hundred roubles he has embezzled, they would leave him alone. Only nine hundred roubles!"

"What nine hundred roubles?" Pasha asked in a low voice. "I—I do not understand—I have not taken——"

"I do not ask you for the nine hundred roubles. You have no money, and I do not want what belongs to you. I ask you for something else. Men generally give costly presents to such as you. Return me only those trinkets which my husband has given you!"

"Madame, your husband has never given me any trinkets!" screamed Pasha, who was at last beginning to understand.

"Then where is the money? He has squandered all I had, and has taken that of others. Where has it all gone to? Listen to me, I beg of you—I was excited and said many unpleasant things, but I beg your pardon. You must hate me, I know; but if you are capable of feeling pity you will understand my situation. I implore you to return the things to me!"

"Ah, yes——" said Pasha, shrugging her shoulders. "I would gladly do so, but may God punish me if I have taken anything from him. Upon my conscience! But let me see," and the chorus girl suddenly became confused. "Some time ago he did bring me two trinkets—if you care to have them I will return them to you."

Pasha pulled out a toilet-table drawer and took out a tawdry gold bracelet and a thin gold ring set with a cheap ruby.

"Please take them!" she said, handing them to her visitor.

The lady flushed deeply and her lips quivered. She was very much offended.

"What is this you are giving me?" she asked. "I have not come here for charity. I have come for what does not belong to you—for what you, taking advantage of your position, have forced out of my husband—the weak, unfortunate man! On Thursday, when I saw you with him in the arbour, you wore costly brooches and bracelets, so it is no good playing the innocent with me! I ask you for the last time: will you or will you not give me the things?"

"Lord, how funny you are!" said Pasha, beginning, in her turn, to feel offended. "I assure you that I have not received from your Nikolai Petrovitch anything other than this bracelet and little ring. He used to bring me only sweet tarts."

"Sweet tarts!" The stranger smiled bitterly. "At home the

children have nothing to eat, and here we eat sweet tarts! Then you refuse finally to return the trinkets? ''

There was no reply. The lady pressed her handkerchief to her face and burst into tears.

'' I implore you! '' she cried through her sobs. '' You have been the ruin and undoing of my husband; I implore you to save him. You have no pity for him; but the children, the children— what have they done that this misfortune should fall upon them? ''

Pasha pictured to herself the little children standing in the street and crying with hunger, and began crying herself.

'' What can I do, madame? '' she said. '' You say that I am a wretch and that I have ruined Nikolai Petrovitch, and yet I swear to you, as if I were standing before God Himself, that I have not in any way benefited by your husband's visits. In all our chorus there is only Moti who has a rich admirer.''

'' I ask you for the things! It is the things I want of you! I weep, lower myself—if you wish I will fall on my knees to you! ''

Pasha cried out in sudden fear and wrung her hands. She felt that this pale lady, who spoke in the high, refined language in which people generally express themselves on the stage, would make good her threat and really fall on her knees before her. She would do that out of pride and nobleness, knowing that it would elevate herself and degrade the chorus girl.

'' Well, I will give you the things.'' Pasha began to bustle about, wiping her eyes. '' You can have them. But they are not from your Nikolai Petrovitch. I got them from my other guests. But, as you please! ''

She pulled out the top drawer of the bureau and took from it a brooch set with diamonds, a string of coral, several rings, and a bracelet, and handed them all to the lady.

'' Take them if you want to, but I tell you again, I had no benefit whatsoever from your husband. Take them, and get rich on it! '' continued Pasha, who was deeply offended at the lady's threat to fall on her knees to her. '' And if you are an honest and lawful wife to him, you had better keep him in hand near yourself, that's all! I did not call him—he came himself.''

The lady looked at the jewellery through her tears. '' These will not do,'' she said. '' There is hardly five hundred roubles' worth here.''

Pasha impetuously threw out of the bureau a gold watch, a cigar-case, and a pair of cuff buttons, and cried, with a fling of her hands:

'' And now I have nothing more left! You may even search me! ''

The visitor sighed and with trembling hands wrapped the trinkets in a handkerchief, and without saying a word, without even the slightest bow, she left the room.

The door of the next room opened and Kolpakov appeared. He

was very pale, and his head shook nervously, as if he had just swallowed something bitter, and tears were in his eyes.

" What kind of things have you given me? " Pasha fell upon him. " When, I ask you? "

" Things—nonsense, who speaks of things! " said Kolpakov, shaking his head. " My God! She cried before you, lowered herself——"

" I ask you: what things have you given me? " screamed Pasha.

" Good Lord! She, noble, proud, pure, she wanted to go down on her knees before—before this hag! And I brought her to this! I allowed it! "

He caught his head in his two hands and groaned.

" No, I will never forgive you this! Never! Get out of my sight, you dirty beast! " he shouted, backing away from Pasha with disgust.

" She wanted to go down on her knees, and to whom? To *you*! Oh, my God! "

He dressed himself quickly, avoiding contact with Pasha, and turning to the door went out.

Pasha lay down and began to cry bitterly. She was already regretting the trinkets she had so thoughtlessly given away, but she felt, too, deeply offended. She remembered how a merchant, about three years before, had given her a beating without any provocation, and cried still more bitterly.

# THE AVENGER

### Anton P. Chekhov

As soon as Fedor Sigaev found out that his wife was unfaithful to him, he decided to revenge himself, and for that purpose he paid a visit to the shop of Schmucks & Co., dealers in all kinds of firearms, and asked the man to show him a good revolver. His face expressed anger, sorrow, and irrevocable decision.

" I know what I am about to do," he thought. " My honour has been trodden in the mud, the sanctity of the family outraged, and wickedness is triumphant; therefore I, as a good citizen and an honest man, must appear as the avenger. First I shall slay my wife and her lover, then myself——"

He had not, as yet, bought a revolver, nor had he shot any one, but his imagination already pictured to him the ghastly wounds he would inflict, the crowds of people and the scenes at the inquest. With the malignity of a deeply offended man he imagined the horror of his relatives and the public in general, the mortal agony of his faithless wife, and even saw in his mind's eye the large headings in the papers and the long editorials treating of the breaking up of family life.

The shopman, an active little man with a paunch and white vest, displayed before him on the counter several revolvers, and with a deferential smile upon his lips, continually scraping with his feet, said:

" I would advise you, sir, to take this splendid revolver. The newest make of Smith-Wesson. It is the latest thing in firearms; it has six chambers with an extractor. Just look at its beautiful workmanship. The very latest, sir. We sell dozens every day for defence against marauders, wolves, and the wreckers of family happiness. The bullet strikes surely and powerfully, can hit at a considerable distance, and kills outright the faithless wife and her lover. As to suicides, I can assure you, sir, that I know of no better make——"

The man lowered and lifted it in the air, pulled the trigger, took aim, and handled the weapon lovingly as if he could not contain his enthusiasm. Looking at his rapturous face one could think that he would gladly have sent a bullet through his head if he only possessed a revolver of such beautiful workmanship as Smith-Wesson's.

" What is the price of one? " asked Sigaev.

" Forty-five roubles."

" M-m! It is too expensive! "

" In that case I will offer you one of another make, a cheaper one. We have a large assortment at different prices. For instance, this revolver is of a French make. The price is only eighteen roubles, but—(the man's face expressed contempt)—this make is an old-fashioned one, it is bought now only by intelligent proletarians and by women cranks. To commit suicide or to shoot one's wife with such a revolver is considered now a sign of vulgarity. Polite society recognises only Smith-Wesson."

" I am not going to kill any one or to commit suicide. I simply need a revolver to frighten away thieves from my summer cottage," Sigaev gloomily lied.

" It is none of our business what you are buying a revolver for," said the man, modestly lowering his eyes. " If we should try to find out the reasons in every case we should be compelled, sir, to close our shop. For frightening away thieves this revolver is no good, sir, because it produces a dull, weak sound. I would suggest that you buy one which is generally used, the Mortimer pistol or, as it is commonly known, the duelling pistol."

" Would it not be a good idea to call him out? " ran through Sigaev's head like lightning. " But no, that would be too much honour—such a beast ought to be killed outright like a rabid dog."

The man, gracefully turning and scraping his feet, put before him a whole heap of revolvers without ceasing to smile and to chat. But somehow a Smith-Wesson seemed to Sigaev more desirable and imposing than the rest. He took one of them in his hands and sank into thought. His imagination pictured to him how he would fire through her head and the blood would pour in torrents from the wound, over the carpets and parquet-floor, and how the dying traitress would writhe in mortal agony.

" That would not do," he thought. " I should do much better to kill him and myself—her I will spare. Let her live and suffer all the harrowing pangs of remorse, and suffer the contempt of all who come in contact with her. That would be much worse for a nervous, over-sensitive nature like hers than death."

And he pictured to himself his funeral: he, the offended one, was lying in his coffin with a gentle smile on his lips, and she, pale and worn-out with remorse, walked in his funeral cortège like a veritable Niobe, and did not know where to hide from the contemptuous glances the highly indignant people threw at her.

" I see, sir, that you like Smith-Wesson best," the clerk suddenly disturbed him in his dreams. " If the price seems too high to you, I am willing to let you have it five roubles cheaper. Besides, we have still other makes, slightly cheaper."

The little man turned gracefully to the shelves and took down another dozen revolvers.

" Here is one for thirty roubles. That is not dear, if you consider that our currency has fallen terribly and the import duty on foreign makes is becoming higher with every day. 'Pon my honour, sir, I am a conservative by nature and even I begin to grumble! Judge for yourself, sir, things have come to such a pass that only the rich can allow themselves the luxury of a good revolver! The poor must satisfy themselves with revolvers of cheap Russian make, namely, those which are made in Tula, and the Tula make is a—misfortune! You fire at your wife with such a revolver and hit your own shoulder."

Sigaev suddenly felt very sorry that he would not live to see the sufferings of the traitress. Revenge is only sweet when one can see and gloat at one's enemy's sufferings. What good would his revenge do him when he would lie in his grave and not see the havoc it had wrought?

" Would it not be better," he thought, " to kill him first, be present at his funeral and only kill myself afterwards? But I should be arrested long before that and my revolver would be taken away from me. And so: I will kill him, her I will spare, and I—I will not commit suicide at first, but will let myself be arrested instead. There is always time enough to kill oneself. An arrest would give me an opportunity to show the jury and society in general the whole baseness of her conduct. If I should be fool enough to kill myself she would probably succeed, with her characteristic boldness and natural aptitude for lying and prevaricating, to clear herself of all guilt and put all blame on me, and society would perhaps justify her action, and—who knows?—probably laugh at me; if, on the contrary, I should remain alive, then——"

A moment later he thought:

" Yes, and besides, if I should kill myself I should probably be accused and suspected of being prompted by a petty impulse. And, in truth, why should I kill myself? Besides, to shoot oneself would be to confess cowardice. And so: I will kill him, and will leave her alive. As to myself, I shall be arrested. On the trial she would have to figure as a witness. I can easily imagine her confusion when questioned by my lawyer! The sympathy of the press and the public would in such a case undoubtedly be on my side."

He considered, and the salesman continued to display before him his goods and dutifully to entertain his customer.

" Here are some revolvers of English make which we received but a short time ago, but I assure you that they pale to nothing before the Smith-Wesson. The other day—you, of course, have seen it in the papers—an army officer bought from us a revolver of the Smith-Wesson make. He fired at his wife's seducer and— what do you suppose?—the bullet went right through his chest, then it went through a bronze lamp, then the piano, from the piano it rebounded, killing a spaniel and wounding the wife. A splendid feat, and one which does honour to our firm. The officer is now under arrest. Of course, he will be found guilty and sentenced to a number of years of penal servitude in Siberia. That is, first, because our laws are too antiquated, and, secondly, because the jury is almost in every instance over-partial to the seducer. Why? Because the judges, jury and public prosecutor all have a weakness for breaking the tenth commandment, and they do not care in the least if there be one husband less in Russia. As to society—I really believe it would enjoy nothing better than the deportation of all husbands to Saghalin. Oh, sir, you cannot imagine what a feeling of indignation fills my heart when I think of the deplorable state of our contemporary morals! Why, to love the wife of another is just as much in vogue as to smoke some one else's cigars or to read some one else's books. Our trade is falling off every year more and more—that does not mean that family life has become purer and the breaking of the tenth commandment rarer—but simply that the husbands are reconciled to their fate and are afraid of the courts and of penal servitude."

The clerk looked about cautiously and whispered:

" And whose fault is it, sir? Why, only the Government's! "

" Where is the wisdom of going to Saghalin on account of such a hog? " thought Sigaev. " If I should be sent to Siberia my wife would be free to marry again, and to betray her second husband; she would be triumphant. And so: her I shall not kill; myself, also not; *him* I shall also not kill. I must find another way to revenge myself—one more sensible and more painful. I will pay them with contempt and will institute against her divorce proceedings in which her scandalous conduct will be shown before all the world and she will be for ever disgraced."

" Here, sir, is still another make," said the man, taking down a new dozen of revolvers. " I ask you to turn your attention to the peculiar mechanism of the lock."

Sigaev, after his decision, no longer needed a revolver, and wished nothing better than to get out of the shop. The salesman in the meanwhile waxed more and more enthusiastic, and did not tire of displaying his goods.

The offended husband felt conscience-stricken at the sight of the salesman, who was giving himself so much trouble displaying his wares, smiling, turning, scraping, and trying with all his might to please him, the customer.

" Very well, in that case," he muttered, " I will call later on, or—or will send some one."

He endeavoured not to see the expression on the shopman's face, but, to smooth out at least a little the awkward position to which he had brought himself, he felt it necessary to buy something. But what? He looked around the walls of the shop, wishing for something cheap, and his eyes rested upon a net which hung near the door.

" This—what is this? " he asked.

" That is a net for catching quail."

" What is the price of it? "

" Eight roubles, sir."

" I will take one." The offended husband paid the eight roubles, took the net, and left the shop.

# NATALIA VLADIMIROVNA

## Anton P. Chekhov

### I

ONE evening, nine years ago, at the time of the hay harvest, a friend of mine—Peter Sergeitch, a lawyer—set out with me to ride to the station for letters.

The weather had been perfect, but on the way home we began to hear distant thunder, and to perceive an angry black cloud advancing to meet us. Against its dark background the church and the house gleamed white, and the tall poplar-trees silver. All the air was full of the scent of rain and of new-mown hay. My companion seemed to be in the best of spirits, and, among other things, observed that it would be a fine stroke of luck if suddenly we were to come upon some old mediaeval castle, with castellated battlements and moss and owls complete, where we could take shelter from the rain, and let the storm beat upon us until the close of eternity.

Then a first spurt of rain came sweeping over the fields of rye and oats, and the wind plucked at us, and the dust circled high in mid-air. Peter Sergeitch laughed, and spurred his horse forward.

" Splendid! " he cried.  " Splendid indeed! "

Infected by his gaiety, I, too, laughed, without giving a thought to the matter of whether or not I might be soaked to the skin or killed by a stroke of lightning. How the whirlwind and the gallop caught one by the throat, and made one feel as though one were moving swifter than a bird! How they fired and tickled one's breast! Yet by the time we had reached home the wind had fallen, and great drops of rain were pattering down upon the grass and roofs.

## II

In the stable-yard not a soul was to be seen.

Peter Sergeitch himself unsaddled the horses, and led them to their stalls. Meanwhile, I stood at the door of the stable, and gazed at the rain-soaked ridges of hay. The luscious, rousing scent of the crop was even stronger here than in the open. Everything had become a blur of mist and damp.

" What a peal that was! " said Peter Sergeitch as he approached me just when a particularly loud, reverberating clap of thunder had seemed to split the very heavens in twain. Panting with the swift motion of the ride, he stood beside me on the threshold, and looked at me. And as he did so I could see that he was in love with me.

" Natalia Vladimirovna," he began, " I would give the whole world to stand here for ever and gaze at you! You look to me so beautiful to-night! "

His eyes were full of mingled rapture and entreaty, his face was pale, and on his beard and moustache there were glistening rain-drops which, to my fancy, seemed also to be gazing at me with eyes of love.

" I love you! " he went on.  " Yes, I love you, and the very sight of you makes me happy. I know that you can never be my wife, but I wish for nothing, I have need of nothing, except that you should *know* that I love you. Do not speak, do not answer me, do not take the least notice of what I say. Only learn that you are very dear to me, and permit me to continue looking at you as I am doing now."

His passion communicated itself to me, and as I gazed back into his inspired face, and listened to the murmur of his voice as it mingled with the sound of the rain, I felt as though I were bewitched, and could not stir. Nevertheless, I could have remained there for ever—for ever I could have looked at his shining eyes and listened to the sound of his voice!

"Do not utter a word," he said again. "Continue only to be silent, and all will be well."

And, indeed, all was very well with me just then. For sheer joy I laughed—then started to run towards the house through the pouring rain. He, too, laughed, and, darting forward, pursued me. Noisily as children we clattered, wet and panting, up the stairs, and flew into the drawing-room. My father and my brother, who were not used to seeing me full of laughter and gaiety, stared at me in astonishment—then joined in our merriment.

### III

The storm-cloud had passed away, and the thunder had ceased to roll; yet on Peter's beard there were still glistening a few raindrops. All that evening, until supper-time, he sang, whistled, and played with the dog—chasing it from room to room until he came near to upsetting a servant who happened to be entering with the tea-urn. At supper-time, too, he ate enormously, talked a great deal of rubbish, and assured us that to eat fresh cucumbers during the winter season gave one a foretaste of spring.

When I went to bed I put out my candle, and opened the bedroom window. My soul was full of a vague, indefinite feeling. I recalled the fact that I was free, healthy, rich, and well-born, as also the fact that I was beloved. Yes, above all things I recalled that I was rich and well-born. My God, how good that seemed! Then, shivering slightly with the chill which was rising from the garden, I endeavoured to decide whether or not I loved Peter Sergeitch! and, without deciding either way, fell asleep.

Next morning, on seeing the sunbeams and the shadows of the lime boughs playing over my bed, the events of the previous evening returned vividly to my recollection. Life seemed to me bounteous, varied, and full of delight. Singing softly, I dressed myself in haste, and ran down into the garden.

### IV

What happened afterwards? Nothing happened. True, next winter, when we were living in town, Peter Sergeitch paid us an occasional visit; but country acquaintances are interesting only in

the country and in summer-time, whereas in town, and during the
winter, they lose half their charm.  Should they be taking tea with
you, they seem to be wearing strange garments, and to be stirring
their tea overlong with the spoon.  Though Peter Sergeitch would
discourse in a general way on love, he was quite a different being
from what he had been in the country.  In town we were more
conscious of the barrier which stood between us.  I was rich and
well-born, whereas he was poor, and not even of gentle rank—a
mere deacon's son who had happened to attain the post of a public
prosecutor.  Both of us—I through youthful ignorance, and he for
God knows what reason—looked upon the barrier in question as too
high and too broad ever to be surmounted.  When visiting us, he
would laugh in a forced manner, and criticise Providence; yet,
should any one else chance to enter the room, at once he would
become moodily silent.  True, no barrier existed which could not
have been broken through; but the heroes of contemporary romance,
as I know them, are too timid, too unenterprising, too slothful, too
diffident of their own powers, ever to perform such a feat.  They
are too ready to accept the idea that they never will succeed, and
that life has cheated them; wherefore, instead of striving, they
criticise, and call the world base—forgetting that, through that very
criticism, they themselves are merging into baseness.

For myself, I had kinsfolk who showed me affection, and prosperity lay all around me.  I lived hand in hand with happiness, and
sang as I pursued my way through life.  Never once did I try to
understand myself, or to know what I was looking for or wanted
in life.  I simply let time pass by.  Affection hemmed me about,
bright days succeeded warm nights, the nightingales began to sing,
and soon the hay was giving forth its sweetness.  Yet all these
things, astonishing and delightful to the senses though they were,
passed from me as they pass from all human beings, and vanished
as a cloud might do.

V

At length my father died, and I found myself growing old.
What, that summer evening, had so pleased me, and charmed me,
and bidden me hope—the sound of the rain, the pealing of the
thunder, the thoughts of happiness, the talk of love—had now become for me a mere memory.  Before me there lay only a dreary,
empty waste, on the horizon of which not a living soul was visible.
Yet on that horizon there was looming something dark and terrible!

A ring at the bell! . . . Peter Sergeitch had called! . . . When,
in the winter-time, I see the trees, and remember how, in the
summer-time, it was for me they donned their greenery, I whisper
to them, " My dear ones! "  Similarly, whenever I chance to
encounter some one who has been with me in the spring-time of

my life, my heart feels sad, yet warm, as I whisper to that person words of like import. . . .

Not long before, my father's influence had procured for Peter a post in town. He had grown a little older and a little greyer. Also he had ceased to hold forth on the subject of love, or to talk nonsense. He had no great enthusiasm for his work, but seemed to be ailing, to be disillusioned, to be shaking his fist at life, to be living against his will.

Entering the room, he seated himself by the fire, and gazed silently into the flames. And I, not knowing what to say, asked him:

" Well—what? "

" Nothing," he replied; and again the firelight played upon his sorrowful face.

Then I remembered the past; and suddenly my shoulders began to heave, and my head to sink forward, and I burst into a storm of tears. I felt sorry beyond measure both for him and for myself. I felt a passionate yearning for what was gone, for what life had denied me. Nor had I a thought in my head about my being rich and well-born.

Continuing to sob convulsively, I pressed my hands to my temples and murmured:

" My God, my God! I have ruined my life! "

Meanwhile he sat without speaking. Yes, he forbore to say to me, " Do not weep "; for he knew that I *must* weep, and that the time had come for me to do so. Yet by his eyes I could see that he was sorry for me. And I too was sorry for him, as well as angry with him for having been so faint at heart—for having so little understood how to order my life and his own.

VI

When, later, I saw him to the door, he seemed purposely to be a long time putting on his overcoat. Twice he kissed my hand in silence and gazed into my tear-stained face. I have an idea that during those few moments he was recalling to his memory the thunder, and the rain-soaked ridges of hay, and our laughter, and my face as it had looked that day. Lastly, he tried to say something—something which he seemed very much to desire to say— but he could not do so. He just nodded his head and pressed my hand. May God be with him!

After seeing him depart, I returned to the study, and seated myself upon the hearthrug in front of the fire. The red coals had turned to ashes, and were beginning to die out, and the frost was knocking louder and louder at the window-panes, and the wind was singing in the chimney.

A maid-servant entered, and, thinking that I was asleep, called me by name.

# THE CHAMELEON

## Anton P. Chekhov

The police sergeant Achumyelof, wearing his new cloak and with a bundle under his arm, is walking across the market-place. He is followed by a red-haired policeman carrying a sieve filled to the brim with confiscated gooseberries. Quiet reigns all around. Not a soul in the market-place. The open doors and windows of the shops and public-houses gaze out sadly upon God's world like hungry mouths wide open. Not even beggars are hanging around.

Suddenly Achumyelof hears some one shouting: " So you want to bite, you accursed beast! Children, don't let him! Nowadays dogs are not allowed to bite. Stop him! Oh, oh! "

The howling of a dog is heard. Achumyelof looks in the direction from which the sound comes and sees a dog, limping on three legs, run out of Pinchugin's timber-yard. A man in a starched calico shirt and with a vest unbuttoned is chasing him. The man is close at the dog's heels; suddenly he lurches forward, falls to the ground, and takes hold of the dog's hind feet. Again the dog's howling is heard and the cry, " Do not let him! " Sleepy faces appear at the windows of the shops, and at the timber-yard a crowd quickly gathers as though it had grown out of the ground.

" Do you think it can be a riot? " asks the policeman.

Achumyelof turns to the left and walks toward the crowd. Near the gate of the timber-yard he sees the man with the unbuttoned vest holding up his right hand and showing the crowd a bloody finger. On his half-drunken face there is an expression as though he were saying: " Wait, I will make you pay for this, you scoundrel! " And the finger itself looks like a trophy. In this man Achumyelof recognised Khriukin, the goldsmith. In the centre of the crowd, with his forefeet spread out and trembling from head to foot, sits the author of the whole row—a young white greyhound, with a pointed muzzle and a yellow spot on his back. In his watery eyes there is an expression of distrust.

" What is the matter? " asks Achumyelof, making his way through the crowd. " Why are you here? What is the matter with your finger? Who has been screaming? "

" I was just walking along, sir, not touching anybody," says Khriukin, coughing into his fist, " to see about the wood for

Dimitri Dimitriyevitch, when suddenly this vicious cur bites my finger. You will excuse me. I am a man who works; I have very particular work to do, and somebody will have to pay me, for I won't be able to use this finger maybe for a week! There is nothing in the law, sir, about having to stand things from animals! If they are all going to bite it would be better not to live in this world!"

"Now," says Achumyelof sternly, moving his eyebrows up and down, "now, whose dog is this? I shall not allow this matter to rest. I will teach you people not to let your dogs run about loose! It is time that something were done about people who won't obey regulations. When I punish the scoundrel he will find out what it means to let dogs and other animals roam about. I will show him who I am! Yeldyrin," turning to the policeman, "find out whose dog it is and draw up a report. The dog will be killed. Make short work of it! He is probably a mad dog anyhow. Whose dog is it?"

"He looks like General Yigalof's dog," says some one in the crowd.

"General Yigalof's? H-m! Yeldyrin, take off my cloak; it is terribly hot! It is probably going to rain. There is one thing that I do not understand: how could that dog bite you?" says Achumyelof, turning to Khriukin. "He does not come up to your fingers. He is such a little dog, and you are such a big man. You have probably torn your finger on a nail, and afterwards the idea of the dog occurred to you and you are trying to extort money. I know you people; you are devils!"

"He teased the dog by putting a cigarette in his face; but the dog is no fool and went for him, sir."

"You lie, squint-eye! He did not see it, sir! What does he want to lie for? You, sir, can tell whether a man is lying or talking according to his conscience as in the sight of God. But let the judge decide whether I am lying! The law says that nowadays we are all equal. I have a brother myself among the gendarmes. If you——"

"Stop talking!"

"No, that is not the general's," observes the policeman pensively. "The general does not have dogs like that. His dogs are mostly setters."

"Are you sure of that?" "Yes, sir, quite sure."

"I know it myself, too. The general has high-priced thoroughbred dogs, but this is—the devil knows what! He has neither hair nor shape—just a common cur. For any one to keep a dog like that! What are you people thinking of? If such a dog should show itself in Petersburg or Moscow, do you know what would happen? They would not stop to look up the law, but just simply —and that is the end! Khriukin, you have suffered pain, and I will not let this matter rest. I must give them a lesson! It is about time! ''

'' But perhaps it is the general's dog after all,'' the policemen thinks aloud. '' It is not written on his muzzle. The other day I saw a dog like that in the general's yard.''

'' Of course it is the general's,'' says a voice in the crowd.

'' Yeldyrin, help me put on my coat. It is draughty around here; I am shivering. Take the dog to the general's and find out there. Say that I found him and sent him. And tell him not to let the dog out in the street. It is probably an expensive dog, and if every fellow is to hit him on the nose with his cigar, he will soon be ruined. A dog is a delicate creature. And you, blockhead, put down your hand! It is not necessary to exhibit that stupid finger of yours. It is your own fault! ''

'' There is the general's cook. Let us ask him. Hello, Prokhor, come here a minute! Look, is that dog yours? ''

'' That dog? We never had such a dog in our lives! ''

'' He is not worth asking questions about,'' says Achumyelof. '' He's a tramp dog. There is nothing more to be said. If I say he is a tramp dog, he *is* a tramp dog! He will be killed.''

'' That is not ours,'' continues Prokhor. '' That dog belongs to the general's brother, who has recently arrived. My master is not a lover of greyhounds, but his brother is fond of them.''

'' So his brother, Vladimir Ivanovitch, has arrived? '' asks Achumyelof, and a rapturous smile spreads over his face. '' Well, well, and I did not know it! He is here on a visit? ''

'' Yes, sir, on a visit.''

'' Well, well, he probably was home-sick for his dear brother. And I did not know it! So it is his dog, you say? I am very glad. Take him! A nice little dog! A quick little dog—*Snap*, and he has hold of the fellow's finger. Ha-ha-ha! Why are you trembling, you dear little thing? That man is a villain! '' Prokhor calls the dog and walks away with him from the timber-yard. The crowd laughs at Khriukin. '' I will catch you some time! '' Achumyelof threatens him, and wrapping himself in his cloak, he continues on his way across the market-place.

# A WORK OF ART

## Anton P. Chekhov

Sasha Smirnov, only son of his mother, entered the office of Dr. Koshelkov, carrying under his arm something wrapped up in No. 223 of the *Bourse Gazette*.

" Ah, my dear lad! " the doctor greeted him. " Well, how do we feel? Anything new? "

" My mother sends her respects, Ivan Koshelkov, and commands me to thank you," said Sasha Smirnov in a highly excited voice, placing his hand on his breast. " I am the only son of my mother, and you have saved my life—cured me of a dangerous illness, and —we, both of us, do not know how to thank you for it."

" That is enough, young man! " the doctor interrupted him, beaming with pleasure. " I did only what every one else would have done in my place."

" I am the only son of my mother," Sasha continued. " We are poor people and of course cannot pay you for your services, and —we are pained—our conscience is not at ease, doctor, and we, that is I and my mother, whose only son I am, beg you to accept as a mark of our esteem and gratitude—this object—which object is very valuable, of antique bronze—a work of art."

" There is really no necessity," the doctor frowned. " Now, where is the need of it? "

" No, but you must not refuse it, please," Sasha continued to mutter, unwrapping the parcel. " You will greatly mortify us, my mother and myself, by a refusal. It is a nice thing, this—of antique bronze. It was left us by my late father and we kept it as a dear heirloom, a remembrance. My father used to deal in old bronzes, you know, buying them when chance offered, and selling them to lovers of fine art. My mother and myself are now in the same business."

Sasha took the object out of its paper wrappings and solemnly placed it on the table. It was a very small candelabrum of old bronze and of very artistic workmanship. It represented a group: on a pedestal stood two female figures in the costume of Mother Eve. The figures smiled coquettishly and, on the whole, gave one the idea that if they were not in duty bound to support the candlestick they would at once jump down from the pedestal and turn the room into such a scene of revelry as would make you, reader, blush with shame at the mere thought of it.

After the doctor had examined his present he scratched his ear, chuckled and blew his nose.

" Yes, it is really very beautiful," he continued; " but how shall I best express myself? It is that—You know what I mean—improper—That is no longer what they call décolleté, but the devil only knows what——"

" I do not know why you should think so."

" Why, the Arch-Tempter himself could not have invented anything worse! To put a thing like this upon a table means to pollute the whole dwelling! "

" How curiously you look upon art, doctor! " Sasha said in an offended tone. " Why, this is a *chef-d'œuvre*! Just look at it more closely—why, it is of such an exquisite beauty that the heart is filled with a feeling of deep reverence and tears well up to the eyes. When you see such loveliness you forget everything earthly! What grace! What expression! "

" I understand that very well, my dear boy," the doctor interrupted; " but I am a family man; the children are always running about and ladies often visit me——"

" Of course, if one looks at it from the standpoint of the crowd," said Sasha, " then, of course, this highly artistic work appears in a different light. But, doctor, you must rise above the crowd, all the more so because by your refusal you will deeply grieve myself and my mother whose only son I am—you have saved my life—and we present you with the most valued object in our possession, and—I am only sorry that we have not the companion to this candelabrum."

" Thank you, my dear boy. I am very grateful—and wish that you greet your mother for me. But, really, 'pon my honour! Judge for yourself—my little ones are always running about these rooms and ladies are often calling. But, well, let it stay! You are not to be convinced! "

" And there is nothing of which to be convinced," Sasha said joyously. " Just place the candelabrum right here near this vase. It is too bad that there is no mate to it! Such a pity! Well, good-day, doctor."

After Sasha left, the doctor contemplated the candelabrum for a long time, scratched his ear, and thought.

" The candelabrum is a splendid piece of workmanship—that cannot well be denied. It would be a great pity to throw it away. But it is quite impossible to leave it here! M-m! There is a nice problem for you! To whom could I present it? "

After he had considered the matter for a long time he suddenly remembered a great friend of his, the lawyer Ukhov, to whom he was indebted for conducting a law-suit.

" Why, that is a splendid idea," decided the doctor. " It is kind of awkward for him on account of our friendship to take money from me, and it will be only proper on my part to make him a present. I will take this piece of devilry to him myself. By the way, he is a bachelor and very giddy."

Without letting the grass grow under his feet, the doctor dressed, took the candelabrum, and went to see Ukhov.

"How are you, comrade?" he greeted the lawyer, glad to have found him in. "I called upon you to thank you, little brother, for the service you did me, and as you do not care to accept payment in money, you must at least accept a present. This, little brother, is an object of art—a veritable gem!"

At the sight of the candelabrum the lawyer was transported with joy.

"Oh, what darlings!" he laughed. "Ah, the devil take them all, what won't they invent! Why, it is marvellous! Delightful! Where did you get such a beauty?"

After he had admired the candelabrum to his heart's content and poured out his rapture, he looked fearfully at the door and said:

"Only, brother mine, you must take this thing back with you. I will not accept it!"

"Why not?" the doctor asked in affright.

"Because—my mother comes to see me sometimes, and the clients—besides, I would not like the servants——"

"No, no, you must not refuse my gift!" The doctor waved his hands. "I will not hear of it! Why, it is a work of art! Just look how much feeling and expression! I do not want to consider a refusal at all! I'll feel very offended!" And the doctor almost ran out of Ukkhov's house, glad to have got rid of the unwelcome present, and went home.

After the doctor left, the lawyer looked attentively, from every side, at the candelabrum, and even touched it with his finger. Then he began to rack his brains over the question of what to do with the present.

"The thing is really beautiful," he reflected. "It would be a great pity to throw it out, but it is not at all a proper object to keep in one's house. The best thing to do in such cases is to present it to some one. I will take it this evening to Shishkov—the comedian. The rascal loves this sort of thing, and, as luck will have it, to-night is his benefit."

Ukhov was as good as his word, and that same evening the carefully wrapped up candelabrum was presented, among many flower offerings, to the comedian. The whole evening the artist's dressing-room was besieged by men who came in to admire the present.

After the performance the comedian shrugged his shoulders, gesticulated and harangued:

"Now, what in the world am I to do with this thing? I am living in a private family! Actresses often come to see me! And this is not a photograph—you cannot hide it away in a bureau-drawer!"

" Do you know what I would advise you to do, sir? " said the hairdresser, who was just then helping him to divest himself of his wig. " There is an old woman by the name of Smirnov—every one knows her. She deals in old bronzes, I would sell it to her."

Some two days later Dr. Koshelkov sat in his study and, with his finger to his forehead, was thinking deeply upon the bile-pigments. Suddenly the door was thrown open and in flew Sasha Smirnov. He smiled and his whole figure breathed forth happiness. In his hands he held something wrapped up in a newspaper.

" Doctor! " he began breathlessly. " Just picture my joy! As your luck would have it, we succeeded in obtaining the mate to your candelabrum! Mother is so happy! I am the only son of my mother; and you have saved my life! "

And Sasha, trembling with the feeling of gratitude, placed the candelabrum before the doctor. The doctor opened his mouth, wishing to say something, but could not utter a word; he had lost the use of his tongue.

# THE SLANDERER

## ANTON P. CHEKHOV

SERGEY KAPITONITCH AKHINEYEV, the teacher of calligraphy, gave his daughter Natalya in marriage to the teacher of history and geography, Ivan Petrovitch Loshadinikh. The wedding feast went on swimmingly. They sang, played, and danced in the parlour. Waiters, hired for the occasion from the club, bustled about hither and thither like madmen, in black frock coats and soiled white neckties. A loud noise of voices smote the air. From the outside people looked in at the windows; their social standing gave them no right to enter.

Just at midnight the host, Akhineyev, made his way to the kitchen to see whether everything was ready for the supper. The kitchen was filled with smoke from the floor to the ceiling; the smoke consisted of the odours of geese, ducks, and many other things. Victuals and beverages were scattered about on two tables in artistic disorder. Marfa, the cook, a stout, red-faced woman, was busying herself near the loaded tables.

" Show me the sturgeon, dear," said Akhineyev, rubbing his hands and licking his lips. " What a fine odour! I could devour the whole kitchen! Well, let me see the sturgeon! "

Marfa walked up to one of the benches and carefully lifted a greasy newspaper. Beneath that paper, in a huge dish, lay a big fat sturgeon, amid capers, olives, and carrots. Akhineyev glanced at the sturgeon and heaved a sigh of relief. His face became radiant, his eyes rolled. He bent down, and, smacking his lips, made a sound like a creaking wheel. He stood a while, then snapped his fingers for pleasure, and smacked his lips once more.

" Aha! The sound of a hearty kiss! Whom have you been kissing there, Marfushka? " some one's voice was heard from the adjoining room, and soon the closely cropped head of Vankin, the assistant school teacher, appeared in the doorway. " Whom have you been kissing here? A-a-ah! Very good, Sergey Kapitonitch! A fine old man indeed! Alone with a woman! "

" I wasn't kissing at all," said Akhineyev, confused; " who said I was, you fool? I only smacked my lips with pleasure at the sight of the fish."

" Tell that to some one else! " exclaimed Vankin, whose face expanded into a broad smile as he disappeared behind the door. Akhineyev blushed.

" The devil only knows what may come of this! " he thought. " He'll go about tale-bearing now, the rascal. He'll disgrace me before the whole town, the brute! "

Akhineyev entered the parlour timidly and cast furtive glances to see what Vankin was doing. Vankin stood near the piano, and deftly bending down, whispered something to the inspector's sister-in-law, who was laughing.

" That's about me! " thought Akhineyev. " About me, the devil take him! She believes him; she's laughing. My God! No, the matter mustn't be left like that. No! I'll have to make it so that no one will believe him. I'll speak to all of them, and he will only appear a silly gossip in the end."

Akhineyev scratched his head, and, still confused, went up to Padekoi.

" I was in the kitchen a little while ago, arranging things there for the supper," he said to the Frenchman. " You like fish, I know, and I have a sturgeon that long. About two yards. Ah, ha, ha! Yes, by the way, I had almost forgotten. There was a good joke about that sturgeon in the kitchen. I entered the kitchen a little while ago and wanted to look at the food. I glanced at the sturgeon and, for pleasure, I smacked my lips— it was so piquant! And just at that moment the fool Vankin entered and says—ha, ha, ha!—and says: ' A-a! A-a-ah! You have been kissing here! '—Marfa! Just think of it, the cook! What an invention, the blockhead! The woman is ugly, she looks like a monkey, and he says we were kissing. What an absurd fellow! "

" Who's an absurd fellow? " asked Tarantulov, as he approached them.

" I refer to Vankin. I went out into the kitchen——"

The story of Marfa and the sturgeon was repeated.

" That's what makes me laugh.  What an absurd fellow he is. In my opinion it would be more pleasant to kiss the dog than to kiss Marfa," added Akhineyev, and, turning round, he noticed Mazda.

" We have been speaking about Vankin," he said to him. " What a queer fellow.  He entered the kitchen and noticed me standing beside Marfa, and immediately he began to invent different stories.  ' What? ' he says, ' you have been kissing each other! ' He was drunk, so he must have been dreaming.  ' And I,' said I, ' I would rather kiss a duck than kiss Marfa.  And I have a wife,' said I, ' you fool.'  He made me appear ridiculous."

" Who made you appear ridiculous? " inquired the teacher of religious knowledge, addressing Akhineyev.

" Vankin.  I was standing in the kitchen, you know, and look-ing at the sturgeon——"  And so forth.  In about half an hour all the guests knew the story about Vankin and the sturgeon.

" Now let him tell," thought Akhineyev, rubbing his hands. " Let him do it.  He'll start to tell them, and they'll cut him short: ' Don't talk nonsense, you fool!  We know all about it.' "

And Akhineyev felt so much appeased that he drank, for joy, four glasses of brandy over and above his fill.  Having escorted his daughter to her room, he went to his own and soon slept the sleep of an innocent child, and on the following day no longer remembered the story of the sturgeon.  But, alas!  Man proposes and God disposes.  The evil tongue does its wicked work, and even Akhineyev's cunning did him no good.  A week later, on a Wednesday, after the third lesson, when Akhineyev was standing in the teachers' room discussing the vicious inclinations of the pupil Visyekin, the director approached him, and, beckoning to him, called him aside.

" See here, Sergey Kaponitonitch," said the director.  " Pardon me.  It isn't my affair, yet I must make it clear to you, neverthe-less.  It is my duty—You see, rumours are on foot that you are on intimate terms with that woman—with your cook.  It isn't my affair, but—You may be on intimate terms with her, you may kiss her—You may do whatever you like, but, please, don't do it so openly!  I beg of you.  Don't forget that you are a schoolmaster."

Akhineyev stood as though frozen and petrified.  Like one stung by a swarm of bees and scalded with boiling water, he went home. On his way it seemed to him as though the whole town stared at him as at one besmeared with tar.  At home new troubles awaited him.

" Why don't you eat anything? " asked his wife at their dinner. " What are you thinking about?  Are you thinking about Cupid, eh?  You are longing for Marfushka.  I know everything al-ready, you Mahomet.  Kind people have opened my eyes, you barbarian! "

And she slapped him on the cheek.

He rose from the table, and staggering, without cap or coat, directed his footsteps toward Vankin. The latter was at home.

" You rascal! " he said to Vankin. " Why have you covered me with mud before the whole world? Why have you slandered me? "

" How; what slander? What are you talking about? "

" Who told everybody that I was kissing Marfa? Not you, perhaps? Not you, you—murderer? "

Vankin began to blink his eyes, and all the fibres of his face began to quiver. He lifted his eyes toward the holy image and ejaculated:

" May God punish me, may I lose my eyesight and die, if I said even a single word about you to any one! May I have neither house nor home! "

Vankin's sincerity admitted of no doubt. It was evident that it was not he who had gossiped.

" But who was it? Who? " Akhineyev asked himself, going over in his mind all his acquaintances, and striking his chest. " Who was it? "

# FEÓDOR SOLOGUB
B. 1863

# THE WHITE MOTHER

I

EASTER was drawing near. Esper Konstantinovitch was in a perplexed, weary mood. It began, seemingly, from the moment when at the Gorodischevs he was asked: "Where are you greeting the festival?"

Saksaulov for some reason delayed his reply.

The hostess, a stout, short-sighted, bustling lady, said: "Come to us."

Saksaulov was annoyed. Was it with the girl who, at her mother's words, gave him a hasty glance and instantly averted her gaze as she continued her conversation with the young professor's assistant?

Mothers of grown-up daughters saw a possible husband in Saksaulov, and this irritated him. He looked upon himself as an old bachelor, and he was only thirty-seven. He replied coldly: "Thank you; I always spend this night at home."

The girl looked at him and asked with a smile: "With whom?"

"Alone," Saksaulov replied, with a shade of surprise in his voice.

"You are a misanthrope," observed Madame Gorodischev, with a somewhat sour smile.

Saksaulov valued his freedom. It seemed to him strange, whenever he thought of it, that at one time he had been very near to marriage. He had grown accustomed to his small but tastefully decorated flat, to his own valet, the aged, sedate Fedot, and to the latter's no less aged wife, the good Christine, who cooked his dinner for him, and tried to convince himself that he did not marry out of a desire to remain true to his first love. In reality his heart had grown cold from indifference, born of his lonely, purposeless life. He possessed an independent income, his father and mother were both dead, and he had no near relations. He lived a quiet, regular life, was attached to some Government department, was intimately acquainted with contemporary literature and art, took an epicurean

746

pleasure in the good things of life, while life itself seemed to him empty, meaningless. Were it not for one pure, bright dream that visited him at times, he would have grown quite cold, like so many others.

## II

His first and only love, that had ended before it had time to blossom, would sometimes, in the evenings, wrap him in strange, sweet fancies. Five years ago he had met the young girl who had produced such a lasting impression upon him. Pale, delicate, with slender waist, blue-eyed, fair-haired, she seemed to him almost a superhuman creature, born of the air and mist, and blown by fate for a brief space into the city din. Her movements were slow; her clear, tender voice was soft, like the murmur of a brook rippling gently over stones.

Saksaulov—was it accident or otherwise?—always saw her dressed in white. The impression of white had become inseparable from his thought of her. Even her name, Tamara, always seemed to him white, like the snow on the mountain-tops.

He began to visit at the house of her parents. More than once he had resolved to say those words to her that bind one human being's fate to another's, but she would never let him speak. Fear and anguish were reflected in her eyes. She would get up and leave him.

What did she fear? Saksaulov saw in her face the unmistakable signs of maidenly love. Her eyes would light up at sight of him and a faint blush would spread over her face.

But on one memorable evening she listened to him. The time was early spring, soon after the river had broken up and the trees had clothed themselves in soft green leaves. In a flat in town Saksaulov and Tamara were sitting by an open window that looked over the Neva. Without considering what he was to say and how to say it, he began to speak tender and what seemed to her terrible words. She turned pale, gave a wan smile and rose. Her delicate hand trembled on the carved back of the chair.

" To-morrow! " she said softly, and left him.

Saksaulov sat for a long time in tense expectancy, staring at the door that had hidden Tamara. His head was in a whirl. A sprig of white lilac caught his eye; he picked it up and went away, without so much as taking leave of his hosts.

That night he could not sleep. He stood by the window staring into the dark street, that grew lighter with the dawn. He smiled and kept on pressing the sprig of lilac in his hand. In the morning he noticed that the room was strewn with petals of the white lilac, and this struck him as both naïve and absurd. He took a bath and felt refreshed; then he went to Tamara.

They told him she was ill—had taken cold somewhere. And Saksaulov never saw her again. In two weeks she was dead. He did not go to her funeral. Her death left him almost unmoved, and already he wondered whether he had loved her, or if it had merely been a passing fascination.

He would muse about her sometimes in the evening; then he began to forget her. Saksaulov had no portrait of Tamara. It was only last spring, after several years had gone by, that he was reminded of her by a sprig of white lilac in the window of a restaurant, sadly out of place among the rich eatables. And from that day he again loved to think of Tamara in the evening.

Sometimes he would fall into a light sleep and dream that Tamara had come. She would sit down near him and look at him with caressing, longing eyes. And it was painful to feel Tamara's expectant gaze upon him and not know what it was she wanted.

Now, as he left the Gorodischevs, he thought timidly: " She will come to give me the Easter greeting." Then a feeling of fear and loneliness took such hold of him that he thought, " It might be well to marry, so as not to be alone on holy mysterious nights."

Valeria Michailovna—the Gorodischev girl—came into his mind. She was not a beauty, but her dress always suited her to perfection. She was well disposed towards Saksaulov, and would hardly refuse him if he proposed.

The noise and crowd in the street distracted him, and his thoughts of the Gorodischev girl soon became tinged with the usual shade of irony. And could he be false to Tamara's memory? The world seemed to him so petty and vulgar that he longed for Tamara— and Tamara only—to give him the Easter kiss. " But," he thought, " she will again look at me with that strange expectancy. The white, gentle Tamara, what is it that she wants? Will her soft lips kiss me? "

### III

With tormenting thoughts of Tamara, Saksaulov wandered about the streets. The coarse faces of the grown people disgusted him. He reflected that there was no one with whom he would gladly exchange the Easter kiss. There would be many kisses on the first day—coarse lips, knotted beards, an odour of wine.

It was much more pleasant to kiss children. The faces of children became very dear to him.

He walked for a long time, and when he grew tired he went into a church garden off the noisy street. A pale boy, sitting on a seat, looked up at Saksaulov apprehensively, then continued sitting motionless, staring straight before him. His blue eyes were sad and caressing like Tamara's. He was so small that his feet projected in front of the seat. Saksaulov sat down beside him and began observing him with a pitying curiosity. There was something about this lonely little child that created sweet, stirring memories. And he was the most ordinary boy, in ragged clothes, a white fur cap on his fair little head, and worn, dirty boots on his feet.

For a long time he sat on the seat, then he got up suddenly and began to cry pitifully. He ran out at the gate into the street, then stopped, set off in another direction and stopped again. It was obvious that he did not know which way to turn. He cried quietly to himself, the big tears rolling down his cheeks. A crowd gathered and a policeman came up. They asked the boy where he lived.

" Gluhov House," he lisped, in the manner of very young children.

" What street? " the policeman asked.

But the boy did not know and only repeated: " Gluhov House."

The policeman, a good-natured young fellow, reflected for a moment. He knew there was no such house in the immediate neighbourhood.

" With whom do you live? " asked a gloomy looking workman. " With your father? "

" I have no father," the boy replied, looking up at the crowd with his tearful eyes.

" No father! dear, dear! " the workman said solemnly, shaking his head. " But you have a mother? "

" Yes, I have a mother," the boy replied.

" What is her name? "

" Mother? " the boy replied; then, after a moment's reflection, added, " Black mother."

Some one in the crowd laughed.

" Black? I wonder if that is their surname? " the gloomy workman suggested.

" First I had a white mother and now I have a black one," the boy attempted to explain.

" We shall never make head or tail of you, my boy," the policeman said decisively; " I had better take you to the police station. They will make inquiries on the telephone."

He went up to a gate and rang, but the house porter had already caught sight of him and was coming towards the gate, broom in hand. The policeman ordered him to take the boy to the police station, but the boy bethought himself and cried out: " Let me go; I will find the way myself! "

The porter's broom may have alarmed him, or perhaps he had indeed remembered something; at all events, he ran away so quickly that Saksaulov nearly lost sight of him. After a while, however, the boy slackened his pace. He walked from street to street, running from one side to the other, searching in vain for his home. Saksaulov followed him silently. He was shy of talking to children.

At last the boy grew tired. He stopped by a lamp-post and leant his shoulder against it. The tears glistened in his eyes.

" My dear boy," Saksaulov began, " haven't you found it yet? "

The boy looked at him with his sad gentle eyes, and suddenly Saksaulov realised what had made him follow the boy so persistently. In the face and glance of the little wanderer there was something wonderfully like Tamara.

" What is your name, my dear? " Saksaulov asked in a tender, agitated voice.

" Lesha," the boy replied.

" Do you live with your mother, Lesha, dear? "

" Yes, with mother. Only she is a black mother; before I had a white one."

Saksaulov concluded that the black one was the step-mother.

" How did you manage to get lost? " he asked.

" I was walking with mother, a long way; then she told me to sit and wait and she herself went away. I began to get frightened."

" Who is your mother? "

" Mother? She is—so black and cross."

" What does she do? "

The boy reflected.

" She drinks coffee," he said.

" And what else does she do? "

" She quarrels with the lodgers," Lesha replied, reflecting for a moment.

" And where is your white mother? "

" They took her away. They put her in a coffin and took her away. And father, too, they took away." The boy indicated the distance with his hand and burst into tears.

" What shall I do with him? " Saksaulov thought. But suddenly the boy ran on further. After passing several houses he slackened his pace and Saksaulov caught him up again. In the boy's face there was an expression of mingled fear and joy.

" Here is Gluhov House," Saksaulov said, indicating a hideous five-storeyed building.

At this moment, from the gate of the " Gluhov House " a dark-haired, dark-eyed woman appeared, in a black dress and black shawl with a white pattern. The boy shrank back apprehensively.

" Mother," he whispered.

The step-mother stared at him in astonishment.

" What are you doing here, you little scamp? " she shouted. " I told you to sit on the seat. Why have you come back? "

She was about to strike the boy, but observing that a gentleman was looking at them, very severe and grave of aspect, she softened her tone.

" Can't I leave you for half an hour but you must run away?

I have run myself off my legs, looking for you, you young scamp! I feel fit to drop."

She seized the child's little hand in her broad one and dragged him into the yard. Saksaulov made a note of the address and went away.

Saksaulov liked to listen to Fedot's sound judgments. When he returned home he told him about the boy Lesha.

"She left him on purpose," Fedot announced. "What a vicious woman, to take the boy so far from home!"

"But what was her motive?" Saksaulov asked.

"Who can tell? The stupid woman must have thought that the boy would wander about the streets until one or other would pick him up. After all she is a step-mother. What is the child to her?"

"But the police would have found her," Saksaulov said incredulously.

"That is possible, but then she may be leaving the town, and how could they find her then?"

Saksaulov smiled.

"Really," he thought, "my Fedot should have been an examining magistrate."

Sitting near the lamp with a book that evening, he fell asleep. In his dreams he saw Tamara—gentle and white—she came and sat beside him. Her face was wonderfully like Lesha's. She gazed at him steadily and persistently, as though expecting something. It was painful for Saksaulov to see her bright, pleading eyes and not know what she wanted. He rose quickly and walked over to the chair where Tamara appeared to be sitting. He stood before her and demanded imploringly, in a loud voice: "What do you want? Tell me!"

But she was no longer there.

"It was only a dream," Saksaulov thought, sadly.

IV

Coming out of the Academy exhibition on the following day Saksaulov met the Gorodischevs. He told the girl about Lesha.

"Poor boy," Valeria Michailovna said softly; "his step-mother simply wants to get rid of him."

"One can hardly say," Saksaulov replied, annoyed that both Fedot and the girl should take such a tragic view of a simple incident.

"It seems obvious," Valeria Michailovna went on warmly. "There is no father; the boy lives with his step-mother, to whom he is simply a nuisance. She will get rid of him one way or another."

"You take a very gloomy view," Saksaulov said with a smile.

" Why don't you adopt him? " Valeria Michailovna suggested.

" I? " Saksaulov asked in surprise.

" Why not? " she persisted; " you live alone and have no one belonging to you.  A good deed at Easter is well done.  You will at least have some one with whom to exchange the Easter greeting."

" But, Valeria Michailovna, what could I do with the child? "

" You could get a nurse.  Fate seems to have sent the child to you."

Saksaulov looked at the flushed, animated face of the girl in wonder and unconscious tenderness.

When Tamara appeared to him that evening he seemed to know what it was she wanted, and in the stillness of his room he heard her clearly pronounce the words: " Do as she bids you."

Saksaulov got up, rejoicing, and passed his hand over his sleepy eyes.  On the table lay a sprig of white lilac.  Where had it come from?  Had Tamara left it in token of her will?  And suddenly it dawned on him that in marrying the Gorodischev girl and adopting Lesha he would be fulfilling Tamara's wish.  He breathed in the fragrant perfume of the lilac joyously.

Suddenly he recollected that he had bought the sprig of lilac himself that day.  " But it makes no difference," he thought.  " It is significant that I should have wanted to buy it and should have forgotten afterwards that I had done so."

v

In the morning he set out to find Lesha.  The boy met him at the gate and took him to his home.  Lesha's mother was drinking coffee and quarrelling with her red-nosed lodger.  Saksaulov learnt something about the boy's story from her.

He had lost his mother when he was three years old.  His father had married this dark woman and died too, within a year.  The dark woman, Irina Ivanovna, had a year-old child of her own. She was about to marry again.  The wedding was to take place in a few days, and immediately afterwards they were to go into " the provinces."  Lesha was a stranger to her and in the way.

" Give him to me," Saksaulov suggested.

" With great pleasure," Irina Ivanovna said with a malignant joy.  " Only you must pay for his clothes," she added, after a pause.

And so Lesha was installed in Saksaulov's house, and the Gorodischevs' girl helped him to find a nurse and in other details relating to the boy's comfort.  This necessitated her presence in Saksaulov's apartments.  Seeing her thus busy with these homely cares, she seemed a different being to Saksaulov.  The door of her soul opened to him.  Her eyes grew tender and radiant and she was permeated with almost the same gentleness that was so characteristic of Tamara.

VI

Lesha's stories about his white mother touched Fedot and his wife. When putting him to bed on Easter Eve they hung a white sugar egg at the head of his bed. "This is from your white mother," Christine said; "only you mustn't touch it, darling, until the Lord has risen and the bells begin to ring."

Lesha lay down obediently. He stared at the lovely egg until he fell asleep.

And Saksaulov was sitting alone. Near midnight an unconquerable drowsiness closed his eyes, and he was glad that he would soon see Tamara.

And she came, radiant, all in white, bringing with her the joyous distant sound of church bells. With a gentle smile she bent over him and—unutterable joy!—Saksaulov felt a light touch on his lips, and a gentle voice pronounced softly: "Christ has risen!"

Without opening his eyes Saksaulov stretched out his arms and embraced a slender, gentle body. It was Lesha, who had climbed on to his knee to give him the Easter kiss.

The church bells had awakened the boy. He had seized the white egg and run to Saksaulov.

Saksaulov awoke. Lesha laughed and held up his egg.

"The white mother has sent it," he lisped. "And I will give it to you and you must give it to Auntie Valeria."

"Very well, my dear, I will do as you say," Saksaulov replied.

He put Lesha to bed, then went to Valeria Michailovna with Lesha's white egg, a gift from the white mother, which at this moment seemed to him a gift from Tamara herself.

# THE INVOKER OF THE BEAST

### FEÓDOR SOLOGUB

I

IT was still, tranquil, neither joyous nor sad. There was an electric lamp in the room. The walls seemed impregnable. The windows were covered with heavy dark green curtains, darker in tone even than the green of the wall-paper. Both doors, the large one to the side and the small one at the other end, opposite the window, were tightly shut. And there, behind them, it was dark and empty—

in the broad corridor, as well as in the spacious cold and desolate drawing-room, where drooping plants yearned for their native soil.

Gurov was lying on the couch. A book was in his hand. He was reading. Now and again he would pause. He mused and meditated during these pauses, and it was always about the same thing; always about *them*.

They were all around him. This he had noticed long ago. They were hiding. They were incessantly near him. They rustled quietly. For a long time they were not visible to the eye. But one day, when he awoke tired, pale and suffering, and wearily turned on the electric light to banish the dense gloom of an early winter morning, he suddenly saw one of them.

Small, grey, lightly alert, he flashed above his head, muttered something—and vanished. From that day, in the morning and in the evening, Gurov would see these small, elusive house-sprites running past him. To-day he was certain they would come.

From time to time he felt a slight headache, then a sudden flash of heat and then cold again. Then from the corner emerged the long, gaunt Fever, with her ugly yellow face and dry bony hands which she entwined about him, as she lay down beside him, and began laughing and showering him with kisses. And these quick, passionate kisses of the cunning Fever and these slight periodical headaches were both pleasant.

Weakness and languor spread over the whole body. This, too, was pleasant. The turmoil of life seemed to have receded into the distance. And people, too, seemed far away, uninteresting, unnecessary. He wanted to be alone with these sly, timid house-sprites.

Gurov had not been out for some days. He had locked himself securely in the house. No one was allowed in. He was alone, thinking of them, awaiting them.

## II

The weary waiting ended in a strange, unexpected manner. There was the slamming of a distant door and from the drawing-room Gurov could hear the sound of measured footsteps. Some one was coming, drawing nearer, with light, assured tread.

Gurov turned his head towards the door. A cold draught came into the room. Before him stood a boy of a strange and wild aspect. He was draped in a linen cloak. He was half nude, barefooted, swarthy, and sunburnt. He had black, wavy hair and bright black eyes. A wonderfully perfect, handsome face; so handsome that it was almost awe-inspiring to gaze at its beauty. The face expressed neither good nor evil.

Gurov was not surprised. A powerful sensation took hold of him.

He could hear the house-sprites running away to hide themselves.

And the boy began to speak.

"Aristomachos, have you forgotten your promise, or is this the way of valiant men? You left me when I was in mortal danger, you made me a promise which you seemingly did not intend to keep. For a long time I have been seeking you, and now I find you living in idleness and in luxury."

Gurov looked at the handsome, half-nude boy in perplexity; a confused recollection awoke in his soul. Something long since submerged and forgotten began to assume vague form, and tormented his memory that could find no solution to this strange apparition; a solution that seemed so near and so intimate.

And what had become of the invincibility of his walls? Something had happened around him, some mysterious change had taken place. But Gurov, absorbed in his vain exertions to recall something that was kindred to him, yet was slipping away into the tenacious clutch of ancient memory, was not yet fully conscious of the change that he felt had taken place. He turned to the wonderful boy.

"Tell me, dear boy, simply and clearly, without unnecessary reproaches, what is it that I promised you, and when did I leave you in time of mortal danger? I vow by all that is holy that my honour would never have permitted me such a black deed as that of which you accuse me."

The boy shook his head. In a voice as musical as the sound of a stringed instrument, he said:

"Aristomaches, you have always been a man skilful in words, and no less skilful in matters requiring daring and prudence. If I said that you left me in time of mortal danger, it was not to reproach you, and I do not understand why you speak of your honour. Our undertaking was a daring and dangerous one, but who can hear us now? Before whom do you seek to prove with your crafty, wily words and your dissembling ignorance of what happened this morning before sunrise that you had not made me a promise?"

The light of the electric lamp grew dim. The ceiling seemed dark and lofty. There was a smell of grass—its forgotten name had at one time been soft and joyous. A cool breeze blew.

Gurov rose and asked: "What is it that we two had undertaken? I deny nothing, dear boy, only I do not know what you are speaking of. I cannot remember."

It seemed to Gurov that the boy was looking at him and yet not looking at him, that some one else was present, some one as foreign and wonderful as this curious stranger, and, that the form of this marvellous person was in some way inseparable from his own. Some ancient soul seemed to have entered Gurov's body and enveloped him in the long-lost freshness of his vernal impressions.

It was dark; the breeze grew fresher and colder; in his heart arose the joyous ease of pristine existence. The stars shone brightly in the dark sky. The boy spoke.

" We had undertaken to kill the Beast. I tell you this under the multitudinous gaze of the all-seeing heavens. It may be that your fear confounded you. And no wonder! We were going to do a mighty daring deed so that our names should be famous through the generations."

The soft, monotonous, gentle murmur of a stream could be heard in the nocturnal stillness. The stream was not visible, but the sense of its nearness was sweet and refreshing. They stood under the broad shelter of a tree and continued their conversation begun at some other time.

Gurov asked: " Why do you say that I deserted you in your moment of mortal danger? Who am I that I should get frightened and run away? "

The boy laughed. The sound of his laugh was like music, and like music were the words that he uttered, the laughter still rippling in his voice.

" Aristomachos, how cleverly you pretend to have forgotten everything! What is your motive in doing it, and doing it so well as to bring reproaches on yourself that I had not even intended? You left me in a moment of mortal danger because it had to be; you could not have helped me otherwise than by forsaking me at that moment. And will you still persist in your denial when I remind you of the words of the Oracle? "

Gurov suddenly remembered. A brilliant light seemed to illuminate the dark domain of things forgotten. In a wild ecstasy, loudly and joyously he cried out:

" One shall kill the Beast! "

The boy laughed, and Aristomachos asked:

" Did you kill the Beast, Timarides? "

" With what? " Timarides exclaimed. " However strong my hands, I am not the one who can kill the Beast with a blow of my fist. We were imprudent, Aristomachos, and unarmed. We were playing on the sandy bank when the Beast fell upon us suddenly and pinned me with his heavy paw. It fell to my lot to offer up my life as a sweet sacrifice to glory and a noble cause, and to you to carry out our plan. And while the Beast was rending my defenceless, unresisting body, you with your long legs, Aristomachos, could have run for your lance and killed the blood-intoxicated Beast. But the Beast did not accept my sacrifice. I lay beneath him quiescent and still, looking into his bloodshot eyes. He held his heavy paw on my shoulder; his breath was hot and quick, and he growled softly to himself. Then, with his broad, hot tongue, he licked my face, and went his way."

" And where is he now? "

Strangely tranquil, and in a voice that sounded strangely melodious in the gentle stillness of the humid air, Timarides replied:

" He followed me.  I do not know how far I have come to find you, but he followed me.  I led him on by the scent of my blood. I do not know why he has not touched me.  But I have enticed him to you.  Get your weapon that you have hidden so carefully and kill the Beast, and I in turn will run away and leave you alone in your moment of mortal danger, eye to eye with the infuriated Beast.  Rejoice, Aristomachos! "

With these words Timarides set off at a run.  For a short while his white cloak glimmered in the darkness.  Already he was out of sight.  And at this moment the terrible roar of the Beast could be heard, and the sound of his heavy tread.  The bushes parted, and the enormous, hideous head of the Beast appeared, a livid fire flashing out of its huge flaming eyes.  And in the dark stillness, beneath the nocturnal trees, the black and furious Beast bore down on Aristomachos.

Aristomachos' heart was filled with terror.  " Where is my lance? " flashed across his brain.

And at this moment, by the sense of the cool night air that beat against his face, Aristomachos knew that he was running away from the Beast.  Its heavy bounds and broken roars grew closer and closer.  And when the Beast reached him, a loud cry rent the stillness of the night.  It was Aristomachos who had cried out.  And recalling some weird ancient words, he began an incantation to the walls.

And thus conjured, the walls began to rise about him. . . .

### III

The bright, enchanted walls stood firm, and the wan light of the electric lamp seemed dead against them.  Gurov was in his usual surroundings.

Again the Fever came lightly and kissed him with her yellow, dry lips, and caressed him with her dry, bony hands, which diffused heat and cold.  The same thin little book with the white leaves lay on the table by the couch on which Gurov had lain contentedly before in the arms of the amorous Fever, while she showered quick kisses upon him.  And again the tiny little house-sprites laughed and rustled around him.

Gurov pronounced loudly and indifferently:  " The spell of the walls."  He stopped.  But what was the spell?  Had he forgotten the words, or had they never existed?

The little grey mischievous house-sprites danced around the little book with the deadly white leaves, repeating in their silky little voices:

" Our walls are strong.  We are in the walls.  No harm can come to us from outside."

In the midst of them stood one just as small as the rest, but different from them. He was black all over. His garments fell about him in folds of smoke and flame. His eyes flashed like lightning. Gurov was seized by terror and then by a sudden joy. He asked: " Who are you? "

The black guest spoke.

" I am the Invoker of the Beast. In a long past existence, on the banks of a forest stream, you abandoned the lacerated body of Timarides. The Beast forged himself on the beautiful body of your friend—he ate of the body that should have tasted to the full of earthly happiness; a creature of superhuman perfection had perished to satisfy for a moment the ever ravenous and insatiable Beast. And the blood, the wonderful blood, the sacred wine of joy and happiness, the wine of superhuman bliss—where is this blood? Alas! the thirsty, ever thirsty Beast drank of it for a moment and is thirsty anew. You abandoned the lacerated body of Timarides on the banks of a forest stream, you forgot the promise made to your valiant friend, and the words of the ancient Oracle failed to banish the fear from your heart. And do you imagine that you are safe, that the Beast will not find you? "

His words were harsh and cruel. While he was speaking the house-sprites ceased their dancing; the little grey creatures stopped to listen to the Invoker of the Beast.

And Gurov said: " What do I care for the Beast! Have I not put a spell on my walls for ever? The Beast cannot penetrate to me here."

The little grey creatures rejoiced; their voices rang out in a merry laugh. Again they took hands and made ready to form a ring, when the Invoker of the Beast spoke, and his voice sounded harsh and austere:

" But I am here. I am here because I have found you. I am here because the spell of the walls is dead. I am here because Timarides is waiting, incessantly imploring. Do you not hear the gentle laugh of the valiant, trusting boy? Do you not hear the roar of the Beast? "

From without the walls the threatening roar of the Beast could be heard drawing nearer.

" The Beast roars without the wall, the invincible wall! " Gurov exclaimed in terror; " my walls are enchanted for ever and their barrier is impenetrable."

And the Dark One spoke in a commanding voice:

" But I tell you that the spell of the walls is dead. If you wish to save yourself by the spell why not try and repeat the incantation? "

A cold shiver ran down Gurov's back. The incantation! But the ancient words were forgotten. And what did it matter? Was not the ancient spell dead—dead?

And every object in the room confirmed with irrefutable evidence that the spell of the walls was dead, because the walls, and the light and the shadows, all grew dim and wavering. The Invoker of the Beast went on speaking terrible words. Gurov's head ached and ached, and the importunate Fever tormented him with her hot, passionate kisses. The terrible words rang out, scarcely reaching his consciousness; and the Invoker of the Beast grew larger and larger, diffusing hot vapours and grim terror. Fire flashed from his eyes, and when at last he grew so tall as to screen the light of the lamp, his black cloak suddenly fell from his shoulders. And Gurov recognised him—it was the boy Timarides.

" Will you kill the Beast? " Timarides asked in a ringing voice. " I have enticed him, brought him to you, destroyed the spell of the walls. The base gift of a hostile god, the spell of the walls had turned to naught my sacrifice and shut you out from your deed. But the ancient spell of the walls is dead; be quick and take up your sword and kill the Beast. I was only a boy before, now I have become the Invoker of the Beast. The Beast drank of my blood and is thirsty anew; he ate of my flesh and is hungry again, the cruel insatiable Beast. I have brought him to you and you must fulfil your promise and kill him; or die yourself."

He vanished. A terrible roar shook the walls. A damp cold draught filled the room.

The wall, exactly opposite the spot where Gurov lay, opened, and out came a ferocious, monstrous, hideous Beast. With a savage growl he walked up to Gurov and laid his heavy paw on his breast. The pitiless claws penetrated to the very heart. A sharp pain pierced through his body. With flaming, bloodshot eyes the Beast bent over Gurov, and crunching his bones with his teeth, began to devour his palpitating heart.

# A SOOTHING DREAM

## Feódor Sologub

SERIOJA died.

It was Passion week. In the house, preparations were being made as usual for the festival—preparations that were a joy to the children and pleasant to the adults. Eggs were coloured with cochineal, saffron was prepared for the rolls, and cream whipped for Easter visitors; there was a smell of vanilla and cardamom.

The floors were polished, dirt and dust was everywhere removed, the windows were cleaned. The servants were tired out. The girls,

Serioja's sisters, dreamt of pleasant kisses, and shuddered at the thought of the unpleasant ones.

And Serioja lay in his room, which was bare, so that the furniture should not absorb the fresh air in the room where there was a sweet smell of tallow.

He was only fifteen, bright and gay, and loved by the family. It was the beginning of Spring, just before Easter Sunday, and Serioja's sisters wanted pleasures only, and were afraid to think of death.

Serioja's death was so out of keeping with the rush and bustle of preparation for the festival, that they wanted to deceive themselves and imagine that he was recovering for it.

He had been ill for some time, and they had decided to take him away somewhere, but it was put off because they could not make up their minds where to take him. And suddenly, no one knew why, his lungs got worse quickly, and he grew so weak that it was impossible to move him; the journey would have been too tiring, and besides, the warm climate could not then have saved him.

The young doctor said to Serioja's distracted father:

" Not more than a month, now."

The old doctor said wearily and indifferently:

" Six weeks at the most."

Serioja's father conducted them politely to the door. His face was red and confused. His mind would not grasp the fact that Serioja was about to die. His thoughts were slow and dazed.

He stood by the fireplace in the dining-room, and mechanically looked at himself in the mirror hanging above it, straightened his tie that had slipped to one side, and with trembling fingers stroked his moustache that was beginning to grow grey.

In an awkward, apologetic manner he walked up to the table where his wife was peeling almonds. Thrusting his hands into the pockets of his short house-jacket, he stood behind her back, and suddenly, by some intuition, by the manner in which she bent over, by her suppressed bodily suffering, by the trembling of her lips, he realised that she knew the worst.

It struck him painfully that she was not lying among her soft pillows weeping bitterly, but was sitting there with the young boys, apparently so calm, yet suffering cruelly. And the boys, helping their mother, laughed and talked carelessly.

The sight of her lonely suffering sent an acute pain through him. A lump rose in his throat, and with small, quick footsteps he walked away from her, the tap-tap of his heelless shoes resounding on the polished floor. Small and grey he went along the empty corridor to his study—to throw himself on the couch, his face to the high back, and toss about with sighs and groans on the dark green leather.

Hearing his footsteps behind her, his wife grew redder than before, and her face twitched, but she sat straight and calm. The almonds were all finished; she wiped her soft white hands on a towel, and went slowly into her husband's study.

And there they sat, side by side, weeping bitterly in their despair, no consolation in sight. . . .

II

It was the Saturday before Easter. Serioja was asleep. He was dreaming—a strange but soothing dream.

It was a sultry day, he dreamt. Before his eyes there stretched a valley golden in the bright rays of the sparkling sun. He sat on the threshold of a poor hut. The broad leaves of two palm-trees threw a shade on his sunburnt legs and on his white linen clothes. He was small, as he used to be ten years ago, and very happy. His tiny body, scarcely covered by the white linen, was as light as that of an earthly angel. Everything made him gay—the earth so hot and firm beneath his bare feet—the air so sultry yet fresh,— the sky so blue and high, yet so near that it seemed to touch the earth—the quick flight of the birds—the cries of the children playing by the neighbouring huts—his mother's mellow, unexpected voice as she chatted merrily with other women by the well in their white garments, swarthy and barefooted.

Now she was returning. On her shoulder was a long narrow-necked pitcher. Her bare, swarthy arm was raised to support it. The sunlight played on her rosy cheeks, her lips were half-parted in a smile, her eyes gazing at the child from beneath long lashes sparkled and shone with pleasure. She was proud of her boy while he ran, laughing and joyful, to meet her. In his hands was a toy he had made himself out of clay—a bird,—a clay bird, but it seemed alive.

The wonderful little artist had modelled it out of heavy clay— his fingers had been quick and deft, and the clay seemed to wish to come to life, and the little bird trembled in the warm, childish fingers full of the will that creates life.

The mother passed him in her haste to relieve herself of her burden. Smiling, without a bend of her neck or a motion of her head, she cast a glad look at her son from her deep black eyes.

The boy put out his left hand, and catching hold of her sunburnt foot, cried:

" Look, mother! "

He was a little surprised at his foreign speech, but soon forgot it, and left off wondering at the strange tongue and the fact that he was understood.

His mother stopped and laughed. She asked:

" Well, what is it, my son? "

The boy raised the clay bird and said gaily:

" Look, mother, here is a bird I made myself; it sings like a real one."

He put his lips to the tail of the bird where it was formed like a whistle and blew into it, and from the clay back of the bird there issued a soft whistle. Modulating his breath, the boy blew into his clay whistle creating real musical sounds.

The mother laughed and said:

" What a clever boy to make such a wonderful bird! Look after it, hold it firmly in case it should fly away."

She went into the hut and about her work. And the boy sat on the perch gazing pensively at his bird, and stroking its feathers with his slender fingers.

" Do you want to fly away? " he asked softly.

The little wings moved slightly.

The boy asked again:

" Do you want to fly away? "

The little heart began to beat in the bird's breast.

For the third time the boy asked:

" Do you want to fly away? "

The little body trembled all over, it spread its feathers and flapped its wings—the bird twittered and turned its head from side to side.

The boy opened his hand and the bird flew away. And in the light blue sky its joyful song receded farther and farther.

The sultry sun rose higher and closer grew the still air.

### III

Serioja awoke bathed in a cold sweat.

There was a horrible pain in his chest and breathing was difficult. But where was the little bird, the little bird that he had made?

There it was by the window, twittering, beating its wings and flying away.

" My bird! "

" And who am I? "

Serioja raised himself, but fell back on the pillows again. He murmured in his delirium:

" And who am I? "

The mother bent over him, but Serioja did not see her. He did not see the walls of his room, they had gone off again and left him alone.

### IV

He was on the top of a hill.

The country spread out before him sparkling in the sultry noonday sun.  His clothes were poor and worn, his weary feet were covered with dust, and dust was in his short, golden beard.

His companions remained below in the shade of the olives, sleeping off their fatigue.

Around him the light grew brighter, and more majestic grew the broad sparkling heavens.  Floating through the transparent air, and bringing a cool heavenly breeze with them, two men in resplendent flowing garments came up and spoke to him.  He asked them:
" Who am I? "
" Do not be afraid," they answered him.  " On the third day you will arise."

His clothes were already a fiery red, and a fiery halo was over his head, and the fire in his blood made his blood course through his veins, and a shout of unutterable joy escaped him.

## V

He awoke.  His cry brought them, frightened, to his bedside.  A thin stream of blood flowed from his mouth, coming out from the left side of his pale lips.  His face was deadly white, the frightened eyes gazed above the dear ones gathered at his deathbed, wide-open eyes motionless with terror.

Black and sightless, with terribly shiny white teeth, there approached an inexorable figure bringing with her an eternal cold and eternal darkness.  She was enormous.  She took all the air from Serioja, and like a dark cloud, shaking the heavy folds of her garments, she bore down straight at Serioja.

But, loud as thunder, the voice of the resplendent man was heard:
" On the third day you will arise."

And behind the black mantle of the deadly guest could be seen the golden lighting of the Resurrection day, a glad sight to Serioja's eyes.  His pale face lit up with the joyous golden lighting, and in his eyes was a quiet triumphal look.  He whispered, catching his breath:
" On the third, I will arise."
And he died. . . .

## VI

On the third day he was buried.

# THE HOOP

## FEÓDOR SOLOGUB

EARLY one morning, in a deserted street on the outskirts of a town, there walked a lady and a boy of four. The boy was gay and rosy, the lady was young and well-dressed. She smiled in her happiness and looked anxiously at her son. The boy was bowling a hoop, a large, new, yellow one. He ran after it with awkward childish movements, laughing joyfully, stamping his chubby feet, displaying his bare knees and waving his stick. It was not at all necessary to raise the stick so high, but what would you have!

What joy! A short while ago he had no hoop, and now there it was bowling along so swiftly! And everything was so jolly!

There was nothing there before—for the boy—it was all new—the morning street, the bright sun, the distant murmur of the town. To the boy all was new, pure and joyful.

Yes, all is pure; children never see the impure side of things until their elders show them where to look.

## II

A shabbily-dressed old man, with coarse hands, stood at the crossing and drew himself up against the fence in order to let the lady and her son pass. The old man looked at the boy with dim eyes, and smiled dully. Slow, vague thoughts began to creep into his bald head.

" A gentleman's son," he thought. " A nice little fellow. How he enjoys himself. A child—a gentleman's child, mind you! "

There was something he could not understand, something that seemed strange to him. A child: but children are pulled by the hair. Petting indulges them: children are always in danger of being spoilt.

And the mother did not repress her son—did not shout or threaten. How well-dressed and beautiful she was! What did she want for? She evidently lived in peace and comfort.

When he—the old man—was a boy he had led a dog's life! It was not too sweet even now, although he was no longer beaten or went hungry. In those days it was hunger, cold, and blows. In those days there was no such indulgence as hoops or other such toys of the gentry. Thus his whole life had passed in poverty, care, and bitterness. There was nothing to remember—not a single joy.

Smiling with toothless mouth at the boy, he grew envious. He thought: "A stupid amusement." Envy made him weary. He went to his work—in the factory where he had worked from childhood, where he had grown old. All day he kept thinking about the boy.

Effortless thoughts: it was so easy to remember the boy running, laughing, stamping, chasing his hoop—and his legs were so chubby and his knees so white. . . .

The whole day, amidst the din of the factory machines, he thought of the boy and the hoop. And at night he dreamt of the boy in his sleep.

### III

Next morning dreams again possessed the old man. The machines rattled, the work was mechanical, and it was not necessary to think about it. The hands performed the accustomed task, the toothless mouth smiled at the absorbing dream. The air grew cloudy with dust, near the ceiling the belts with a sharp hiss glided from pulley to pulley. The far corners were enveloped in noisy gloom. People moved about like ghosts—human speech was drowned in the resounding song of the machines.

And it seemed to the old man that he was a little boy, that his mother was a lady, that he had a hoop and stick with which he was playing, bowling the hoop with his stick. He was dressed in white —his legs were fat and his knees bare. . . .

Day after day the same work and the same dream.

### IV

When returning home one evening, the old man saw in the street a hoop from an old barrel—a rough, dirty hoop. The old man trembled with joy, and tears started to his dim eyes. A sudden, almost unconscious desire entered his soul. He looked round cautiously, bent down, and with trembling hands seized the hoop and carried it home, smiling shamefacedly.

No one saw him, no one asked questions. Besides, what business was it of anyone's? A little ragged old man carrying an old hoop of no use to anybody—who would notice him?

But he carried it stealthily—in fear yet smiling. Why he had picked it up, why he was carrying it home he himself did not know. It was so like the boy's toy, so he had taken it.

To see, to touch, was more real than that dream, dimmer than the din and roar of the factory, hazier than the noisy gloom. . . .

For several days the hoop lay under the old man's bed in his poor crowded corner. Sometimes he would take it out and look at it—the dirty grey hoop comforted him, and the ever-present dream of the happy boy became more real.

### V

On a clear, warm morning, when the birds in the shelter of the town trees were singing more gaily than usual, the old man rose very early, took his hoop and walked out of the town.

Coughing, he wound his way among the old trees and clinging branches through the woods. The silence of the sombre trees with dark, dry barks was incomprehensible to him. The scents were strange, the insects amazed him, and the pearly dew was as in a fairy tale. There was neither din nor dust, and a wonderful soft darkness lay behind the trees. The aged legs glided over the carpet of leaves and stumbled against the ancient roots.

The old man broke off a dry twig and put it through the hoop.

A meadow, bright and still, lay before him, the many-coloured, countless dewdrops sparkling on the blades of the newly-mown grass.

Suddenly the man struck the hoop with his stick and set off at a run; the hoop rolled softly over the meadow. The old man laughed with joy and ran after the hoop like the boy. He threw out his legs, caught the hoop with his stick, and raised the stick high above his head as the boy had done.

It seemed to him that he was a little boy once more, gentle and happy. His mother was following him and watching him with a fond smile. Like a child he felt a little chilly at first in the dark wood, on the gay grass and the soft moss.

The grey, goat-like beard on the worn face shook and laughter and coughs issued together from his toothless mouth.

### VI

The old man loved to come to the wood in the morning and play in the glade with his hoop.

Sometimes he feared that someone might see him and laugh, and at this thought an unbearable sense of shame possessed him. The shame was akin to fear; his legs grew weak and gave way under him. He looked around cautiously and shamefacedly.

But no—no one saw him—no one heard him. . . . And having played to his heart's content he walked peacefully back to town, a light glad smile on his lips.

### VII

And so, no one saw him; and nothing more happened. He played peacefully for several days, and one dewy morning caught cold, took to bed, and died. When dying in the factory hospital amid strange, indifferent people, he smiled serenely.

He was comforted by the thought that he, too, had been a child, had laughed and gambolled on the fresh grass under the shady trees while his dear mother looked on.

# ACKNOWLEDGMENTS

TO MESSRS. GEORGE NEWNES, LTD., LONDON

In arrangement with whom "The Snow-Storm" and "The Queen of Spades" by Pushkin, and "A Fair Smuggler" by Lermontoff, are here reprinted from *The Strand Magazine*.

TO MR. WILLIAM HEINEMANN, LONDON

For permission to use Mrs. Garnett's translation of Turgeniev's story "The Singers," from the collected edition published by Mr. Heinemann.

TO THE WALTER SCOTT PUBLISHING CO., LTD., LONDON

For their courtesy in permitting the reprinting of Schedrin's "The Self-Sacrificing Rabbit," and Uspensky's "The Village Schoolmaster," from their volume *The Humour of Russia*.

TO THE EDITOR OF "EVERYMAN"

For his permission to use the translation of Chekhov's "In the Coach-House" and "Natalia Vladimirovna," from *Everyman*.

*Made and Printed in Great Britain by*
*Hazell, Watson & Viney, Ltd., London and Aylesbury*